Goodreads Praise for

SPELLCASTER WILD CARD

"You don't want to miss this coming-of-age tale that gives pop culture a paranormal twist."
—Wendy Higgins, NYT Bestselling Author of *Sweet Evil*

"**I devoured it in 3 days!** It hit on all emotions. AND the plot twist, WHAT??? Didn't see it coming from a mile away."
—Jax Britt

"Nikki Jefford is back and doing what she does best: writing about a **strong female character who triumphs against all the odds."**
—Sharon

"*Spellcaster Wild Card* by Nikki Jefford is an **electrifying** blend of supernatural intrigue, teen drama, and a reality TV show twist that had me hooked from the first page!"
—Nessa's Book Reviews

"This isn't just about a competition or spellcasting. It's about family and love and trust, bigotry, heartache, loss, murder and metamorphosis."
—Michelle Helen Fritz, author of *A Court Of Broken Dreams & Curses*

"For fans of the supernatural genre, this book is a must-read. Jefford not only introduces a strong female lead in Haylee, but also delivers a plot brimming with **suspense and unexpected twists."**
—Bookish_Mum

"Haylee is one of the best FMCs I have read this year who doesn't need anyone to save her; she can save herself."
—Abbie

"*Spellcaster* is a macabre take on a magic-focused reality show competition that delves into deep societal hardships, including celebrity obsession with elite vampire cliques and species relations/tensions, which comes with stereotyping and bigotry, competitor alliances and, in turn, hate crimes and hazing, all played out with a full cast of unique, relatable, and vibrant characters—and lots of action amidst gut-wrenching emotional turmoil."
—L.B. Carter, author of *Body Snatcher*

"This is definitely **my favorite read of the year** and probably for a while."
—Mima

"If you loved the voice TV show and you love magic and supernaturals then you will love this book."
—AM

"Every page and chapter had me stunned and speechless."
—Belinda Clemons

SPELLCASTER WILD CARD

NIKKI JEFFORD

SPELLCASTER WILD CARD

First edition.

Cover design by Najla Qamber
Interior format and design by Nada Qamber
Character Art by Surya Handoko and Deo Louis Bukit

ISBN: 979-8-9869761-9-8

www.NikkiJefford.com

For those left behind.

“Why fit in when you were
born to stand out?”
- Dr. Seuss

PROLOGUE

THIS IS WHERE I take my last stand, atop the acclaimed *Spellcaster* stage.

Purple lights rim the circular platform and outline the large pentagram filling the center. The glow spreads outward, illuminating the edges of wide stairs leading to the four purple velvet high-backed chairs. The auditorium is empty except for the vampires surrounding the stage and their master. He leans forward in one of the chairs, his tailored suit and Italian leather shoes as black as his soul. He's selected a front-row view for my execution. To add insult to injury—with which I am riddled—his Evilness has hijacked Malachi Rayne's chair. It's going to need reupholstering. Scratch that. They're going to have to burn it to ash and then replace it altogether.

Seated beside him is the traitor.

Without the cheering audience, camera crew, stagehands, band, Colt Cohen, and coaches, the auditorium feels like a mausoleum at midnight. I suppose this is to be my final resting place.

Blood and bone matter spatter the glossy stage. Dim overhead lights gleam against the reflective surface where I stand in rhinestone-studded black ankle boots, crimson crushed-velvet high-rise pants, a black eyelet camisole, and a cropped moto jacket. At least I'll go out in style. Sorta. One of my gold-tone dangle earrings has been shot off, along with my earlobe. The outfit I so carefully put together is in tatters. Some of the bullets clipped me, while others tore straight through my body as though I were a piñata dripping guts. If I were still human, I'd already be dead. This is just a warm-up for the goons. The rehearsal before the big production. In addition to their guns, the master's lackeys hold weapons that can end me for good: a semiautomatic assault rifle, chainsaw, flamethrower, katana, spiked baseball bat, and a good old-fashioned wood-splitting ax. Maybe I should feel flattered to have become such a stellar threat that they had to bring in a whole arsenal to take me down, along with the master himself to oversee it. He was a no-show for my family, but I've got his undivided attention now.

"Not feeling so superior now, are you?" His diabolical voice burns through me.

He's managed to turn my world upside down all over again with his sickening reveal. I avoid looking at the occupant of the seat beside him.

I'm sure they're all feeling smug in the knowledge that if the situation were reversed, they would be able to self-heal.

I touch the delicate gold disc pendant, engraved with the letter *H*, hanging at my neck. It feels like a shiny penny I'm about to make a wish on before tossing it into a fountain of forgotten dreams. I've worn this necklace during the best and worst moments of my life. I can't decide if it's good luck or bad. I guess it's all just life, which is beautiful, ugly, and endlessly unfair.

I don't answer to this monster. He's not *my* master. No one is. Somehow that makes me grin through the pain.

Manicured nails press into the velvet armrests, gripping the edges. Yep, Malachi is definitely going to need that chair burned to cinders. Not that he'll know it needs replacing.

There is no one coming to rescue me. I have no wand to save myself. But I do have one last trick up my sleeve. The final performance of Haylee Hutchins.

No one will ever see it, but it's better this way. I don't want to be remembered for what I'm about to do.

It's highly unlikely I'll make it as far as the purple velvet chairs, but at least I will be numb to the carnage. Popular opinion has it all wrong. I'm not some rag doll who feels no pain. The gunshot wounds burn and throb like bullet-sized horseflies took chunks out of my flesh while a swarm of wasps stung me repeatedly with venom. Even my high tolerance for physical suffering isn't enough to entirely shield me against this level of brutality. I'm still standing, but everything inside of me is on fire, like I'm about to go up in smoke.

The stage might as well be an iceberg with killer whales closing in from the dark shadows of the ground-floor seating. My stomach knots at the sight of their crude weapons.

I didn't sign up for this.

I like glamour and glitz, not anguish and gore.

I want to break free of this nightmare spell—some sick prank a caster is playing on me. To go back in time. I want to wake up on Christmas morning and join my family downstairs in our living room decorated with garlands, multicolored string lights, and a fragrant noble fir tree with pretty packages waiting to be opened. I want to gorge on empty calories: maple-glazed donuts, blueberry pancakes, cupcakes with buttercream frosting, chewy chocolate chip cookies, creamy peanut butter cups, key lime pie atop a graham cracker crust, waffle fries, and pizza—especially pizza.

Even if I had my wand, there is no going back.

I aim a haughty gaze at the master vampire in Malachi's chair as I slip off my jacket. It plops to the stage, revealing my bloody arms. On my right shoulder, my wild card tattoo is still intact.

Yep, I *literally* have a trick up my sleeve. I get one spell. One chance. That is all. I press two fingers into the tattoo with a mixture of confidence and horror. And then I open my mouth, daring to be the first spellcaster in the history of magic to launch this spell.

There is no going back.

Someone ought to chisel that onto my gravestone. Not that they'll give me one. My kind aren't welcome in cemeteries.

Well, this is it.

In five. Four. Three. Two.

CHAPTER ONE

THERE IS NO reason to feel this nervous, and yet my stomach threatens to erupt.

I've done this hundreds of times before. Still, no matter how many videos I record, pressing the *Go Live* button on my phone always feels like pulling the pin from a grenade.

I breathe in through my nose and out through my mouth, then give the camera a full-lipped, red-tinted smile with Bite Back, my new favorite shade from Spark Cosmetics.

@HeyHeyHaylee is LIVE on JingleJam
989,027 Followers

"Hey, hey. Hello, beauties. It's Haylee. Today, I am going to show you an effortless hairstyle you can literally throw together in under three minutes. I'll be using two mini elastic hair ties and finishing the look with this vintage beaded pearl hair clip from Hoodoo Emporium. Follow the link in my post to receive fifteen percent off your first order."

@jean_e_sw Hey, Hey, Haylee!

@tricia_moon_goddess 👋

@foxyroxy HEY!!!

The face reflecting back from my screen is round and fair-skinned with dark eyebrows, gray-blue eyes that pop with black eyeliner, and straight ash-blond hair landing an inch south of my collarbone. My halter top matches my lip color and leaves a generous amount of skin for my delicate gold disc pendant to settle against my chest.

Because of my flawless skin, my followers are constantly telling me that I would make a gorgeous vampire. It's a huge compliment in the beauty world. Vampires are the epitome of glamour and style. A lot of people would do just about anything to be remade. Me? I'm proud to be a genuine living, breathing member of humanity and content with my big, beautiful, plus-sized bod.

I lift the beaded hair clip in front of the camera for my ring light to catch the smooth synthetic pearls strung over the gold barrette.

"Isn't it pretty?" Once I'm recording, I am in my element, having fun with my followers.

@janettepnrfantasybookclub Need!!

@queentiff I know where my next paycheck is going.

@jean_e_sw Thank you for the discount, Haylee!

@foxyroxy So pretty!

@tricia_moon_goddess pearly

@deissy_daisy OMG! Heart that hair clip so much!

"Wait until you see how pretty it looks with this style," I say. "First, part your hair. As you know, I like my part from the left." I use my comb to make the part, then set it down and grab a clear elastic band. "Leave a section of hair at your forehead and gather the section behind. Secure it with the first band, and then thread your hair through. Gently pull the hair loose up top. Next, do the same to that front section of hair, like so, and then secure both pieces with a pretty clip above the ear."

The barrette snaps into place. I tilt my head to the side and smile into the camera. "See? Easy. Now you're ready to step out, turning heads everywhere you go."

@queentiff You're gorgeous, girl!

@tricia_moon_goddess wowwwww

@hotbabe1010 Fake pearls can't hide your FAT ass!

@angel_leah Need now!!

@irishpam I am so doing this for my bridesmaids.

@foxyroxy @hotbabe1010 Big is Beautiful you Moluccan cockatoo!

@deissy_daisy @hotbabe1010 Don't you realize how pathetic you sound? 😟 #sad

@queentiff When does the discount expire?

I latch onto the question, ignoring the battle taking place between my beauty brigade and my number one hater.

"There is no expiration date on that discount, Queen Tiff. As long as my link is up, Hoodoo Emporium will take fifteen percent off your first purchase when you use my affiliate link."

My image in the camera is super glam. No way is **@hotbabe1010** gonna get me down. I just wish she would find a more productive use of her time and stop tainting my feed with her bad juju. Every time I block her, she comes back under a different user account, so now I ignore her. Some of my followers have a harder time with her insults, but I love that they've adopted my "Moluccan cockatoo" lingo. Also known as the salmon-crested cockatoo, the species is one of the loudest birds in the parrot world. I don't believe in calling women the *B* word—not even a nasty, raging *BLEEP* like MC1010, as I've nicknamed her. No matter what username she appears under, it always ends in "1010." All I know is that she needs a lesson in Social Media Etiquette 101. The extra 0 at the end represents my zero-tolerance-for-bullying policy. I have no clue what the numbers mean to her, but that's what they mean to me.

"And now for the finishing touch." I pick up my most prized possession, a dark brown wand the length of a ruler. Anyone can perform magic . . . if they can afford a Lignum Vitae wand. Even then, not everyone should be using wands, the way some people aren't meant to sing outside of the shower. Unlike bad singing, slipshod spells can do actual damage to the spellcaster and anyone who happens to be around them. Luckily for me, casting comes as naturally as breathing.

I loosen my jaw, spin my wand with my right hand, and sing out, "*Ringawhirl.*" Relaxed, wavy curls tumble from the right side of my hair. Switching the wand to my left hand, I repeat the spell, completing my signature style.

There are plenty of cheap knock-off wands, but all they're good for are props and Halloween costumes. The smooth wood of a Lignum Vitae wand is rich and luxurious, needing no added paint or polish. Carved designs go from elaborate to simple, but they all do the same thing. I've always been happy with the classic wand my parents gifted me as a child.

"Now, I know a lot of you don't have wands lying around, but I've got some seriously exciting news. Guess what, beauties? I'm about to reach a million followers," I squeal. "You guys, I never dreamed my account would grow this fast. It's all because of your amazing support. To celebrate, I am planning my most epic giveaway ever. One lucky follower will be winning their very own genuine Lignum Vitae wand. I will tell you how to enter in an upcoming video."

Comments flood through my feed. I do regular giveaways of beauty bags filled with goodies supplied by sponsors, but for this mega milestone, I am dipping into my personal affiliate earnings. A Lignum Vitae wand will take a massive chunk out of my account, but the reason I have that money to begin with is because of my fabulous followers, and this is my way of saying a big thank you back.

I lift my wand and flick it around, casting mini fireworks that explode into bursts of color that shimmer before fading. "*Baloominate. Propellets. Glintle flare. Flicktilla glowbeam.*" After showing off the fun that can be had with a wand, I set mine down and say, "Who knows? Maybe the winner will use their Lignum Vitae to audition for *Spellcaster*. How cool would that be?"

I would totally freak if any of my followers got on the show. And you can bet I would be rallying the troops to vote for them during the live episodes. Have I fantasized about competing on the show myself? Only since Season 1! Maybe after I graduate from high school, I'll muster up the nerve to audition.

"Speaking of *Spellcaster*," I say, "what color do you think Malachi should dye his hair next season?"

@deissy_daisy Red!

@queentiff Teal purple combo

@theamazingmichelle rainbow

@missmima back to black

@jean_e_sw Malachi Rayne would look hot in any hair color.

I grin. "Oh, I agree, Jean E. Malachi Rayne would probably even look good bald." I press my lips together and think on that a moment. "Meh. I prefer him with hair."

@foxyroxy ORANGE!

"Orange?" I grin. "Great suggestion for Season 13."

Malachi is the only vampire bold enough to pull off bright new hair colors, which he rocks during every season of *Spellcaster*. Also, he was turned right before the show first launched—not one of those younger-looking vampires who have been around for decades or centuries, which is so gross. They're like creeper online catfishers, only worse because those old-timers don't have to use a fake photo.

@jean_e_sw You should audition for *Spellcaster*.

@tricia_moon_goddess yassss, girl

@theamazingmichelle Four wand lift for sure.

@missmima Team Malachi!

@irishpam What about Brody Morgan? He's won more seasons than Malachi.

@bookbel I'd go Team Cleo. Witches know magic better than werewolves and vamps.

@deissy_daisy MALACHI!!!

@foxyroxy We'd vote you all the way through to the finale!

I laugh. "Oh my gosh, you beauties are the best! If I was on *Spellcaster*, you know I'd choose Malachi Rayne as my coach in a heartbeat." The thought of it makes my grin broaden. "See you all in the next recording, where I will be kicking off Haylee's Holiday Looks. You're going to flip out over the limited-edition beauty sets releasing for the season. Also, I'll show you how to add color pops that will jazz up your hair. Until next time, be bold, be beautiful, and always be yourself."

I end my live feed, heart still pounding from the adrenaline rush. A flurry of likes adds up into the hundreds. Twirling my wand, I watch the comments pour in. My best friend, Ellie, is among the first to give my video a heart. Then I see a name that makes me drop my wand.

Colt Cohen.

I sway, wand at my feet like maybe the smoothly carved piece of Lignum Vitae is now twirling me.

COLT! COHEN!

It can't be. I'm hallucinating.

With jerky hands, I detach my phone from the clip holding it in the center of my ring light and jab my finger to view all my likes. And there it is. *The* Colt Cohen—not some impostor, fan account, or name twin.

I scream like a banshee, barely hearing the pounding footsteps that follow my freak-out. When my parents throw open my door, I am jumping up and down with my phone held high in one hand like a winning lottery ticket. "Colt Cohen liked my video! Colt Cohen!"

Dad's salt-and-pepper hair is askew, and his tortoiseshell glasses are slipping down his nose. They're cool frames he let me pick out, unlike the nerdy button-up collared shirts he wears underneath plain sweaters. He could fill his closet with designer clothing and shoes on his earnings as one of the world's top divorce attorneys, but—as Mom likes to remind me—truly successful people have the confidence to dress casually.

For me, it's simple. Look good. Feel good. Style is the essence of life. What we wear affects the way we think, feel, and behave, as well as the way people react to us. It says who you are without having to speak.

Dad pushes his glasses up the bridge of his nose and looks at Mom, who is eight years younger than him and pulls off casual chic with way more style. "Who is Colt Cohen?"

"Dad!" I screech. Seriously? Dad doesn't watch anything that's not the news or a documentary. That's if he has any free time at all—but still. Come on!

"He's the host of *Spellcaster*," I bluster over the stampede of wild stallions pounding in my ears.

"Werewolf," Mom supplies to Dad.

He frowns. "Hm. I thought maybe he was a boy at school."

"Dad!"

"What?" He looks to Mom like he needs her to translate teen talk, specifically mine. My dad and big sister can debate for hours on end. Not so much with me.

Mom clears her throat. "Haylee has no interest in any of the young men at Brookdale."

"Young men?" I snort. "They're a bunch of obnoxious, unhygienic trolls."

Dad's frown deepens the way it does when he listens to one of his doom-and-gloom docudramas about how another endangered species is on the cusp of extinction—not that it matters much, since a solar flare may or may not wipe out humanity, shifters, and witches within the next ten years. Unless it doesn't. I can't keep up with all of the doomsday scenarios. I don't want to.

As Dad scratches his chin with one finger, his gaze appears to have traveled light-years away. "You have a crush on an adult werewolf?"

"Dad! No!" I slap my hand to my forehead. "*Spellcaster* is my all-time favorite competition. How do you not remember this?"

"Oh, okay then." He shrugs.

I know it's pointless, but still I try to explain. "It's only one of the most popular shows in the country—and the entire world, with its foreign versions."

"That's exciting, sweetie," Mom says in a tone that seriously needs dialing up on the Pep-o-Meter.

I huff out a breath. "Where is Kendra when I need her?"

Mom instantly brightens. "Your sister will be home next week."

There's no way I can wait until next week to tell my sister about Colt. After my parents retreat, I open Telepatch, which is Kendra's favored social media outlet. She's built her own following with her no-apologies commentary that accompanies the disturbing images she shares. I look for anything new before I call. My sister has always been supportive of what I do (even though her beauty routine consists of a ponytail, nude shade of lipstick, and quick coat of mascara). I make a point of supporting her back.

I scroll through her latest photo exposé. Yep. More zombies. In the first photo, a young twenty-something female zombie with matted hair sits at an intersection holding a cardboard sign that reads *STARVING*. Her eyes have sunken in while the rest of her body pulls taut against a bony frame. I put my excitement on ice, forcing my finger to swipe to the next photo and the next. There's a zombie slumped beneath a bridge with bullet holes riddling his torn shirt, shorts, and brown skin. A zombie wearing a baseball cap trying to cover a rotting wound above his eye. A *NO HORDING* sign splattered in blood on a brick wall. A female zombie who can't be much older than I am, lying in a street with tire tracks across her lower legs.

My stomach churns around a pit in the center. I read my sister's short post.

> Do these images disturb you? Good. It means you have a functioning heart.
>
> Contact your local officials and demand equal rights for zombies.
>
> #Rightsforzombies #Zombiesaresentient #WhatIfThisWereYou

I always feel weird liking Kendra's posts, because I don't like what's happening in the photos—it's cruel—but I admire how much my sister cares for the downtrodden. Likes are a good thing, so, as always, I push past the discomfort and tap the heart attached to her post. Then I call, and she answers after the second ring. "Haylee!"

My face lights up. Kendra makes me feel like I'm her best friend in the whole wide world, even though she has no trouble amassing admirers and companions alike.

Melodic birdsong trills in the background. I can picture my sister in the quad at Blakely College, doing her homework in the shade of the trees over in sunny California. I got to visit her once, and it was one of the best weekends of my entire life.

"Heya!" I match her enthusiasm syllable for syllable. "Oh my gosh. I have the most exciting news ever. Like ever, ever!"

"What is it?" Kendra gasps.

"Colt Cohen just liked my live JingleJam."

"Colt Cohen, host of *Spellcaster*?" Kendra demands.

"The one and only."

Her scream is so loud I have to hold the phone away from my ear.

"No, I'm okay," Kendra assures people on her end. "My little sis just told me the most exciting news. Holy crap," she says to me—I think. "Hold on a sec. I need to pull up your video and see. Colt Cohen liked my sister's video." Now she *is* talking to someone else. "Cameron's with me," she supplies.

"Hi, Haylee," her fiancé says.

"Hey, Cameron."

My sister managed to do the impossible—find a guy not only worthy of her but also approved by every member of the family. He adores my sister, 'cause he's smart. He's also super sweet, cute, and clever—the whole package. Kendra and Cameron. Even their names sound adorable together. They're getting married after they graduate from college at the end of next semester. It's going to be the most beautiful beach wedding ever. I'll make sure of that.

Kendra reads names aloud as she searches through my likes. It sounds like she has me on speaker. The birds have gotten louder. "Wait a sec. Wait. Oh my gosh! Here it is! Cam, look! Colt Cohen. Legendary talent scout, radio announcer, and host of America's number one hit TV show."

"I feel like I should howl or something," Cameron says.

"Sounds like my sister's already drawn enough attention," I chuckle.

Kendra scoffs. "Let them look. This is a big deal. Were you talking about *Spellcaster* when Colt liked your video?"

"Yes."

"What were you saying?"

"I asked my followers what color they thought Malachi should dye his hair for Season 13 . . . and said I will always be Team Malachi. Naturally."

"Naturally," Kendra repeats with a laugh. "Hey, what if Malachi watches your videos?"

"No way," I intone as my heart lurches. "He's Forever 23. They don't like anything outside of their club."

"Doesn't mean he doesn't watch."

"Why would the world's sexiest spellcaster watch some human nobody's JingleJam video?"

"Hey!" Kendra says sharply. "You're not a nobody. You're about to reach a million followers. Let me repeat that. One. Million. Followers! Not to mention you're better than all of those F23ers combined."

I'm not sure about that, but I appreciate my sister's loyalty. I sigh. "All I'm saying is he's big time."

"So is Colt Cohen."

"That's different."

"How?"

"It just is," I say. "Colt's backdrop fame. Malachi's spotlight stardom."

Kendra clucks her tongue, never one to back down. I can practically see her shaking her head. "All I'm saying is that if Colt has seen your videos, then maybe the *Spellcaster* coaches have too. You're always hashtagging the show and bringing extra publicity to their competition. Cam, back me up here."

"Your sister's right," Cameron says. "Their show is popular because of super fans like you."

"I guess," I hedge, "but that doesn't change the fact that Malachi Rayne doesn't know I exist and never will."

At least not until I make it onto the show.

CHAPTER TWO

WHEN I STEP outside early Monday morning, a damp late-November chill fills my lungs. There is tranquility in the ten minutes I wait for my school bus to bustle down the street. This is the calm before the social storm that is Brookdale High.

The lawns lining the two-story homes in our Virginia neighborhood have turned into the Everglades, and the sidewalk is wet, but it's not raining at the moment. My maroon-and-black trench coat looks as cute as a dress attired over a pair of my favorite comfort plus-sized bootcut pants for women with curves. The material is stretchy but looks like dress-up slacks with a faux front fly with no zipper. I have them in five colors. Today, I'm wearing a pair in black that matches my sleek faux leather tote bag. Phone in hand, I join the three other students waiting near the curb. We keep our heads down, eyes scanning our screens. I'm not sure when we stopped saying "hello" or "good morning" or making any kind of eye contact, but I'm all for early morning quiet time.

Socialite Phoenix Starr is all over the headlines again, along with photos of her latest scandal. The gorgeous redhead flashes a saucy grin for the cameras at one of her father's fancy charity events. The bigwigs in the background are all dressed to the nines. Phoenix Starr is not. The twenty-eight-year-old is wearing a long shimmery red see-through gown with empty blood bags instead of a bra, and a gold, glittered straw sticks out between her cleavage.

"You're crazy, girl," I whisper in awe.

Phoenix has always been vocal about wanting to become a vampire and is one of the few humans with enough status, money, and power to be made if only her father would give his permission. He claims he never will, and he happens to be one of the few humans the vampires don't want to piss off.

This is the first time I've seen Phoenix portray herself as a vamp snack. It's no secret that her relationship with her father has deteriorated since he denied his only child her greatest desire to join Forever 23. Maybe this is a new attempt to push him to relent. F23 is no longer possible, but she's still young and beautiful. Wouldn't Alexander Starr rather his daughter become a high-class vampire than a blood sack? Along with the rest of the media, all I can do is speculate as to her motives.

I switch over to JingleJam to check for new followers (I'm up to 989,238) and look over the latest comments beneath my videos. Would Colt Cohen ever post a comment or emoji? Nah. Of course not, but it would be crazy cool if he did. My earbuds are stuffed snugly inside my ear canals, playing short bursts of music and narratives.

My best friend Payton has posted a new video. I don't know why I still call her "best" or even "friend." She stopped being either of those things sometime during summer break. Frenemy is more fitting. Her and Ellie. Mom told me that it's normal for friendships to dissolve during senior year of high school.

"You'll make true and lasting friendships in college," she assures me.

The text on Payton's new post reads: Does this lipstick make me look like a whore? #FashorTrash

I know I shouldn't do it, but I watch Payton's video.

@BrunetteBeautyQwn

"What up, babes? Ready to start a new school week?" She pouts at the camera. "Me neither, but at least it's only three days until Thanksgiving break. Oh my gawd, I am sooo tired after a crazy weekend. I had to wake up an extra ten minutes early to apply foundation. I'm not going to school with blotchy skin and bags under my eyes like some rundown old hag. Gross! As you can see, my base layer is smooth and slightly bronzed." She turns her head from side to side and fluffs her long, shiny brown hair around her face. "So, I've got my hair, face, cheeks, brows, and eyes done. All that's left are lips. I thought I would try Spark's lip stain in BITE BACK." She holds the square-shaped cosmetic and wrinkles her nose. "Oh my gawd, that is like really red. Like really in your face stop sign, red light, breakout pimple red. But let's give it a try and see if it's less obnoxious once it's applied." Payton unscrews the top, sniffs, and wrinkles her nose. "Well, it certainly doesn't smell good." She coats her lips in the bold shade and barely glances at her mouth before flipping out in an overly rehearsed display of disgust. "Oh, hell no! This color makes me look like a hooker. Oh, wow, it's actually even worse on." She smacks her lips and winces. "And what is that aftertaste? It's like sweaty gym socks stuffed with old cheese. Ew! Babes, this is trash, not fash."

And she wonders why beauty brands don't reach out offering her samples and sponsorship. Not to mention this feels like an indirect slam aimed at me. She's always been jealous that companies send me their new beauty lines to review before they're released to the public, but this is next-level nastiness.

I squeeze my phone, my nostrils flaring.

@fabbab Total trash!

@pur_t_gurl My slutty cousin would love that color.

@thatgirl19 no no NO!

Payton's savage group of followers parrot her animosity in comments.

I'm almost certain MC1010 is one of her followers and found me through Payton, but I don't spot her as I scan the comments. I stopped commenting on Payton's videos sometime over summer break, and she quickly returned the favor. I'm tempted daily to unfollow her. In the end, I don't think it's worth the repercussions. Not when we have only one more full semester of high school left together.

On screen, Payton blots her lips hastily, tossing tissue after tissue with a flick of her pastel purple nails. "Oh my gawd, you guys. I'm going to be late for school, but better late than showing up looking all skank. I usually like Spark cosmetics, but this shade gets a big, red N-O from this brunette beauty queen."

The video ends. Heat flares through me. I can practically feel it steaming off the top of my head. My finger shakes as it hovers above *Unfollow @BrunetteBeautyQwn*. I want to do it. I want to so bad. The skin tightens around my eyes and sweat drips down my sides. I feel like I'm about to cut the wrong wire on a ticking time bomb that will blow up in my face.

I'm not ready to take the risk.

I release a harsh breath, close JingleJam, and lift my head, clutching my phone, which is like having a portable security blanket that fits in the palm of my hand.

The bus grumbles from down the street. Brakes squeal as the bus stops in front of us, and students shuffle in with their eyes glued to their screens. I take in one last deep breath of cool Virginia air before boarding the school bus. It smells like a locker room on wheels. A tempest of body lotion, hair spray, perfume, deodorant, wet hair, and BO. After taking my seat along the right near the middle-front, I pull back the sleeve of my trench coat and the sweater beneath, bring my wrist to my nose, and inhale the comforting scent of vanilla, cocoa, and musk. BlossUm's limited edition holiday scent is holding up to its claim of a cozy, decadent aroma. It's not enough to bliss out on a bus, but it reminds me of nicer things.

I reopen JingleJam and find a fresh stream of comments coming in this morning. My beauty brigade is the best. They remind me of what real support looks like.

If only I could weed Payton from my life right now, but it's too late to make new friends. Cliques were established freshman year. Scratch that. They transferred over from middle school, and probably elementary. I'm the interloper who came along freshman year after we moved across town to my aunt Chloe's district for Mom to support her younger sister through a rocky marriage my aunt can't seem to shake.

I could have attended Dalbury Academy from either district—with a private car and driver to chauffeur me to and from school—but Dad says Dalbury is an incubator for narcissistic grandeur. He says it cuts privileged kids off from the real world and what it means to be a full-fledged, caring member of society.

Maybe he was afraid of Kendra and me meeting our future husbands at Dalbury. It's where Dad met his ex-wife, Cressida Angelise Beckwith, before falling for Mom and discovering his true calling. I've never actually met Cressida. That was a long time ago, and our families move in entirely different circles. I have seen her online, though not as much since her modeling heydays or since her second husband, pro football player werewolf Jael Doren, suffered a concussion forcing him to retire early.

Unlike Phoenix Starr, I'm okay with my dad's desire to keep my sister and me grounded. I'm proud of what I've accomplished through my own hard work. I prefer connecting with real people online—not a bunch of privileged pricks. Then again, there is no shortage of pricks no matter where you go.

Caleb Lawrence is the worst prick of all. He lives in the neighborhood behind our high school, and I swear he arrives early just so he can heckle students as they stream in from the double doors leading from the bus lane into Brookdale.

Like every morning, he's leaning against his locker, picking food out of his teeth with his fingernail and then flicking it into the hallway as he surveys the influx of students. His best friend, Lewis, stands half a head shorter at his side, scratching at his nose. Acne dots Caleb's chin, and his overuse of hair gel makes his muddy strands look greasy.

He's always there in the corner of my eye as I arrive, like a retinal detachment casting a dark curtain along his side of the hall. The jackal jeers as I walk past him, eyes fastened to my chest.

"Damn, Haylee. Your hips look bigger than last week. Did you spend your entire weekend eating cookie dough straight from the tube again?"

I lift my chin higher and keep walking.

Caleb peels himself off his locker to follow me. "Haylee. Hey, Haylee. Hey! Hey!" Caleb's friend Lewis erupts into laughter, but I detect something dark in Caleb's undertone. He hates being ignored. It's like he turns into a cyclone when he jogs ahead to try and block my path. That oily gaze of his goes straight for my chest again.

I zip right around him and barrel over to my locker, happy—for once—to see Payton there running a brush through her already silken hair as she stares into the small mirror affixed to the inner door of her locker.

Caleb's sneakers squeak on the linoleum floor as he storms over with a cruel curve of his upper lip.

"Get lost," I snap, as he opens his mouth to speak.

Caleb's face turns as red as his pimples. "You think you're all that, but you're nothing more than a fatty in fancy clothes and makeup. Try not to eat the entire turkey this Thursday."

I glower. Could Caleb be MC1010? Somehow, I doubt he would make it through beauty tutorials long enough to pester me.

Payton surprises me when she stops brushing her hair to wrinkle her nose and wave her hand in front of her face. "Ew, what is that disgusting smell of moldy pizza? Oh, it's Caleb. You should try using soap when you shower and a toothbrush more than once a month."

"Shut up, Payton," Caleb sneers. "You're a whiny little wannabe Botox bitch."

My fingers twitch. "You're lucky wands aren't allowed at school," I hiss at him.

They're considered weapons by some institutes. Never mind that witches and wizards can do magic without the use of a wand. Supernaturals have their own schools. All we get are zombies. One per grade after the latest law to prevent hording. My sister says it's more political propaganda meant to further isolate a minority group. Zombie hordes are no joke, though. They'll attack and tear a human apart with their teeth. But thanks to modern magic, getting bitten by a zombie is no longer a death sentence by insanity. We're taught safeguard spells in Beginners Spellcasting in elementary school for a variety of unlikely situations. It's not all that helpful, seeing as fake wands are used to practice the spells in class, though it does give teachers an indication of which students have an aptitude for casting. Those who appear to have a knack for it go on to take Intermediate and Advanced Spellcasting. Schools with bigger budgets have loaner wands for in-class use only. The emergency stuff isn't as fun. It's more like first aid and CPR. I should really practice these spells every year, just in case, but I always put it off.

Payton pulls out a pink bottle of body mist and pumps it at Caleb. He jumps back with a curse. For one glorious moment, it's like the good old days when Payton and I were united. It feels like a warm hug that's over too quickly.

"Witch wannabe," Caleb snarls at me as he retreats.

I open my locker, hang my trench coat from the hook inside, and organize books and binders for my upcoming classes into my tote. Malachi Rayne flashes a reassuring grin at me from the picture sticking to the inside of my locker door in a magnetic photo frame. It's a black-and-white shot of him slouching in a black leather chair, wearing dark jeans with his legs spread, a white T-shirt, a wand loose in his fingers resting against his thigh, and an impish gaze. Oh, Malachi, if only there were more men like you. Shockingly, he's single at the moment. The tabloids have been after him all year about whether he's dating anyone or has plans to move on from his last breakup with Charliese Darlington, another F23 vampire. Before closing my locker, I take in his smile one final time.

Payton continues spritzing herself with a heavy finger on the pump. The fruity scent of her mist makes my head ache. I take a step away. She pauses, bottle suspended by her neck, and a pout on her pink—not "hooker red"—lips. "What?" she demands.

"Nothing. I don't want to get caught in the mist."

Payton narrows her eyes. "You got a problem with my scent?"

"Of course not. I just don't want it masking my perfume."

Payton rolls her eyes. "Oh, your superior *perfume*."

"That's not what I'm saying." Now I really do have a headache. It's way too early in the morning for this crap.

I think we're both relieved when Ellie shows up. Her bus is one of the last to arrive, which has her jogging up to us, auburn ponytail swinging, before she peels off her navy backpack. "Hey, gals," she says breathlessly as she spins her locker combo. "Everything good?" Her gaze darts between us before she unzips her backpack and stuffs books inside her messy locker.

Payton huffs. "It was until Creepy Caleb followed Haylee over. You just missed him. He's like obsessed with Haylee." She wrinkles her nose. "So gross."

"He's not obsessed with me," I say in horror. "He heckles everyone. That's what loser bullies do."

Payton looks me over, a vicious smile stretching across her lips. She sprays herself again before setting her mist inside an acrylic makeup caddy on the top shelf of her locker. "He would totally go out with you if you let him."

"Ew!" Ellie and I cry at the same time.

Payton makes duck lips and shrugs.

"I'm seriously going to be sick." My stomach is roiling and everything.

"Me too," Ellie says, clutching her middle for emphasis.

The warning bell rings. Payton and Ellie hurry to close their lockers and scurry away with a "See you later." It hasn't helped our trio that those two have three periods together, and I don't share any classes with either of them this semester.

I take off in the direction of my first-period psychology class.

Usually, I sit in the middle of the classroom, but today, I take a front row seat to get as far away from Caleb as possible. He and Lewis stink up the back row. And that is how I have to start every school day this semester. Unfortunately, I will still have psychology first period second semester with those two jokers after Christmas break.

Something hits my back. I turn around and glare at Caleb, who chuckles. "I thought you might be hungry since it's been almost an hour since breakfast."

I flip him off before facing the front again. I don't have to look at the ground to know he's pelted me with a piece of candy. The cretin does not have an original bone in his gangling body. Miss Grady walks in and not a moment too soon.

As soon as first period ends, I hurry out of class and check my JingleJam account.

989,255 Followers

That brings a smile to my lips as I collide with another body. With the morning I'm having, is it any wonder it's a zombie?

CHAPTER THREE

MY HEAD JERKS up as Rosie Clemons, Brookdale's freshman zombie, flies backward and falls to the ground. She is a petite, skinny girl with wide, puppy-dog eyes that always appear to be begging for love.

"I'm so sorry!" Crap. I should reach out my hand to help her up, but I really don't want to touch her. I don't want to appear mean, either. Hopefully, she knows this was an accident.

"That's okay. I'm fine," Rosie assures me with a sheepish smile.

Loud applause explodes near my ears. Caleb claps. "Five points for Haylee for taking down a zombie before second period." He whistles and claps harder. Students slow as they pass, some stopping to see what's going on.

"I didn't do that on purpose," I snap at him.

Rosie scrambles to her feet and grabs her pastel and cloud print backpack off the ground.

"Did I give you permission to get back up?" Caleb sneers cruelly before shoving Rosie to the floor. A couple of seniors on the basketball team snicker as they pass.

There are no tears in Rosie's eyes. I've never seen a zombie cry; maybe they're incapable of producing tears. But the hurt look on her face makes my chest tighten. Rosie makes no move to get back up, like a puppy who has been kicked and doesn't know what to do next.

"Don't listen to him," I tell her, but she stays where she is.

"Zombie corpse knows her place," Caleb says. I want to slap the smug grin off his face, but that would involve touching him, which is more grotesque than touching a zombie. Nothing against zombies. It's just a phobia, like touching a snake. I've heard their skin feels cold and squishy, like it's about to rot off their bones.

Zombies don't have the awesome healing powers of vampires. They have to eat brains regularly in order to avoid turning into decomposing body sacks. The school cafeteria provides animal brains through a government-run program that also oversees the regular human food—which doesn't look or smell any better than the brains.

I stick my phone in my tote and clench the straps, one boot tapping anxiously on the hard, lacquered hall flooring. Rosie isn't moving, and neither is Caleb, though Lewis has disappeared. I can't leave her like this. I'm the one who bumped into her.

"Don't you need to get to second period?" I snap at Caleb.

"Don't you?" he challenges. "Go ahead, Haylee. I'll make sure the carcass doesn't get back up."

I no longer see Rosie's sad eyes. I see Kendra's disappointment. What am I supposed to do? Tackle Caleb? I'm not into violence or physical fighting. Instead, I pick up Rosie's backpack like that will get her to stand. It doesn't.

"What the hell is this?" Georgia Keller demands as students scurry by to get to second period. She bounds over, short, dark curls whipping against sharp cheekbones on flawless, fair skin. Her dark brown eyes glare from a thin outline of black eyeliner, and her lips purse. Somehow the pale pink shade she wears works on her, accenting the firm line between her lips. The loose metal buckle on her black moto jacket swings above her gray jeans before stopping when she plants herself in front of Caleb.

Most lucid zombies are timid. Georgia is the exception. When someone annoys her, she looks at them like she wants to bash their head in with a baseball bat and then eat their brains straight from their skull. She's Brookdale's junior zombie.

"You killed Myles, and now you're going after Rosie," Georgia shouts for everyone in the hall to hear.

Caleb grimaces. "You're crazy," he hisses.

I gape. Myles Castillo is our senior year zombie. He went missing a few weeks ago—not that anyone's concerned. Myles wouldn't be the first zombie to drop out of high school. It never occurred to me that something might have happened to him. I look at Caleb and shudder. Is he capable of murder? Can offing someone who is undead be considered murder? The law is a bit gray when it comes to zombies.

Georgia sneers at him. "You're such a pansy you have to go after a freshman girl. That makes you feel like a big man, huh?"

Caleb folds his arms. "I didn't push her. Haylee did."

Georgia's gaze snaps to me, and a tremble runs down my legs.

"It was an accident," I say.

"Sure, it was," she says in disgust. The dark curls in her short hair seem to shake in disbelief.

"It was! I was staring at my phone when I collided with her."

Georgia gets up in my face. I wince. It's all I can do to hold my ground. Her dark eyes bore into mine. I doubt she would try to bite me. It would mean her immediate extermination but having a zombie this close sets off all of my fight-or-flight alarms.

Georgia raises a dark brow and leans back slightly. "Best watch where you're going from now on." She chomps her teeth, and I gasp before I can stop myself. Georgia smirks but doesn't laugh. She backs away, eyes not leaving mine. When she reaches Rosie's side, she orders her to get up.

Rosie hurries to obey. Once the freshman is on her feet, Georgia yanks the pastel backpack from my fingers and shoves it at Rosie.

"Thanks," Rosie squeaks.

"Get to class, and steer clear of these two," Georgia commands, keeping Caleb and me locked in her gaze.

"It was an accident," I repeat.

Georgia huffs. "If you say so."

What the hell? Does she know who my sister is? I'm the last person who would push a zombie down for the fun of it.

Rosie hurries off as the warning bell rattles the metal lockers lining the hallway. Georgia pivots and takes off, curls bouncing against her head like they're egging her on.

"I'd wash my hands if I were you." Caleb juts his pimpled chin at my hands. "You touched the maggot's backpack."

I narrow my eyes before beelining down the hall for second period Spanish, hating that I do feel like washing my hands. There's a small bottle of hand sanitizer inside my bag, but I wait until I reach Spanish—as the final bell echoes—to pull the bottle out and squeeze some of the liquid onto my palms.

I don't see Payton and Ellie again until lunch at our table near the windows. They have fourth period together near the cafeteria, which is why Payton decided a couple of weeks into the new school year that rather than wait for me at our lockers, they should get us a table. That part was fine. But soon they were eating before I arrived with my pink-and-orange plaid Kate Spade lunch tote. Whatever. At least I have company while I eat and share my news about Colt.

Payton pulls out a tube of shimmery pink Lola & Lizzy lip gloss and points it at me like it's a finger. "You know that wasn't really Colt Cohen, right?"

I set the last quarter of my ham and cheese sandwich down and frown. "What do you mean?"

"It's one of his PAs, obviously. Colt's like your dad's age. Do you really think he spends his time scrolling through JingleJam? The wolf probably has an entire marketing team to handle such trivial activities."

My sandwich turns to sawdust inside the blender that is my stomach. All of the hurt and anger steaming inside my head feels like it's stamped across my face in red ink, but Payton doesn't look at me. She unscrews the white top on her lip gloss. After running the gooey pink tip over her lips, she smacks her mouth and turns to Ellie. "Do my lips look fuller than they did last week?"

My jaw loosens. Since when does she ask Ellie for beauty insights? Ellie's idea of makeup is a tube of cherry soda–flavored Lip Smackers. Payton and I used to tease her about it all the time.

Ellie fiddles with the end of her ponytail and offers a sweet smile. "Your lips look great."

Payton pulls a compact mirror from her purse and holds it up to her lips. "I guess this plumper really works. I'll do a video about it during holiday break."

I could be a Moluccan cockatoo and talk about how I will be doing my one million follower giveaway post, but I decide to be the bigger person. It's not as though Payton and Ellie aren't aware of my upcoming milestone, though they never bring it up, as if it's an awkward situation—like an unplanned pregnancy or STD. What would it be like to have friends who were happy for me?

"Is your whole family getting together for Thanksgiving?" Ellie asks me.

Small talk it is. Lately, it feels like the only option short of becoming a loner senior year.

"Yeah, I might need a Xanax," I force myself to joke. My immediate family is the best. It's my Uncle TJ who's the loser and Uncle Alvan who butts heads with my mom. My little cousin Joni is nice, but it's hard to get anything done when she comes over.

Payton snorts.

"You must be so excited to see your sister, though," Ellie says.

She has no idea.

Payton picks up her phone from the table, a smug smile appearing over her lips as she stares at the screen. Ellie lifts her own phone and begins swiping with her finger.

Conversation over. Fine by me.

I grab my phone and open JingleJam.

989,601 Followers

I grin and sit up taller.

"Oh, gross." Payton gasps before holding her screen out to Ellie.

"Ew. Why did you show me that after I just ate?" Ellie groans.

Payton laughs and pulls her phone back without looking at me. I'm not about to take the bait. College can't come soon enough. I wish Kendra and I could have one year together. She'll be on her way out when I'm on my way in at Blakely. I'm not going to miss Brookdale. That's for sure. As I look over the students clustered at square tables in the cafeteria, my gaze passes over Georgia standing in line for food, one hand on her hip.

I should leave it alone, but I can't help myself.

"I'll be right back," I say.

Payton keeps her attention on her phone and doesn't answer.

"Okay," Ellie says.

I clutch my phone but leave my plaid lunch tote and last piece of my sandwich on the table. Once on my feet, I breeze past tables and walk straight up to Georgia, who is now first in line, waiting for her lunch tray. Brookdale's lunch ladies work from behind counters with a small window to slide food trays through. There are five counters, and you can't see through to the kitchen and mystery food beyond. I'd rather starve than eat the school's lunch slop.

"Hey," I say, stopping a good few feet away from Georgia.

Lunch hour is more than half over, and the lines have mostly emptied.

Georgia turns and slouches against the counter, looking me up and down. "Yeah?" she challenges.

"Like I said before, I didn't push Rosie down."

Georgia rolls her eyes. "I heard you the first time. What do you want—an award for not pushing a zombie?"

I scowl. "No. I want you to know that I would never do that."

"Okay. Sure." Georgia shrugs one shoulder and faces the counter again. "What's going on back there, Agnus? You better not be spitting on my brains unless you want me to get a taste of you."

"My big sister advocates on behalf of zombies, you know," I say.

Georgia shakes her curls. "Your sister. Good for her," she says sarcastically before slamming her fist on the counter. "Agnus!"

A stout middle-aged woman in a hair net appears on the other side of the window. She sets a yellow plastic tray down with a *clack*, giving Georgia the stink eye. My stomach turns at the sight of the brain sitting on a paper plate. It's got light pink ridges and a grotesque sheen with bright red jagged lines filling the crevices. I lift my hands to my mouth and make a gagging sound.

Georgia's attention is on her tray as she carries it to the nearest table where two freshmen are seated. The moment Georgia sets down her meal, the freshmen get up and hurry to leave while Georgia digs in with her bare hands, pulling apart brain matter and stuffing it into her mouth.

Disgusting!

I turn away so quickly I nearly give myself whiplash. Clutching my roiling stomach, I storm off while trying to erase the image from my mind. I lift my wrist directly to my nose and inhale deeply. I make it back to the table and stop short when I notice my friends are gone—as is my Kate Spade lunch tote.

I group text Payton and Ellie.

Haylee: Where did you guys go?

Payton: Bathroom.

Haylee: Do you have my lunch tote?

Payton: No.

Haylee: So you left my stuff?

Payton: You're the one who took off.

Ellie: Oh, no. Is it missing?

When I don't respond, Ellie sends me a direct text.

Ellie: I'm sorry, Haylee. I can't believe someone would take your tote while you were right there in the room.

Well, believe it, false friend. I close her text, sit down with a huff, and check JingleJam. There are no new followers since the last time I checked. I jump over to Telepatch and check out the latest #SpellcasterSeason12 posts. The network has posted a photo with the four coaches posing around their purple velvet high-backed chairs.

@UTVSpellcaster If you received a 4-wand lift, which Coach would you pick? 🪄🪄🪄🪄 #Spellcaster

@HeyHeyHaylee Team Malachi 4ever

I get up and head out of the cafeteria. As I pass through the student center on my way to my locker, Colleen Hansen bounds over with my Kate Spade tote in hand.

"Hey, I saw your tote was left at a table and grabbed it for you."

"Thanks," I say with a grateful smile.

"It's cute. I figured you'd want it back." Colleen smiles with crooked teeth. Her periwinkle collared sweater looks like something her grandmother passed down. "By the way, congratulations on reaching a million followers on JingleJam."

"I'm not quite there but thank you."

"I'll be trying for the Lignum Vitae wand."

I look at Colleen closer. "Do you like magic?"

"I love magic!" Colleen gushes. "I don't know if I'm any good at it, but I would love to try."

"Well, good luck, and thanks again for returning my tote."

Colleen smiles and nods before joining her group of band friends. I stand watching them for a moment as they tease one another and laugh. No one is on their phone or making pouty faces. I take a step toward them like all I have to do is go over, and I'll have a new group of genuine friends. A cold sweat comes over me, and I sway on my feet. I can already see their smiles turning into confusion—can feel the burn of humiliation before it happens. They may be nice, but the band group is another clique that's been together since grade school. Also, I don't play an instrument.

I'm stuck with Payton and Ellie, which makes me laugh because it's the other way around. They're stuck with me, and I'm ashamed of how terrified I am that they'll cut me out altogether before graduation.

I don't know how I would get through high school alone.

CHAPTER FOUR

@HeyHeyHaylee is LIVE on JingleJam
998,993 Followers

"HEY, HEY, HELLO, beauties. It's Haylee. My account is almost one thousand away from one million followers. I want to thank all of you beauties for your amazing support, and welcome our newest members to the beauty brigade! My one million followers grand prize giveaway is now posted to my account. If you haven't already seen it, make sure to enter for a chance to win your very own Lignum Vitae wand. That's not all. Spark, BlossUm, Color Case, and Diversions have put together beauty bundles for me to gift in celebration of this milestone. Make sure to check my account this week and next for chances to win one of these amazing beauty hauls filled with products from some of my favorite brands. I will be announcing winners for the beauty bundles within a week of posting, and the grand prize wand winner before Christmas. Just in time to add an extra touch of magic to one lucky winner's holiday. Until next time, be bold, be beautiful, and always be yourself."

I sign off, heart racing with excitement. My room looks like Christmas morning with tissue paper spewing from open boxes on my floor and bed. Colorful bottles, tins, compacts, brush sets, nail polish, creams, powders, hair clips, and more fill the boxes and padded envelopes. I've kept our mailman busy with the mountains of packages flooding in from companies sending me their holiday kits, scents, shades, and gifts to review on JingleJam. Forget homework. I have so many products to test and videos to make that there is little time for anything else. Usually, I organize my review posts by the order in which I received the items, but right now, everything is pretty much arriving in an avalanche all at once. Luckily, my mom understands I won't be able to help out in the kitchen with our Thanksgiving meal. She could hire someone to prepare a feast for the whole family, but when it comes to holidays, Mom is old-school hands-on nostalgic.

"Hey, Sis."

I turn around and shriek, "Kendra!"

My sister's grin lights up the room. She's got a healthy tan and natural bronze highlights from the California sun. A long blue-and-white scarf is tied loosely around her neck, draped casually over a fitted long-sleeved white tee. Layers of auburn hair frame the scarf. Kendra doesn't need to wear makeup. She's naturally pretty with an inner glow that highlights her cheeks.

I throw my arms around her, and we hug tightly. "I didn't think I'd see you until tomorrow."

Kendra chuckles and continues hugging me. "I finished all of my essays and exams and caught an earlier flight. You never know when the airlines will cancel, and I absolutely had to come back this Thanksgiving to celebrate Dad's big win in person. Well, that and your upcoming one-million milestone. Our family is unstoppable."

"I'm so happy you came early." I squeal and squeeze her tighter.

"Me, too, though Cameron was bummed out that he had to stay behind. His grandmother's health hasn't been too great. This could be her last Thanksgiving." Kendra pulls away and gives a sad shake of her head.

I force myself not to roll my eyes. "Cam's cool and all, but pretty soon he'll get to spend the rest of his life with you. I think he can survive four days without you."

"Five with the earlier flight," Kendra corrects. This time, I do roll my eyes. My sister flashes me one of her knowing smiles. "One day you'll meet someone who will make the hours apart feel like days, and days like weeks."

I scoff because I never see that happening. Not for me. I don't have a magnetic personality like my mom and sister, who each found great men to idolize them without even trying. Dad and Cameron are the best of the best and totally, one hundred percent devoted to these strong women. No guy has ever flirted with me, let alone asked me out.

Kendra looks around my room, still grinning. "I guess it's a good thing I didn't get you makeup for Christmas."

"You already have my gift?"

"Cameron and I picked it out together. Custom-made." Kendra's straight teeth line up into a beautiful smile.

Now I'm curious and excited, but I'll have to wait until Christmas to see what it is. Also, I need to find something extra cool for Kendra.

My sister looks around my room and whistles. "Is all this for you to review?"

"Yeah. I mean, it's the most I've ever received at one time. Holiday season." I shrug.

"That and your nearly one million followers. I'm so proud of you." Kendra beams.

"Aw, thanks, Sis." I mean, I'm not saving the world or whatever with lip gloss, but I'm trying to make it a little brighter. "Do you want to watch *Spellcaster* with me? It starts in"—I check my phone—"nine minutes."

"You go ahead. I'm going to catch up with Mom and Dad." Kendra squeezes my arm and gives me another smile before walking out of my room.

I commandeer the living room as the *Spellcaster* lives begin broadcasting. With the holiday weekend, they moved Friday's results night to Tuesday for Enchantment Week. I've been voting for Gianna Woods ever since she turned the stage into a magical garden of blooming flowers, butterflies, and a rainbow that spread across the audience during her blind audition. Cleo Killian and Zen Renko raised their wands for her from behind the judges' screen that makes contestants appear as gender-neutral silhouettes. The shadow figure puts all contestants on equal footing, making the contest all about the magical talent. The judges don't have a clue as to the performer's appearance, gender, or age until the screen is lifted at the end of the performance. Same goes for the live audience, but television viewers have an unobstructed view of the performer's audition from the start. The *Spellcaster* hopeful must get at least one of the coaches to lift his or her wand before they finish their act.

Gianna Woods surprised me by choosing Zen as her coach. Not only is he old, but he's human and about as flavorful as petroleum jelly. But I have read that Zen is helpful when it comes to getting his team members magical gigs and opportunities after their time on the show. Only one contestant can win immortality, along with the one-hundred-thousand-dollar grand prize and one-year world tour contract each season. Having other doors open is not a bad outcome for a runner-up.

The *Spellcaster* theme music starts over a dark screen as the show's symbol lights up in purple and glowing white. It's a circle inscribed with a star, a keyhole over the top point. Symbols rim the curving outline. They look like ancient hieroglyphics, but they are actually the alphabet of wand motions that form the basis of all spells.

The camera zooms in on Colt Cohen and his magnetic smile. Colt is a tall, lean Black man who always appears laid back while classy in a black suit standing in front of the stage while the live audience screams in excitement.

Hey, buddy, I think with a smile. Even if it was Colt's PA who liked my post, it's still really cool to be noticed by someone from his official account.

"Good evening, everyone, and welcome to results night of Enchantment Week. We have an exciting show for you with guest performances by Itrix Onyll, the Apostles, and our very own Tyler Shaw, winner of Season 6. But first, please welcome our Season 12 coaches: Wand Hall of Famer and Forever 23 socialite, Malachi Rayne; CEO of LVW Inc. and sorcery sensation, Cleo Killian; twenty-time Wand Master champion, Zen Renko; and our favorite werewolf whose new world tour, *Howl-ology*, is already sold out, Brody Morgan."

More screams erupt. A woman yells, "I love you, Brody!" Another shouts, "Bite me, Malachi!" "And me!" another voice booms.

Colt Cohen chuckles. "We have a frisky audience tonight. And now, please welcome our remaining ten casters to the stage, where I will announce the first two advancing to next week."

The audience applauds as the contestants take to the stage. Gianna Woods is dolled up with shimmering silver eyeshadow and a billowy white blouse cinched with a thick white glittered belt over white jeans. I totally cried over her audition story. Gianna dropped out of high school in Kentucky to work three jobs and help feed her family after her mother died of breast cancer. She grew up playing with sticks, pretending they were magic wands, and practicing runes in what little free time she had even though she didn't have the means to execute the magic. For her sixteenth birthday, some of Gianna's former teachers surprised her with a Lignum Vitae wand so she could audition for *Spellcaster*. After she dropped out of school, her teachers spent nearly two years raising funds to buy Gianna her wand. My eyes mist every time I consider that level of support and belief in someone, and the hardships Gianna endured before making it on *Spellcaster*. I am super privileged in a world where most humans aren't.

Gianna Woods is not among the first two casters Colt announces that are advancing to next week, but I'm not worried. She blew the roof off the stage with her *Through the Looking Glass* performance the night before.

Guest performer Itrix Onyll takes the stage. I was lucky enough to see him live in New York two summers ago. Itrix is an incredibly gifted animator. He's a thirty-something-year-old human with mad talent. Tonight, he strides onto the stage in a navy pointed wizard's hat printed with golden stars. Itrix steps onto a stool and lifts his wand as though he is the conductor of an orchestra. Music from Fantasia begins.

Oh, fun," I say, and stand with my wand in hand.

Itrix brings his props to life, making brooms, buckets, mops, and rags move about the stage. I flick and swirl my wand and animate the coffee table's legs to walk in a small circle in the middle of the living room. "*Lavitamay*," I cast at the window curtains to get them swaying with the music. I aim my wand at the tall floor lamp. "*Lifteena, elona veed!*" The metal base splits into two short legs that send the lamp walking across the room. I'm rocking the animation thing, if I do say so myself.

I grab my phone and record my living room coming to life with Itrix performing on TV in the background. At the commercial break, I direct everything back into place with my wand and then post my video on JingleJam.

@HeyHeyHaylee Performing with **@ItrixOnyll** live from my living room. 🪄 😉 👏 #SpellcasterLives #SpellcasterSeason12

Spellcaster returns, the remaining nine casters filling the screen.

"From Team Malachi . . ." Colt pauses and lets the music build tension. The camera cuts from the two remaining members of Team Malachi to their coach, who leans forward in his purple velvet chair. Malachi's hair is swept up nearly two inches above his head, dyed red, yellow, and orange. It looks like flames and is seriously badass. He's wearing a fitted suit over a white V-neck that outlines his toned chest. A black woven bracelet circles his wrist. My heart beats a little faster.

"Devon Torres," Colt announces.

The twenty-two-year-old from Chicago lifts his wand in the air triumphantly before swaggering off stage. Malachi gets out of his chair to clap Devon on the back as he heads backstage. Devon has been vocal from the beginning about his dream to win *Spellcaster* and be made when he turns twenty-three so that he can join Forever 23. Even if he wins, which I hope he doesn't because Gianna deserves it more, it's not a golden ticket into F23. They're super selective. I highly doubt that winning *Spellcaster* is enough for them to allow Devon, or anyone else for that matter, into their exclusive club. The reason I'm not a fan of Devon is because he treats spellcasting like it's his way to becoming made. I don't think he loves magic enough. Like, if he wins, I could see him putting his wand aside to vamp out. He didn't grow up clutching a twig in his hand, pretending it was a real wand. That's real passion. But Devon's good looks and unwavering confidence have gone over well with thousands of voters. Also, his dad is some big theater director who hired a publicist to post incessantly, reminding fans to vote for Devon.

"The next caster to move on, from Team Zen," Colt announces, "is Gianna Woods."

"Yes!" I lift my hand above my head. At least my girl Gianna is advancing. I mean, it would be crazy for her not to go on, but you never know. There's one more week until the semifinals. I'll be all over it. #VoteGiannaWoods

After the show ends, I scroll through *Spellcaster* posts on Telepatch, finding one of Gianna grinning backstage, wand cradled in the palm of her hand.

@Gianna_Woods Thank you for voting me through to another week! #Thankful #Grateful #Blessed #SpellcasterSeason12 #TeamZen #ILoveMagic

@HeyHeyHaylee Congratulations! Your casting is out of this world. I can't wait to see what you do next week!

I lose track of time scrolling through Telepatch and then JingleJam, where my following has jumped to 999,200. I'm off the couch doing a shimmy, phone in one hand, wand in the other.

"Only eight hundred more follows to go," I announce.

"What's that, hon?" Mom calls from the kitchen.

I dash in to join her and Kendra. Mom is stretching plastic wrap over a casserole dish filled with corn pudding while my sister saws bread into slices, which she then cubes, tossing them into a bowl.

"I'm up to 999,200 followers!"

"That's incredible," Mom says.

"It really is," Kendra agrees. "You've made a voice for yourself. Imagine if you used your powers for good," she adds in a teasing tone.

"That's exactly what I'm doing. A well-coiffed head of hair, touch of makeup, and spritz of perfume does wonders for a woman's confidence." I pat the loose curls on the right side of my face.

"You always look beautiful," Mom says, "but I admire your entrepreneurial spirit. You'll go far in life with that kind of hard work and talent."

I set my phone and wand on the counter and aim beseeching eyes at my mother, palms pressed together. "Speaking of which, can I skip school tomorrow? It's only one day, and I don't have any tests or homework to turn in. Everyone just goofs off waiting for break to start. Even the teachers don't bother trying to teach. Please?"

Mom sighs. "I suppose it wouldn't hurt for you to miss one day."

"Thank you," I squeal, giving her a quick hug before scooping my phone and wand off the counter.

"Does this mean you'll help me and your sister with meal prep?"

"Mom," I gasp. "I have hundreds of products to review."

"You can't be posting during school hours," Mom says.

"Of course not. I'll be recording videos and taking pictures to schedule later."

Kendra sets the knife down on the cutting board and nods. "Bread is cubed and ready to dry out for the stuffing."

"Thanks, sweetie," Mom says.

"Well, looks like you have everything under control." I dart out of the kitchen and run upstairs to my room to select some products to try out while discussing *Spellcaster* results on JingleJam.

When I'm finished, I check Malachi Rayne's Telepatch account, where he's posted a smiling selfie backstage with his two remaining teammates.

> **@MalachiRayneF23** #TeamMalachi is pure magic with **@DevonTorres** and **@AveryWalsh** lighting up the stage week after week.

For a moment, I imagine myself in a ballroom gown with Malachi's arm around me, a proud smile on his lips, and his caption, which reads: She crushed it again! **@HeyHeyHayley** there are no words to describe how much I enjoy having such a talented and beautiful caster on my team!

Yeah, total fantasy land.

Even if I got an audition, I would probably drop my wand before I completed my performance. Knowing that Malachi was watching—even not seeing me until the screen came down—would seriously mess with my head.

It's not as though I want the immortality prize, not unless it was a package deal that included my family. They would never go for it, so it's a moot point. Mom pretty much believes that a person loses their soul the moment they become a vampire. "Bloodsucking demons" is her more colorful term. Dad takes a more philosophical approach, calling it an unorthodox phenomenon that goes against the natural order of the world, cycle of life, biology, and so forth. Kendra agrees with Mom and Dad, but for some reason, zombies have a soft spot in her heart, which is kind of weird. I guess it's because they are what they are after being victimized. Their making isn't glamorous like a vampire's. It's a horror story.

I don't know how it happened for Rosie or Georgia, but I did hear the gory details of how it went down for Myles on a camping trip with his family. They were all attacked, and bitten, but were lucky enough to have a wand on hand and a mother gifted in casting. At least they have each other or used to before the hording laws got super strict. Is Myles even around anymore? Caleb is a lot of creepy awful things, but I never considered him a murderer.

I frown, recalling the diabolical gleam in Caleb's eyes when he told Rosie to stay on the ground. A jolt of anxiety spreads through me like a rock that's hit a windshield. It forms a crack of doubt that expands the more I think about it.

Zombies freak me out, but I don't wish any of the sane ones ill. Myles seemed like a nice guy. We had science together last year—before his family's unfortunate outing in the woods. I've never been into camping to begin with. Knowing that not all werewolves, vampires, and zombies have their urges under control makes me all the more opposed to nature trips.

My interest is in magic, which I can do just fine as a human.

You don't have to be made into a vampire if you win *Spellcaster*. The champion can take all of the glory and opportunities without giving up their humanity.

But no one who has won the show has ever turned down immortality so far.

I imagine myself winning it all at the end and then saying, "No, thanks. I'm fine the way I am."

I would, however, happily accept the cash prize and year-long contract to perform around the world. I'd put college on hold for a gig like that.

CHAPTER FIVE

@HeyHeyHaylee is LIVE on JingleJam
999,436 Followers

"HEY, HEY. HELLO, beauties. It's Haylee. If you're watching from America, happy Thanksgiving! In the spirit of the holiday, I have on Gratitude by Arbor Botanicals." I hold up the square glass bottle branded with a dragonfly silhouette inside a circle. "This blend of gardenias and jasmine is mesmerizing. Best of all, it is alcohol-free and non-toxic. There are no artificial synthetic scents or colors, only natural ingredients to remind us to bring more appreciation and gratitude into our lives with every breath we take." I lift my wrist and breathe in. "That is lovely and fresh. I can't tell you all enough how grateful I am to have you as treasured members of the beauty brigade. To express *my* gratitude, I am gifting this full-size bottle from Arbor Botanicals to one of you. For a chance to win, tell me what your holiday plans are. One random winner will be chosen by the end of the weekend."

@glitzeegirl17 working waaaaaa

@irishpam Spending it with parents.

@queentiff Have to work.

@jean_e_sw Home with family. Thanks for the chance.

@deissy_daisy Preparing a feast with my family.

@umbrella_k8 Preventing my younger siblings from killing each other. 😂

"Before I sign off to stuff my face with delicious Thanksgiving eats, I've selected five holiday must-haves to add some glitz and glam to your seasonal look." I am already dressed for company in a short burgundy dress with sheer long sleeves that glimmer with matching burgundy sequins. A velvet ribbon pulls the fabric taut below my bosom, beneath which a layer of sequined tulle descends, landing above my knees. I'm wearing skin-toned pantyhose and black Mary Janes, not that my viewers can see anything from my waist down, though they can see my gorgeous braided bun and rhinestone headband. The braid and bun are loose and wispy. I don't like things too tucked in or tight.

Family will be arriving within the next hour, which means I need to get this video finished quickly.

I go through the products I've lined up on my vanity, applying them one by one in front of my phone. "I call this look shimmer and shine. You want to start by keeping the eyes and lips soft to put the focus on your shimmering cheekbones. I'm using pinks and neutrals from Color Pop's First Flush shadow palette and Ravishing Raspberry from Spark on my lips." I sweep three colors of shadow over my lids and use my blending brush until I am satisfied with the outcome. Then I apply the glossy berry lip stain. "Mm, this gloss has a nice flavor. It's making me hungry for cranberry sauce," I joke. I apply eyeliner and mascara next before finishing the look with champagne gold shimmer, rubbing a generous amount onto my cheeks. When I'm finished, I grin at my reflection in the phone. "Now I'm ready to celebrate. Thanks for joining me. Have a wonderful Thursday, a fantastic Thanksgiving, and remember to make grace and gratitude a part of your daily beauty routine. Until next time, be bold, be beautiful, and always be yourself."

I end the recording and scroll through the comments, coming across a new one from @hotbabe1010 that makes my stomach tighten into a fist that punches me directly in the gut.

@hotbabe1010 I bet you smell more like pork than florals. 🐷

"Really, cockatoo? You're seriously bringing out the nasty on Thanksgiving?" I huff out a breath. This chick must have a horrible home or school life or both. "Be bold and beautiful. Don't let her get to you," I remind myself out loud. Taking it one step further, I stand in front of my vanity mirror. My hair, dress, and makeup all look pretty. *I* look pretty. Lifting my phone, I take several selfies and then swipe through them, feeling reassured.

I turn off my ring light and put away the products I showcased. Yesterday, I spent a productive day reviewing and organizing cosmetics and beauty tools into totes and bins neatly arranged on my shelves and in drawers. My room feels so much better when it's picked up. Also, I don't want my ten-year-old cousin, Joni, getting into my makeup. At least she's gotten better about asking first, but I wish she would stay out of my room.

Sure enough, when Aunt Chloe and her family arrive, Joni zips up to my room straightaway. My cousin is wearing a gray and black cheetah print jacket over fuchsia spandex pants. Messy brown hair hangs loosely over both shoulders to her chest, and thick, long bangs cover her forehead. There are shadows beneath her deep blue eyes that a touch of Winky Peepers brightening under-eye concealer would help clear up.

Joni goes straight to my bed, where she tosses her purple crossbody purse with a matching faux fur pom-pom dangling from the zipper.

"Haylee! Guess what? I won my class's rune-a-thon for fastest student to form correct runes. Mrs. McCoy gave me a ribbon. Look." Joni unzips her purse and pulls out an orange ribbon with WINNER running down the length in large yellow print.

"Good job, Joni. Congratulations."

"Mom says I can have wand lessons after I turn eleven. I asked my parents for a Lignum Vitae wand for Christmas so I can start practicing sooner." She sets her WINNER ribbon on my bed and walks around my room, eying the surfaces of my vanity, desk, and dresser. I know exactly what she's looking for. "Want me to show you my protective circle spell?" Before I can answer, Joni darts to her purse and pulls out a small navy hardback copy of *Safety Spellcasting for Beginners*. The cover hasn't changed since I was handed a copy in grade school. An illustrated wand descends vertically down the center like a sword. Behind it, there is a moon within a sun within a circle in gold. Joni flips it open. The dry sound of parchment rasps as she turns pages. "Here it is," she announces, gripping the edges of the book. "Do you have something I can use to show you?"

I fold my arms and smile wryly. "Something as in my Lignum Vitae wand?"

Joni shrugs innocently.

"Here, use this to show me." I pluck a foundation brush from a crystal cup on my vanity and hold it out to Joni.

Rather than take it, my cousin frowns at the brush. "Uh, it would work a lot better with a real wand."

"Well, maybe you'll get one for Christmas." No way am I handing my wand over to an adolescent. She could mis-cast and destroy half my bedroom. Lignum Vitae wands are not toys.

Joni's shoulders sag, and her chin dips. With the dark patches beneath her eyes and the forlorn expression on her face, she looks like a sad, skinny little orphan dreaming of being adopted.

"Hey, how about a touch of shimmer before we go down to eat?" I smile and sweep the brush over Joni's nose.

Her eyes light up when she grins. "Okay. Where should I sit?"

"Over on my vanity chair."

"Really?" her eyes expand.

"Yep. Take a seat." Joni hurries and plops down, staring at the cosmetics I pull out of the vanity's top drawer. "Okay, close your lids," I say. "I'm starting you off with a spritz of primer." Joni sits statue-still with her eyes closed. "Next, I'm brushing a coral matte shade over your lids and topping it with copper shimmer. These colors will make the blues in your eyes pop." I rub the tip of a shadow brush into the pot and then sweep it gently over Joni's lids. A relaxed smile forms over her lips. When I finish with the shadow, I can't help pulling out my tube of Winky Peepers, dabbing it beneath Joni's eyes, and rubbing it in. She has fair skin like me, so the shade blends in well. "Beautiful," I say.

"Can I open my eyes?"

"Yes." While Joni turns around and smiles at her reflection in the vanity mirror, I pull a shiny silver makeup bag out of a tote from my shelf and hand it to my cousin. "Go ahead and pick out a lip gloss."

"To keep?" Joni's eyes widen, and she clutches the bag.

I frown briefly. Kids have a knack for taking me off guard. I'd meant for her to choose something for me to apply to her lips, but I've got more than enough of everything and should have thought of giving her one to begin with. "Yes."

Joni unzips the bag and digs through tubes of gloss. I have extra makeup bags filled with lipstick, tints, glosses, and lip scrubs. I keep the shimmery ones in the shiny silver zipper pouch. I have a whole system for storing cosmetics.

Joni pulls out the glosses, some still in the original boxes they arrived in, and sets them down on the surface of the vanity. She studies them for a long time before saying, "This pink one is pretty."

It is, and I have loads of pink glosses. Beauty companies are always throwing in extra freebies when they send me new products to review. It's like Halloween year-round, with cosmetics instead of candy, and without having to leave the house.

"Let's give it a try," I say. "Want to take it out of the box?" I love unboxing products, and I know Joni will too.

My cousin is surprisingly delicate about lifting the glossy paper free of its top fold. She pulls the shimmering pink gloss out and hands it to me. Once I'm finished applying it to her lips, I return the application wand to the tube and twist the lid closed. "Good color choice," I say as I look over her face. I know she's only ten, but she looks healthier with her mini-makeover.

"Thank you, Haylee." While Joni carries the lip gloss—and the box it came in—to her purse, I return the other glosses to the bag, zip it closed, and place it back in the tote.

The doorbell rings. That will be Uncle Alvan, Mom and Aunt Chloe's little brother. We don't see him as much since he took a job as an executive assistant to a vampire master in New York. Joni follows me out of my room, looking over her shoulder. That inquisitive mind of hers is still probably trying to figure out where I keep my wand. She'll never find it. It's tucked beneath my pillow, which I think is pretty dang clever. No kid in the history of the world ever felt like taking a nap. Little does she know how close her purse and spellbook are to my wand's location. She leaves her things on my bed, hurrying behind me down the hall. We pass my dad's office where he leans over his laptop, his back to us, more at ease in his work than making conversation with Mom's family.

The mouthwatering smell of turkey, casseroles, bread, and apple pie thickens with every step I take down the stairs. Uncle Alvan stands in the entryway wearing a black peacoat and gray cashmere scarf over slim-fit charcoal chinos. He cradles a bottle of red wine with both hands like it's a priceless vase. Aunt Chloe greets him and reaches for the bottle. "Careful," Uncle Alvan says. She narrows her eyes at him briefly as he hands it over and then removes his coat and hangs it from a standing rack. Uncle Alvan is a fit thirty-two-year-old with dense brown hair, a trim layer of scruff, flawless skin, and suave style. Uncle Alvan is employed by vampires, but he's not one of them—though Mom's often muttering about how he would leap at the chance.

"Happy Thanksgiving, Uncle Alvan," I say.

Joni immediately echoes my greeting.

An easy smile lifts Uncle Alvan's lips. "Well, don't you two look pretty."

Joni beams. She looks from our uncle to her mother, but Aunt Chloe appears to have gone into a trance.

"Is that Alvan?" TJ hollers above the TV in the living room. "Grab a beer. You gotta see these jokers with Phillingham United. They're getting their asses kicked up and down the field. It's pathetic."

Uncle Alvan raises a sleek brow at Aunt Chloe, who wrinkles her nose and shakes her head like she can't understand how she ended up married to TJ, either. My uncle takes the bottle of wine back from her.

"Join you momentarily," Uncle Alvan says to TJ.

I follow my aunt and uncle into the kitchen, which smells like a bakery set up shop next door to a cafe. My mouth waters as my thoughts fill with gleeful anticipation.

Kendra turns away from the cheese plate she's arranging to wave. "Hi, Uncle Alvan. Happy Thanksgiving."

"Kendra, it's good to see you. How is Cameron? And school? Still putting your mark on Blakely?"

Kendra chuckles. "You know it. Cameron is doing great, and school is going well. How's life in the Big Apple?"

"Fantastic. Greatest city in the world." Uncle Alvan grins.

Mom's lips flatline when she looks at her brother. She pulls a large wine glass from the cupboard, followed by a bottle opener from a drawer, and sets them on the counter by Uncle Alvan.

"Thanks, Mel. Can I pour you a glass?"

Mom straightens her shoulders. "I'm good."

"There are only five thousand bottles of this vintage in existence. It's reported to contain a fine elegance with beautifully balanced acidity."

"No, thanks," Mom reiterates.

Uncle Alvan's forehead creases.

"I'd like to try it," Kendra announces. My sister wears two hats in life: rebel and peacemaker. She gets out a clear shot glass and sets it down beside the bottle. Okay, so even when she's playing at diplomat, it's with a rebellious spirit. I grin at her antics.

Uncle Alvan shakes his head before smiling. "Sure, why not?" He carefully tips the bottle and fills the shot glass three-quarters full.

Kendra lifts it to the ceiling and studies the dark, ruby-red liquid against the overhead light. "How much would you say this sip is worth? Ten bucks? Twenty?"

"Higher." Uncle Alvan smirks and pours into his glass. He swirls and inhales before tilting the glass back and taking a sip.

"Fifty?" Kendra doesn't wait for his answer as she downs the wine in one go. "Tastes rich," she says as she rinses her glass off in the sink.

I'd rather drink soda any day, but I understand the draw of luxury goods.

"Only a select few get to experience this divine flavor," Uncle Alvan says before taking another sip.

Mom makes a huff of disgust.

Uncle Alvan's eyebrows draw in as he frowns. "Am I not allowed to enjoy the finer things, Melanie?"

"With your blood money," she fires back.

"Working for a vampire doesn't make it blood money," he says in exasperation.

"You do know you work for the devil, right?"

Uncle Alvan sets his glass of wine on the counter and pinches the bridge of his nose, squinting as though in anticipation of a headache. "Not this again."

"Hey, how about we enjoy a delicious meal with family today?" Kendra suggests.

"I think that's a great idea," Aunt Chloe says, absently stroking Joni's head in the corner of the kitchen. My cousin is backed against her mom, who still hasn't noticed the makeup.

TJ notices the moment we all sit together at the large dining table to eat.

"What's that on your face?" he demands, practically snarling at his daughter, whose hand visibly shakes, making the piece of turkey on the end of her fork wobble.

Needle-like points prickle my arms. My stomach presses into the edge of the table as I lean forward like I might physically shield my cousin from her father's glare. "Joni let me try out some new products on her. She's a good sport."

As usual, TJ ignores me.

Kendra sets down her glass of apple cider and flashes me an appreciative smile. I'm happy she's home.

TJ places both elbows on the table and sneers at Joni. "You're too young for makeup. You look ridiculous."

Joni blinks rapidly. Aunt Chloe turns to stone in her chair.

"Come on, Uncle TJ. It's not like it's permanent." Kendra laughs breezily, as though she delights in this jerk's company. "Not like a tattoo," she adds.

TJ grunts and wrinkles his nose. "Don't give her any bad ideas. She has enough of those already—her and her mother." He grabs his fork and knife and saws at his slice of turkey, scraping against the plate.

Silence settles over the table, which only draws more attention to TJ's loud chewing and swallowing as he guzzles down another beer straight from the bottle.

Aunt Chloe picks up her knife and moves food around on her plate. It doesn't look like she's eaten a bite. I'm an emotional eater, but Aunt Chloe is a slender woman who probably loses her appetite every time she sits down for a meal with TJ.

Mom's face is red. She looks ready to explode. Dad sets his fork down and places a reassuring hand above her wrist. Mom's expression and posture soften when she looks at him.

I check my phone, which, unfortunately, gives my mom a new target to snap at. "Haylee, you know the rule. No phones at the table while we're eating."

With a sheepish shrug, I return it to its place on my chair, beneath my leg, which is technically not the table.

"This is exactly why Joni isn't getting a phone until she's old enough to leave the house," TJ says.

Joni blinks back tears. I don't blame her. I'd want to cry all the time if TJ was my father. He's a monster.

After everyone leaves, Mom attacks the dishes in the sink, scrubbing at them like she's sanding wood on a casket while Kendra and I finish clearing the table. Dad stands at Mom's side with a dish towel, drying the plates, cutlery, and glasses as soon as they are rinsed.

"Chloe told me that he threatened to take off with Joni if she ever tries to leave him," Mom seethes.

"We won't allow that," Dad says calmly.

"Her phone went straight to messages all last week," Mom continues. "She texted me claiming she wasn't feeling well, but what do you want to bet the only illness she had was a noxious case of the TJs."

"Why don't I turn him into a toad?" I swirl my finger in the air like it would be that simple.

Kendra snort-laughs.

Mom twists around, soapy foam splattering the floor. "Absolutely not. You are not getting yourself locked up for my sister's mistake—not to mention the unconscionable misuse of power. I already lost Alvan to the dark side."

I roll my eyes. "Mom, I was kidding."

"Were you?" She purses her lips.

"Slippery slope, Sis," Kendra says, sounding amused, unlike Mom, who looks at me as though I might actually go through with it. Even if I was okay with risking my personal freedom, which I'm not, transformation takes more than words and the wave of a wand. It requires rare ingredients and creepy rituals. Not my style.

TJ does deserve to be turned into a toad, though, right before he's run over by a dump truck.

"I'm going to wash my face," I announce.

"Thanks for all your help," Kendra teases.

I mock salute her before leaving.

Shortly after nine the next morning, Aunt Chloe shows up at our house with a swollen eye and split lip, sobbing hysterically.

CHAPTER SIX

JONI IS WEARING the same clothing as yesterday. Kendra ushers our aunt and cousin into the living room. Dad brings them each a glass of juice. Aunt Chloe sets her glass on the coffee table while Joni wraps both hands around hers.

"That's it. I'm calling the police," Mom says.

"Don't bother. He's friends with the chief," Aunt Chloe says bitterly.

"Oh, really? Well TJ isn't the only one with friends in high places." Mom spits TJ's name out like it's an STD.

Silent tears leak down Joni's cheeks. Mom looks at her and then at me, voice turning artificially sunny. "Haylee, I know you still have gobs of product reviews to do. I bet Joni would make an excellent helper."

My mouth hangs open in silent protest. Mom's right about one thing. I'm way behind, but I don't have time to entertain Joni. I have real responsibilities. My account is a mere eighty-seven followers away from one million. Today is the day I reach my first mega milestone. I want to scream my lungs hoarse and celebrate, not babysit my little cousin. Not today.

TJ is terrible, and it makes me sick that he struck Aunt Chloe, but I can't help it if the timing sucks.

Should have let me turn him into a toad.

I sigh. I don't smile on command like Kendra. "Come on, Joni," I say moodily. "If you promise to keep quiet you can watch me record."

Joni gets up so quickly she spills some of her juice. "Oh no!" she cries. "I'm sorry. It was an accident."

It's not her fault. Dad always fills glasses to the brim like they're tanks of gas he's compelled to top off.

"Don't worry about it," Kendra says, pulling a tissue out of her jean pocket. She dabs at the rug. "It's only a drop."

Mom mouths "thank you" as I walk out. I give her the stink eye, not about to pretend I'm happy about the interruption. When I look over at my aunt's bruised and blotchy face, I instantly feel guilty.

Forget the police. Mom should call Uncle Alvan. I'm sure his vampire connections could take care of TJ.

Joni drifts behind me like a ghost. Once we've reached my room at the end of the hall upstairs, I usher her inside and close my door. Joni pulls her crossbody purse over her head, sets it on my bed, and begins crying. She stuffs her fist against her mouth. "I'm sorry," she sniffles. "I'll be quiet. I promise."

"Joni," I sigh. "Don't apologize. It's fine. And it's going to be okay. The adults will figure it out."

She rubs her nose on her cheetah-print sleeve.

"They will?" she asks dubiously.

"Definitely. Don't forget that my dad is a very powerful man."

TJ doesn't stand a chance against my dad, who recently won the largest divorce settlement in the world for his client, going after her shady Russian vampire mega crook billionaire husband. He said it's just the tip of the fang when it comes to rampant worldwide corruption among the "master race," but I've never seen Mom so proud. I only half listened when she told me the case wasn't about the amount of the settlement so much as an opportunity to uncover a master vampire's ill-gained assets.

But going back to the main point. Dad took down a Russian master billionaire. TJ does not stand a chance. My father didn't want to get involved, but that was before TJ hit Aunt Chloe.

Joni sniffles a few more times before clearing her throat. "Can I help you set up for your videos?"

"Sure." I walk over to a tote on a high shelf. "You can put these on my vanity," I say, handing her the cosmetics I'm using for my next makeup tutorial.

"Should I sit on your bed?"

"No. It might creak." I toss a throw pillow from my bed onto the floor. Joni sits on it, crossing her legs, then uncrosses them and draws her knees up, hugging her arms around her legs.

"Don't worry. This isn't live, so I can redo the video if I have to."

It would be a royal pain to have to wash my face and start all over, but obviously not the end of the world.

Joni nods and whispers, "Okay, but I promise to stay silent."

My stomach twists. No doubt she has plenty of practice with TJ.

Before recording, I check my JingleJam account.

999,991 Followers

Holy wow!

Maybe I should wait to record and witness the moment I hit one million. I press refresh.

999,991 Followers

Refresh.

999,991 Followers

Arg. So close, but the number isn't budging. Staring at my screen is having the opposite effect I was hoping for.

"Cousin Haylee? Is everything okay?" Joni releases her legs and leans forward.

"Everything is great," I say with a wide smile. "Ready to watch me do my thing?"

"Yeah." Joni nods vigorously, perking up.

I might as well get glammed up now so that I will be ready to go live with my reaction when I reach one million followers.

I do a final check in the mirror of my dressy and flattering black quarter-sleeve V-neck wrap top.

Joni's attention is on everything I do. At least this helps distract her. I clip my phone into the center of my ring light and switch it on.

"Okay, quiet on set." I wink at Joni, who grins back at me. "Hey, hey. Hello, beauties. It's Haylee with another holiday look. I call this purple-toned pleaser *Stunning Sugarplum*. Plum smoky eyes paired with—" A distant car alarm cuts me off. I huff out a breath of exasperation. Joni grimaces. "At least I was just getting started," I say. The obnoxious alarm continues incessantly. Dogs bark from down the street. I stop recording and tap my polished nails on top of my vanity. I painted them deep berry violet first thing in the morning to match the makeup I will be applying.

Someone really needs to turn off their alarm. I swear it's increasing in volume. Not only that—it's moving closer. What the heck?

I stand and walk to my window as the clamor of car alarms blares up the street. Seriously, what is going on? Joni remains on the cushion, taking the keep quiet thing a bit overboard.

When I look outside, my mind and body freeze over.

ZOMBIES!

A horde of them, maybe fifty, rush up the street, following the sound of the car alarms. I open my mouth and scream, "Zombie horde outside!"

Joni yelps and jumps to her feet. She reaches the window at the same time the horde advances in front of our house. Aunt Chloe's car alarm blares. Every honk of her white Volkswagen Golf causes my heart to jerk. Instead of jumping to the next car on the street, the alarms go off on Dad's electric Mercedes-Benz. They go off and keep going, followed by our doorbell. The TV blares downstairs.

No! I scream inside my head.

CHAPTER SEVEN

THE ZOMBIES RUSH up our driveway with bloodshot eyes, loose skin, open wounds, and patches of flesh decayed or missing over their decomposed bodies.

I whip around as the sound of breaking windows crashes below. Aunt Chloe screams and doesn't stop.

I run to my bed and yank my wand from beneath my pillow before thrusting it at Joni, who stares wide-eyed, not taking it.

"Cast a protection circle!" I order.

"I-I can't remember how."

I leap back to my bed and snatch her copy of *Safety Spellcasting for Beginners* from her purse as a stampede of bodies bombards the first floor. Furniture crashes. Glass breaks. Aunt Chloe's scream makes my heart feel ready to explode. I shove both the book and my wand into Joni's hands. "Do it!"

The book shakes in Joni's hands as she turns the pages. She holds the book open and looks at me with pleading eyes. "You have to be inside the circle with me when I cast it."

"I'll make my own after you," I say, taking a step toward my bedroom door.

An explosion goes off downstairs. Dad's shotgun. "Out back!" he bellows.

Another gunshot.

I rock in place. Dad's okay. He'll protect Mom, Kendra, and Aunt Chloe. He'll give them a head start while he blasts the zombies away. Another gunshot roars. Something thuds up the stairs. What if it's Kendra? What if she's coming to get us or making a run for it to the second floor? Maybe her route to the back door is blocked, and upstairs is her only option.

"Don't leave me!" Joni shrieks.

I'm at my door, but the reason I've frozen is due to the wrongness of the noises traveling up the stairs. It's the clumsy smack and thump of far too many footsteps making their way to the landing. A horrifying dry rasp rumbles from the mass in the hallway—that awful throaty, gurgling bray as they collectively wheeze. My legs wilt like tiger lilies in a bone-dry vase. And then my bones snap back into place, muscles firing to life. I twist the lock on my door as the first zombie rams into it from the other side. Joni shrieks, which makes the zombies in the hallway fling themselves at the door with crazed fervor.

I grab the end of my wooden bed frame and pull it over the carpet with strength born of panic. Once it's near the door, I run to the opposite side and push it the rest of the way against my door.

The groaning on the other side is abhorrent, but not deafening enough that I would miss a gunshot. Why haven't I heard more shots? The horde must have—NO! I stop the thought dead in its decaying tracks. Dad made a run for it. He's right behind Mom, Kendra, and Aunt Chloe. I need to worry about Joni and myself. We're still trapped in the house.

I scan my room for things to stack on the far end of my bed. The totes are no good. I doubt I can Hulk out enough to lift my dresser onto the bed. The zombies aren't just attacking the door, they're pounding and scratching at the outer wall like relentless termites determined to chew their way through. I have to hold them off long enough for a Z Squad unit to arrive and exterminate the monsters. Someone on our block must have called the sighting in by now. If I weren't barricading my room against the tide of flesh-eating mutants, I would be dialing Z Squad now.

The door pounds and shakes in the frame. It sounds hollow. Composite wood. It won't hold up. Wood splinters and cracks apart in the middle. A bloody fist shoots through. This time, Joni and I both scream as mangled fingers with missing fingernails claw through the opening. Pieces of bare bone show through the bloated fingers. My bladder loosens. A burst of wetness soaks through my underwear to my jeans.

If the zombies get through, if they reach us—

"Haylee!" Joni screams, snapping me out of a terror-induced stupor.

I grab the stool from in front of my vanity. From the corner of my eye, I see Joni crouched on the floor with my wand and her spellbook. I leap onto my bed, holding the seat by the metal legs, using it to beat at the sickening hand grasping at the air in my room.

Another hand breaks through. And another.

"Go away!" I scream. "Go away! Go away!"

There's no use trying to be quiet anymore. My bellows barely cover the wet gurgling noise oozing from the zombies' throats.

Come on, Z Squad. Hurry. Please!

The metal-rimmed edge of my stool smashes the hands reaching in, but they do not retract. I hate standing this close to the flesh-eating freaks. Only a few feet separate me from the most horrifying death imaginable. I am also aware of Joni. I have to protect my little cousin—buy her time to complete her circle of protection. It gives me strength I never knew I possessed.

The metal hinges rattle along the frame as fractures form all over the door and rotten flesh punches again and again like a bunch of zombie ninjas are karate chopping their way through. These things are nothing like Rosie or Georgia.

"Did you cast a protection circle?" I yell, as I bring the stool down on the putrid arms.

I thought the sound they made was ghastly, but the smell of them is worse.

"I think so," Joni squeaks.

To every deity out there, please let it be so.

A head with half the skin missing from its skull and matted gray hair bursts through. I slam the seat of the stool against it. At the same time another head breaks in, torso and all. Screaming like a banshee on PMS, I swing the stool sideways into the head protruding through what's left of my door.

Slimy fingers touch my wrist. I shriek and fall backward onto my bed. The first zombie worms its way through the splintered opening, pulling at my blanket and leaving bloody smears over my lavender and gray comforter.

"I have your wand!" Joni yelps.

I roll off the edge of my bed still clutching the bloodied stool like it's a shield that will save me. When I reach Joni, my hand hits an invisible shield as I reach for my wand in her hand. Thank God! Her circle of protection worked. Joni tosses the wand out of her barrier. I catch it and whirl around, stool in one hand, and wand in the other.

More zombies wriggle through the jagged opening and crawl over my bed. They spill into the room. I'm drawing a circle, repeating the words Joni shouts from her book, which are in plain English—another small miracle. Plain English spells are for precision and focus, meant for controlled magical actions.

"With the power of the sacred tree, I call upon thee to protect me. Spirit of magic, energy, life. I call upon thee—"

Zombies swarm me before I can finish. Teeth tear into my arms and neck. Fingers tug at my clothing. It all happens so quickly. Joni is screaming, but it sounds far away. My eardrums are too full of the feeding frenzy—of the spittle, smacking lips, and hoarse, horrifying exhalations. The zombies pile on, suffocating my airways as they consume my flesh. My heart threatens to give out before I'm eaten alive.

Terror turns to rage. Death by zombie? I don't think so! Curse words erupt out of me as I smash the stool into the horde. It doesn't do as much damage one-handed. With my wand, I point at my window and cry out, "*Lavitamay, librawhisksha.*" Two thick gray curtains pull free of their rods and swirl around a couple of zombies, wrapping tightly around their jerking bodies. "*Lifteena, elona veed!*" I cast at my dresser, my vanity, my bed, my nightstand, and my bookshelf, bringing the furniture to life. Totes filled with cosmetics rain down over the carpet. My bedside lamp and mini succulent are dumped to the ground. Furniture comes at the zombies, who scratch and bite at me, some of them clamping their jaws over my jeans, trying to saw their teeth through to my flesh. "*Lavitamay, librawhisksha,*" I cast at my comforter and throw blanket. They wrap more zombies that thrash and flail, trying to free themselves from their entrapping.

Nonsensical words flow from my lips. It's a less-defined magical phenomena that taps into the subconscious and summons magic more intuitively, manifesting in potent ways. In other words, I've gone full hocus-pocus on the horde.

My furniture knocks into zombies, beating them back, away from me. It's a struggle when the zombies continue springing on me the second they get an opening. They snap their teeth. I kick. My large ring light hammers into a zombie girl with bloody drool running down her chin onto her pink tank top with glittered words that read *Daddy's little girl.* My stool butts against decaying legs like it's transformed into an angry goat. My textiles are doing a better job of temporarily mummifying the zombies, so I have my dresser start herding those ones out of my room. The bed walks several feet forward, opening space for the zombies to be forced back into the hallway against the ones still trying to get in. My bed flips up like a Murphy bed retracting into the wall. It blocks the door, but three zombies remain. I swing my wand, and my dresser does a flip, crashing into a zombie before crushing it against the floor. A couple of decayed fingers poking out from under it twitch and then go still. Now is not the time to reinvent the wheel, so I push a zombie backward and send my dresser after it. Blood sprays the carpet after it lands true yet again. One left. I've been kicking at it. Now I tackle the bald male with the missing eye. He chomps his teeth, missing my nose by half an inch. His rancid breath hits me instead.

"Get. Back!" I scream, giving him a shove that sends him reeling back several steps. I swing my wand, bringing it down with a jerk of my wrist. My dresser smashes over the zombie. Bones crunch, and blood sprays.

In the distance, sirens blare. There's less than a second of silence before the zombies thunder down the stairs. They stampede from the first floor to the front yard as the sirens get louder, closer.

Blood gushes from my neck, streams down my arms, and soaks into my shirt. Panic returns. I've been bitten! Not only that. Flesh is missing from my arms, exposing bone. Vomit rises up my throat but doesn't make it out. Maybe it's leaking from the open wound at my neck.

I dry heave and then jerk around, terrified of finding Joni outside of her circle of protection, bitten too. But she's standing untouched, with eyes that look permanently stretched in shock. Her spellbook shakes in her hands.

"I need your spellbook," I say, sounding breathless. Joni lifts her foot to step forward. "No!" I yell. Her entire body jolts. "Toss the book out of your circle. Stay where you are. Just in case."

In case I turn before I can complete the spell of sanity. I have less than ten minutes. If I get it wrong, I'm done for. Joni's lower lip wobbles, but thankfully she does as I say and tosses the book onto the carpet beside me. It lands on the bloody carpet. There isn't much area left that's not trashed or stained in gore.

Without any directions to guide their movements, my furniture bumbles aimlessly around the room. The metal stool keeps running into the wall while the vanity shudders in place. Little drips of blood fall from my ring light as it hops around.

"*Ceasinatage*," I command. My furniture goes still. I return my attention to the book, flipping to the back pages.

SPELL OF SANITY

(For the immediate treatment of zombie bites.)

In the unlikely event that you—or someone in your group—are bitten by a zombie, first get yourself to safety as quickly as possible.

Perform the following spell with a genuine Lignum Vitae wand within ten minutes of being bitten. For best results, cast the SPELL OF SANITY immediately following the attack.

Once the afflicted person(s) has been treated, call Z Squad at SOS (or 767). When help arrives, hold your wand above your head, signaling that you are not afflicted by insanity. The response unit will take you in for treatment and processing.

Note: *Once bitten and the SPELL OF SANITY has been successfully performed, you will remain immune to any and all future zombie bites.

*Zombies are not known to consume the flesh of their own kind, including the class of zombie rendered self-possessed through the use of emergency spellcasting.

Speaking of Z Squad and their team of "rippers," the sirens now blare out front. Howls go up. Z Squadrons are made up of werewolves. Zombies can't infect other supernaturals—not to mention werewolves are exceptionally skilled at ripping apart zombies. Growls erupt outside as the crew gets to work exterminating the horde. I'd better make sure I'm not next.

I set the spellbook on my bloodied vanity and stare down at the words I must cast to save myself from becoming one of those monstrous creatures.

"Mind. Body. Soul. Unite." I point my wand at myself, making a windshield wiper motion, and then circle my wrist slowly three times before pressing my wand between my palms as though in prayer. "Blood congeal. Flesh heal. Preserve, maintain, and keep me real. Mind. Body. Soul. Unite." I repeat the wand motions according to the spell's directions. It calls for the words and wand work to be repeated a third and final time. "Mind. Body. Soul. Unite."

The burning pain in my body dulls. My heart beats out of rhythm before stopping altogether, but I'm still alive, or rather not alive. Undead, or whatever, like a vampire, but not like a vampire because this makes me a freaking zombie. I shove the thought deep down. The only thing that matters is getting downstairs to help my family—unless they already got away safely. If they didn't make it out, they'll need me. I'm the only one with a wand. We'll figure out the rest later.

"Haylee? Did it work?" Joni's voice wavers.

"Yeah. I'm pretty sure."

"Can I come out of my circle now?"

"No. Stay there until Z Squad has finished. It will be over soon. It will be okay." I repeat my reassurance one more time while my mind screams back. *It's not okay. It's so super not okay.*

I grab Joni's spellbook off the vanity, lower my bed with my wand, and walk the frame away from the door.

"Where are you going?" Joni yelps.

"I think my parents, sister, and your mom escaped out the back door. I want to see if they've returned."

"They made it out?" Joni's voice raises hopefully. "I'm coming with you."

"No!"

Joni's face crumples.

"Please, Joni. Just stay in your circle a little longer, and uh, don't look at the floor."

Who am I kidding? After today, she's going to be scarred for life. The sight of bloody, beaten zombies eliminated by my dresser—and I suppose me—can hardly add extra trauma that isn't already there.

"The rippers will kill you if you go out there," Joni says desperately.

I shake my head. "I'll hold my wand over my head the entire time. I promise."

I walk out of my bedroom and enter the hallway. My comforter, throw blanket, and window curtains lie in lumpy piles on the floor runner. The zombies must have cast them off before running outside.

Bloody fingerprints and blood trails smear the walls like psycho finger paintings. I go down one stair and then the next, not breathing, not needing to. When I reach the first floor, I notice the finality of the silence that's fallen inside my home. The snarls outside are frenzied, excited. This might as well be a playdate for the werewolves. I hear their growls clearly, and yet they're a world away.

I pause outside the living room. It's eerily silent.

Don't go in there, a somber inner voice warns.

I consider turning around, returning to Joni. I shouldn't leave her alone. She needs me. I should turn around. But I am standing in quicksand. My body is heavy. Sluggish. My legs drag over the hall runner to the wide opening of the living room. It's like stepping through a picture frame into the scene of a massacre.

CHAPTER EIGHT

BROKEN GLASS CRUNCHES beneath my Sherpa slipper booties. Gem-sized pieces and larger shards litter the room. Artwork is knocked off the wall. The TV is smashed over a section of hardwood floor outside the area rug. The couch and coffee table are turned over.

There are five bodies on the ground. Aunt Chloe is still wearing her plaid coat. It's the only way I can tell that it's her. She's closer to the windows than the rest, as though she was the first to die. Where her head should be there is only bloody pulp. The gore on its own doesn't affect me. Another sign that I'm in shock.

One of the bodies is a zombie with its face blown off, brain matter splattering the rug and the toppled couch. Beside it is a body stretched over the floor on his back with his face chewed off, tortoise shell glasses smeared and bent beside him. Several paces away, two bodies lie side by side as though they were clutching one another. Kendra's knit sweater is mauled and stained with blood. Mom's slip-on clogs are separated—one flipped over near her calf, the other near her feet. Her toes have been bitten off. The moment my eyes reach my mom's and sister's faces, I look away. My brain shatters.

The memory of the last look I ever gave Mom vaporizes my soul. The sob that bursts out of me is an atomic bomb that cannot have possibly originated from a living being.

More sobs follow. I drop my wand and the spellbook and clamp my hand over my mouth trying to muffle the agony erupting from my throat. Under no circumstances can Joni be allowed to see her mother this way. If she hears me wailing, I'm afraid she'll rush down here. This isn't the kind of sight that can ever be unseen. It's too late for me, but not Joni.

I back up and fall against the couch, crumbling beside the gore-stained rug.

I want to die. I did die. We all did. My immediate family is dead. I am dead. My heart stopped. Why can't my brain?

"Doubt there are any survivors," a male voice says. It's as though he teleported inside my home. "This is a hot mess."

"Oh, shit We've got a straggler," his companion answers.

It takes me a moment to realize he's talking about me and that I have broken my promise to Joni. Heavy steps pound my way. The werewolves are dressed in brown pants and short-sleeved khaki collared shirts with large shield patches on the upper sleeve of their uniform that depict a fanged wolf head carrying a severed green zombie hand in its jaws and *Z SQUAD* embroidered beneath. The older one has a crew cut, additional patches, and a badge. "Shift?" he asks casually.

His partner, a muscular, mid-twenties werewolf in a khaki baseball cap and mountain range wrist tattoo with a crescent moon above it purses his lips. "Nah, I just put my clothes back on. One zombie isn't worth undressing for." He pulls a steel baton free of his belt.

"Wait!" I belt out, snatching my wand and lifting it above my head. "I'm a survivor. I cast the spell of sanity. My little cousin Joni is still upstairs in a circle of protection."

"Was she bitten?" the werewolf with the badge and crew cut demands.

"No."

"But you were?"

I stand slowly, lower my wand, and give Captain Clodhopper an incredulous look.

No, I did this to myself. What do you think?

I stuff down my snark. "As you can see," I say.

"Very well, take her in for processing, Terrick. I'll see to the cousin."

Terrick snatches my wand out of my hand.

"Hey! That's mine."

"And it will be returned to you after processing," Terrick says, sounding bored now that bludgeoning me to pulp with his steel baton is off the table. "Let's go."

I step away from him. "I can't just leave my cousin."

"You can see her after processing."

"At least let me go upstairs and tell her what's happening."

"We need to go right now."

I glare at Terrick, but he's not looking at me as he reaches out, grabs my destroyed arm, and steers me out of the living room.

"Joni!" I yell at the stairs as we pass. "Z Squad is taking me in for processing. I'll see you soon."

I'm hauled out into the sunlight, where shredded chunks of zombie are strewn across the yard, driveway, sidewalk, and street. It looks like multiple grenades went off. Blue lights flash on top of a long lime-green truck. There are zombies impaled on the truck's spiked front grille.

Several black SUVs with tinted windows dot the street. A nondescript man with a camera snaps pictures of the yard while another man follows behind him setting numbered evidence markers on the ground. A third man wraps yellow tape around our mailbox post and then unspools the thick roll as he walks to a tree, sectioning off the yard. A group of uniformed werewolves watch the men move around the dismembered zombie parts.

"You hear whose house this is?" one of the werewolves asks his buddies. He lets out a low whistle. "Going to be up to our elbows in paperwork for months."

Nodding, a ripper in wraparound sunglasses notices me. He juts his chin in my direction. "What's this?"

"We've got ourselves a recently converted." The werewolves all turn their heads to stare at me from behind shades and beneath baseball caps like a pack of dogs catching sight of a bone. "There's another survivor upstairs. Little girl. Still human," Terrick adds. "I'm taking this one in for processing."

"Better roll out the red carpet," one of them quips.

At first, I think he's referencing my fame as a JingleJam influencer before quickly realizing he's referring to my father.

Terrick's grip remains firm as he hauls me across the street to a lime-green SUV with *Z Squad* spelled out in blue across the lower half of the vehicle's doors. I am placed in the back seat behind a metal separator made up of small squares that only a finger could fit through.

Terrick starts the SUV, then grumbles when a dump truck blocks the road. He rolls down his window and yells, "Back up. You'll have to wait a bit longer, buddy."

Loud beeping ensues as the dump truck shifts into reverse. Terrick pulls the SUV onto the road, and we crawl forward as the truck backs up slowly, passing the black SUVs and residential vehicles before finding a spot to pull to the side. Terrick lifts his hand out the window as we pass. I read the words printed on the dump truck.

DEAD HAUL REMAINS REMOVAL

"What's going to happen to my family?" I ask.

"What do you mean?" Terrick doesn't look over his shoulder. His tone is indifferent.

"Their bodies!" I barely recognize my hysterical voice. The sight of the dump truck has me in a panic. They wouldn't put my parents, sister, and aunt in with the zombies, would they?

Terrick drives slowly down the street. Neighbors have ventured outdoors now that the threat has passed. They stare or hold up phones, recording the activity. People wave at Terrick as he drives past. He waves back.

"You're a hero," Mrs. Kline yells. Her husband works in accounting while she runs a small alteration business out of their home. Kendra paid Mrs. Kline to fix a busted zipper on her winter coat last year. My neighbor's gaze travels to the back seat, and she squints. I'm grateful for the tinted windows.

Once we've curved our way to the main road, Terrick answers my question. Sort of.

"Your family will be photographed and then processed."

"What do you mean *processed*?"

"Cold storage until your family lawyer produces your parents' last will and testament. They'll either be buried or cremated, depending on their instructions."

I sit back and stare at the cars we pass along the main road. Drivers and passengers look over when they notice the Z Squad SUV passing.

Does Kendra have a will? What happens to her remains if she doesn't? I don't have a will, which means Kendra might not either. She's too young to have a will. She's supposed to have her whole life in front of her.

Oh, God. Cameron. This is going to kill him.

What's going to happen to Joni? TJ isn't fit to take care of a dog let alone a child.

Would Uncle Alvan take us in?

Does that mean we would move to New York, or would he move here? I would rather move to New York. I don't want to stay in Garnet. I'm never coming back to this city. I might avoid the entire state of Virginia for as long as I live. How long will I live? Forever, in theory, but probably less than a mortal with all the violence against zombies. I think of Myles Castillo, missing and presumed extinguished. That leaves a place in senior year for me at Brookdale. No way. I definitely can't return to school. It was bad enough as a human.

There are too many questions and worries clogging my mind like oatmeal stuck inside a sink's strainer. It's as though my brain is overcompensating for my suspended heart. It's fitting that it will never beat again. Today, my world has turned forever inside out.

Terrick parks in front of a Z Squad station. He turns off the ignition, gets out of the SUV, shuts his door, walks around with the swagger of a hotshot werewolf, and opens my door. "Let's go."

Numbly, I follow him into the station.

A uniformed werewolf with short dark spiky hair at the front counter looks at the lacerations and chunks of flesh missing from my arms, then flicks his gaze to Terrick. "Only survivor?"

Terrick taps the counter. "There's another girl—still human—back at the scene. Sgt. Ganon is seeing to her."

The other werewolf nods. "Room C is available."

I suppose it's called Room C because it looks more like a holding cell than a room, with a set of cuffs bolted to a metal table.

"What's going on?" I try to walk backward out of the forlorn room, but a werewolf blocks me.

"Just sit down. Once our agents interview you, we will proceed to the next stage of your processing. First, I'm going to need you to have a seat and place your arms on the table."

This is all hues of shady. Mom would be reaming out the station chief as soon as she heard about this treatment . . . if she were still alive.

I do as Terrick instructs. While I'm at it, I dive headlong into frustration, confusion, and outrage. It's distracting. It's the only thing keeping me from falling apart.

Processing. I need to get through processing, and then I'll deal with the horror, the grief, the absolute end of my life. I'm not talking about becoming a paranormal pariah who eats brains. I mean the death of the people I loved more than anyone on this doomed planet. I don't know how I can possibly go on.

For now, I sit on a cold, hard chair, place my arms on the table, and hold still for Terrick as he cuffs me. Once he's finished, he heads to the door. "I'll be back shortly," he says before closing me in.

As soon as I am alone, I stare from the cuffs around my wrists to the violet nail polish at the ends of my fingers. I think back to polishing my nails at my vanity while Dad was down the hall on his laptop, and Mom and Kendra were downstairs. Maybe if I focus hard enough, I can go back to that moment and warn them about the zombies before it's too late. As far as the world knows, time travel doesn't exist. With all of the amazing magical feats we've witnessed in the modern age, it should be possible to turn back time. Speaking of which—

Terrick is not back shortly. He does not return for some time, during which I check out mentally. I don't mean space out. I'm talking a horse snoozing standing up. No thoughts and, best of all, no feelings. Maybe it's a zombie thing. Maybe I can turn myself off and find the abyss within the same way a Buddhist monk finds enlightenment.

My repose is interrupted when Terrick opens the door and walks in with two lanky males who are wearing "take us seriously" suits. They have trim, boring haircuts and bland expressions.

"Miss Hutchins, I am Agent Lennix, and this is Agent Arnet. We have some questions to ask you about what happened this morning." They sit in the chairs in front of me, not waiting for a reply. A recording device is set on the table. Agent Arnet clicks his pen over a fresh legal pad. Terrick leans against the closed door, arms folded.

"Tell me everything that happened from the moment the zombie horde attacked to when Z Squad found you," Agent Lennix instructs.

Happy to. They need to get to the bottom of this right away. I tell them everything. Every detail I recall. Something's been bothering me from the start. No way was this an accident. Someone sent that horde to our house. A spellcaster had to have made the car alarms go off one by one, leading the zombies up the street and to our driveway.

Agent Arnet jots notes while I speak, showing zero reaction to what I share.

I remember the TV blasting to life, and Aunt Chloe screaming soon after. Acid fills my throat. Who could do something that evil? And why?

I have to know, which is why I want to help the agents out as much as possible.

"And you were upstairs the entire time of the attack?" Agent Lennix prods.

"Yes—with my cousin Joni. How is she, by the way?"

"Your cousin is back home with her father. Safe."

My stomach plummets. She is most certainly not safe with TJ. "You can't leave her with her father. He's a monster. He hit my aunt. That's why she and Joni came over this morning—to escape him. You have to get her away from him."

Agent Arnet clicks his pen closed, then back open, and looks at Agent Lennix, who says, "Sgt. Ganon reported no signs of physical harm from zombies or anyone else."

"I didn't say he hit Joni," I quip, trying to lift my hands, only to scrape my wrists against the metal cuffs. This is lunacy. TJ should be the one chained and detained. "Let me call my Uncle Alvan. He might still be in town."

"Alvan Bates?" Agent Lennix asks.

"Yes," I say in exasperation.

"We've already tried reaching out to him with no luck so far." Agent Lennix looks at Agent Arnet. "Well, I think we got everything we need."

Agent Arnet nods and clicks his pen shut. Their metal chairs scrape back.

"What about my cousin?" I demand.

Agent Lennix gives me a considering look before answering. "She's better off with family than strangers."

The hell she is! I grind my teeth.

"We've left Mr. Bates a voicemail. Maybe he can help you out."

Unless he's dead. Maybe the same villain who put a hit on my family sent someone after Uncle Alvan. TJ is the only one who seems to be fine, which makes him my number one suspect.

"My Aunt Chloe said that TJ is friends with the police chief. Maybe he arranged the attack through him. He threatened to take action if she ever tried to leave him, and he knew my parents had the power to help her get away from him."

TJ is not a good guy. He could have done this. It makes me sick thinking we all sat down to dinner with him last night.

Agent Lennix shakes his head. "TJ Mullins was at work at the time of the incident."

"And he couldn't have hired a spellcaster?" I demand.

Agent Lennix holds my stare and then sighs. "Spellcasting on this scale, not to mention procuring a zombie horde, would cost an exorbitant amount to orchestrate. Your uncle works in construction, does he not?" The lift of the agent's brows and his placating tone say it all. He doesn't suspect TJ of any wrongdoing.

I need Uncle Alvan. He knows what TJ is like. Uncle Alvan will be devastated when he finds out he's lost both of his sisters. He'll want justice as much as I do. He'll demand it.

"I want to try calling my uncle," I say. "Where's my phone?" Did the rippers find it upstairs? Did Joni grab it for me?

"Your phone will be returned to you soon," Agent Lennix says. "You may move her to holding now." He nods to Terrick on his way out of the room.

My mouth opens, anxious to learn more, but the agents know nothing. They're useless to me at this point.

"What happens now?" I ask Terrick instead.

He unchains me from the table but leaves the cuffs binding my wrists. "Come along," he says, leading me from Room C and out of the station. The world has gone dark. Headlights beam over the road outside the station. Red brake lights glow as they pass like demon eyes in the night.

Terrick pulls my arm, which feels numb, and walks me to the building next door with cold metal letters affixed to the exterior: *Z SQUAD DETENTION CENTER*.

"What are we doing here?" I ask in alarm.

"Don't worry. I'll check on you tomorrow," Terrick says, before marching me in and locking me inside a jail cell.

CHAPTER NINE

NOW THAT I'M caged, I'm no longer cuffed.

My twelve-by-twelve-foot cell contains a single bed with a thin mattress. It's like a smear of mayonnaise on a stale piece of bread topped with a blanket the color of a slice of beef bologna. And yes, I am thinking about food. Well, not food in particular so much as eating. I'm hungry. I don't want to really get into what it is I'm craving.

In the corner, there's a metal toilet, minus a seat and lid. I guess zombies still have to relieve themselves? Or maybe this is a multipurpose facility. I don't need a toilet. I need a shower, fresh undergarments, clean clothes, and bandages.

I sit on the edge of the bed, my slippered feet flat against the hard floor. Without my phone, it feels like I'm missing a limb. Also, what am I supposed to do until tomorrow? Why didn't Uncle Alvan answer Z Squad's call? He was probably on his flight to New York—phone in airplane mode. I need him here. Joni and I both do.

I stare at my painted nails and think of stupid things like how washed out my face must look without makeup. But if the choice was between makeup and perfume, I would take the bottle of perfume and douse myself in scent. I can't imagine returning home, but I will need to get my clothing, shoes, jewelry, cosmetics, candles, spellbooks, and the rest of my stuff. There's no way I can continue with Haylee's Holiday Looks. The beauty brigade will understand why. How loyal are they? I must have reached one million followers by now. It's no longer important, but I can't help thinking about it. I need to pick a winner for the Lignum Vitae wand. I wish I had my own wand to help pass the time. Round and round my thoughts go. Between musings, flashes of crazed zombies crash through my mind. I see them burst through my door. Worse, I remember the skull where Dad's face should have been, and Mom's missing toes. And then there is Kendra. A black hole opens in my mind if I get too near that memory.

I launch myself off the bed but don't reach the toilet in time before I retch. It's mostly drool and foam. I've missed lunch and dinner.

I walk around my mess to the toilet and spit into the metal bowl as the facility lights go out. It's not like I have far to go back to the bologna bed. Apparently, a hotel room isn't in the budget. So much for the red-carpet treatment. I lie on my back and reach my mind out toward the abyss. If I am no longer human, then I should not have to feel the crushing weight of human emotions. Maybe I'm in shock or denial, or "shenial." Lying in a dark cell—clothing soiled, wounds untreated, devastated, alone, and starving—I find a way to detach like a piece of driftwood floating toward an unknown shore.

I drift through the night until lights flood my cell and the hall outside, heralding my first morning as a zombie. Yesterday, my parents and sister were alive. Today they're gone. Dead and gone. It's the dawn of a doomed day.

I flip around and bury my face in the limp pillow. Maybe if I press hard enough, I can smother myself. Except I don't have to breathe in order to remain undead. My chest doesn't rise and fall like a human.

I can still cry, though.

Tears stream out the corners of my eyes. I rub my face dry on the pillow. My grief is private. I just need to get through processing, talk to Uncle Alvan, then get inside Dad's car, close the doors, and sob myself hoarse.

I sit up and rub away any lingering moisture under my eyes. The lights are on. Terrick said he would be back for me today. They must have reached Uncle Alvan by now. I'm ready to complete processing and get out of here.

My first visitor is a massive male with the darkest skin I've ever seen. His uniform is gray. The collared shirt is rolled up past his elbows, showcasing thick, muscular arms, and the top three buttons are undone over a white tee outlining the mass of muscles covering his chest. Square, gold earrings glint from his black lobes. A leather lanyard dangles from his thick neck. There's a tattoo on his lower arm that is difficult to make out, given it's done in black ink on his dark skin. He carries a plastic tray with a plate of mashed up bits of—brain?

"What is that?" I ask in disgust.

Thick lips smirk at me. "Breakfast."

I move closer to the bars and read the name on his badge: Maurice.

"That's not what I meant," I say.

"You know what it is," he counters.

I should be at home with my family eating leftover turkey, gravy, casserole, biscuits, and pie. Not being served brains in a cell.

"I'm not eating brains."

"Better get used to it if you want your postmortem body to continue functioning."

"What happens if I don't eat brains?"

"You end up like a late model vehicle without petroleum." When I squint at Maurice, he chuckles. "Let me put it in teenage terms. You would be like a phone with an empty battery. No power, no communication, no stimulating social media." He rolls his eyes, the whites like spotlights in his dark face. "No access to information, no oversharing, no sending, no receiving—capisce?"

I narrow my eyes. "Yeah, I think I got it. Brains do a zombie good."

"Oh good, you do understand."

I huff as he slides the tray through a horizontal opening in the bars. A piece of paper towel and a metal fork rest beside the plate. I make no move toward it. "Why is it all mushed up? You didn't scrape this off the road, did you?"

Maurice belts out a laugh. "Nah, nothing like that. We have a contract with Five Sevens Cattle Company. And to answer your first question, I chopped the organ because I've found that new zombies have trouble eating their very first brain if it looks exactly like what it is."

I purse my lips in thought. That does make sense. "Okay, so how often do I have to eat brains to maintain a *charge*?" I air quote the last word.

Maurice chuckles. "I like you, Haylee. You've got a spark inside I don't see too often among the undead—vampires included." His eyes narrow, which makes his entire face turn dark. Just as quickly, he's smiling again. "Depends on the size of the brain. I don't recommend rodents. Too much trouble for too few calories."

"Ew," I groan.

Maurice continues as though I never interrupted. "Small mammal brain—dogs and cats—will keep you up and running for a couple days. Something large, say a human or cow, can last you up to a week."

"Wait—human?" My upper lip curls.

"Organ donors—if you're lucky. Which reminds me, you can also consume organs and raw flesh."

"Oh, thank goodness. I was afraid I had limited options," I quip.

"At least your kind can handle liquids: water, soda, juice, blood, and alcohol. I'd stay away from smoothies and dairy, though."

"What about eating regular human food?"

"Not unless you want to give yourself the most explosive stomach flu of your life." He snorts. "I've seen it, and it's not pretty."

"But eating raw flesh is so appealing," I huff.

Maurice shrugs. "I'm a werewolf. Doesn't bother me. Now are you going to eat your meal or not?"

"Are you going to watch me?" I fire back.

He grins again. "Nothing like seeing a new zombie take her first bite of brain."

"Gee, I'm so glad I am able to entertain you," I say sarcastically. For real, though, suddenly I feel like I'm the newest addition in a zombie zoo.

Maurice's grin widens. "I imagine you are many things to be standing here now. Your file says that you fought off a zombie horde and performed your own Spell of Sanity. But I understand your frustration. This twenty-four-hour holding law to ensure you're truly sane is bureaucratic bull. We all know it. The vampires keep pushing us to up the wait time to a full week.

They're still lobbying for it in Congress. Be grateful we've got a werewolf as president. Now stop stalling and eat the brain. I promise you'll enjoy it."

"Doubtful. What kind of brain is this, anyway?"

"Maurice's secret blend." I scowl as Maurice busts out a laugh.

Not about to give him a front row viewing, I pick up the tray and carry it over to my bed, sitting on the edge. Tray on my lap, I pierce a chunk of brain with the fork. I want to be grossed out, but I'm not. It's not like my mouth is watering either. I lift the brain matter to my mouth and make a show of plugging my nose with one hand as I use my other hand to feed it into my mouth with a fork and chew.

After the first swallow, my body takes on a life of its own, casting me aside as easily as a shadow. I devour the rest of my meal like it's a plate full of homemade pasta marinara with fresh ground parmesan and basil. When I'm finished, I stare down at the empty plate in confusion.

Maurice chuckles. "Happens every time." He rubs his chin. "Though I've never seen anyone eat as fast as you."

Great. My ravenous appetite is tagging along into zombiehood.

"I'd bring you seconds if it wasn't against protocol." Maurice puffs out a breath of air. I'm pretty sure he thinks that's bull too.

"Thank you," I say, meaning it. Mrs. Kline called Terrick a hero, but Maurice is mine. He's the first person who took the time to help me understand what's happening to me. And he fed me. I wipe my mouth on the paper towel, carry the tray back over to the wall of bars, crouch, and slide it through the opening.

Maurice nods and takes the tray. "Pleasure to serve." I can't tell if he's being sarcastic or sincere. He sounds honest, but I can't imagine anyone finding satisfaction with this gig.

I take a closer look at Maurice's face and notice a tribal design buzzed into his coiled hair. He looks way too cool to be detention center staff. I tell him as much. "I'm surprised you're on meal duty instead of out crushing crazed zombies to pulp with your biceps or whatever."

Maurice stretches his neck to one side. It makes a popping noise that has me grimacing. Maurice smirks. "I was taken off Z Squad for not being a team player." I frown, but he doesn't look upset in the least. Maurice lowers his voice. "Don't tell anyone, but I prefer being a cuisinier over an attack dog." He winks, laughs, and starts backing away.

I don't want to be left alone.

"Cool tattoo," I say quickly, jutting my chin at the moth inked on his arm. The design is encased in a card-shaped frame with pretty embellishments in the corners. I squint. "Is your tattoo ensorcelled?" Magical tattoos are rarer than Lignum Vitae trees. They require crushed jetnite, which costs a small fortune. I prefer my skin unblemished; otherwise an ensorcelled tattoo would have been at the top of my wish list after getting a wand.

Maurice flashes me a smile that's all teeth. "This here is a *ny scelta,* otherwise known as the wild card."

"I've heard of it," I say, sounding every bit as awestruck as I feel. It seemed more like a myth. I didn't think anyone would go for something so impractical and expensive. You can use it for any spell you choose, but it's only good for one use. "What's it for?" I want to know.

Maurice continues grinning. "My baby girl. If there ever comes a time that I can't protect her with fangs and claws, I've got backup. Had to spend my entire inheritance to get it done, but money is something I can earn back."

"That's really sweet." A lump forms in my throat. Could I have saved my family if I'd had a *ny scelta* tattooed on my body? Everything happened so fast, but maybe I could have sent out a protective circle across my whole house. Not that I've ever had enough money to afford a jetnite tattoo of any type.

"It also makes other supes think twice about messing with me," Maurice states.

"You don't need a tattoo for that." I snort.

Maurice chuckles as he walks off with my tray. Before disappearing down the hall, he turns to look at me over his broad shoulder. "Keep your power charged, Haylee Hutchins."

Morning wears on. My physical body buzzes with anxiety. It doesn't help that I have no outlet to work any of it out. Time drags, trips, falls, stumbles, and drags on longer. The only reason I know that days aren't passing is because the lights have remained on. Finally, boot steps thud down the hall, coming closer at a slow, leisurely pace.

Don't hurry on my account.

My legs hang off the edge of the bed. I fold my arms behind my head and rest against them. If Z Squad wants to play it cool, so be it. Dressed in uniform, Terrick steps up to the bars. I stand and fold my arms.

"Congratulations, Miss Hutchins. You are officially of sound mind. We'll get you cleaned up and registered."

"Has someone spoken to my Uncle Alvan?"

Something unreadable flickers in Terrick's eyes. "He's unreachable at this time."

A sob escapes my lips. I don't care if it makes me sound pitiful. "Do you think he's dead?"

Terrick grits his teeth and glances sideways down the hall.

"Just tell me," I half demand, half plead.

Terrick's forehead wrinkles. Just when I'm convinced he's not going to tell me anything, he does. "He's in New York, and he's fine but unable to take calls at the moment. That's all I can tell you."

"But—"

Terrick full-on growls. We glare at each other through the bars. "Perhaps you would prefer to spend another night in here?" he suggests.

"Where else am I gonna go?" I counter. "Caribbean vacation? Rent myself one of those over-the-water bungalows? I bet they include a toilet with an actual seat and lid."

Terrick grunts and shakes his head before unlocking my cell. "Come with me." I follow him out of the hall of holding cells, through a set of double doors that lead into another hall with no natural lighting, and into a small room that looks like the ones at hospital clinics. It's got the padded geriatric chair, side sink, and metallic instruments lining the counter.

A thirty-something woman in a white lab coat and a short brown braid walks in after us, which surprises me. I had fully expected to be kept waiting again.

"This is Dr. Anju. She is going to treat your wounds," Terrick announces, leaning his back against the wall.

I frown at him. "Ever hear of doctor-patient privacy?"

"His presence is part of protocol," Dr. Anju informs me. "Have a seat." She nods at the geriatric chair.

"So long as I don't have to remove any clothing," I say like I have a choice. I seat myself on the edge of the chair, a thin layer of white paper crinkling beneath me.

Dr. Anju isn't one for conversation. She brings over a plastic bin with supplies and gets to work disinfecting my wounds and gashes. She wipes away the dried blood, throwing soiled tissues into a small trash bin. Once each wound is clean, she dresses it with gauze, wrapping bandages securely in place around my arms and neck. The part-mummy look isn't really my thing.

"Um, I thought you were going to heal these?"

"You're going to need alterations for that," Dr. Anju says.

I'm aware she doesn't mean the type of alterations Mrs. Kline can provide with needle and thread. The realm of zombie services is entirely foreign to me.

"Come on. I'll drive you home," Terrick says.

"Home?"

"Your uncle TJ Mullins has agreed to take you in."

I gape in horror. Take me in like I'm a stray dog. I bet he's not above kicking me either, especially now that he's lost his punching bag.

Before I can object, Terrick adds, "This is your only option—for now."

"For now?" I repeat.

"You can sort the rest out with Alvan Bates once he's available."

"Fine," I say, because Terrick is right. I'm fresh out of options at the moment. But this also presents an opportunity to search for evidence of TJ's involvement in my family's murders. I can watch his behavior and go through his phone while he's asleep. I'm also desperate to check on Joni. "What about my wand?"

"We'll get it from the station and then be on our way."

In addition to returning my wand, I'm handed a book with a torn cover.

RULES AND GUIDELINES FOR ZOMBIES

The narrow spine is cracked, and the corners of the pages are dented. I wonder how many zombie hands have held this worn guidebook and why Z Squad can't hand out fresh copies. Budget cuts?

I follow Terrick outside into the crisp daylight. The sky is blindingly blue without a trace of warmth.

As we approach the lime-green-and-blue SUV, I ask, "Do I get to ride up front this time?"

"Not in those clothes," Terrick says.

I scowl at him. Cold-blooded criminals are treated better than zombies. They, at least, get clean clothing and a shower. I suppose I should be grateful they bothered feeding me.

Once I'm seated—in back behind the barrier—I flip through the beat-up rule book. "Do werewolves have a handbook?"

"We don't need a handbook."

Yeah, because werewolves are grandfathered in. Not only does the law allow them to pass down their supernatural gifts to family members and spouses, but they're also there to guide the next generation through their first transformation.

"Shouldn't other supernatural creatures have their own special rule book?" I press. Terrick starts the SUV and guns it out of the parking lot as though he can get away from me and my questions if he drives fast enough. "Well?" I demand when Terrick is forced to stop at a red light.

"Those rules are in place to protect civilians from hordes and crazed zombies."

I rub my thumb over the bent page edges. "I don't think crazed zombies will be reading this handy, dandy guide or any other literature for that matter." Where sarcasm ends, despair waits to swallow me whole, which is why I keep the quips coming. I flip through the book some more. "Gross. There's a hair in my copy." I close the book and stare out the window at the drivers and pedestrians going about their business like it's any other day. "Can we swing by my house first?"

"It's being fumigated."

"What?" I screech. "What about my clothes and things?"

"Everything inside has been removed and incinerated."

My scream makes Terrick jolt forward and grip the steering wheel like a sea captain entering a white squall. "Jesus!" he yelps.

"Everything?" I demand.

At the next red light, he hits the brake hard and whips his head around to glare at me. "You need to calm down. You almost made me rear-end the truck in front of us."

I don't back down. I'm not calm. I'm freaking out. "You're telling me that all of my things have been destroyed? My clothing? My laptop? My equipment? My cosmetics?" The light turns green, and I keep going as the SUV lurches forward. "My spellbooks? My candles? Perfumes? Lotions?"

"Yes!" Terrick yells. "All of it."

"Oh my god. My phone! Did someone get my phone for me before incinerating all of my worldly possessions?"

"I don't know. Maybe Sgt. Ganon grabbed it while retrieving your cousin."

A kernel of hope pops into my head—not that the Z Squad sergeant bothered to save my phone—but that Joni nabbed it and stuffed it inside her purse on her way out. We're going to need that phone to contact Uncle Alvan ASAP.

My mind reels for the remainder of the drive to TJ's. What am I supposed to wear? How can I record videos without my equipment and products? It hits me again and again that my life as a beauty influencer is over and that I don't care. Lipstick, hair clips, and followers don't mean anything when my family was killed in the most gruesome way imaginable. Whoever is behind their murders has to pay. That's all that matters now.

The sight of TJ's one-story ranch house fills me with purpose and dread. Terrick pulls into the driveway, remaining in the driver's seat, engine running.

"Not walking me to the front door?" I ask sarcastically while batting my lashes in an overexaggerated display.

"You're not a child," he answers.

No. I'm not. I'm a teenage zombie. Forever seventeen.

As soon as I'm out of the SUV, the door closes behind me, Terrick backs out. The front door to TJ's house flies open, and Joni runs out. "Haylee!" Her smile looks all wrong in her blotchy, tear-stained face.

TJ is right behind her, snapping, "Lower your voice!" Never mind that he says this louder than Joni. My cousin freezes in place, her mouth ajar.

I frown, unable to hide my disgust for this man.

"Hurry inside before you scare the neighbors," he snaps at me.

CHAPTER TEN

I GNASH MY TEETH and fume with every step I take up the driveway. TJ thinks he can order me around? I want to give him the finger and storm off, except that would be a stupid thing to do right now. Knowing I am stuck to do as he says makes me even angrier.

I walk inside TJ's house, followed by Joni and then the ogre. He closes the door, turns, sniffs the air, and scowls. "What is that awful smell?"

Your rotten soul, I think, which lifts the corners of my lips slightly.

Not waiting for an answer, he looks me up and down with a sneer. "Listen up, because I'm only going to say this once. You're in my house now. My rules. My authority. We'll sort out custody with your parents' fancy lawyer on Monday. In the meantime, my friends are coming over any minute to help out, seeing as Chloe got herself killed by going over to your meddlesome mother's house when she should have been home taking care of her own family. Now I'm left to raise not one, but two girls on my own." The sound of a vehicle pulling into the driveway lifts TJ's chin. He's no longer looking at me or the burning hatred raging in my eyes. His gaze lands on my gauze-wrapped neck. "Go to Joni's room and stay out of sight until my friends leave. They want nothing to do with a zombie, and I don't blame them."

Gladly! If I have to stand here listening to this stinking pile of crap a second longer, I'm going to bite first and ask questions later.

When Joni tries to come with me, TJ snaps at her. "Where do you think you're going? We have guests taking time out of their busy lives to check on you. You will be on your best behavior."

This means I have to wait until after TJ's friends leave to talk to Joni. I hurry to her room—a trail of angry fumes following—close myself inside, stand in place, and stew, wand and handbook still clutched in my hands.

I'm in desperate need of a shower, but I already feel vulnerable enough without undressing in TJ's bathroom while he has guests over. I'll wait until they're gone and my uncle and cousin are asleep tonight. In the meantime, I cast an anti-stink spell over myself, but I still feel gross.

TJ's vicious words break apart like pieces of a puzzle that don't form a clear picture no matter how many times I try to fit them together. He sounded genuinely put out that Aunt Chloe is dead rather than smug over punishing her and my parents. And why in the world would TJ want custody of me?

On Monday morning, his motivation behind custody becomes as clear as tears.

Aunt Chloe's gray turtleneck feels like a noose around my neck even after I used my wand to up the size. The sky is as bleak as the sweater on the rough truck ride over to the Law Offices of Dirk and Sunder.

Joni already left for school after TJ told her he would not tolerate any wallowing at home feeling sorry for herself. Unfortunately, Joni did not think to grab my phone before Sgt. Ganon led her out of my bedroom—an oversight for which she has apologized over half a dozen times.

I'm not mad. How could I be? I'm just drowning in an ocean of plastic waste and disappointment.

Anger, sorrow, and despair have kept me up the past two nights at TJ's. Last Monday, my parents and sister were alive. I had my own bedroom—with an actual bed—not a sleeping bag on the floor. Joni said maybe I could use her mother's craft room as my own, but her voice had wobbled and her chin trembled. When I told her I'd rather share a room, she'd hugged me so tightly I knew it was the right choice. My cousin then offered to give me her bed and take the floor, but I'm not about to boot her out of her single-mattress platform bed with its zebra print blanket. I'm not even sure that I need sleep. But I do need brains, which means returning to the last place I want to set foot—Brookdale High. TJ has made it clear that if I want to eat, it's not going to be on his dime. He's already had to put in for a vacation day to accompany me to this morning's appointment.

Inside the sitting room of the lawyer's office, a gorgeous woman with layers upon layers of brown highlighted hair leaps up from her seat in the waiting room, which is impressive in stilettos and a short black leather skirt. She's tall and skinny, with a bust pushing the laces of her silky olive V-neck near snapping. She comes at me like she means to tackle me to the thin layer of taupe carpet.

"My poor, dear girl!" she cries out, long slender arms wrapping around me with surprising strength. I stand dumbfounded as flashes go off and a young man steps forward from a corner, camera lens aimed at us. "When I heard what happened to poor, sweet Laurence, my heart broke to pieces," the bombshell sobs against Aunt Chloe's turtleneck before pulling back and dabbing at her eyes, makeup still perfectly in place. Maybe she's wearing waterproof mascara.

TJ swings around midway to the secretary's desk. "What the hell is this?" he demands.

The woman pulls away from me—while sticking close—and glares at TJ through long, curling lashes. "I am Haylee's stepmother, Cressida Angelise Beckwith."

"The hell you are," TJ sneers.

For once, I have to agree with TJ. I've never met this woman until today. She's my dad's ex. He remarried and so did she. In what universe does she presume to have any relation to me?

When TJ steps toward the woman, a beast of a man moves in, curling the fingers on his left hand into a fist.

An older gentleman emerges from the hall leading back to several offices and strides into the waiting room. He peers around the room from above wire-rim glasses. His silvery hair is as immaculate as his black suit. "Good. You're all here. Follow me. Family only," he adds, directing the last part at the photographer, who looks at Cressida. She gives a pout with her full, plump lips before nodding at the photographer. Cressida then glides forward as though she was born with spiked heels attached to the soles of her feet. Her bodyguard takes up the rear and keeps glancing around like he expects our group to be tackled from behind at any moment. The nameplate on the door the lawyer leads us to reads *CHARLES DIRK*.

Inside the lawyer's office, Cressida is the first to take a seat in front of a large mahogany desk. She pats the chair beside her and smiles at me. "Haylee, darling, come sit beside me."

TJ loses it. "Don't go anywhere near that woman," he snaps at me, then at the lawyer. "Why is she here, and what's with the muscle?"

The linebacker in question grunts, whether in amusement or annoyance it's difficult to tell.

Cressida bristles, giving TJ a full-on pout. "That is Jael Doren," she informs him. "My husband, former defensive midfielder, and four-time World Cup champion with the Hamlet Hounds."

TJ narrows his eyes. He hasn't taken a seat, and neither have I, not because he forbade it, but because this is a woman Dad wanted nothing to do with after their divorce. I can't even believe he married her to begin with. That's not something I can remotely picture inside my head.

"Why are either of you here?" TJ demands.

Cressida places one manicured hand over her chest. "Who better to take care of sweet Haylee than the woman her father first married?"

TJ laughs harshly. "Oh, I see now. You're after the rest of your ex's money."

"Careful," Jael warns, taking a step toward TJ that goes no further.

That's when it fully hits me. These clowns seem to be under the impression that custody of me means access to my family's fortune. I suppose the checks aren't coming in the way they did before Jael's injury forced him into early retirement.

I look at Mr. Charles Dirk, who has settled into his leather office chair. "Firstly, I would like to express my condolences," he says. "Laurence Hutchins was well respected by everyone in our profession."

Cressida's head bobs like it's attached to her shoulders with loose hinges. "I always knew Laurence would make a name for himself, just like my Jael." She flashes kissy lips at her husband and winks. "Even back in high school, Laurence was a high achiever—voted most likely to succeed."

"Well, he certainly didn't succeed in protecting my wife from zombies," TJ complains.

Cressida gasps and then shoots TJ a venomous glare. "How dare you disrespect the deceased?"

I've had enough of their bickering. "What does my father's will say?" I ask Mr. Dirk.

The lawyer inclines his head. "Let's get to that, shall we?" He opens a file folder and pulls out a stack of typed documents, handing us each a copy. Cressida snatches hers first and scans it like she's a human photocopy machine.

"Ah-ha! You see here?" She jabs a long white-tipped nail at the paper. "It's up to Haylee to choose her guardian."

Head bent over his copy, TJ's chin moves back and forth like that will help him read faster. With a growl of frustration, his head jerks up. "You're not even blood-related."

"Neither are you," Cressida fires back, sounding triumphant.

"You're a stranger to Haylee," TJ says, dropping an F bomb before "stranger."

Cressida raises one dark, sculpted brow. "That's no language to use around a child."

Child? Ohhh. I loathe them both.

"You know nothing about child raising, you greedy b—"

"Does this guardianship thing last until I graduate from high school?" I speak up.

That quiets both TJ and Cressida, who turn their attention to Mr. Dirk as he folds his age-spotted hands on top of his desk. "Normally, yes. Once you turned eighteen, you would then become your own legal guardian and have access to your family's assets. Unfortunately, you will never physically reach your eighteenth birthday." My jaw unhinges, but my outcry doesn't make it past the lump in my throat. Mr. Dirk continues. "On the plus side, you have the authority to select the person by whom all assets will be controlled on your behalf—your legal and lifetime guardian. In the event that your chosen guardian perishes before you, you are then able to appoint a new guardian."

Mr. Dirk's mouth is a whirlpool I'm stuck in. I can't be hearing him correctly. My brain is scrambled. No way. Just no freaking way this is happening.

"It's for the best, dear," Cressida says from much too close after moving from the perch of her seat to place her hand with its long nails on my arm. "What you need is a mother figure. I'll treat you like the daughter I wished for back when your father and I were together. Raising a family together was one of our earliest dreams." Jael's eyes are half-lidded, arms hanging loosely at his sides from his position near the closed door. He doesn't react in any way to his wife discussing her child-rearing fantasy with her ex-husband. Cressida takes my hand before I can step back. She must really want my father's fortune to sully her baby-soft palm on a zombie. "Think of all the fun we'll have, us gals going out on shopping trips and spa treatments, traveling." Her fingers begin squeezing too hard. "I know what you need, sweetie. Distraction from this terrible tragedy and someone who will love you just the way you are."

Her script is pretty good—if I were a member of her wide-eyed, gullible audience.

I pull my hand out of hers and address the only sane person in this room. "What about my Uncle Alvan?"

Mr. Dirk hasn't opened his mouth before TJ spits, "Alvan has no time nor interest in raising a teenager."

I'm a rubber band that's been stretched too far. I snap at TJ with a curled lip. "I'm old enough to look out for myself. And we shouldn't even be meeting today without Uncle Alvan—an *actual* blood relative of mine."

Cressida shakes her head and tsks in disappointment like she's trying her parental authority on for size. She's delusional.

An ugly laugh burbles from TJ's lips. "You can cross Alvan Bates off of your guardian list this second, niece. Let me tell you why your gallant uncle couldn't make it. He's a vampire now."

At first, I'm sure I misheard. White noise fills my head. My mouth dries out. The lump returns. I shake my head.

"Oh, yes," TJ crows. "Alvan is not to be disturbed during his making—not even over the death of his sisters. His boss's lackeys told me not to call again." TJ taps a dirty fingernail below his lower lip. "I suppose the vamp is no longer his boss so much as his master."

My ears pound, and my vision tunnels over Mr. Dirk's desk. I feel like grabbing his stapler and throwing it against the wall. Did Uncle Alvan's boss even give him a choice, or did he force my uncle into serving him forever? Mom was right. He works for the devil, and now he is doomed to obey his master for centuries.

Body heavy and fingers numb, I look at Mr. Dirk for guidance. The lawyer rubs a finger over his age-spotted hand. "Miss Hutchins raises a valid concern. As her last remaining adult blood relative, Mr. Bates should be included in these proceedings—regardless of his current circumstances."

Cressida lifts her chest and grins at me like I'm a rare collector's Gucci handbag she intends to walk out with at any cost—or snatch up with her one-inch-long nails if it comes to that.

"Alvan Bates is such a bad boy." She giggles. "As much as we all love Al, he's not a family man."

"You know my uncle?" I ask, surprised.

"Oh, yes." Cressida's eyes light up. "My friendship with Alvan goes way back. It's how Laurence met your dear, sweet mother. They likely would have never met if not for me." Cressida arches a brow, and I think I know what she's implying. I wouldn't have been born if not for her supposed matchmaking. "It was all for the best," she goes on, tossing a smile over her shoulder. "If not for our breakup, I wouldn't be married to my beloved Jael. I cared for Laurence very much, of course, but Jael is my soulmate."

"Love you, babe," he says.

She blows him a kiss.

I don't know how much more of this sticky sweet, phony bootlicking I can listen to. "Before I decide anything, I want to talk to Uncle Alvan," I announce.

TJ's nostrils flare. He shoots me a menacing glare that has me wanting to walk home. Cressida sees it and smiles smugly. "Take all the time you want, dear, and think about who could give you the best afterlife. Let me remind you that my Jael is a werewolf. Our household is inclusive and eclectic. Your poor parents, God rest their souls, would want you to be looked after by someone who cares and understands supernaturals."

"If you love supernaturals so much, why didn't you become a werewolf?" TJ fires off.

Cressida gives her hair a lazy toss and lifts her nose. "Because I'm perfect just the way I am."

"Love you, babe," Jael says.

Cressida makes a kissing sound his way and then smirks at TJ.

"Very well," Mr. Dirk says, standing up. "We shall reconvene at a time when Mr. Bates is available to join us. My secretary will make arrangements. Until then, good day." He nods at the door, dismissing us from his office.

Cressida and Jael leave ahead of me and TJ, but not before Cressida gives us a cheerful wave and says, "See you soon."

On the truck ride home, TJ floors the gas pedal down the roads and slams the brakes at stops. "If you choose that harpy as your guardian, you can forget about ever seeing Joni again," he threatens.

"What if I choose Uncle Alvan?"

TJ makes a sound of disgust deep in his throat. "You just don't get it, do you? Alvan doesn't want responsibility for a teenager. He only cares about himself."

"That's not true!"

"Fine. See for yourself after he completes his luxurious transformation process and finally gets his ass over here to pay his respects to my dead wife. He was always selfish. Chloe said so herself. He'll be even worse as a vampire. Wait and see."

CHAPTER ELEVEN

LAST TUESDAY MY parents and sister were alive. Today they're gone. Dead and gone. I'll never hear their voices, never see their faces, never hug them again.

Last Wednesday my parents and sister were alive. Today they're not. I took the day off from school last week—back when I was still human. I take it off again today. I'm never going back to that hellhole.

It's Thursday. A week ago, everything was right in the world. Well, not everything, obviously, but my family was alive, and they were everything to me, which made everything right.

While Joni's at school and TJ's at work, I lie on top of my sleeping bag, closed up inside my cousin's room either curled up crying or zoning out.

Joni's walls are painted lavender. There's a zebra-print accent wall that matches her blanket, throw pillow, and floor rug—though the rug is now mostly covered by my sleeping bag. Her fuchsia-and-mint-green dresser, bed frame drawers, desk, and wall shelves look like life-sized dollhouse furniture. The blinds are closed over her window with fuchsia curtains too sheer to hide the PVC slats. There's a small plastic pink chandelier hanging low in the corner, along with framed pictures of African animals.

I sit up and rub the smooth wood of my Lignum Vitae wand back and forth against my palm. It's my last worldly possession. I only get it out when I'm alone in the house. Otherwise, it's hidden at the bottom of my sleeping bag.

My stomach rumbles, hunger pangs digging in with sharp pointed nails.

I can't go back to Brookdale. I'm still holding on to hope that Uncle Alvan will come through for me and Joni. TJ said vampires have a week-long transformation process. I bet it doesn't involve a jail cell, cuffs, and a tattered guidebook.

If Uncle Alvan doesn't want to take me and Joni in, fine. I just need him to assume the title of legal guardian and get me access to my family's fortune. With funds, I can buy a house for me and Joni where we can dictate our own terms and cry as often, and as loudly, as we want.

The thought cheers me up. I don't need Uncle Alvan. I only need my inheritance.

Feeling slightly less suicidal, I open up the zombie handbook.

INTRODUCTION

How to Integrate Back into Society after Becoming Undead: Rules and Guidelines for Zombies

After becoming one of the cognizant undead (classification zombie), readjusting to society-standard life can be challenging. This guidebook provides recommendations, resources, and rules to live by. (Full list of rules and regulations appear in the following pages.)

After successful completion of the Spell of Sanity following a zombie bite, former humans face a much different world than the one they previously inhabited. Post-human life can be difficult for many zombies. Attitudes and obstacles can be depressing. This handbook is intended to guide former humans to focus on meeting society-set standards under their new conditions.

Get Started on the Right Foot

> Maintaining a normal routine is a key aspect of successful reintegration, whether that is returning to school or work. Assessing your strengths and weaknesses will create a framework for remaining a productive member of society going forward. Consider your assets in life: relationships, social networks, and undeveloped talents, and see how those can impact your life after undeath.
>
> Your condition heavily affects relationships, and if you want a successful reintegration, retaining amicable exchanges with family and friends is key.

Blah. Blah. Bull. Why is it all on *me* to make the effort? I return to reading the *encouraging* introduction.

> Make sure that you locate helpful local resources. From how to find sustenance that meets your dietary needs to alterations and physical treatments, these resources for zombies are a necessity. If you can determine where you can turn for aid, it will help lessen the stress and anxiety of resuming your life.
>
> Finally, do your best to serve your community. Contributing to society takes time, effort, and intentionality, which helps the cognizant undead build a constructive future for themselves. Volunteering with appropriate organizations will reincorporate you with your "new" world and help you build positive relationships with others. You can carry the skills you learn in these scenarios into many other areas of your life as well.

I flip to the rules section, which has a huge **BITING = EXTERMINATION** warning graphic. No exceptions. No do-overs. Only death—the forever and gone kind.

Delightful.

There's a page torn out near the front. Hope it wasn't something I needed.

I do find something interesting at the back of the book.

SPELL OF SANITY TURNABOUT

"What the?"

I lift the book to my face.

SPELL OF SANITY TURNABOUT

(For the immediate reversal of the SPELL OF SANITY.)

WARNING: Once spoken, this spell cannot be undone. Effects are IMMEDIATE. Do NOT, under any circumstances, perform the Turnabout Spell in public or in the presence of humans or other creatures.

The Turnabout Spell was created by Bentley Sagan as a way for sane zombies to give Z Squad permission to exterminate their life. It ONLY works on the zombie who speaks the incantation and **cannot be reversed once completed**.

IMPORTANT: Before performing the SPELL OF SANITY TURNABOUT, contact Z Squad at SOS (or 767) to arrange for a holding cell or to disclose the secure, or remote, location you have chosen for your reversal. If you do not own, or have misplaced, a Lignum Vitae wand, one can be provided for you at a Z Squad detention center on loan while you are securely locked in a cell during your casting of a turnabout. Performing the Turnabout Spell inside the safety of a Z Squad cell is the recommended method.

So much for feeling less suicidal. "Has the world gone mad?" I ask aloud. Do they want all zombies to be crazed and killed? Apparently so. It's like, "Hey, here's a spell. Don't have a wand? We'll loan you one. Problem solved." Maybe they want an excuse to wipe zombies off the face of the Earth guilt-free. Is it even possible to exterminate zombies permanently? Would I care? Is that what happened to the previous owner of this manual? I scoff. It wouldn't surprise me in the least if Z Squad recycled the guidebooks of zombie suicides.

I read the spell. Five lines of casting—that's all it takes to turn me into one of those crazed horrors that ate my family.

Body. Mind. Soul. Divide.

Flesh decay. Remains waste away.

Body. Mind. Soul. Divide.

Thoughts move on. Memories gone.

Body. Mind. Soul. Divide.

A cold shiver runs through me, like just reading the words silently might undo the spell holding me together. At the same time, I'm drawn to the spell like a vampire to an artery. It would be so easy to end this unbearable suffering once and for all. I have everything I need.

The wand work starts with a windshield wiper motion first, followed by aiming the wand inward. Instead of a triple spiral, it has the instruction for making a flinging motion with the wand. I look at the instructions closer. Oh, wow. The spell actually calls for releasing the wand as it's flung aside. Never seen that before. Then again, I suppose performing this spell means the wand is no longer of use to the zombie caster.

A glance at my wand makes my stomach plunge over a cliff and somersault halfway down before deep diving into a bottomless lake.

I smack the manual shut. It's almost as though it's calling to me. Would someone have spelled the print to get inside the reader's head? Maybe I should take the guide out back and torch it inside TJ's grill. However, it does have some useful information, like the page dog-eared by the guide's previous owner about alterations. A professional alterationist is a mix between a sorcerer, or a licensed spellcaster, and a plastic surgeon. It would be nice if I had my phone or laptop to look up the web addresses listed in the guide.

Huffing, I shove the guidebook aside and lie on my back. TJ's house is more comfortable than Z Squad's detention center, but it feels just as prison-like with a worse warden.

I take hold of my wand and bring a memory to mind of my long weekend visit to Blakely College. Pointing my wand at the ceiling, I cast. "Memory, memory, on the wall. Show me what I wish to see most of all."

The memory plays out like a projection over the textured white paint above. In the past, I used this spell to show Mom how Payton had acted toward me at a football game we had gone to together at the beginning of the school year, and what she said, how her voice sounded. I was quite proud of my ability to conjure it all back up. But Mom had frowned and told me I needed to let that stuff go, not obsess over it with replays, allowing it to fester.

I don't want to remember Mom's disappointment. I don't want to remember how my last feeling toward my brave, beautiful, amazing mother was annoyance.

Instead, I watch Kendra give me the campus tour on a sunny California afternoon between classes. We grab our lunches to go from the cafeteria and take them outside to eat on a picnic table beneath the shade of oak trees. After we're finished eating, Kendra glances at her white smartwatch.

"Next class starts in fifteen. Do you want to wait for me out here or back at the dorm?"

"Can I come with you?" I ask. Every moment of this memory is projected from my mind's eye. I can't see myself, other than my arms resting on the outdoor tabletop across from my sister.

Kendra's brows lift. "Are you sure you want to sit through a political reporting lecture?"

"Why not? I'm interested in media stuff."

"How about politics?" Kendra laughs.

"Eh, not so much." But it doesn't matter what class she has. I just want to hang out with my big sister every second I have left of my West Coast visit.

Kendra gets up from the table and smiles at me. "Well, it's never too late to educate yourself and get involved."

I watch my sister take our paper plates and biodegradable wooden forks to a nearby compost bin—one of many around campus that she explained get collected by students in the horticulture and gardening program.

I'm more interested in a business degree, specifically to help me launch my own beauty line. Advertising classes will help too, though I have a head start on the social end of marketing.

Kendra slings her backpack over her shoulder and grabs her water bottle off the picnic table. Her back turns, sunlight catching natural highlights in her unbound hair. I watch myself follow her to class while tears run in rivers down my cheeks from my spot on the floor looking up at the past.

It's results night on *Spellcaster*, but I couldn't care less who leaves the show and who stays.

Saturday morning, I help Joni with her homework at the kitchen table. Understandably, she's been having trouble concentrating. TJ isn't helping with the volume on high while he watches a game on TV from the living room. Our chairs are pushed together. My arms, covered in another one of Aunt Chloe's long-sleeved sweaters, rest on the table. It took less altering with my wand. After not eating for a week, I'm down a size, maybe even two. I try not to slump. While Joni was having breakfast with her dad earlier, I cast a silencing spell on my rumbling stomach. My energy is all but depleted. I'm just holding on for tomorrow's funeral. Holding on for the moment I see Uncle Alvan in the church or graveyard—whichever comes first—and am finally able to throw myself at his mercy.

When TJ issues a string of curses, I assume it's because his team lost a point, but he stomps into the kitchen, phone in front of his face, swearing up a storm. Joni drops her pencil on her notebook and quickly picks it back up, keeping her face down, letting her hair curtain her face. TJ snatches another beer out of the fridge and storms over to us, setting the can down roughly beside Joni's textbook.

"Your uncle is a real piece of work," TJ carps.

"You heard from Uncle Alvan?" My head jerks up. I eye TJ's phone hungrily—along with the fingers holding them.

TJ sneers. "He *texted* to inform me that he has only just emerged from his transformation phase and that he has to consult with his master before he can see any of us. The bastard won't be making the funeral tomorrow. His own sisters' memorials, and he can't be bothered."

"What?" My mouth hangs open, and my heart stops. Wait. No. It already stopped a week and one day ago. I swear I feel it stop again and mummify inside my ribcage. If it had started, it would break all over again.

Uncle Alvan has forsaken us.

Scenes from last year's Christmas break play on Joni's ceiling Sunday morning.

It turns out zombies aren't allowed at memorial services. Too dangerous. Too upsetting to other attendees. Whoever came up with these harsh and discriminatory laws can bite my rotten flesh (since I'm not allowed to bite theirs).

With the last of my energy, I throw my own memorial—one in which my family and I are together again for one last holiday.

Sunday night, Joni and I lie awake. She's on her zebra bed. I'm in my sleeping bag.

"Did Uncle Alvan show up?" I ask, even though I know the answer.

"No," Joni whispers.

If TJ hears talking, he'll either shout from his bedroom or storm in with his threats. I've gotten to know his sleep pattern in a short time, though, and have waited long enough for normal speaking voices to be safe.

"Was Kendra's fiancé, Cameron, there?" I ask next. Joni never met him, but Kendra showed her pictures on her phone. Joni had called him "handsome," which Kendra thought was so cute.

Joni leans over her bed, which makes her look like a sad little lump in the dark. "Yeah," she whispers.

I turn onto my side and peer at my cousin. "Really?"

"He was there, and he was looking for you. He said he had something for you."

Now I'm sitting up. "What is it? Did he give it to you? What did he say?"

Joni shakes her head. "Dad said whatever it was, he would pass it on to you, but Cameron said he wanted to give it to you himself. Dad told him you're not allowed to have visitors inside his house."

I bite back a curse. Damn TJ to the seven circles of hell!

"What did Cameron say?" I demand.

"He got upset. He said Kendra would have wanted him to check on her sister. Dad reminded him you're a zombie and said you don't feel the same kind of sadness or pain as humans." Joni gave a little sob of distress. "I'm sorry, Haylee. I know that's not true."

"It's okay. Cameron would never believe that," I say. "What happened next?"

"The memorial service was starting, so we sat down. I only saw Cameron once after that. After the service, he walked out crying." Joni's voice breaks. She stuffs her face in her pillow. Muffled sobs ensue.

I dig my wand out from the bottom of my sleeping bag and give her a gentle tap on the shoulder. "Hey, want to see a meteor shower?"

Joni lifts her head, eyes wide. "You still have your wand?" I know TJ is usually deep asleep by now, but I still wince at Joni's high-pitched surprise and press two fingers to my lips. Joni grimaces and whispers, "Sorry."

"Look above you," I whisper back, and then, "*La kizzy. La solaverse. Wirl a la cosmosta. Expand.*" I make little tapping motions with the tip of my wand pointed at Joni's ceiling. Stars appear, glowing overhead in a dark blue sky. Constellations shimmer into existence. A hazy band of purple, pink, and white-blue light forms the Milky Way.

Astronomy was my favorite class junior year. If I had been allowed the use of spellcasting for our final project, I bet Mr. Harris would have added an extra plus to my A.

"*Macro. Solario. Torped-a-flash.*" I make several slashes with my wand, and meteors streak across the ceiling in flashes of white light. "*Down. Down. Down*," I encourage, and they drop from the ceiling, showering Joni's bedroom in cosmic wonder.

I shake my wand at the universe I've created, bringing my stars to life by adding twinkles that pulse overhead. "*Glint. Flare. Flame rindle.*" I add touches of color to my meteors' tails.

The flashes light up my cousin's face. The tears have dried on Joni's cheeks. Her lips are slightly parted.

Spellcasting takes concentration. I can't lie on my back and watch my own work, or it will fade away. I wouldn't want to slack off. Casting makes my nerves buzz with exhilaration. It's a magnificent art form that feeds my soul.

"Hold out your hand," I whisper to Joni.

She cups her palm over the edge of her bed. I draw an invisible line from the ceiling to her outstretched hand and whisper a spell. A meteor with a zebra trail jets from the ceiling to her hand, leaving a small, gray, lumpy piece of space rock in her palm. It's an illusion, of course, but Joni stares down at it like she's just been handed the world's largest natural diamond.

"Amazing," she murmurs. She lifts the meteorite fragment in front of her face to examine it closer. Her fingers curl in. There's nothing for her to feel, but when she spreads her fingers open again, it's still there where I cast it to remain. Joni tips her hand over, and I spell the fragment to fall as though it is a physical object. Unlike a real rock, it goes straight through the floor, disappearing from sight. Joni looks up at the ceiling again. "I wish Mom's ashes could be released into space."

My wand shakes slightly in my hand. The stars dim overhead.

"What happened to their ashes?" I all but whisper.

"Dad said Mom, Aunt Melanie, Uncle Laurence, and Cousin Kendra were all incinerated together. He said he didn't have the kind of money to pay to separate Mom's ashes. Their ashes were buried in a mass grave in All Saints Memorial Park." Joni sounds detached. Numb. She stares at the ceiling, so I keep the meteor showers going despite wanting to drop my wand, cover my face with both hands, and sob.

My wand feels fused to my hand. The celestial show continues until Joni drifts off and her measured breaths fill the room. Once my cousin is soundly asleep, the meteors burn up, the Milky Way fades away, and the stars wink out, pitching me in darkness.

CHAPTER TWELVE

THE LAST THING I feel like doing Monday morning is going to school, but gnawing hunger forces me out the door. I don't want to expire before I get a chance to contact Uncle Alvan and Cameron.

I step outside in another one of Aunt Chloe's turtlenecks, a cowl scarf, and a pair of her slip-on sneakers. Kids are waiting for the bus across the street a few houses down, so I join them. Two of them look up from their phones, frowning with foreheads that wrinkle like discarded candy wrappers. They shoot me dirty looks and then cross the road. The rest of the kids soon follow until they are all on the opposite sidewalk. I guess the entire school has heard about what happened to me by now. Zombie attacks make headlines. It's big-time gossip if it happens close to home.

I'm under no illusions of Payton and Ellie sticking loyally by my side, but this early preview of what it feels like to be a leper makes me want to return right back to TJ's house, crawl into my sleeping bag, and stay there until I'm nothing but a bag of bones.

Another thought hits me. What if Cameron tries to come by during the day while TJ's at work? Maybe this really *isn't* the day to go back to Brookdale.

The appearance of the bus turning the corner roots me in indecision. I already went to the trouble of getting dressed and lugging myself outdoors.

Also, the cafeteria serves brains. Brains do a body good. I snort to myself. It's not like anyone is standing around to hear me.

Then there's the real prize—the school computer lab. I am desperate to get online. I'd stay at the computer all day if Mrs. Marshall let me. I don't actually have computer lab this semester, and I doubt Mrs. Marshall remembers me from freshman year, but I'm optimistic I can slip into one of her classes. Like her students, Mrs. Marshall spends her class periods glued to the screen at her desk. If anyone needs assistance, they have to get up, go to her, and ask. Otherwise, everyone just does their own thing, clacking away at the keyboard, staring at their own screen. I'm hoping this hasn't changed.

Lunch and computer lab are two big incentives to brave the halls of Brookdale.

The bus slows sooner than needed and eventually stops in front of me. The door swings open, and a middle-aged male driver hacks out a cough, sending spittle over the steering wheel. (And, supposedly, I'm the gross one.) He looks across the street to where his usual passengers wait, and then narrows his eyes on me. "You a zombie?"

"Umm, yeah. I am now."

"Already got a zombie on my route. Can't let you on."

My jaw drops. "How am I supposed to get to school?"

He coughs again and shrugs. "Not my problem." The driver honks the bus horn, which makes a sad bleating noise. The kids waiting across the street jog over, hurrying to board the bus while I watch. The doors shut, and I'm blasted by the bus's exhaust pipe as it rolls away, leaving me behind.

Well, I tried. Maybe I can eat one of my fingers. Oh, wait. Zombies don't eat zombie flesh.

As I cross the street, one of TJ's neighbors backs his white van out of his driveway onto the street . . . and continues backing up toward me. The van speeds up. I have to sprint to the sidewalk to avoid being hit.

"Watch where you're going!" I yell.

The van screeches to a stop, and a bald man in his mid-forties gets out, face red all the way to his faded hairline and beyond. His hands form fists as he starts toward me.

Oh, crap!

My legs spring into action, and my arms pump to assist. I run like I'm training for a marathon, flashing past homes, parked cars, and mailboxes.

"Get back here, zombie trash," my pursuer bellows.

Yeah, right. My legs and arms kick into high gear. I've never moved anywhere near this quickly. It's not like my heart is going to burst or I'm going to run out of breath. So, I run for my life.

Steps beat against the sidewalk behind me. They taper off and fade, but I keep running until I'm a block from school. I guess my legs were taking directions from my stomach.

I glance over my shoulder, overcome with relief to see the coast is clear. The man is nowhere to be seen, nor is his white van.

I hoof it the remaining block to the brick structure that makes up Brookdale High and walk in the front entrance rather than the bus drop-off in back. While I'm at it, I avoid my locker. I have two objectives today—message Uncle Alvan and make it to lunch. Maybe if the serving is filling enough, I can wait another week before returning for more.

I'm all too happy to skip first period with Caleb and Lewis. Instead, I head straight for the computer lab and take a seat in the farthest corner from Mrs. Marshall's desk. A quick glance over my shoulder confirms her attention is divided between her screen, her breakfast muffin, and her steaming cup of coffee.

I sit with my back to the teacher and press the space bar to wake the computer monitor, rushing to log in to my email account. Scrolling through my inbox quickly, I locate the save-the-date wedding message Kendra sent out to our entire family and Cameron's. It's only thanks to my sister that I have Uncle Alvan's email address.

To: AlvanBates@futuresforeverglobal.com
From: heyheyhaylee@kemail.com
Subject: HELP!!!!!!!!!!!!!

My nose practically touches the screen as I tap out letters. I could message him quicker using a phone. Computer keyboards are so antiquated.

Uncle Alvan!

I don't have my phone, and TJ won't let me use his. We went to the lawyer's office last Monday, and my dad's ex-wife and her husband were there. She's trying to get custody of me. So is TJ. They just want to get their hands on—

"Hey, you're in my seat."

I hit "send" before looking up, taking a small amount of comfort in the sight of my message disappearing into the ether. Maybe the way it cuts off will help Uncle Alvan understand the urgency of the situation. Then I look up at a lanky boy with a freckled nose and backward baseball cap.

His brows lift. "Wait a sec. I heard you're a zombie now."

Several students look over. Perfect. The last thing I need is for their attention to drag Mrs. Marshall away from her breakfast muffin. When I planned this out, I had been banking on the teacher not noticing me. What I really should have factored in were the students.

I get up and abandon the spot, hustling out of the lab before a mob has a chance to gather around me and call me out. I'll have to try again next period. My chest tightens at the thought of repeating this whole song and dance all over again. My best bet is to try slipping in after everyone else, but not after the final bell, and hope there is an available computer not directly in front of Mrs. Marshall's desk. AND that everyone is too distracted logging in to notice me. I need to become a zombie ghost.

Or I could bring my wand to school tomorrow and make myself an actual ghost—in the invisible sense. I like that idea better. If they can't see me, no one has to know I brought a wand to school. It's not like I care about my attendance record any longer. No promising future for this zombie chick.

The halls are emptying, which causes as much anxiety as relief. Thinking quickly, I make a dash along the shiny mopped floors for the library and enter as the final bell finishes its ring. The computers in here, unfortunately, only access the school's book catalog and educational sites. Head down, I take purposeful steps past the small circulation desk where young Miss Tregger is mercifully preoccupied with her phone as she sips from a travel tumbler. I make a beeline for the back rows of shelves and plop down on the floor, utterly exhausted. My muscles tremble all over, mini quakes going off beneath my skin.

I try to go into a zen state—or zomb state, rather—as I prepare to wait through four periods to reach lunch hour. But my mind is awake and active from the morning's adrenaline. I pull a hardback from the bottom shelf beside me.

Words Unspoken: Poetry of Grief and Loss.

At least I have something cheerful to read.

I crawl down the aisle looking for something that won't reduce me to tears. It's bad enough that I have no makeup. I don't want to step into the cafeteria with a splotchy face.

Scanning the spines of the books, it appears I have entered the nonfiction section. Great. Just what I need right now. More reality.

I lean against a shelf and try to get comfortable, quickly deciding the floor offers better back support. As calm as the library is, school is not the place I would ever let my guard down by zombing out. When boredom gets the better of me, I pull a book with two wolves on the cover from the bottom shelf.

Never Cry Wolf by Farley Mowat.

At first, I'm afraid it's a werewolf autobiography, but it turns out it's about wild wolves and conservation. Tearjerker for sure, which is why I'm surprised to find myself laughing as I read the opening chapter. This Farley Mowat guy is a hoot. I lose myself in someone else's past life as first, and then second, periods come and go.

When the lunch bell finally rings, I shelf Mr. Mowat's book back in its place, stand up, and stretch out the kinks in my joints.

The cafeteria is conveniently located beside the library. While students travel from fourth period to their lockers, I breeze into the empty cafeteria and walk straight up to Agnus's window. The lunch lady isn't waiting to take my order. I peer in through the small slat at the kitchen behind the wall, where women in hairnets bustle around stainless-steel counters and equipment. Food sizzles in fryers, steam spews from tall pots, and pizzas bake inside commercial convention ovens. The combination of smells is gag-inducing. This isn't food. Where do they keep the brains? The fridge probably.

I clear my throat. The cafeteria ladies either don't hear or choose to ignore me.

"Hey, there," I call out pleasantly. "I'm the early bird this lunch hour." *And I want brains.* My arms grip the metal counter, ready to launch myself through the window, tackle any hairnet who gets in my way to the fridge, and loot cold storage for organs.

Agnus looks over, not even cracking a smile. "Be with you in a moment."

"Okay, thanks. Also, I'm a zombie now, so I'm going to need brains."

Her expression and tone remain dull. "All new zombie students need proof of species before they can be served organs. You have to go to the office and get a permission slip."

I glance over my shoulder. Students are trickling in, but they're still on the opposite side of the cafeteria. With shaky fingers, I pull down my scarf and turtleneck to uncover my neck wound. "There's proof for you," I say angrily, baring my neck until Agnus has gotten a good long look. The woman still doesn't react. And supposedly zombies are the ones who are zonked out.

"You're still going to need a permission slip from the office before I can serve you remains."

"Are you kidding me?" I grumble.

Agnus goes back to the fryer. I pull my turtleneck up, shove myself off the small square counter, and storm across the room into the student center on my way to the front office. Of course, Caleb is right outside the cafeteria doors, as are the students who eat their sack lunches in groups inside the student center.

The second Caleb sees me, he cups his hands around his mouth. "Dead girl walking, everyone! Dead girl walking!" Lewis is pretty much Caleb's only friend, but that doesn't prevent onlookers from chuckling, staring, grimacing, or backing away. Like always, I ignore Caleb for as long as I can. Unfortunately, he falls immediately into his pattern of following me. "What's the matter, Haylee? Cafeteria brains not up to your standards? Portions too small? You're going to need elephant brains to feed that big appetite of yours." Laughter ensues, which only encourages the cretin. "Come on, be a good sport and show us your wounds. Are they super gnarly? Where all did you get bitten?"

I quicken my speed. Caleb follows suit and doesn't back off until I reach the front office. He takes one look at the front desk lady's scowl and then falls back.

The wait for the permission slip is excruciating. The front desk lady can't help me. It has to be either the vice principal or principal—whichever one gets off the phone first. It ends up being Vice Principal Rogers, who tells me I need to make an appointment with one of the school counselors as soon as possible. At least she hands over the permission slip that serves as my special diet lunch ticket.

Slip in hand, I run down the hall and through the student center. A group leaving the cafeteria jumps aside as I barrel through the double-open doors. The tables inside have mostly cleared. I spot Georgia in the far corner. After Agnus looks at my slip and hands me my tray, I pull out a wad of recycled paper napkins from the dispenser on the counter and take them and my lunch over to Georgia's table. She raises her brow as I sit. I forego pleasantries and dig into the brain. It's not cut up all nice the way Maurice prepared it back at the detention center, but I'm so hungry at this point I wouldn't care if it was still attached to the cow or sheep or whatever animal it came from. The fact that it's intact doesn't slow me down. As with my first brain, this one disappears in minutes, or maybe seconds. All I know is it's gone, and I feel charged up.

I wipe my mouth with napkin after napkin, wadding each one and tossing them onto my empty plate.

"What a messed-up morning this has been," I gripe. "First the bus wouldn't let me on because there was already a zombie on that route. Then the neighbor tried to run me over with his van and then, after missing his target, came after me while I ran for my—"

"What do you think you're doing?" Georgia rudely interrupts.

"What do you mean?" I fire back.

Georgia looks me over and scoffs. "You think now that you're a zombie that makes us friends?"

I sit back in the metal chair and fold my arms. "Who said anything about friendship? I'm just making conversation. I didn't realize I needed a permission slip to sit here."

Georgia holds my gaze for several seconds before a snort escapes, followed by a laugh that sets me off with her. My arms loosen to my sides. Our hilarity doesn't last long, but it feels like a truce. Cafeteria stragglers look over and gawk. Three younger girls a few tables away scoot their chairs back abruptly and practically jog out of the lunchroom. There's a suppressed instinct within me that itches to pursue them and, well, there's no delicate way to say this, bite into the flesh above their beaded bracelets and layered necklaces.

Georgia smacks the table, snapping me out of my hunger fog. "You can't stare at humans like they're snack packs. It's impossible enough staying under the radar without making people more nervous."

"Yeah, thanks. I'll keep that in mind. They were too skinny, anyway. Not much meat on their bulimic bones."

Georgia doesn't laugh this time. "What's wrong with you?"

"I'm an emotional eater, and my uncle's been starving me, so you know . . . I'm really hungry."

"Well, the school is obligated to feed you, so I suggest you don't skip."

"What am I supposed to do during Christmas break?"

"Raw Tasty Meat Co. offers organs in exchange for a couple hours of cleanup. Other butcher shops have similar under-the-table arrangements, but Raw Tasty is the closest shop in the area."

I nod eagerly. This is valuable information. I need more tips on zombie etiquette and survival—the real-life, practical stuff that's missing from the pages of the handbook. Georgia would make a killer mentor, but before I can ask if she has any more advice, the bell rings, signaling the end of lunch hour, and Georgia gets up with her tray. I follow her to the bin, where she dumps the disposable plate before setting her tray on the stack above. "Same time tomorrow?" I joke, meanwhile thinking, *Please, please, please say you'll let me sit with you again.*

Georgia faces me, sighs, and shakes her head of short dark curls. "You don't get it, but you will soon enough."

I hang back as she leaves the cafeteria. I'm not about to follow after her like a sad puppy. I don't want to look lost, like Rosie. I may be Brookdale's newest zombie, but I'm still a senior.

Students run down the halls to get to fifth period before the final bell. I head for one of the back doors. Now that I've eaten, I don't see any reason to stick around waiting for school to end. But before I make it out, the intercom system crackles, and a booming voice announces to the entire school, "Haylee Hutchins to the principal's office."

CHAPTER THIRTEEN

"HAYLEE HUTCHINS TO the principal's office," the voice repeats.

I wince as the words echo across the entire freaking school. Every speaker. Every classroom. Every student hearing my name shouted.

So much for staying under the radar. In one of those rooms Georgia is probably rolling her eyes or shaking her head or rolling her eyes *while* shaking her head. Unless she's not in class. Does she have a secret school hangout? I should ask her tomorrow. In the meantime, I have business to take care of.

Back at the office, I wait on a bench outside of Principal Wallace's office to be summoned. I've never been called in before. Now I'll have seen both the vice principal and principal in the span of an hour. I suppose it's too much to hope that the reason I've been called in is because Principal Wallace doesn't realize Vice Principal Rogers already took care of my permission slip for the cafeteria. If he gives me another one, does that mean I can go back for seconds?

I watch the large hand of the round wall clock *tick*, *tick*, *tick*. I wonder if I have time to grab Mr. Mowat's book from the library to help pass the time while I wait.

Finally, I am told to go into Principal Wallace's office. He's a balding, rotund middle-aged man with a desk covered in file folders, stacks of printed pages, a notepad, scattered pens, napkins, an empty food container, and a bag of chips that have left crumbs.

Principal Wallace smacks his lips as he looks at me. "Miss Hutchins, I received an alarming report that you were seen sitting at a table with another zombie in the cafeteria this afternoon."

Oh, so that's what this is about. Boy, that didn't take long.

"It was the closest table to the lunch window," I reply with a shrug. "Location is everything."

Principal Wallace scowls. "Did Z Squad provide you with the official rule book for zombies?"

"Yeah, they gave me a copy."

"Perhaps you think you're above the rules, Miss Hutchins. I assure you, you're not."

I counter with, "There was a page missing from my manual. Perhaps that was the one about not consorting with fellow zombies."

Principal Wallace narrows his beady eyes. "Handbook or not, you know the rules. Since this is your first day back to school as a zombie, I'm going to let you off with a warning. If it happens again, I'll have to call your guardian and suspend you from school for one week."

Now there's a real threat. The only guardian Principal Wallace could reach at this point is TJ. And suspension means two things to me: no food service and no computer lab.

I swallow the burning lump of indignation lodged inside my throat and say, "I understand, sir," in the most demure tone I can muster. It makes my stomach cramp like I just ate a whole head of raw cabbage with beans.

Principal Wallace nods. "Very well, you may return to class now."

When I move to leave, Principal Wallace calls out, "Oh, and Miss Hutchins, be sure to make an appointment with one of the school guidance counselors. They can provide you with a fresh rule book, as well as advise you on your options after graduation."

Yeah, I'm gonna have to pass. I can't imagine there are many exciting opportunities awaiting a forever seventeen-year-old zombie after graduation.

I exit the principal's office and keep walking without making any kind of appointments.

It's tempting to vacate the premises through the set of double doors to my right, but I don't want to be seen ditching school early by the front desk lady, just in case she reports me to Principal Wallace. The last thing I need is for him to call me in again tomorrow.

I'm halfway to the back entrance when the intercom crackles along the deserted hallway. Foreboding slows my steps.

"Haylee Hutchins to the front office. You have a visitor."

All of my previous grumblings evaporate from existence as I sprint the way I came, rocketing down the hallway. I don't slow for a second, not even when I reach the corner.

Cameron has come! It must be him!

I run faster than I did this morning when Scary Van Man came after me. I run like I'm about to miss the final boarding call for an all-expense-paid trip to Fiji. Soon, I'm charging toward the front desk, coming in like a runaway jetliner. The rubber soles of Aunt Chloe's sneakers squeak as I skid to a stop. I turn my head from side to side frantically. No one is waiting at the front desk or anywhere in the vicinity. Where is Cameron?

I throw myself at the front counter. "I'm here. Where's my visitor?"

The front desk lady peers at me through her rimless frames. "He had to leave but—"

"Leave?"

My screech earns me a frown. She starts over, slow and deliberate. "He had to leave, but he left you something."

I push off the counter and race for the double doors to the parking lot in front. I can still reach Cameron in time. I have to.

The pathways leading up to Brookdale are empty. No one is walking to or from any of the parked vehicles. There aren't a lot of spaces at the main entrance. I hustle along the row of cars in case Cameron has a rental and got in before I ran outside. But I don't hear any engines. The cars are all empty. I must have just missed him.

Without warning, tears burst from my eyes.

Has the universe conspired against me? Did I commit some unspeakable wrong in a past life?

I blink and rub my eyes before returning to the front desk. The secretary sets a package roughly the size of a twelve-pack of canned food on the counter. It's gift-wrapped in white paper with red printed words repeating, "Ho Ho Ho" with the third "o" in every line a red heart. It's tied with a red-and-white-striped bow.

Fresh tears leak from my eyes.

"He also left this." She sets an envelope on the counter with *Haylee Hutchins* handwritten on the front.

I snatch the envelope and gift and dash into the nearest girls' bathroom. A leaky sink drips steadily in the corner. Alone inside the drably tiled room, I wipe off a section of the counter and set the package down before ripping open the envelope. I don't bother drying my eyes when I'm certain the note will wring more tears out of me.

I unfold a piece of notebook paper, checking the end first to verify that it's from Cameron. His name is signed at the bottom. Tear stains smudge the ink in various spots.

Dear Haylee,

I am deeply sorry that you were unable to attend your parents' and sister's memorial. I would have gladly come up with the money to separate and save your family's ashes but was informed that it was too late, and it was not my decision to make in any case. I am heartbroken I was unable to preserve this last part of Kendra and your admirable parents. I am sorry I missed seeing you, but I must get back to California to speak with Kendra's professors and pack up her belongings—all of which I was unable to face this past week.

Once I've had a chance to sort things out, I will contact you.

I've left the gift Kendra got you for Christmas. She would have wanted me to ensure it reached you. Dropping it off at your school seemed like the best option. Kendra was beyond excited when she found your gift. She was so proud of her talented little sis. She always said that you would make your mark on the world in a spectacular way.

I hope this gift reminds you of Kendra's love for you and of her belief in your greatness.

With profound condolences,
Cameron

Tears fall in big, fat heavy drops. I push my arm holding the note away before my onslaught has a chance to mingle with Cameron's and smudge the ink worse.

Drip, drip, drip, drip, drip.

Tap water provides unnecessary sound effects to my sorrow. I try to tighten the metal faucet, which only makes the leaking worse.

Drip, drip, drip, drip, drip, drip, drip, drip, drip, drip, drip.

I lift the handle then close it, which helps a little.

Drip. Drip. Drip.

This isn't the twentieth century. It's a waste of a precious resource. The threat of climatic catastrophe is one of the big reasons vampires frequently spout as explanation for why they had to come out of the shadows. They claim responsibility for sustainability laws and implementing fundamental changes before the planet becomes uninhabitable for all beings. But really it was a rogue group of sorcerers who outed the existence of supernaturals. Vampires, wizards, and werewolves came together to bring order back to the world—and assert their dominance. Vampires prefer control over chaos, as do most witches and wizards. Like the other supernatural groups, werewolves prefer to stick to their own kind and were content to live under the radar until the sorcerers messed everything up, which is another reason why the wizarding community is not looked upon kindly. They've tried, on multiple occasions, to burn down all of the Lignum Vitae trees to prevent non-wizards from having access to their powers.

Natural born witches and wizards have no need of wands in order to cast. Coach Cleo Killian only uses a wand on *Spellcaster* during the blind auditions when she lifts hers to show that she wants a contestant on her team and while working with her team members in demonstration.

Then there is the newest group of supernaturals: zombies. *Mutants*. *My* kind. The public doesn't know the true origins of zombies. Some media outlets claim the mutation was created in a lab. Others believe that following a worldwide pandemic, a series of nasty viruses spread and mutated, and one rare mutation, known as TTZ, created the first zombies. Still other reports suggest scientists in America were working on a way to become a vampire without requiring transformation from the creatures themselves. They managed a cure for mortality, but it came at a terrible price no sane person would willingly pay. That one is the favored theory among witches. They love using it as a reminder that magic will always trump science.

Anyway, no one cares about the planet more than vampires. They're the ones who will inherit it after all. They're the ones hoarding over half of the world's wealth, and they get to keep it FOREVER . . . so long as humans don't go extinct and take away their food supply. Werewolves and witches age at the same rate as humans. I suppose werewolves should count themselves lucky they don't age like canines.

Zombies could live forever like vampires if everyone wasn't out to exterminate us, crazed or not. There are no millionaire or billionaire zombies. As far as I know, zombies are all broke and dependent on some type of guardian. I could be a millionaire zombie if it weren't for the stupid law. Mr. Dirk said that being a minor means I cannot inherit money, or anything else, from my parents, but he didn't say anything about my own earnings.

I really need to get back to the computer lab and check my Payoneer account. There's probably enough in there to buy a new phone and hire an alterationist to get me back into tank tops before spring.

After drying my eyes with toilet paper, I carefully refold Cameron's note, return it to the envelope, and stuff it in my back pocket. I grab the package. Whatever is inside the box weighs maybe a few pounds. Not too heavy but not super light. This is the last gift I will ever receive from my sister, and I'm not about to open it in the girls' bathroom. I wonder if I should save it for Christmas. It's not like I can expect any other gifts. Unsure what to do, I head to my locker to store the package. It's the only space that is mine. But I need to hurry before fifth period ends and students come spilling out into the hallway. I had planned to be back at TJ's by now.

There's a skull and crossbones spray-painted in white over my locker, along with the word "MUTANT" in dripping green paint. I spin the combo lock and open the metal door. Staring inside, it hits me that the last time I opened this locker, I was human. My parents were alive. Kendra was alive. I stand frozen, having difficulty—yet again—truly believing something this horrible happened to me. My parents and sister are dead. Nothing left of them. Not even ash.

Malachi Rayne grins lazily at me from his black leather chair. For once, I don't smile wistfully back.

A white-and-light-gray-striped button-up hooded cardigan sweater hangs from a hook. I set the gift inside my locker vertically and then pull out the sweater, hug it against my chest, and go into a temporary trance as I breathe in the smell of home. Eyes closed, I try to return to that place of love and safety.

The bell rings. Crap!

I slam the door closed, spin the combo lock, and then try the latch, verifying that Kendra's gift is locked securely inside.

Students spill from doorways along the hall. I hurriedly unbutton my cardigan, stuff my arms through the sleeves, and pull the hood over my head as I walk away from my locker. Luckily, my classmates are distracted in their rush to get to their lockers and check their phones before they have to put them away during final period. I go unnoticed as I move with the crowd. Payton appears down the hall, engrossed in whatever conversation she is having with another senior girl named Tina. They walk close together. Payton flips her hair back and says something with a smug smile. A flash of anger jolts me. I wonder if she feels any sympathy over what happened to my family and me. Neither Payton nor Tina looks my way as they pass, but I catch Payton's next words like loose hairs in a mesh drain catcher.

"I heard she was seen in the cafeteria at the end of lunch hour. The only reason she wasn't eaten alive like her family is probably thanks to her fat ass. The zombies got too full before they could finish the rest of her."

I stop as though I just ran straight into a light pole. This level of nastiness is beyond disgusting. It triggers something else. Payton sounds a lot like the 1010 user who keeps changing their name every time I block them.

I whirl around, pull the hood off my head, and storm after her. By now, Tina has parted ways, and Payton has her locker open. Before she has a chance to see me standing behind her, glowering, I demand, "Are you hotbabe1010?"

I expect Payton to startle at the sound of my voice and my accusation, but she doesn't so much as jerk. Instead, she pivots slowly and wrinkles her nose. "I thought I smelled something off."

"That would be your rotting soul," I snap.

Payton narrows her eyes and purses her lips. "You're one to talk. You're no longer human. You're a dead thing."

"Do I look dead, you Moluccan cockatoo?"

"That is such a stupid thing you came up with. You think I care?" Payton rolls her eyes. "I don't care, especially not coming from a fat-ass zombie mutant."

"Wow, original," I answer sarcastically. The name calling doesn't hurt the way her cruelty does.

Payton lifts her chin and looks down her nose at me. "I *am* unique and original. I don't need magic to make me interesting or beautiful. Oh, and the 1010 is because I'll always be a ten out of ten—unlike you."

My mouth opens and closes like a guppy stuck inside a shallow vase. I'm drowning in disgust. Before I can say anything more, Ellie shows up, doing a double take when she sees me. She stops, not approaching me or her locker. Her phone shakes in her hand, drawing my gaze to that coveted piece of technology and communication.

"Oh, um, what are you doing here, Haylee?"

Really? I put a hand on my hip. "Going to my locker. Attending school," I say impatiently.

The next thing I know, Payton whips out a bottle of Febreze and blasts me with its spray. Artificial peach scent gets inside my mouth and seeps into my cardigan. Is it weird that I can still smell and taste without breath? The chemicals sting my eyes. Worst of all, she's probably obliterated any lingering scent of home. Ellie coughs, as do the students at neighboring lockers. Mark Anton, senior and captain of the basketball team, slams his locker shut and snaps at Payton, "Don't be spraying that shit around me."

"It's her fault," Payton points a finger at me and pouts.

Mark Anton looks from her to me and says, "You should request a new locker someplace else. Somewhere far from mine." With that, he stomps off.

Payton smiles smugly. Ellie chews on her bottom lip, avoiding eye contact—glancing down at her phone in her hand, instead.

Her phone!

Desperate times call for desperate measures.

"Can I borrow your phone?" I ask. "I will return it to you right after final period." It's not like she can use it in class, whereas I desperately need to get in touch with Uncle Alvan and Cameron. I don't know their phone numbers, but maybe I can search for them online—along with the nearest alterationist while I'm at it. This could be an extremely productive hour in the library.

Ellie clutches her phone and grimaces. "I'm sorry, Haylee, but I can't lend you my phone or anything else. I shouldn't even be speaking to you. I have to think about my personal safety. I never know when you might turn on me."

"You mean the way you're turning on me right now?" I hiss between clenched teeth.

Ellie's eyes widen, and she makes a strangled sound before fleeing.

"Now look what you've done," Payton shouts at me, slamming her locker and hurrying after Ellie.

Students watch and whisper to their friends, frowning at me like I tried to assault my former best friends.

Tears coat my throat as if they're running inward rather than out. I gulp them down while staring at the rows of gray metal. It's tempting to open my locker and leave with Kendra's gift. I could really use some cheering up. But it's only a present. It's not my sister. I can't open it in front of her or call and thank her. I don't need a gift. I need my family. So I leave the mystery package in my locker and go.

Reaching TJ's house takes longer when I'm not running for my life. I take shuffling steps, and the bottoms of Aunt Chloe's sneakers drag over the concrete sidewalk. The neighborhood is quiet at this time, at least. I retrieve the spare key from beneath a flowerpot and unlock the front door before putting the key back.

With the time it took to walk from Brookdale to TJ's, I have less than two hours before Joni's bus drops her off. I go to her bedroom—to my sleeping bag. I know it's not healthy, but I don't care. I want to see my family. To be together in any capacity, even when they're not really here.

I drop to my knees beside my sleeping bag, unzip the side, and then reach to the bottom, expecting my fingers to close around my wand. When they don't, I pat around. As panic rises up my neck, I move my hand around frantically before unzipping the whole bag and pulling it open.

My wand is gone.

CHAPTER FOURTEEN

HOW COULD JONI do this to me after everything I've done to try to cheer her up?

I pull my cousin's bed apart, checking the pillow first, as though she might have stolen my secret hiding spot along with my wand. After searching her drawers with no luck, a terrible thought occurs to me.

What if she took it to school to show off to her friends?

There's nothing left to do besides pace by the living room window, waiting for Joni's bus.

The moment she walks through the door, I pounce.

"Where did you put my wand?" I demand.

Joni drops her backpack on the entryway floor and gives a little yelp. She gawps at me before finding her voice. "I didn't take your wand." Her bottom lip trembles. Tears spill from her eyes, followed by full-on, chest-heaving sobs that prickle beneath my skin. "I sw-swear, Haylee. It wasn't me. I-I-I would never do that to you." She runs to her room, crying.

Well, good one, Haylee. I should have asked more nicely, or maybe she's telling the truth.

I go to the kitchen and pour Joni a glass of juice to take to her room as a peace offering before I try talking to her again. After returning the juice to the fridge, I notice a crumpled Burger Boys bag on the kitchen table that wasn't there when I left for school.

Then it hits me like a rockslide dropping boulders over my head and fracturing my skull.

TJ took my wand.

Now I'm waiting for my no-good, dirty thief of an uncle to pull into the driveway. It's the first time I've wanted him to return home from work. I'm fixated on the road outside while Joni hides in her room. I already apologized before growling out that it was TJ who took it.

I'm waiting near the window again, staring outside with the tenacity of a Rottweiler awaiting an intruder. I wish I could tear TJ apart without consequences. How is it fair that my kind and generous parents and sister and Aunt Chloe were brutalized to death while an abusive, greedy waste of oxygen like TJ gets to keep on living?

When his beat-up truck rolls into the driveway, something in me snaps. In that moment, I'm not only aware that I'm no longer human, I can feel it in my bones. It's like my fear receptor has been cut off from my brain permanently.

Or maybe this is merely the volcanic rage of a teenager grossly wronged.

I push the sleeves of Aunt Chloe's turtleneck above my elbows to remind TJ that he's not dealing with his human niece any longer. There's a monster inhabiting his house, one that's come out from under the sleeping bag to confront him. I look at the bandages covering the exposed bones along my lower right arm. I'm a freaking zombie. TJ should be the one walking on eggshells. Not Joni. Not me.

When he walks through the front door, I storm over, stop, and put my hands on my hips. He doesn't drop his keys or anything else the way Joni did, but he looks at my arms, and I swear I see a flicker of fear before he covers it swiftly with a glare and curl of his upper lip.

"Give me back my wand," I say in a chilling voice.

"I don't have your wand," TJ fires back. "And watch your tone with me."

"If you don't give it back—" I let the end of the warning hang around his neck like a frayed noose doused in kerosene. I can't go saying the words out loud. According to the zombie guidebook, the mere threat of biting someone is considered grounds for extermination.

But I do want to bite TJ.

First, I want to punch him in the face on behalf of Aunt Chloe. Then, I want to kick him in the nuts for Joni. Finally, I want to bite him—for me—and for the rest of the world, which would be better off if he went insane and was exterminated by Z Squad.

"Careful," TJ responds in a low warning.

He's the one who needs to be careful, and from the clench of his jaw—and the way he's keeping his distance—I'd say he knows it, too.

"All I'm asking is that you give me back what's mine," I say.

"I told you; I don't have your wand." Our eyes lock, and suddenly, TJ's shoulders relax. A nasty grin replaces his tight jaw. "I sold it this afternoon."

"You did what?" I ask in horror.

TJ sneers. "Your no-good, undead uncle is taking his sweet time transitioning. Meanwhile, I've got bills to pay. That stick of wood bought you an extra week under my roof."

"A week?" I ask shrilly. "A week? A Lignum Vitae wand is worth three months of your salary." I don't actually know what TJ's income is, but I'm betting I'm not far off. "And what expense am I costing you? You don't even feed me. I cost you less than a dog or a cat or even a goldfish."

TJ's face turns red. "Enough!" he blasts. "I told you, my house, my rules. Do you want to try your luck out on the streets? I doubt you would last a day."

"If you throw me out, you can kiss my family's fortune goodbye," I counter. I can't believe I'm arguing to remain under this thief's "care." No matter what, I'm not choosing TJ as my guardian. The moment he got his grubby hands on my parents' bank account, he would turn right around and toss me out anyway. Maybe he can't legally, but I have no doubt he would find a way to make me disappear. He'd have enough money to hire a freelance zombie hunter.

TJ's shoulders relax. He huffs out a breath. "So, you've come to your senses and realized I'm your best option for legal guardian."

No surprise that TJ is as stupid as he is sinister. Let him think what he wants for now. I'll buy myself a new wand once Uncle Alvan becomes my guardian. I'll buy backups. I'll buy one for Joni, too. Maybe *I'll* hire someone to take out TJ while I'm at it.

I pull down the sleeves of the turtleneck, fold my arms, and walk to Joni's room, with TJ following several feet behind. My cousin is seated cross-legged on her bed, hugging a stuffed zebra to her chest, crying softly. TJ looms in the open doorway, sneering at his daughter. "Stop your sniveling, Joni. You think I wanted this? You think I'm happy to be left with the care of two ingrates?" My eye roll earns me a piercing glare. TJ quickly turns his attention back to Joni. "Now do something useful and make dinner." He storms out and stomps his way down the hall.

My cousin drops her stuffed zebra and scurries off the bed to do TJ's bidding. I sit on the floor and try to channel the abyss, but I am way too enraged. Images of a bloodied TJ—guts spilling out of his cleaved chest—flash through my mind. Anger rots the space where my heart used to beat. It eats away like maggots devouring my remaining tissue. I check my arms just to make sure larvae haven't appeared in my open wounds, but the magical seal is still holding up.

That night, Joni and I stare up at a dark ceiling. Not speaking. Not making a sound. As though we've entered a black hole.

I step into the abyss and wonder whether, if I was exterminated, there would be white light and warmth waiting for me instead of this deep, dark, all-encompassing cold?

I don't go to school the next day or the next or the next.

I force myself to show up Friday in order to fill up on brains before the weekend.

By now, a new caster has won *Spellcaster* Season 12, but I don't know who. I haven't posted on my JingleJam account since Thanksgiving. I wonder what my beauty brigade is saying. Do they know what happened to me?

I've never felt so cut off from the world.

At school, I steer clear of my locker. There is a new **NO HORDING** sign posted in the student center and cafeteria.

How do Georgia and Rosie get through each day in this hellhole?

After lunch, I leave, because what more does this place have to offer?

On Saturday, Uncle Alvan finally calls. TJ shocks me by handing me his phone to speak with him, but when I head to Joni's room for privacy, TJ snaps, "Talk to your uncle at the kitchen table or not at all."

At this point, I don't care. I plop onto a chair with TJ's phone shoved against my ear. "Uncle Alvan!" It's hard not to sob.

"Hey there, kiddo." Tears drip down my cheeks at the sound of his sympathetic voice. I turn away from TJ, who blatantly eavesdrops while drinking a beer at the kitchen counter. "I am so sorry about your parents and sister. When I found out what happened to them—" Heavy seconds pass until Uncle Alvan sighs. "Being remade helped me get through the grief."

"Did your boss push you to become a vampire?"

"No. I chose this. My master is benevolent. He gifted me eternal youth."

"But—"

"I also have access to immense resources. The first thing I'm doing is looking into what happened that morning."

I grip the phone. Now we're getting somewhere. I need Uncle Alvan's help, and every advantage he has at his disposal on this. As miserable as TJ is, I no longer believe he arranged the attack, and if he didn't, I don't know where to begin looking. But Uncle Alvan will. He works for a powerful vampire. He's joined their ranks. Maybe this isn't such a terrible thing, especially since I won't be aging, either. It will be nice to have my uncle around for the long haul.

"Okay, good," I say. "Do you have any leads?"

"Not yet, but I will let you know as soon as I have any new information."

"Thank you," I whisper. I glance sideways at TJ, who looks straight back at me. I turn away from him and lower my voice. "What about the other matter. Did you receive my email?"

"I did," Uncle Alvan answers slowly. "Cressida is a master manipulator. You can't trust her. Do not allow her to gain legal control of your father's assets."

"I have no plans to. I choose you as my guardian, Uncle Alvan." The words rush out of me in case TJ tries to wrench his phone from my fingers. Surprisingly, he remains still and silent.

The pause that follows is the longest yet. My stomach drops in trepidation.

"Haylee," Uncle Alvan sighs my name. "I cannot be your legal guardian."

"Why? Is it not allowed?" I demand.

He's quiet again before answering, "One of the reasons my master chose to remake me is because I have no children, no partner, no attachments. I am not in a position to take care of you."

"You wouldn't have to," I argue. "I'm seventeen. I can look out for myself. I only need you to be my guardian on paper and to get me access to my family's funds. I'll take care of the rest."

"Haylee." Another sigh. His use of my name is no longer a comfort. It's irritating. I don't think I'm asking for a lot here. My freaking family died. They were murdered. The least Uncle Alvan could do is give me my independence. "It's complicated," he continues. "You're a zombie. The world is an unforgiving place for your kind. You can't make it on your own. I know you don't want to hear this, but you need a caretaker. I can't be that for you. My master won't allow it." He stops talking and waits for a response, but I can't speak at the moment.

I'm deadly quiet. His words are raspberry seeds stuck between my teeth. It's like trying to get them unstuck with my tongue when what I need is a piece of floss or a toothpick or a hammer to hit him over the head for abandoning me to the buzzards.

"What am I supposed to do?" I ask bitterly.

"Stay with TJ." My soul shrieks at his suggestion. "I know this isn't what you want to hear, but Joni needs you, and TJ is family. If I know Cressida, she'll promise to be your best friend and that the two of you will have all the fun in the world, but that woman will say anything to get what she wants. Don't fall for it. At least with TJ you know what you're getting."

"A cruel, negligent, thieving bastard." The moody words blast between my lips like black smoke from an exhaust pipe.

"Careful," TJ warns in the background. I'm too distraught to care or worry about how he'll react once I get off the phone.

"Just remember he is more scared of you than you are of him," Uncle Alvan says.

I'm not scared of TJ. I'm angry. I'm mad at him *and* Uncle Alvan. Mom would be livid.

"Joni needs you," he says again. "She's still human. Vulnerable. I'm counting on you to look out for her. Chloe would want that too."

And what about me? I want to scream. Am I not vulnerable? Or does being a zombie mean I don't count?

My teeth clench. The phone shakes in my hand.

"It will be awfully hard to look after Joni once TJ gets my money and offs me." I don't hold back my bitterness.

TJ takes a leisurely sip of beer like he presumes this is a done deal. He's getting what he wants. I have to hold back a scream.

"He won't," Uncle Alvan says firmly. "I had Mr. Dirk send me a copy of the paperwork. It clearly states that your legal guardian would lose access to the funds should you meet with a premature death or—in your case—extermination."

"What's to stop him from taking the money all at once? Won't matter much if I'm out of the picture if he already drained the account."

"There are provisions for that, as well. Withdrawals cannot exceed five thousand a month, unless he petitions for special circumstances—say, your college tuition or a big event like a wedding."

This is insane! We both know I'm never going to college or getting married now. It only makes me angrier because Kendra and Cameron are the ones who should be exchanging their vows and starting their happily ever after on the beach of California this summer. Tears sting my eyes. They flood my vision. I'm drowning in my own sorrow and bitter rage.

"Look, kiddo. I have to go, but you'll be all right. You'll get through this. I promise." Oh, he *promises*. Well, in that case, I guess everything really is going to be okay. "Give Joni a hug from me. We'll talk again soon." Uncle Alvan hangs up.

I remain seated, phone pressed to my ear. As far as TJ knows, my uncle is still speaking to me. I never said "Bye." I never said "Talk to you later." I never said "Screw you, Uncle Alvan! Did your master remove your heart along with your soul when he remade you?"

I sit and sit, not planning to give TJ his phone back until he figures out I'm done with my call and demands its return. Another thought enters my mind. Could I dial another number fast enough while the phone is still in my possession?

This thought is quickly followed by despair. Who would I call? My shoulders slump.

Well, there's one more thing I've been wanting to look at—just to torture myself.

"Hold on a sec, and I'll look," I say into the phone for TJ's benefit. Then I pull his phone away from my ear and hold it in front of my face. With a speedy finger, I open the app store, find JingleJam, download the free app, and press "install."

"What are you doing with my phone?" TJ demands as the app finishes installing. I've barely hit "open" when TJ snatches the phone from my fingers and lifts it to his ear. "Hello? Alvan?" he asks tentatively, which makes me snicker. TJ's eyes narrow to slits. He lowers his phone, face turning red when he looks at his screen. "What is this crap you've downloaded to my phone?"

"It's an app. Don't worry. It's free."

"I don't want your junk app on my phone."

"Here. Hand it over, and I'll remove it." I hold out my hand and smirk.

"I don't think so." TJ storms back to the kitchen counter and jabs his finger at his screen. His snarl communicates the success he's having. Eventually, he tosses his phone on the counter and folds his arms. "At least the matter of guardianship is settled. Alvan might be a narcissistic upstart, but even he understands I'm the only option. You will remain under my permanent care. You're lucky you have me. Who else would want to look after an undead ingrate? You've already wasted my time waiting on Alvan to set you straight. Of course, it's Saturday. I'll have to wait until Monday to call Mr. Dirk's office and make an appointment to settle a matter that should have been settled two weeks ago." TJ kicks the half wall beneath the kitchen counter.

Even when he gets his way, he's pissed off.

This man. This vile being can't be my only choice of guardian. For life!

Think of Joni, I tell myself. Do this for your little cousin. Watch over her until she graduates high school. It's only nine years.

I'm a zombie. Nine years is nothing.

I'm a teenager. Nine years is an eternity!

I can't stop thinking *no*. No to TJ becoming my guardian and getting the money. No to Uncle Alvan choosing to serve the needs of a vampire master rather than his own flesh and blood. No to having no control over MY life and having to do as the adults say just because they're older. They certainly aren't wiser.

CHAPTER FIFTEEN

MONDAY MORNING. ANOTHER turtleneck to cover my outer wounds. It's the last week before the long holiday break.

I head to school early, shuffling along the sidewalk. The only reason I'm headed to Brookdale is to fuel up on my kind of food.

The route I take is in the opposite direction from Scary Van Man. I leave before him now, but just to be safe, I walk down the street and circle around the block.

Homes light up along the street as adults prepare themselves for the start of the work week and kids get ready for school. Merry wreaths hang from doors. Multicolored bulbs glow along the edges of rooftops and from net lights arranged over bushes. Large shiny red bulbs dangle from an awning. Front porches have been transformed into enchanting entryways.

I can see into some of the living rooms that are dimly lit by adjacent kitchens. Sometimes I catch movement as I drag one foot after another. Behind the window of a brick home, a young woman in a white bathrobe holds a mug away from her body as she kisses a young man dressed in a shirt and tie.

I peer into one house after another, as though window shopping for the life I want back.

A door opens after I pass, and running footsteps have my arms lifting to my sides, ready to start pumping as I make a run for it. I take a quick glance over my shoulder and see a bright green umbrella with a smiling frog face coming at me. Two large frog eyes poke out at the top. The umbrella obscures the face below, but the legs running toward me—in cute Christmas leggings—are skinny.

"Haylee!" The girlish voice is non-threatening.

I stand in place, still ready to run. It's a good thing I no longer need a functioning heartbeat because I'd likely have a stroke at this point from being on edge all the time.

"Haylee. It's me. Rosie." Though it's not raining, she doesn't lower her umbrella, even when she reaches me. I crouch beneath the happy frog face to find Rosie staring at me with wide eyes. "I heard that my bus driver won't allow you on because I was on his route first. I'm sorry." She grimaces. "I'm so, so, so sorry you lost your family. We can trade off riding the bus if you want. I can walk to school half the week, or every other day, or however you want to do it."

Tears fill my eyes, and wind typhoons through my eardrums like my very soul is about to erupt from my ears. This sweet girl, this freshman, this "dead thing," is the first student to offer her condolences. It's enough to make me cry all over her umbrella, but I don't. I bottle it right back up and screw a lid over it. *It* being my shattered, weeping soul. And the lid being the kind that screws on so tightly it takes two people—and multiple expletives—to open.

Something else fills me. Something unexpected. Love. I didn't think it was possible for that warm glimmer to breach my undead, brokenhearted body. I feel it in my soul, and it's profound because it's a reminder that I still do have a soul. It makes me wish I could shout to Kendra, "You were right about zombies!" and that my message would echo and reach her all the way into the afterlife. Of course she was right. My sister was the smartest person I knew, along with my mom and dad.

I smile at Rosie, then duck out from under her umbrella before the lid loosens, and I end up pouring my grief onto the pavement—or the jar shatters altogether. "Thank you for your condolences, and for the offer of ride swapping, but I don't mind walking. I could use the exercise." I don't add that it's probably a good thing to keep limber for the next time someone wants to harm me for what I am. Rosie has enough to worry about without me reminding her. "So, this is where you live with your parents?" I glance over her umbrella to the house she darted from. Giant plastic candy canes line the drive and walkway leading to the front porch, which is draped in garlands and red bows. A steel-framed sled and a team of reindeer light up the yard, and snowflake string lights dangle from tree branches above.

The frog eyes turn to the side as Rosie twists to follow my gaze. It's like she has to verify her home hasn't vanished. When she faces me again, I can only see her from her neck down.

"I live with my adopted parents. My real parents—" Her voice trembles. She swallows. "They didn't want me after I became not human."

I frown.

"It's okay," she rushes to say. "Mr. and Mrs. Stockton are so nice, and now I'm the youngest. It's nice to have protective older siblings."

"How many kids do your adoptive parents have?"

"Four. Two of their own, Keaton, and me. They want one more."

"Is Keaton like us?"

The frog head bounces slightly. I don't know if she's nodding or shaking her head. "Keaton is human. He's a freshman in college. Molly and Mike—the twins—are sophomores in college. Mr. and Mrs.—I mean my parents—don't want to be empty nesters. That's why they want to adopt more kids."

"I'm glad you found a good home." I mean every word. Rosie reminds me so much of Joni.

"Rosie," a woman in a red-and-green-plaid plush bathrobe calls from the doorway. Light brown hair falls just past her shoulders. Despite the robe, her hair is styled and makeup applied. "Rosie, you need to finish getting ready for school." The woman puts one hand on her hip, but her stern gaze is entirely on me.

"Coming, Mom," Rosie says, projecting her voice without yelling. She lifts her umbrella briefly to smile at me. "See you at school."

Rosie jogs back to the holiday wonderland that is her home. Her frog umbrella bobs with every bounce of her steps. She looks like a normal young teenage girl. Thanks to magic, we're not mindless monsters or decaying body sacks.

Mrs. Stockton waits on the porch, not going inside until Rosie closes her umbrella and leaps through the doorway. Joni and I need a Mr. and Mrs. Stockton. That's when an idea hits me. I wish I had thought of it sooner!

I hurry the rest of the way to school, still making it early enough to beat the buses. I go straight to the computer lab, which, as luck would have it, is unlocked and empty. Before I even sit, I press the space bar on the nearest keyboard, awakening the screen. Then I plop down, open an internet search, and type in: Cameron Ward.

I sift through multiple Cameron Wards until coming across Cameron's Telepatch account. My fingers grip the mouse as I move the arrow to his link. There is still someone who cares about what happens to me. Cameron's graduating. He can be my guardian. We can stop TJ from grabbing up my family's fortune—no thanks to Uncle Alvan. Cameron to the rescue. Just in the nick of time.

I click the link. It feels so weird doing this on a computer rather than a phone. The site asks me for my login information. Telepatch wants to send a text or email passcode to verify this is really @HeyHeyHaylee since I've never logged on from this server.

I go into my kemail account next, get the code, and make it onto Telepatch, quickly finding Cameron.

Square photographs appear. His most recent post makes my stomach tighten. It's a photo of Kendra on the beach at sunset, the light hitting her in a way that makes her appear ethereal. The arrow shakes over the photo before I click down.

Cameron's post is short and heartbreaking.

@cameron.w.cole I miss you so much.

I type out a private message to him.

Cameron! I received your note and Kendra's package. I wish I could have seen you before you returned to Cali. I need your help ASAP!!! My uncle TJ is about to take hold of my inheritance unless I can find someone else to be my guardian. Uncle Alvan is a vampire now and refuses to help. The only reason Aunt Chloe died is because TJ hit her the morning she came over to my house for help. Please,

Cameron. Help me and Joni. You are literally our LAST HOPE! We'll be no trouble. I'm old enough to take care of myself and Joni. I just need someone I can trust to transfer monthly payments to me from my father's account. You are the only one I trust. Please contact Charles Dirk with the Law Offices of Dirk and Sunder and tell him I've asked you to be my legal guardian. I'll check back with you tomorrow morning. I've had to sneak into the computer lab to get in touch. Thank you, Cameron!

I thank him like it's a done deal because I trust my sister's fiancé to do the right thing.

Voices in the hall become more numerous and vocal. I'm not giving up my computer time until the first student enters the computer lab. I click back to the photo of Kendra, scrolling through notes of condolences.

so sorry man

💔

She was a kind & beautiful soul. The world has lost a shining light.

Prayers.

I still can't believe it.

😭

Z Squad needs to kill every last zombie!!!!!

I'm still in shock.

Absolutely horrifying and tragic!

The most recent comments take a different tone, one that has my torso pressed against the desk and face paling in the white glow of the monitor.

Sending healing prayers to Cameron and his family.

Hang in there, buddy.

Prayers!

We can't lose you, too, Cam. You're a fighter.

What's going on?

Yes, exactly. What the H is going on? And then I find the reply.

Cameron tried to commit suicide over the weekend. He's in the hospital in critical condition.

My world stops turning so abruptly, I nearly fall onto the keyboard. I'm back in my bedroom as the zombie horde closes in. All I can think is *no. No. No. No.* Over and over again. This isn't real. This isn't happening.

Two girls enter the computer lab. Their chattering dies off when they see me. I log out and rush out of the room. The hallway is a blur. Everyone is a blur, like I'm going blind. I bump into someone who snaps, "Watch it, you reanimated corpse" in a deep voice before shoving me against a locker.

I hear my back hit metal, but I don't feel it. I can't see who pushed me. This moment is made up in gray-toned watercolors that are bleeding together and dripping down the edges. I have to get out of here and do something. Jump off a bridge. Step in front of oncoming traffic. Stop existing.

I've tried so hard not to give up, but hearing what Cameron did kills me all over again.

I stumble along the hall and fling myself from the nearest double doors into the dark, chilly early morning. There is no sunset on the horizon. Gray clouds matte the sky.

All hope is lost.

I take lumbering steps along the sidewalk, leaving Brookdale behind. I don't want to be there, but I don't want to be at TJ's house either. For now, I lurch across the street and make my way to a small urban park with a pavilion, play equipment, and trail circling the grassy wooded area. It's deserted at this hour. It's quiet until the first whimper leaves my lips, followed by sobs.

My sneakers scrape against loose gravel on the trail as I set my sights on a bench beneath a tree where I can crumple and fall apart. Before I make it there, someone rams into me from behind, and I lose my footing. My chin hits pavement, and my front tooth goes straight through my lip before breaking in half. Concrete and gravel scrape apart my palms.

"Even undead, you've got a sweet ass," Caleb drawls.

I roll over as though on fire and jerk into a sitting position. "You asshole!" I seethe. "You broke my front tooth!" I press the pad of my thumb against the jagged edges. Blood dribbles down my chin.

Caleb's pupils dilate when he looks at his nasty handiwork. His grin makes me sick. "Let's see the rest of your wounds—the ones the zombies gave you. You still have them, right? That's why you've been wearing turtlenecks and scarves to school?" He sounds excited. Demented.

"Screw you." I spit out a mouthful of blood and start to stand, only to be pushed back down. I've had it with the shoving.

My death glare ought to make Caleb take a step back. Instead, he pulls out a pocketknife and snaps open the blade, which is shorter than my index finger but probably bigger than his teeny, tiny—

Caleb drops over me and jabs the blade into my belly. I scream in horror. Shock. Outrage. Caleb draws it back out and stares at the spot where he stabbed me with a glazed expression. "Stop screaming. I know it's nearly impossible to hurt your kind," he says calmly.

It's a dull prick, but I still felt it, and why does he think he knows what does or doesn't hurt a zombie? He stabs me again near the first spot. I try to punch him in the face, but he leans away, grabs my wrist, and slams my hand to the ground, then brings the blade down, piercing straight through my hand.

My scream burns my throat.

The feel of the blade as Caleb pulls it back out sends shivers of dread through my body.

"Show me your zombie wounds, and I'll stop," he says like it's the most reasonable request in the world.

"You killed Myles, didn't you, you psychopath?" I spit the words at him.

Caleb purses his lips for a moment, eyes going foggy, but not long enough for me to scramble away from him. He grabs the back of my neck in one hand and holds his blade against my throat with the other. I don't scream this time. Hate rises from the pits of my forsaken soul and spills like black ink from my pupils. I direct it all at him.

"Are you scared?" he asks. "You should be." He licks his lips. "Things didn't go so well for Myles when he displeased me. Show me your wounds, and I'll let you go."

I continue glaring at him. Caleb's manic gaze shows how deranged he is. He should be more careful around a zombie. If I bite him, I'm dead, but if I don't, he might kill me. Not the best options, but at this point, I wouldn't expect anything more from life. I don't trust him to let me walk away even if I do what he wants. Maybe he will today, but what about tomorrow or the next day?

What did he do to Myles?

Poor Myles probably held back biting because he hoped to see his family again.

Well, my family is dead, jackass. I won't make the same mistake Myles did. If I'm going out, I'm taking Caleb with me. I don't need a weapon. I don't need a wand. I am the weapon.

The abyss falls over me like a predatory shadow descending over prey. My soul shrinks away as the monster in me rises to the surface. I run my tongue over my broken tooth and then smile.

"Fine. I'll show you."

CHAPTER SIXTEEN

"YOU MESSING WITH me?" Caleb asks in a teasing tone, like we're flirting. Sick jerk.

"Nope," I say. "But it's really gross. Are you sure you can handle it?"

"Blood, guts, and gore have never bothered me." Caleb puffs up his chest.

"What about bones?"

His eyes light up like neon Christmas bulbs. Without further ado, I pull up my right sleeve. Caleb's gaze seems to caress the open wound. The hand holding the knife lowers. He seems almost to go into a trance as he stares. That's when I make my move. I grab the knife from his now loose fingers. It's mine before he can react. Then I open my mouth wide and lunge at his neck like I'm part vampire.

He's wearing a jacket. Where else am I supposed to bite him? A finger maybe? It doesn't matter. Caleb pushes me back before I can dig my broken tooth into his greasy skin. He scrambles away from me, feet and hands on the cold ground. We stand up at the same time. Caleb pants like he just ran eight laps around the gymnasium. It makes me grin a bloody, broken-toothed smile.

"You can't do that," Caleb says, looking stunned.

"Why not?"

"They'll exterminate you."

"So?"

He can threaten and harm me, but he can't scare me.

At last, he seems to recognize that I'm not going to roll over without a fight. A thin smile spreads slowly across his face. "I want to see the rest next time."

"You're insane," I spit.

The problem is the manic gleam has not left his eyes. He'll be more prepared next time, mark my words. Bigger knife. Zip ties. Duct tape. Ball gag. I wouldn't put anything past his warped mind. My own morbid imagination takes off. I know what monsters are capable of.

Caleb nods at the pocketknife leaving an imprint on my knuckle. "Keep it," he says with a nod, like it's a special gift from a deranged admirer. "I've got more at home."

Inwardly, I curse TJ yet again for selling my wand. If I had my Lignum Vitae, I wouldn't have to threaten Caleb with my teeth. I could lift him thirty feet in the air and then drop him—preferably over a barbed wire fence or active volcano.

Yeah, they'd exterminate me for that, too, but at least I wouldn't have to sully my tongue on his putrid flesh.

Eyes still on me, Caleb bends, picks up my broken piece of tooth from the ground and pockets it as though he's found himself a rare pearl. He backs away, looking more reluctant than frightened. Before he disappears around the wooded bend, he sweeps one last gaze up and down my body.

I remain rooted to the spot with his pocketknife firmly in hand. I'm still standing in that same place—same pose—long after Caleb has gone. The murky light of dawn is a diluted ink stain across the sky.

I am frozen by a grim realization. Payton is right. Caleb is obsessed with me, and it's hazardous now that I'm a zombie. He can stab me, and far worse, without consequences. I'm his ultimate gift. I refuse to let him get the better of me. The problem is, if I avoid school, I'll starve. If I do go, he's going to stalk me until he finds a way to ambush me again. Ending Caleb means ending myself, which means leaving Joni at TJ's mercy. I have to ensure her safety. Maybe there's a reason I'm still here. A final purpose before I join my family. If I'm taking anyone out before I go, it has to be TJ. Maybe Mr. and Mrs. Stockton would adopt Joni. She and Rosie could be sisters. Joni deserves a protective guardian who wears a holiday-themed bathrobe and buys a frog umbrella for her adopted zombie daughter. I'll leave a note for Joni to hand-deliver to Mrs. Stockton—The Final Wishes of Haylee Hutchins. And another note for Mr. Dirk saying I bequeath my inheritance to my cousin. I'm better at expressing myself on video, but for Joni, I'll take up the pen and bleed my heart out.

I head to Mystic Wand Haven, my favorite local magic supply shop, which is about two miles away. Two miles to think my decision over. Two miles to change my mind.

I follow the neighborhood streets to a main road, striding with purpose. Cars blare their horns as they pass me. My bloody face and hand scream ZOMBIE! Humans don't walk around bleeding. Too many vampire attacks in the past. Now, if a human gets injured, they get a ride—or drive—straight home or to the hospital.

Someone throws a paper cup half full of coffee out their window. It hits my arm, soaking through my sleeve and splattering over me and the ground at my feet. I concentrate on the slight burning sensation as my sweater absorbs the hot liquid through to my skin.

"Thank you for making this decision so much easier," I say to the coffee tosser, who has already sped away.

I continue to thank every car that honks. Every driver who gives me the finger. Every passenger who sticks out their tongue.

"Go back to the grave!" a young bearded man in a Jeep yells.

I never was in the grave, Einstein, and they don't allow my kind there to begin with. When did people get so stupid and spiteful? I don't want to be a part of this ugly world.

I don't have to be.

The coffee is cold against my shoulder when I reach Mystic Wand Haven. They don't open until 11:00 a.m. on weekdays. I don't know what time it is. Eight-thirty? Nine? As much as I want to get rid of Caleb's pocketknife, I pocket it for now—just in case. I keep my back to the street and stare at the crystals displayed in the window with spellbooks and candles. I go into a trance, only vaguely aware of the vehicles and occasional pedestrians passing by.

"Good morning," a woman calls out cheerfully.

Stella. Her familiar voice wakes me from my standing slumber. I blink and turn. Stella gasps, lifting a hand with midnight blue polished nails in front of her mouth. Feathered hair extensions in blue, violet, and black mix with her brown dreads and braids. She's dressed in dark plaid shorts layered over fishnet stockings, an oversize black cotton jacket, and a black tee with a large dreamcatcher pendant hanging from her neck. Tattoos peek from the edges of her clothing at her neck, arms, and thighs.

"Haylee, you gave me a fright."

"Hi, Stella." I force a smile, which makes Stella's eyes widen.

"You've been hurt."

"Just some jerk at school with no life. It doesn't hurt," I mutter.

Stella frowns and shakes her head. "I saw what happened to your family on the news. I am so sorry. Here, let me unlock the door and get you inside. I hope you haven't been waiting too long. Sorry I'm late. Sadie made quite the mess earlier."

I wouldn't have known if she was early or late. And I can't remember whether Sadie is a child or a pet. I follow Stella into the shop, then stand near the entryway like an awkward guest while Stella sets her purse and keys on the counter beside a small laptop.

She disappears into the back room before returning with a damp washcloth and small jar of salve. I almost tell her not to bother, but when she dabs gently beneath my lip, my throat wells up at the loving attention.

"Did you report this boy to the principal?" Stella asks while brushing the lukewarm wet cloth delicately over my chin like I'm made of porcelain rather than dead meat.

"Not yet." When Stella raises a brow, I add, "It didn't happen on school property."

"Doesn't matter," Stella says. "People shouldn't be allowed to attack sentient beings."

Ethics aren't going to save the day, but I keep my mouth shut, especially since Stella is now smearing my lower lip with salve. She finishes and tends to my hand next, then heads to the back room, returning with a Lignum Vitae wand.

"I'm not an alterationist, but I can spell you temporarily to appear uninjured so you won't be harassed on your walk home." She moves the wand from side to side in front of my face. "*Ignus ception farage.*" Stella repeats the wand movement and spell over my hand before lowering her wand, looking me over, and nodding. "You shouldn't draw unwanted attention for the rest of the day. Oh, and—*Ignus ception farage.*" She flicks her wand at the coffee stain, and it disappears, and then does the same to the blood stains in my turtleneck.

"Thanks," I say softly.

"I wish I could do more," Stella says with a sad smile. "You've always been one of my best customers."

"Well, you haven't lost me yet," I say. No need to tell her that I'm here for my final purchase. "I want to hire you for an enchanted tattoo."

Stella frowns. Her eyes dart to the front door. Only a select group of licensed practitioners are legally allowed to tattoo enchantments, but I've put two and two together over the years, catching whispered negotiations between Stella and customers.

This past summer, I was at Mystic Wand Haven, sorting through crystals—holding each prism to select the one that called to me—when an attractive young woman in a black-and-white-striped power suit entered the shop and began haggling with Stella for a rune tattoo. I picked up the words "birth control" and "preventative," along with the young businesswoman's huff and grumble of "the amount you're asking is outrageous."

"The rune can be used as often as you need," Stella had reminded her.

That's how magicked rune tattoos worked—unlimited use, except that they were limited to the specific type of rune. For a human to afford even one rune meant they had the kind of career that came with extra zeros tacked onto their salary. That or a seriously loaded benefactor. Affording more than a few runes is virtually unheard of. The magic only works if it's been tattooed with a mixture of crushed purple iolite and jetnite ink. Otherwise, it's just art. Cool, but of no practical use to a spellcaster.

Stella is still frowning.

"I can pay you."

At least I hope I can.

Stella considers me. I'm a big spender. My parents bought my Lignum Vitae from her, and I have been coming in for regular supplies of crystals, herbs, charms, candles, and spellbooks ever since. Not all spells can be executed with a flick of a wand.

Stella looks from the door to me. "What kind of rune are you wanting?"

I chew on my bottom lip. "Actually, I wanted a *ny scelta*."

Stella's frown deepens. "That's a tarot tattoo only good for a one-time use."

"I know."

"You don't want an illusion rune or invisibility? I know teleportation has a limited radius, but it could come in handy given your condition."

I shake my head. "I need the wild card." There isn't a rune for what I'm going to do.

Stella raises her slender brows. "You have sixty grand?"

I jut my chin at her laptop. "Can I log into my Payoneer account?"

Stella nods, disbelief in her hazel eyes. It's three times the price of a Lignum Vitae wand.

My stomach twists as I log into my account. The funds I've earned through affiliate links and sponsorships amount to $53,238.79.

"Would you consider a loyal customer discount and do it for the sum total of all I'm worth?" I ask, turning the laptop to show Stella the screen.

She cranes her neck to look at my account. Her frown deepens. My stomach plunges deeper. I'm about to beg when she says, "Yes. I'll do it."

I would jump for joy if this tattoo wasn't to be my mark of true death. Also, Stella is grim-faced. I can't tell if it's because I'm nearly seven thousand dollars short or because she has a sixth sense about my intentions.

Shoulders squared, Stella walks to the front door and locks it. She twists the hanging window sign around. I've seen the sign before. It reads: *Be Back When I'm Back.*

"It will take me about fifteen minutes to prepare," Stella says.

"Who do I make the transfer to?" I ask.

Stella pulls a card from her wide jacket pocket, sets it on the counter, and points to an account that's not under the shop's name: MagicInkSS3@independent.com.

While Stella sets up. I make the transfer and watch as my account goes from over fifty-thousand dollars to zero in one click. No turning back. I only wish I'd had enough left to buy Joni a Lignum Vitae wand. I would have gift-wrapped it and left it beneath her pillow. If only her dick of a dad hadn't sold mine.

"I'm ready for you," Stella soon calls from the back room. It's a cramped space filled with wall-to-wall bookshelves stuffed with an assortment of books. "Go ahead and have a seat on the chair." Stella indicates a worn armchair with stuffing pushing at the threadbare seams.

I sit and pull off my turtleneck, which leaves me in my bra.

Stella gasps. "You've been stabbed! I didn't realize that was blood on your shirt."

I lower my chin and take a look at Caleb's handiwork. "Oh, right." The blood around my stomach wound has congealed. If I were human, it would probably still be pouring out.

Stella cleans me up again but doesn't use her wand where illusion isn't needed. I'm not about to flash my belly to the world, even though it has shrunk on my limited diet.

Stella sets a metal chair beside me and then a stool, where she places a small pot of glowing purple ink and a tattoo gun.

"Set your arm on the rest." She outlines the moth's wings on my upper right shoulder. When she tattoos the otherworldly ink into my skin, the glow fades. "This might hurt a little."

"Not for me."

Stella keeps her eyes on her work. "Sorry, I keep forgetting. I've never inked a zombie before."

"It does tickle a little," I offer, not wanting to fuel false beliefs that zombies feel nothing. The tattoo gun is more like a massage compared to Caleb's violent stabs. There's a slight leftover burning sensation where he wounded me. My lip has that bloated feeling, like I just got work done at the dentist's office. "What happens if the tattoo gets cut? Will it still work?"

"Tarot tattoos have built-in protection. They're virtually indestructible." Stella's eyes remain on the design she's tattooing as she answers.

"What if my entire arm got chopped off?"

Stella pulls the tattoo gun away from my skin and frowns as she looks me in the eyes. "You could still use your one spell as long as you're touching the tattoo when you cast."

"Cool," I say.

Stella switches the tattoo gun off, sets it down, and stands. "If you don't mind, I'd like to add a little more color to the design. It won't interfere with its magical properties. I'll make it extra pretty."

"You really don't need to bother," I say.

"I want to," Stella insists. "Maybe you'll want to keep it longer this way."

Not happening, but I can't tell her that. Instead, I ask, "What happens after it's used for a spell? Does it disappear or something?"

"I've read that it goes away, but there were no details on whether it's instant or gradually fades."

Guess I'll find out.

Stella grabs extra colors and starts back on the design, adding teal, pink, and white in with the purple wings. It's beautiful. Too bad I won't be enjoying it for long.

The iolite and jetnite mix with my blood and hum with power in my veins.

When it's finished, I feel stronger. The design cannot be undone. No one can steal this from me. It feels like more than a tattoo. It feels like a dark secret all of my own.

Stella sends me home with a jar of ointment and instructions to apply it over the tattoo three times a day. I don't have the heart to tell her I won't need it.

I am grateful for Stella's illusion spell when Joni's bus trundles up the street.

As soon as she comes inside and shuts the door, I hug her tightly. Joni wraps her slender arms around my middle, and we hold one another for a long time until I pull away and ask, "How was school?"

"It was fine. Mindy brought me one of her mom's homemade fruit rolls."

"Which flavor?"

"Apricot."

"Yum."

Joni smiles, but it doesn't reach her eyes.

I've written her a letter with instructions for what to do after my true death. I hate that, like Cameron, all I can offer is a note. I don't want to leave her alone, but I don't see what choice I have. At least this way it will be on my own terms, and I can make it count.

For now, I help her with her science homework at the kitchen table. It's not astronomy, but I still find it interesting. Maybe it's weird to be into spellcasting and science, but to me they're both about discovery, mystery, and awe.

The worksheet Joni brought home tonight is about biospheres. There are clues and spaces beneath black-and-white illustrations for Joni to write in which is which.

She skips to number three, announcing, "This one is easy. Mountains!"

"Very good." I nod.

Joni reads the next clue aloud. "Dry, grassy plain dotted with trees and shrubs. Home to many large animals, including elephants, lions, and zebra!" she finishes in excitement. "That's a savanna. Oh, wait, or is it a desert?"

"Which one do you think?"

She chews on her bottom lip. "Um, what does a savanna—" Joni's voice cuts out at the sound of TJ's truck as it growls into the driveway and sputters to a stop.

All too soon, his key clangs overly loudly in the lock. The front door opens, and TJ walks in whistling. He enters the dining room holding a box of pizza with a salad and bag of bread sticks balanced on top in one hand. In the other hand, he holds a six-pack. TJ puts the food on Joni's math book and then takes the beers to the fridge.

"Your father's fancy lawyer can squeeze us in tomorrow at one," TJ announces.

Joni darts a glance my way.

"Guess you're celebrating early," I say.

"Watch your tone," TJ snaps.

"You watch yours," I backtalk, grinning at how easy it is to get under his skin. He can't see it, but I feel like a deranged jack-o-lantern with my broken tooth. My new tattoo makes me feel fearless. It's giving me a daring rush I wasn't expecting.

TJ squares his shoulders. "Once I'm officially your guardian, you better change that attitude of yours."

I just smile and wonder if there will be enough of me left to enjoy his screams after I reverse the spell of sanity. TJ shoots me another glare before backing into the kitchen. The fridge opens and shuts. A lid pops off a bottle.

Joni stares at the pizza box on her math book. I stand and reach over to push it off. "Asshole," I mutter under my breath. He'll be dead soon enough.

After Joni and TJ have turned in for the night, I lock myself inside the bathroom and pull off my sweater to stare at the wild card in the mirror's reflection. My skin's red and raw-looking around the design, but I don't feel any discomfort. Out of respect to Stella, I apply ointment over the design. While it soaks in, I go over the plan again. I think of the maimed zombies Kendra shared photos of on TelePatch. At least I won't be one of them.

I would rather go out as a monster than a victim.

CHAPTER SEVENTEEN

I START SCHOOL TWO hours before Joni, which is a good thing since she's still sleeping when I slip out of her room to "get ready."

The glamour will be gone, and I can't have my cousin see my swollen lip. At least I don't feel my wounds any longer. I might not be self-healing like a vampire, but my pain tolerance exceeds that of a human. I can't feel the tattoo either. Locked inside the bathroom, I admire Stella's beautiful work on my wild card before pulling on some clothing. Before leaving the house, I put on a winter jacket, hat, and gloves. For the finishing touch, I wrap a scarf around half my face.

This is the last holiday tour of Haylee Hutchins. I walk in the opposite direction of Brookdale, weaving around neighborhood blocks. Without a phone or watch to tell me the time, I pay attention to people leaving for work and kids getting ready for school. When buses appear filled with elementary school children, I head back to TJ's.

His truck is gone, but he told me to be back at the house well before the appointment. He thinks he's picking me up and striking it rich. TJ is in for the shock of his life. I'm going to give him a small taste of the horror my family and Aunt Chloe experienced after Thanksgiving.

With slow, deliberate movements, I take off the winter gear until I am left standing in a scoop-neck, short-sleeved black top. Even though I am down another size, it's snug. Aunt Chloe was skinny. Wearing her clothing has shown me just how thin she was.

I return to the bathroom and pull out a floral makeup bag from the bottom drawer. Using my dead aunt's makeup felt off-limits before. Today is different. Today is special. Putting on my face is a ritual of calm, and I want to look nice before Z Squad puts me down.

Aunt Chloe has a suspicious amount of foundation. I start on the scar forming below my lip. My aunt's skin tone was slightly darker than my own, so I rub it all over my face and neck, taking time to massage it into my skin and smooth out any streaks. Aunt Chloe's selection of eyeshadow isn't too exciting. She has a palette of taupes and nudes. I brush on layer after layer to darken it up. At least she has a black eyeliner pencil and mascara. I twist open three tubes of pink lipstick before finding a darker shade. When I'm done, I feel more like me than I have since the day after Thanksgiving. I stare at my reflection, and it's like staring into the past. The exposed bones on my arms and neck remind me of what I am and what I have to do.

I bring a piece of paper and a red marker to the kitchen table where I write:

Do NOT Enter! Crazed zombie inside. Call SOS immediately!

I set the warning face down on the end table nearest the front door in the living room, along with an envelope with Joni's name on it and a roll of tape. Once TJ is inside, I will tape both to the front door and then lock myself in with my uncle before activating the wild card.

I don't need my zombie handbook. I have the spell memorized.

The time on the digital microwave clock reads 10:43. I have less than two hours before TJ swings by to pick me up. I pace inside the kitchen, glancing at the clock way too often until the sound of a vehicle pulling into the driveway stops me dead in my tracks. Guess TJ was too excited to wait until his lunch break.

My stomach twists.

I'm not ready.

It's too soon.

I rub my fingers over the sleeve covering my tattoo. It's not like it's going anywhere.

So what if TJ gets guardianship today? I can take him out just as easily after he's gotten his hands on my father's money. Riches won't do my uncle any good once he's experienced death by zombie. I should at least wait until after Christmas for Joni's sake. Unless Caleb, Scary Van Man, or anyone else tries to take me out sooner. I'll just avoid school. But without brains, how will I make it through the holiday? Butcher shops. I can look into that.

My thoughts whirl, and acid burns my throat.

There's a loud knock at the door. TJ wouldn't knock. What if it really is Scary Van Man? What if he saw me wandering back home or had someone on "neighborhood watch" report my activities? I do not want to waste my wild card on a stranger. A bigot. No way!

The pounding is relentless. I approach the door with caution. When I'm four feet away, I call out, "Who is it?"

A high-pitched and impatient voice announces, "Alexander Moore with *Spellcaster* recruitment. Can you please open the door?" My jaw about hits the floor. "Hellooo?" he calls more insistently.

While my mind processes, my body takes over, unlocking and opening the door. Standing in the frame is the most gorgeous man I've ever seen. He is in his late twenties with flawless skin and soft pink makeup. He looks as though he's been airbrushed or photoshopped—or both. His peachy, slightly gold-tanned skin, forms a heart framed by dark brown hair, swept and styled about an inch above his scalp. Trim, dark stubble descends from his earlobes to the tip of his chin, finishing off the bottom half of his heart-shaped visage while showcasing a stunning jawbone structure. Long lashes curl toward the heavens. The pink on his lids and cheeks makes his face appear to glow. Glossy, full lips pucker as he looks me directly in the eyes. I'm still finding my voice, still admiring the pink mesh turtleneck printed with large red roses and green leaves that complement his makeup beautifully.

When I finally find my voice, it's less than eloquent. "Um, who did you say you were?"

"Alexander," the man intones, placing a hand on his chest. The sleeve of his floral shirt covers his knuckles, and his fingernails are polished pale pink.

"You're gorgeous," I blurt.

"Thank you," he says like it's obvious. "May we come in?"

We? I was so blinded by Alexander's beauty I hadn't noticed the two slightly older men behind him. Next to Alexander, they look drab in cargo pants and dark jackets. They're holding camera bags.

"What's going on?"

"Sweetie, you have been hand-selected by yours truly to audition for Season 13 of *Spellcaster*." Those pale pink nails move to Alexander's chest again.

Wait. What?

"But—I'm not human," is about all I can manage to say.

"Don't worry. I'll explain everything." Alexander winks before looking over his shoulder. "Follow me, boys."

I stand aside, allowing Alexander to sweep into the living room. Both of his hands lift to his shoulders like he's trying not to get them dirty as he does a small lap around the living space.

"The lighting in here is dreadful. Max"—Alexander snaps his fingers—"fix it."

A man in his mid-thirties gives me a cursory nod as he enters the living room, sets his bag down, and unzips it, pulling out an adjustable tripod stand. He sets to work pulling it open and then attaching a ring light.

I glance at the exposed bones on my arms and frown.

"Don't worry about that," Alexander says with a flick of his fingers. "That's perfect." He studies my face and purses his lips. "I'm not loving what's going on up here, though, hon."

"This was all I had to work with," I say in a daze. This is too surreal.

Alexander nods sympathetically. "It's okay. I never travel without a makeup kit. Jimmy—"

"On it," a man with a scruffy chin says on his way to the front door.

The other guy, Max, pulls a large handheld video camera out of a second bag. My stomach bottoms out.

"Wait. What's happening?"

Alexander's hands reach out and take me gently by my shoulders. He's a vampire, I think. It's like a sixth sense I can't explain. The men with him are human. They look and smell appetizing, whereas Alexander lacks any kind of fleshy odor. Light brown eyes peer into mine from beneath his long lashes. "You, hon, have been chosen to audition for *Spellcaster's* first all-supernaturals special! Isn't it exciting?" He releases me and gives a little squeal.

"I—what?"

There's a light tap at the door before Jimmy reenters toting a Kate Spade blue multicolored jacquard striped makeup bag. I'm still processing. I don't think I'll ever stop. This is all too crazy. I was supposed to die today.

Alexander walks to the table where I left my notes and tape.

"Wait—" I start to say, but he moves them to the coffee table, still face down, before taking the makeup bag from Jimmy and setting it on the now cleared end table. Alexander extracts a face wipe from his bag and starts toward me. I back away. "I can't audition for *Spellcaster*."

"Why not?" Alexander puts a hand on his hip.

I look around the living room, at the camera guys who continue to set up.

"My cousin needs me."

"You'll only be away from your cousin during travel and performance days, and not gone long at all if you don't make it to the next round, but I'm rooting for you to go all the way to the finals and win this thing, girl!"

I gape at him. "But why would you want me to win?" I thought vampires were supposed to hate zombies.

Alexander's hand remains propped on his hip. He waves the face wipe at me like it's a handkerchief. "Girl, I'm a loyal fan of Hey, Hey, Haylee. You were my personal pick to audition for a future season. I wasn't counting on it being Season 13, but now that you're supernatural, we don't have to wait for Season 14."

Wait a minute. "Did you like one of my posts last month under Colt Cohen's account?"

Alexander smirks. "I sure did, honey. I'm Colt's executive assistant."

I guess Payton was right. It's still exciting, especially coming from someone who appreciates beauty. Now that I think about it, I can't imagine Colt noticing anything to do with makeup, hair, or fashion when he wears the same style of suit every season, not to mention the fact that he's bald. The tall African American werewolf has a friendly yet no-nonsense vibe about him that remains steadfast season after season.

Then it truly hits me like a meteor hurtled from outer space. Alexander scouted me. I could have been on *Spellcaster* Season 14, or at least auditioned for it. Could have performed in front of Malachi Rayne and the other judges. It's all part of an alternate universe, one I wish I could transport myself to. The world of lost dreams.

Alexander gives me a considering look. "You're protective of your cousin," he states.

"Yes," I say, relieved that he seems to understand.

"That is so sweet. It makes me love you even more—and so will the audience." My shoulders slump. He's not getting it. But once again, Alexander seems to read my mind. "Not to worry," Alexander announces. "I know we can work something out, but first we need to get you ready for your pre-audition interview with Colt."

"Colt Cohen?" I gasp.

While my mind goes spastic, Alexander sets to work swiping my face with the cleansing face wipe. "Colt's on standby back at the hotel. Once we have you ready, we'll call him over." Colt Cohen! I'm about to meet Colt Cohen! I sway. Alexander steadies me with a chuckle. "Don't worry, Colt's a down-to-earth wolf. He'll guide you through the interview." When Aunt Chloe's makeup has all transferred from my face to the face wipe, I can't read Alexander's expression as he studies me. "We'll need an alterationist to fix that tooth before your audition. For now, an illusion will have to do." He drops the cloth on the end table and extracts a wand half-studded in silvery rhinestones from the tote. Alexander quickly performs the same spell Stella did over my mouth region and gives a nod. He drops the wand back in his bag and pulls out eye shadow palettes along with brushes, which he arranges along a cloth like a dentist about to get to work on a patient.

Alexander applies foundation over my face and then dabs and swipes with a blending sponge while I hold perfectly still. Next, he rubs primer between my upper lashes and brows before grabbing the eye shadow palette and a small brush and getting to work on my face like an artist painting a canvas. Shimmering white powder presses gently into the corners of my eyes. Vibrant purple goes on next. He blends with expert strokes. Every so often, Alexander stops and takes a step back to look over his work. Once finished, he pulls out setting spray. He doesn't need to tell me to close my eyes. This is the most normal I have felt since the attack and my transformation. It's therapeutic and calming.

For his last touch, Alexander pulls the wand back out and adds soft waves to my hair. It makes tears prickle at the backs of my eyes, which I hold in as much for the makeup as for the privacy.

"Gorgeous, girl," Alexander announces. "Go take a look in the bathroom."

I do as he says, leaving Colt's executive assistant and the cameramen in the living room while I shut myself briefly inside the bathroom. Alexander's artistry is beautiful. Striking purple covers my lids with a hazy pink and peach border. Electric blue eyeliner pops along my upper lids while a thin layer of purple accents my lower lids. Dark mascara thickens my eyelashes. It's like seeing an old friend in the mirror.

I return to the living room with praise on my plum-painted lips, stopping short when I notice the coffee table cleared of my notes and TJ's sports magazines, replaced with a set of mini succulents that are either an illusion or were brought in. They were probably spelled, like the dingy cream couch, which has been replaced with a geometric gray-and-white pattern.

Before I can freak out, I notice the magazines and my notes—still facedown—on a chair opposite the couch. The camera guys have their lights aimed at the couch.

Alexander's makeup bag is already packed up, though he's left his wand out beside it.

"Thank you for making my face look beautiful again," I say.

There's an odd expression on Alexander's face when he looks directly into my eyes, seeming to stare straight into me rather than at his handiwork. His brows pinch together momentarily before relaxing again. He waves an airy hand and says, "Girl, you are always beautiful. Don't you forget it. And Colt is on his way."

"Uh." My thoughts go hazy and I sway in place, afraid I might pass out.

"You'll be great," Alexander sings out. "You're a natural on camera. Just think of it as a friendly one-on-one conversation with Colt. He'll talk a little bit about what you've been through and ask you some questions about your love of magic, who you would want to coach you—stuff like that—though I know who you would choose as your coach." Alexander winks. "Team Malachi Rayne. I get it, girl. He's not bad for a vampire."

"Um, aren't you a vampire?"

"Look whose supernatural instincts have kicked in," Alexander says in delight. "And to answer your question, I am indeed a member of the vampire race, as much as I wish I were a werewolf."

"You do?" I try not to gape too much. I feel like I've done enough of that already.

Alexander frames his head with his hands. "With this face, I was destined to remain forever young, I know, as does my master. But I can't help being attracted to werewolves, and unfortunately, they, like all of the species, pretty much stick to dating their own kind." He sighs dramatically and lowers his arms. "I'm just a beauty queen destined to live out his life breaking hearts and having his broken in return. What can I do?" He sniffs and shrugs.

"Sorry," I offer.

"Me, too, girl. Me, too." When he holds me in his solemn gaze, I feel like he's offering me condolences rather than the other way around. I can't imagine there are a whole lot of cute AND sentient male zombies on the market.

Is that what my dating option will be for the rest of my life? Why am I even thinking about this? It's not like I dated before. But that doesn't mean I wouldn't have been open to it if the right guy ever came around. I always imagined it happening the way it did for Kendra—meeting my dream guy in college.

Now what's the criteria? Good at remaining undead—opposed to extermination—enjoys zoning out and eating organs? I look at the chair with my note and frown. Why am I even thinking about this kind of thing?

I don't think there's any getting rid of Alexander and his crew—not to mention Colt Cohen is on his way. I just need to let them do their interview and then reassess my plan. Talk about an enormous, hippo-sized hiccup.

I moisten my lips, mindful of the pretty stain. "So, I'll sit on the couch talking with Colt?"

"Don't worry," Alexander reassures me again. "It will be over before you know it."

I am hit by the irony of his words. Wasn't I just telling myself that for an entirely different reason?

There's a rumble in front of the house, one I recognize as TJ's truck. It's a good thing I've got the foundation and touch of bronzer Alexander put on. Otherwise, I'm sure my face would be pale. I walk swiftly to the window and confirm it. TJ has parked along the sidewalk on the road. His truck door flies open, and he jumps down, immediately glaring at the SUV in the driveway before storming across the lawn.

"My uncle TJ is here," I whisper, seconds before he stomps through the door.

"What the hell is going on?" he demands. "Who's parked in my driveway? Who are these people?"

Alexander's upper lip curls back. He looks at Max, the burly camera guy. It's like some kind of silent command, because Max is the one to answer TJ.

"I'm Max, and this is Jimmy and Alexander. We're crew members for *Spellcaster* setting up an interview between your niece and the show's host, Colt Cohen."

"You're what? Why didn't anyone call and ask my permission first? What did you do to my couch?" TJ blusters.

"Not to worry, it's only an illusion spell," Alexander says calmly. "Your homely couch will be just as it was after we leave."

TJ's beady eyes turn to flint. "You all need to leave. Now." His face is so red it looks like he's running a fever.

"You don't want your talented niece to audition and compete on the show?" Alexander raises an eyebrow.

"What show?" TJ demands.

"*Spellcaster*," I say in exasperation. "It's a televised magic competition."

Alexander takes a step to stand next to me. I don't feel so alone with him beside me.

"All travel expenses to and from Hollywood, including hotel and food, are provided during Haylee's participation in the competition," Alexander says.

"Hollywood!" TJ blasts. "Absolutely not. Haylee isn't going anywhere. You and your crew need to pack up and leave immediately. We have an important legal meeting. You need to go now."

The tears return, burning the back of my eyeballs as I hold them in.

Max and Jimmy look at Alexander for direction. "You heard the man," Alexander says calmly. The gorgeous vampire struts over to the end table and threads his pink polished nails around the handle of his makeup tote. TJ folds his arms and lifts his chin like an overlord watching underlings do his bidding. Alexander picks up his wand by the rhinestone-studded handle and, quick as a bull whip, points it at TJ and casts. "Alexander says behave. Obey. Accept my words as your will today." Alexander turns the tip of his wand to himself quickly and then back to TJ before arcing in a wide oval as though framing my uncle within a transparent picture frame.

I'm speechless, staring in shock at Alexander's bluntly worded spell and then at TJ as his entire body jerks as though hit by lightning. My vocal cords can't even squeeze out a gasp.

"You will allow your beautiful and talented niece to audition for *Spellcaster*," Alexander tells him.

TJ blinks and says, "Of course, Haylee can audition. Magical talent like my niece's should be showcased." He looks around the living room, confusion writ large across his face.

"I couldn't agree more," Alexander says, setting his tote and wand back down on the end table.

"Can I get you anything to drink?" TJ asks. "I've got beer and water. There might be a little bit of grape juice left. Sorry, not well stocked."

"How about you get the boys each a beer," Alexander suggests.

TJ's lips quiver like he's trying to frown but can't. "Beer, sure."

As soon as he walks out, I turn to Alexander and throw my arms forward. "What did you do to him?"

CHAPTER EIGHTEEN

ALEXANDER ROLLS HIS eyes. "He was interfering in your interview. The spell will wear off when he wakes up tomorrow—unfortunately."

Max snorts and then lifts his hand over his face, clears his throat, and drops his hand. "Sorry."

TJ returns with two beers and a bottle opener, which he uses before handing a bottle to Jimmy and then Max.

"Thanks," Jimmy says, taking a tentative sip before setting the bottle on an end table, which TJ fixates on.

"How long will this take?" my uncle asks.

"As long as it needs to," Alexander answers.

The muscles in TJ's face appear to spasm. Eventually, he nods. "I should call Dirk and Sunder and tell them we need to reschedule."

My chest lifts. I might feel more elated at the delay of guardianship than the interview with Colt Cohen.

"You do that," Alexander says dismissively, "and then I'm going to need you to turn off your phone so it doesn't go off in the middle of filming."

"Oh, right," TJ says, sounding almost sheepish. "I'll wait inside my truck." He starts toward the door and then stops, scratches his head, and turns around. "Actually, if you don't need me here, I'll go on back to work."

"Even better," Alexander says with a grin.

"Okay." His eyes dart from Alexander to me. "Well, then, good luck with the interview, Haylee."

"Um, thanks?" I look at Alexander like *What the hell?* but the vampire is peering through the camera lens and then saying something to Max that has him moving the tripod an inch to the right.

"See you tonight." TJ pulls his keys out of his pocket and swings the ring around his finger as he walks to the front door. It's unnerving.

The moment he's gone, I raise my arms in exasperation. "What if he reports you? He's friends with the local chief of police."

Alexander lifts his manicured nails over his mouth and mimes a yawn before lowering his arm with a graceful sweep. "And I'm friends with a powerful master—not to mention I'm a spellcasting vampire." He grins wickedly.

"I mean, can't you get in trouble?" I stammer.

Alexander laughs. "You're cute."

I huff, which gets more laughs out of him.

I suppose it's a good distraction because when Colt Cohen arrives minutes after TJ has left, I'm still so flabbergasted by the spell Alexander put over my uncle that I forgot to go back to the cold sweats in anticipation of meeting a TV celebrity face-to-face.

Alexander is the one to announce, "Colt is here." The vampire opens the front door as though this is his house. "Excellent timing," he calls out. "We're all set up in the living room."

Colt ducks his head as he enters with an easy smile and bright eyes. Dressed casually in a jean jacket and white shirt over blue jeans, he's even taller in person.

"Haylee," he says, immediately zeroing in on me. "It is a pleasure to meet you."

"Well as you," I blurt, and then grimace. "You, as well," I correct.

Colt doesn't chuckle or smirk. He slips one hand in his front jacket pocket and nods all casual and chill. "Alexander has told me all about your talent and following. You already have an impressive fan base on JingleJam."

"I—" I look at Alexander for help. He stares back and tilts his head at Colt in a *go on girl, you've got this* gesture. So I do. I look Colt square in the eyes. Well, first I crane my head back so that I can reach the giant's gaze. "I used to, anyway. I don't know if my account is still active."

"Oh, it is, hon," Alexander butts in. "Your account has been blowing up with comments. Folks are heartbroken over what happened to you and your family."

I feel a little weepy again thinking of the beauty brigade's concern. "I don't have a phone," I say.

"Don't worry. I'll help you with that." Alexander bats the air.

"I, uh, don't have a wand, either." I look at the ground. Better to tell them now in case it's a deal breaker for the audition.

"Didn't you use your wand to save yourself?" I startle at Colt's deep voice, feeling, yet again, as though I'm dreaming he's here inside TJ's living room.

"My uncle sold it." I shrug.

Alexander gasps. "That cad! He sold the wand you used to save your cousin and then yourself." The vampire huffs.

Colt purses his lips. "It would have been great for the interview." He rolls his shoulders back and lifts his chin. "No matter. We'll get a shot of it during auditions. Alexander, I trust you can track it down?"

Alexander nods vigorously. "Happy to."

"Excellent. Now, how about we sit and get to know you better." Colt directs me to the couch. Again, it's an out-of-body experience of being on set rather than in TJ's living room.

I sit on the couch and set my hands in my lap, pulling at my fingers. Colt settles beside me on the edge of the couch, leaning forward and slightly to the side to face me. He threads his fingers together and smiles kindly. "Pretend like it's just the two of us having a friendly conversation." Does he think that will make me less nervous? He's Colt Cohen! "Max here will keep the camera recording for later edits. Sound good?" I nod. "Excellent. So, what first got you interested in magic?"

Oh. Easy. I relax a little as I answer, "It was after watching *Les Trois Magiciens* perform live on tour."

Colt's eyes light up. "Phenomenal group of spellcasters," he says reverently. "How old were you when you saw them perform?"

"Six." I still remember the wonder, the discovery of magic introduced by the French trio: Jean, Cecile, and Vincent. They came through Virginia the summer before I started first grade. Mom and Dad took Kendra and me to see them. I hold that information back, knowing how these interviews work. Every season has contestants who have experienced hardship—spellcasters who have lost a parent or a close family member, lost their home and all their belongings to a natural disaster, or who battled a life-threatening disease. Those kinds of things. But no one is going to cry over a zombie.

"Six years old," Colt muses. "You caught the bug early. Did your parents get you a wand after that?"

"For my seventh birthday," I answer, feeling the threat of tears.

"Do you remember the first spell you performed?"

A memory inflates inside my head, the way my first spell expanded out of control. I wince. "Yeah, it's embarrassing."

Colt's smile widens as he leans closer. "Now you really have to share."

"Okay, but remember I was seven years old at the time."

"I will," Colt says with a chuckle. He's as good-natured in person as he is on camera. Alexander was right; it didn't take long for Colt to set me at ease.

"I had this cute teddy bear about this big." I hold my hands apart a little over a foot tall and then rotate them horizontally roughly seven inches from palm to palm. "I thought it would be fun to spell him into a giant-size stuffed bear—I'm talking maybe five feet tall—so I tried out an expansion spell."

"Uh-oh." Colt's cheeks dimple with his grin.

"Yeah," I say with a smile. "Teddy ended up filling my entire bedroom. I think the ceiling, floor, and walls were the only barriers stopping him from spreading across the entire state." Colt and I share a brief laugh.

"Did your parents take away your wand afterward?"

I shake my head. "No, they hired me a tutor."

Colt could dig more into my parents and their early support of my magic, but to my relief, he keeps things light.

"And what happened to Teddy?"

"My tutor taught me a reversal spell, though I was kinda sad. What seven-year-old doesn't want their bedroom stuffed with a plush bear?"

Colt's eyes shine when he chuckles. Making him laugh feels good. Charisma and character are as important to a contestant's success as the actual spellcasting. The world is filled with talented casters, so it's important to stand out.

"Seven-year-old me would have been on board for that—if it was a giant soccer ball I could have kicked down the street I grew up on," Colt says. He turns his head to the camera. "Kids, don't try this at home—at least not without an experienced spellcaster supervising." He chuckles. It's infectious. Colt leads the interview in a new direction. "You recently surpassed one million followers on your JingleJam profile. Congratulations. Tell me more about your passion for combining beauty and magic."

I sit up straighter. "Thank you, Colt. For me, beauty and magic are about transformation and expression. I use them both to jazz up my appearance and my life. Life is what we make of it. I happen to want to live in a world that never loses its dazzle."

Colt looks at me for several beats before bobbing his bald head, white teeth flashing from a wide grin.

I think we're both surprised by that awesome soundbite. The words are flowing through my lips as though I had weeks to rehearse. It's really thanks to countless hours of talking on camera to the beauty brigade. Little did I know it would lead to this moment.

"Wonderful words to live by," Colt says. He pauses for several seconds before commenting, "You're doing fantastic, Haylee."

I blink a couple of times, realizing we've reached an "edit out" portion of this chat.

"She's a natural," Alexander boasts. "What did I tell you?"

The skin crinkles around Colt's brown eyes when he smiles at his executive assistant. "You were right, Alexander. A diamond in the rough to be sure."

I glance at my arms. I suppose that my being a zombie is the rough part.

"Time to change location," Colt announces, taking long strides to the door. "Meet you there."

"See you soon," Alexander replies.

Max and Jimmy pack their gear faster than they set up. Meanwhile, Alexander ushers me to the door.

"Where are we going?" I ask.

"Your old house," Alexander answers.

I come to a dead stop, my body shaking. "What? Why?"

Alexander's lashes flutter. "It's for your back story. That will be a big theme for Season 13 interviews—how contestants became supernaturals. Except for witches and wizards, naturally. Boring." Alexander mock yawns.

I walk outside with the crew and find myself getting into the back of a black SUV with Alexander. Jimmy drives with Max beside him. My stomach twists and cramps. I swear it's overcompensating for my dormant heart.

Home.

I'm going home.

But I'm not really going home. I can never truly go back home.

Tears swarm my eyes as I stare out the window. I feel betrayed—not that I blame Alexander or Colt. They're not my friends. They have a hit show to produce. I allowed myself to forget that while Alexander applied makeup and Colt chuckled with me in TJ's living room. Of course they want the horror story on top of the fluff. It's for Season 13, after all.

Blinking away my tears, I face forward and ask, "Since we're already supernaturals, what is Season 13's grand prize?"

Alexander's eyebrows jump. "That, Haylee, is a surprise I am not allowed to share. You'll find out before the blind auditions, though. We have a whole big publicity announcement planned."

I forget about my tears. What could it possibly be? For so long the show's been about competing for a chance at immortality that I can't imagine what they could have come up with for creature contestants.

"Can you give me a hint?"

Alexander chuckles softly. "Nice try, hon."

"Fine. At least tell me who won this season."

"You don't know?" Alexander demands, sounding horrified.

"You met my uncle, right?" I ask sarcastically. "Nothing gets in the way of his evening sports."

"Unforgivable," Alexander announces. "Well, I know it's not the same to hear it after the fact, but Devon Torres, Team Malachi won the show."

Ugh. There really is no justice in the world. I hold in a huff. "Are they allowing him to be made at twenty-three?"

"He wishes." There's a touch of scorn in Alexander's voice. "Devon should consider himself fortunate just to be made. He can go through the transition at twenty-two or wait until he's twenty-four—or older for all anyone cares. In all my years as Colt's assistant on the show, I have never met a more demanding finalist."

I nod. "He wasn't my favorite." It's easy to confide in Alexander.

"I wanted Gianna Woods to win," Alexander states.

"Me too!"

"Well, hopefully this new season, my first pick wins it all. That's you, in case you've forgotten."

"I didn't realize you started recruiting this early."

Season 12 has barely ended, and the holidays are around the corner.

"Our casting director is always recruiting. It's not my job to find talent. I just got lucky when I came across you. And you're right. We don't usually film interviews at the end of the year," Alexander acknowledges. "Colt made an exception for you." He grins like it's a huge honor, but it only makes me more curious.

"Why?"

"Well, for one thing, your kind has a less than impressive survival rate." When I scowl, Alexander says, "Sorry, hon, those are the stats. Also, now that your parents' home has been fully fumigated, there's no telling how soon the house will be put on the market. This might be our last chance to film on location."

I pitch forward like I've been punched before quickly righting myself. As excruciating as it is to go back, it's even more distressing to think of a new family moving in—as though my parents and sister never existed.

"Wait a minute? Who is selling my house? Don't they need permission?" The questions fire off my tongue like bullets.

Alexander gives me a sidelong glance. "I assumed whoever becomes your guardian will want to offload it after the holidays. Take it from me, letting go of the past is the quickest path to setting yourself free."

Given the choice, I could never live there again, but it's still painful. Maybe that's what Alexander is talking about.

Sighing, I say, "I don't suppose you know of any great guardians for hire?"

"What about your uncle?"

"You mean TJ?" I blast. When Alexander gives me a nonchalant shrug, I scoff. "You met him. Would *you* want him as your guardian, or master, or whatever?"

"Use the spell I put over him. It has to be cast every morning. High maintenance, I realize, but also highly effective."

My jaw feels about ready to detach from all the gaping I've done in the past hour—ever since Alexander knocked on the door and took me on this whirlwind campaign.

"Isn't mind manipulation illegal?" I demand.

Alexander inspects his nails. "Don't worry. He won't be able to tell anyone. It's a precaution built into the spell."

"He's friends with the local police chief. What if he, or one of his coworkers, notices that something's off?"

The knots forming inside my stomach have frayed edges that scrape against my internal organs.

"Doubtful," Alexander replies breezily. "Humans are too caught up in their own problems to bother examining what's going on with others too closely. They'll make time to judge people, sure, but only on a surface level. After a while his behavior will become the new normal. Just don't forget to spell him before he gets a chance to stop you."

I jerk upright. "Will he remember that you spelled him?"

"He's already aware—not that he can do anything about it or voice his displeasure until he wakes up in the morning. The spell requires that he sleeps it off. At least three full sleep cycles," Alexander adds. "There are no napping shortcuts."

I press my palms against my forehead. "He's going to be furious."

"Another good reason to keep the spell going."

"I don't have a wand, remember?"

"I'll provide you with a backup."

"You'll give me a Lignum Vitae wand just like that?"

"The show has a sizable budget," Alexander says. "Besides, your cousin will need it while you're in Hollywood competing. I hope she inherited your talent for casting."

Joni! With all the hubbub, I momentarily forgot about her.

"You can't expect a ten-year-old to perform an illegal spell on her father." As great as it sounds, I'm supposed to protect Joni—not get her involved in unlawful activities. Then again, having TJ under our control would make everything a million times better. It's beyond tempting.

"Talk it over with your cousin first," Alexander says. "She could keep it up until she graduates from high school. After that, I know multiple experts in memory wipes."

Oh my gosh! I can't believe he's openly talking about this like it's no big deal to manipulate and wipe a person's mind. I glance up front, but Jimmy and Max don't so much as pause their banter. I'm paying as little attention to their conversation as they are to mine, apparently.

As familiar houses flash past, my throat tightens, and I can no longer speak. We pass Mrs. Kline checking her mailbox. She stops to stare as the SUV passes, but other than her, there is no one out in the cold. Most of my old neighbors will still be at work and school.

When my house appears, I feel as though I am staring at a mirage across an endless desert. The yard has long since been cleared of the carnage, but caution tape still surrounds the property.

While most of the homes on the block have been decorated for Christmas, my old home looks as though it hasn't moved on from Halloween. It might as well be a haunted house for all I want to go in there.

Jimmy pulls in along the curb and parks behind a white compact car. He and Max get out, go to the back of the SUV, open the trunk, and pull out their equipment bags. I stay where I am, clutching my hands in my lap.

"You can do this," Alexander coaxes.

But I can't. *This* isn't an on-camera interview with a celebrity TV host in TJ's living room. This is everything I want to forget.

I gaze out, feeling as though I am staring through an airplane window at a distant suburb within sight, but out of reach. Jimmy and Max move around the yard, recording the outside of the house from different angles. Holding his camera steady, Max walks toward the front windows. They've been replaced, as though zombies never crashed through and murdered my family.

A moving vehicle catches my attention as it comes in from the opposite direction. How can it not, with its obnoxious lime-green-and-blue paint? The Z Squad SUV slows before pulling into my driveway.

"What are they doing here?" I demand.

CHAPTER NINETEEN

ALEXANDER DOESN'T HEAR my question over his squeal. He flips open a compact mirror and checks his face before quickly snapping the compact shut and stuffing it into a bag. The vampire is out the door in a flash, zipping over to the driveway to greet the four werewolves as their doors open simultaneously. They're all dressed in brown pants and short-sleeved khaki button tops with their horrid Z Squad logo patch on the upper sleeve. Werewolves, like vampires and zombies, don't require extra layers of clothing in winter. Terrick emerges from the passenger's seat. A werewolf with wraparound sunglasses and one wearing the Z Squad baseball cap step out of the back seats. Sgt. Ganon's head pops up from the driver's side.

Hot, liquid rage scalds my brain. What are *they* doing here? I throw open my door, get out, and then slam it shut.

I step over the yellow tape, heading across the yard where Z Squad has joined Colt Cohen and are taking selfies with him—with my house as a backdrop. Seriously? What the H-E-L-L?

At my approach, the ripper with the wraparound sunglasses growls.

"Down, boy. You know Haylee is harmless." Alexander swats the air playfully.

Terrick lowers his phone. "Thanks, man," he says to Colt, before heading toward me. The ripper in the baseball cap takes his place beside Colt and holds up his phone. Terrick walks over to me, stopping a few feet away. "Hey." He jerks his chin. "How you holding up?"

"Aw, because you care so deeply for a zombie's welfare," I say sarcastically, making a point of looking at the steel baton hanging from the belt against his hip.

"Pretty exciting to get an opportunity to interview with Colt Cohen and audition for *Spellcaster*," Terrick counters.

"I'd rather have my family back," I snipe.

"But you can't."

Those three brief words make my vision swim. An ocean of grief rushes over me.

Creases ripple across Terrick's forehead. "I didn't say that to be cruel. It's just how it is."

I turn my head away from him, blinking rapidly, fighting for control over the wind rushing my ears and rain threatening to fall from my eyes. It's like being caught in a storm when seconds before, there wasn't a cloud in the sky.

I lock it down like a pro baseball player knocking curve balls left and right with the crack of a bat.

"I know," I tell him.

Alexander flounces over, tapping the tips of his fingers together in excitement. "This is perfect!" he exclaims. "Max, get over here. I want shots of Haylee with her local Z Squad heroes."

I glare silver stakes at Alexander. "No," I snap. "No way."

Alexander looks at Terrick and chuckles before threading his arm around mine. "If you'll excuse me a moment while I speak with our rising star. We sprang all this on her earlier, and she's still a bit overwhelmed by the attention." He continues smiling until he's dragged me clear across the lawn to the yellow line of tape dividing my family's property from the Wilson's yard next door.

Before Alexander can lecture me, I yank my arm out of his grip and spout off. "They aren't heroes. Killing zombies is sport to those animals. They would have killed me too, if I hadn't spoken up in time. Wouldn't surprise me if that's happened before. What if a newly casted zombie was in shock and unable to communicate in time?" I put my hands on my hips, getting warmed up. "They have no decency. My parents, sister, and aunt lay torn apart at my feet when Z Squad came in and dragged me away like I had committed a heinous crime just for surviving the attack. They wouldn't allow me to check on my cousin. They cuffed me and interrogated me at their station before tossing me into a cell." My voice wobbles. My ruined arms wrap around my middle and the dam breaks. Tears drip down my cheeks.

I want to run from Alexander, from the rippers gathered in my yard, from Colt, from the crew, from the ghosts of my past.

I'm about to run—leave them all behind to film without me—when I notice tears sliding down Alexander's face. I stare at him in utter shock. He sniffles and forces a weak laugh. "Damn you, Haylee Hutchins. You're ruining my makeup."

"I'm sorry," I say in genuine horror, which makes us both laugh.

"Come back to the SUV with me. We both need a touch-up," Alexander says gently.

We walk side by side to the parked SUV, going around back to the trunk. Alexander lifts the hatchback and grabs the Kate Spade bag. "Mind if I go first?" he asks.

"Not at all," I say. "Can I hold a mirror for you?"

"Yes, that would be fantastic. You're such a doll. If you weren't already a zombie, I would beg my master to turn you into a vampire."

"Thanks," I say politely, even though the offer holds no appeal. While I fetch the compact, Alexander sets out brushes, palettes, and a pot of blush. Alexander taps the blush into his cheeks with his finger pads, freshening the pastel glow over his skin. "That is such a pretty shade of pink," I say, holding the compact up at an angle.

"Thanks, girl." Alexander finishes his touch-ups in no time and says, "You're next." He dabs under my eyes with a wet wipe.

"Sorry," I say.

"Hon, you have absolutely nothing to apologize for, but let me offer you some advice. When life throws you a bone, bite it."

"Meaning?"

Alexander swipes a wide brush over bronzer and then sweeps it over my face in gentle strokes. "These wolves are salivating at the prospect of national recognition. We'll be sending a press release to your local media outlets about how their resident zombie girl was the first supernatural chosen for a blind audition to compete in Season 13. It wouldn't hurt for your community to see you chummy in photographs with Z Squad. The message is clear. Anyone bothers you, they're going to have wolves tracking them down."

"Oh," I say. "I hadn't thought of that."

"That's what I'm here for," Alexander boasts. "I've been doing this for a long time. I'll guide you."

"Thanks, Alexander."

"Mm-hmm." He finishes touching up my face and has me take a look in the compact mirror. I pull my lips back from my teeth to double-check that the illusion is still in place hiding my broken tooth.

Alexander puts everything away and then places a hand on his hip. "Ready to cozy up to some hot werewolves?" I wrinkle my nose, which makes Alexander laugh and shove me playfully on the shoulder. "Pretend that you're posing with Malachi Rayne."

My cheeks instantly flush.

"Yes, girl. Just like that."

My stomach twists the way it did when Colt Cohen first walked in, because it's hitting me again. All of this is leading to a live performance in front of Malachi and the rest of the coaches. If I flub my audition, I'll never live it down.

For now, I let Alexander take over. I become the perfect model, following directions, holding poses, and smiling for the camera as though life is peaches and cream. When Alexander directs Terrick and me into the living room for Max to photograph us in the spot where Z Squad first found me, I repeat "for Joni" inside my head over and over. I don't have to leave her to fend for herself. Alexander's right. A Z Squad photo shoot gives me the appearance of having powerful, supernatural friends. Alexander is getting me my wand back. I can protect myself and Joni. He'll hook me up with a phone. We'll be okay as long as I play along. This opportunity isn't one to be squandered.

"Ready to go upstairs, Haylee?" Colt asks.

"Yes," I answer like a marionette. The bones exposed in my arms make me feel like a skeleton on strings.

"Thank you for your service and assistance," Colt says to Sgt. Ganon and his team in a voice that conveys both gratitude and dismissal. "Alexander will keep in touch to let you know about publication dates, and I certainly hope you will watch Season 13 when it airs and vote for your gal here." A charismatic smile fills his face.

"It was an honor to meet you," Sgt. Ganon says. "Thank you for spotlighting my department."

"I've watched every season. I'm a huge fan," the ripper in the baseball cap says.

"Glad to hear it," Colt says. "We're big fans of Z Squad, aren't we, Alexander?"

"Huge fans!" Alexander squeals.

"Why don't you escort our friends back to their vehicle and answer any questions they have," Colt suggests to his executive assistant.

Alexander puffs out his rose-accented chest. "With pleasure."

Colt nods to me and jerks his chin toward the stairs. Dread drags each of my steps like quicksand rapidly pulling me into a pit of terror.

Colt waits at the bottom of the stairs for me to go first, like he's being chivalrous or something. Max and Jimmy lower their cameras, coming up behind Colt—holding back. All of them are waiting for me to face my fears.

I take the first step up and then the next. Memories of decayed flesh, hissing, biting, and bloody fingers grasping at me flash behind my eyes. Someone flicks on the overhead hallway light from below. The walls have been repainted a pristine eggshell white.

Two steps from the upper landing, I realize that I'm no longer scared of zombies. I *am* a zombie, and I pity those poor crazed beings trapped in a mindless state. I wouldn't wish that on anyone.

Someone used the horde to come after my family. I can't believe I considered suicide and letting the real culprit get away with their crime. It might be the best reason of all to audition for *Spellcaster* and use whatever resources they can provide.

I go to my now-empty bedroom—also repainted eggshell white—and wait for Colt and his crew to enter before announcing, "This was my room. This is where I became a zombie."

Without my furniture and things, it's a barren space without character. No beauty. No fashion. No style. Certainly no giant stuffed teddy to comfort a heartbroken girl.

I'm too old for plush toys, anyway. Dark magic never interested me until now. A month ago, I would have never considered illegal spellcasting, either. Those sentiments belonged to human Haylee. Zombie Haylee will do anything to keep her cousin safe and get justice for her family.

The real battle has only just begun.

After we're finished with the interview, Colt thanks me and says he looks forward to my blind audition in the spring. He joins Jimmy and Max inside the SUV while Alexander beckons me to the white compact car Colt drove in earlier.

"I'm taking you to get a phone and a wand," he announces.

He said that he would, but I am still flabbergasted.

Alexander doesn't just get me a phone; he purchases the latest Vampton Galactic 16. Stella's eyes practically pop out when Alexander struts into Mystic Wand Haven announcing, "We need a Lignum Vitae." He sets a credit card on the counter and says, "Haylee insisted we purchase one from your shop. She was just filmed with Colt Cohen for her pre-*Spellcaster* Season 13 audition interview."

"*Spellcaster*!" Stella exclaims.

Stella clutches the large quartz crystal hanging from her neck. She looks from Alexander to me. "Haylee, are you auditioning to compete on the show?"

I nod. "Season 13 will be the first all-supernatural competition. They wanted a zombie, so . . ." I shrug.

"Supernaturals performing, what a fantastic idea!" Stella exclaims.

"Isn't it, though?" Alexander agrees with a lift of his chin.

Stella glances at my sleeve covering the rune tattoo she did yesterday. A smile lights up her eyes. She's probably thinking the tattoo has something to do with auditioning for the show. If that's her belief, all the better.

"I'll be right back with the Lignum Vitaes," Stella says, hurrying to the back room.

Alexander taps two of his polished nails on the counter and watches me as I continue setting up my new phone. The first thing he insisted I do was add him to my contacts . . . along with personalizing his ringtone with an upbeat tune that sounds like something a DJ would play in a nightclub.

Stella returns with a small carved wooden box and sets it on the counter before inserting a key and twisting open the lock.

"I apologize for the lack of choice," she says, before pulling out one wand, followed by a second and setting them on the counter.

"It's for my cousin," I say, picking up the one with a swirling handle. My fingers close around the smooth wood. It feels good to hold a wand again. The second wand has a rounded knob at the end of the handle. I prefer the swirly one, and I'm pretty sure Joni would too.

"That one?" Alexander asks, like he's reading my mind again, or—more likely—because it's the one I'm clutching.

"Yes. Thanks."

Stella places the second wand back in the box, closes the lid, locks it, and sets it aside. When she reaches beneath the counter, I tell her, "I don't need a bag."

Stella smiles warmly as she takes Alexander's credit card and gives it a swipe. The transaction goes through immediately. Stella thanks Alexander as he signs off on the purchase.

"Congratulations, Haylee," Stella says.

"I'm not on the show yet," I answer with a grimace. "Maybe none of the coaches will lift their wands for me." If they don't, will I still be able to keep my phone and wand?

Alexander's head snaps up. "Impossible," he intones. "The real question is how many wands will lift for you. I'm betting all four."

Stella nods. "I'd make that bet."

My cheeks heat. "Well, that's nice of you both to say."

"Nice has nothing to do with it," Alexander says. "Ready to go?"

By the time Alexander pulls in front of the house, I'm ready to jump out before he's turned off the ignition.

"Haylee, we need to talk." His use of my name, and the serious tone of his voice, makes my stomach bottom out. This is it. This is where he tells me I've been pranked. Did I really believe they would allow a zombie to audition for *Spellcaster*?

I clutch my new Vampton Galactic 16 and the wand in a death grip.

"What?" I ask, unable to mask my defensiveness.

Alexander's long lashes flutter. He sighs dramatically. "I found your note while moving things around earlier."

My stomach rises right back up, along with the steam in my head. "You read my note to Joni?"

"No, but I saw your crazed zombie message. Were you planning on pretending you had become crazed so that Z Squad would take you out? Or perhaps you had no intention of pretending." He flicks a glance at my shirt sleeve covering my wild card as though sensing the powerful tattoo and lifts a shapely brow.

"I'm not a coward," I say.

"I certainly hope not," he says, all cynical.

I narrow my eyes. Yet again, Alexander isn't fully grasping the perils of being the creature at the end of the alphabet. I set the phone and wand in my lap, holding up the hand that Caleb stabbed. Illusions cannot hide the ugly truth.

"A classmate came after me yesterday. He gave me this and this." I point to my mouth. "And this." I poke at the wound on my belly. "He already killed another zombie at our school. I'm next on his list."

Alexander purses his lips but shows no other signs of worry. "Tell me his name, and I'll take care of it."

"What do you mean, 'take care of it'?" I ask.

"Better if you don't know," Alexander says dismissively.

I shake my head. "He's my problem to deal with."

Alexander places his hand on my right shoulder, near the *ny scelta* hidden from view, and gives me a gentle squeeze. "If this boy interferes in your ability to audition this spring, then that makes him *Spellcaster's* problem."

I shake my head again. "He caught me off guard and without a wand. I'll be ready next time. I'll—take care of him myself." I'm not sure what I mean by that, but it makes Alexander beam.

"I knew you were special, Haylee. It's a shame you're not a vampire. You would have done my kind proud."

Because zombies can't be badasses? I keep my quip to myself. I know Alexander means well, and I now have a phone and a wand thanks to him, so I'll dial down the snark . . . or try to, anyway.

The following morning, I stand at the foot of TJ's bed waiting for his alarm to go off. He's on his side, one arm slung over the edge of the bed with the blanket and sheets dragged halfway down his bare back, which is freckled and hairy around his shoulder blades. It's disturbing, but it's about to be more so for him than me.

TJ's a mouth breather. It reminds me of the sounds of the zombie horde as they closed in, but it doesn't trigger any fear. Joni, on the other hand, is a bundle of nerves beside me, twitching like she drank a gallon of coffee. She pulls at her pink-and-white-striped sleep tee with its cute koala face that matches the drawstring pants in baby blue with smaller koala faces printed all over. The shirt reads DREAMER AT HEART.

I'm dressed for school. Alexander is going to pick me up at Brookdale after lunch and take me to an alterationist to fix my broken tooth and the wounds Caleb gave me. They want me to keep the injuries I sustained from the zombie attack during my televised audition for the whole Season 13 supernatural stereotypes. I don't see why the interview wasn't enough. It totally sucks that Malachi Rayne and the other coaches are going to see me all skeletal and gross. I'll just have to distract them with a phenomenal performance. Great makeup and hair go a long way too.

As extra incentive, Alexander says that *Spellcaster* will arrange and cover the cost of full alterations after I officially make it on the show. He's sorta like a fairy godmother who comes with terms and conditions—and I'm the one with the magic wand. Speaking of which, I hope Alexander will have my wand this afternoon. Hope someone else hasn't beaten him to whatever pawn shop TJ likely sold it to. Even if someone purchased my wand, I have no doubt Alexander could track it down like a bloodhound on the scent.

While I ponder, Joni's fingers move to the drawstrings of her pants and tug. The beep of the alarm clock causes her to jolt in place. TJ groans. His hand lifts from where it was dangling over the bed and feels around his nightstand for several seconds before silencing the alarm.

With another groan, he flops onto his back and rubs his eyes before sitting up. I ready the wand, the carved swirls secure within the curl of my fingers, and point it at my uncle. TJ's jaw loosens when he notices me.

"What are you doing in here?" His eyes widen in realization. "Don't you dare try and spell me, you little bi—"

"Haylee says behave. Obey. Accept my words as your will today." I repeat the motions Joni and I practiced with Alexander yesterday before he left to join his crew at their hotel. Luckily, the spell isn't complicated. It's a little alarming that a piece of carved wood and words hold this amount of power. I mean, it's cool, but it depends on whether the caster is using that power for good or evil. I'm inclined to believe that spelling TJ into compliance is for the greater good.

As with yesterday, TJ's entire body jerks.

"We don't use that kind of language here," I say as I lower the wand, "especially not toward family. You will respect me, TJ."

He clutches his bed sheets and grimaces. "Sorry about that. I'm cranky first thing in the morning."

I purse my lips, nod, and think it over before answering, "Apology accepted." TJ sighs with relief, falling forward slightly. Joni's eyes bug out. "We'll leave you to get ready for your workday." I nod for Joni to follow me out.

Once back inside her room, I announce, "And that is how it's done."

CHAPTER TWENTY

HOHOHOHOHOHOHOHOHOHOHOHOHOHOHOHOHOHOHOHO HOHOHOHOHOHOHOHOHOHOHOHOHOHOHOHOHOHO

HoHoHoHoHoHoHoHoHoHoHoHoHo.

The gift from my sister sits on the coffee table in the living room with a few smaller wrapped presents arranged around one of the succulents Alexander's crew left behind. Turns out they brought in real house plants for the home interview.

TJ earns enough to get by each month without much extra for extravagances like a Christmas tree. I could cut off his beer fund, but I've found that he is less likely to fight the spell's control over him at the end of the day if he is allowed to drink. The beer is nearly as effective as the wand. Alexander quickly succeeded in retrieving my wand, which was at the nearest pawn shop. He also got my broken tooth and stab wounds fixed as though they were never there. Thank goodness for alterationists!

My inheritance remains inaccessible. Dirk & Sunder closed their office early for the holidays, and I'm still struggling with the idea of allowing TJ to be my legal guardian even if I can keep him under my control.

He sits with us in the living room in an armchair, sipping a beer, while Joni and I munch popcorn on the couch and watch a romantic holiday comedy. According to the calendar, it's Christmas Eve. For me, it's just December 24th. Another day without my sister, Mom, and Dad.

TJ's phone rings. I lean forward on the couch to grab the remote and mute the sound on the TV while TJ sets his bottle of beer on the side table by his chair, trading it for his phone. My wand rests against my thigh, always within reach. The extra wand is next to the presents. I thought Joni would be more excited about it, but she's been treating the wand like it's a loaded gun and she's afraid to shoot off her toe or accidentally kill someone.

TJ clears his throat before answering. "Hello? Oh, hi, Alvan." Joni looks at me in alarm, but she needn't worry. TJ sounds like his typical surly self. I don't think Uncle Alvan would care that I've spelled him. It wouldn't matter anyway. I don't care what Uncle Alvan thinks. He left me and Joni to fend for ourselves. This is the result. "The girls are fine." TJ is quiet for several beats before responding, "Sure, hang on a sec." TJ gets out of the armchair and walks over to me. "Your uncle wants to speak to you."

"Sure," I say as I take his phone. "Hey, Uncle Al," I say brightly.

"Hi, Haylee," Alvan answers in a slow, perplexed voice. "You sound like you're doing well."

I filter the sarcasm and bitterness from my voice when I answer. "Why shouldn't I be?" I only lost my family and humanity last month, but three cheers for the holidays and being left with Uncle Scrooge and Uncle Undead.

"Um—" Uncle Alvan leaves himself hanging in confusion, which only encourages me.

"Happy Christmas Eve," I say. "Oh, or do vampires not celebrate the holidays?"

"Yeah, we do," Uncle Alvan says slowly. "I'm a day early, but I wanted to wish you and Joni a merry Christmas."

"Thanks. I'll tell her. Unless you want to?"

"No. No, that's fine. You can let her know for me. How is Joni?"

I cross my legs and sink back into the couch. "She's fine. Eating three meals a day. Going to school. Doing her homework. The usual."

"Good. I'm glad to hear that. And everything is okay with TJ?"

"He'll never be father of the year, but we're managing to coexist." TJ tries to narrow his eyes at me from his spot on the armchair and fails.

Anytime he gets peeved, he looks like he's having a stroke. He grabs his beer bottle instead and gulps it down.

"Is he in the room with you?" Uncle Alvan asks sharply.

"Yeah, we're all hanging out. Holiday family time, ya know?"

"I feel like there's something you aren't telling me," Uncle Alvan presses.

This time, my annoyance filters through the barrier. "I've told you everything you need to know."

A heavy sigh blows through the line. "Haylee, I'm sorry I can't be there for you and Joni."

"Nothing to be sorry about," I quip. "We don't need you."

"I know. I'm just sorry my sister isn't there to take care of you."

"TJ can manage."

"Are you sure?"

"Yep." Funny how Uncle Alvan is only asking now that I'm no longer begging and pleading with him. Never again. I've taken responsibility for myself and for Joni. I only wish I was eighteen and human so that I could be both independent and Joni's legal guardian.

"Well, good." Uncle Alvan's voice loosens. "I wanted to send gifts, but I wasn't sure if you would be celebrating this year."

"Uncle Al, don't sweat it," I say, proud of all the teenage chill I am channeling. "Anyway, we're in the middle of a movie marathon. Thanks for calling. You have yourself a merry little Christmas and a happy New Year." I smirk into the phone. "Talk later. Bye." I end the call before he has a chance to respond.

TJ snorts and lowers his beer. "What a schmuck."

For once, I'm inclined to agree with TJ.

Uncle Alvan doesn't call back after I hang up on him. I don't expect him to. I don't expect anything from an undead underling. There's nothing glamorous about what he's become. He's a minion. A pawn. A parasite. Unlike Uncle Alvan, I have no master.

I look at Joni, who chews on her lower lip. Offering a sardonic smile, I say, "Uncle Alvan says hi and merry Christmas."

"Is he okay?" Joni asks softly. She's way too sweet.

"He's a vampire," I say, as I stand and walk TJ's phone back to him. If Uncle Alvan doesn't care enough to show up for family funerals or bother sending gifts (whether we're in the mood for them or not), then he doesn't deserve my direct phone number. "Let's return to our movie before we miss any more of the show." I plop back down on the couch and turn the sound on. It's still early afternoon, and I plan on numbing my mind as much as possible with back-to-back showings of old holiday flicks.

Dinner that night is pre-made chicken and sides I instructed TJ to pick up from the deli the day before for himself and Joni. With school closed for holiday break, I also had him get me a couple of cow brains from the butcher's shop. I sit at the table with Joni and TJ watching them eat. I'll have my meal in private later. I don't want to spoil my cousin's dinner. At the end of the meal, I tell TJ to leave his plate on the table. "Joni and I will clean up. Why don't you get ready for bed? I doubt Santa will bring you anything, but if you continue behaving, I'll let you have some milk and cookies tomorrow."

As soon as TJ leaves the dining room, Joni gapes at me. "Haylee! I don't know how you can talk to him that way."

"Easy." I shrug.

"You know it will only make things worse if he ever breaks free of that spell," my cousin presses.

I lean my elbows on the table. "Which is precisely why we have to spell him first thing every morning."

Joni squeezes her arms against her sides and hunches in her seat. "What if I mess up, or he grabs my wand from me before I can finish the spell?"

"We just need to cast quickly." And by "we," I mean Joni whenever I'm in Hollywood. "We'll practice the spell together until performing it becomes second nature," I assure her. "In fact, let's practice right now."

She blinks several times. "Really?"

"Yeah. What else are we going to do? Sing carols?"

Joni's frown pulls my stomach lining loose and double wraps it in guilt. I remind myself she's lost her mom, too. She's still young. Human. Sensitive and vulnerable. It's my job to ensure she's able to protect herself.

It's been so long since I first picked up a wand that it's easy to forget about all of the stumbling blocks and mistakes I had to navigate when I began my magical training. On top of everything else, Mom and Dad hired me a pro in the field.

I'm no Lewis Carney, but I did learn from the best and will impart every piece of spellcasting I learned from my late and great instructor unto Joni. I lead my cousin into the living room and jut my chin at the coffee table. "Go ahead and grab your wand." When her eyes dart in the direction of the wand, I add, "Remember, without words to accompany it, the wand is only a stick of wood." Joni nods and gets her wand. "Now, pretend the armchair is your dad and cast the spell."

Joni steps in front of the armchair and points her wand at the cushion. "Joni says behave." She flips the wand, smacking the tip against her chest. "Oops."

"It's okay, keep going."

"Obey," she continues softly. "Accept my words as your will today." Joni points her wand back at the chair and then swings her arm in a wide oval.

"Excellent. Do it again." I have Joni practice the spell six times. Mr. Carney was all about lucky prime numbers. For now, I'm going with lucky number seven, which is why after Joni's sixth go, I say, "Now try it on me."

Joni's face blanches. "I can't do that to you."

"It's okay. You have my permission." I glance at the dark window. Christmas bulbs light up the homes across the street. "It's getting late," I reason. "I'll sleep it off soon enough."

"What if I get it wrong?" Joni asks.

"Then you'll try again. Besides, it will be good for me to understand the effect it has firsthand." It really would help to know what kind of hold it has over TJ and whether there are any weaknesses in the magic that I should be aware of. I swear sometimes he looks like he's going to break out of the spell before the end of the day. It's equal parts comical and terrifying.

When Joni hesitates again, I assure her that I am impossible to harm.

"Better to use me as your first-time guinea pig than TJ. If you mess up, I won't ground you," I joke.

Joni moves the wand from her right hand to her left, flattens her palm, and spins her wand over her hand with her opposite fingers, watching the motion closely.

"I know you can do this, Joni. Know how I do?" She looks up and shakes her head. "Because you're the only member of this family whose eyes lit up any time I performed a spell. You've got the passion. Now it's time to master your gift."

Joni stops fiddling with the wand. She takes a deep breath, holds it for several seconds, and then releases. "I'm ready."

I smile. "Good." I walk over to the armchair, plop into it, and set my wand on the side table. "Go for it," I tell her.

I've never had anyone else point a wand at me. It makes my tattoo itch. I close my lips over my teeth to hide the fact that I'm gritting them.

"Joni says behave. Obey." The wand tilts toward her, then back to me. "Accept my words as your will today."

Electricity flashes through my brain, and my muscles spasm all at once. It doesn't hurt. It could be because I'm a zombie. I'm not overly concerned about TJ's humane treatment, though. So much worse is done to dogs, and they are good, kind, loyal creatures—unlike the TJs of the world.

I grin, sure the spell has worked. When I open my mouth to praise Joni, my lips move soundlessly.

Her eyebrows furrow. "Haylee?"

I stare at her, waiting for an instruction, a command, directions of any kind.

"Haylee!" Joni repeats my name shrilly. I stare at her blankly, unsure of what she wants. "Oh my gosh. I did something wrong." Joni throws her wand on the ground. Her face tears up.

I want to go to my cousin and comfort her, but I can't. When I try to lift myself out of the armchair, my muscles lock up. Every time Joni blinks away tears, then looks at me sitting silently, she starts crying again.

"Haylee, say something please."

"Holy crap," I gasp.

Joni's next sniffle cuts off. "Haylee?"

I stand up and flex my fingers. "Yeah, all good. I think I figured out the next part of the spell. You have to follow it up with an instruction of some sort for the subject to begin functioning."

Would have been nice if Alexander clarified that bit, but here we are.

Joni presses the heel of her palm to her forehead. "Thank goodness. So you're okay?"

"Yeah. Fine. It felt like an electrical shock, but that part is over quickly." Joni grimaces. "Doesn't bother me," I assure her. Hopefully zapping her dad won't cause her to hesitate.

"Do you feel any different?" Joni asks.

"I'm fine." I smile, then frown. "Is there some other way you want me to feel?"

Joni's pupils dart from side to side. "Um, I don't know if you're being serious."

"I would never mess with you," I say. "You deserve better than that."

"Okay, thanks." Joni looks at the wand by her feet.

"Do you want me to pick up your wand?" I ask.

"I've got it." Joni bends and snatches it up. "What should we do now?"

"What sounds good to you?" I ask.

"I don't care." She rubs her chin and stares off for a moment then returns her attention to me. "Uh, actually, would you mind singing 'Rudolph, the Red-Nosed Reindeer'?" A smile stretches across Joni's cheeks.

"Sure," I say. It's a silly request, but I'm not about to deny her. I sing the first lines, my voice rising when I get to the introduction of Rudolph. As Joni rocks from side to side, I grab my wand and touch my nose with a quick "*rosilla*," making it turn red. I tried it on my cheeks once, but never my nose. I even have a glow spell. Again, never used it on my nose until tonight, but it goes perfectly with the song. Joni's delightful squeal fills me with glee. I dance around the living room as I sing.

When I finish, I start again, and Joni joins me, only stopping to say, "I want a red nose, too."

I give her one. I'll give her anything she wants.

After the third round of Rudolph, Joni throws her arms above her head and says, "Let's do 'Frosty the Snowman' next." I give us both black button nose illusions. We swing our arms as we circle the living room, singing. If anyone was to drive past the house and look in, they would think we were a joyful family celebrating Christmas.

They couldn't be more wrong.

My heart might as well be a lump of coal inside my chest. It's fitting that I'm a zombie. No more heart to break.

If that's the case, then why does another piece of it shatter every time I wake up and start a new day without Kendra, Mom, and Dad? I wish I could sleep through tomorrow. I don't want to wake up to my first Christmas without my family.

For once, I sleep soundly. Maybe it was all the exercise in the living room singing holiday tunes with Joni. At any rate, sweet oblivion ends all too quickly when rough hands grab me by the throat.

"Wake up, bitch."

CHAPTER TWENTY-ONE

MY EYES FLY open, and a wet gurgle passes through my lips as TJ looms over me, squeezing my throat. It's not as though he can choke me to death, but it doesn't feel good.

Joni wakes up screaming. "Dad, stop! Let Haylee go. Please!"

His fingers tighten, and he leers into my face. I grab his wrists and attempt to pry his hands off, but I'm up against a full-grown man who works in construction. I jerk and squirm beneath him, rage engulfing me at being accosted by my uncle while I was sleeping. I go for his eyes with my nails, which does the trick. He releases my neck and leans back before I can scratch his eyes out.

Before I can scramble out of my sleeping bag, TJ's fist socks me in my left eye. Stars explode behind my skull.

Joni's scream rips through the house.

Merry bloody Christmas!

While TJ's weight is off me, my fingers grasp inside the sleeping bag until I find my wand. Before I can pull it out, TJ's scuffed-up slipper comes down over my wrist. He puts his full weight into crushing me. I feel at least one bone snap and scream in fury. TJ leans into his weight, wrenching another scream from my lips.

"Stop it! Stop hurting her," Joni yells between hysterical sobbing.

TJ swings his leg and kicks my face like my head's a football. I fall on my back, my vision sinking into a dark sea where sharks wait to finish me off.

"You're going to pay for performing your hocus-pocus on me," TJ seethes.

There is no warmth, no light. If only there were no sound down here in the darkness. I don't want to hear my uncle's awful voice ever again. Hate consumes me. There is no fear. Only burning wrath. I no longer want to cast spells over TJ. I want to kill him. I already have a wild card tattoo and a plan to pull it off. If only Joni weren't inside the house with us.

TJ's dirty hands close around my throat again, lifting me to my feet by my neck.

"Dad, no!" Joni shouts again.

It's like he can't hear her. His eyes are bloodshot and crazed as he sneers into my face. "Let's move this to the kitchen, shall we?"

Great, I bet I will soon experience the stab and slice of another knife. Sadistic males are nothing if not unoriginal.

TJ yanks me with him into the hallway, and there isn't a thing I can do about it. Even if I decided it was worth wasting my wild card on a teleportation spell, I wouldn't be able to cast with my windpipe being crushed. I'm dragged halfway to the kitchen when Joni's bellow echoes down the hall.

"Joni says behave. Obey. Accept my words as your will today." There isn't a moment's hesitation. I almost don't recognize my cousin's voice. It's angry and fierce. "Let Haylee go, Dad." My uncle's hands loosen before falling to his sides. He's no longer looking at me. "Go to your room and stay there until I tell you that you may come back out," Joni commands.

I don't really have a room. I suppose Joni's room counts as the closest thing, so I head for her room as TJ heads for his.

Joni's lips part in confusion as I pass her and go into her room. She follows right behind me. "Oh my gosh! Did I hit you with the spell too?"

I stare at her through my right eye. The left one has swollen shut. "It seems so. I didn't realize that was possible." Though I suppose it makes sense given my proximity to TJ when Joni cast her spell. "Thanks for stopping him." My voice comes out small. I thought I had TJ under control. I let myself get too cocky. My bruised throat, damaged wrist, swollen eye, and aching skull are sharp reminders that even with my wand back, I am powerless.

Tears stream from my left eye. My uncle beat on me like I was a rag doll. He punched me, same as he punched Aunt Chloe—and on Christmas day, no less.

"Haylee, don't cry. It's okay," Joni says so sweetly that I stop crying at once. "Oh! I mean, cry if you want to. Don't listen to me. Do whatever you feel like."

"I feel like dying." The words slip past my lips. It's like trying to stop the gush of blood from an open wound by putting pressure over it with only your pinky. It cannot be held in.

I expect Joni to start crying, but she surprises me by squaring her shoulders and lifting her chin. "I am going to clean you up, and then I am going to make breakfast and hot chocolate."

"Okay," I answer without enthusiasm.

"Can you come with me to the bathroom?"

"Sure."

I follow my cousin to the bathroom and stand as still as a medical human skeleton on a roller stand while Joni flips through her *Safety Spellcasting for Beginners* spellbook, which is open on the counter beside the sink. I already am part skeleton, with my open arm and neck wounds. At least with my wand back, I've been able to cast an illusion spell instead of having to wear long sleeves, turtlenecks, and scarves. After Joni finishes with me in the bathroom, I'll grab my wand from her room and make myself presentable.

Joni slips through more pages before stopping and announcing triumphantly, "Here it is! The Owie Wowie Spell. Provides relief from minor accidents involving scrapes, cuts, burns, or blows . . . *and* speeds up recovery time. Let's give it a try, shall we?"

"If you want." I shrug, maintaining my Sam the Super Skeleton pose.

Joni grabs her wand from the counter and waves it at my wrist, neck, and head. "Tissue, muscles, bones defend. With this spell, injuries dull and recovery attend. Tissue, muscles, bones mend."

Where I felt dull aches before, they disappear altogether. "It worked," I say.

Joni smiles. Her elation fades in the next instant. "You're not just saying that?"

"I'm not. I can't feel a thing anymore." I glance in the mirror and find I am able to see my reflection through both eyes. "Even the bruises are fading." My cousin's grin mirrors back at me. "Great spellcasting, Joni." I wish I could put more enthusiasm into my praise, but TJ snapped more than my wrist bone.

There is no way I can ever leave my cousin alone with TJ. Without Aunt Chloe or me as his punching bag, he will likely go after Joni next. That means there is no point in auditioning for *Spellcaster*. I need to figure out a way to break the news to Alexander after the holidays. But before then, I have to allow TJ to become my guardian so that I can spell him into giving me a monthly allowance that I can use to pay *Spellcaster* back for my phone and wand—and Joni's wand.

I groan. With the monthly allotments Uncle Alvan mentioned, it's going to take years to pay *Spellcaster* back. What if they demand the return of our wands? We need at least one to keep TJ from killing us in our sleep.

As though sensing the direction of my thoughts, Joni waves her wand in front of me. "It's okay, Haylee. I've got the spell down."

"Yes, you do." I nod slowly. I'm still not leaving her alone with that monster.

"You don't have to worry about me while you're in Hollywood," Joni insists.

It's a relief. She's right, of course. I don't have to worry about her while I'm away. She can handle the spell on her own. *Don't worry*, I tell myself. *I'm not worried. It's okay. We're both okay.*

I keep Joni company in the kitchen while she makes cinnamon rolls from a pre-made refrigerated tube that includes an icing pack. Once the oven reaches temperature, Joni pops the tray of raw rolls in and sets the timer. She pulls a carton of eggs and a pack of bacon from the fridge next.

"How can I help?" I ask.

"Um, can you make scrambled eggs and bacon?"

"Sure." I'll try, anyway. Cooking has never interested me, but it can't be that complicated to throw eggs and pre-sliced strips of pig meat into a frying pan.

I begin with breaking eggs over the side of a bowl.

Joni watches me for several seconds and then says, "Sorry, I know you can't eat them. Are you sure you don't mind?"

"I don't mind at all," I answer automatically.

It's not like I have anything better to do. That, and Joni asked for my help, which means she wants my help, and I feel compelled to do as Joni wants.

So, not only was I beat up on Christmas, but now I'm spending the day at my cousin's beck and call. My bitterness isn't fair to her. I'm in a dark place, spelled or not. What I do know is that no ten-year-old should have to wake up on Christmas morning to her father's brutality. In spite of everything she's been through, she faced her fears this morning and came to my defense. I would do anything for Joni with or without a spell of obedience. Scrambled eggs and fried bacon is really no big deal. It doesn't get much easier in the way of breakfasts—short of pouring a bowl of cereal with milk or spreading cream cheese over a bagel.

Joni sets a small saucepan on the stove beside the frying pan, and then pours in milk, followed by several heaping spoons of powdered cocoa mix. The smell of cinnamon and sugar fills the kitchen as the rolls bake.

"Joni!" TJ yells.

I drop the fork I was using to whisk the eggs. The whole thing slips into the goop. My left eye twitches.

"What is it?" Joni calls back, not abandoning her spot stirring the milk and cocoa with a wooden spoon while it heats above electric coils.

"Can I use the bathroom?"

Yesterday, I might have laughed. This morning my sense of humor was kicked out of me.

"Yes," Joni speaks with a raised voice. "You don't have to ask to use the bathroom."

He's not a complete puppet unable to make everyday decisions for himself. It's like he's toying with us.

The sound of his footsteps creaking through the hall makes me cringe.

I fish the fork out of the eggs and shake it gently over the bowl before rinsing it in the sink.

"Joni?" TJ soon calls.

"Yes?"

"I'm hungry."

"Go back to your room, TJ. I'll let you know when breakfast is ready."

TJ narrows his eyes. "I'm your father."

Joni shrugs. Luckily, he leaves without saying anything more.

I hate how his voice makes me flinch. Hate that he put his hands on me. I can't stop thinking about it. The morning plays in an endless loop inside my busted brain. I want to grab my wand and use it to toss him around his room—see how much he enjoys being the victim of violence. Give him a taste of what it's like to feel defenseless. Not that it would change him. Violence begets violence. His act of cruelty is already twisting my soul, and I cannot allow that to happen.

I imagine my hatred burning up with the grease sizzling around the bacon slices in the pan. I make my voice sound pleasant when I ask Joni, "Want to sing Frosty again?"

She looks over with a grin. "Really?"

"Or Rudolph. Doesn't matter to me." I turn over the pieces of bacon.

"Let's do Frosty," Joni says.

And so we sing and cook. When breakfast is ready, Joni dishes up a plate and takes it to TJ for him to eat inside his bedroom. After she finishes her meal and cocoa, I section off a chunk of cow brain and wolf it down. These are my rare happy Haylee moments—right before, during, and immediately following brain consumption. That's the extent of my capacity for joy.

After my delicious meal, I brush my teeth, shower, and rub ointment over my tattoo before changing out of Aunt Chloe's sleep tee and pants into jeans and a short-sleeved blouse. I sit on my sleeping bag and roll my wand over the fabric, pushing it absently along with my finger.

Joni hovers in the doorframe. "Do you want to open your gift from your sister?"

I place my hands into my lap, still focused on my wand. "No," I answer. "Not today." Maybe not ever. The moment I unwrap it, that's it. I will never have another gift from Kendra again.

"Uh, so, what do you want to do? Watch movies all day?"

"Yeah," I say, looking up at my cousin. "That sounds perfect."

We spend most of the day in the living room with the TV for company. When the final hours of Christmas finally come along—and TJ does his final business before bed—I spell Joni's dresser to walk into the hall and settle securely in front of my uncle's closed door.

The next morning, I startle awake to a realization as harsh as yesterday's strangulation.

I blink and stare at the ceiling from my sleeping bag on the floor and remember why I can no longer audition for *Spellcaster*. I'm no longer under the influence of a spell. No more illusions.

TJ is a manic dog. The moment he slips free of his collar, he'll rip us apart. Before, he might have blamed the casting entirely on me. But now that Joni has spelled him, he'll be gunning for her too. I can't leave her alone with him. I lost my mother, my father, and my sister. I won't risk losing my cousin.

I stare at the ceiling, stuck in a box I won't be able to escape for years. Not that I'm in any hurry. What happens after Joni graduates from high school and goes to college? Will *Spellcaster* ever do another supernaturals special? Even if they do, I doubt they'll want to invite me ever again after I throw this opportunity back in their faces. I don't want to think about it. Anytime I do, I feel like wailing. I'm waiting until after New Year's to tell Alexander. That, and accepting TJ as my guardian, aka human ATM.

I grab my phone from the floor beside me and do something I've been avoiding the same way I've been avoiding Kendra's gift—I open JingleJam and go to my account.

@HeyHeyHaylee
1.6M Followers

The number is just that. It means nothing now. Why did I ever think it did? A number. Nothing more.

With the volume on mute, I scroll through past posts, skimming comments, but mostly staring at a beautiful, plus-sized, cheerful girl who is no longer me. Tremors rack my body. The phone shakes in my hand. I bite my tongue to silence a sob. It's all about to burst out of me.

I don't debate or reconsider. I just do it. Delete my account.

You are about to delete account @HeyHeyHaylee. Continue?

I jam my finger against the delete button. That action immediately signs me out of the app. My stomach swoops and a sick thrill shoots through me before dissipating—a short-lived sugar rush followed by a crash.

@HeyHeyHaylee is dead on JingleJam.

CHAPTER TWENTY-TWO

HAIR PULLED BACK in a low ponytail, I aim the nozzle connected to the industrial steam cleaner and blast the metal worktable inside the spacious workroom at Raw Tasty Meat Co. Hot white mist pours out, enveloping the metal table in a cloud of sanitizing heat. I move to the equipment next, giving the racks, tray holders, ovens, cutting boards, and processor machines the same treatment.

It's Wednesday, midweek of a new semester—for Brookdale students, anyway. Not me. I'm a high school dropout. Mom would be rolling in her grave. If she had one.

In the past, I would have imagined butcher shops as gross, dirty places. I'm here to tell you they're not! Brock, the shop's owner, takes sanitation and safety as seriously as quality cuts. Most meat is grown in labs, which makes businesses like Brock's an establishment offering rare luxury foods.

Once finished with disinfecting equipment surfaces, I change tools and work on removing oily residues from the walls. I clean the floor last. When I'm finished, everything looks brand spanking new. I stand up taller in my white overcoat and thick rubber gloves, taking pride in my work. Cleaning beside an industrial fridge that stores brains and organs, along with the meats, is highly motivating for a zombie. It's peaceful back here, too, after hours, having the workshop to myself. This space feels like my personal safety zone.

Brock is the only person around in the late afternoon. He hangs up his black apron and catches up on accounts in his office. I've only had this gig since last week, but I feel like I've gotten the hang of it.

I spray the counters with disinfectant and give them a final wipe down before putting the cleaning equipment and supplies away. I rinse my thick rubber gloves in scalding hot water and soap before hanging them to air dry over the edge of the sink. My white coat sleeves cover my arms. They're spelled with an illusion, anyway, but I need to save up for an alterationist once TJ gains access to my inheritance. We're scheduled to see Mr. Dirk on Friday afternoon. Having my arms and neck fixed are yet another item to add to my growing tab.

Once guardianship is finalized, I'll let Alexander know that I can't audition. I'll wait until after the weekend. Put it off a couple more days. I'm totally dreading it, but it has to be done. Just not this week.

The door to Brock's tiny office is open. My boss is a big, bearded dude with tattoos covering his arms and a chill personality. He doesn't care that I'm a zombie so long as his kitchen is spotless at the end of the day.

I tap lightly on the doorframe. "All clean."

Brock looks up from his laptop and offers a grin through his beard. "Let's take a look." He hefts himself out of his squeaky wheeled chair and lumbers into the workshop, where he inspects the surfaces closely. I stand back while Brock circles the room, often stopping to lean in and take a closer look at the equipment. If I had any breath, I'd be holding it. Instead, I grip my fingers and pull at them. Brock has yet to deny me my payment of animal organs and brains, but that doesn't prevent me from worrying that one day he'll find a speck of grease I missed and send me home empty-handed.

Brock makes his way to the stainless-steel fridge and wraps his thick fingers around the handle. Saliva gathers in my throat. I've been told that if I ever open that fridge without permission, my position will be revoked, and I will be banned from the shop for life. It sounds worse than a death sentence.

Brock opens the fridge and pulls out two large lumps wrapped in white butcher paper sealed with masking tape. One is marked in black ink with the letter B, the other with the letter M. I'm not only paid in brains but cold cuts for my cousin and uncle. I am literally bringing home the bacon. Well, TJ does his part with the bills, of course.

"Good job, Haylee," Brock says as he walks over and then hands me the packages.

I snatch them from him and hug the cold lumps against my stomach. Not only am I getting the food I need, but it's quality brain from grass-fed cattle. "Thanks, Boss. Same time tomorrow?"

He nods. "Same time."

I grin. The shift is Tuesday through Saturday. It's late enough in the day that I could still attend Brookdale, but I don't see any point in going back to that hellhole. To top if off, not going means no run-ins with Caleb.

This is my life now. It's as good as it gets for someone like me.

TJ is waiting in his truck out front. Once he sees me, he starts the engine. I let myself into the passenger side and hoist myself onto the bench, setting the packages onto the middle spot between us. TJ's pupils dart down. He licks his lips. "At least you've managed to make yourself more useful."

My eyes narrow. Spell or not, he's always less pleasant come evening—like a caged panther testing the bars holding him back—searching for a gap or an unlocked door within his enclosure.

"Why don't you do your part and drive us home?" I say between clenched teeth.

TJ puts the truck in drive and pulls onto the road, heading for home. "I'm out of beer," he grumbles.

"Already?" He should have nine left to get him to the weekend as part of his evening half-pack allocation.

"It's gone," TJ insists.

I haven't been taking daily stock. It's troublesome that he managed to drink more than what's allowed.

"Fine, you can pull into the mini mart on the way home and get another six-pack, but you'd better make it last until Saturday." I fold my arms. Ever since TJ punched me, it makes my skin crawl hearing his voice or being anywhere near him. I swear I don't know how I'm going to get through the next nine years without wanting to vomit every time I have to talk to this abusive monstrosity.

"You can't contain me forever, you know." The sidelong smile he shoots me is sinister.

"Watch me," I say, sounding far more confident than I feel.

TJ leans back and steers one-handed, looking far too smug for someone who is spelled. I could wipe that grin off his face with a command—tell him to stop smiling—but like everything else, it feels pointless. Let him smirk and drink so long as he keeps his hands to himself.

After TJ gets his six-pack, he whistles a tune for the remainder of the drive home.

When we walk inside, the smell of steak fills my nostrils. TJ hurries in front of me, going straight for the kitchen. He sets a beer on the counter, puts the rest of the pack in the fridge, and then plants himself in the kitchen, drinking while he watches Joni finish making dinner. My phone, which Joni and I share, is propped against a spoon holder on the counter. Joni uses it to follow recipes. Tonight, it's Salisbury steak with instant mashed potatoes and peas.

We could spell TJ to make meals, but Joni says she enjoys cooking. It's probably for the best. I wouldn't put it past TJ to spit in her portion, not to mention he's likely a lousy cook and no spell can change that.

As has become our routine, we all sit at the dinner table together. We've started allowing TJ to watch TV after dinner. It's too eerie having him wait quietly inside his room until bedtime. Joni insists on cleaning up while I eat my meal alone. After she's finished, I help her with her homework at the table.

Tonight, she spends more time looking at me than at her math problems. "So, Friday you go back to the lawyer's office?" she asks tentatively.

"Yes," I answer slowly, glancing at her sideways. Why is she asking when she already knows?

"Just checking."

I purse my lips, feeling suspicious but not coming up with any scenarios or motivation for Joni to interfere. My cousin doesn't know that I am going to turn down my audition with *Spellcaster*. She would only plead with me to reconsider. It's best to tell her once it's already said and done—no turning back.

During a commercial break, TJ yells from the living room, "Are you going to open your present from your sister?"

"Not yet," I call back.

"Then you should move it out of the living room."

"Not yet," I say again, this time through clenched teeth.

"You know you're going to have to remind me again tomorrow," TJ announces triumphantly, like he just scored a point.

It's enough to make me wonder if I should reconsider my original plan of biting him. Alexander's obedience spell needs an upgrade that includes a personality change. The effects are becoming far too diluted for my liking. I could try tweaking it, I suppose. I've got plenty of free time and nothing better to do. Maybe I should add in a new feature that causes TJ to slap himself in the face if he backtalks. The thought brings the ghost of a smile to my lips.

In the past, I've stuck to experimenting with beauty, illusions, and movement spells. Perhaps it's time to widen my magical repertoire.

My mood darkens once more—smile twisting and drifting away like gray smoke from an extinguished candle.

Spellcaster would have been the greatest opportunity I could have hoped for to learn from the best casters in the country and work on my craft. I wonder if Malachi would have lifted his wand for me.

Thursday morning, my phone wakes me with its vibrations.

I keep the alarm as quiet as I can so that I don't end up waking TJ in the process. Usually, I shake Joni awake gently or leave her to sleep—or I used to let her sleep, anyway. Ever since TJ attacked me, we've made a pact to double-up on him as a precaution. Unfortunately, the obedience spell cannot be cast through doors. We have to face the monster to tame him.

Joni is already fully awake, sitting with her legs dangling over the edge of her bed. I blink away the morning brain fog and then shimmy out of my sleeping bag. It's doubtful the sound of the zipper would wake TJ, but these days I'm paranoid.

When my eyes meet Joni's, she gives me a determined nod before getting up silently and grabbing her wand from her nightstand. I take up mine, leaving my phone on my sleeping bag.

We creep into the hallway like a couple of early-morning burglars. I point my wand at Joni's dresser stationed in front of TJ's door and whisper, "*Alioop a la returna.*" I swing my wand in the direction of Joni's bedroom, and the dresser's legs inch along the carpet, uncovering TJ's bedroom door little by little. Unlike me and my cousin, the dresser doesn't know how to be quiet. Its weight makes the floorboards beneath the carpet creak with every shuffle.

Joni and I keep back, our wands pointing at the door. Two days ago, TJ burst from it and tried to tackle me, but my spell was faster. I've practiced it so many times during the day I could enter a speed-casting competition.

"*Oop-vo-ren,*" I command, spelling the door open. No way am I getting close enough to open it myself.

I crouch as the door flies open, ready to duck if TJ comes at me with his fists. But all is quiet. Too quiet.

I look at Joni and point for her to stay behind me. She nods. We creep forward. All the while, I'm white-knuckling my wand. If TJ comes at me now, I might stake him with it in a moment of blind panic. Wrong uncle—TJ's not the vampire; he's the monstrosity.

Unable to take the suspense any longer, I clear the final distance in two wide steps, reach the door, and look inside. Today, TJ is face down on his bed, head beneath his pillow, and his arms lifted in what looks like an attempt to cover his ears. Well, that's new, not to mention unhelpful.

"*Lifteena, elona veed,*" I cast at his bed, which tips up by the headboard and dumps TJ on the ground.

His arms flap around for purchase, and his eyes round.

After I begin the spell of obedience, TJ squeezes his eyes shut only for them to pop back open. I can feel it like a nibble on a hook—not that I have any experience fishing, but that's how I imagine the sensation of hooking and reeling one in.

"Accept my words as your will today," I finish, and then step aside for Joni, who repeats the spell with her wand. We've experimented and found that if we both perform the spell, we can both command him throughout the day. Nifty and necessary. Two wands are better than one. I really need to come up with a way to pay them both off, along with the phone. I could make TJ leave his at home, but it's gross, and I'd rather have my own—plus a way to contact him at work just in case. We make him leave his device on the kitchen counter every night before bed so he can't wake up early and call his police buddy—or anyone else—for help first thing in the morning.

My uncle gets ready for work, eats, grabs his phone and keys, and leaves. Usually, Joni isn't far behind him in departing for school, but this morning she announces over her bowl of cereal, "I'm not going to school today."

I fold my arms and lift my brows from across the table. "Why not?"

"It's a surprise." Joni tries to hide a smile and fails.

"Joni," I drag her name out, "what's going on?"

"You'll see," she chirps, and then grabs her glass of grape juice and drinks it down.

I tap my foot beneath the table. "I hate surprises." Can anyone blame me?

"You'll like this one," Joni insists.

"All the same, I'd like to know what it is."

"You'll find out in a couple hours."

I grit my teeth. It's great that Joni is learning to hold her ground. I'd just rather she doesn't do so around me.

"I don't want to celebrate my birthday," I say. What else could the surprise be? I would have been turning eighteen on January 11th next week.

"Oh," Joni says, her lips briefly forming a wide O. She blinks several times. "I, uh, forgot about your birthday. Sorry."

"Well, it's not here yet, and I don't care about it, anyway," I grumble. If this isn't about my birthday, then what the heck *is* it about?

My cousin takes her bowl, spoon, and glass to the kitchen where she washes, dries, and puts them away. Sighing, I go to our room to look through my drawer of Aunt Chloe's clothes and pick out jeans and a cream cable-knit sweater. In the bathroom, I touch up my face with her makeup and place an illusion over my exposed neck.

I hear the TV in the living room. With nothing better to do, I join my cousin to watch a soap opera. Well, I'm not really paying attention—not like Joni, who sits on the edge of the couch leaning forward. I keep a tight grip on my wand and phone, having no clue what manner of surprise to expect this morning.

Oh, God. What if Alexander is back in town and arranged to check in?

That's probably it. Joni likely intercepted a call from him during her phone usage hours, and for some reason, they think it would be a great idea for Alexander to surprise me . . . again!

The timing is awful. I'll be forced to pretend like everything is on track for me to audition this spring. It's going to be excruciating lying through my teeth. I can't even zomb out when I am this on edge. Nor can I get into the tragic love triangle taking place on the television screen.

Later, during a commercial break, Joni asks, "What time is it?"

"It's *time to tell me what's going on* o'clock," I quip.

Joni merely smiles a little too big for my liking. Ugh, the suspense is way more intense than what's going on in the soap opera.

At the next commercial break, Joni asks me to tell her the time again, and I do. "Twelve to ten."

Joni's eyes light up, and her grin returns. It hasn't really left all morning. Something is way up. I wouldn't think a visit from Alexander would excite her this much, which worries me.

The soap ends, and another starts up. A little over halfway through, Joni's head jerks away from the screen. She jumps to her feet and rushes to the window, remote still in hand, and gives a little squeal. "He's here."

She turns off the TV and tosses the remote onto the couch. Holding back a sigh, I get up, preparing myself to face Alexander. Joni opens the front door, bouncing on her toes as she waits inside.

The guy who walks in isn't Alexander. It's Cameron.

CHAPTER TWENTY-THREE

MY SISTER'S FIANCÉ is alive, and he has facial scruff, which goes with the dark circles beneath his eyes, making his entire face appear shadowed.

He walks in with a huge duffel bag, dropping it in the entryway.

"Thanks for coming," Joni says, before closing the door and locking it behind him.

Cameron gives the barest nod, but he isn't looking at her at all. He stares at me for several seconds before tears spill from his eyes. Right on cue, I start crying. Cameron strides over and envelops me in his arms, hugging me tighter than I've ever been hugged in my life, which makes me cry harder. I hear Joni start sniffling. The tears pour out of me. Every time I try to rein them in, they start anew. Finally, I get a hold of myself enough to pull free of Cameron's hug and punch him in the shoulder.

"How dare you try to off yourself," I say in a watery voice.

Cameron's jaw tightens as he blinks away his tears. "Moment of weakness. I'm sorry."

He doesn't sound sorry. He sounds resigned. Like I'm one to talk, but my circumstances are different, and I never actually made the attempt, so it doesn't count.

"Just don't do anything like that ever again," I scold.

"I won't."

"Promise."

"I promise."

I study him for several seconds before shifting my gaze to Joni and then back to Cameron. "What are you doing here? How long are you staying?" This has to be about my birthday. Joni must have been pretending to forget. Well, if that's what it took to see Cameron, then so be it.

But Cameron truly surprises me with his answer. He runs a hand through his hair, which is disheveled and in need of a trim—not the clean-cut Cameron I remember. "I'm here to become your legal guardian," he announces, "and stay for however long you and Joni need me."

"But—" My mouth gapes open. "What about college?"

"I've arranged to finish my degree via correspondence. I only have one semester left, anyway."

"I don't expect you to uproot your life for us," I say.

"What life?" Cameron asks darkly, and I get it. I really do. His eyes are vacant, and he's way too thin. I see him the way no one else possibly can, and we do need him; I'm just not sure how he's going to hold up.

"Did you get breakfast on the plane? I can make you something," Joni offers brightly, eager to please.

"I'm fine, thanks," Cameron answers.

"You should eat something," I say. "You look like a husk."

Cameron shrugs. "Sure, if it's not too much trouble."

"None at all." Joni takes off for the kitchen.

Once we're alone, Cameron's jaw tightens. "Joni told me her father hit you."

I wrinkle my nose and frown, not wanting my sister's fiancé to look at me like I'm a victim. What a joke, being a zombie and all.

"We've got him back under control," I say tightly.

"He should have never struck you." Cameron's voice has an angry rumble that's entirely new. The sweet young man my sister fell in love with is gone, replaced by this morose figure who looks capable of killing—not only himself but my uncle.

"He won't do it again. I won't let him," I insist.

"If I had any aptitude for spellcasting, I would put him in a wheelchair," Cameron says, all dark and disturbing. He sounds like he means every word.

I shake my head. "Then he would be stuck at home. He needs to go to work, earn his keep." I attempt to crack a smile, but it comes out feeling ghoulish.

Cameron grunts in a way that's difficult to read. He moves on from TJ, though. "Joni told me about *Spellcaster* recruiting you for Season 13. I looked into it, and from everything I've read, it's legit. They're planning their first all-supernaturals competition."

"Yeah, pretty sure it's the real deal when Colt Cohen flies out for an interview," I say.

"Hm." The sound Cameron makes is laced with mistrust. I'm touched by his concern.

"Colt and his assistant Alexander were really nice," I offer.

"Hm," Cameron murmurs again.

I roll my eyes because it hardly matters. "I was planning on telling them I'm not auditioning after I get access to my inheritance so I can pay them back for my wand and Joni's, and the phone they bought me. Now that you're here, it should be no trouble getting the money, right?" I tap my foot—covered in a thick, fuzzy, burgundy sock—over the beige carpeting.

Cameron's lips pinch while I talk. "You can't quit *Spellcaster*."

I scowl. "It's not quitting when I haven't even started."

"Why?" he demands.

"Joni needs me."

"I'm here now. I'll look after her while you're in California."

I snort. It's pretty ironic that Cameron just came from California so that I can head that way when it comes time for auditions. I fold my arms and arch my brow. "And who will look after you?"

His face reddens. "I'm a grown man. You don't have to worry about me."

"Well, I do worry about you."

"I have no intention of trying to kill myself again." His arms hang at his sides, and he stands very still. Even though he looks like a hollowed-out shell, the intensity in his eyes says he means every word.

"Breakfast is ready," Joni calls from the kitchen.

Cameron blinks several times, as though coming out of a daze. He doesn't move until I lower my arms and lead the way to the dining table, where Joni is setting a steaming plate of food down, along with a fork. "Scrambled eggs, toast, jam, and bacon from Raw Tasty Meat Co., where Haylee works."

Cameron looks from the plate to me with a tight frown. "They treat you well there?"

I nod. "Brock, my boss, is nice. I don't really have any coworkers. Cleanup crew, party of one."

"Nevertheless, I want to introduce myself to your boss as your legal guardian and make sure he understands what will happen if he so much as looks at you wrong."

"No way!" I cry, as Cameron takes a seat at the table and thanks Joni, who beams in pleasure before taking a seat beside him to watch him pick at his food. I plop into the chair across from Cameron. "I have a good job, and Brock's cool. I don't need you threatening him and then having him annoyed at me or worse—coming up with a reason to let me go."

Cameron pushes scrambled eggs around on the plate with his fork. "I wouldn't threaten him." Cameron sets his fork down and sighs. "How about I come in for a friendly hello and thanks for giving my sister-in-law a job? That way he'll see that you have family looking out for you without me spelling it out. Would that be acceptable?"

I nod, too choked up to speak. It's not worry over the job that has my throat clogging up. It's the all-too-rare feeling that there's still someone in this world who cares about me. He called me family, his sister-in-law. I might as well be.

"Cameron? Aren't you going to try the eggs?" Joni leans over the table, watching Cameron like he's an exotic animal at the zoo.

He scoops eggs from his fork into his mouth, chews slowly, and nods. "It's very good. Thank you, Joni."

"What about the bacon?"

"It looks nice and crisp, but I'm not very hungry." He levels Joni with a shrewd look. "I appreciate the welcome and breakfast, but after today, no more missing school, okay?"

"Okay," Joni agrees immediately.

My cousin and I spend the rest of the morning packing up yarn, knitting needles, and unfinished projects in Aunt Chloe's craft room. There's a set of hand-knit personalized Christmas stockings that never made it to whoever ordered them from her online Etsy store. We stuff things into clear totes, seal them with lids, and stack them against the wall, making room for Cameron.

There's a small desk with an old computer, printer, and labels. At least Cameron has a spot to work on his correspondence. The room is missing one important part, though . . . a bed.

"Do you think there's a spare blanket in TJ's closet?" I ask Joni.

She looks at the floor and grimaces.

"Don't worry about me," Cameron says in the doorframe, causing Joni and me to jump in place. "I'll get everything I need in the next few days."

"In the meantime, you can't sleep on the floor," I say. "You can borrow my sleeping bag."

"Not necessary," Cameron answers flatly, and then turns and leaves us alone.

There isn't much left to do, so Joni and I hover around the dining table, darting looks Cameron's way as he scrolls and taps at his phone.

Usually, I'm glad to get out of the house and head over to Raw Tasty's, but today my feet drag as I get ready. I brush my hair and secure it in a low ponytail, rub ointment over my tattoo, and put on my white work coat over jeans. I carry my wand with me. Invisibility spells are especially useful during the two-mile walk to work. I don't mind walking one way while TJ finishes his work shift.

It's no surprise when Cameron insists on escorting me, so I keep myself corporeal. Having his company brings the kind of fireside comfort I've been missing from a life made up of ashes and coal.

"Thanks for coming out to Virginia and helping us," I say as soon as we're outside.

Joni watches from the window. When she sees me looking, she waves. I wave back and then start the walk to Raw Tasty's. Cameron matches my stride.

"I'm sorry I wasn't here sooner." His gruff voice still sounds foreign. I can't imagine him ever smiling or laughing again. Kendra wouldn't want this, but she's not here, and that's why Cameron is broken beyond repair. He's here, but he's not, which sends a wail through my head and fills my soul with loneliness.

A selfish side of me is more than willing to take what I can get. Even a vacant Cameron is better than no Cameron.

"You're here now." I shrug and continue leading the way down the sidewalk, purposely stepping on cracks.

Cameron drifts along, speaking absently. "I've ordered bedding with overnight shipping. I'll take the couch tonight. I'm going to need to find a car."

I try to hide my grimace, which isn't hard when he isn't really looking at me or anything else. It's as though he is walking through the veil, and nothing around him is real.

I chew on my lower lip for a moment. "Um, just let me know how much everything costs so I can start reimbursing you." My IOUs are burying me faster than an avalanche.

Cameron looks over at me and blinks. "You don't need to reimburse me. I can cover myself."

What a difference from TJ and Cressida with their greedy intent. Cameron is too far on the opposite end of the spectrum. Guilt swirls through my gut. It feels like it will remain trapped there until I am able to repay Cameron, or at least compensate him beyond bacon—which he didn't even touch.

I'm not sure what to say to him. On the one hand, it's something of a novelty to have company. On the other, Cameron's like a ghost, here with me, yet not really.

And then it hits me. "My parents' house!" I exclaim. "We can sell it and use the money to cover your expenses and mine for years to come." Alexander was right. Better to let go and move on. I don't ever want to step inside that house of horrors again.

"I'll make arrangements, but whatever we get from the sale of your house is yours alone."

"But—"

"I'm not taking a cent," Cam says gruffly.

I want to argue further, but not at the risk of offending him. Not when he picks up his pace as though ready to run away if I bring it back up.

Two blocks from Raw Tasty's, Cameron comes to a sudden stop and stares through the glass wall of a gym filled with ellipticals, weight machines, and other stuff I would never be caught sweating on dead or alive. Cameron continues to stare in. I check the time on my watch. I always give myself an extra fifteen minutes, but it doesn't make me any less antsy about arriving at my usual early time. This job is one of the few things that's been keeping me going.

"Uh, Cameron? You thinking of joining a gym?"

He blinks and looks at me. "I am now. I need to beef up."

If he wasn't so somber, I would make a joke about how I could work in the beef shop while he beefs up. Ha. Ha. Ha.

We start walking again. Cameron looks over his shoulder one more time. "I'll check it out after I drop you off. The next time your uncle decides to pick a fight, I want to be ready for him."

"That's what the wands are for," I remind Cameron.

He balls his fingers into fists. "I won't be using a wand on that bastard. The only thing he deserves is a taste of his own medicine."

My stomach plummets. I shake my head. "I don't want you to fight him." Cameron rotates his neck like he's already warming up. "It would upset Joni," I add.

Cameron looks at me, making no promises.

That evening, after my shift, Cameron waits out front on the sidewalk, hands in his jean pockets. TJ waits in his truck, as usual, but when I get inside after Cameron, I see my uncle has a black eye. My jaw unhinges as I look from TJ to Cameron, but neither of them says a word. Cameron has taken the middle bench seat.

"Buckle up," Cameron says.

"I don't need to," I reply.

"Yes, you do," he insists.

My stomach flutters with a mix of appreciation and unease. Once my buckle has snapped into place, Cameron juts his chin forward. "You can drive now."

TJ's jaw looks clenched tightly enough to break over the tiniest pothole. He says nothing on the drive home. Once he's parked in the driveway,

Cameron turns to me. "Can you put an illusion over his face? We don't want to upset Joni."

For a moment, I can't speak or move. I feel like I'm sitting next to a stranger. Then I remember the feeling of helplessness when TJ attacked me.

I pull out my wand and sit up straight before turning my shoulders to face TJ. "*Veez a la—*"

"Bitch," TJ snarls between clenched teeth.

Cameron socks TJ in the face so fast I give a squeal of surprise. He shakes out his hand. "Better do both eyes," he tells me.

I glare at TJ. "I thought I told you no name calling."

"I'm sorry. It's been a long day, and then this joker showed up." TJ grips the steering wheel even though the truck is parked and the ignition is off.

"Cameron is living with us now, and he's going to be my legal guardian."

"We had a deal," TJ seethes.

"No, we didn't. I never wanted you as my guardian, TJ, especially not after you broke my wrist and punched me. You don't deserve to take care of a dog, let alone a teenager and a young girl. We've got two wands and Cameron. You're outnumbered, so you might as well make things easier on yourself. Go to work, eat your meals, drink your beer, watch TV, go to bed, and keep your foul comments to yourself."

Cameron nods. "We can do this the easy way or the hard. Makes no difference to me."

"I'm not paying to feed and shelter this jackass," TJ fires back.

Cameron laughs darkly. "I don't need anything from a piece of filth like you."

My uncle jerks around and reaches both hands toward Cameron's neck.

"TJ, stop!" I yell. My uncle freezes. "Keep your hands to yourself. You are going to walk inside and mind your manners the rest of the evening. First, hold still and keep quiet while I conceal the bruises on your face."

TJ lowers his arms and purses his lips, doing as I say. Cameron watches closely as I finish the spell, and TJ's face seems to return to normal.

Afterward, we all go inside and sit down for dinner.

After TJ turns in for the night, Joni and I check on Cameron in the living room, where Joni did her best to make the couch comfortable. She found a spare set of bed sheets and a couple of throw blankets. A couch cushion serves as a pillow for now.

"I have everything I need," Cameron insists.

Joni throws her arms around him. "Thank you for coming."

Tears fill my eyes as I watch her hold on like he'll disappear if she lets go too soon. Cameron pats her head gently. "I'm not going anywhere, Joni. You won't be thanking me when you hit your high school years and I sit your dates down for interrogation."

Joni erupts into a fit of giggles. She loosens her arms, steps back, and tilts her head to look into Cameron's eyes. "I don't mind," she says with a grin.

Cameron gives her a quick hug and musses up her hair playfully. "I'm going to remind you that you said that when you're a teenager. Now, off to bed. You've still got a school day before the weekend."

"Good night, Cameron," Joni says happily.

"I'll join you soon," I tell her.

My cousin nods and swings her arms as she leaves. Once she's had time to reach her room, I raise my brows at Cameron. "Are you really planning to stick around for Joni's high school years?"

When Cameron locks eyes with me, it's like being caught in a steel trap—his expression harsh yet reassuring. "I'm exactly where I need to be."

I fold my arms. "After I'm eliminated from the competition, I'll be around full-time to see Joni through to graduation. Who knows how long I'll last on the show—if I even make it through auditions." I shrug.

Cameron pierces me with stern blue eyes the color of a clear winter sky on a negative-two-degree day when only the hardiest of souls brave stepping outdoors. "You're going all the way to the finale, Haylee. You have the talent to win the whole thing." I blink a couple of times. "*Spellcaster* is about the magic, right?"

I nod.

"Well, you've got the magic. Keep believing in yourself, and the world will too."

Tears spill over and run down my face. I'm so touched and amazed that Cameron is capable of giving me this heartfelt pep talk. "I swear I don't usually cry this much." I force out a chuckle as I swipe the tears away with my fingers.

Cameron grabs the present from the coffee table and holds it out to me. "Open your gift."

I stare at the Christmas wrapping and frown. "I'm waiting," I say, not taking it.

"For what?" Cameron asks.

"I don't know. Next Christmas or my birthday next week." I shrug again.

"Or you could open it now," Cameron says, "for Kendra," he adds in a soft, sorrowful voice.

Well, now I have to. The poor guy looks like he's going to relapse if I don't unwrap the gift. I take the package from Cameron and sit on the edge of the recliner, placing it on my lap. I stare down. In my mind's eye, I see my sister's fingers wrapping and taping the gift with gleeful excitement. A flash of her chewed-up skeletal fingers after the zombie attack comes in and out of focus like a strobe light going off inside of a haunted house. *No*, I tell the memory. *You are not allowed inside my mind.* I blink it away and carefully pull the taped edges of the present free.

I turn it over and pull up the tape along the back seam before taking the edges and spreading them open like a book. Inside is a shiny purple jacket. I hold it up. On the front there's a small embroidered *Spellcaster* symbol. Embroidered on the back—

TEAM HAYLEE

That's not all. The inside of the jacket has a snake shaped in the infinity symbol printed on the tag. It's the logo from Uraeus Spellweaves, which means Kendra really splurged, because the witch-run company specializes in personalized jackets that are indestructible and only unzip for the person they're intended for.

"You have to audition. Do it for her." I hear Cameron's voice, but I don't look at him. I'm deep inside my head.

This is about more than competing. Someone silenced my parents and my sister, but they didn't snuff out the Hutchins name altogether.

I realize that I'm the most unlikely member of my family to make noise, but I can't think of a better stage to do so than *Spellcaster*. This isn't only about the competition. My family is still in need of justice. I've lost my faith in Uncle Alvan. He claims to have powerful connections. Well, I'm going to wow the coaches in Hollywood and make my own.

CHAPTER TWENTY-FOUR

I WAKE UP IN darkness. A figure looms in the doorframe. "It's time," Cameron says, in the same sober tone he's used every morning for the past two weeks since moving in.

I slide one leg after the other over the single bed frame and mattress Cam had delivered along with his own bed. He paid for both and won't let me pay for mine, which is frustrating when I have a monthly stipend thanks to his guardianship.

The blanket on the opposite side of the room twitches, and Joni stirs from sleep. Her voice comes out muffled. "Is it already time to get up?"

I grab my wand, which stays with me in my bed while I sleep, and stand up. "You can rest another five or ten minutes while I take care of TJ."

"Joni needs the practice for when you're gone," comes Cameron's firm response.

"She's been practicing for weeks. Can't she snooze for one day?"

"It's okay. I'm up." Joni flings her blanket aside and snatches her wand off her nightstand as she bounds out of bed in her koala PJs.

Fifteen minutes later, my cousin and uncle are dressed for the day, hunched over the table shoveling down the bacon breakfast casserole Joni made on Sunday for reheating. Meat is in no short supply in our household thanks to my job—though it's no use to Cameron, who is vegetarian.

When Joni offered to start cooking all vegetarian recipes, TJ nearly broke through the control spell like a wolf trying to get at a bone. But Cam told Joni he doesn't want her to cook anything special for him. He bought a blender and starts his day off with a protein smoothie mix . . . unless he skips breakfast altogether, and it appears to be that kind of morning today. He sits at the table with a menacing far-off look. Even with the control spell cast over TJ, Cameron doesn't like leaving him unsupervised at home, which has made the morning glower part of the breakfast routine. TJ ignores Cameron as he scarfs down his square of breakfast casserole. I'm glad I can still enjoy the smell of food. There's a dinged-up thermos filled with coffee in front of TJ that he drinks on his drive to work.

After my uncle and cousin leave, Cam goes to his room and closes the door. I assume he's studying or working on assignments to complete his college degree.

I wander into the living room to practice magic. My *Advanced Levitation* book is still resting on the coffee table, along with three other volumes of cutting-edge spells.

I flick my wand at the book and cast, "*Recisocation.*" *Advanced Levitation* flies at me, smacking me in the chest before hitting the ground. Oops. I guess I'm still a bit groggy. I point the tip of my wand at the book on the floor and start with, "*buoy tri air hover sif ascond*," saying the words slowly. This time, the book rises leisurely from the floor, heading straight for the ceiling until I snatch it with my free hand. I squeeze the book and smile.

The light thud of a door opening and closing again is followed by Cameron, who walks by the living room dressed in an unzipped gray hoodie with a fitted white T-shirt beneath. His eyes are on the front door as he says, "I have an errand to run. I'll be back before your shift."

I toss my book on the couch and join him in the entryway, where he stuffs his feet inside his sneakers.

"I'll come with you." I slip into a pair of Aunt Chloe's flats and resize them with my wand. I will be so happy when the shoes and clothes I ordered online show up. It's not a lot, but it's a start as I start over. My old clothes wouldn't have fit me any longer, anyway. Zombie Haylee seems to have settled into a size six. I call it "The Zombie Diet." Brains and organs with lots of fasting, manual labor, and spellcasting. At least I've been able to check running for my life off the list since Cameron moved in.

He lifts his hand to one side of his head and digs his fingers into his hair. His head bends to one side as he looks at me through blue eyes. "I need to do this alone."

"Do what alone?" I challenge. When he purses his lips, I lift my eyebrows. "Where are you going?"

Cameron's fingers tighten in his hair. He sighs and breaks eye contact, releasing his hold on his head and dropping his arm to his side. "I'm going to your father's law office to start searching his files for vampires who would have wanted him dead."

My eyes widen. "You think it was a vampire?"

Cameron lifts his chin. "They were the ones most threatened by him."

Phantom snakes slither through my ribcage, wrapping my bones in a cold shiver. Snippets of conversation between my parents and Kendra speed through my mind—stuff I found boring at the time. Warnings from Uncle Alvan. "You're making enemies of the wrong beings." Mom answering, "He's not doing this to befriend those tyrants, but then you'd understand that if you believed in serving a higher purpose."

"His last case," I whisper. "He was able to drain a vampire master of billions of dollars of ill-gotten gains by representing the master vampire's wife."

Cameron nods grimly. "Kendra told me all about his case against Vlad Dobrolyubov. Vlad was supposed to be the first domino—one of the few ways to expose vampire corruption is by gaining access to all of their assets as part of the divorce proceedings. Mr. Hutchins already had more females contacting him for representation right after he won the case for his client. Unfortunately, it made him a threat against all of the filthy rich vampire masters of the world. God forbid they give up one cent from their bottomless treasure trove." Cam's face is red, and he bares his teeth like he wants to bite back at all of those nefarious fangers.

I pinch the bridge of my nose and groan in frustration. "No wonder Uncle Alvan doesn't want to help. He threw his loyalty in with the vampires by working for them. He never wanted my dad to go after the creatures he idolized—and now he's one of them," I say bitterly.

Cameron grits his teeth. "You can't tell Alvan I'm looking into the murders. He can't be trusted."

I fold my arms and huff. "You don't have to tell me twice. He'd report it directly to his master, anyway."

"You can't tell TJ or Joni, either. The less they know, the better. I'll tell you if I find anything, but you need to stay away from the firm. Your parents and Kendra were killed by one—or more—of these demons. If they discover someone's looking into what happened, I don't want anything blowing back on you."

A volcano of frustration and rage burns up my neck and spews from my mouth. Cameron isn't the one I'm mad at, but I direct some of that anger at him as I squeeze my wand so tightly it feels like a sixth finger bone grinding into my palm.

"It already did blow back on me!" I don't mean to shout, but he's treating me like Joni, like I'm some little girl who needs to be kept in the dark for her own good. "It *devoured* me." Worse than my anger are the sobs that follow. I rub away my tears like they're made of graphite that I can erase from my face. "I have to know who did this to me and my family."

I can still hear the sound of the horde breaking through the window and stampeding up the stairs in vivid detail. The feel of their slimy, bony fingers grabbing at me. The pain of teeth tearing through my flesh. The ghastly quiet afterward. Stepping inside the living room, I wonder if the memories will ever fade.

Cameron's lips look glued together and remain that way for seconds that drag on after my outburst.

"I know you do," he answers in calm, measured words. "You also have your audition to think about."

"I care more about solving my family's murder than some competition," I scoff. I mean, I care about both. It's not like this has to be an either or, but still. I lift my chin. "I'm coming with you."

Cameron's right eye twitches. "Fine," he says, "but let me do all the talking."

I shrug as I step in front of him to open the front door. Cameron locks up behind us.

Infernal dark gray clouds fill the sky, looking heavy enough to fall to Earth and turn the world into a dystopian wasteland. It sends a shudder through me, like the vampires are on to us. Unease tugs at my lips. There was always tension between my mother and Uncle Alvan, but I used to brush it off as the sort of sibling rivalry I happily never had to worry about with Kendra. But disagreeing was one thing. Now that Uncle Alvan's been remade, does that make us enemies? That would really suck, because he and Joni are the only family I have left, and I used to think he was cool. But if Uncle Al doesn't demand justice when Cameron and I expose the vampires who killed my family, then he truly is dead to me.

Maybe the culprits aren't vampires, but I'm with Cameron on this. I think they're the most likely suspects. Not that I'm blaming it on their entire species. I'm not going to generalize the way people and creatures do for my kind. I'm more evolved than that.

Cameron doesn't seem to notice the demonic clouds overhead as he strides to the used Nissan Versa parked on the street. He purchased a gray compact car yesterday. His parents must have sent him money. Kendra said his family was well-off—not wealthy like ours, but far more comfortable than most humans since the decline of the middle class. I still wish Cameron would let me contribute to his costs.

My body buzzes with energy as we drive through the neighborhood. I finally have help from someone who wants to get to the truth as much as I do. And Cameron's smart. I didn't think of going to Dad's law office.

"Is Vlad our prime suspect?" I ask. I mean, even his name sounds like an evil Russian vampire master. (No offense to any nice Vlads out there.)

"One of them." Cameron grips the wheel and keeps his eyes on the road.

We enter the highway and join traffic headed into the city. Cameron maneuvers the vehicle across lanes, squeezing between cars and navigating his way through clusters. I'm afraid to distract him with conversation, seeing as he eyes the road and surrounding trucks and cars as though they're part of a video game he intends to beat. He weaves from lane to lane and back again, ignoring the honks from other drivers. Intent on the road, he doesn't bother to even toss back a curse or a rude gesture.

If I had any breath in me, I'd be holding it. I've never been in a car with someone who drives aggressively. Has Cameron always driven this way, or is this part of his new *Out for Vengeance* package? Or maybe Californians are just crazier on the roads.

After watching him a little longer, and determining that he's calm and in control, I venture to ask, "What should we do when we discover the culprit? If it's a vampire master, he'll find a way to get off the hook. And if he knows we're the ones outing him, he'll have us killed." I glare at the SUV in front of us with its *happy family of five and a dog* stick figures bumper sticker. This time, when Cameron migrates into the open space on the left and then swerves back over in front of the happy family van, a little thrill shoots through me.

"Not if we have him killed first," Cameron says in a deadly serious voice.

It's hard to look away from the windshield, so I don't as I watch the next group of vehicles Cameron closes in on.

"How are we supposed to kill a master vampire?"

"I'm working on it," Cameron answers cryptically.

"Dynamite," I suggest, and then shake my head and sit up taller. "No. A remote-controlled bomb. Have it delivered inside a medical cooler labeled *BLOOD* and then *boom*! Vampire master becomes vampire blood and guts. It will have to be a large blast, so he has no chance of self-healing."

From the corner of my eye, I see Cameron grin.

Good. I want him to know I'm not afraid to get my hands dirty. In fact, the dirtier, the better. Justice served cold and cruel—creature style.

"Or if we wanted to go the eye-for-an-eye route, I could eat him. I wonder what vampire brains taste like?" I muse, as I look out the window at the cars we pass. "Probably like rotten meat," I decide aloud.

Cameron jerks his head away from the windshield to look at me, adding to the seriousness of his tone. "You're not risking extermination over a single one of those fanged fascists."

I've come to hate the word *extermination*, like no matter what I do, I'm a pest to society, existing only on borrowed time. I'm supposed to be immortal, not disposable supernatural garbage.

Cameron speeds up again before crossing over two lanes and exiting the highway. The sidewalks are lined with oak trees and brick buildings. I can't remember the last time I saw Dad's office, let alone stepped inside. He kept his work life separated from his family life as much as possible, but Mom used to pass it on the way to my casting lessons in the city. The first time I asked if we could go inside and say hi, Mom explained that Daddy was busy and they didn't want his employees involved in his private life, including interacting with his children.

Now, I wish I had known at least some of his staff, so they'd recognize me on sight and help us out without question.

Cameron finds a spot to park a few blocks away. As with the highway, he moves quickly down the sidewalk. I hurry alongside him to keep pace. When we reach my dad's law office, our mouths hang open, dumbstruck.

The bronze letters that used to spell out *HUTCHINS LAW FIRM* on the outside of the brick building have been replaced with the raised outline of a white tooth and blue letters announcing *OAK STREET DENTISTRY.*

CHAPTER TWENTY-FIVE

CAMERON STORMS INSIDE the building. By the time I dash in after him, he's already reached the front desk, where he demands, "What happened to Hutchins Law Firm?"

A heavyset, thirty-something woman in tortoise-shell glasses cups the receiver of the phone pressed against her ear. "Sir, I'm on the phone with a patient."

"Tell them to call back," Cameron growls. He grips the front counter and leans in closer.

The woman's eyes widen behind her round lenses. "I'm sorry; I'm going to have to call you back," she says into the receiver, before setting it down with a heavy *thud*.

There are three people seated in the waiting room. Two of them lower their phones to stare at Cameron, while the other peers at him over the edge of a magazine.

The woman levels a stern glare across the counter. "Sir—"

"I want to know what happened to my father-in-law's office." Cameron raises his voice over whatever she was about to say.

A door with a frosted glass window opens, and a young woman in light blue scrubs and a long brown ponytail hurries out. "What's going on?"

The woman in glasses glowers. "He wants to know what happened to the previous tenant—says it was his father-in-law's practice."

The young hygienist's forehead wrinkles. "Why don't you ask him?"

"Because he's dead," Cameron snaps.

The hygienist's body jerks as though Cameron's anger gave her an electrical shock. She recovers quickly, keeping impressively calm as she says, "I'm sorry for your loss. I don't know anything about the previous occupant. If you leave your name and number, I will have Dr. Myers give you a call."

Cameron pushes away from the counter and folds his arms. "I'm not going anywhere until someone tells me what happened to Laurence Hutchins's case files—not to mention his employees."

Clouds darker than the ones outside storm my mind. I hadn't considered Dad's office staff. Were they offed too?

The hygienist sighs. "Wait here."

"I'm not going anywhere," Cameron says sarcastically to her retreating form.

She leaves silence in her wake. No one says a word. The front desk clerk doesn't call back the patient she had on the phone. She's got her tortoise-framed hawk eyes all over Cameron.

I shift from one foot to the other, scanning the pale moss-colored walls, which look unmarked and freshly painted.

The hygienist who hurried away doesn't hurry back. When she returns, it's with a piece of paper in hand. She gives it to Cameron. "This is the name and number of the leasing agency who rented us the space. As I said before, we don't know anything about the previous tenants." Not waiting for a response, she turns on her heel, heading for the frosted door.

Cameron grips the piece of paper and turns in the opposite direction. It's a relief to get out of the tension-filled waiting room and back outside under the oppressive clouds. Yeah, real cheerful inside and out.

Back in the car, it doesn't surprise me when Cameron uses his phone not to call the agency but to put their address into the GPS and zooms his way through downtown to reach Totello Property Management.

Our waiting room encounter at the leasing office is colored in shades of déjà—dental—vu. But this time, we're allowed beyond the plastic entrance chairs to speak with Henry, the leasing agent who handled the listing of my dad's office.

I take a seat on a padded chair in front of the dark wood desk in Henry's small, windowless office. Cameron remains standing, looming over the room like he's the sharp edge of a scythe.

"You had no legal right to lease Mr. Hutchins's office without our permission."

Henry dabs at his balding forehead with a cloth handkerchief and then stuffs it back inside his pocket. "We were told the practice had been dissolved after the unfortunate death of Mr. Hutchins. We even made a special exception to terminate the lease early given the circumstances."

Cameron takes two steps to Henry's desk and leans over it. "Who made the request?"

"Mr. Hutchins's brother."

I narrow my eyes. "My father doesn't have a brother."

"We verified his identity," Henry says defensively. "He had the proper authority."

The snakes return to wrap around my ribs, slithering and tightening like they mean to crack me apart like a wishbone. "Do you mean his brother-in-law, Alvan Bates?"

My insides turn into tar as Henry nods. "Yes. Alvan Bates. He made the arrangements."

I'm on my feet. I don't remember ever getting out of the chair. One moment Henry's shifty eyes are in front of me. The next, the bald patch on his head shines with sweat below my nose.

"Was he here in person?" I demand.

Henry's forehead wrinkles when he lifts his head to look at me. "Yes."

The burning rage rising up my chest sends the snakes descending for cover.

Uncle Alvan couldn't bother with the memorial or my guardianship, but he had no problem making time to shut down my father's law office. 'Cause that's not at all suspicious.

Heat burns from my chest into my fingers, neck, and face. I feel like biting someone.

Cameron sounds way too calm when he asks, "Do you know what happened to the case files Mr. Hutchins kept, or to his employees?"

"You'd have to ask Mr. Bates." Henry pulls the handkerchief back out to dab at his forehead again.

"Is that a no?" Cameron presses.

Henry lowers the handkerchief and shakes his head. "I have no knowledge of what became of Mr. Hutchins's personal effects, nor the goings-on of his former employees."

"Did Alvan bribe you or compel you?" Cameron asks in disgust.

The practice was outlawed decades ago, but it's not as though someone would be able to report a vampire if they were a victim of mind compulsion. It would be like trying to preserve a snowflake on their tongue.

"Neither, I assure you," Henry answers quickly. "I'm sure if you talk to Mr. Bates, he'll address all of your concerns."

I snort. And to think that TJ was my first suspect. I had the wrong uncle.

"Fine, I'll talk to Uncle Al," I say moodily. I look at Cameron. "Can we go now? Something tells me Henry has nothing useful left to share."

Cameron frowns deeply at Henry before giving a slight nod.

Outside, I kick a lamppost. "How could Alvan do this? How could he allow his own sisters and nieces to be attacked?"

Cameron's face is tight, his brows drawn together. "We don't know that for sure."

"But he has to be involved, right?" I want to call him up right now to scream, shout, and demand answers. But if he's mixed up in this, then I don't want him to know we're onto him. I don't want him having Cameron killed, either. I'm not sure I could survive that.

"His master may have ordered him to cover it up," Cameron says. He shoves his hands in his pockets and walks over the sidewalk in measured steps that don't match the urgency from earlier.

"And what? He's compelled to go along with it?" Tears burn the backs of my eyeballs. *How could Alvan do this?* I think again. How in the world could Uncle Alvan be involved in something so heinous? "What do we do now? How are we supposed to find anything out when the information we need belongs to a *creature* under suspicion?" That's what Alvan is now. A creature. No longer human. No longer family. He answers to one being.

"We don't need Alvan to tell us what happened to Laurence's practice."

I blink several times at Cameron's assurance. How can he sound so confident at a time like this?

"What do you mean?"

Cameron lifts his chin. "All I have to do is track down at least one of your father's former employees and ask them what happened."

"You don't think they're dead?"

"No. It would be too obvious—draw too much unwanted attention." Cameron looks over at me. "Also, Kendra told me that Laurence paid for everyone who worked for him to get resistance runes to protect them against vampire compulsion."

I chew on my lower lip. It makes sense that Dad would take precautions when he went after a master.

Cameron has the glazed look of someone staring inward rather than out. "Kendra had the rune, as well. So did your mom and dad."

"Wait. What? Why didn't I get one?"

I don't expect Cameron to have the answer, but he does. Of course he does. He and Kendra talked about everything together.

"Your parents wanted you to have a carefree teenage life. You didn't need the rune because you weren't a threat to anyone."

My feet thud against the pavement, and my neck heats.

Once again, I feel like I wasn't part of my parents' and Kendra's special "change the world" club.

"Well, I'm a threat now," I say. I've got my own secret tattoo. And I don't have to worry about mind control. It doesn't work on other supernaturals. I stop walking and face Cameron, scanning him from his head to his shoes as though able to see through to his skin. "Do you have the resistance rune?"

Cameron presses his hand against his chest. "Kendra and I got them done together. When she told me she was getting the tattoo, I said that I would too." He smiles briefly with a faraway look only to crumple a second later, blinking rapidly, the edges of his lips curling inward like a brittle fall leaf catching on fire.

I feel like the only thing holding back my pain is a single finger, and if I release the pressure even a little, there's a deep well waiting to spill over. Unfortunately, that's exactly what happens. My hold over it slips. Hot tears streak down my face. They flow from my eyes as wind fills my ears. The sadness inside of me is a storm rushing in from a swirling abyss. I am out at sea, clinging to the wreckage of a ship that sunk, leaving me behind as one of the sole survivors. Storm clouds surround me. Rain and wind batter my body. I am alone with no land in sight.

Warm, steady hands take me by the shoulders. Cameron gives me a gentle squeeze. "Today wasn't a total bust. We uncovered more than I expected. This is our first good lead. Why do you think Alvan's master hired him in the first place?"

I blink back the next gush of tears pooling in my eyes and swallow past the lump in my throat. "To keep tabs on my dad?"

"It's just a theory at this point," Cameron says, releasing my shoulders to press his hand against his head. "He might not have known it at first—might not have realized his true purpose until his vampire employers had him under their thrall. Then they made him one of them to ensure his obedience. It could have been worse. They could have kept him human and then killed him after he took control of Laurence's law firm and whatever incriminating files might have been left there. They have no reason to kill him now that he's theirs to command."

Maybe. But I can't say I'm overly concerned for Alvan's safety. Not if he took any part in my family's death. Not if he's helping cover it up. I don't care if he was compelled. No excuse in the world could make up for this loss. And I haven't forgotten how he idolized vampires before he ever worked for them. His fixation could be the reason the vampires got to us.

If it was vampires.

It has to be vampires.

CHAPTER TWENTY-SIX

THERE HAVE BEEN a lot of spring storms and rain, but not today. Today, the sun lights up the streets as Cameron pulls into a parking spot before walking alongside me to Raw Tasty's.

Tomorrow is my last shift before I fly out to Hollywood for my blind audition. Brock's given me the rest of the week off to travel for the show. I am a bundle of nerves. It will be good to put that energy into cleaning the tables, walls, and equipment today. After months of hard work and showing up to every shift early, Brock pays me an hourly wage on top of the brains and beef. My boss and Cameron are even buds. They do dude stuff together, like axe throwing, barbecuing, and gaming. I'm glad Cam has a friend—and activities outside of investigating my family's murders. Plus, I'm pretty sure it's the reason why I get a paycheck. Not that Brock was trying to cheat me, but he's mentioned several times that he feels like he can count on me long-term, knowing I have a strong and committed guardian looking out for my well-being.

Yep. My guardian is strong, all right. If he spent as much time studying as he does working out, he could be valedictorian. Probably not through correspondence, but you get the idea. I think he's working out his frustrations over all the dead ends we've hit.

The former employees Cameron tracked down all have the same story. After my father's death, they were offered positions at other firms. Oddly, all the jobs have taken them out of state, and no two employees are with the same law firm, as though they were purposely displaced. None of them knows what became of my dad's old case files.

Despite the setback, Cameron says he's not giving up, and neither am I.

We pass a couple of young women on the sidewalk who crane their heads to check Cam out. He's dressed in gym shorts and a black fitted T-shirt. He's got muscles now. Working out motivates him to eat three full meals a day, and power bars, for which I'm grateful. He buffed up quickly, and the ladies eye him like he's Mr. July on a hot dudes swim calendar. They don't stand a chance, of course. Cameron walks past them as though they're fire hydrants covered in dog urine.

I pull my fingers as we walk. Cameron looks over and stares at my fingers as I tug on them, which makes me stop what I'm doing and press my palms into my thighs.

"You're going to blow the judges out of their purple chairs," Cameron assures me. "You've been practicing nonstop. You've got this."

"Or maybe I'll mess up and make a fool of myself on national TV."

"You won't." Cameron says this like a command.

I clench my teeth. There's another reason I'm nervous today. Well, nervous and excited. Tonight, *Spellcaster* is announcing the highly anticipated grand prize for Season 13's winner.

I've been waiting for months to find out what it is. I spend my shift wondering. Later, I sit through dinner wondering and unable to pay attention as Joni talks about her school day. After tonight, I will no longer have to spend my time speculating.

At 7:50 p.m., we gather around the TV. TJ drinks a beer straight out of the bottle in his recliner while Joni, Cameron, and I share the couch. Joni and I have our wands in our laps. I always watched *Spellcaster* with it, so it feels natural to have it with me during Colt's interview. That, and no place feels safe to hide it whenever TJ's around, even though he's been commanded not to touch them.

"Maybe the winner gets a million dollars," TJ says.

"The winner from every season gets a hundred thousand dollars. They'll have something more interesting to go with the cash prize," I say as I run a finger along the smooth wood.

"Not like you'd share, or win it to begin with," TJ mutters.

Cameron glares at him. TJ takes another swig of beer, keeping his attention on the television screen.

"Maybe the prize is turning you back into a human," Joni says. She picks up her wand and gives it a quick twirl.

I blink several times. "I—don't think that's possible." I look at Cameron as though he might know. He purses his lips and shrugs.

Dare I hope? What if they did have a way to reverse my condition? Magic has come a long way over the past decade. If I could be made human again, I could come of age, become my own guardian, and release Cameron from this duty. I stop poking at my wand to steal a sideways glance at my sister's soulmate. I've gotten used to having Cam around, and so has Joni. I can't imagine him leaving us—selfish as that may be.

"Why would a werewolf or a vampire want to be made human again if they won?" TJ sneers at Joni.

My cousin lowers her wand into her lap and shrinks into the couch, mumbling, "I don't know."

"Well, I think it would be an amazing prize, not to mention next-level spellcasting the likes of which have never been seen before." I nudge Joni's shoulder with my own. It brings a brief smile to her lips.

"Only zombie trash would think so," TJ says, with his eyes still on the TV.

Cameron stands up and curls his fingers into fists.

"Apologize, TJ!" I command, before Cameron has a chance to go over and punch my uncle. It wouldn't be the first time, and I'd rather limit Joni's exposure to violence.

"I apologize," TJ says to the TV.

"Look at Haylee, and say it like you mean it," Cameron snarls.

TJ flicks a gaze Cameron's way, noting the color rising up his neck, the flexed arms and tight fists begging for a reason to strike. Cameron didn't cast the spell of obedience. TJ doesn't have to obey him, but my uncle turns his head to me and says, "I am sorry, Haylee. That was insensitive. You didn't choose to be this way. Nobody would."

"Yeah, well, thanks for your sympathy," I answer sarcastically.

TJ returns his attention to the TV and his beer. Cameron remains standing, glaring at my uncle.

"Cam, it's about to start," I say.

It takes Cameron a moment to sit down. His fists don't relax, and he continues to fixate on TJ with a murderous expression. Sometimes it's hard to believe that this is the same sweet guy my sister was engaged to. That's just the thing, though. He's not the same guy and never will be.

An insurance commercial ends on TV, and a broadcaster announces, "*Spellcaster* is renowned worldwide for magical performances by humanity's most talented casters. Each season, contestants compete for a chance at immortality. But this year, *Spellcaster* is doing something entirely different. Tonight, we bring you an interview between Hugh Marin and *Spellcaster* host Colt Cohen, for a thrilling preview of Season 13, which airs this fall."

I lean forward on the couch as the TV cuts to a montage of moments from past seasons before settling on Colt Cohen seated on a cushy chair across from Hugh, a middle-aged, white, male reporter. Colt wears jeans and a button-up shirt, open over a fitted gray T-shirt. He appears as relaxed as he is when he's the one doing the interviewing.

"Thank you for joining us for this exclusive first look into Season 13," Hugh says from his chair.

Colt grins. "The show's producers and I are excited to try something different."

Hugh nods. "Tell us more about that."

"For the first time in our show's history, we are doing an all-supernaturals season of *Spellcaster*," Colt says.

Hugh tilts his head back and to one side as he looks at Colt. "So your contestants will be vampires, werewolves, witches, and wizards."

"And zombies," Joni tells the TV—almost at the same time as Colt Cohen. Joni beams.

"Zombies?" Hugh's barely visible, white-blond eyebrows furrow.

"*All* supernatural beings are welcome to audition," Colt answers firmly.

"But isn't that dangerous?" Hugh presses.

Cameron presses his fists into his thighs and aims his glare at Hugh.

"No more dangerous than competing alongside werewolves, vampires, and witches," Colt says.

"But a zombie's bite—"

"Is harmless to other creatures, not to mention illegal, the same way it is for werewolves."

Hugh scoffs. "You're not really comparing your species with zombies, are you, Mr. Cohen?"

"No more than relating zombies with vampires." Colt continues while Hugh's jaw hangs open. "Like a werewolf, a zombie's condition is spread through a bite. Of course, zombies—sentient or otherwise—are not allowed to transmute humans into one of their own kind. As per the law, if a human is not a family member, werewolves must file for permission—usually involving a spouse—but even then, it is extremely difficult to get approval. We werewolves also have the unfortunate disadvantage of getting old. When it comes to the non-aging process, zombies are more like vampires."

Joni and I suck in a breath. Vampires are going to be enraged when they hear Colt Cohen compare them in any way to zombies, because as much as they believe themselves superior to werewolves, it's nothing compared to their abhorrence of zombies. I wouldn't be surprised if Colt gets harassed after this.

Cameron huffs and crosses his arms like he's unimpressed. Hugh visibly sweats and dabs at his forehead with his hand before saying, "Uh, and there will be no human contestants in the new season."

"All supernatural," Colt repeats.

"Will the blind auditions be entirely blind, or will the coaches know the species of the contestant performing?"

"Entirely blind," Colt says with a grin. "Our coaches will have no clue as to the species or gender of the contestant until the screen lifts at the end of the performance."

"Do you think contestants will be more inclined to choose a coach of their own species?"

"One way or another, they might not have a choice," Colt answers, "but it will be interesting to see what happens."

"Indeed so," Hugh acknowledges, relaxing back into his chair. He looks into the camera and smiles as he says, "When we return, discover more shocking revelations you can expect from Season 13 of *Spellcaster*, including all-new combat rounds that might be more literal than you think."

"What does he mean by that?" Cameron asks, as a cartoon commercial for toilet paper fills the screen.

I'm not thinking that far ahead, though. My mind is on auditions and coaches.

I chew on my lower lip. There is no option of a zombie coach for me, so that won't be a factor when I make my decision. It wouldn't matter if there was, or if that coach raised a wand for me. If Malachi raises his wand, there's no question who I'll choose as my coach. I won't even make a show of mulling it over, struggling on stage to pick. As soon as Colt asks me to choose, I'll belt out, "Team Melachi!"

If I make it, that is.

As long as I don't mess up, I don't see how at least one coach won't raise his or her wand for me. My audition routine is next level, out of this world. Cameron was even able to get me practice time in Joni's school auditorium on weekends to perfect my routine. The awe on Cam's and Joni's faces when I was ready for them to watch buoyed me as much as their praise. My routine is the stuff of four-wand lifts . . . not that I'm taking it for granted. Nothing is guaranteed, as my lifeless heart reminds me daily. Could it ever beat again? Doubtful, but I'm on the edge of my seat to find out what the heck this mysterious grand prize will be.

When the TV cuts back to the interview, the reporter presses one elbow into his armrest and leans forward. "With supernaturals competing in the next episodes of *Spellcaster*, Season 13 will be the first magic competition of its kind. Tell us, Mr. Cohen, what other variations—if any—can viewers expect to see during the show? One would guess that you have more surprises planned this season."

Colt languidly crosses one long leg over the other and chuckles softly. "It will be like none other. That's for sure, but I don't want to give away too many spoilers."

"Can you at least tell us about the combat rounds? Typically, they are a combined performance in which two contestants from the same team work in unison to wow their coach for a chance to continue to the live cast-offs. We've heard rumors that for Season 13, the combat rounds won't be as coordinated or harmonious as previous seasons."

My body tenses as Colt's teeth gleam from a wolfish grin he flashes Hugh.

"As you know, competition among supernaturals is fierce. We want to give our creature contestants an opportunity to flex more than just their magical abilities."

"Say what?" I ask Colt's televised image. "I don't want to fight off werewolves, vampires, and witches. I want to do magic."

A laugh filled with menace and delight leaves TJ's lips. It's no surprise my sadistic uncle's eyes gleam, and his attention is glued to the TV as though this interview has suddenly turned into one of his favorite sports matches.

"I don't like the sound of this," Cameron says darkly.

Joni grimaces. "Do you think it's unsafe?" Her voice wobbles.

Now that my mind is made up to compete, I'm all in. I sit tall and listen carefully to everything Colt says—anything that can help me prepare for this unexpected inconvenience.

At the next commercial break, I glance over at Cam and my cousin and announce, "It's fine. I faced a zombie horde. I think I can handle a few bloodthirsty, fanged fur balls and biters. As for witches and wizards—they're basically humans who don't require the use of wands." I shrug. "No biggie."

My inner monologue doesn't match the assurance I speak aloud.

Oh, my gosh! What the heck, Haylee? You have no supernatural abilities. Werewolves can transform into freaking beasts! Vampires have super speed and superior senses and are self-healing. Witches and wizards don't require a piece of rare wood to cast spells. What can you do, besides go into a trance that leaves you even more vulnerable?

They can't hurt me! I shout back before sobering. *I mean, they can, but I can take it. I'm ageless. Way harder to hurt or kill. The zombies weren't able to finish me off. I won't let the werewolves, or vampires, or witches do me in, either.*

When another round of commercials airs over the screen, TJ huffs and turns his head in my direction. "Why don't you wave your wand to skip over the ads?"

"It doesn't work that way," I answer.

"Then what's the use of magic besides pissing me off?"

Cameron's eyes narrow on TJ. "*You're* pissing me off."

Thankfully, the commercial break ends. The camera zooms in on Hugh.

"And now, the moment we've all been waiting for—the Season 13 grand prize mystery we've all been dying to uncover. What will the winner of *Spellcaster*'s all supernatural competition walk away with? The time has come to reveal the astonishing reward that awaits Season 13's champion."

The camera pans to Colt, who looks off screen. "How about we *show* viewers the prize?" Colt suggests.

I scoot to the edge of the couch, gripping my wand, my eyes stuck to the television screen.

A young man in slacks and a button-up top wheels out a metal rolling cart, pushing it to rest between Colt and Hugh before walking off screen. The top shelf is waist high and has a dome-shaped object that's draped in teal fabric covered in gold stars.

"Care to do the honors, Hugh?" Colt asks.

"Gladly," Hugh says, as he stands and walks behind the mystery prize. "I'm sure our viewers are as curious as I."

"Way more than you, Hugh," I tell the screen.

Joni grins and nods. Cameron's steely eyes continue glaring at the screen as though he expects a snake to shoot out from beneath the cloth.

Hugh pinches the fabric at the top of the dome and smiles into the camera. "And now, the moment we have all been waiting for." He yanks the fabric, uncovering a glass dome and the prize within.

"What the hell?" Cameron says.

"Is that a—?" Joni covers her mouth with one hand.

TJ lowers his beer bottle.

I stare and stare and stare before murmuring reverently, "Oh, my God. It can't be. Can it?"

CHAPTER TWENTY-SEVEN

THE GLASS DOME reminds me of the one encapsulating the enchanted rose in *Beauty and the Beast*.

Only, in this case, the red object inside is a beating heart.

"Is that a human heart?" Hugh squats to peer inside the dome.

"It's a witch's heart," Colt says, "and not just any witch. We located it in the lost tomb of Egyptian Queen Yapsut. Anyone who has studied supernatural history knows that creature origins date back to ancient times. Some of those beings weren't as discreet as others." Colt pauses to chuckle. "Queen Yapsut used her natural-born powers to rule over her people as a goddess, though she was not content to age and die the way of mortals. It is rumored that she had a vampire lover named Mosi and that, together, they conspired to find a way to share both immortality and power. Remember, this was before the discovery of Lignum Vitae trees' magical properties. Ancient records recount a celestial event in which bright, oblong circles appeared in the night sky. Supernatural scholars believe that Yapsut and Mosi performed a complex ritual at the time when this phenomenon took place in the heavens. We do not know what ingredients were used, sacrifices made, nor spells cast. All anyone had to go on were rumors passed down from Mosi. It was said that the vampire bit and drained Queen Yapsut, believing their ritual would make her immortal with his bite, and that her blood would give him power." Colt pauses and raises one brow. "It did not. Queen Yapsut died in all ways but one. Her heart continued beating while her body decayed. Mosi believed her beating heart to be a sign that all was not lost. He reportedly tore hearts from countless young Egyptian beauties and shoved Yapsut's heart in their place, believing Yapsut would claim the new body and self-heal as she took possession of her vampire abilities. Over and over, Mosi failed to bring back the witch queen. It became an obsession—one he believed he had all the time in the world to solve."

Hugh returns to his seat to listen as Colt continues the story.

"Eventually, Mosi hid Yapsut's heart in a vessel, which he sealed in a secret tomb while he traveled the world in search of the missing piece of their master plan. With the heart securely hidden, and no written record of the ritual, Mosi set out to make inquiries of the most powerful wizards at that time. Here, the story takes an interesting turn."

Colt's brows jump. "After decades of searching, Mosi stumbled across a drunken wizard who admitted that Queen Yapsut was not the only witch to try an immortality ritual during the celestial event, which they referred to as 'the circles of immortal fire.' In this case, an old wizard had performed the spell, hoping to cheat death. Nothing happened . . . until he was attacked by a vampire a year later. Vampires were much more violent creatures in those days, and this one not only drained the wizard but tore out and ate his heart—leading to the first vampire with powers, however short-lived." Colt chuckles. "The doomed vampire had no understanding of magic. The few spells he cast were sloppy and accidental, drawing the attention of the wizards, who beheaded him and then burned his body. Hearing this tale, Mosi realized that he could never get Yapsut back, but he could consume her heart and gain her powers."

My eyes are wide, and my pupils go haywire darting between Colt and Queen Yapsut's heart. This is a thing of legends! Only magical geeks like me have any notion of such an anomaly.

When I turned thirteen, my mom gave me a beautiful, illustrated book of magical myths. One such story was that of Queen Yapsut and the beating heart she left behind. When I read that particular tale, I was more intrigued by the romance between a witch and a vampire than the legend of the ceaseless heart. In the illustrated book's version of the story, Mosi was consumed by grief and guilt, which led him to build Yapsut a secret tomb, where he hid her heart before sealing himself inside with the last piece of his true love before ripping out his own heart and dying on the stone floor as Yapsut's heart beat on.

It had seemed so romantic and tragic when I read the tale of the star-crossed lovers. Never mind that Mosi could have self-healed after pulling out his heart. It was a fairy tale. Now, Colt was sharing a very different account of how the story supposedly ended.

"Mosi never made it back to Egypt." Colt pauses for dramatic effect. "Researchers' best speculation is that the drunken wizard who shared the story sobered up, alerted members of his coven, and they hunted Mosi down and killed him before he had the chance to consume Yapsut's heart—though not before sharing this new discovery with other vampires who attempted to locate the hidden tomb over the centuries. Supposedly, Mosi was in his cups when he let the story slip—which is why I don't drink." Colt grins and winks.

"Your loss," TJ says sarcastically, and takes another swig of beer.

"Following that second close call, the witches and wizards formed a secret society to prevent any such ritual from being attempted again and to recover Yapsut's heart. They, too, were unsuccessful in their search for the hidden tomb."

Hugh's mouth gapes open. "How did your team find it?"

Colt's grin widens. "Teamwork. The idea for Season 13 has been years in the planning. We knew we needed an extraordinary prize. The producers brought our coaches in on the brainstorming. It was Malachi Rayne who brought up the legend of Yapsut's enchanted heart. I have to admit I became somewhat obsessed with having that heart as Season 13's grand prize."

I press my hand against my chest and feel my cheeks warm thinking about Malachi Rayne coming up with this epic reward.

Colt chuckles. "In fact, all four judges became fixated on finding the heart. I can't give away all the details, but it was something of a treasure hunt; we would have never found it without our combined efforts."

Hugh's brows furrow. "And no one was tempted to take the heart for themselves?" His gaze locks onto the heart, and I wonder if he'd considered grabbing it and making a run for it. Sure, it would end his career, but if he ate the thing, he would possess Yapsut's power. Then again, stealing the heart would paint a target on his back.

Colt's grin turns wolfish once more. "I ensured that wasn't an option. As soon as we located the tomb, I had my most trusted assistant ensorcell the vessel, enclosing the heart you see here. Only the winner of Season 13 can lift the dome to reach the heart. The glass is shatterproof. Immovable. Indestructible. Whoever wins Season 13 wins the heart and the power locked within the organ."

"By eating it," Hugh says.

"Yes."

Not a problem. I can eat a heart, and it would mean I could protect myself and Joni without needing a wand or rune tattoos. Not only that, but it would also give me the ability to help others like me. Rosie is the first to come to mind. It's too late for Myles, but how many more sentient zombies are in desperate need of aid? Images from Kendra's Telepatch flash through my head. I could honor my sister's memory by doing something about the cruelty shown to my kind. I could be a guardian angel of sorts, maybe even create a zombie sanctuary.

And I'd be even more unstoppable when it came to hunting down and exposing those responsible for murdering my family. I twist my wand in my palm as my thoughts turn while listening to the interview.

"But why would a witch or wizard want to compete to win Yapsut's heart when they already have that kind of power?" Hugh wonders aloud.

"Excellent question," Colt says. "You will recognize the sorcerers' secret society by their modern organization: Agents of Night. They are putting pressure on members of their species to compete for a chance to win the heart and destroy it once and for all. Such a feat would brand them a hero among their kind." Colt shrugs like it makes no difference to him whether the heart is consumed or destroyed.

I clench my teeth. It would be such a waste of power—preserved for centuries—if Queen Yapsut's heart was to be obliterated. Truly tragic. I want to win that heart! And I want to make Malachi proud because, of course, he has to be my coach. The heart was his idea, so it's only poetic that a member of his team brings home the prize.

"Mr. Cohen, thank you for joining us." Hugh faces the camera. "Don't miss Season 13 of *Spellcaster* this fall on UTV. Watch as creatures compete against one another on stage for the first time. Who will fare best during the magical combat? Which species will win Queen Yapsut's legendary heart? Don't miss the exciting and jaw-dropping performances. Blind auditions air this September."

A commercial follows Hugh's conclusion. My nerves are wreaking havoc on my stomach. Sure, the auditions are aired in September, but they're about to take place starting this week.

TJ lowers his beer bottle. "Well, for once I'll be rooting for the witches. The last thing we need is vampires with more power than they already hold over the world. Or, if not a witch, then a werewolf. It would serve the vampires right if a werewolf won."

"I'm rooting for Haylee," Joni says.

"We all are." Cameron aims a menacing glare TJ's way.

I shake my head. "I don't need TJ to root for me. I'm winning the show and the heart."

"In your dreams," TJ says. "The only reason they want you to audition is to cover all their bases without some do-gooder raising a stink about discrimination. Wake up, Niece. Other than these two fools, no one's gonna want you to win."

Tears prick the backs of my eyeballs, but I'm able to will them away as I stare down TJ. "Guess I'll have to change viewers' minds by dazzling them with my astounding performances."

"You're going to blow the roof off the place, Haylee," Cameron says with conviction.

He says it again when he drops me off at the airport. It's more reassuring than "Good luck."

I repeat his words in my head like a mantra as I wait in line to check my bag.

I'm wearing the purple jacket Kendra got for me, and the illusion spell I cast over myself makes me appear human. I'm nervous enough without having to worry about passengers freaking out over being confined in an airplane with a zombie. At least I can go back to see an alterationist after my audition. I'm more than ready to repair my original wounds from the zombie attack. I don't need any extra reminders of that horrific day.

I wheel my suitcase to the front of the line and wait until a pretty woman with tan skin, bronzed cheekbones, and long, shiny brown hair in a low ponytail waves me to the counter.

I hand over the ticket Alexander sent me, along with my ID, and then place my suitcase on the belt. The name tag on the woman's navy blazer reads *Kristy*. She types on a keyboard and stares at the monitor, her fingers going still.

"Haylee Hutchins." She turns away from the monitor to beam at me. "You've been upgraded to first class."

"I have?" I blink several times. "Um, awesome. Thanks," I say, even though I know Kristy didn't personally upgrade me. It must have been Alexander. He really is the dream assistant or, in my case, show advocate—proving that not all vampires are bad.

Kristy smiles with straight white teeth. "Your electronic boarding pass has been updated. Would you like a print copy as well?"

"Electronic is fine, thanks."

"Just the one bag?"

"Yeah."

Kristy prints a barcoded baggage label and fastens it around the nylon loop of my black canvas rolling suitcase. I used to have a vintage three-piece luggage set of hard case suitcases in sky blue with pearl-white straps. Cameron found this one at our local thrift store. It turns out people aren't jumping at the chance to make an offer on a home where a zombie massacre took place, and even with a trusted guardian, we're limited to the monthly allowance and have to be careful. True to his word, Cam only uses the money for me. He set up savings accounts for both me and Joni. There isn't much left over from TJ's paycheck to put aside for Joni, but Cam says even a little adds up over time. I wish he'd take some of my monthly stipend out for himself, but he insists he doesn't need it.

"You're all set," Kristy says. "Have a nice flight."

I force a smile, but I am all nerves, which makes it impossible to enjoy my spacious seat in first class or the liver served especially to me on the flight. It's sliced thin atop a bone china plate with silver cutlery. At least I'm able to consume organs and maybe pass for a werewolf. The man in the suit next to me is served steak with a side of herb-roasted fingerling potatoes and charred green beans. He scrolls through a report with pie charts and graphs on his tablet while he eats. Not interested in making conversation. A complete relief.

I saw off tiny bits of liver and chew them slowly while staring out the window into a sky full of clouds. My mind wanders from the auditions to my family.

After finishing my meal, I continue to gaze into that fuzzy space outside of the plane. As the flight progresses, the clouds clear, revealing a bright blue sky. I swear I hear Kendra's voice inside my head saying, "Come fly with me. I am the sky."

I wish I were on my way to see her. I wish she were meeting me in Hollywood to watch my audition from the private viewing room alongside the stage. There will be no one to wait with me at the studio until my name is called to perform. No one cheering me on during my audition while simultaneously urging the coaches to lift a wand. No one to celebrate with afterward. I've never seen a contestant that didn't have at least one family member or friend along for support.

I am on my own.

For all my practice and bravado, all I want to do right now is turn right back around. Things aren't so bad with Cameron and Joni for company. I'm at ease at my job. TJ's right. Viewers aren't going to vote a zombie through. The magic won't matter. People are going to vote for their favorite creature contestants. I shouldn't have deleted my JingleJam account. Maybe the beauty brigade would still support me as I am.

I pull the zipper on my purple jacket up and down, then stop when the man in the suit sighs his irritation. The jacket is too big, since I've been unable to eat carbs or sugar, but I haven't spelled it to fit the way I did with Aunt Chloe's clothing before I was able to order my own outfits. I don't want to mess with Kendra's last gift to me.

I turn my back to my prickly neighbor and peer out the window, hoping to commune with my sister again, but she's gone silent. The transmission felt one-way and disconnected to begin with. Like a message in a bottle. It doesn't matter. My mind probably made it up. I'm all alone, reaching out for any signs of my family's continued existence in some other form when all I really have of them are my memories and thoughts.

By the time we land, I feel like an emotional wreck.

There's a chauffeur waiting outside of the terminals with my name on a clipboard. He accompanies me to baggage and wheels my suitcase to a black Mercedes-Benz sedan parked near the entrance of the parking garage. He's about as chatty as suit-dude was on the plane. Again, no complaints.

I am dropped off at the Solace Hotel, which he tells me is near the *Spellcaster* theater. He says he will pick me up tomorrow morning at six to drop me off for my audition.

Alexander has me booked in a penthouse, but like with first class, I'm unable to truly enjoy it. I pace from room to room, wand in hand, stopping briefly in front of a large mirror to tell my reflection, "You've got this. You've practiced. You're going to blow the roof off the place."

After wearing myself out, I lay on the bed and zomb out until four in the morning.

At 5:45 a.m., I'm dressed in stretchy silver sequined pants, waiting out front for my ride to the theater. My top is a fitted white tee with one big silver metallic star printed on front. My shoulder-length hair is wavy with several thin braids added in. It all looked fun and pretty in the mirror, but I'm still not used to this slim version of myself. Then there is the missing flesh and bones still exposed in my arms and neck. Part beauty, part nightmare. The young woman in the mirror might as well be someone else staring back at me.

As much as I'd like to bring the jacket Kendra gave me along as a security blanket, it's too bulky to wear during my performance, and I'm too afraid of it being grabbed if I set it aside during my audition. A would-be thief would later discover they couldn't wear it, but that wouldn't make it any less gone. Instead, I fold it up carefully and tuck it inside my suitcase.

At 6:23, I'm at the theater, waiting in line to check in. And then I'm wandering across a large, open lobby full of supernaturals waving their wands in excitement while grinning and chatting with parents, siblings, friends, and romantic partners.

The witches and wizards have gathered in a corner of the lobby, forming one big clique. They fold their arms and whisper to one another while glowering at everyone outside their species.

They taunt a lone werewolf who walks by. He stops and growls at their group, only to have his wand fly out of his hand and zip across the auditorium. The group of young sorcerers erupt into laughter. When the werewolf begins to shift, a security guard arrives with a wand in time to prevent him from turning full beast. Another guy hurries over with a handheld camera. He's been going around talking to contestants and their families while filming.

I haven't seen Max or Jimmy . . . or Alexander for that matter. They're probably too busy operating the main stage.

I scan my surroundings, looking for a place to settle in. The production aides told us to expect to wait for hours—if not all day. Depending on how the auditions move along, some of us will have to return with tomorrow's group of contestant hopefuls.

All around me, I pick up on different species. I'm not used to being around supernatural creatures, let alone a warehouse-sized theater packed with paranormals. It's overwhelming and fascinating how I can tell what each one is. Which, unfortunately, goes both ways. A female vampire with raven hair, tight black leather pants, and a crimson lace-up bustier lifts her nose in the air as I pass.

"Gross, a zombie."

I roll my eyes because she's a vampire fashion cliché. It's sad.

From what I've seen, the werewolves have the coolest style. A crew member films two young female shifters seated on a couch. One has gorgeous blue highlights running through her brown hair. A thick braid sweeps across the back of her head before twisting past her right shoulder blade. Black-and-white-plaid skinny capri pants cling to her long legs, ending in black combat boots. She's got on a white crop top and moves a tattooed arm with water-colored moon phases as she answers questions on camera.

"You love cats?" the camera man asks in surprise.

"We already have enough canine energy in our family," she answers in a Québécois accent.

The young woman beside her chuckles. "That we do."

"This is my sister," the blue-haired female says. "Her name is Kat, by the way," she adds with a smile in her golden-brown eyes.

"I'm her biggest fan," Kat says.

I hurry away from the werewolf sisters as tears threaten. This is not the time or place for a breakdown. I'll save it for after my audition. Well, hopefully I'll be celebrating after my audition.

Alone.

Without my sister.

I blink rapidly and hurry toward an empty armchair beside a potted palm, making my way past the hyper groups of contestants and their close-knit circles. I reach the chair only to be shoved aside by a young guy who snarls. He's short but has no shortage of muscles bulging from his fitted gray T-shirt. He plops into the seat and pats his lap. A skinny female in a cropped faux-fur jacket and skin-tight black suede pants seats herself in his lap. She swings her legs so that they hang over one side of his legs, wraps her arms around his neck, and starts making out with him like she intends to devour him on the spot.

I wrinkle my nose and hope that whichever one of them is auditioning doesn't make it on the show. Several feet from the rude werewolves, a blond dressed in a silver sequined romper holds court with two drop-dead-gorgeous guys. Dead as in *undead*. I recognize one of the guys as Ace Callan, who is Forever 23. Payton had a black-and-white poster of him shirtless on a beach on her bedroom wall. The other guy and the female look vaguely familiar. They're most likely F23, as well. That group sticks together like caramel popcorn.

Great, just what I need—a popular F23er competing in *Spellcaster*. The public will vote them all the way to the live finals whether or not they deserve that spot. I wonder which one of them is auditioning. I hope not all three.

At least they don't send dirty looks my way. Not that that's saying much. The F23 trio ignores everyone else, which makes it tempting to stare a moment longer as I shuffle past them. They all have flawless skin, naturally. A dainty chain necklace swoops just below the female's collarbone. Her sequined romper is a V-neck without showing cleavage. The sleeves are long and wide at her wrists. The shorts reveal long, skinny, fair legs that are bare before ending in dark red ankle boots. Dark blond, unbound hair falls in lazy waves that end just below her chest. Half of it drapes over her shoulder like a fancy scarf. The other half is behind her back. She holds a wand horizontally at her waist as though it's a clutch, which confirms my fears that at least one member of their elite group is auditioning.

While other contestants find couches and seats to settle into, the trio stands poised like they're ready to be photographed.

Well, this sucks. At least the auditions are blind, so she won't get special treatment for being fabulous.

There are more vampires inching closer, gaping at the trio.

"That's Carolina Bellmore," a teen female vamp whispers reverently. "She's so pretty."

"You're pretty, kitten," a human male reassures her.

I increase my speed to get away from the vampire cluster. Someone ought to make a rule about vampire hordes.

For the thousandth time, I wish Cam could be here. I'm a whale out of water. I don't fit in with these creatures.

There's a less crowded area near a set of wide double doors where yet another gorgeous, young female vampire stands as though posing in a short, light-pink halter dress. She looks Indian, maybe nineteen, with long dark brown hair parted down the middle and irises to match. Not only is her skin flawless, it's bronzed and has a healthy, natural-looking glow. Her short nails are painted milky white, full lips glossy pink, and her eyes are penciled in a thin, dark shade. She doesn't need much makeup to look stunning.

The only indication that she's not completely at ease is the way she grips her wand like she might snap it in half.

Unlike the F23 trio, this vampire looks through the crowd as though assessing the competition. A white, middle-aged male vampire with thick salt-and-pepper hair stands beside her in a suit, scrolling through his phone.

If I had to guess, I'd bet the male is her master.

I look from him to the female, only to find her eyes boring into mine. Her expression doesn't change. She continues staring, so I stare back like we've entered a contest. I don't know why it matters, but somehow it does. If I look away, I feel like I'm conceding that she's at the top of the food chain while I'm future roadkill. For this competition, I plan to stand on equal footing with all the other supernaturals. I am a Hutchins. We rise to the challenge.

The male at her side pulls his gaze away from his phone and follows her gaze to me. Out of the corner of my eye, I see his lips move and then hers respond. I swear her mouth forms the syllables that sound out, "Haylee Hutchins."

CHAPTER TWENTY-EIGHT

"*DIOS MÍO*! HAYLEE Hutchins!"

I startle as a young woman steps in front of me, ending my staredown with the Bollywood Biter. I blink. How do any of these supes know my name?

"I love your beauty and magic tips on JingleJam so much," the girl squeals.

Oh, right. That. I'm sure Kendra would laugh if she knew that my life no longer revolves around posting videos and gaining followers.

Being recognized isn't my only surprise. My fan is a zombie. Instant relief floods me that I'm not the only supernatural of my kind. This girl might even be my age. It's hard to tell when her face is painted like the Day of the Dead and her thick brown hair is gathered on top of her head, fastened with a flower crown headpiece. She's dressed in a black-and-white skeleton catsuit with a floral lace bustle skirt that ties in front with a purple ribbon. Fake purple and red flowers accent the lace on her shoulders and along the open lining of her skirt.

Seeing me gape, she strikes a pose—hands on her hips. "Why not, right?"

Her comment tugs a laugh from my lips. "You're awesome," I say. "What's your name?"

"I'm Mariana, and you have to meet my family."

Before I can agree, Mariana takes me by my arm and tugs me over to a couch where three adults are seated. A younger teenage girl sits cross-legged on the rug in front of them, staring at her phone, and there's a young couple on a loveseat pushed in close to the couch. They're all human.

Mariana pulls me onto the rug in front of them. "*Escucha a todos.* This is Haylee Hutchins." Six pairs of eyes stare at me. I have to relax my jaw. I'd better get used to this kind of attention if I hope to make it through the judges' scrutiny. "She's a mega beauty influencer on JingleJam and a crazy talented spellcaster." Mariana turns to me and grins with her reddish-black lips that have been painted to appear stitched at the corners. "No surprise that you're here to audition. How lucky is it that they're doing a supernatural season? Anyway, this is my mother, Adelita; aunt, Bonita; uncle, Juan; my little sister, Amora—"

"I'm not little," Amora says, barely looking up from her phone.

"—cousin, Petra, and her boyfriend, Carlos."

I smile politely. "Quite the entourage you have." Tears sting the backs of my eyes as I look into the faces of Mariana's family members.

"The guest limit is six." Mariana shrugs, and I imagine there would have been many more couches to carry over if all of her family members were allowed to accompany her.

"Nice to meet you, Haylee," Mariana's mother says.

"Carlos, go bring another chair," the uncle says.

"Oh, that's okay," I say, but Carlos is already on it.

I don't know how he does it because seats are scarce, but he returns with two stackable chairs with padded seats.

"Thank you," I say, sitting beside Mariana.

Her aunt stares at me. "Is anyone here with you?"

I bite down on my lower lip to keep it from quivering before swallowing and answering, "I'm here alone."

"You must come out to dinner with us tonight to celebrate," Mariana's mother says.

"If a coach bothers to pick Mari," the sister says.

"Amora!" Adelita snaps. "*No hables asi. Se amable con tu hermana mayor.*"

"It's okay, Mami," Mariana says with a grin. "Amora's just jealous."

Amora rolls her eyes and lowers her phone. "We both know I've got the most magical talent in the family. The only reason you're auditioning and I'm not is because it's creature season."

"And because I'm awesome," Mariana adds, patting her floral crown.

"You wish."

Adelita leans forward, all business, as she shakes her finger. "*Chicas, basta ahora.*"

Their aunt shakes her head and tsks.

"*Sí, Mami.*" Mariana and her sister say in unison.

Mariana turns in her seat to face me. "How cool would it be if we got on the same team?"

Looking around the room of poised vampires, snobby witches and wizards, and rambunctious werewolves, I think it would be pretty fantastic. Dare I hope?

"We could be roommates." I don't want to get too excited only to be let down, but it's too late.

"Okay, let's make a pact. I know Malachi is your first choice, but what if he doesn't lift his wand for us?" Amora snorts. Mariana ignores her. "Who would be our second choice of coach?"

"Brody," Mariana's mother and aunt say, followed by a giggle.

"I was thinking Team Cleo," Mariana says.

"Yeah, I don't know," I say slowly.

"Just don't pick Team Zen. He's boring," Amora offers.

"Better Team Zen than going home," Mariana's cousin says. Her boyfriend leans over and kisses her cheek. She grins and turns to give him a peck on the lips.

"What do you say, Haylee? First pick Malachi; second choice Cleo?"

"You know what? Sure. Let's do it." It doesn't matter. I'm going to make sure Malachi lifts his wand for me, but saying I'd go for Cleo second gets a smile out of Mariana that looks cheerful in spite of her skeletal face makeup. I don't suppose she has any real bones poking out, or she wouldn't need the catsuit.

"I wonder if there are any other zombies here." Mariana cranes her head, looking around.

"We're far too outnumbered," I say, adding, "At least they don't seem to have any stupid 'no hording' rules here."

"Right?" Mariana says. "It's completely unfair to isolate us when all the other species get to have their own communities and support networks. What's their justification? They know sentient zombies are harmless." Amora snorts, but Mariana ignores her. "Anyway, I'm just happy you're here."

I return Mariana's smile.

Amora snorts again, but this time it's not directed at her sister. The younger teen is watching two cute werewolves standing on chairs. The one with the loose man bun holds out his phone and pans across the crowd before turning the screen to himself, and the other guy with a crew cut leans in to talk into the phone.

"Hopefully, they don't burn down the stage," Amora quips.

"Who are they?" Mariana asks.

"Cody and Jake Miller, total pyros."

Mariana squints in their direction. "Are they twins?"

Amora snorts. "Yeah, used to be identical before Jake's hair caught on fire. Idiot."

"How do you know them?" I ask.

Amora shoots me a sassy young teenage girl look. "JingleJam. Hashtag *Spellcaster* Season 13 auditions."

"You don't have to be rude," Mariana chides.

But I don't blame Amora for rolling her eyes. I should be on top of *Spellcaster* social. Deleting my account might not have been my brightest idea. I can make a new account to at least follow what's going on with the show. Ugh, starting over with zero following is depressing.

"Do you know who anyone else here is?" I ask Amora.

"No," Mariana says at the same time her sister answers, "Yes." Mariana sticks her tongue out at her.

Amora sets her phone in her lap to point at a petite girl with shoulder-length pink hair dressed in an orange crop-top sweater, short jean skirt, and striped platform shoes. "That's Izzie King. She auditioned for Season 5 and didn't make it. Now that she's been turned into a werewolf by her family, it looks like she gets another shot at auditioning—not that being part-beast will make her casting any better."

"Amora!" Mariana says.

I take a closer look at Izzie. Her hair was blond when she auditioned for Season 5, which is probably why I didn't recognize her immediately. If I remember correctly, the teams were filling up when she auditioned, making the judges pickier about lifting their wands.

"The blond with the curly hair on the red couch is Tripp Peters and his girlfriend, Alice, who encouraged him to audition," Amora continues. "She handles his social."

"Is he any good?" Mariana asks.

"He'll probably get a four-wand lift," Amora says. "He's a werewolf. They both are."

"Well, I knew that," Mariana says.

"Right. Your utterly amazing new superpower." Sarcasm drips from Amora's words.

Mariana sits up tall and touches her temples. "You know what? It's working right now. I sense a critter of the annoying brat variety seated on the floor in front of me."

"Girls!" their mother scolds, though I don't know how effective it is.

"Do you know who that girl in the pink prom dress is?" I ask quickly, before Amora has a chance to pick up her phone and go back to ignoring us.

Amora takes one look at the vampire and impresses me yet again with her social knowledge.

"Suhani Das, India's undefeated spellcasting champion. She's recently made. That's her master looming beside her. The rumor going around social is that the vampires recruited her to win the heart."

"But the prize was only announced last week." My words turn to dust on my tongue. Of course vampires would know about the heart before the public. They *always* have the advantage.

Amora lifts her brows like she's thinking the same thing. "Anyway, Suhani will definitely be in the final three, and very likely win the whole thing."

I clench and unclench my teeth. "No way. Vampires already act like they're the superior species. We can't let those smug bastards win the heart."

Mariana nods vigorously. "It's not even fair that they went scouting and turned gifted humans for their own glory. How many other contestants were recently made for that purpose?"

A brief silence settles over us as we look around the auditorium.

"Suhani Das, please proceed to door A," a woman announces over the loudspeaker.

Suhani and her master don't have far to go, since they stationed themselves in front of the double doors from the start. A young male wearing a headset opens the door and holds it for them to enter.

Mariana's mouth hangs open dramatically. "She even gets special treatment."

"Good luck following up her act," Amora says.

Mariana stands and shakes her hands out in front of her. "I'm so nervous. I feel like I'm going to pass out."

"Then sit down and have a snack," her aunt suggests. Mariana's mother nods her agreement and pulls out a stack of metal food canisters from a tote bag beside her ankles.

Mariana clutches her stomach and makes a gagging sound. "No thanks. My stomach is already rioting. I don't want to be barfing brains on stage during my audition."

"It would be funny if you threw up on national television," Amora says.

"Not helping," Mariana snaps.

"Well, maybe Haylee would like a snack," Mariana's mother says. "I prepared cubed cow tongue, sliced pig liver, and sautéed lamb brains. Not to worry, I didn't add anything to the sauté. We learned the hard way not to include any vegetables or seasoning."

"Don't remind me," Mariana groans.

"I'm good. Thanks," I say with a smile.

"Zane Barrett, please proceed to door B." The room quiets following the announcement, heads craning to see who has been called next.

A guy in matching midnight blue slacks and an open blazer with a black top buttoned to his neck swaggers across the auditorium. Blond hair sweeps to one side of his head and azure eyes stare ahead, not sparing anyone a glance. There's no wand in his hand.

EXIT

"Show these cretins how it's done, Zane!" a guy shouts from the group of sorcerers, who snicker in response.

Amora lifts her phone, aiming the screen at Zane.

"Amora," Mariana chides.

"What? He's hot and famous. Not that you'd know, being a nerd and all, but Zane Barrett models for all the top fashion brands, luxury goods, and cologne."

As Amora follows Zane with her camera, Mariana rolls her eyes. "You know you have zero chance with a wizard," she says.

"I'm making a recording, not planning our wedding," Amora huffs.

"I'm so happy to be going out with a real man," their cousin says sweetly, before nuzzling against Carlos's shoulder.

"Hey, we should exchange numbers," Mariana says.

"Yeah," I pull my phone out of my pocket and see I have a new text. With the collective noise, I never heard it chime.

Cameron: How's it going?

I exchange numbers with Mariana and then reply to Cam.

Haylee: I met another zombie. She's nice.

Cameron: Good. I wish I could be there. So does Joni.

Haylee: Me too, but it's ok. My new friend's family invited me to join them for dinner tonight.

Cameron: Are you getting the nourishment you need?

I already told Cameron about the first-class upgrade and liver, and the special room service menu left on the table of my hotel suite. As ever, it's touching that he worries.

Haylee: More than enough.

Cameron: That's good.

Haylee: I'll text you after my audition.

Cameron: Call.

Haylee: ok

Cameron: Be safe. And knock 'em dead.

Haylee: Will do.

I tuck my phone in my pocket as static precedes the next announcement over the loudspeaker.

"Cody and Jake Miller, please proceed to door A."

Howls go up.

"Time to get lit!" Cody hollers. He and Jake hold their wands above their heads as they strut to door A.

"Morons," Amora mutters, but her cheeks flush all the same.

The Miller twins are flanked by what appear to be their parents and three younger siblings. After the family disappears behind door A, the next contestant is called to door B.

Hours pass. More names are called. My palms sweat, which makes me worry about my wand slipping out of my hand during my performance.

A familiar pattern develops as contestants are called backstage. Werewolves have the largest groups of supporters accompanying them when their names are called. The vampires glide to the doors escorted by an immaculately dressed vampire I assume to be their master, or with a couple of gorgeous vampire friends or a boyfriend or a girlfriend. The witches and wizards stride in alone, like they're above bringing in a cheer squad.

For the hundredth time, I wish I wasn't going back there alone.

"Dominic Monroe, please proceed to door A."

Another wizard struts his stuff across the auditorium like he's a model on a runway. With his thick, dark curly hair, brooding gaze, and toned towering frame, I wonder if he, too, does commercials for luxury cologne and clothing companies. I'm not the only one who notices. Amora aims her phone at him as her cousin huffs. "I thought this competition was supposed to be about magic, not looks."

Amora finishes snapping pics and then lowers her phone and looks over her shoulder at her cousin. "It's not like there's a lot of ugly supernaturals."

"Rude, but true," Mariana says, patting her floral crown with one hand.

"Nathaniel Duke, please proceed to door B."

"Jeez, even their names are fancy," Mariana's cousin says.

Her boyfriend's eyebrows jump. "Ahem, is Carlos not a suave and romantic name?"

"You forgot sexy." She grins and kisses him. They turn to hold one another and kiss on the couch.

I look away and try not to blush. There's no way I'd be comfortable making out in public . . . in front of my parents if they were still alive. But the rest of the family doesn't seem to notice or care.

My attention drifts across the theater's lobby and the remaining contestants. The room is still full of posturing paranormals. Carolina's arms are folded while Ace and the other male thumb through their phones. The she-vamp pouts each time her name isn't called.

"Daphné Melanson, please proceed to door A."

The brown-and-blue-haired werewolf I saw talking to the camera earlier heads to door A, her sister Kat striding beside her.

Even though I won't have family to cheer through my audition, I'm relieved to have found a new friend and her family to wait with. Wand on her lap, Mariana tugs at a fake flower on her skirt. There's a nervous energy buzzing all around us.

"Izzie King, please proceed to door B."

An adult male and female werewolf accompany the pink-haired weregirl to the double doors, where they hug her before entering.

"Mariana Caraballo, please proceed to door A."

Mariana stands up so fast her wand rolls off her lap onto the carpet. Amora leans forward to pick it up and lifts the wand for her sister to retrieve.

Mariana's mother gets up and hugs her daughter tightly, issuing a string of Spanish that sounds heartfelt and encouraging. I stand and wait until Mariana is out of her mom's arms to wish her luck. She sucks in a breath and nods.

"Team Malachi or Team Cleo. Here goes nothing."

Mariana's family grabs their bags and follows her to the double doors marked "A."

I remain standing, watching Mariana, ready to wave if she looks back my way. But Mariana is probably too nervous. She walks through the double doors without ever turning back. I don't blame her.

My stomach hollows with the all-too-familiar pang of loneliness. A group of werewolves moves in on the vacated couch. I walk over to a wall, lean my back against it, pull out my phone, and text Cameron.

Haylee: My new friend was just called in. I hope she makes it.

Cameron: Me too. Where are you now?

I blink back tears when I see Cameron's immediate response. Is he hanging around all day with his phone in case I text or call? I wouldn't put it past him.

Haylee: Standing by a wall, waiting. Hopefully I won't have to come back and do this all over tomorrow.

Cameron: Anyone bothering you?

Haylee: No. We're all waiting around for our names to be called in to audition.

Cameron: The judges haven't seen anything yet.

I think of Suhani Das and chew on my lower lip. If she's as good as Amora claimed, they've probably already been wowed ten times over. Not to mention the wizards with their natural-born abilities.

Cameron and I text back and forth until the next set of contestants are called back.

Haylee: Hey, I'm going to text my friend and see how her audition went.

Cameron: No prob. I'm around whenever you need me.

Haylee: Thanks, Cam.

Cameron: Anytime.

I blink back more tears. Kendra found one of the good ones. I'm happy she got a chance to experience true love before she died. It's a small comfort that also breaks my heart.

I open a new message for Mariana.

Haylee: How did it go? Team Malachi or Team Cleo?

I stare at my screen. Long minutes drag by with no response. She's probably on her way back to her hotel to wash off her face paint and change.

I imagine her family's collective voices on their ride from the studio to their rooms. We can catch up tonight. My chest bursts with gratitude that I'll have friendly, familiar faces to celebrate with rather than an empty suite to hole up inside at the end of a long, stress-filled day.

My phone rings with a request for a video call with Mariana. My lungs fill with air, ready to scream in excitement that she made it on the show. Grinning, I hold up my phone and swipe over the video icon.

"Heyyyyyyy . . ." My cheerful greeting drags out and dies as a tearful Mariana sobs on screen. Her hair is a frizzy mess, floral crown missing, and black makeup running down her face. There's a tiled shower in the background.

"Mariana! What happened?"

"They played the wrong music for my audition," she cries. "I tried to do my routine anyway, but it didn't go with my performance at all. It completely threw me off. Haylee, it was a disaster. My ghosts came out looking like mist. The tombstone illusion flickered out altogether. I forgot to create a night sky. It's no wonder I didn't receive a single wand lift." Sobbing, Mariana grabs a white hand towel off a towel rack and scrubs her face, smearing the paint into a blotchy mess and staining the towel black.

My dead weight of a heart sinks into my stomach. "Did you tell the coaches what happened?" I demand.

She lowers the towel, lower lip quivering, and says bitterly, "I didn't have to. At the end of my performance, Colt Cohen came on stage and said that random contestants are having their music changed without their knowledge as an added Season 13 surprise to see how well the unlucky contestants can pull off their routine when their soundtrack is switched on them." Mariana's sniffles cut off as she scowls. "I bet they didn't pull that crap on Suhani Das or the werewolf twins or any of those hotshot wizards or vampires."

"That's not fair," I say, as I white knuckle my wand.

"Colt Cohen said it was part of the suspense or whatever. I'm so embarrassed. I might as well have barfed brains all over the stage." Mariana returns to sniffling.

I wish I could say something to make her feel better, but I'm too outraged. Cheap tricks aren't what *Spellcaster* is about. They're taking the Season 13 theme too literally.

"Well, if they did that to you, they're definitely going to do the same to me," I huff.

Mariana swallows and lowers the hand towel. "That's why I called. At least I can give you a heads-up. We can't let them get away with taking our species out of the running."

"No," I say absently, as my mind wanders into a wasteland of hurt and betrayal. I thought Colt and Alexander genuinely wanted me to compete on the show. Did they really go through all that trouble of recruiting me only to set me up for failure? To make a mockery of me? I grind my teeth. "I was looking forward to being roommates."

"Me too," Mariana says. "We can still go out to dinner tonight. You shouldn't have to celebrate alone."

"I might not be celebrating at all," I mutter while looking around the auditorium. Why does everyone else look so confident?

"Yes, you will! You have to—for all our kind." Mariana's conviction draws my attention back to my phone. Her face makeup is smeared, but she looks dead serious at the moment. "Promise me you'll get on the show." I look into the screen and promise Mariana. "And let me know as soon as you've finished your audition."

"I will," I promise. Right after I call Cameron. After we say our goodbyes, I open a new text to Cam, only to close it and pocket my phone. I need to mentally prep.

What if they play heavy metal or country for my performance instead of "Celestial" by Ed Sheeran? I'll just have to tune it out and sing the song in my head. I pace the auditorium, running the lyrics on repeat through my brain. Having a different soundtrack would totally take away from the beauty of my performance, but I guess that's not what the producers want this season. They want a carnival of creatures. A freak show. Magical warfare between species. It sucks! I'll just have to rise above it all as best I can. Make my family proud, even though they're no longer around to see me.

The day wears on. It's late afternoon. Maybe I should be worrying more about getting any kind of audition than whether they switch out my soundtrack. What if the teams fill up and I get sent home without having a chance to ever compete?

At this rate, there will be nothing to celebrate at dinner. Mariana and I can sulk together.

"Avery—" The voice on the loudspeaker cuts out. Then the woman comes back on and announces, "Haylee Hutchins, please proceed to door A."

CHAPTER TWENTY-NINE

BEHIND DOOR A, there's a small open room with a camera and lights aimed at a teal sofa. Four large posters of the coaches hang from thick purple frames on the wall to the left of the sofa. There's a short hall that way with double doors stenciled with the word STAGE.

For a second, I swear I feel my heart beat again.

There are two young men, humans, in the room with me. One stays behind the camera. The other holds a clipboard and smiles at me.

"Hi, Haylee. How are you feeling?"

"Like I've been waiting in line for the world's tallest roller coaster all day, and now it's my turn to ride to the top before plummeting into a series of speeding curves, upside-downs, free falls, and spirals."

The guy with the clipboard chuckles. "This is an exciting moment."

"Try terrifying," I counter.

"You'll do fine."

Easy for him to say. He's not the one performing in front of four celebrity casters, a live audience, and cameras.

"Better than fine. Try amazing!" Alexander squeals as he strides in from a dark hall to the right. That vampire hearing of his must be nice.

"Alexander!" I cry.

He looks fabulous, of course, dressed in tight red denim jeans, a skinny black belt, and a long-sleeved black-and-red mesh top unbuttoned below his neck, showcasing his silver chain necklace. In a flash, he's air kissing my cheeks. "I had to come see you before you go on stage. Oh, and no pressure, but Brody only has one spot left on his team."

"Seriously?" My mouth hangs open a moment.

Alexander releases a dramatic huff. "I had to go find out what was taking so long for them to call you in for your audition. You can't receive a four-wand lift if the teams are full before you get your shot to perform. Someone dropped the ball, but I got it straightened out in time." He lifts a proud nose in the air.

"Uh, Alexander, we're running out of time," clipboard guy says.

"You do your thing, hon," Alexander tells him. To me he says, "See you on stage, girl." He zips away before I can answer.

"Haylee, please have a seat on the couch," clipboard guy says. As I walk to the couch, he adds, "Cool outfit. Are you wearing it for luck?"

"Every little bit helps," I say as I sit. Not that I believe in luck or wishing on stars. You have to fight to get what you want. I have to fight just to survive another day.

Once I'm settled, clipboard guy stands near camera guy.

"I'm going to ask you a few questions before you go on stage for your audition. Sound good?"

"I'm ready," I say.

"Great. Why don't you start by telling us who you want as your coach and why?"

"If I could choose any coach, it would be Malachi Rayne because I've been a mega fan of his since Season 1. Not only is he an incredible spellcaster, but he's got such cool style. It really sets him apart. It's refreshing to see a vampire break out of the mold. He's like his own species of awesome."

Way to go full-on fangirl. Am I saying this out loud? Are they going to air all of this for Malachi and the rest of the world to hear? Well, it's not like I haven't gushed about Malachi over the years on JingleJam. This is different, though, because he'll probably actually see this, but the words have already left my mouth.

"And you are performing with the same wand you used to save yourself during a zombie attack?"

"Yes." I look down at my wand clutched in my hand.

"What would winning the show mean to you?"

I've heard the same answer spoken over the years. It would mean the world. Again and again, contestants parrot those words. What does that even mean?

I stare into the camera, unblinking. "I want to win Season 13 to show all of the species and humanity that a zombie can wield a wand just as well, if not better, than any other caster. Maybe then we'll start being treated like equals with the compassion and respect we deserve."

Clipboard guy looks at camera guy, who gives him a thumbs-up.

"Okay, that was great. You can head to the stage doors now and wait. Someone will get you when it's time for you to go on for your performance. Good luck."

The coaches' eyes seem to follow me as I walk past their posters. Cleo Killian looks intense with black eyeliner and purple eyeshadow lining her eyes. Her silky brown hair is parted down the middle and pulled back tightly, showcasing tanned, glowing skin and pouty lips stained dark purple. Brody Morgan smiles at me with a boyish grin. His skin is a light shade of brown, and his thick hair is wavy on top of his head and trimmed and buzzed on the sides. He's wearing a tan hoodie with a tribal print over the top half. Zen Renko's thick hair is silvery white and gray with a beard and mustache to match. His voluminous locks end just below his ears. He looks dapper in an open blazer and gray suit vest. His blue, unflinching eyes are a reminder that he may be old and human, but there's a reason he's a coach on the show. And finally, there's Malachi Rayne in a slim-fit burnt-orange ribbed velvet turtleneck. A pentagram hangs from a long pendant around his neck, and his hair is midnight black.

It hits me again that I'm about to perform live in front of them all. This is not a drill. I repeat. This is not a drill.

After reaching the stage door, I stand, staring at it while squeezing my wand. All too soon, the door cracks open, and a woman with short black hair and a headset slips through holding a small clear tote with handles.

"Haylee Hutchins?" she asks in a low voice. I nod. "Please put your phone and anything else you don't want on stage with you inside the tote to collect after your performance."

I squeeze my phone for several seconds before placing it inside the tote.

After that, I'm led through the stage door. My feet become heavier with each step. I have a clear view of the stage from the side.

"Better luck next time, Mal." Brody's voice echoes through the theater's sound system followed by a single howl that is instantly answered by a chorus of howls beyond the stage.

As soon as the clamor dies down, Malachi says, "Yeah, well, the next one is mine."

"Why's that?" Brody challenges. "Are your Spidey senses telling you a vampire is about to take the stage?"

"Maybe I'm sensing true power," Malachi says.

"Oh, so it's a witch back there," Cleo quips.

Brody's laughter fills the theater. "I don't care what kind of creature it is. If they impress me, I'm completing my team."

"We'll see about that," Malachi says.

I stand frozen. What made me think I could perform in front of these power legends?

My stage escort says "Ready" into her headset.

Wait. No! I am so not ready.

"Quiet on the set," an announcer's voice booms over the speakers. The lights dim, and the theater quiets.

"You're up." I barely register the woman's words. She looks from me to the stage.

I don't want to do this.

Yes, I do!

I can't.

I can!

It doesn't matter. I have to. The coaches and audience are waiting. It's the only option.

My feet tap against the surface of the stage with each step I take to the spotlight in the center. The light shimmers over the silver sequins on my pants, sending glittering light in my wake.

I only have seconds to look at the hazy, gray screen hanging directly in front of the coaches. The veil of anonymity works both ways. I can't make out their features, though I know where each one sits from watching the previous seasons.

Large cameras are trained on the stage from my side of the screen. There are more cameras on the other side aimed at the coaches to capture their reactions. As I settle onto my spot, I notice Max behind one of the cameras. Before I can give him a little wave, the music starts.

It startles me to hear the familiar Ed Sheeran track when I spent the last few hours anticipating a switch in songs.

The time for agonizing is over.

I swing my arm and cast softly, allowing the song's lyrics to fill the audience's ears. Shimmering stars appear above my head. Earth, as seen from space, forms beneath my feet with its swaths of green continents and blue oceans. Clouds form above my head. I send them billowing beyond the screen into the audience. Beyond the clouds, planets appear among the stars.

I stare into the clouds and reach out my free hand, using my wand to levitate from the stage as though invisible fingers are pulling me up. As always, I imagine Kendra tugging me beyond the clouds.

Gasps arise from the audience as I step onto Uranus before leaping onto Neptune.

This routine takes not only advanced skill but also concentration. Levitating on its own is an extraordinary feat of defying gravity. Casting lifelike illusions of space is astounding. Doing both at the same time is rarely attempted during a *Spellcaster* blind audition.

Some clichés have merit, and mine happens to be "Go big or go home."

A string of spells flow through my lips as though my throat is a spigot that's been turned wide open. Jumping from planet to planet is challenging when I'm not touching anything solid from which to propel. I use my wand to give me a lift from Neptune to the rings of Saturn. I lift my feet to make it appear that I am strolling along the glowing rings before stepping onto

Jupiter. Gravity works in my favor when I drop off the solar system's largest planet onto Mars.

I'm falling too fast. I belt out the next spell and stop myself in the nick of time before my body has the chance to slip through Mars and crash to the stage. With one final leap, I land back to Earth. Back to the stage and solid ground. I arch my wand over my head, and a comet flares into view, streaking across my head and then into the audience.

Usually, contestants wait until later into the show before casting into the audience, but like I said, I went all out planning, practicing, and perfecting this routine.

The music ends. My stars wink out. Planets fade. The Earth and clouds dissipate.

Thunderous applause echoes through the theater. It quakes below my feet. It's like seismic heartbeats, reverberating through my chest. All four coaches are standing with their wands lifted high above their heads. I didn't dare look their way during the performance—even the slightest distraction would have been too risky. I wonder who raised their wand first.

A tear streaks down my face. I tilt my head back and stare into the space where my universe burned bright seconds before and whisper, "We did it, Kendra."

The screen lifts, revealing the coaches and crowd beyond. All four coaches are still standing. Seeing them face-to-face is surreal, especially when I see Malachi wearing a white sweater covered in silver stars. Holy crap! We match! The stars literally feel aligned in that moment.

The cheers from the audience die off. The clapping stops. The coaches gape at me like I'm a five-headed hydra from another planet.

Cleo flops onto her high-backed purple chair with a huff of annoyance. The guys lower themselves into their chairs, wincing like someone has stuck nails on their seats.

Whispers of "zombie" rush through the audience.

Colt Cohen hurries onto stage holding a cordless microphone. "What an amazing performance by Haylee Hutchins!" Excitement fills his voice and echoes through the speakers.

I wish his big smile could make up for the coaches' grimaces, but it doesn't begin to settle the nerves that feel as though they've been yanked out like strands of hair.

Colt reaches my side and puts his arm around me, hugging me against his towering frame. Malachi and Brody exchange a puzzled look as Cleo narrows her eyes on Colt and Zen scratches his beard. Colt releases me and beams into the theater.

"A four-wand lift—and no wonder. I can't remember an audition that impressive from any previous seasons. What do you think, Brody?"

"I, uh. Yeah, that was certainly out of this world." Brody chuckles soflty. He doesn't look at me. He stares at Colt.

"What made you lift your wand for Haylee?" Colt urges.

Brody glances down the line of purple chairs at his fellow coaches. "Well, we all did," he says.

Colt's sigh is so low I wonder if I'm the only one who hears him. "Malachi?"

After years of loyally fangirling the vampire, it crushes me to watch the way Malachi's eyebrows pull in and nose wrinkles. His hair is dyed all black this season, like a crow coming to pick at bones. He studies me as though I am carrion before answering, "I've never seen anything like this before."

Cleo snorts from her chair beside him. "No, we certainly have not seen anything like *this*." Dark eyes flick my way when she says *"this."* She turns to face Malachi. "You should take her, Mal. You're already wearing matching shirts."

"You lifted your wand first," Malachi counters.

"He's right, you did," Brody says, in a rare show of solidarity with his on-air nemesis.

Cleo turns a withering glare Brody's way. "And might I remind you that you said you planned to complete your team if this performance impressed you, no matter what the creature. Are you all bark, wolf man?"

"I know the rest of you need help filling your teams. Trying to be helpful here," Brody says quickly. He shrugs and picks at his nails.

Zen glowers like he's a put-out grandpa forced to listen as his grandkids bicker. He taps his long fingers against his armrest before lifting his wrist to look at his watch.

My tears of elation vaporize as though the planets I conjured for my performance are now burning inside my eyes. Sweat drips down my sides, and my wand shakes in my fist.

How dare they? I gave the performance of a lifetime, and now no one wants me. Well, it's too damn late. They all lifted their wands. The only question is, which of these A-holes am I going to pick as my coach?

Malachi Rayne is dead to me. Both he and Brody Morgan can bite me. Cleo Killian is being a Grade A Moluccan cockatoo. That leaves only one coach.

I turn to Colt and reach my hand out for the microphone. At least when the werewolf frowns, it's at the coaches. When Colt notices what I want, his forehead wrinkles.

"Haylee, have you decided on a coach?"

I nod and take the microphone from him. "I choose Team Zen."

I don't bother looking at my chosen coach as I return the mic to Colt. The woman who escorted me in waits offstage, on the opposite side from where I entered. She's holding the tote with my phone. As I move toward her, I feel an urge to flip off the coaches as I walk across the stage, but I manage to maintain my composure, head held high.

I've barely made it behind the black curtain when I hear Cleo chuckle into her clip-on mic. "Well, if she bites Zen, we'll become an all-supernatural panel of judges."

CHAPTER THIRTY

BACK IN MY hotel suite, I see a missed call and text from Alexander.

Alexander: Girl! You were PHENOMENAL! 4-wand lift! I knew it! Zen is one lucky old man. Malachi blew his chance at winning Season 13. So did Brody. I can't even look at either of those two after they were such brutes when the screen pulled away. Cleo's always been a catty witch, but the boys let me down. They should have been on their hands and knees BEGGING you to join their team.

I'm not ready to respond. Cameron's waiting to hear from me, so I text him.

Haylee: 4-wand lift.

My phone rings several seconds later with his name appearing on my screen. I don't feel like talking, but I have to. At least he's not screeching with excitement.

"You did it. I knew you would," Cam says matter-of-factly. "I take it you went with Team Malachi."

"No, actually. I decided to go human."

"Is that Haylee?" Joni yells in the background. "Did she audition?"

Cameron's voice is muffled as he answers her, like he's lowered his phone. "Yeah. Four-wand lift. Team Zen."

"Did you say Team Zen?" Joni asks in surprise.

"Give me a moment to speak to Haylee."

"Oh, right. Of course! Sorry."

"Hey, it's okay. I just need a moment, and then I'll hand Haylee over to you," Cam says sweetly.

My stomach tightens. He would have made the absolute best dad. He and my sister would have been the dream parents. And I would have been the fun aunt.

No. Stop. I tell my brain. I can't let myself go there. Those thoughts only bring pain and despair, and I already have plenty of turds on my plate.

It's quiet for several seconds. I imagine Cameron moving to his room. His voice is low when he says, "Tell me what happened."

With Cameron, I don't have to sugarcoat anything. I tell him everything, and when I'm finished, he says, "They're a bunch of dicks. You were right to choose Team Zen."

I swallow. "You think so?"

For so long, I dreamed of what it would be like to learn magic from Malachi Rayne. He did lift his wand for me. Have I passed up the opportunity of a lifetime? Then I remember how he didn't offer a glowing performance review or fight for me to be on his team, as is custom during auditions. No. He did the opposite. He argued for another coach to take me on their team rather than be on his.

At least Cameron is reassuring when he says, "From what you told me, Zen was the only coach who didn't make a complete ass of himself. That makes him your best option."

I flop down on the king-size hotel bed, lying on my back, head pressed against the covers. I'm zipped up in my purple jacket like Kendra's gift has the power to cocoon me from all of life's hurt and disappointments. If only it had that power.

"It's just going to be so humiliating when the auditions air on TV, and everyone sees the way the coaches treated me like some kind of wand-wielding freak of nature."

"Listen to me. They're the ones who are going to look like fools," Cameron says sternly. "*Spellcaster* is supposed to be about the magic, and without a doubt, you gave the greatest performance those assholes have ever had the privilege of witnessing on that stage. They're going to lose respect with the fans when their pitiful reactions are televised."

I doubt that, but it does make me feel better hearing Cam say so.

"Are you up for talking to Joni?" Cameron asks. "She's been on pins and needles all day waiting to hear how it went."

I sit up on the bed. "Yeah, of course."

"And hey, congratulations. Don't let those assholes ruin your victory."

"Thanks, Cam. Thanks for everything."

"Don't thank me. That was all you."

"Yeah, but still."

He's quiet a moment before saying, "Anytime."

I blink back tears before they can enter my voice while Cam takes his phone to Joni. I didn't realize zombies were so weepy. I don't think it's being undead, though. It's having lost loved ones and carrying that grief inside of me forever. It's knowing that this isn't just a rough patch or a bump in the road. This is my life.

Everything goes back to normal after I return home from my audition. Which is weird.

I got a four-wand lift! I made it onto *Spellcaster* Season 13!

And yet, I'm back to scrubbing down tables, appliances, and walls at Raw Tasty's. Not that I'm complaining or think I'm suddenly above working the job. But I feel like I should be freaking out with my friends over my upcoming appearance on the show. I'm only allowed to tell immediate family I made it on at this point.

I wonder if Payton and Ellie will be sorry when they see me on TV. Or maybe they'll be as scornful as the judges. I bet their remarks will make Caleb happy.

I can't think about that.

Brock walks back with heavy steps and a frown beneath his beard. "Haylee, your uncle is here to see you. He's up front."

I set down my rag and rub my forehead with my arm before peeling off my gloves. What is TJ doing here? My shift isn't over for another hour. A shiver runs through me. What if something happened to Joni or Cameron? My body goes rigid.

"Is everything okay?" I'd rather hear bad news from Brock first.

But my boss shakes his head and folds his arms. "I don't know. He's waiting."

I've never seen Brock so stiff. After he shuts himself inside his office, leaving me alone to face TJ, I pull my wand out of my purse just in case. Except it's not TJ waiting on the narrow strip of linoleum that makes up the front of the closed butcher shop. It's Alvan. He's dressed in a tailored suit and has his hair slicked back. It's the first time I've seen him since he gave up his humanity.

"Uncle Al, what are you doing here?" I ask, forcing blandness into my tone. I'm not sure if I should join him or keep the counter between us. The case is empty. The meat that didn't sell today has been returned to the fridge in back. I remain behind the counter and clutch my wand as I fold my arms.

Alvan looks me up and down with an air of detachment. "We need to talk."

"You could have called."

"What I have to say isn't safe to voice over the phone."

I lift my brow. "And what's that?"

"I know you went looking for your dad's old case files. You have to stop poking around."

"Why?" My voice rises in anger.

Alvan's eyes flash. "Because it's not safe!" he belts out, matching my ire with his own. "I told you I'd get to the bottom of things, and that's what I'm doing, but when you show up at Laurence's old office building asking questions, it jeopardizes my investigation and puts us all at risk." He glowers over the counter at me.

Alvan looks and sounds more annoyed than scared, but maybe vampires are incapable of fear. This one seems to have lost the ability to apologize for being an asshole uncle. Even if he really is helping find my family's true killers, that doesn't change the fact that he abandoned me and Joni when we needed him most.

My arms remain twisted across my torso like I'm a tightly woven pretzel.

"So? What have you learned so far in your quest for the truth?" I challenge.

Alvan narrows his eyes. "That your father pissed off a lot of powerful beings."

I unfold my arms, set them on the counter, and slouch forward. "Oh, gosh. Really? I thought lawyers were supposed to make everyone feel like they'd won the lottery."

"No one forced him to go after a vampire master," Alvan fires back. He rubs his eyebrow as though to ward off a headache. Good. I hope it pounds at his skull like brass knuckles. He's forgotten that he's dealing with a teenage girl.

I scoff. "Poor, defenseless master vamp. They should all be allowed to do whatever they want without consequences."

Alvan's face turns red. "Vampires are saving the planet."

"Oh, please. Everything they do is for their own benefit." I roll my wand back and forth over the counter with my index finger.

Alvan's fingers curl into fists. "That's not—" He starts toward me, then stops and blinks. His eyes flick to the gold and onyx cuff links adorning his sleeves. He lifts his head, jaw and shoulders relaxed. "I didn't come here to argue with you, Haylee. You're still my niece, and I will do everything in my power to protect you—even if that means protecting you from yourself." He pulls a phone from the front pocket of his slacks and taps across it quickly. "TJ gave me the direct number to your new phone. I just texted you mine." He slips his phone back into his pocket and then stares at me expectantly.

My phone's not on me. It's in my purse hanging from a hook in back. I'm not about to run off and fetch it for his benefit.

I snatch up my wand and push up from the counter. "Is that all?"

"I guess so," Alvan says, like I'm the one letting *him* down. "You have my number. I'm trusting you not to call or text about anything pertaining to the murders. All I'm asking for is that you trust me in return. I will find out who is responsible for my sisters', Kendra's, and Laurence's deaths and make them pay. We will have vengeance, Haylee."

"And you'll let me know when that happens?" I prod.

"You will be the first to know." Alvan offers me a smug smile and stares into my eyes. His are gleaming. He thinks he has me convinced. Adults are so clueless. I don't trust vampires, and I don't trust him. Maybe he means what he says, but I have no way of knowing for sure, and that's not something I'm willing to accept.

For now, I nod my head. "Okay. Thanks for stopping by. I'd invite you over for dinner, but I'm afraid we're all out of caviar and champagne. Give us a heads-up next time so that we can have fresh truffles flown over from France."

Alvan's sigh blows the smile off his lips. "It's fine. I have a flight back home in a couple of hours."

In and out. What a kind and caring uncle Joni and I got left with.

After Uncle Alvan takes his leave, I lock the front door behind him, tuck my wand back inside my purse, knock on Brock's office door, let myself in, and apologize for the interruption.

"I'll stay longer," I offer.

Brock clasps his thick hands and rests them over his desk. "Haylee, the kitchen is already spotless. I'm happy to have your help for however long I can before you go off and become a big spellcasting superstar."

Right, so I let Brock know I made it on the show. He can keep a secret.

I give him a half-laugh. "I don't know about superstar."

"Well, you have my vote."

"Thanks, boss," I say with a smile. Then I get back to work, giving the appliances and countertops an extra rubdown while my mind turns over everything Uncle Alvan said like each word is a rock with bugs skittering underneath.

I still can't believe he showed up out of the blue.

"Maybe he really does want revenge," I say to Cameron on the drive home from my shift.

"He should," Cam answers.

I nod. "He's the one with the connections and resources."

"I still want to talk to Laurence's former paralegal," Cameron says.

"Yeah, just be careful."

"I will." It sounds like an automatic response, which worries me because humans are fragile, and he's one of two left in my life whom I care about.

At least I'm busy. When I'm not working, I'm practicing from advanced spellbooks and creating spells of my own, which I jot down in a blank spell journal I got at Mystic Wand Haven. I still have the use of the empty auditorium at Joni's elementary school. It helps to practice using a similar space to what I'll have on the *Spellcaster* stage. I think Joni's teacher, Miss Elms, has a crush on Cameron, which helps too. She says it's "thrilling" to have a *Spellcaster* contestant practicing in Harmony Hills's auditorium even though it's still hush-hush. It sorta went to her head that we let her in on the secret, but it's worth it for the private use of the school's space.

"Butterflies" by Kacey Musgraves fills the auditorium Saturday morning as I conjure a rainbow with my wand, walk through the colorful arch, and then spin and spin while setting off an illusion of butterflies detaching from my body, fluttering high into the air. The effect is going to look amazing with the orange dress I'll wear with a full skirt and tulle beneath. Who doesn't love rainbows and butterflies? My winged creations flit into the bleachers, as they will in the *Spellcaster* auditorium.

Cameron's chest puffs out as he watches every magical moment as though he's an NFL coach helping his star player win the Super Bowl. Miss Elms is too busy sneaking glances his way to appreciate my casting. She rubs her lips together and smooths out her floral skirt.

I continue spinning like an Olympic figure skater until I reach the tape we put down to mark the edge of the stage. There, I stop and cast another illusion spell. Large orange, black, and white spotted wings unfold at my sides.

"*Lifteena. Buoy tri air hover sif ascond.*" I levitate from the gymnasium floor. The swarm returns from the bleachers to join me. A field of wildflowers erupts into bloom below my feet. My wings flutter as I drift into them and crouch on my knees within the colorful petals. The regular-sized butterflies swarm me, piling on until they dissolve into my skirt. I lift to my feet and back up until I am standing in the center of my rainbow arch. I lift my wand and cast, "*Expellis, ealah, ealah, veed.*"

The rainbow explodes into a mass of butterflies in every color. I swing my wand arm toward the bleachers, and they flutter away before disappearing as the music ends.

Cameron is on his feet applauding as the last note fades. Staring at him, Miss Elms gets up and does the same.

"Beautiful," Cameron calls over the clapping. "Perfection."

I grin, feeling as though my butterflies have returned once more—swarming my stomach this time. Aside from my audition, this will be my last chance to plan my own routine for the season's opening performances. After earning a spot on the show, a confidential email was sent to all contestants informing us that *Spellcaster* would kick off Season 13 with their usual "cast-off" eliminations. It's like a dance-off for casters. Coaches pair their team members to go up against one another in the televised cast-off in a battle to keep their spot on their coach's team and the show.

I need to ensure Zen picks me over the caster he pairs me against. I have to get my routine perfect. My performance has to be phenomenal. I can't expect a fair fight after the coaches' reactions. Zen Renko didn't outright dismiss me, so I have no idea what to expect from him, but hopefully it will help that I no longer have exposed bones that scream ZOMBIE CHICK!

I smile gratefully at my enthused audience of two. "Thanks. And thank you, Miss Elms, for allowing me the space for practice." Even though it's more likely for Cameron, I'm still thankful.

The pretty young teacher is fawning over the wrong guy, but at least the smile she flashes me is genuine.

"You have an amazing talent, Haylee," she says in her encouraging teacher's voice. "I'm looking forward to watching your performance on the show."

My stomach tightens, crushing the butterflies into a mass of broken wings that continue to twitch and cause my arms to jerk. "Hopefully, I won't mess up." I grimace.

"You'll be great," Cameron says.

Miss Elms nods. "We should have a viewing party at my house." Her gaze slides over to Cameron, but he's pulled out his phone and is frowning at the screen.

"Where is he?"

"He who?" I ask suspiciously.

Cameron's still staring at his phone. His jaw relaxes right before he stuffs the phone in his back pocket. "Daniel just parked and is heading in."

I fold my arms over my chest. "Who is Daniel?"

"Your new magical combat instructor," Cameron announces, as he steps down from the bleachers and eyes the wide double doors. He smiles as a lanky young guy in square-shaped glasses walks in with a small duffel bag slung over his shoulder.

"Are you Cameron?" the guy—Daniel—calls across the gymnasium.

"Yep." Cam waves him over. "And this is my sister-in-law, Haylee."

Miss Elms frowns.

While Daniel crosses the gym, I close in on Cameron and hiss, "What is this?"

Cameron jerks his chin up. "Whatever this combat crap is for Season 13, we're going to make sure you're ready to take down any of the contestants they pair you with."

My mouth hangs open in silent protest. This is not the type of magic I'm interested in. But therein lies the problem. I don't have a choice.

When Daniel reaches us, he pushes his glasses up by the bridge. "Hey, nice to meet you, Haylee. Congratulations on making it onto *Spellcaster*."

"Um, thanks." I look the guy over. He's all limbs and no muscle. He doesn't look like he should be teaching any type of combat.

Daniel slides his duffel off his shoulder onto the lowest bleacher bench, unzips his bag, and extracts a file folder and pen. Returning to Cameron, he slips out a piece of paper covered in typed text, sets it on top of the file, and hands it to him.

"I'll just need you to read and sign this waiver before we begin." He clicks open the pen and hands it to Cameron.

I press against Cam's arm and lean forward, reading snippets about how Daniel isn't liable if I get hurt during training. Well, that's reassuring.

Cameron takes his time reading the waiver. After what must be at least the fifth read-through, he lowers the waiver and pierces Daniel with irises that look like jagged glaciers. Maybe I'll be dodging a magical bullet.

"I want Haylee to learn combative spellcasting, but I don't want you to hurt her," Cameron all but growls.

"That's not the intention," Daniel answers calmly. "This waiver is just a precaution. Until now, all my students have been humans—none of whom have ever been seriously harmed. They're more likely to hurt themselves using their wands incorrectly." He pushes his glasses up the bridge of his nose and taps his finger on the waiver. "As you see here, Haylee can ask me to stop at any time, and I will halt our session."

Daniel looks over at me and asks, "Are you comfortable with that, Haylee?"

"Yeah," I say, because what choice do I have? I won't be able to ask my opponent to stop on the stage. Until then, I'd better learn what I can while I have the option to call a ceasefire.

Cameron presses the tip of the pen to the signature line at the bottom of the waiver. Before signing, he says, "Just remember that Haylee isn't some rag doll to zap with your wand. She has feelings, understand?"

"Cam, I'll be fine." Oh my god, this is getting embarrassing.

"Understood. Now should we get started?" Daniel asks, not sounding intimidated by Cameron in the least. With that kind of confidence, maybe he is good at combat casting. I know better than to judge people based on their appearance, but I still can't help myself.

"I'm ready," I say quickly, before Cameron can grill him more, even though he's the one who called in the wand nerd. The more I look at Daniel, the less nervous I feel.

"Great, I'll get my wand." Daniel takes the paperwork and pen from Cameron and heads to his duffel.

Miss Elms closes in on Cameron and touches his arm. "I love how protective you are of the girls," she gushes.

I turn my back to hide my scowl at being lumped in with Joni, who actually is still a little girl. Usually, my cousin accompanies us to practice, but today she has a cold and is stuck at home with TJ. I miss seeing her face light up as I practice my routine. She's also a great buffer between Miss Elms and Cameron. I'm afraid Miss Elms is going to ask Cameron out and that after he rejects her, she won't be so keen to arrange my practice space. She knows he's not my actual brother-in-law. That he never got the chance to marry my sister. That he's single.

I squeeze my wand, which always gives me a sense of security.

Daniel returns with a wand that's short and simple. He stands around seven feet away, facing me. "*Recisocation veed*!" The spell strikes lightning quick, nearly ripping my wand from my fingers. It would have, if I hadn't already been gripping it so tightly. "Impressive," Daniel says. "You're my first student who managed to hold on to her wand when I started with a surprise disarming spell. "Very good."

Miss Elms is seated back in the bleachers, but Cameron stands in front of the stadium seating with his arms folded, ready to run in at a moment's notice.

Daniel holds up his wand. "Now, you try it on me."

I know it's fruitless. He's expecting it, plus he's supposedly great at this whole magical combat thing, but I try anyway, because he's the instructor. So, whatever.

I point my wand at his and cast, "*Recisocation veed.*"

As expected, nothing happens. Daniel's arm doesn't so much as jerk. Frowning, he says, "Try harder."

I sigh inwardly. Guess that first impression I made is fading into a less impressive category.

"*Recisocation veed!*" I shout. Again, Daniel's arm remains still. "*Recisocation veed!*" I shout louder, and then I scream it at the top of my lungs.

Daniel shakes his head, pushes his glasses up his nose, and lowers his wand. "Your spell is getting weaker each time you cast. You're putting too much intention into the volume of your voice and not enough into the spell."

"Ugh," I groan.

"Concentrate on your intention. You should be able to whisper the spell and still make it work." Daniel demonstrates, and dang it, I'm so distracted by my inefficiency that the scrawny caster manages to flick my wand right out of my fingers and send it flying across the auditorium.

Cameron's sneakers squeak over the glossy floor as he jogs to retrieve my wayward wand and return it to me.

"Thanks," I say with a pout.

At least Daniel doesn't gloat. He pushes up his glasses, all business. "We'll move on to blocking spells for now, but you're going to want to practice casting disarmaments before our next session."

"Okay," I say. I spend the remainder of our hour taking Daniel way more seriously—and trying to keep up.

At the end of our session, I'm sweating like we just used the auditorium to play sports. Daniel packs up his duffel bag and then slinks off. Cameron's standing in front of the bleachers, avoiding eye contact with Miss Elms.

"Tell Joni I hope she feels better soon," she says. "I'm going to miss having her in my class this fall. Are you sure you don't want me to bring over some homemade soup?"

"We've got it covered. Thanks," Cameron says, still not looking at her. "Ready, Haylee?" he asks, glancing from me to the doors leading out to the parking lot.

Yeah, I'm just as ready as he is to run from Miss Elms's sad attempts to reel him in. I am not, however, ready for combat. Not even a little. If I can't hold my own against a lanky human, how am I supposed to fight off a vampire, werewolf, wizard, or whatever Zen pits me against?

CHAPTER THIRTY-ONE

MY NEXT FLIGHT to LA is in economy class—and it's the red-eye. There's no driver waiting to pick me up and no hotel suite. I received an email with instructions, including my roommate assignment at the Solace Hotel, where all contestants are staying whenever we come into town to perform on the show.

I take an Uber to the hotel, where I have just under an hour to stash my luggage in my room and meet my roommate. The email included her name (Blair Monroe), species (witch), and the team she's on (Team Cleo).

Well, at least I don't have to worry about getting into a biting match with a werewolf or a vampire.

After checking in and getting my keycard at the front desk, I ride the elevator to the eighth floor and find my room for the next five days. I could have checked in yesterday afternoon, but I chose to spend one more night at home. It's not like I have to worry about lack of sleep the way a witch or werewolf does.

I knock on door 809 before slipping in my keycard and walking in. The curtains are drawn, making the room appear as inviting as a dark cavern. There's a smoky, lingering scent of burning sage.

I don't get the sense that anyone's here, but I call out, "Hello?" all the same while feeling around for a light switch. Both beds are empty and made up, but the one closest to the door has a midnight-blue throw blanket in the center with protective rune symbols stitched into the fabric in silver thread. Tiny figures carved out of gemstones take up space on the nightstand, including an obsidian owl facing my side of the room.

Right, well, this isn't friendship camp, so whatever. Blair's probably having breakfast with the other witches and wizards before heading over to the *Spellcaster* studio, where the lucky spellcasters who made it through blinds have been instructed to arrive no later than 10:00 a.m.

I shoot Mariana a quick "Wish you were here" text. She's been so sweet to send me encouraging messages, gifs, and emojis leading up to the competition. I've promised to keep her up to date behind the scenes. The roommate report will have to wait.

I don't mind having the bathroom to myself as I freshen up my makeup and hair. I'm dressed in a floral, bohemian blouse with long, puffy sleeves over blue jeans. My hair is pulled back softly from my face and gathered in a loose bun near the top of my head. Brown liner and mascara make my gray-blue eyes pop. My cheeks have a bronzed, sun-kissed glow, and I've used a natural shade of pink lipstick that gives them an attractive blush. Large hoop earrings practically touch my shoulders. The gold tone matches my round "H" pendant hanging over the loose blouse.

With my new figure, I could dress in a miniskirt and crop top, but in my head, I'm still two-hundred-twenty pounds. Besides, miniskirts and crop tops aren't my style, and I'm in love with the new top I'm wearing now. It has an apricot, ivory, and light pink floral print over green and feels light and breezy against my skin. I don't need to dress up until I perform in front of the cameras, but that doesn't mean I don't plan on looking cute during coaching.

Today, we've been told we'll be paired up with another teammate by our coaches, who will then help us with our routines before we perform on stage in front of the cameras and studio audience. Speaking of which, it's time to hustle over for an exciting first day on *Spellcaster*.

It feels surreal entering the theater as a Season 13 contestant.

A female vampire wearing a headset over her smooth black shoulder-length hair approaches me with a clipboard and checks off my name. She's flanked by two buff werewolves. "We will be addressing all contestants in the auditorium shortly. You may go find a seat there now." She flicks a finger in a general direction I don't quite follow.

Guess I'll be showing myself in.

My stomach feels like a tunnel that echoes with each footstep. It's a relief when I notice two familiar faces walking in ahead. It's the werewolf twins, Jake and Cody. The one with the crew cut yanks out his brother's hair tie and slips it around his wrist. His brother shakes his loose hair from side to side, laughing.

I hurry to catch up as they step through a set of propped-open doors.

"You should keep that around your wrist until your hair grows back long enough to use it."

"Maybe I'll keep the crew—makes me look more manly." I remember Mariana's sister telling me that the twin who burned off his hair was Jake.

"You wish," Cody ribs.

"So do you."

They shove each other as they enter the auditorium housing the *Spellcaster* stage with its stadium seating. When I see the stage from this angle, my head turns fuzzy with wonder and disbelief, like this is all a dream. The theater lights are on, but the coaches' chairs and the stage are dark. I squeeze my brown leather clutch against my thigh. It's just large enough to stash my phone, wand, wallet, and a few beauty items in case I need any emergency touch-ups. It's not Alexander's mega kit, but it's enough to work with until we get our own makeup crew for performance days.

Jake's and Cody's voices boom and echo in the quiet theater. Contestants turn in their seats near the stage to see who is making the ruckus. My stomach hollows out as their hostile gazes find me trailing in behind the twins. So much for a stealthy entrance. The only attention I want is awe and rapture from the judges and audience when I'm on stage. Behind the scenes I just want to be left the hell alone.

"Raise your hand if you're Team Brody," Jake hollers.

Several hands lift. I recognize some of the contestants from audition day, including Tripp Peters and petite, pink-haired Izzie King. There's also Daphné the cat-loving werewolf, whose blue highlights are tucked into a low messy bun that shows off several hoop earrings along her ear and multiple piercings in her lobes, but she doesn't raise her hand. A guy sitting beside her waves the twins over. "Sit over here."

The twins bound toward them while I slow my steps, feet dragging as I scan the seating situation.

"You didn't raise your hands. Are you not on Team Brody?" Cody asks a couple of the werewolves in his loud voice.

"I'm Team Zen," Daphné says with a shrug.

That makes her not only my teammate, but potential competition if Zen pairs us during cast-offs.

The male beside Daphné grimaces. "Unfortunately, Brody didn't raise his wand for me. I'm on Team Cleo."

A witch in a short-sleeved black V-neck stands up. She's got thick brown bangs that cover her eyebrows. The rest of her hair is twisted and secured in a hair claw. A long, beaded tassel necklace hangs past the opening in her shirt, where shorter necklaces are layered. Tassel earrings dangle from her lobes and multiple corded and beaded bracelets circle both of her wrists.

She glares over at the group of wolves. "You're lucky to be coached by the best."

"You wish," a female voice mocks.

"Who said that?" the witch demands.

"I did."

The witch squints and scans the surrounding contestants. A slender, pale arm lifts lazily before descending. Carolina Bellmore sighs audibly. "I forgot how inferior a witch's eyesight is."

The vampires seated around her chuckle.

The witch's eyes flare like a camera flashing as it captures an image in the dark. She lifts her beaded wrists, palms facing up, and moves her lips in a silent chant. Her tasseled earrings sway.

"Blair, save it for combat," says a wizard with thick curly hair. I recognize him as one of the swaggering males from audition day.

Blair? Great. I should have known I'd get a Moluccan cockatoo for a roommate.

Blair pouts but listens to Mr. Hot Shot Wizard. What was his name? I think back to the names called over the loudspeaker while I waited to perform. Dominic Monroe. That's the one. With the same last name, he and Blair must be related, but not a duo act since he got called in alone.

The ornery witch sits back down. I notice the blond head of Zane Barrett several seats away from her. He slouches against his chair as though he's one of the coaches on a high-backed purple throne.

Cody and Jake are in a group seated closest to where I hover, unsure of where to sit. It's become clear that contestants are forming cliques by species. Oh, goodie. I inch along the rows of seats and sit in an empty aisle. Zombie, party of one. Boy, do I wish Mariana had made it on the show.

I've barely settled when the wolves howl, startling me in my seat. They're using their beastly vocals to fill the auditorium. It makes the hair rise on my arms.

Blair jumps up again. "Will you cut that out?" she yells.

The wolves' chorus mellows.

"Just testing out the acoustics," Jake says, with a snicker the other wolves share.

At least the other species are too busy glaring at one another to spare me a second glance. Maybe they'll take each other out, and I'll be the last zombie standing.

But I'm not the only contestant to isolate herself from the cliques.

Suhani Das sits front and center on her own. Her dark, silky hair is pulled over her shoulder. All I see is the back of her head because she never turns around—just maintains forward focus on the darkened stage in front of her.

Although I haven't seen her perform yet, from what Amora told me, Suhani is my biggest competition.

More contestants arrive and sit with their species. I notice several male werewolves and vampires walk by with their wands stuffed in their back jean pockets like it's a drum stick rather than a prized object of power. They've got privilege written all over them.

A low growl accompanies the hard brown eyes of a werewolf who passes me. I wish it didn't make me feel like breaking out into a cold sweat. Werewolves are pack animals. Being around so many at once makes me think of Z Squad and dismembered body parts.

I've barely had time to shove down a panic attack when a silky male voice drawls, "Well, what do we have here?"

His face is symmetrical perfection with a medium-toned complexion, full lips—also well-shaped—a slight dimple in his chin, luscious dark eyebrows, and thick black hair. But the vampire's gray eyes are lifeless.

I instantly recognize him for what he is—another Caleb, only in prettier packaging. Well, I have plenty of practice dealing with the Calebs of the world.

Squaring my shoulders and lifting my chest, I stare right into the vampire's deadened eyes and muster up more courage than I feel. "You're looking at the upcoming winner of Season 13. Maybe you should ask for an autograph while you still have the chance."

His jaw slackens, and he stands there looking dumbstruck that he just got sassed by a zombie.

The wolves burst into laughter.

"Oh, slam. Vampy just got dissed by a zombie," one of them says. This sets the wolves off into a fresh wave of hilarity.

The male hisses as his fangs descend.

Well, that's not good. I jump to my feet, wand at the ready, extremely grateful in this moment for Daniel's training. Didn't think I'd need it until the combat rounds, but here we are.

"Fight! Fight! Fight!" the wolves chant.

The vampire's full lips frown. I can practically read his thoughts. He doesn't want to do as the wolves command, but he also wants to save face.

I clutch my wand. I'm not about to get kicked off the show for attacking a vampire, but if he makes the first move, no one can blame me for defending myself.

Those bitter gray eyes stare at my wand. He reaches around to his back pocket—another douchebag who keeps his wand stuffed where he might accidentally forget and break it in half when he sits. Not that Lignum Vitae is prone to breakage, but still, a wand should be handled with respect.

As soon as the vampire's wand appears from around his back, I strike.

"*Recisocation veed*!"

Not only does his wand fly out of his hand, but it zips over the stadium seats all the way to the dark stage, where it lands with a wooden clack.

Whoa. Guess I was a bit worked up. I'm not sure whether Daniel would be proud or lecture me for my lack of control when I'd only meant to knock it out of his hand and into the aisle maybe a few feet away.

The auditorium has gone deadly silent. The witches and wizards are all looking over at us with furrowed brows. Not only do they lack werewolf and vampire hearing, but their group is seated the farthest way, so they probably have no clue what led to this altercation.

Zane Barrett stands. Maybe the blond mega-hunk wants a better view. If I were still human, watching Season 13, I might have drooled a little over Zane, but he's likely another Caleb who wants to see me squirm. Only, whereas the vampire's eyes are abandoned wells filled with putrid water, Zane's are oceans brimming with life and curiosity. As he stares at me, his lips part slightly. It makes my stomach flutter against my will. When our eyes meet, I have to remind myself to breathe, then promptly chastise myself for forgetting for a split second that I'm undead. Also, I have an angry vampire seething in front of me and wolves who have gotten over their surprise and are once more laughing like hyenas.

"That was awesome!" Cody bellows.

His voice breaks the momentary spell of dazzling blue eyes, which is not literally a spell, but just as alarming. I tear my gaze from Zane's and point my wand at the vampire as he starts toward me. He moves slowly, like he's still unsure of what to do or, more likely, uncertain what he can get away with. If he wanted, he could already be on me with his vampire speed. Still, there's no mistaking the murderous intent in his eyes.

"Don't make me hurt you," I warn.

The wolves' laughter is deafening.

"*Le crétin sait même pas tenir sa baguette,*" Daphné says, pointing at the wandless vampire.

"Baguette?" Cody asks.

"It means wand in French," Daphné supplies.

"Then maybe you should go back to France," the vampire snarls.

Daphné lifts her nose and narrows her eyes. "I'm from Quebec."

A deadly looking African American shifter covered in tattoos cracks his knuckles and says in a threatening voice, "You better watch how you speak to my friends, fanger."

A piercing whistle makes all of us wince and brings silence to the auditorium. "Settle down," the booming voice of an adult werewolf calls from the back of the stadium seats where we all first came in.

I glance up that way to see the female vampire and the two werewolves making their way down.

While there's still distance between them and the contestants, Carolina Bellmore addresses the vampire sending me the death threats with his stormy eyes. "Don't listen to those fleabags or the flesh eater. Her brain is as rotted as the rest of her." Carolina and the rest of her minions laugh cruelly.

Even without a heartbeat, my ears pound. I want to tell Carolina Bellmore that she's a blood-sucking parasite, but facing mean girls has always felt more hazardous than dealing with jerks. Plus, no one insults a member of Forever 23 without consequences.

A male vampire from Carolina's group stands and spells the lost wand from the stage to levitate and return to its dreadful owner. He strides toward it and snatches it from the air before joining the group of vampires without so much as a thank you to the vamp who retrieved his wand. But his species obviously gives him a free pass to behave like a prick and still be welcome in Club Undead. He drops into his seat so violently, a metal snapping sound follows. He gets back up and sits in the next chair over, which likely means he broke the first one with the mere force of his body. Wonderful. He looks over his shoulder and shoots me a glare filled with dark promises. Hopefully he gets eliminated during the cast-offs.

Surprisingly, Suhani looks over at the group of vampires with a narrowed, hateful gaze. From what Amora shared, she's not a vampire by choice. There are laws prohibiting turning a human against his or her will, but vampires have a number of ways of getting what they want. It could be something as callous as the promise of status, eternal youth, and wealth or as nefarious as a threat to family members. I wonder which category Suhani falls under.

Lights flood the stage. The vampire with the short dark hair stands in front of the stage and looks over us with a cool gaze. "My name is Jovi, and I am the show's director. This is Kurt and Dennis. They are supervising producers. We've got a lot of filming to do this week, so I'll get right to it. Congratulations on making it onto *Spellcaster*'s first all-supernatural magical competition. At the end of the week, half of you will be eliminated during cast-offs."

"Not me," someone says, which produces soft chuckles that abruptly cut off when Jovi glares.

"Each coach has one steal and one save, giving you an opportunity to remain in the competition if you do not win your first cast-off. In the past, the use of jetnite tattoos has been prohibited during any of the cast-offs, combats, or on-stage performances. Since we now have witches and wizards in the competition, that rule does not apply to Season 13. Your coaches have already paired you up for the cast-offs. They will be working with you two at a time. The first group to be coached is Team Zen. The rest of you need to gather your things and wait in the lobby until your team is called in for practice."

I remain in my seat as the other contestants leave the auditorium. After the long wait to be called to the stage for my blind audition, I expected the same today. Guess I was wrong. Team Z is up first.

CHAPTER THIRTY-TWO

ONE OF THE way-too-hot wizards stays behind while Zane and his crew vacate their seats. The guy's wearing a tight T-shirt that shows off his lean, muscular arms. He props his legs on the seat back in front of him like he doesn't care that he's not part of the Team Cleo entourage.

That must mean Cleo didn't raise her wand for him, but I won't know for sure until they air the blind auditions.

The only familiar face on the team is Daphné, who sits between two male werewolves.

"We're ready for Zen," Jovi says into her headset.

"I'm already here," Zen drawls.

Daphné gasps as we all turn in our seats to find Zen Renko seated behind us, one arm resting on the next seat back as he rubs his thumb and forefingers over his wand. He totally teleported! For an old man, he knows how to make an entrance.

Zen stands regally and makes his way to the front of the stage. He has a suave and casual look going on with his light-blue buttoned dress shirt, gray tweed button vest, and jean jacket with a fleece-lined collar. He's also an old man who kept all his hair. It falls in thick, silvery waves to the nape of his neck while his cheeks and chin are covered in a thick matching mustache and beard.

Jovi hands Zen a file before she and the werewolf producers step aside, giving Zen space to address us.

"Welcome to Team Zen. You are here because of your magical aptitude and talent, which I look forward to seeing grow as you progress on the show. Our group has been selected as the first to perform in front of a live audience in the televised cast-offs. I can only choose one of you as the winner from each pairing. As with prior seasons, each coach is allowed one save from their own team, and one steal from another coach's team. It is your job to make my decision difficult or to entice another coach to use their one steal on you if you are not the winner of your cast-off. Does anyone have any questions so far?"

When no one raises their hand, Zen continues. "I will call you up to the stage in pairs to practice your routines, which will be followed up with my suggestions on how to improve your casting. These sessions will be filmed but treat the camera crew as though they are not here. Once I dismiss you, see Kurt to schedule a time to practice on stage in front of me one final time tomorrow." He uses his wand to point in the producer's direction. "Afterward, you may return to the hotel to practice what you can from your rooms. While the rest of you await your turns, please remain silent to prevent sound interference during filming. Good. Now, let's start with the first pairing. First up, we have Nathaniel Duke and Haylee Hutchins."

The buffed-out wizard pulls his legs off the chair in front of him and stands.

I try not to choke on my tongue.

I don't want to go first while the rest of the team watches. Not only that, Zen's paired me with a wizard—a hot one with dreamy olive eyes and gravity-defying chestnut brown hair.

I swallow past the thickening of my throat.

My body feels as though it has gained back all of my previous weight as I hoist myself out of my chair. Nathaniel reaches Zen way before I do and shakes his hand. They both smile. When I make it over, I hover awkwardly, not knowing if Zen, being human, will want to touch a zombie. To avoid humiliation, I keep my arms at my sides, and offer a smile, instead.

"Hi, I'm really excited to be on your team."

Zen nods. "Let's go up to the stage and see what you've prepared."

I can feel the rest of my teammates watching every step we take to the stage. It doesn't matter how many times I've practiced; running through my routine in front of this group of competitors feels terrifying. I'd be more comfortable performing in front of an auditorium filled with viewers than enduring this excruciating scrutiny. Why did Zen have to call me up first?

On stage, Zen plucks a sheet from the file and sets it on top, lifting it inches from his face. "Nathaniel Duke. Wizard. Two-wand lift. You will be performing a disappearing act to 'Disappearing Syndrome' by Hail the Sun. And Haylee Hutchins. Zombie. Four-wand lift. You will be performing a nature illusion and levitation to 'Butterflies' by Kacey Musgraves."

My back straightens, and a satisfied smile pulls up my lips when I hear that Nathaniel received half my number of wand lifts. He blinks rapidly before giving me a wrinkled nose and scowl.

From side stage, Jimmy and Max enter with large handheld cameras. My chest lifts. I want to smile and wave at them, but Zen just said to pretend they're not there, so I return my attention to my coach.

"Nathaniel, you're up first," Zen announces. "Haylee, wait on the side of the stage for your turn."

"Okay," I say as I move aside, feeling relieved that Nathaniel is going before me.

Once Jimmy and Max are in place with the cameras, Zen says to Nathaniel, "Tell me why you chose a disappearing act for your cast-off performance."

"Because it's a favorite among humans," Nathaniel answers with a winsome smile. "This season, fans get to see how a wizard does disappearance."

Zen strokes the bristle beneath his chin. "Let's see it, then. Lift your wand, or rather hand, when you are ready for your music to begin." He, along with Jimmy, moves to the opposite side of the stage, while Max joins my side. I really can't say hi now, though. The camera is propped on Max's shoulder, lens aimed at Nathaniel.

As soon as the stage is clear, Nathaniel doesn't waste time. He raises his hand and hard rock booms from the auditorium speakers.

The young wizard snaps his fingers and disappears. Another snap, and he reappears on Jimmy's side of the stage. Nathaniel faces me and leaps into the air then disappears. Reappears. Disappears. In and out of focus as he strobes across the stage. When he reaches the center, he does a back flip, disappears, and then reappears back on his feet. Great, so he's an acrobat in addition to a wizard.

Nathaniel strobes toward me again. I lose count of how many times he disappears. There's no way a non-wizard could cast this quickly. But if I win the heart, maybe I could be the first.

When the music ends, Nathaniel vanishes. Silence and seconds fill the stage while he remains incorporeal. Perhaps he thinks he's above receiving feedback from a human. All the better for me if Nathaniel offends one of the world's greatest casters.

Zen walks onto the stage with Jimmy several steps ahead, filming him. Nathaniel reappears with his thumbs in his pockets and a smirk on his lips.

"Well executed. Your timing and pace were right on the nose," Zen says matter-of-factly. "I especially enjoyed the flickering effect. It displayed great skill that you maintained the affectation while remaining in constant motion."

Nathaniel's chest expands. Zen strokes his beard. "I'm not sold on how your act ends, however. You might leave the audience floundering with nowhere to focus while they applaud."

Nathaniel remains puffed up. He even smiles. "Your suggestions would be appreciated."

Nope. The wizard isn't going to give me any advantage with Zen. Nathaniel's not only on *Spellcaster* to perform. He's here to play the game, as demonstrated by deferring to his coach.

Zen strolls across the stage as he speaks. "Audiences love the unexpected, so how can you surprise them?" He turns to face Nathaniel. The young wizard's smile wavers. Zen looks from him to the auditorium and then back. "Do you have the power to transport me?"

"Of course, I—" Nathaniel swallows his indignation and alters his tone to one that's respectful. "Yes, I do."

Zen nods, appearing indifferent to the wizard's uppity predisposition. He's probably used to it from filming twelve prior seasons of the show with Cleo Killian, not to mention his lifelong career in magic.

Zen grins through his beard. "Let's try something. I'm going to sit on my coach's chair. I want you to transport me to the stage while simultaneously teleporting yourself to my chair where you will reappear to end your performance."

"Yeah, that would be really cool," Nathaniel says, nodding vigorously. His enthusiasm is genuine, and no wonder. The audience will eat up this ending. Now he'll have both flair and humor. Leaving viewers with a laugh on their lips goes a long way. Dang it!

Zen lifts his wand and brings it down quickly right before teleporting to his purple chair. "Try it without the music," he instructs.

Nathaniel focuses on Zen. Without uttering a word, Nathaniel makes our coach disappear before he, too, flickers out of sight. Zen is the first to reappear—on the spot where Nathaniel stood seconds before. The wizard reappears in Brody's chair, grinning from ear to ear. His smile fades when he notices he's in the wrong seat. I have to bite my tongue to keep from laughing as an image of Nathaniel winding up in Brody's lap during the performance flashes through my head. That would be awesome!

Nathaniel quickly teleports back to the stage.

Zen scratches his beard with one finger. "You'll need to work on your timing—and placement." Zen looks at me. "Your turn, Haylee."

Despite my harried nerves scraping me raw, I walk to the back center of the stage and put my watchful teammates out of my head.

There is only the stage. I can do this. I'm ready. I'm magic.

I lift my wand.

As my soundtrack plays, I arch my wand and cast a rainbow, but as I walk beneath it, my inner critic whispers that my stripe of orange looks brown. I don't want brown. I want happy orange to match the dress I'll be wearing, and the monarch butterflies I'm about to unleash.

I start spinning. Unfortunately, my mind whirls with me. I've fallen into a mind trap with no way out. What does Zen think of me? My species? Is he sorry I chose him as my coach? What do my teammates think of me? Were they impressed when Zen announced that I received a four-wand lift? Ugh. Why do I care?

I spin and spin. Crap! The music's moved on without me. Now my timing is all off. I have to rush the butterfly illusions. They don't make it past the edge of the stage before blinking out of existence. Nathaniel had the disappearing act. Not me!

Get it together, Haylee.

I cast my wings and lift from the ground. My thoughts are so jumbled I'm not able to conjure my swarm back to life, which means it's just me flitting around all alone above the stage. I cast the field of wildflowers below and drift down among them, landing harder than usual. I crouch, tucking in my head, which gives me a couple seconds to give the stage a bug-eyed look of frustration. My wings fold in, but I still have no butterflies to call back. At the very least, I need to nail the finale.

I get to my feet and back away until I'm under my rainbow.

"*Expellis, ealah, ealah, veed,*" I cast with the lift of my wand.

The rainbow erupts into multicolored butterflies. I swing my arm, and this time send them fluttering into the auditorium.

Zen walks up to me and tells me what I already know. "You need to work on your timing. Otherwise, it was a charming use of illusions."

That's all I get before Zen dismisses me and Nathaniel. While our coach calls up the next two contestants, Nathaniel and I schedule tomorrow's final stage practice.

CHAPTER THIRTY-THREE

BACK AT THE hotel, I drop my clutch onto my bed before falling backward onto the covers with a groan. I slap a hand against my forehead.

Being called to the stage first gives me plenty of alone time in my room to berate myself for getting distracted during my first session with Coach Zen. I can't even blame it on outside interference.

The flub was all me.

"Good going, Haylee," I say to the ceiling.

Cameron told me to call him with updates when I'm able, but I'm not in the mood to talk just yet.

I should do something productive—like practice.

I reach for my clutch and pull out my wand. "*Ignus ception butterfly monarch*," I say, conjuring a monarch butterfly to life, followed by, "*Ignus ception replimation thirty*," which is a multiplication spell. Once I have my swarm, I sit up and direct them around the room. They flit over Blair's bed.

"Watch out for Witchy Witch's territory." I snort before duplicating the spell several more times until butterflies fill the room. My stomach clenches, remembering the way I crammed my childhood bedroom with my teddy-gone-wrong spell.

It brings the past back to me in a rushing wave, which distracts me. The butterflies fade.

I grit my teeth and shake my head. "Focus, Haylee. *Ignus ception butterfly monarch. Ignus ception replimation fifty.*" The butterflies return. This is actually good practice. I should think of other distracting thoughts and work on keeping the illusion going while I do.

I picture Vampire Caleb and the stunned expression on his face when I pitched his wand across the front of the auditorium and over the stage. Giggles tickle my throat. The butterflies flicker, which reminds me of Nathaniel's performance. I straighten up. Our cast-off is in two days. I have to beat him.

I stand up and hold out my arm while casting, calling the butterflies to me. They land on my fingers and continue swarming up to my shoulder. Beating wings flash below my nose, covering my blouse like they're trying to get to the flowers on the print. They gather around the bun on my head and land on my legs. Once I am covered in the illusion, I spell them to dissolve.

"And that is how it's done," I say aloud.

Now that I'm in better spirits, I call Cameron and then text Mariana. I'd like to find out how things went with my roommate, but—big surprise—she's not inclined to share.

The moment Blair enters our room, she places her hands on her hips and narrows her eyes on me. "If you tried touching any of my things, then you already know that was a big mistake."

I roll my eyes from where I'm currently resting against my pillows and the headboard.

"Um, hi. I'm Haylee. Nice to meet you," I say sarcastically. "P.S. I didn't touch any of your stuff."

"Be sure that you don't," Blair intones. She crouches in front of her suitcase, unzips it, and looks inside before closing it back up as though making sure.

"Feel free to borrow any of my things. There's some concealer in my cosmetic bag in the bathroom that might help with all those frown lines," I say sarcastically.

Blair stands up straight and scoffs. "Like I'd touch something that belongs to a mutant, let alone put any of your products on my body."

"Suit yourself." I shrug, grab my phone, and open Telepatch. I scroll through the feed and gasp.

Blair huffs, stomps into the bathroom, and locks the door. It's only background noise as my nose nearly touches the screen of my phone.

Phoenix Starr lays in a puddle of blood—naked aside from her lacy black bra and panties. Written in blood on the white marble floor beside her are the smeared words: ***It's too late now.***

It takes me a moment to realize this is another one of Phoenix Starr's shocking stunts.

Her post reads:

Unless you want to walk in and find me this way one day soon, you better grant me immortal permission before it's too late.

Everyone who follows Phoenix Starr knows that the "you" she refers to in her posts is her father. The socialite is addicted to airing her grievances against her dad publicly. Mr. Starr neither answers nor demands that any of it be taken off social media—at least not that I'm aware of. He sounds to me like a stereotypical elite parent who doesn't bother with consequences when his child throws a temper tantrum.

Comments on her post are blowing up.

@lillylit WTF?????????

@sportychick201 Girl, you nearly gave me a heart attack!

@lunabeautyglow What kind of father denies his only child everlasting life?

@starlit3 Alexander Starr sucks!

@gildedgoddess06 Love ya, babe. Call me.

@siren77 Nooooo! Don't you dare!

@neondreams Phoenix Starr is HOT dead or alive.

@glamtech25 I literally screamed when I saw this pic.

@darronhughs Seek help.

Blair emerges from the bathroom with her phone to her ear. "Hey, you want to go out for lattes? It's not like we need to practice magic like the creature contestants." Blair laughs rudely. "Okay. Sure. I'll wait for you in the lobby. I don't want to breathe stale mutant air any longer than I have to." When I glare at her, she turns away. "I know, right? Okay. See you soon."

After Blair finishes her call, she grabs a small purse and a green cardigan. It's no surprise when the witch walks to the door without saying goodbye. Guess I'm not invited.

"Have fun," I call after her. "I'll try not to accidentally touch any of your things with my zombie hands."

Blair spins around and stomps her way closer. "You better not."

"I said I'll try." I shrug.

Blair's eyes narrow. "I'll know if you do."

"Sure thing, roomie."

"Don't call me that." She scowls and storms out, slamming the door behind her.

"Good times," I mutter to the empty room.

I wish I had someone to go out exploring the streets of Hollywood with. With the cast-off coming up, I'm too nervous to venture out alone and risk any kind of incident that might prevent me from performing. That leaves lots of alone time in my room until it's time for me and Nathaniel to go through our routines with Zen one more time.

The following day, I keep my mind on my illusions during practice, and everything goes smoothly. It will look even better when I'm dressed up. Nathaniel also has his timing perfected for the swap-out at the end of his routine. But seeing his act again, it seems lacking in complexity. He's basically running across the stage and flickering while doing acrobatics. I've seen way more impressive performances by humans over the years.

An email instructs Team Zen and Team Cleo to arrive at the studio early on Thursday. With the number of contestants the show starts out with, we've been broken into two teams for two performance days in front of a live audience and all four coaches.

The good thing about performing first is we get to return home a day early for the weekend before flying back out for combat week. I miss Joni and Cameron something fierce. Being separated from them makes me appreciate that I still have family who loves me, and whom I'd do anything for.

Walking into the auditorium, looking for a place to sit among the gathered contestants, feels as awkward as the first time. The witches are already congregated in their posse, which includes Blair, Dominic, Zane, and Nathaniel.

Guess it's right back into isolation.

When I walk past the werewolf section, it's quieter than the first day—probably because the pyro twins are absent. A werewolf with dark brown skin, Afro-textured hair, and tattoos covering both arms, hands, and neck watches me with keen eyes while rolling his wand behind his thumb and forefingers.

"Yo, Z," he calls. His tattooed arms take up both armrests, and his legs are spread wide.

"Hey," I say and keep walking.

"Yo, wait up, Z."

"Dude, leave it," I hear one of the werewolves tell him.

But the guy is on his feet and by my side in an instant. "I'm Kace."

Oh my gosh. I just want to be left alone. I wait for the catch, the insult, or whatever prank he must have planned. The entire front of his neck is inked with a wolf face. When he lifts his thick brows expectantly, I clear my throat and ask, "Ace?"

He shakes his head. "No. Kace with a K, as in cool."

"Um, I've never heard that name before." Nor seen cool spelled with a K, but there's a first time for everything, including this bizarro encounter. "I'm Haylee."

"Cool," he says, which would apparently be spelled with a K if he were texting. "Nice to know you, Haylee."

"Really?" I continue toward an aisle seat.

Kace puts his arm around my shoulder, stopping me in my tracks. He does realize he's touching a zombie, right? I suppose it's not as big a deal for werewolves, who enjoy close proximity to prey.

HELL WAS BORING

The *HELL WAS BORING* printed in a gothic font on his oversized black shirt isn't reassuring, but Kace sounds sincere when he says, "Me and you are going to be good friends, Haylee."

"Really?" I ask again, trying to figure out what's happening here. Kace is extremely difficult to read—and even more intimidating. I glance down at the arm not currently draped over me and see the all-capped words in thick black ink that read: ***EAT SHIT DIE***. Every one of his fingers has a small animal skull inked in black—with a human skull on his thumb.

Kace steers me to an empty row of seats and juts his chin for me to go in first. *Such a gentleman*, says the sarcastic and nervous voice inside my head. I slip out from under his heavy arm and settle into the seat four over. Kace plops down right beside me and makes himself comfortable, leaning back and taking the armrest.

His grin is all mischievous when he says, "You showed that fanger who's boss on day one. I dig it."

Oh. Right. That.

I've been so focused on the cast-off performance that my orientation encounter feels like it happened weeks ago rather than on Monday.

"Thanks?"

"No, thank you, Z," Kace says with enthusiasm. "If one of us wolves had humiliated a fanger like that, it would have turned into a bloodbath in here. Could have been the end of Season 13 before it ever started. Know what I'm saying?" His teeth gleam. Not really, but I nod anyway. Kace's eyes seem to go out of focus when he stares at the stage and frowns. In the next instant, he blinks and grins at me. "If I wanted violence, I would have stayed home, ya know? I'm here for the magic."

I relax slightly. "Me too. So, you're on Team Cleo?" I glance over at the wizard posse and smirk to think of Kace on their team of pretty boys and uppity witches.

Blair keeps her head turned away from the rest of the creature groups, leaning in close to talk to a Native American witch—probably the one she meets up with for lattes at night. Nathaniel talks with a group of guys, but keeps darting looks at the stage and furrowing his brows. Then there's Zane Barrett. His eyes meet mine and remain locked. I don't mind being the first to look away, especially now that I'm no longer alone. I don't know what Zane's deal is. It's as though he's never seen a zombie before. I guess that makes me a rare unicorn. The thought makes me smirk.

"Yep. Team Witch," Kace says. "Not for long. Coach hates me."

I snort and then cover my mouth.

Kace chuckles. "I had to choose between Cleo and Malachi. The wolf in me can't take instructions from a fanger, so . . ." He shrugs.

"Well, if you outperform your competition in the cast-off, she should put her personal feelings aside."

"Not happening, Z. She paired me with golden boy Barrett over there. He was a four-wand lift." Kace scratches his neck.

I look over at Zane, who looks back at me. Has he been staring this entire time? His lips lift into a slight smile. What's that about? I don't return it. Instead, I turn my attention back to Kace. One of these times, I'm going to wait until Zane looks away first.

"That bites," I say.

"Bites, yeah," Kace chuckles.

"You could still beat him."

"I appreciate your vote of confidence, Z, but no way is Barrett going home."

"Well, then she can keep you both."

As Kace scoffs, a rumbling sound escapes his throat, like a low growl of frustration. I can hear the underlying tension in his voice, a mix of irritation and determination.

"Nah, she's been side-eyeing me like leftover Pad Thai she discovered growing mold in the back of her fridge—something she doesn't want to keep around."

"I don't want you to leave the competition," I say, surprised by how much I mean it. Of all the species, werewolves have shown me the closest thing to kindness, and this one has turned out to be cool—with a K and a C!

"Believe me, it's the last thing I want either, Z, which is why I'm hoping Brody will steal me."

"My name's Haylee, you know," I say with a huff.

Kace smirks. "I know, but I like calling you Z."

I roll my eyes. "What happens if you befriend another zombie? What do you call them?"

"By their name. Z's already taken." He winks at me.

I fold my arms. "Maybe I'll start calling you W or K."

Kace's grin widens. "Hey, switch those around and you've got my initials. My name is Kace Warren. I could even go by KW, but it's your call, Z."

I huff and roll my eyes again. "Well, I won't be calling you anything if you don't win your cast-off."

Kace clutches his chest, pressing his wand over his heart. "Ouch, so you're saying there's no chance Cleo will pick me. That hurts, Z."

"Whatever." I laugh. "Your words, not mine. At least our teams are performing first. Brody can have first dibs on saving you."

Kace bobs his head, stops and looks over his shoulder, then looks at me and lowers his voice. "I have to make sure I outperform Tanner back there. Cleo paired him with that douche wizard Dominic. You know he's not going home, either. If Brody saves Tanner, I'm screwed."

When voices quiet around us, I look to see what's going on and sit up in my seat as Colt Cohen walks onto the stage in the black suit I'm used to seeing him host the show in.

This is real! This is happening. Today!

Unlike my pal KW, I have zero chance of being saved by any of the other coaches if Zen doesn't choose me.

CHAPTER THIRTY-FOUR

COLT IS ACCOMPANIED on stage by Alexander, who wears a pink silk suit with large silvery gray blossoms printed in various spots. He wears a white collared shirt beneath it and a large pink oval pendant.

"Good morning, Team Zen and Team Cleo," Colt greets in his booming voice. "Are you excited to perform in front of a live audience and the *Spellcaster* judges in Season 13's first televised cast-off?"

The werewolves howl in answer, including Kace. I get a good, close look at his wolf tattoo while his head is thrown back, neck exposed. I'm certainly glad he wants to be friends.

"That's what we like to hear." Colt walks to the edge of the stage and stops. Alexander stands slightly off to his side. "Your teams are the first to participate in this season's first round of eliminations. I know that none of you wants to go home, so give it your all on the stage today. The order in which pairs will perform has been posted backstage, where our talented makeup and costume crew is waiting to get you ready for your performance. Your live audience is already lined up outside, thrilled to be the first group to watch this season's creature cast-offs. So, let's make history, casters!"

The wolves chorus again while the rest of us clap and cheer. Getting caught up in the excitement, I fist my wand and thrust it above my head. Kace looks over with a smile before doing the same. He looks over his shoulder and nudges me. When I look back, I see the werewolves have all lifted their wands, and for a moment, I feel the warm fuzzies, like I'm part of the pack.

Colt sticks his fingers in his mouth and issues a shrill whistle. Once everyone quiets, he claps his hands together and rubs them. "All right, Team Zen and Team Cleo. Time to get ready backstage. Good luck." Colt leaves the stage while Alexander remains behind.

The werewolves are the first to leap from their seats and bound up the stage steps, disappearing behind the curtains. Meanwhile, the witches and wizards seem to be making a point of taking their sweet time vacating their seats. The vampires swagger toward the stage like they don't want to appear overeager.

Kace and I follow the pack up. I am so excited to put on my dress and makeup!

Alexander steps in front of me and Kace and squeals. His upper eyelids shimmer with white powder that blends into a light pink on his lower lids.

"Oh my gosh! When did this happen?" He turns his head from me to Kace before staring at us both with what I think are happy tears that glisten but don't fall.

I grin. "Hi, Alexander. That suit is gorgeous on you."

Alexander preens for a moment before slapping my compliment away. "Yes, yes. No one pulls off Celestia couture like me. Just give me a moment to finish freaking out that my two *Spellcaster* recruits are together."

I turn to Kace. "Alexander recruited you as well?"

Kace grins. "Well, he does have great taste for a fanger."

Alexander gasps with mock indignation.

I put my hands on my hips and say jokingly, "I thought I was your one and only."

Alexander lowers his head and winces at me. "Yes and no. Girl, when I saw this steaming cup of cocoa on the news after he rescued a child with his wand, I had to make room for one more."

I lift my brow and look at Kace with new appreciation. "Fair enough, and it's true Alexander has great taste."

Alexander lifts his arms and hands and does a little shimmy in place that ends with one hand pressed over his chest. "My two dark horses. Make Daddy proud today."

"Nope!" Kace hollers, and hurries backstage while I laugh.

Alexander tilts his head and bats his eyelashes. "Did I just scare off the big Black wolf?"

I nod and dab at the corners of my eyes with my fingers. "Yeah, I think you did."

Vampire contestants look over at us as they pass, but Alexander ignores them entirely.

"I'll be cheering you both on from the sidelines. At least you're not going up against one another. Now that would have broken my heart." He clasps his chest again.

"Well, thanks. It's nice to know someone is rooting for me."

Alexander tsks and waves a finger back and forth in front of me in a scolding motion. "Girl, you have more fans than you know, and your following is only going to grow. Now hurry on back and get yourself dolled up for the stage."

My cheeks heat. I nod and smile before darting backstage feeling all light and fluttery. I'm in such high spirits that when I come across Blair behind the stage, I say a heartfelt, "Hey, good luck out there today."

"I don't need luck, you wand-waving mutant freak!" She stomps off, leaving my head pounding and chest tight.

Why does she have to be such an MC? I should have kept my mouth shut. She ruined my good mood. I shouldn't let her, but it's not exactly a choice.

"Why do you waste your breath?"

I nearly jump out of my skin as Suhani Das detaches herself from the black stage curtains gathered to the side. She's dressed in a long black embroidered tunic over black silky pants that leave her ankles bare above a pair of beaded slip-on flats. Her dark hair is pulled back in a low bun.

Her unexpected comment and appearance startle a joke out of me. "I don't know, because I have plenty of breath to spare?" Suhani surprises me by laughing softly. My brows furrow. "What are you doing back here, anyway? You're not on Team Cleo, are you?"

She's not on Team Zen, but she wasn't sitting in the auditorium with the rest of us, which leads me to believe she's either on Team Malachi or Team Brody. My bet's on Malachi.

"My benefactor arranged seats in the audience to watch today's teams perform," Suhani informs me.

Her master, she means. Great. Not only is she talented but cutthroat as well. No doubt she's here to assess the competition.

I frown. Speaking of performing, it's time to get dressed and done up.

"Okay, well, see you later."

Suhani gives me an assessing stare before saying, "Maybe."

I sigh heavily and walk away. She's nowhere near as rude as Blair, but she's not exactly nice, either.

"There you are!" Jovi exclaims. "Females on that side." The vampire director quickly points and rushes off to speak with the human crew dressed all in black.

It hits me again, with each step, that I'm performing on the *Spellcaster* stage for the second time. Millions of viewers will see my illusion spells once the cast-offs are aired. We were also reminded, by group email, that the blind auditions will begin airing next week. I wish I could watch them with Joni and Cameron, but if I make it to next week, I'll be back in Hollywood preparing for combat.

I wrinkle my nose as I enter a hall backstage and follow the shrill pitch of female voices ordering the human hair and makeup crew around. The crew continues to brush, clip, and spray hair without comment. They're total pros—not to mention saints for putting up with a roomful of supernatural divas.

There's a large flat screen on the wall that lists the order of performances. Thankfully, Nathaniel and I don't have to go first, though third to perform is still really soon.

I find my orange dress hanging from a rolling rack that's mostly empty and take it to an empty vanity station to get changed.

"I said matte, not gloss," a vampire with silky brown hair snaps at her helper from the vanity beside mine.

A blond with a ponytail hands the vampire tissues to blot the glossy red lipstick. The vampire does so and then throws the wadded tissues in the blond's face. My entire face cringes at her disgusting behavior before returning to prettier things like my amazing dress. The A-line gown is a dreamy ensemble made of orange tulle and loose, short sleeves that flutter above the elbows. I absolutely love the embroidered 3D butterflies lining the two thin straps attached to the corset-style bodice that cinches at the waist with orange ribbon before flaring out.

I have never felt more beautiful as I stare into the vanity mirror and see myself in the fairytale dress. I feel nearly as excited to show off the gown on stage as my magic.

My smile fades as I look around at the activity. I'd hoped that by the time I finished changing, a crew member would have come over to help. There seems to be one helper per contestant, except in the case of a golden-haired witch who has two helpers weaving braids into sections of her lengthy hair.

Another helper begins cleaning up after securing a white lace headband in Daphné's brown and blue hair. It matches the short white lace dress she's wearing with a pretty ribbon around her waist and stunning layers of tulle that ruffle from her hips to her knees.

"Could I get some help?" I call out in a courteous tone.

No one comes over or responds.

"Now my teeth are stained!" the vampire next to me snaps, before grabbing more tissues and rubbing furiously at her front teeth. "Get it right this time, or it will be your blood staining my teeth rather than lipstick."

"We're not allowed to harm the crew, Tori," another vampire calls over.

"Says who?" Tori demands.

"It was in the email."

"Fine. Whatever. Just do your damn job, human."

I clear my throat and raise my voice. "Could someone please help me with my hair and makeup?" Don't get me wrong—I've put in enough hours doing it myself, but having help with my hair would be nice.

When I'm left hanging again, Blair scoffs from where a crew member powders her face across the room. "Don't you get it? No one wants to touch a disgusting brain eater." Her witchy gal pals snicker. Tori flicks her gaze my way and hisses when our eyes meet before she snaps her fingers at her helper.

The crew stays focused on the other contestants.

Fine. I'll do my own hair and makeup. I've got my very own built-in pro to get the job done. I pull open the drawer on the vanity to see what they've given me to work with when a frog jumps out at me with a loud croak. I shriek and jerk backward—more afraid for my dress than about the amphibian. It continues straight for me . . . and then disappears.

It was only an illusion.

My relief is short-lived when the other females burst into hysterics. They've all turned in their seats to laugh at me. A few of the crew members look like they're biting their tongues not to join in.

"Real original," I huff. It's the kind of illusion that brings to mind juvenile boys, not professional spellcasters who have made it onto a premiere competition.

But whatever. Vampires suck. Werewolves bite. And witches are Moluccan cockatoos.

Humans are plain old disappointing.

A woman in her mid-twenties runs in, breathing heavily. Her shoulder-length brown hair is held in place by a simple headband, and a small, glossy shopping bag dangles from her fingers. She stops to take in a gasping breath before saying, "Sorry, I'm late. Where's Haylee Hutchins?" Everyone stares at her dumbfounded, me included. "Oh! Never mind. I see her." She hurries my way with a wide grin. "The dress looks even more gorgeous on!" she gushes, and sets the glossy bag on the vanity table before holding out her hand. "I'm Anya. Alexander assigned me as your personal beauty helper."

I stand corrected, I think as I shake Anya's hand.

"Some helper. Can't arrive on time," Tori grumbles beside us.

It's nice to see the tables turned as Anya ignores the vampire beside us entirely. She plucks packs of golden butterfly pins from the glossy shopping bag and sets them on the vanity top.

"Oh my gosh! These are perfect," I gasp.

Anya nods eagerly. "They're going to look gorgeous in your hair. I apologize again for being late, but when I saw your dress, I remembered seeing these at Starstruck Styling Studio last month, so I called to check if they still had some, and when they said they did—*eee*—I just had to have them for your hair!"

"Thank you," I say.

Anya is all smiles. "My pleasure. Now, please have a seat, and I'll get you done up."

Once I'm seated, Anya's expression turns serious in the vanity mirror's reflection. She opens a drawer, pulls out a brush, and gets to work. I hold perfectly still, watching her progress in the mirror.

Jovi pokes her head in for a quick announcement. "Seats are nearly full. Show will start on the hour." She ducks out, leaving a tense silence in her wake.

Anya remains intent on my hair. Once she's finished, she hands me a mirror. "Take a look."

A small section of my hair is pulled up in the back. The rest shines with volume and soft waves. The pretty butterfly clips ornaments my tresses along the left side of my head.

"Anya, it's beautiful," I gasp. I stop myself from asking if I can keep the pins after the performance. Priorities! Right now, I need to focus on the cast-off—not free gifts.

"The audience—and judges—won't be able to take their eyes off you," Anya says, moving on to my makeup. She pulls out shades of pink, violet, and orange—brushing and blending each layer with expert care. With a thick brush, she sweeps shimmer over my cheekbones. When she's finished, she shakes the can of hairspray and gives me a final mist.

I smile at Anya's reflection in the mirror. "It's beautiful. Thank you."

"Good luck out there, Haylee."

"Thanks."

I wait until Anya's excused herself from the room to use my wand to spell my hair into a permanent hold until I release it from my command. I'm going to be moving around and levitating. I wouldn't want to hurt Anya's feelings by implying that her pin and spray job isn't secure, but I'm not taking any chances.

I stare up at the order and list of cast-off pairings, wishing I could spell Zen into saving Kace. It would be so nice to have a friend on my team. Sadly, Kace is right. There's no way Cleo will choose him over Zane. I chew on the inside of my cheek as I stare at Zane's name on the flat screen. Guilt niggles at my mind because I don't want Zane to go home either, and I can't explain why. Ugh. It's those magnetic blue eyes. Maybe he's got some kind of enchantment woven into his gaze. Well, I'm banishing Zane Barrett, and his eyes, from my mind. I can't let him, or anyone else, get inside my head and mess me up during my performance.

"Paula, we're ready for you backstage," a crew member announces.

The room is quiet again, but not for long. "It's about time the coaches started eliminating some of the dead weight," Blair announces.

I ignore her, knowing full well she's likely staring directly at me. Instead, I pretend to busy myself touching up my lips with gloss in front of the mirror.

The next pairing are both males. Being third means a crew member arrives to collect me all too soon.

I stand to the side of the stage, not listening to the critiques the coaches give the werewolf and wizard who just finished their cast-off. Somewhere on the other side of the stage, Nathaniel is waiting to perform against me. What if the audience goes wild for his little switcheroo trick at the end of his performance? It's a cheap thrill, if you ask me, but I'm not the one in the coach's seat.

There are now butterflies in my stomach, in addition to my dress and hair.

"Zen, who is the winner of this match?" Colt's voice echoes from the speakers.

"The winner is Luke."

A howl of excitement follows.

Colt chuckles before announcing, "Coaches, let me remind you that Rhett is available to save or steal. Rhett, is there anything you would like to say to your coach?"

"Thanks for lifting your wand and having me on your team. I'd love the opportunity to show you my combat skills next week."

A short pause ensues followed by Colt announcing in a booming voice, "Rhett Sullivan has been saved by his coach!"

I miss the next exchange as my stomach twists and sours like those moldy noodles Kace was talking about. My coach seems a lot nicer than Cleo, but that still doesn't make me his prime choice—and he just used his one and only save on a wizard, which means I have to win my cast-off if I have any hope of continuing in the competition.

“Congratulations, Rhett,” Colt says. “Next up, from Team Zen, we have the wizard from Seattle. Please welcome Nathaniel Duke.”

Applause explodes from the audience. Everything inside of me tightens like a bowstring prepared to launch onto stage.

“Going up against Nathaniel is the zombie from Virginia. Let’s hear it for Haylee Hutchins.”

“You’re up,” a stagehand whispers urgently into my ear.

CHAPTER THIRTY-FIVE

I WALK ONTO THE stage amongst cheers. Maybe the audience has been spelled not to boo. One of the many things I have always loved about the show is its positivity and encouragement.

I make my way to a stool in the corner of the stage, where we've all been instructed to sit while our opposing teammate performs. Careful with my dress, I sweep my hands over the tulle skirt behind me before settling onto the stool. Then I sit up tall, holding my wand in my lap, and steal a glance at the coaches while the auditorium is lit up.

I can't help staring at Malachi in his khaki trousers and fitted white T-shirt. It's the shirt unbuttoned over the tee that draws my attention the most. Half of it is printed with pink flamingos. The other half is a pink-and-white vertical striped print. His black hair isn't as fun as other seasons, but at least his top is lively.

Farthest from Malachi, Brody Morgan is spruced up in an olive blazer buttoned over a geometric collared top and black tie. He has beautiful light brown skin, a jovial trademark smile, lush lips, gorgeous almond-shaped eyes, and thick dark brown hair teased at the top of a smooth, square forehead. The whites of his straight teeth flash when Cleo leans over her purple armrest and says something to him. The witch is wearing a long, sheer black-and-maroon shawl with a fringe over a short black dress with black tights and black heeled boots that lace above her ankles.

Zen's dressed in a black suit with a lime green shirt underneath and matching handkerchief peeking out of the breast pocket of his blazer. I don't know whether he uses products or magic to make his gray-and-white hair lift off his scalp and wave above his shoulders. He has the perpetual look of a man who's been out cruising in his convertible along the coast with the top down—minus the tangles.

My eyes shift back to Malachi and find he's staring at me with a dark gaze that does not match his shirt. I don't look away. Maybe I shouldn't be making it a habit of staring down vampires, but I can't help myself. They're not superior creatures or demigods. They're undead—like me. Plus, he sucks for lifting his wand during my blind audition and then failing to fight for me to choose his team.

I'm still in an eye-lock with Malachi when the lights dim. Only then do I blink and move my attention to my teammate.

The hard rock soundtrack begins, and Nathaniel flickers around. The audience claps several times, but when he goes to do his back flip, he remains invisible the entire time.

I suck in air.

Nathaniel reappears, but it's too late. The audience and coaches missed his acrobatics. There's no indication on his face that he even realizes everyone missed one of the more impressive parts of his routine. He does get the end correct, though, which earns him a loud round of applause.

After Zen appears on the stage, Brody laughs and says, "I didn't know you were competing for Queen Yapsut's heart, Zen."

Zen flashes a wry smile before casting himself back to his chair and Nathaniel back on stage.

I stand up and walk to my starting spot on the stage. The dazed, dream-like feeling of performing in front of the audience, coaches, and cameras returns in full force. Nathaniel plops down on the stool and stretches out his legs, crossing one ankle over the other.

My soundtrack begins, and I give myself over to the performance. This is my element. I perform best when it counts. Once I get going, it's as though I'm possessed and addicted to magic.

The audience gasps in awe as wings unfold from my back. They applaud when I levitate. When my butterflies burst from the stage into the theater, the applause is deafening. My winged beauties multiply in a flurry of bright orange wings. I send one to land on each of the coaches' arms—a totally impromptu addition. Brody lifts his arm and smiles at the winged illusion clinging to his blazer.

There is only me on that stage. No one else to cloud up my mind. It's clear skies with butterflies and rainbows. My illusions bring a physical and mental lightness into the theater's auditorium.

I finish with my exploding rainbow of butterflies to a thunder of applause. My heart feels near to bursting from the thrill and adrenaline still buzzing through my veins.

Colt strides across the stage to join me and Nathaniel, who teleported rather than walked the less than twenty steps to face the judges.

"Cool performance," I whisper to Nathaniel, who lifts his nose and ignores me.

"Those were some spectacular performances," Colt says into his microphone. "Let's start with Brody. What did you think?"

"Nathaniel, my man, that switch at the end of your performance was a riot." When Brody chuckles, Nathaniel grins. "And I lost count of how many times you disappeared and reappeared."

"Maybe you should have completed elementary school and learned things like the alphabet and counting," Malachi jabs.

"Count this," Brody says, and gives Malachi the middle finger.

Cleo laughs derisively.

Brody clears his throat, "As I was saying before F-twenty-*flea* over there interrupted, I thought it looked really cool. Gave me dance club vibes." Brody makes a sound like bass thumping through speakers, lifting his arms and swinging them in the air.

Cleo scoffs and rolls her eyes.

"Thank you," Nathaniel says, puffing out his chest.

Brody lowers his arms and looks at me. "And Haylee, wow. Those butterflies were beautiful, and so is your dress. That was a nice touch sending me and the other coaches our very own little fluttering critter—though I think you should have magicked Malachi a flamingo to match his tacky shirt."

The audience chuckles while Malachi glares at his on-air nemesis. I force a smile, trying my hardest not to let it show that my feelings are hurt in any way that Brody called my dress beautiful—not me.

"Cleo?" Colt says.

Cleo turns her attention to the stage and sits up straight. "Yes, those butterflies were certainly pretty. We've seen a lot of lovely illusions on this stage. Invisibility and teleportation is more advanced magic—both of which Nathaniel executed exceptionally."

I force myself to continue smiling for the cameras and audience even though Cleo Killian is clearly playing favorites with her own species.

Zen strokes his beard as he listens to the other coaches' opinions on the performances.

"Malachi, what did you think?" Colt asks.

My smile feels ready to flit off my face like one of my butterflies when Malachi speaks. It turns to shock when the vampire coach says, "I find levitation requires more skill to maintain than invisibility or teleportation." Brody nods in agreement. "Haylee, your performance was an enchanting display of gravity-defying magic and life-like illusions. I think it's safe to say the entire audience loved it."

I gape at him, not quite believing my ears now that I'm finally having my moment in the spotlight.

Malachi shifts focus. "Nathaniel, you disappeared an impressive number of times."

"And exactly how many times would that be, Count Dracula?" Brody jabs.

Shaking his head, Malachi continues. "You kept up a good pace, and that was a fun bit with your coach at the end. But I guess I expected a little more from a wizard."

Cleo narrows her eyes, and Nathaniel bristles beside me.

"Let's hear from Coach Zen," Colt says.

Zen strokes his beard several more times, staring slightly off into the distance as though gathering his thoughts.

My wand feels slick against my sweaty palm.

Zen lowers his hand and crosses one leg over the other as he aims his bright blue eyes at me and Nathaniel. "You both did a fantastic job of spellcasting and put in the work with practice. This decision is never easy, especially when we have such talented casters in the competition."

"Zen, who is the winner of this match?" Colt asks.

Zen lifts his hand to his beard and strokes it again while Nathaniel and I stand rigidly, awaiting his decision. The auditorium is silent. No one so much as coughs.

"I'm going to have to go with my gut on this one," Zen says. "The winner of this cast-off is Nathaniel."

My heart drops at those words. Beside me, Nathaniel fist-pumps the air before swaggering to the stairs on the side of the stage while waving to the audience.

A cannonball weighs down my stomach, and my hands shake. Forcing a smile is impossible at this point.

Colt moves in closer to me. "Coaches, let me remind you that Haylee is available to steal." He turns to me with a kind smile. "Haylee, is there anything you would like to say to your coach?"

I stare at Colt, not Zen. I know the lines I'm supposed to say. I gave it my all. I appreciate this opportunity. I learned so much and grew as a spellcaster. A bunch of bullcrap clogging up my throat. But I've got verbal constipation. I keep looking at Colt.

"What is there to say?" I ask in a low voice.

The crazy thing is that Colt is glaring at Zen . . . or maybe Brody? But why would he glare at Brody? I'm not about to look at any of the coaches. I hate them all.

Fisting my wand, I head off stage, not waiting around for Colt to dismiss me. I'm not going to humiliate myself any longer than I have to. I hurry down the stairs. Applause thunders from the stands. Oh god, the audience is cheering my departure.

I trip over an electrical wire. It doesn't matter that it's behind the cameras, which are still trained on the stage. I feel like the whole world has seen me stumble. My entire body trembles. I just need to get out of here.

"Haylee Hutchins has been saved!" Colt's voice booms from the speakers. I'm still stumbling off with blurred vision. "Haylee! Haylee, get back here." Colt chuckles. He sounds relieved.

My body stops, as still as my unbeating heart. I blink and blink again. The nearest camera man looks at me and then points in the direction of the stage.

I've been saved? Impossible. Did Brody save me? Is that why Colt was staring intensely at him?

I still can't move.

"Haylee!" Colt bellows again.

I turn around and sway. The stage tilts like a balancing scale, and I nearly choke out a laugh. I should be racing back to the stage, jumping up and down with unabashed excitement. But Zen's rejection is still too raw. My mortification shattered the last scraps of my dignity. Part of me still wants to storm off, but of course, I don't do that.

My body returns to the stage while my consciousness catches up.

I'm standing in front of the coaches, cameras, and audience with Colt showing off his white teeth as he grins. "Congratulations, Haylee. You're now a member of Team Malachi." My jaw drops as Colt turns his attention to the vampire in the flamingo shirt. "Malachi, what was it about Haylee's performance that made you use your one and only steal on her?"

Malachi slouches in his seat, one long leg crossed over the other above his knee. One elbow presses into his armrest as he rubs his thumb across his index finger in slow circles.

"Zen has obviously gone senile. That was the best performance we've seen so far this evening," Malachi says.

And I must have larvae in my ears, because I had to have heard Malachi wrong.

Brody laughs. "Maybe Zen got his contestants' names mixed up."

"His loss," Malachi drawls.

What is happening? Malachi and Brody agreeing on something? Malachi saving me? I feel as though I've entered an alternate universe.

"Congratulations, Haylee," Colt says again, but this time it's in his dismissive voice as he prepares to introduce the next pairing.

CHAPTER THIRTY-SIX

THE STREETS OF Hollywood light up in the dark and streak past the window as my Uber gets ever closer to the theater.

My hair is tucked back in a short pull-through braid, and I have on the sportiest outfit to ever cover my body. It's a set of matching leggings and a long-sleeved top in a black, white, and burgundy block print with stretchy, comfortable material. It's still cute and stylish enough as far as exercise wear goes. But what really sold me on the set is the long, thin, stretchy outer pocket specifically for carrying a wand.

It's the beginning of a new week. Combat week—thus my adventures in sports attire. Blair is still in the competition and still my roommate. I guess that's the way it will remain until one of us is eliminated. Her team met earlier. Malachi has the stage reserved last.

There are security guards at the lobby doors, but no more checking in. I know the drill. Know what awaits me in the auditorium. Another team that wants nothing to do with me. This one turns out to be a zillion times worse.

As soon as the group is within hearing distance, I'm hit with the knowledge that Malachi's team is made up entirely of vampires. Wonderful. Way to diversify.

Malachi stands near the stage with Jovi, frowning. There are crew members mopping the stage. The overhead stage light catches the roped ends of a mop when it's lifted from the floor and is tinged pink, which makes me think someone from Team Brody bled during practice, since his group was scheduled before us.

A cold sweat breaks out beneath my sports top, which makes me grateful I went with something in a breathable material. There are still parts of my body that behave like a human's. It doesn't seem fair that I still sweat when I no longer breathe. Someone really ought to dedicate a section of the zombie handbook to our biology or "zoology," as they'd more likely classify a non-human creature.

I tread slowly toward my new team in my white sneakers. Suhani sits alone in the front row. Like me, she's pulled her hair back. Her tresses are secured in a long, dark braid. The rest of the vampires are clustered together in several rows of middle seats.

I'm unable to slink into a chair behind them unnoticed because they're turning their heads and wrinkling their noses.

A male with short, spiky brown hair purses his lips. "What is she doing here?"

The vampires don't bother lowering their voices.

Carolina stands and tosses her hair over her shoulders. Her white shorts and taupe tank top seem better suited for the beach than practice, but to each their own. Carolina's eyes drill into mine. "You must be lost, zombie. This is Team Vampire."

"Yeah, mutant, the dumpster's out back."

My stomach tightens upon seeing and hearing the wretched male whose wand I punted on orientation day. Being on the same team with someone like him sucks.

Another male echoes Carolina, "This is Team Vampire."

Malachi's head jerks. He storms away from Jovi and plants himself in front of the group, arms folded. "This is team sit down and shut up."

I lower myself into the nearest seat as the vampires do the same—all except for Carolina, whose lips pout. Malachi stares directly at her and continues to glare into her eyes until she takes a seat.

"Welcome back," Malachi says sardonically. "You made it to the combat rounds, but that only means you have to work harder. I expect excellence. My human contestants worked their asses off, which means you lot should put in twice the effort. I'm talking all-nighters refining your spells and then perfecting them even more."

"Our team has to be number one," Carolina butts in, as though she's Malachi's co-coach.

He frowns.

When Vampire Caleb raises his hand, Malachi briefly squeezes his eyes shut and rubs the center of his forehead with two fingers like he's trying to blot out a headache.

"Yes, Vincent?"

"What's with the zombie trash?"

I bare my teeth at the fanged jerk—not that he sees me.

"Haylee is now a member of Team Malachi, which is all the more reason to give this everything you've got, because she gave the best cast-off performance of the season."

Several vampires hiss. I slouch into my chair. It's a little difficult to bask in Malachi's praise when all it's really done is paint a larger target on my back. Suhani turns in her seat and sends me a chilling challenge with her darkened eyes.

"Cast-offs and combat are two entirely different beasts," Vincent grumbles.

"By the end of the week, half of you will be going home for good," Malachi's voice booms over us. "There are no steals during battle rounds. If you don't want to be one of the losers taking his or her last flight out of Hollywood, then you'd best decide where you plan to put your focus this week. Hey, if heckling a female teenager means more to you than winning *Spellcaster*, then by all means enjoy your petty indulgence before you leave the show. Now, are there any more questions, or are you ready for combat?"

"Combat!" The vampires yell in unison.

I chew the inside of my cheek.

"Good. Before I pair you up, I want to work with each one of you individually to assess your skills so that I can ensure that you're as evenly matched as possible."

Well, that's something at least, but it doesn't stop me from gnawing on my inner cheek and picking at my cuticles. Somehow, the extra sessions I crammed in with Daniel don't feel like nearly enough.

Malachi looks at Jovi, who nods. He returns his attention to our group. "The stage crew needs more time to cleanse the stage."

"The smell is making me thirsty," the male with the spiky hair says. His buddies chuckle.

Another male vamp calls out, "What happened, Coach? Did someone from Team Brody get killed during practice?"

Vincent looks over his shoulder at me with a nasty gleam in his eyes. I'm too nervous to glare at him. Malachi wouldn't be so cruel as to pair us together, right? Then again, I'd likely have a better chance at beating Vincent than Suhani. Those two top my list of vampires I do NOT want to go up against. Make that three. The last vamp I want to be paired with is Carolina Bellmore, because Malachi would never, and I mean NEVER, choose me over his F23 compatriot.

Carolina points at the stage and announces gleefully, "First fatality of Season 13."

Malachi's jaw tightens. "No one was killed, but two contestants had to be sent home and eliminated from the competition. And before you get any ideas, let me make myself clear. This is *magical* combat. Wand work. You want to rip out throats? You're in the wrong place. If I wanted to bloody the *Spellcaster* stage, I'd have chosen werewolves for my team. Are you animals, or do you have self-control and magical prowess? Do you want to give the witches and wizards the satisfaction of brawling like beasts in front of millions of viewers?"

That shuts the vampires up. They straighten up with tall backs and give Malachi their undivided attention. Malachi folds his arms and scans each of their faces, all except mine. I suppose I'm not included in the warning. He doesn't have to worry about me going after anyone with my teeth. I'd be more than eliminated from the competition. I'd be exterminated from existence.

"We're here to cast, Coach," the spiky-haired vampire says.

"Glad to hear it, Oliver," Malachi answers. "Now go wait in the lobby until you are called to the stage for your one-on-one session with me."

My throat constricts as Malachi turns away from us. After a quick word with Jovi, he strides to a side door and exits the auditorium—leaving me alone with his team of bloodsuckers.

On instinct, I pull out my wand and cast myself into invisibility, and just in time, because Vincent is the first vampire to stand up and turn my way with a snarling upper lip. His expression changes from one of vengeance to confusion, forcing me to bite my tongue to keep from laughing. I'm not in an especially comical mood, but his nonplussed stare makes him appear moronic.

"What happened to the zombie?" Oliver asks. His sleeveless black shirt has a fake zipper pattern running across it at an angle, along with a fake pocket and extra zipper pulls. Tall combat boots are pulled over dark gray pants with white stripes along the side. It's grunge chic. He looks like a musician. It wouldn't be the first time the show had a multitalented caster.

Carolina scans the area where I sit frozen and wrinkles her nose. "She may have teleported or fled, but her stench is still here." She faces the stage. "Hey, you up there. When you're finished, we need a cleanup in aisle Z."

The vampires laugh, all except for Suhani. She lifts herself regally from the front row and makes her way to the main aisle. As she passes my row, I swear she looks directly at me before lifting her nose and continuing to the lobby.

"Blackthorn's new pet is such a killjoy," Carolina remarks with a flip of her hair.

"Can she even speak English?" another female asks.

"How about you ask her to suck your dick, Vince, and find out?" a male suggests.

The males laugh while Carolina rolls her eyes. She leaves her row and heads toward the exit Malachi went through rather than the lobby.

"Where are you going, Carolina?" a female asks.

Jovi looks over and frowns.

The blond F23er puckers her lips and lifts her chest. "That's nobody's concern." She arches a challenging brow at Jovi. The show's director rolls her eyes and turns away like Carolina's not worth the headache. Carolina smirks and then slinks off after Malachi.

I look at the rest of the team taking their time leaving the auditorium. Several keep glancing at the stage, licking their lips. It makes my stomach knot into ropes.

"Better pray Malachi doesn't pair you with the zombie, Vince, or you won't have a wand to defend yourself."

Several males crack up with laughter.

Vincent bares his teeth at them, cheeks turning red. "She caught me off guard is all. Next time, I'll repay the favor."

"Next time?" Oliver taunts.

Vincent puffs out his chest. "After Malachi calls me in for practice, I'm going to request he pit me against the zombie."

"Right. Sure thing, Vince. Cause Coach is in such a lenient mood."

"I'll give him a good reason to pair us," Vincent insists in an even voice that chills me. Gone is the hotheaded loudmouth from earlier, replaced by a facade of calm determination.

He and the other vamps leave the auditorium. I stay behind, eying the theater's side door exit.

If Vincent can request Malachi pair us up, then I have every right to request he doesn't.

CHAPTER THIRTY-SEVEN

I THROW MYSELF AGAINST a wall backstage, narrowly avoiding collision with a stagehand who rushes around the corner with a jug of bleach.

I'm not supposed to be back here, so I leave on the spell of invisibility as I pass two young, human, female crew members headed for the stage. One holds a black mug with the *Spellcaster* pentagram logo printed on the front. The other has a wand squeezed in her fist. I smell blood as they pass.

"I knew a supernaturals season was a bad idea," I overhear one say to the other, before they're too far to hear any more.

I hope Kace made it onto Brody's team and, if so, that he's not one of the contestants who got sent home for whatever led to the stage cleanup.

The halls are quiet after the crew members rush off. I wander around until I come across a hall with doors marked with the coaches' names. I see Cleo's door first and stop, swaying in place. What the hell am I doing sneaking around backstage? Malachi's obviously in a mood. For all I know, invading his privacy will have the opposite effect. He could pair me up with Vincent just to make a point.

Good going, Haylee. Well, he hasn't seen me, so I can turn right around and find a corner of the lobby to hide out in until Malachi calls me in for our one-on-one session.

I'm extra glad there's a special wand pocket on my stretch pants. It frees up my hands to wring my own neck for being such an idiot. My body goes from cold to hot at the mere thought of working with Malachi alone. This is what I always dreamed of, right? Getting coached by the legendary Malachi Rayne. In this moment, I think I prefer the fantasy.

My head spins, and my vision darkens. No. Please, no. Don't let me pass out in the hallway. With my luck, Malachi will trip over my unconscious, invisible body on his way back to the stage.

How am I supposed to calm myself when my lungs are incapable of breathing exercises? Can I spell myself into a state of bliss? I wish!

Then I remember my go-to zomb-out practice. I focus on Cleo's door before letting my eyes glaze over and shoulders relax. Muscle by muscle, my body becomes lighter. My lips part as my jaw loosens. My fingers uncurl.

I'm approaching the void when Carolina's shriek snaps me back to reality.

"What the hell, Malachi? How could you pick that undead thing over one of our own?"

I blink and look over to where Carolina's outcry originated. There's no slinking away now, not when I'm the topic of conversation. Instead, I inch closer to the next door, which is propped halfway open. It's marked *Malachi*, not that I need to read the name plaque with his raised voice coming from within.

"This is a spellcasting, NOT a species competition, Carolina, and Haylee clearly won," Malachi intones.

I swallow. Malachi's praise makes me feel lightheaded again. Be still my unbeating heart.

"She doesn't deserve to be on the show," Carolina snarls.

"She deserves it more than you."

Silence smothers the hall like a black bag yanked over the head right before a body goes missing. It is shortly broken by a resounding slap. I clench my teeth.

Malachi's voice is low and lethal. I have to strain my ears to hear him. "You dare strike me after I bent the rules to allow you on the show."

"*Allowed* me," Carolina says shrilly. "You forget yourself, Malachi. I've been a member of Forever 23 a lot longer than you."

"I didn't realize rank existed in F23," Malachi answers mockingly.

"Exactly! We're all equals and loyal to one another above all else. You know the damn rules." Carolina scoffs in disgust.

"When it comes to *Spellcaster*, you're on my turf and will not question the decisions I make on the show," Malachi says with equal scorn.

"Be grateful you don't have a master to reprimand you, Malachi, but just remember you still answer to F23. We're a unified group—now and forever. So, enjoy your sense of authority on your stupid show, but remember who got you into your purple chair in the first place."

I barely move out of the way in time before Carolina storms out of Malachi's dressing room. She stomps off in a burst of speed. There's a bang inside the room that sounds like a wall taking a kick from Malachi's foot.

"I never asked to be in your stupid, narcissistic snub club," Malachi growls to himself.

Snub club. That's a good one—not to mention shocking coming from an F23er. He has to be the first vampire in history who isn't on cloud nine that he belongs to the most exclusive club on the planet.

I start backing away. Yeah, now *really* doesn't seem like a good time.

When Malachi pokes his head out of his dressing room, I freeze in my tracks. The doorknob turns violently as it's twisted from inside, but then Malachi goes still. I grit my teeth as the vampire sniffs the air. He releases the door and steps into the hallway, narrowing his eyes in my direction.

"Haylee, I can smell you."

I'm too furious to worry about being caught eavesdropping. I unspell myself and put my hands on my hips.

"Why? Because I reek of zombie?"

Malachi's shoulders lift and fall on a heavy sigh. "No, it's your perfume. It's nice—whatever it is. I smelled it on you earlier."

"Well, that's just—" It takes my brain three words to catch up and realize that Malachi Rayne is in fact telling me that I smell nice. My cheeks fill with heat. "Um, thanks. It's called 'Beautiful Moments' by Midnight Reverie. They did this lovely blend of bright orange, warm vanilla, and caramelized sugar. What else? There were a couple other florals. Umm. Maybe some rose and something else. What was it?" I stare at the ceiling, uncomfortably aware of the gorgeous celebrity vampire staring at me.

"What are you doing here, Haylee?" Malachi punctuates each word.

I blink. "Oh, right, well, um—"

Before I can finish sorting out the tumbleweed that is my train of thought from whirling across a desert highway, Malachi's brown eyes drill into mine. "I trust you won't share what you overheard with anyone."

"Me? No, of course not! I barely heard anything, anyway. No vampire hearing, remember?" I chuckle nervously and dart sideways glances, briefly worrying that another spellcaster might come along cloaked and overhear *this* awkward exchange.

"But you do have ears, right?" Malachi's jaw loosens, making way for a smirk.

"These?" I tug on my lobes and shrug.

Malachi full-on smiles. I must be hallucinating. In the next instant, he looks stern. Yep. My eyes are playing tricks on me, but not my ears! He said I smelled nice. No take backs.

"Did you need something from me?" His voice oozes annoyance.

Yet again, I want to disappear and take off, but it's too late now. I've been caught thanks to my amazing scent—though I don't think this counts as a beautiful moment.

"I overheard Vincent saying he was going to request you pair him with me and—"

"I don't take requests," Malachi interrupts roughly.

My head bobs like a buoy in the wake of a passing trawler. "Good. I mean, you shouldn't. This is your turf." I wince and hope he doesn't think I was being glib in using his phrase to Carolina earlier.

But Malachi shakes his head and mutters, "Barely heard anything at all."

"Just a random word here and there—like 'turf.'"

"Haylee, I'll see you at our practice session," Malachi says with finality before retreating inside his dressing room and yanking the door roughly shut behind him. I turn and leave, hearing heavy metal blast from his quarters several seconds later.

I can hardly blame him. I'd want to blow out my eardrums, too, if I was stuck with Carolina Bellmore for life.

I've never heard of an F23er wishing they weren't part of that illustrious club. I guess there's a reason Malachi wants me to keep that information to myself. It makes me like him a little better—that and him complimenting my perfume. I'm still put out over how he behaved during my blind audition, but this takes some of the sting—or rather bite—out of it.

Unlike Malachi, I don't have a sanctuary backstage to await our practice session. It's back to the lobby until I'm called on to face him again.

Oh, joy. What a fun evening this is turning into.

One-on-one time with Malachi doesn't mean we're alone. Jimmy and Max are filming everything, and a couple of crew members are controlling the music and stage lights.

At least Jovi and the cleanup crew have left the theater, and "Team Vampire" is waiting in the lobby.

Malachi called me in first. I don't know if he did it as a kindness or to get our session over with.

Jimmy stands in front of the purple chairs with his camera aimed at the stage while Max is stationed on stage, pointing his lens at me walking down the aisle to join my coach on stage.

Malachi's eyes feel like spotlights, exposing every inch of me. It doesn't matter that I'm trim. The formfitting leggings and top feel too tight beneath his scrutiny. I'm not exposing much skin, but that's hardly comforting when every curve and outline of my womanly frame is visible in these snug clothes. At least my body had a chance to develop before I was zombified—unlike poor Rosie and all the other child zombies. It's annoying enough being treated like a teenager, never mind if I had to spend my life being a kid.

"Take your place on the X," Malachi instructs.

I walk to the X taped on the stage and face my coach. "Combat begins when the music starts and ends when it stops. Any casting before or after will result in your disqualification. You have three minutes to defend yourself against your opponent."

"Defend?" I pull my wand from its side pocket and frown at Malachi's lack of faith in me. Here we go again. The underestimated underdog. It's getting to be an old routine.

"Three minutes," Malachi repeats gruffly. The vampire's jaw is set, but he has a loose hold on his wand, which is way too tempting.

The second the music starts, I blast his wand right out of his hand. It sails over the edge of the stage and lands near Jimmy.

I think I hear Max snort out a laugh, but before I can gloat, Malachi flies at me in a burst of vampire-speed. My muscles contract, bracing for an impact that never comes. Malachi snatches my wand and whirls around to point at me and cast.

A tornado surges to life around me. My short braid whips against my neck and wind stings my eyes as it engulfs me in a cyclone. I can barely see through the savage swirl or the tears dragged from my eyes; it's as though it means to suck out every last drop of moisture from my body.

I have to get out of this thing.

When I make my leap, the vortex sucks me up and hurls me at least twenty feet above the stage, where I'm spun round and round, faster and faster until I'm dizzy and ready to hurl. The worst part is that if it stops, I have no way of saving myself from becoming a pile of broken bones on the stage.

CHAPTER THIRTY-EIGHT

OF COURSE, MALACHI is going to drop me.

I wounded his pride by getting the jump on him, and now he's turned my own wand against me.

Everything is spinning. My body. My vision. My brain. I clamp my mouth shut to keep from vomiting. The cleaning crew just got the stage cleaned. Then there's the second reason I keep my lips pressed tight. I refuse to beg Malachi for mercy.

My hands flail and grasp for something to hold on to, but the wind rushing between my fingers is no help. If this is what flying feels like, then it's highly overrated. I lean forward in an attempt to go vertical, which has the ill effect of pitching me forward so I catch a brief view of how far I am from the stage. My body flips around another time. I don't want to land on my feet and crush my ankles. I certainly don't want to land on my head and shatter my skull. I don't want to break anything on my body!

If I won the heart, I could defend myself instead of swirling helplessly like the roof of a house caught in a tornado.

The wind rips out my hair tie and blows my braid out in an instant. Blond hair whips me in the eyes. My body begins to descend slowly, while the spinning continues in full force. The tornado fades little by little into the stage until I am set down gently and it disappears altogether. I try to remain standing while the theater seats and stage continue to spin, but I tilt to one side and misstep. *Thump.* I fall to the stage, sprawled out on my side. It could have been worse, though. Way, way worse.

It's a little hard to feel grateful as partially digested brain rushes up my throat. I swallow it down, and it's just as gross as I remember bile tasting as a human.

Malachi stomps over. "What the hell was that, Hutchins?"

Great. He's using my last name. The coaches never use contestants' last names. I must be in trouble.

It's a serious effort to get to my feet, which takes outstretched arms to keep my balance, but I'm not about to listen to this lecture in a crumpled heap on the stage.

My loose hair tickles my cheeks. I swallow again and cover my mouth with my hand. Malachi's not in my face, but I don't want him scenting my vomit breath. Well, not technically breath, but whatever foul waft might originate from the leftover taste on my tongue.

Malachi doesn't wait for me to answer his question before drilling into me. "First rule of magical combat—never lose hold of your wand."

"You lost yours," I mutter, which is the wrong thing to say.

Malachi hisses. I don't know why humans associate vampires with bats. It really ought to be snakes, with the way they hiss when they're angry. They also have fangs, cold blood, and lightning-fast strikes in common. Just saying.

My coach squeezes my poor wand in his fist. "If this had been your real combat performance, your opponent would not have hesitated to drop you from two stories high."

"Why didn't you?" I demand.

Malachi's lips part, and he blinks several times. "I'm your coach," he answers, sounding genuinely confused by my question. I give him a *yeah and?* kind of shrug, which makes the swaying worse.

He stares at me for several seconds before releasing an exasperated sigh, which is only slightly less irritating than his hiss. Malachi Rayne sighs a lot for a man who, like me, doesn't breathe. Does it take effort? Does he do it for the sole sake of communicating his annoyance?

"My job as your coach is to give you pointers to help you win." He says this slowly as though I'm dimwitted. I narrow my eyes. Malachi narrows his back. It's hard to focus when my vision is still recovering from its spin cycle. "I saved you during cast-offs, didn't I?" Malachi snaps.

He comes into sharp focus as anger freezes my vision. Mythical brown eyes. Thick eyelashes. A proud nose. Full lips. Why does he have to be so hot? It doesn't matter, because I'm mad too.

"This season's competition is completely unfair and speciesist," I gripe. "I shouldn't have needed saving."

The muscles cord in Malachi's neck. "Well, you did, and it likely won't be the last time. Now take this and try to hold on to it for the remainder of our session."

I yank my wand out of Malachi's hand and swiftly back up several steps. There's still the whole mouth vomit issue. Confusion briefly flickers over Malachi's face when I withdraw as though he's the icky one I'm trying to avoid, which is hilarious.

My vampire coach storms down the steps to fetch his wand off the ground, several feet away from Jimmy, who films the whole thing. Noticing him, Malachi straightens up and glowers straight into the lens.

"Erase that," he says. Malachi turns to the stage. "You too," he commands Max.

Max lowers his camera, frowning. "It won't be aired," he says.

"I don't care. I want the footage destroyed immediately."

Momentarily forgetting my vomit mouth, I gape at Malachi. "Are you compelling them?"

"Of course not; that's illegal," Malachi snaps at me. "But Max and Jimmy know it's better to stay on my good side."

Well, there go the last of my illusions of Malachi being one of the rare decent males of his species. I suppose not flinging me into the auditorium chairs could be considered a kindness as far as Malachi Rayne is concerned. I clamp my mouth shut and narrow my eyes while Max and Jimmy turn away to presumably rewind the spectacle that's been my first training session with Malachi—so they can record over it. Nope, no illegal activity happening here, just a good old-fashioned threat.

The cameramen share a look before Max announces, "Ready when you are, Malachi."

The vampire nods curtly and stalks toward me. "When the music begins, you will have three minutes to either take down your opponent or outlast their onslaught." His tone is chilly and crisp. "Which approach do you want to take? Offense or defense?"

"Defense," I say through tight teeth. As much as it pains me to voice the word, I'm nowhere near ready to use my wand for violence. All that matters is making it to next week, which means I need my coach's help avoiding fun things like treacherous twisters.

Malachi nods. "Let's see what you've got. I want you to block my attempt to knock you down. *Hufta gamal veed*!"

The blast of wind that hits me feels like a brick wall. I land on my ass with a heavy thud, which makes Malachi grin. I bet this part ends up on TV. Jerk!

"At least you managed to hold on to your wand," Malachi says while I get up. "Better to take a hit and hang onto your only source of magical defense than to stay upright but have your wand whisked away."

My nostrils flare. "Well, maybe I'd just have to tackle my opponent and steal their wand if that happens."

Malachi tsks and lifts his chin with an air of superiority. "That kind of maneuver is most likely to fail for anyone other than, say, me."

Now he sounds like the pompous F23er he'll always be. I glower at him. A grin lifts his cheeks before it's gone in a blink, and my coach gets back to business.

"Do you know how to shield?" he asks.

"Yeah," I grumble.

"Then show me. Here, I'll even give you a three-second warning. Three. Two."

"*Sheltaward!*" I shout, right as Malachi finishes his countdown and slams another wall of air at me. My invisible shield blocks his ill wind. Malachi swings his wand arm as though he's about to pitch a baseball. "*Ramfend*," I say to strengthen my shield.

Malachi points his wand above me and casts. "*Vitanate arachno halluce aphobia.*" Spiders rain down over my head. Hundreds of them land on my chest, arms, and legs, clinging to me with hairy legs.

I shriek like a banshee and wave my arms, but the spiders hold on. A few dangle and begin climbing their way back up.

Somehow, I keep hold of my wand despite the tarantula that's appeared over my hand and looks to be prying at my fingers.

Then a blast of wind comes at me from across the stage, once more knocking me down. Thankfully, it blows the spiders away as well. They turn into bits of black smoke that drift away and disappear. I still feel itchy all over.

"You have to focus," Malachi says. "Look what happened with a small distraction. You lost hold of your shield. Also, you left yourself vulnerable from above." I narrow my eyes. I hate that word. Malachi purses his lips. "Glare at me all you want. Three minutes is a long time, and so far, you're barely holding out for three seconds." He glances at his wristwatch, which has me scrambling to my feet. Malachi's right. I'm struggling, and he doesn't have all night to work with me.

"How do I defend myself from top to bottom and all sides?" I ask in a rush of words.

Malachi lowers his arm. "I have a bubble barrier spell. It takes longer to cast, but it's all-encompassing."

"I'd love to learn it." Malachi's brows draw in like he's suspicious of my enthusiasm. I tuck my hair behind my ears. "Please," I add with a smile.

Malachi searches my face, taking his time before nodding. "Very well. Come here."

Heat sweeps up my neck. I pinch my pendant between my fingers. "Er, aren't I close enough?"

This earns me one of Malachi's exasperated sighs. He briefly grips the hair on his head. "For Pete's sake, I'm not going to bite you."

"I know you're not going to bite me." I huff and roll my eyes. "I'm just trying to be respectful of your space."

Malachi blinks, and his jaw loosens slightly as though he finally understands what I'm getting at. He straightens his spine. "Haylee, when you're on this stage, you're one thing and one thing only—a spellcaster."

"That's not how you looked at me after the screen lifted at the blinds," I remind him.

"I had all vampires on my team and knew you'd clash."

"Then why save me?" I demand.

"Because I couldn't let a caster with your potential walk away. Now come here."

I approach Malachi cautiously. He stuffs his wand in his front jeans pocket and turns me around by my shoulders so that my back is to him. His hands are surprisingly warm and gentle. My throat goes dry as he takes my wand arm and guides it above my head.

"*Norda*," he says in a deep voice inches away.

My body tingles all over. "Uh—"

"Repeat my words," Malachi instructs.

"*Norda*," I repeat, trying to focus on the words and not his strong, but also soothing, hold on me. This is more distracting than the spider illusions. Malachi's fingers pressing against me are all too real.

My coach brings my arm to one side, followed by the other—finishing with it by my side, wand pointed at the floor.

"*Suda*," he says before releasing my arm.

"*Suda*," I repeat.

My neck feels hotter than ever. He's no longer touching me, but he's still right behind me. If there was breath in his lungs, I'd probably feel it against my ear as he murmurs, "Good. Now try it on your own."

I turn around as Malachi backs away and pulls out his wand.

"How will I have time to complete the spell before my opponent throws something at me?" I ask.

"Shield first. Bubble second. Most spellcasters will first come at you with a frontal assault. It's the quickest and easiest form of attack." Malachi huffs like it's magical child's play that doesn't impress him in the least.

I nod. "Okay, thanks for the tip."

I expect Malachi to throw a spell at me, but his wand remains at his side while he watches me cast the spells.

"Good," he says. He looks across the theater seats and raises his voice. "Now let's try it with the music."

I repeat Malachi's spell over and over in my head while we face off waiting for the first note of the music.

When our session ends, I still can't hold out for three full minutes, but I'm up against Malachi freaking Rayne, and I've made vast improvements—praise from the vampire's own lips—so that's something. But is it enough to win my combat round?

CHAPTER THIRTY-NINE

THE NEXT EVENING, I've got the hotel room to myself and a tray with plated brain, liver, and a crystal glass a quarter full of blood. I guess the kitchen staff wasn't sure what to give me to drink from the supernatural section of their menu. Can't imagine they get too many zombies in their fine establishment ordering room service.

I sit cross-legged on my bed with my tray and the TV in front of me. A perk of being on Team Malachi is that I no longer have to perform with the first two groups. Also, the blind auditions are now airing, which gives me a chance to evaluate my competition.

My phone is face up on the blanket beside me with Cameron and Joni on speaker so we can watch the blinds "together."

"That's so cool," Joni says over the phone as Tripp Peters casts a pack of wolves onto the stage.

Her tone changes when a deer materializes and is subsequently chased down and torn apart in a bloody display by the phantom wolves.

"Oh, no. That poor deer," Joni cries.

"It's not even real," comes a huffy retort. Ah, yes, TJ. He's on speaker too. Unfortunately.

Malachi and Brody raise their wands. Even if I weren't already in the know, it would be obvious that Tripp would pick Brody. That doesn't stop Malachi from trying.

"I know you've already made up your mind, but what if you changed things up and surprised everyone?" Malachi suggests from on screen.

Brody chuckles. "This is just sad. Tripp, go ahead and set the vamp straight. You know you belong with me and my pack."

"You mean *team*?" Cleo huffs.

"Isn't that what I said?" Brody asks innocently.

Malachi leans forward in his chair with his attention still trained on Tripp. "On Brody's team, you'll be competing against other werewolves. I don't have anyone like you on my team."

"Anyone awesome, you mean?" Brody jabs.

"Can someone please put a muzzle on him?" Malachi returns.

The camera goes to Colt, who speaks into his microphone. "Tripp, which team do you choose?"

"Team Brody," the werewolf says without pause.

The camera cuts to the coach's chairs where Brody stands up and claps his hands together. "You made the right choice, my man. Let's take this all the way to the finals, Tripp!"

Malachi slumps back in his seat and folds his arms.

Nathaniel Duke auditions next. I frown the entire time, still sore that Zen announced the wizard as the winner of our cast-off. Cleo doesn't lift her wand for him, which is ironic, seeing how she praised his cast-off performance.

Zen raises his wand. As Nathaniel's performance ends, Malachi raises his wand just before the final note.

There's no hesitation when Colt asks Nathaniel which team he chooses.

"Team Zen," the young wizard speaks loudly into the microphone.

Brody points at Malachi and laughs. "Rejected again. Ouch. They better bring out some vampires soon, or you'll have no one on your team."

It's weird not seeing Malachi as the popular coach from the previous—human—seasons. The *Spellcaster* species show has turned the competition on its axis.

Cleo laughs along with Brody. "Maybe there aren't enough vampires with the kind of magical aptitude to audition on *Spellcaster*."

"Oh, burn," Brody says with a wide grin.

Maybe I'd feel bad for Malachi if he hadn't been such a brute after my four-wand lift. Okay, I've got a little more sympathy after he saved me during cast-offs and said I smelled good and treated me like a spellcaster—not a zombie. My cheeks burn as I remember his hands on my arms.

My eyes shift to the mirror beside the TV, where my hot Haylee face reflects back at me.

During the commercial break, I take a tentative sip of blood. It goes down easily, so I drink the rest. Like brains and organs, it might be good for me. It makes me feel more alert, anyway.

After swallowing the last of the blood and setting the crystal glass back on the tray, I wipe my mouth on the back of my hand before picking up my wand.

"*Vitanate arachno halluce aphobia.*"

Spiders appear all over the room, dangling from the ceiling, crawling over the dresser, covering the mirror, and—my favorite—creeping all over Blair's blankets and pillows. I'm not ready to have them on my bed with me yet, but I plan to build up to it. I need to mentally prepare for my combat round. Face my fears.

"*Vitanate repetillian halluce serp*," I cast, adding snakes to the floor. They slither over the carpet.

I scoot into the center of my bed, seriously doubting I'll be able to bring the creepy crawlies and slithering snakes onto my cover with me before I go to sleep.

After commercials, the show launches into the backstory of the next contestant—Carolina Bellmore. Oh, goodie. At least the show helps distract me a little from the frightful illusions slithering and crawling around the room.

Texas born and bred, Carolina is the daughter of the now deceased investment tycoon Robert Bellmore. After he helped his vampire clients make millions, a group of vampire masters offered Mr. Bellmore the opportunity to choose one of his five children to be made.

"I was always Daddy's little girl. I miss him so much." Carolina sniffles during her interview with Colt.

"It must be hard being the last of your siblings still around," Colt says gently.

Carolina's tears dry up in an instant. She sits up straight and purses her lips. "Oh, they were dead to me before they all died. My Forever 23 brothers and sisters are the only family I need."

The interview cuts to Carolina's audition. Almost as soon as her pop music starts, Malachi lifts his wand. His face fills the screen for barely a second, but I swear I catch him grimacing. Carolina points her wand above her head and an illusion of a disco ball appears. It would be more dazzling if she added fractured bits of light to the stage and made them spin, but she doesn't. She casts images of blurry club goers and then spends the rest of her performance dancing in the middle of the hazy crowd.

At the end, Malachi is the only coach holding up his wand. He lowers his arm when the music fades.

Colt strides across the stage to join a beaming Carolina. "A high-energy performance from Carolina Bellmore. Wouldn't you say so, Cleo?"

The screen cuts to Cleo, who flashes a frosty grin. "Yes, well, you have the perfect coach to work with you on the show."

"I do, don't I?" Carolina responds immediately with an arched brow.

Colt turns to the blond vampire and grins with the same good-natured smile he offers every contestant. "Congratulations, Carolina."

The audience applauds as Carolina catwalks across the stage, waving and blowing several kisses.

A male whistles from the audience. Another shouts, "Take me as your slave, Carolina!" She smirks and struts off the stage.

"Vamp tramp," TJ comments snidely through the phone speaker.

As the camera pans across the coaches' chairs, I catch another brief glimpse of Malachi, whose lips have flatlined like a dying human after his final heartbeat. Watching his reaction to Carolina's audition gives me a teetering sense of time traveling into the past. I mean, this is the past as it happened before I overheard the two F23ers engaged in hostile conversation.

It seems obvious to me that Malachi knew what music to listen for—and of course, the studio wouldn't dare switch the soundtrack on an esteemed member of F23 the way they did for Mariana. She's already texted me a half dozen times claiming she'll never live down her audition after it airs.

Cameron huffs over the phone. "Malachi's lucky he got the opportunity to snag you from that old coot Zen."

His compliment alleviates the thorns poking at my belly, making it feel fuzzy again.

"Thanks, Cam."

Obviously, he was less than thrilled when I told him about my new team, but I feel better about it after working with Malachi one-on-one. I was hoping Cameron would too, but all he said was, "I still wish a different coach had stolen you. Better yet, Zen should have held on to his best team member and chosen you as the winner or used his team save more wisely. Foolish old man."

I don't tell Cameron the truth. I'd rather be on Malachi's team. Zen didn't believe in me. I mean, Malachi's not exactly cheering me on, but he's doing something better—coaching me.

He's given me extra motivation to win my combat round tomorrow to stay on his team and on the show.

And he's rekindled the crush I used to have on him—something I'm most definitely NOT sharing with Cameron or anyone else. Ever!

At the next commercial break, I dangle my leg over my bed and grit my teeth. A snake curls up inches below my foot. When its forked tongue flicks out, I pull my leg back to the safety of my bed.

"It's just an illusion," I tell myself. "YOUR illusions!"

I prefer butterflies.

I grab one of my pillows and toss it on the snake. The pillow passes through the illusion. Before I can chicken out, I launch myself over my bed and walk through the spiders and snakes. Having the phone on speaker is a good exercise in holding back my scream. I don't want to alarm Joni or Cameron.

My feet pass through the illusions. There's nothing there. Emboldened, I run my hand over the spiders on the dresser—and suppress the urge to yank my arm away from all those hairy little legs. My face itches, causing my nose to twitch in an effort to let the feeling pass without scratching my face.

A werewolf takes the stage on screen. When "Barbie Girl" by Aqua begins to play, the young twenty-something male freezes up and gapes into the audience.

I know it's wrong, but I laugh and text Mariana.

Haylee: At least you're not the only one they pulled that 💩 on.

"This isn't my music," the werewolf mouths. He continues to stand in place and yells, "Hey! You're playing the wrong soundtrack."

Haylee: He's not even making an effort.

Mariana: I have to admit, I'm relieved they didn't air my fiasco first.

The male growls over the chipper Barbie song, throwing his wand to the stage.

Mariana: Holy 💩. Is he going to shift?

I look between my phone and the TV in shock as the werewolf goes full beast and snarls in the coaches' direction. The image on the screen cuts to Malachi looking amused as he glances over at Brody and lifts a brow. Brody shrugs and says, "Clearly he's not a Barbie kind of girl."

"Or boy," Malachi says.

The werewolf lunges toward the edge of the stage, snapping his fangs. Audience members gasp.

Cleo stands up. "Enough of this." She snaps her fingers and the werewolf disappears. Cleo sits back down in her purple chair and says, "Next."

The following day, I'm back on the *Spellcaster* stage in front of a live audience, the coaches, and the camera crew.

Colt has called me and a vampire named John Gable to the stage for our combat round. John was in his mid-twenties when he was turned. According to the backstory they ran on him last night, he was a heartthrob actor in the 1950s. After being nominated for Best Actor for his role in his most famous film, *Thundering Hooves*, in which he played a charming outlaw, he received an invite into the world of immortality. He was turned before the Academy Awards and received the Oscar as a newly made vampire—not that humans knew it back then. John went on to win more awards over the years before disappearing from the silver screen. According to John, this was because vampires weren't free to be themselves back then, and he couldn't expose his kind by continuing to act while clearly not aging.

"But paranormal creatures have been out in the open for over two decades now," Colt had prodded. "Why haven't you returned to acting?"

That's when John admitted that his master had found his behavior too similar to the rebellious characters he played in films and forced him into servitude as punishment.

Spellcaster is John's comeback performance thanks to his new master.

Something I recently learned about vampire hierarchy is that if a master's underling manages to off their maker, they take over as their clan's master. Lucky for John, a more progressive member of his clan took the reins.

John must be feeling nostalgic, because he's wearing cowboy boots, a thick leather belt with a large buckle, along with a long-sleeved western shirt in an Aztec pattern. He faces me on the stage like we're about to draw guns rather than wands and have ourselves an old-timey shootout.

I'm wearing white platform Dr. Martens boots over snug light purple pants with patches of pink and dark purple. It matches my long-sleeved top that's zipped down to my collarbones.

John and I could not clash more. We're different species from completely separate eras. But after seeing John's audition, I'm glad Malachi paired us. John was a one-wand lift, and lucky to receive that much. The Oscar winner said it himself during his televised interview; he's new to spellcasting.

I'm not sure whether to be relieved or insulted that Malachi paired me with a newbie caster.

Now that I'm standing on stage, palms sweating, the answer is definitely relieved.

I'm wearing tight clothing again. A dress is out of the question for combat. I don't need to go flashing the audience and cameras unintentionally if John ends up using wind magic with even a fraction of Malachi's force.

Anya arranged my hair into a low bun with strands of purple hair extensions woven in to fun it up.

I'm as ready as I'll ever be—which isn't ready at all.

All too soon, Colt announces, "Let the combat begin," and walks swiftly off stage. Heavy metal blasts from the speakers—Malachi's choice.

John points his wand at me and yells, "*Veeda reciso lifteena*!" A bullet rockets straight for me.

Yeah, no surprise he's a *cast first, ask questions later* kind of spellcaster. But I'm expecting this and already have my front shield up in time to block his bullet. The projectile doesn't disperse like Malachi's spiders. It ricochets off my shield and hits the stage with a metallic ping.

What the hell? I gape at the bullet rolling across the stage when I should be finishing off Malachi's bubble spell.

By the time I point my wand above my head, there's a rope swirling overhead before dropping past my defenses. My next spell is cut off by the rope around my throat as John lassos me like cattle. He tries to pull me to him, but my shield is still in place, which means I smack against it so hard I see stars.

The audience laughs at my expense, and it's not the first time. I already had to relive the humiliation of being blown over and shrieking like a girl in the selected replays of my training session with Malachi and the spiders right before Colt called me and John to the stage for combat.

My platform boots leave the stage once more as John lifts me. I try to spell myself free of his rope, but the damn thing is choking my vocal cords. John raises me higher, which makes a cold sweat break out over my skin as I remember the feeling of helplessness when Malachi sucked me into his vortex.

I'm knocked against my shield again, but John's forehead is wrinkled like this isn't his intention. He looks like he wants to lasso me in, not dangle me like a pink and purple Christmas ornament.

Meanwhile, the audience is going nuts over his maneuver. Sure, cheer for the zombie lynching. Good thing I don't need to breathe. But I do need the use of my throat.

John grits his teeth like he's physically hoisting me off the stage. And it sucks because it's working. It's slow, but the stage is most definitively getting farther from my platformed boots. In a panic, I kick out only to hit my shield. How high up does it go? I don't want to find out.

John lifts his hand, dragging me farther up, and pulls another bullet out of his pocket, holding it ready in his open palm. Images of zombies used as target practice flash across my mind from Kendra's Telepatch shares. I can't let anyone see me that way, especially not Joni and Cameron . . . or my coach.

John tosses his bullet and then uses his wand to shoot just above my head. My barrier holds. I start to fall before John stops my descent with a jerky wave of his wand. From the way sweat glistens on his face, it seems performing two spells at once is a strain on him. He pulls out another bullet and aims it higher. This one crosses without trouble. John smiles. He's found where my shield ends roughly four feet from where I currently dangle. His wand swings upward, lifting me to the gap in my shield one foot at a time.

CHAPTER FORTY

MALACHI IS GOING to groan when he sees what I do next, but I have no choice. I need both of my hands right now.

Unfortunately, I don't have a handy wand pocket in my performance pants, which means stuffing it down them—secure against the elastic band.

Once both of my hands are free, I tug at the brittle, unforgiving rope. All it does is chafe my skin. I reach behind my head, locate the knot, and twist the rope around the rough lump. Ignoring the burning in my fingers, I twist vigorously until the knot loosens enough to get my head free of the noose. I'm still hanging on and about a foot away from being shot in the face.

My muscles quiver as I hold on to the rope with one hand while extracting my wand from my pants with the other.

"*Levadrift grav lanta.*"

I let go of the rope and float down to the stage. The sound of my platform shoes returning to the stage is a beautiful melody in my ears.

Lightning quick, I cast a complete protective bubble around myself—not looking to see what John is up to until I've finished the spell.

With a tight frown, John stuffs his next bullet back inside his pocket. His rope still dangles in the air. He spells it back to him before wrapping it into a corded circle that he threads over his shoulder.

The heavy metal soundtrack thuds against me like a heartbeat. Where are we on the clock? How much longer do I have to hold out?

I steal a glance Malachi's way, and my stomach drops as realization hits. If I want to win combat rounds, I can't just hole up in a protective bubble. At this point, John is the clear winner. He got through my defenses right away and came close to taking me out.

Across from me, John folds his arms, purses his lips, and waits. I'm guessing Malachi told him that if his opponent managed to secure herself—the coward's way—he should allow the music to play out and win the round.

Did Malachi know about the rope and the bullets?

I gnash my teeth. Of course he did. He's John's coach. Why didn't he ask me if I wanted props to aid in my magical combat? Oh, right. I chose defense. But still, it would have helped to bring an object like, oh, say a folding knife to cut through rope!

I lift my wand, preparing to release my protective bubble. Sadly, the shield works both ways. I can't shelter myself and attack John at the same time. When I open my mouth to undo my spell, the words dry up in my throat. Sweat beads above my lips. My legs tremble. The moment I release this bubble, I am no longer safe.

A guitar screeches through the speakers. I'm running out of time. It's do or not die—but go home. I know this, but still, I'm frozen.

Then I hear laughter and blink. John points a finger at me in a motion like he shot me and then blows on the tip like it's a smoking gun. He repeats the gesture to the delight of the audience.

"*Evapostray*," I say softly while John's not paying attention. My spell goes unheard while the audience laughs. I point my wand at John and cast, "*Vitanate repetillian halluce serp*."

The rope around his shoulder turns into a snake. I wish the python was real, but at least I can use his horrid rope against him. It moves and rubs over him slowly, winding its tail-end around his arm.

John's head jerks, and he yelps as the audience gasps.

Taking steps toward him, I yell, "*Halluce serp veed*!" with all of the pent-up rage exploding from within my battered body.

The python lashes out, striking John's neck. He jumps backward, but my snake rope is wrapped around him tightly. I line up John's neck in the sight of my wand tip and rotate my wrist. The python wraps around John's neck.

How does it feel now? I scream inside my head.

When John reaches for his neck, I spell my python to strike his hand. John shrieks, which brings a smirk to my lips. What kind of vampire is afraid of snakes?

I cast a growth spell on the python, making it expand around John. He falls to the stage as though his mind can't tell the difference between what's really there and what he's seeing.

A cruel kind of satisfaction builds inside me.

Why choose defense when offense is so much sweeter? Is this how vampires feel all the time? Top of the food chain? Untouchable? Rulers of the world?

Well, step aside suckers, because Haylee Hutchins is taking her place atop the mighty peaks of world dominion.

I take three more steps toward John and point my wand where he struggles on the floor. "*Hance span.*" I magnify my spell until John is entirely wrapped within the thick scales of my python.

After Metallica screeches to an end, a silence as dense as coastal fog fills the theater.

My python disappears on its own, leaving John fighting his own length of rope on the ground. His wand has been abandoned next to him. John blinks, flings the rope away, and snatches his wand before standing with a hiss directed at me.

I bat my lashes and smile at him.

John narrows his eyes and pushes the tips of his fingers into the pocket with the bullets. I ready my wand.

Colt strides onto the stage with his microphone. "Let's hear a round of applause for that exciting combat round between John Gable and Haylee Hutchins, everyone." The audience claps as Colt motions for me and John to join him at the front of the stage. "Brody, what did you think?" Colt asks.

"Well, as you can see, I was on the edge of my seat." Brody motions with his hand to where he's positioned on his purple chair, leaning forward like he's about to fall out.

The audience chuckles as images of him appear on large screens facing into the theater.

"Zen, how do you think your former team member performed?" Colt asks.

It's an effort not to frown when Zen talks. He scratches his beard first while looking at me without meeting my eyes. "Haylee clearly demonstrated that she can both defend herself and attack in a magical combat situation."

Okay, so that was acceptable as far as comments go.

"Cleo?" Colt asks.

Cleo breathes heavily into her clip-on mic before imparting her witchy judgment. "I see why Malachi paired the two of you. I'm going to have to disagree with Zen. I don't think either of you demonstrated the ability or skills necessary to thoroughly defend yourselves against a competing caster. As far as I'm concerned, you both failed to protect yourselves. You both managed a strike against the other; only John had the misfortune of casting his first, and as everyone knows, in combat you have to be the last caster standing." Cleo leans back in her chair and lifts her nose.

Beside me, John's fingers curl into fists. At least his ire is aimed elsewhere—if only for those scathing seconds Cleo drops her criticism over us like bitter word bombs.

"Malachi?" Colt asks our coach.

Unlike Brody, Malachi sits fully in his purple chair, thumb rubbing over his wand. His frown is impossible to read.

"Cleo's right," he says.

My mouth gapes open. Say what? How can he agree with that miserable witch?

"Neither of you had control over your casting. Your magic was"—Malachi wrinkles his nose—"sloppy." I narrow my eyes. If only I could cast a python onto his lap without the risk of being sent straight home. "John, you got too ambitious for your level of casting. If you had stuck with your rope, you very well might have succeeded in getting your opponent past her barrier. Haylee, you lost focus the moment John attacked, and it cost you. Also, you always want to keep hold of your wand no matter what. You should have been able to free yourself with your wand and magic. You got lucky."

My eyes turn to flint, and my lips curl.

Lucky? Does he have nothing to say about the way I turned my opponent's own prop into a badass freaking python?

"Malachi, who is the winner of this combat round?" Colt asks.

"The winner is Haylee," Malachi announces. At least he doesn't keep me in suspense, but that fact is a little hard to appreciate after he dismissed my skills as luck.

"Thank you, John. Congratulations, Haylee," Colt says. "Next up, from Team Malachi, we have Suhani Das and Darren Harmen. Take a look."

The theater darkens as clips from the casters' one-on-one training play over the stage screens. I'm halfway across the stage with John storming in from behind.

Once we're behind the curtains, he hisses at me.

I whip around and raise my wand. "Combat's over. You lost, but if you want a little souvenir to take back to your room, I'll conjure that python again for you."

"You got lucky, flesh eater, but that luck is going to run out soon." With a final hiss, John stomps off.

His ominous warning bounces off me like his wayward bullet.

I won combats. I made it to next week. Now I have to make sure I secure one of the four coveted spots when Malachi chooses who to take with him to the live cast-offs.

Back at the hotel, the werewolves are drinking and laughing in the lobby. Pints are raised. Cocktail glasses clink. Cody and Jake are engaged in a mock duel with their wands near Izzie King, who wears a hot-pink-and-black short skirt with little buckles at the hips and black tulle peeking from the hemline. She holds a champagne flute in one hand and her wand and phone with its glitter case in the other.

I only spare the group a brief glance before heading toward the elevators.

"Yo, Z," a familiar voice calls. "Where you off to in such a hurry? Not packing, I hope."

I can't help smiling when I turn around and spot Kace seated on the top of a couch back, his high-top sneakers on the cushion. He grins back and lifts a highball glass filled with ice and golden liquid with a lemon peel curled over the rim.

"So Brody saved you?"

"Yup." Kace's grin widens. "Couldn't let a good thing go. The dark horses are still in the race—Alexander's words, not mine."

I laugh, practically hearing Alexander's voice inside my head.

Beside Kace, my old teammate, Luke, scowls. "Why are you talking to her?"

Kace's expression turns deadly as he snarls at Luke. "Get lost, mongrel."

Luke looks from Kace's murderous eyes to the wolf tattoo on his neck and flees to join Daphné and the female wolf with a mohawk.

"Look at that, a spot just opened up." Kace's brows jump.

I walk over and hesitate. Tripp Peters is seated on the next cushion over, leaning forward as he texts.

Kace follows my gaze and huffs. "Peters doesn't care if you sit with us. Do you, Peters?"

Tripp taps his phone several times before glancing up. I might as well be a mannequin for all the interest he shows. "It's fine," he says, and then returns to his phone.

Kace rolls his eyes before pointing at the cushion. As soon as I've taken a seat, he drops down beside me. "We're celebrating besting our opponents during combat rounds."

"Congratulations," I say with a wide grin.

"What about you, Z?"

I lift my chest. "Combat champion."

Kace howls and offers me his fist to bump. I go for it. "That's my girl," Kace says. "Let's get you a celebratory drink."

I wince. "Oh, uh, no thanks. I want to keep a clear head."

"Blood?"

"Um."

Kace flicks his wrist, drawing my attention to the collection of tattooed skulls on his fingers. "It's okay, Z. Blood doesn't gross me out. It's like sauce with my meat." Kace smacks his lips. Tripp looks over, frowns, and then gets up and moves to a secluded chair nestled against a potted palm. Kace chuckles. "Don't worry about it. I'm the one he doesn't want to be seen with. He's a whipped wolf—getting instructions day and night from his girlfriend. I'm pretty sure he'd rather be alone in his room on video with her, but she doesn't want him to appear as a lone wolf on social. Anyway, tell me who you thrashed in combat?"

"John Gable."

Kace hoots and slaps his leg. "John Gable the Hollywood legend?" When I nod, Kace's grin widens. "You are badass, Haylee Hutchins."

"You know it," I say jokingly. "What about you? Who did you beat?"

"Like literally?" Kace smiles wickedly.

"No, not literally." I give him a playful shove, which doesn't move his armor of muscles an inch. I'm happy he got onto Brody's team and held his spot during combats.

Kace lifts his glass, avoiding spillage, then laughs and takes a sip. "Showed up a witch. She didn't take it too well."

"Neither did John."

We both laugh.

Cody and Jake stop clacking their wands against one another and race over. "What's so funny?" they ask eagerly.

Kace smirks. "Whipping witches and fangers at combat."

"Now that's what I'm talking about," Jake says. The twins turn to one another and high-five.

Kace snorts. "The pair of you went against another wolf."

Cody folds his arms. "Hey, man, we don't pick who we combat. You know we'd take down a witch, wizard, or vampire over a wolf any day of the week." Beside him, Jake nods.

I smile, grateful my species wasn't on the twins' list of preferred takedowns.

"I'm curious what you used against your opponent, since fire was off the table," I say.

To my delight, the twins lap up my attention.

"Oh, we still used fire," Jake says, puffing out his chest.

"Fire illusions," Cody clarifies. He points his wand at Izzie King and casts. Her short skirt appears to go up in flames. Izzie shrieks and drops her glass, which shatters against the floor.

Cody and Jake burst into laughter. Izzie uses her wand to make the illusion disappear from her skirt and then stomps over to Jake. "Real mature," she snarls into his face.

"Hey, it wasn't me," Jake laughs.

Izzie narrows her eyes. "I'd set you on fire if I didn't know you'd enjoy the heat."

Jake's eyebrows jump. "Oh, yeah?" he asks huskily.

"Sorry, Izzie. I'm the one who cast the spell," Cody speaks up.

Izzie continues glaring at Jake for several more seconds. "You owe me a drink," she snaps before spinning around in a swirl of pink hair and '80s plaid. She storms off and plants herself near Tripp, where she begins scrolling through her phone.

"Sorry, dog, I'm the one she wants," Jake says to his brother.

Cody pats the bun on top of his head. "Maybe I should shave my hair."

"Dude, no. That's my thing now," Jake says.

Tripp stands up and issues a shrill whistle that gets all of the wolves' attention. "Hey, everyone. There's a hot club four blocks away. First round is on me."

Yips and howls arise. Anyone who is seated, including Kace, stands up and moves toward Tripp. Kace sets his half-finished drink on a table and stretches his arms over his head, muscles flexing against his snug black tee. He lowers his arms, smiles, and juts his chin at me. "You coming, Z?"

My stomach turns to lead. I'm not part of the pack. That's just the way it is. "I don't drink, remember?"

Kace folds his arms. "Do you dance?"

Heat creeps into my cheeks. I've never danced with a guy before, and just thinking about it makes me feel faint.

I stand up and look at the elevators. "I'm actually tired, and I need to call home."

Kace lifts a brow. "If you say so, Z."

"Have fun, and congratulations." The words rush out of me as I start for the elevators.

"See you next week, Haylee Hutchins," Kace calls after me.

Loneliness swoops through my stomach as I watch the werewolves head out. A hotel employee passes me swiftly, carrying a broom and dustpan. I get into an elevator alone and press the button for the eighth floor. Loneliness closes in on me with the doors. For a brief moment, I felt like I belonged.

Maybe I should have joined the wolves at the club—or at least gotten the name of the place so I could meet up with them after changing into something less sporty. Yeah, right. I'd have more confidence going up against another vamp on stage than dancing with Kace. The wolf no doubt has worldly experience with women. What if he wanted to get down and dirty grinding on the dance floor? My face full-on flushes. I can practically feel my tears sizzling across my cheeks as they stream from my face unbidden because I don't have my sister or mom to talk to about this kind of thing. Cameron and Joni are great, but this is so not a topic I'd ever discuss with a guy who feels like a brother, and definitely not with my little cousin.

As the elevator slows to a stop, I swipe the tears from my cheeks and blink rapidly.

The doors open, and I step out, not immediately noticing Vincent leaning against the wall watching the elevators—staring at me specifically—as he rolls his wand between his fingers with a twisted smile.

I try to dive back into the elevator, but it's too late. The doors clamp shut, leaving me in the hallway of floor eight, alone with a vengeful vampire.

CHAPTER FORTY-ONE

I TWIST AROUND JUST in time to see Vincent rushing me at warp speed. He tackles me against the walls of steel, blocking my escape.

The back of my skull hits hard enough to send my eyeballs spinning in their sockets—or maybe that's my vision spiraling like a loose hubcap across the pavement after a head-on collision.

Vincent tries to pull my wand out of my hand, but I fisted it the moment I caught sight of him. His fruitless attempt makes laughter erupt from my lips.

"Your casting's so terrible that you have to come at me with brute force," I taunt. Yep, I've officially gone insane. I blame the head trauma.

Vincent snarls, takes a step back, and lifts his wand. "I'm going to turn you inside out with my casting. Your luck just ran out, mutant."

"*Sheltaward*," I say, throwing a shield up between us. I don't need Malachi's bubble spell in the hall when my barrier has enough stretch to expand from the floor to the low ceiling.

Vincent walks up to the barrier and tsks. He taps the tip of his wand against it three times and says, "*Dizappo, elapse, poof.*"

My eyes widen in horror as he punches his fist through as though it's made of air. The entire thing pops like a soap bubble.

Vincent grins with smug satisfaction. "I asked Coach to work with me on breaking through barriers. Handy trick, isn't it?"

I don't respond. I run like a drunk, unable to steady my gait with my vision still dizzy. If I were still human, that blow to the head would have probably given me a concussion.

Cruel laughter echoes through the hallway.

I stumble around the corner and point my wand at the nearest door.

"*Entra.*"

A clicking sound follows my spell. I don't have time to worry—only hope—that the room is unoccupied. I yank the handle toward me, dive inside, and shove the door closed—adding the chain lock for extra measure.

When I turn to face the room, I'm met with a pair of quizzical blue eyes beneath raised eyebrows. Zane Barrett sits on the edge of the far bed dressed in faded blue jeans and a T-shirt, holding a guitar.

Kill me now.

Of all the rooms I had to choose to hide out in, only I could end up in Zane's—while he's in it. It brings a hysterical burble of laughter to my lips. The ground is uneven beneath my platform boots. The bed next to Zane's is empty. If only I could lie down for a moment and recoup from Vincent's assault.

Zane lifts his brows.

"This isn't my room," I say jokingly.

"Clearly," Zane answers. He stands and puts his guitar away in a case against the wall.

I wet my lips, looking between Zane and the door before quickly deciding I'd rather take my chances with the cute wizard inside his hotel room than the deranged vampire in the hallway.

Zane cocks his head to one side and locks eyes with me.

"I'll be out of your hair as soon as I catch my breath." I pause for laughter, which never comes. It appears Suhani has a better sense of humor than the golden boy wizard.

Zane shrugs. "Take your time." He moves back to his bed and flops down, leaning against the headboard.

My throat goes dry. He keeps looking at me, saying nothing. What's his deal?

"Why are you always staring at me?" I demand.

Zane runs a hand through his hair, never taking his eyes off me as he says, "It's just I thought all zombies were supposed to be gross, and you're"—he looks me up and down—"not."

My face flushes at his roundabout way of admitting he finds me attractive. At least, that's my takeaway. I could get offended, but as far as compliments go for a zombie, this is about as good as it gets. I think. I mean, it's better than Malachi saying I smelled nice. That was more about the perfume than me. Also, I was totally right about Zane! I don't think he's ever seen a real, live zombie before. How sheltered is this guy?

I fold my arms and purse my lips. "Like what you see, do you?"

Zane shrugs. "Pretty much. So, want to tell me what you're really doing here?" He arches an eyebrow.

I press my lips together, not wanting him to see me as the underdog the other contestants are out to get. Then again, that smug smile of his might be insinuating something worse—that I broke into his room to get close to him.

I relax my shoulders and arms. "Just a *friendly* little game of hide and seek with a competitor. Next time, it will be his turn to hide."

Zane strokes his chin. "Who is this *friendly* competitor?"

"Just a dick with fangs."

Zane's lips twitch with amusement. "Hmm. I see. I hope it's not Vincent."

My stomach tightens as cold dread twists like a knife through my ribcage. "Why's that?"

"Well, he's my roommate—unfortunately."

I barely hear the last part. My muscles tighten on instinct, ready to run. There's a scream trapped inside my throat with nowhere to go, like I'm underwater and if I try to release it, my lungs will be flooded. I have to get out of here now!

I run to the door, which clicks and opens an inch before catching on the chain when I'm within reaching distance.

"What the fu—" Vincent's brutish voice stops me dead in my tracks. I need to get away from the door. Hide. But I'm momentarily frozen in place. "You know I can break this lock in less than a second, Zane."

"Go away. I've got company," Zane calls back, sounding closer, like he's heading for the door.

I'm still stuck in place, like a damn deer in the headlights.

"You and your wizard pals can hang out in someone else's room," Vincent snarls before breaking the chain and barging in. His eyes round when he sees me.

My feet finally start working, but there's no getting around him, so I turn and run straight into Zane. He's clearly not expecting it as I end up tackling him to the ground and landing on top of him. Those cerulean eyes are only a couple of inches from me, and now I'm the one staring because Zane Barrett truly has the most gorgeous eyes I've ever seen. Our bodies are pressed together, which is the most intimate I've ever gotten with a guy. Zane's gaze drops to my lips. If only there weren't a crazed vampire getting ready to rip me apart.

"Well, well, well. What do we have here?" Vincent sounds diabolical in his glee.

I scramble off of Zane and flip around, only to have my wand yanked from my hand. The scream I'd been holding in lets loose.

"Give that back!" I yell as I get to my feet.

I can't believe this asshole managed to get my wand from me. I'd rather he'd ripped off a finger. Appendages can be repaired. My wand is my lifeline.

"Come and get it." Vincent chuckles and holds my wand over his head.

Zane stands. I don't see his expression with my attention on the vampire.

"Give Haylee her wand back," Zane says in a cool, detached tone.

Vincent frowns at Zane. "This doesn't concern you. Go hang out with one of your witchy friends and come back later."

"No." Zane moves closer, standing beside me. In that moment, I'm not sure if I'm more at risk of dismemberment from the asshole vampire or falling for the hotshot wizard. "Now, you can hand Haylee her wand back willingly, or I can make you," Zane drawls.

Vincent scowls. "If you insist on staying and trying to help her, I'm going to tell everyone I caught you hooking up with a zombie."

Zane shrugs. "Do what you gotta do, man." Then he turns to me and says, "Want to get something to drink at the bar? Three's company—especially when one of those three is a vampire."

"Oh, you're so going to regret this, Zane," Vincent seethes.

"Wand," Zane says firmly, holding out his hand.

Vincent's jaw clenches. His eyes blaze with fury as he looks at Zane's hand like he wants to rip it clean off.

"*Granite limb. Hold him. Body prone. Frozen stone,*" Zane drawls, turning Vincent into a murderous, living statue. Zane tugs my wand from Vincent's stiff fingers and hands it to me. "This belongs to you."

"Uh, thanks." I blink in disbelief.

Zane swings his arm forward in a gesture for me to head out. I hurry past Vincent, nervous he'll break free of Zane's spell and grab me, but the vampire stays put.

It's not until I've opened the door—the hall a step away—that I look back inside the room. Zane is several feet behind me. He turns to address Vincent.

"Now, count down from one thousand, and once you reach zero, you're free to run around telling everyone how your roommate hooked up with a hot chick."

I storm into the hallway, only to whirl around as the door to Zane's room clicks shut behind him. "Seriously?"

Zane offers me a pleased grin. "I'm controlling the narrative."

"Yeah, well you're a guy."

"And you're a zombie," Zane says, sounding confused that I'm not doing backflips down the hall that everyone on the show is going to think I jumped a wizard—and not just any wizard, but Zane "Golden Boy" Barrett. And way to spoil the mood. I'm getting really sick of being defined as a species rather than as an individual.

"Wait. What? I am?" I say with mock surprise and rounded eyes, pressing a hand against my chest. This brings a smile to Zane's lips like we're all good, which we're not. He did help me in my hour of need, so I decide against telling him off. But I'm not going downstairs for drinks with him either.

Supernaturals can drink alcohol at any age. Trying to impose an age limit would be futile when IDs, or the wait staff themselves, can be so easily spelled or manipulated.

I lower my hand and shake my head. "All of this excitement has made me want to relax in my room, but thanks for your help." I rub my finger over my wand, reminded—yet again—how crucial it is to win the heart.

"Well, *I* could use a drink," Zane says, and walks ahead of me.

We round the corner, continuing in silence to the elevators. Zane snaps his fingers, and the down button lights up. I don't know whether he's mad at me for turning him down or trying to show off.

He stands in front of the elevator and watches the doors.

I head down the hall for my room and then stop. "Aren't you afraid he's going to kill you in your sleep?"

Zane turns and meets my gaze. "I have a protection spell over my side of the room. You should too, if you don't already."

Right. I think Blair is more concerned with keeping me away from her than getting anywhere near me or my things. But I keep that to myself.

"Okay. Well, see you next week."

Zane nods and turns away from me as the elevator arrives. I remain in place, watching him get inside. He turns around, meets my gaze, and lifts a brow right before the doors close.

Yep. Next week is going to be a hoot and a holler when everyone thinks we hooked up.

I groan inwardly and rush to my room to pack before my early morning flight.

Haylee, this is the captain speaking. Brace yourself for turbulence.

CHAPTER FORTY-TWO

THE FOLLOWING WEEK, I have the same room number and roommate. Blair isn't around when I arrive from the airport early Monday morning, but her setup is all there—gemstone statues watching my side and all.

After the Vincent incident, I don't mind having a raving witch between me and the door.

I wheel my suitcase against the wall by my bed and check the time. All teams were instructed to meet inside the theater in a little over two hours. My chest tightens. After what happened last week, my nerves have felt like a tangle of short-circuiting wires. At least I was able to pass it off as performance jitters in front of Cameron and Joni—who know nothing of Vincent's ambush or Zane's assistance. I wish I could keep it from the other contestants, but I fully expect Vincent to make good on his threat.

My stomach's all twisted up, and my throat is dry. I sit on the edge of my bed and pick up the phone. When I open my mouth, my lips stick to my teeth. I set the receiver in the cradle and drink water from the faucet in the bathroom before trying again.

I press "0" to be connected to the front desk.

"Hi, yes. This is Haylee Hutchins in 809. Could you please transfer me to Kace Warren's room?"

I'm not sure if the woman on the end of the line will go for it, but she does without pause. "One moment, Miss Hutchins. Transferring you now."

As the phone rings, I wrap the curly phone cord around my finger.

There's a moment of static before a gruff voice answers, "Yo."

I sit up straight. "Hey, uh, it's Haylee."

Kace's voice warms in an instant. "Hey, Z! You missed a fun time at the club last week."

"Oh, well, maybe next time," I say, clenching my teeth.

"So, what's up?"

"Do you want to share a ride to the theater?" Sweat slicks my palms. I hope I'm not being too forward. I mean, I'm not asking him out. I really just want to show up with a friend before everyone casts stones at me for my supposed involvement with Zane Barrett.

"Yeah, cool," Kace answers. "Meet me in the lobby at nine."

"Okay. See you then."

"Yup. See you soon."

I hang up the phone and press my fingers against the clammy skin on my forehead. My experience with guys is so limited that simply calling one makes me feel like passing out. I've never had a guy friend before, not until Cameron, but he's more like family.

Kace Warren is a whole other beast—literally. He's a big, Black, tattooed werewolf. If I'd seen him walking toward me on the street when I was human, I would have hurried to cross the road while trying not to be too obvious about it. Now, I'm thanking my lucky stars he wants to share an Uber with me.

With the time I have left before we meet in the lobby, I take a quick shower and put my energy into makeup. I go dark on the liner with a blend of copper and gray shades to create a smoky look over my eyelids. The nude pink lipstick I apply keeps the attention on my eyes. My smooth, fair skin requires no foundation, but I do brush on a touch of bronze highlights over my cheekbones. I keep my hair down straight.

I choose a long-sleeved knit V-neck sweater that's cream with narrow black stripes from the bust down. The V-neck zips with a silver ring zipper pull. I add a short gold-toned chain necklace above my "H" pendant, along with a pair of thick gold-tone earrings the circumference of quarters. The sweater is loose and comfy while looking sexy and chic over dark skinny jeans. Lastly, I strap on a retro pair of gray-and-yellow high-heeled T-straps that buckle on the sides.

My reflection in the mirror makes me smile.

Hot chick. That's what Zane called me.

I don't want to make it look like I'm trying to impress him in a dress or skirt. However, I am somewhat of a pro at what I call the "casual celebrity chic" look.

My gaze slips down to my slender waist. I still can't believe this smooth belly and these lean legs belong to me. I always felt comfortable with my appearance. Now I'm like a stranger in a strange body, but I do like feeling lighter on my feet, especially on stage . . . or running for my life.

I pull my sleeves above my wrists and spritz on Beautiful Moments, rubbing the scent below my ears as well. Now I'm a hot, great-smelling chick. I chuckle with my reflection and then wait around until there are ten minutes left to meet Kace in the lobby before grabbing my wand and a black crossbody purse with a gold-toned chain strap.

Before leaving, I grab my purple TEAM HAYLEE jacket for courage. It's the closest thing to having Kendra with me. Finally, I stash my phone and wand in the purse, spell myself invisible, and then leave my room. Boy, am I glad I cloaked myself, because Zane Barrett, Dominic Monroe, and Nathaniel Duke are all waiting in front of the elevators.

I hang back, cursing myself for putting on perfume. The last thing I need is for the wizards to catch a whiff of me the way Malachi did. They don't have vampire or werewolf senses, but it would be pretty hard to miss if I rode down in the elevator with them. Their voices are lowered. I'd really like to know what they're saying, but I don't dare get close enough to eavesdrop. I study their faces and body language instead. Dominic runs his fingers through his thick curly hair. Nathaniel lifts his hand to cover a yawn. Zane looks bored. There doesn't seem to be anything to eavesdrop on, as their mouths don't move much while they wait. As far as I can tell, Vincent's rumor hasn't reached the wizards—yet. I feel only mild relief.

When Zane checks his phone, I do the same and grimace. I'm supposed to meet Kace in five minutes, and I still have to wait for the next elevator.

When the elevator finally arrives, Dominic and Nathaniel wait for Zane to walk in first. As the doors close, Cody and Jake come barreling down the hall, arms pumping.

"Hey, hold the elevator!" one of the twins yells.

"*Veed*," a voice casts from within, closing the doors faster while the wizards erupt into laughter.

Cody and Jake glare at the steel doors.

"Assholes," Jake snarls.

"They won't be able to hear you with their weak wizard ears," Cody huffs.

Before I have a chance to retrieve my wand and spell myself out of invisibility, the next elevator over stops at our floor. With no time left to waste, I hurry in after the twins.

"Stupid jerks," Jake grumbles, as he jams his thumb against the button for the lobby.

Cody nods, which makes his bun bob along with him. "Worse than vampires." I step aside as Cody leans against the elevator wall where I'd been standing a millisecond before. He sniffs the air. I tug at my sweater, ready to explain myself. "Haylee must have ridden down before us," Cody announces.

Jake takes several loud sniffs before agreeing. "Must have been right before us."

"She's cool—for a zombie," Cody says.

I clench my teeth. Announcing myself now would feel really embarrassing.

"Way cooler than wizards or vampires," Jake says.

Cody rubs his chin. "Do you think all sentient zombies are like her?"

Jake shrugs. "Never met any before her. Hey, do you think I should ask out Izzie King?"

Cody folds his arms. "Dude, seriously? We're here to compete."

Jake huffs. "You're just saying that because she chose me instead of you."

"Whatever. The only reason she danced with you was because she was drunk. I bet she ignores you completely today."

I have to press myself against the elevator wall as Jake lurches forward and gets in his brother's face. "Oh, yeah? How much you want to bet?"

I've never been happier for an elevator to reach the lobby. As soon as there is enough room to squeeze through the doors, I rush out.

Kace stands near the lobby's entrance door, looking at his phone. His black sweater has a white, manic smiley face design with an X and an O for eyes and an open smile slashed with stitches. In a sloppy, handwritten font below is the word *smile*. His black jeans ride low on his hips, and his wand hangs from a chain attached to his belt loop.

I creep up behind him and whisper, "Boo."

Kace's chuckle is a rumble. He lowers his phone. I guess there's no surprising a wolf.

"Yo, Z. You ghosting me, girl?"

"Nope, I'm right here." I pull my wand out of my purse and spell myself back into sight.

He looks me over with a grin. "Looking good. Ready to win the next round and move on to the lives?"

I give him a thumbs-up.

Kace lifts his phone to his face and smiles. "Our ride is here." He opens the lobby door for me, followed by the door of a silver compact car.

"Thank you," I say, before he shuts my door and circles around to get in on the other side.

Kace glances sideways at me. "I watched the interview replays over the weekend. Sorry about what happened to your family."

I blink back tears, fiddle with the zipper on my jacket, and mutter, "Thanks."

"Did they ever figure out what a horde was doing in your neighborhood?"

"No, but I'm going to find out the truth no matter what it takes."

Kace purses his lips and strokes the tattooed wolf on his neck. "The truth could get you killed."

"Already dead, remember?" I laugh humorlessly. For some reason, Kace's face lights up with a grin. I tilt my head and eye him with suspicion. "What?"

Kace shakes his head and smirks. "It's a surprise."

Now I'm really curious. "A good surprise?"

"Just a surprise."

"When?"

"Later."

"Ugh." I press my palm onto my forehead, briefly closing my eyes as Kace chuckles.

But if Kace wants to be friends, I can't think of a better bodyguard/bud to make other contestants think twice about harassing me.

It's such a nice change to have someone to walk in with after we're dropped off at the theater. I stick to Kace's side and avoid looking at anyone else as we join the wolves in their usual section.

Once more, I wish Kace and I were on the same team so I wouldn't have to face the vampires alone, especially now that Vincent has decided it's not enough to try to physically attack me.

My reputation is on the chopping block.

When one of the werewolves looks up at us and laughs, I think, *Oh no, here we go.*

CHAPTER FORTY-THREE

A MUSCULAR WHITE GUY with highlighted, shoulder-length brown hair grins mirthfully. An amulet pendant of a wolf head surrounded in runes hangs from a leather cord around his neck, and he's wearing at least six woven bracelets on each wrist.

It takes me several seconds to realize that wolf-boy is focused on Kace's sweater, not on me.

"Hey, Kace," he says, and juts his chin.

Kace towers over the guy. "Aren't you going to say hi to Haylee, Noah?"

Noah looks at me and says, "Hey." Unless he has a stellar poker face, he doesn't appear annoyed by the threat in Kace's voice.

"Hi," I say back.

"Hey, Haylee," the Miller twins say in unison from their seats.

"Hi, guys."

Izzie King looks over with a pout.

Jovi stands up front, talking with the producers. According to the clock on my phone, we have another twelve minutes before she addresses us. I sit quietly, listening to the wolves converse while I wait.

"My ex won't stop trying to win me back now that he's seen me audition on national television," Daphné says.

A female with dark roots and an ash-blond mohawk scowls. "Don't you dare take him back. You'll have your pick of males now that you're on *Spellcaster*."

Like a lot of the werewolves, she's got tattoos. There's a full wraparound mountain and forest scene—complete with sky, clouds, moon, and stars—inked in black around her upper left arm. The strappy gray crop top she's wearing shows off a pattern of lines, dots, crescent moons, and rune characters covering her chest.

"Tripp, my man, didn't you get like thirty thousand new subscribers over the weekend?" someone else asks.

"Almost fifty," he answers.

"Dang! That's nuts."

"Better watch out," Luke says. "Tripp's going to beat us all with his growing fan base."

I frown. Luke has a good point. I wonder if my beauty brigade will support me when they see me on the show. I hope their loyalty transcends species bias.

"If anyone's getting points with the public, it's Kace," the female with the mohawk says. "He's the big bad wolf with the heart of gold."

Kace chuckles softly and rubs his hand over his chest.

During this banter, I steal a quick look around the theater. It's a little too fast, so I have to do a second scan, which makes me relax in my seat. The groups are all talking among themselves. No one is staring at me—not even Zane. Maybe he did a memory wipe on Vincent. I hope so.

At promptly ten o'clock, one of the producers releases a shrill whistle, and all eyes turn to Jovi.

"Good morning, everyone. We have a long day ahead of us. As you know, this is your last training and performance before the live shows, and before we take a three-week break. A third of you won't make it to the lives. Each coach has one final steal. Those of you who win the next rounds, or get stolen by another coach, will have three weeks to practice and prepare. Once we go live, the audience will determine who moves forward and who goes home. This is also Halloween week on *Spellcaster*. Not literally, of course, but this week will be aired the last week of October. For Season 13, your costumes will reflect the stereotypes of your species." When groans arise, one of the producers whistles again. Jovi narrows her eyes. "It's only for one performance. Deal with it. Otherwise, there's the door." She nods toward the exit in back. Obviously, no one takes her up on leaving. Jovi lifts a clipboard and glances at it briefly. "Team Zen and Team Cleo, you will wait in the lobby to be called to the stage or the studio to work with your coach in pairs. Team Brody and Team Malachi, you're headed to the dressing rooms to finalize your costumes, as well as hair and makeup choices."

Fun part first . . . or so I think, until Anya shows me the selection of zombie cheerleader and zombie bride costumes—complete with splattered blood across the fabric. I clench my teeth and fold my arms. Across from us, Carolina slips into a crimson velvet body suit over wide fishnet stockings. A tight black bustier laces in front, with a collar that fans out behind her layers of blond hair. It has long black lacy sleeves and a beautiful black lace train. Beside her stands a tall, skinny brunette whose helper fastens a black-and-red choker around the female's slender neck. The colors match her red silk bustier and long, clingy skirt with small black roses stitched on the top. Her shoulders and arms are completely bare, showing off porcelain skin. She's not on "Team Vampire", which means she's on Brody's team.

Anya pushes another one of my rejects along the rack before grabbing an equally hideous gown by the hanger. It's a blood-splattered bubblegum-pink dress complete with a *PROM QUEEN* sash. I stick out my tongue and give it a thumbs-down.

There are only a couple of witches and vampires on Team Brody. From what I saw on the televised auditions, it was only when there was no other option that they ended up with a werewolf coach. Like the vampires, their costumes are short, black, and sexy. A witch with golden-blond hair rolls her eyes when her assistant hands her a pointed hat. She takes it anyway and sets it on her head. Even though it's cliché—she pulls it off.

The werewolves have the cutest costumes, with furry fingerless gloves that match their leg warmers. Izzie King is already fully costumed in an adorable red, black, and white plaid short skirt with a jagged layer of tulle that drops just below her hemline. Her short-sleeved top has red slash marks along the side like it's been clawed, and she's wearing an adorable furry hat with ears.

As the other contestants get fitted, the pain in my jaw grows tighter. They all look sexy or cute—or both. This is so unfair.

Suhani is the only other contestant struggling with her options. Her helper lifts hanger after hanger of velvet, lace, and silk only for Suhani to lift her nose and shake her head at each outfit.

Well, her choices are a hell of a lot better than what I'm looking at. Maybe there's time for me to put something together myself. I'm thinking ripped tights with a distressed short dress on top. Would white make me look like a mummy, though?

I glance around at all the black fabric the witches, werewolves, and vampires are wearing. I want to stand out from the other contestants—but in a good way.

Anya places the pink zombie prom queen costume back on the rolling rack and chews on her bottom lip. Her eyes dart around the room before she takes a step closer and lowers her voice. "I know a guy who designs bodysuits for festivals. He does a lot of psychedelic and superhero prints. Me and my BF got alien bodysuits from him for an "Out of this World" rave last year. We were the hottest-looking extraterrestrials at the party. He has pretty much anything you could imagine. Skeleton bodysuits, cyborgs, robots, comic heroes, voodoo dolls, and . . . zombies." Anya takes another look around the room before bringing her voice so low I have to strain to hear her next words. "It would make everyone else look basic."

I lean in and whisper back, "Yes, please."

Anya's eyes sparkle as she nods. "I need to take your measurements. How about we have a little fun and throw everyone off by having you put on one of these lame costumes and pretend like we're checking the sizing." A grin stretches across her cheeks.

"Why not?" I snort and grab a zombie cheerleader costume by the hanger.

I undress and put on the tight white blouse and baby-blue plaid short skirt. There's a matching tie that tucks into the blouse and a baby-blue button-up vest with a bloody handprint in addition to the fake blood smears all over. They're splattered all over the white knee-high socks I pull on last.

I stand in front of the mirror and share a secretive smile with Anya as she wraps a measuring tape around my bust, followed by my waist and hips.

Most of the other females in the group have moved on to makeup. Luckily, everyone is too preoccupied fine-tuning their performance looks to engage in gossip. That doesn't stop them from checking out what the competition is wearing, though. Wandering gazes swivel around the fitting room and bounce off the mirrored glass. I'm given a passing glance as though I don't matter. Carolina Bellmore receives the most attention as she drapes her body against a chair and gives her assistant hair and makeup instructions. The female beside her has a drop of fake blood painted at the corner of her red lips. From what I've seen so far, Carolina is keeping it classic without any of the horror add-ons.

Jovi rushes in, clipboard in hand, and announces, "You have thirty minutes to finish up and get dressed. There will be refreshments waiting in the greenroom."

Anya wraps the measuring tape around my thigh and then adds numbers in her mini spiral notebook. She circles the tape around my ankle next. Now that's something I never thought I'd need measured.

Anya glances up at me. "Okay, last measurement. I need to get your inseam. Mind lifting your skirt?"

I grimace, glance around, and remind myself that this is part of show business. My knees pull together on instinct as I lift the skirt. Anya waits patiently for me to give her room.

"Here, you hold this end at your crotch." My cheeks are now on fire. I do as Anya asks while she stretches her end of the measuring tape to the narrowest part of my ankle. My excitement is mixed with nerves. I'd gotten so caught up in the stand-out designer costume thrill that I sorta glossed over the bodysuit part. It's right up there with a string bikini in terms of clothing I never imagined I'd wear in public.

I try to distract myself by chanting like a cheerleader inside my head to match my temporary costume. *Give me an M. M! Give me an A. A! Give me an L. L! Give me an A. A! Give me a C. C! Give me an H. H! Give me an I. I! What does that spell? Malachi!*

"Okay, you can change back into your clothes now," Anya says. "This is going to be wicked." She raises her brows in excitement, then presses a finger to her lips, glancing from side to side with exaggerated pupil motion.

I laugh. "Thank you so much, Anya. I don't know what I'd do without you."

"Cartwheel across the stage with pom-poms," Anya jokes, squeezing more laughter from my lips. Her eyes light up. "Well, you're the most fun contestant I've gotten to work with, so thank *you*."

"One of a kind," I joke.

"That's for sure." Anya bobs her head. "If you don't mind, I'm going to get these measurements to Leandro for a rush job."

"Sure, of course." I tug the plaid tie free from the white blouse. "Um, how do I pay him for the costume?" I'm going to assume *Spellcaster* won't foot the bill for something not already on the rack.

Anya waves my question off with the notebook in her hand. "Don't worry about it."

"I have money. I can pay the extra," I insist.

"Well, you'll have to take it up with Alexander, but you try telling him no." Anya winks at me.

My jaw slackens. "Wait a minute. Did Alexander buy the butterfly clips for my first performance?"

Anya finds the look on my face amusing. She laughs huskily and leans in one more time to say, "At least you know he won't be expecting you to put out."

With that, she leaves me standing in the fitting room with my cheeks likely as red as the bloody prints and splotches on the cheerleader costume.

I change back into my regular clothes and then sit in the chair in front of the vanity to await lunch break. Suhani is the last one dressed up in a black Victorian gown. With a flick of her wand and a spell, she returns to her embroidered pink kurta with its matching pants. Her choker is beautifully beaded with pink rubies and matching earrings that hang bell-shaped from large, jeweled squares at her lobes. The jewelry looks fit for an Indian princess.

Talk about being a kept woman. Better her than me is all I can say.

I'm not the only one who notices. Carolina looks at Suhani and narrows her eyes. Is it possible that Miss Fabulous F23 feels threatened by the undead Indian beauty?

If it takes some of her censure off me, I'm all for it.

There's a banquet table set up in the greenroom laid out with paper plates and napkins on either end. The rest of the table is filled with finger foods and plastic cups containing blood. A smaller table holds a large plastic cooler filled with bottled water, sodas, and other fizzy drinks nestled in ice.

Team Brody and Team Malachi males have arrived ahead of the females—no surprise—and are already chowing down or sipping blood. The werewolves have grouped themselves near the table while the vampires preen in the corner. As soon as I notice my male teammates, they look back at me with nasty smirks and begin whispering to one another. I guess it was too much to hope that Zane wiped Vincent's memory.

My heart drops to my stomach. That's all it seems good for anymore—weighing me down like petrified wood.

CHAPTER FORTY-FOUR

CAROLINA SWOOPS IN on the table, grabs a cup of blood, and joins the males. My throat dries out like a corn husk when Vincent inserts himself by her side and whispers into her ear.

I look away, but that doesn't stop me from hearing Carolina exclaim, "No way! I knew wizards were wack jobs, but I didn't realize they had freak fetishes."

Wonderful. So, Zane truly is allowing Vincent to run around spreading rumors about us.

Kace is cramming down buffalo wings, coconut shrimp, bacon wraps, deviled eggs, and mini pizza bites with his werewolf pals. Everything on the table is labeled. I try to focus on reading all of the labels in an attempt to keep calm.

There's a small plate labeled *Brains*. Even this has been carefully cut into bite-sized pieces with toothpicks in them.

I grab a plate and pluck three of the skewered bits of brain before retreating to the wall beside the door. A silent rumble goes through my stomach. Anxiety always increases my appetite. I stick the first brain-bite into my mouth and only chew a few times before swallowing the lump. It feels like a rubber ball going down my throat.

All of the female vampires have now joined the guys, including Suhani, who sips blood from a cup, looking annoyed while the others laugh and look my way.

My brain-bite starts to rise up my throat. It didn't feel good going down, and I sure as hell don't want to feel it come back up. I swallow several times before grabbing a bottle of water from the ice chest and chugging half of it down.

The last thing I feel like doing is eating brains in front of everyone, but Maurice's words come back to me about needing to recharge. I still have to get through training with Malachi.

I pinch the next toothpick and deposit the bit of brain into my mouth. This time, I chew and chew and chew until it's turned to mash that's easy to swallow.

The werewolves have paused from their feasting to watch the vampires with narrowed eyes. Kace follows the source of their amusement, looking from them to me. I grimace, heat filling my cheeks. Kace sets the bacon wrap he's holding back onto the platter and brushes off his hands before marching over to the vampires.

"What's so funny?" he asks in a deep voice that oozes threat.

Vincent flashes him a toothy grin. "Hate to break it to you, wolf, but you've got competition—and I'm not talking about casting."

My mind fuzzes like there isn't enough oxygen reaching my brain. Speaking of which, I suppose it was too much to ask to refuel in peace.

"What are you talking about?" Kace demands.

Vincent looks my way and then returns his attention to Kace. "Your little side piece got down and dirty with Zane Barrett last week."

Kace's snarl is the last thing I hear before all hell breaks loose. The other werewolves move as one. The vampires are slower to react as food is pelted at them. Cody and Jake rush to grab soda cans from the ice chest, shake them up, and then spray the vampires. The brunette female who dressed in the red gown earlier shrieks in outrage as she dives behind Oliver.

One of the show's young PAs runs out of the room. Rolling her eyes, Suhani lifts her wand right before disappearing. I should do the same, but seeing Vincent's white Henley smeared in grease, soda, and sauce is way too satisfying. Instead, I take out my wand and shield myself just in case, which turns out to be a good thing.

Carolina walks straight up to Tripp Peters and flings the remaining blood in her cup into his face. "Post that on social, show dog."

The vampires take their cue from her and throw blood at the wolves. It drips from their faces and stains their clothing.

"You jerks!" Izzie King yells as she pulls her retro crop-top away from her skin by the hem.

Jake takes one look at Izzie before rushing to the ice chest. Instead of soda, he scoops ice cubes into the bowl he's made with the bottom half of his T-shirt and returns to the wolf pack, who reach in and pelt the vampires with ice.

When Oliver rushes to get more blood, Kace beats him there and upends the table.

Most of the food was already chucked at the vampires, but the remaining blood splatters and pools over the linoleum floor like a murder scene.

Jovi runs in, her eyes wide as she takes in the mayhem. She's got a producer right behind her, and he sneers when he sees the mess.

"Everyone stop!" she screams. "Who started this?"

The vampires point at the wolves, and the wolves point right back.

Carolina steps forward and sweeps back her hair. Somehow, she's managed to steer clear of food stains.

"She started it," Carolina intones, pointing a manicured fingernail at me.

Kace scoffs. "You're crazy, fanger. How do you figure that?"

Carolina's chest lifts like it's connected to her high and mighty nose. "She started it by hooking up with a wizard. It's unnatural. Everyone knows it. How did you expect us to react other than with shock and outrage? Season 13 is supposed to be about supernatural species showing all of the races our spellcasting skills." Carolina narrows her eyes. "But what do you think the media is going to focus on if they catch wind of this torrid scandal?"

"There won't be a scandal to report on if a certain vampire stops spreading rumors," I snap. I mean, let's just nip this in the bud right here and right now.

Vincent folds his arms and lifts his brow. "Did I or did I not catch you on top of Zane inside of his hotel room?"

The room is way too quiet as everyone looks from Vincent to me. A vein pulses in Kace's neck as he, too, waits for my answer.

The longer I take to respond, the more triumphant Vincent's smirk becomes. "Well, Haylee?" he coaxes.

I glare at him as I answer, "I ran into him, and we fell."

"Inside his hotel room." He shares a chuckle with the other vampires. "Who knows what was happening before I arrived?"

My throat burns with a rage that's becoming way too familiar. "You know exactly what happened before you came in. You attacked me as soon as I stepped out of the elevators. I just wanted to get away from you. If I'd known it was your room I was taking shelter in, do you honestly think I would have chosen it?"

Kace smacks his fist into his palm and snarls at Vincent. "That's it. You and me outside. No more food fights. Your vamp ass is getting a beatdown."

"No, it's not," Jovi snaps. Her voice evens out as she asks, "Vincent, is this true? Did you attack another contestant?"

"Of course not," Vincent says at once. "She's just trying to save face, or maybe protect Zane. Believe me, I had no idea what I was walking into." Vincent's act of innocence sounds so sincere it makes me want to wring his neck.

"I hate liars," Carolina huffs.

"Me too," I say, glaring at Vincent.

Brody strides in and whistles as he takes in the scene. His hands are on his hips, and there's an amused smirk on his lips. "Wow. Had to see this for myself."

"Yes, well, your team is going to be late for practice, since they're now tasked with cleaning this mess," Jovi says.

"That's not fair," the brunette vampire whines.

"Yeah, we didn't start this," another one of Brody's vampire team members gripes.

"Shut up, Douglas," Kace says.

"Hey, now. That's no way to speak to your fellow teammate," Brody chides. His grin makes it appear as more of a suggestion than a reprimand.

Jovi turns her head slightly to speak into her headset. "Tell Zen and Cleo that their teams are going to have to wait a little longer for lunch. I'm dealing with a situation in the greenroom." Jovi's gaze narrows on the room. "You're all going to have to change out of your soiled clothing and wear costumes for training. Team Malachi, get changed and then wait in the lobby to be called into the theater in pairs." Jovi points her nose at the door. I try to leave first, but Jovi steps in my way. She scans my spotless outfit and says, "That goes for you too, Haylee. In costume. No exceptions."

I hurry out into the hallway, only to have Vincent jog to my side and smirk.

"You know the only reason Malachi saved you is because the producers told him that they wanted a zombie for the audience to boo during Halloween week."

Collective laughter hits my back.

"Well, at least we'll be rid of her before the lives," Carolina says.

Vincent falls back to rejoin the bloodsucking horde.

They gossip the entire way back to the dressing rooms. Every step I take is heavy as I wonder if what Vincent said is true. Why else would Malachi save a zombie? And now I have to dress up as one of the crazed and horrific versions of my species. I never thought I'd have to put that cheerleader costume back on.

I button up the tight blouse and vest, tuck in the tie, pull up the way-too-short skirt, and yank on the bloody knee-high socks.

The brunette vampire from Team Brody stomps in.

"You ruined my favorite top, mutant," she hisses at me, as she pulls off her yellow cardigan stained with soda and grease.

"They should have made her stay behind to help clean up the mess she caused," Carolina says.

This sucks and keeps on sucking when I walk into the lobby, where Teams Cleo and Zen are waiting to be directed to the greenroom for their lunch break.

They whisper to one another and stare as members of Team Malachi walk in dressed in costume. Vincent wears a long black cape that he flips around like he's some kind of superhero rather than a villain.

Carolina has on a different costume. A tight red velvet vest squeezes her breasts into half-moons, and black leather pants are suctioned to her legs. She, too, wears a cape. Hers is red on the inside and black on the outside. All of the vampires on Team Malachi seem to be wearing capes. I wouldn't put it past them to have planned this to make me feel even more like an outsider on the team.

Carolina struts over to Tori and a couple other vampires on Team Zen. Their jaws drop.

It's hard to find a secluded seat or corner in which to hide out when there are three teams currently taking up lobby space. I think of Georgia back at Brookdale High, picking out a table in the cafeteria regardless of its occupants. Maybe she's got the right idea.

I walk over to the nearest couch with space, smooth back my plaid and blood-printed miniskirt, and take a seat at the end. Luke, Daphné, and the female with the mohawk share a look before getting up and walking away. Clearly, they don't feel obligated to hang around me when Kace isn't present. Well, whatever. I have the entire couch to myself now. I set one white sneaker on the table in front of me, followed by the other, crossing my legs with the knee-high socks on full display. Then I pull out my phone to text Cameron. Before I have a chance to tap out a single word, Zane plops down onto the cushion beside me. He's joined by Dominic and Nathaniel.

Zane's black top is buttoned all the way to the collar. His blond hair is swept to one side, and his eyes are as bright as I remember from up close.

I lower my phone. Dominic and Nathaniel wear masks of indifference. They don't look at me. They just sit there like mannequins.

I raise a brow at Zane. "Can I help you?"

"Great costume." He says it without really looking—like he's commenting on the weather.

I uncross my legs and pull them off the table, pressing my knees together. "I have to wear it for training. My real costume is going to be awesome."

"Can't wait to see it." Zane offers me a close-lipped smile and stares directly into my eyes. Trying to decipher Zane's thoughts is like trying to translate html code. "At least you don't have to worry about wearing a robe or a cape." Zane's lips lift higher, making his cheeks puff out in an adorably boyish way.

"Or a pointy hat," I add.

Zane chuckles softly. It makes my stomach flip. His eyes are still locked on mine as he says, "So, I have a question for you, Haylee Hutchins."

I squeeze my legs together tighter and clench my jaw. "Oh, yeah? What's that?"

Zane's still smiling when he asks, "Are you with Kace Warren?"

My whole body loosens as I gape at him. This was possibly the last question I was expecting. I moisten my lips. "Um, we're friends."

"But you're not going out or anything?" Zane presses.

"Um, no."

"Okay. Just checking."

Jovi strides into the lobby and raises her voice. "Team Zen and Team Cleo, you may now follow Amber to the greenroom for your lunch break." She glances over at Zane on the couch beside me and frowns. "Team Malachi, hang back and await your pairings."

Dominic and Nathaniel wait for Zane to stand before they do the same.

"Good luck in practice," Zane says to me.

"Enjoy your lunch and costume fitting," I reply back.

Zane nods, and then he and his friends walk away. I give my head a little shake as I watch them go, chalking it up as another bizarre Zane Barrett encounter. I don't know what I was expecting, but this odd little chat wasn't on the list.

I remain where I am, grateful the vampires have moved to the other side of the lobby and are leaving me alone. Carolina and a male vamp are called into the theater first.

I take out my phone and text Cameron about the secret costume Anya is putting a rush on for my performance.

Cameron: Can't wait to see it.

I stare at his text, which is word for word what Zane said. The more I think about it, the more I find similarities between Cameron and Zane in terms of body height, weight, confidence, and cool composure. Could Zane Barrett be my chance at having a sweetheart of my own?

I drop my gaze to the red handprint on my skirt and scoff at my idiocy.

Yeah, right. Sure. And maybe he'll arrange a surprise proposal at the end of the season on live television with doves erupting from a top hat and thousands of white roses raining down as he serenades me with his guitar. Then there will be the engagement ring with a massive stone and tons of sparkle. I stare at my hand and envision the stunning piece on my finger.

My phone buzzes, and I blink away the fantasy.

Cameron: What's happening now?

Haylee: Waiting to be called in for training.

Cameron: Knock 'em dead.

Knowing Cameron, he wouldn't mind that in the literal sense.

"Suhani and Teo to the stage," a crew member announces.

Teo curses.

Vincent laughs. "Nice knowing you, Teo."

I wish it had been Vincent called in with Suhani. At least there's a weight off my chest knowing I won't be paired with her or Carolina. Time passes and then Oliver and a vamp named David are called to the stage, leaving me and Vincent as the last two members of Team Malachi waiting in the lobby.

My stomach hardens. How could Malachi do this to me?

When it's our turn to join our coach in the theater, Vincent cracks his knuckles and shoots me an evil grin before striding ahead of me.

CHAPTER FORTY-FIVE

MALACHI STANDS RIGID atop the stage with his arms folded tightly, his wand fisted along his lean torso. Five beautiful young women stand slightly behind and to the side of Malachi, staring at him like he's the Messiah. Max and a crew member stand on his other side. Max films while the female crew member holds papers.

"Vincent, you're up first," Malachi says crisply, without looking my way.

The young women aren't the only humans joining us. There are nearly two dozen people seated near the stage. It's mostly guys who look like they're all in their twenties. Knots form in my stomach as I take a seat near them and look up at the stage with pursed lips.

Vincent's cape billows behind him as he practically flies up the stairs and wiggles his brows at the girls while grinning.

Malachi gives me a brief glance, turning slightly so that he's facing both me and Vincent. "For your final cast-offs, you will be performing with extras while casting your stage settings entirely with spells. I'm looking for realistic special effects and lots of them. Not only that—you need to be able to perform with your extras while maintaining the illusions you create on stage. Whichever one of you can manage both the best wins the round and goes on to the lives. Vincent, you will be performing to the soundtrack of

'Closer' by the Kings of Leon. We'll walk through your performance without the music first. Cynthia has a copy of the song lyrics for everyone." Malachi nods at the crew member. She hands a sheet of paper to Malachi, Vincent, and the women. She even walks down the stairs and hands me a copy.

"Thanks," I say, before reading through the lyrics.

"This is a song about a vampire who feels no remorse as he bleeds his victims dry," Malachi announces. Yeah, sounds about right. "Hundreds of years of being driven to drink and kill to the point of exhaustion, but there's no end to the craving. His actions are monstrous, but at the same time, the vampire is lovesick. Vincent, you need to create a full set illusion of the spooky town mentioned in the lyrics while drinking from your victims one by one."

Vincent licks his lips and grins. "Happy to."

"Pretend drinking," Malachi clarifies.

"Can I bite them?" Vincent asks with a wink at the women.

"No," Malachi intones. "Now let's see what you've got."

Vincent lifts his hand and casts a cartoonish haunted house that looks like it belongs on a Halloween card.

"More realistic," Malachi instructs. "Better. Now add more houses. Let's see the street. Okay. Can you add cracks to the pavement? Don't forget the swaying stoplights. Let's see the telephone poles. Add in gray clouds. Bring them down. Make them darker. Open up your sky just enough to reveal a new moon. You're losing control of your backdrop. Remember to weave a pause spell into your casting to free up your concentration."

Vincent clenches his jaw as he twists from side to side, aiming his wand while casting. Malachi keeps on him until he's able to hold it all together.

Malachi takes a step back and looks over Vincent's grim, small-town scene slowly and then says, "Good. Tiffany, you're up first. I want you to stroll up to Vincent on the sidewalk."

Tiffany, a brown-skinned beauty with straight black hair parted down the middle, walks toward Vincent. He licks his lips and looks at Malachi for instruction.

"When you pretend to bite her, I want to see the illusion of a puncture wound at her neck with blood running down when you pull away. Tiffany will collapse into your arms, then you'll lift her, carry her into one of the abandoned houses, and deposit her inside, which will require turning her invisible, then return to the street, where the next woman will come along, and so on. Jessica, you're next." When Vincent leans in toward the brunette's neck, Malachi calls out, "You forgot to put a pause spell on your moon. The clouds are now covering it." Vincent jerks away from the brunette and digs his fingers into his hair. "Keep going," Malachi snaps.

I'd find this a lot more satisfying if I wasn't about to go through the same thing next. I've always performed solo, and now Malachi has a mob waiting to join me on stage. At least I perfected pause spells years ago—thanks to previous seasons of *Spellcaster*. Some people enjoy sing-alongs. I always preferred "cast-alongs" and trying out the coaches' instructions when training sessions aired.

After Vincent completes his second practice run, Malachi has him perform to the music. I hate how haunting it all comes across with the anguished tone of the song. Vincent knows it, too. When the music ends, there's a moment of delight that lights up his eyes and smile. I know that feeling of magical wonder. It sucks to see my archnemesis basking in triumph.

"Great job, Vincent. Thank you, ladies," Malachi says. "Amber will let you know what time you have use of the stage for your final practice run."

"Thanks, Coach," Vincent says.

Malachi nods and flashes him a half smile. "Good work." He's serious once more when he says, "Haylee, you're next. Background dancers, you can head up here too."

I leave my purse and phone on my seat and head toward the closest side of the stage which, unfortunately, is the side Vincent descends. He knocks into my shoulder as he passes me and whispers, "Top that, zombie trash."

The background dancers make a slight ruckus as they get up from their seats and head up the stairs opposite me.

Malachi is waiting on my side. When he looks me over, his pupils dilate and his fangs descend. He quickly clamps his lips shut, scowls, and storms away from me. I stand frozen halfway up the stairs for a moment, wondering what just happened. Is he angry with me, or is it something else? What if a cheerleader covered in blood is some sort of secret fetish of his?

Malachi keeps his back to me as he says, "Thank you for waiting patiently," to the backup dancers. "You will be performing with Haylee to 'Zombie Delight' by Buck 65. Thanks, Cynthia," he adds as she hands out copies, including extra sheets for Malachi and a female with two short brown pigtails.

Once I have the sheet, I lower my chin to speed-read. The lyrics take up both the front and back of the paper. My nostrils flare, and the paper shakes in my hand as I read lines about zombies being on the loose and how they're disgusting, irrational, raggedy, and smelly freaks from hell.

Vincent howls with laughter from his seat.

I don't look at him. I stare directly at Malachi with tears burning my eyes. He frowns before turning his attention to Vincent. "Either keep quiet or leave."

Vincent lifts both his hands in the air with mirth filling his voice as he says, "Sorry, Coach, but your song choice is absolutely perfect for her."

"The soundtracks are stereotypes—just like your costumes." Malachi steals a lightning-fast glance my way before looking away. "Now, let's get started so we can all get out of here. 'Zombie Delight' is a spoof on the zombie apocalypse with a world overrun by zombies and human survivors fighting to survive." Malachi meets my eyes when he says, "My advice is to have fun with it."

I scowl at him. Have fun with it? Is he for real?

Malachi nods at the woman with the short pigtails. "Jan here is coordinating the zombie dance number. Two-thirds of the group will play the part of zombies; the rest will portray street militia with rifles. Haylee, you need to create a dystopian street scene. Go ahead and cast."

Holding in a huff, I swoop my wand over the stage. "*Ignus ception neighborhood street.*"

Having no immediate vision in my head of a post-apocalyptic street scene, I start with a normal one, adding in pauses to keep them in place while I alter the illusion with broken windows and flipped over cars.

Malachi paces the stage, looking over my work. "This is a good start. I'd like to see ash falling from the sky like snow."

I'd rather see butterflies or falling stars, but whatever.

I point my wand above my head. "*Vitanate ash halluce.*"

Flecks of light gray fall like confetti.

Malachi consults his notes. "I need one survivor and three zombies."

"Tom, Kelsie, Alan, and Peter," Jan announces.

Four extras step forward.

Malachi uses his wand to point at the stage. "I need a body on the ground and the other three attacking like vultures."

"Tom, on the ground," Jan instructs. "You three, claw and bite at him."

I stand as stiff as a coffin, watching their sick rendition. My neck feels like an ironing board, and my jaw might as well be wired shut.

This is the exact opposite of how I want the public to see me.

Malachi strides across the stage. "I want someone being chased by four zombies over here on the other side of the stage. And let's have our militia group gather here in the middle."

Jan directs the group as Malachi speaks.

Heat roils through my body. I unclamp my jaw to ask in a scathing voice, "And what will I be doing?"

He'd better not tell me I'm joining in with the fake horde pretending to attack people and eat brains.

Malachi faces me. "I want you to stagger across the stage like the exaggeration of a mindless zombie while casting extra details into the scene. Your extras and backup dancers will be in costumes and makeup for the performance, but you need to add extra gore. Oozing blood. Brains appearing to be removed from victim's heads. Organs. Guts. You get the idea."

"Yeah, I have a pretty good idea," I grit out.

My ears roar. The pause in my spell is the only thing maintaining the street scene and ash falling from above. How could Malachi make me relive the worst moments of my life—and in front of an audience of millions no less? I thought he was different, but it turns out he's just as heartless as all the other bloodsucking assholes.

Malachi steps closer and lowers his voice. "You can pout about this, or you can get into it, face your fears, and turn it into something fun rather than horrifying. Your choice."

I narrow my eyes. He's such an insensitive prick. There's nothing *fun* about being swarmed by flesh-devouring zombies. There's nothing *fun* about bloodcurdling screams and desperation. There's certainly nothing *fun* about finding your parents, aunt, and sister half-eaten on the living room floor.

What choice do I have but to follow Malachi's directions? I don't have fun with it, though. I just go through the motions with a glare in my eyes.

Jan steps in for Malachi when it's time for a ridiculous dance number in the middle of the carnage. It's the only part of the song with non-negative lyrics, which claim that zombies are excellent dancers.

"Haylee, you're front and center," Jan said, tapping a spot on the stage with her tennis shoe. "Everyone else, get into formation." I'm joined by nine background dancers. "Okay, do like me," Jan says. "Arms against your sides and shimmy. Jump to the right. Jump to the left. Right foot back. Right arm up. Left foot back. Left arm back. Swing those hips. Raise both arms. Side to side. Right leg up. Swing your arm. Right leg down. Left leg up. Swing your arm. Let's see it again. Really lift those knees! Rock your hips. To the right. Dance walk in place. Keep it going. Dance walk. Dance walk. Move those arms. You got it."

Sweat beads along my hairline. I can barely keep up. I'm a caster, not a dancer!

Jan does the moves in front of me. "Let's try that again." She moves beside me to dance along and offer encouragement. "That's it, Haylee. You're getting there. It will be easier with the music."

I'm sure I look as out of sync as I feel.

After we've run through the dance number a third time, Malachi resumes the final sequence and then says, "Again from the top without music." There is way more going on in my number than Vincent's. With all of the extras joining me on stage, we could start our own Broadway production—*Zombies: The Musical.*

When we finish the second full round, Malachi lifts his head, scanning over our heads before lifting his hand. "Got my props, Cynthia?" Cynthia walks onto the stage with a duffel bag and sets it beside Malachi, who thanks her before addressing our group. "Those of you playing part of the militia, grab a rifle."

I recoil as extras descend on the duffel bag and pull out rifles.

"That's what I'm talking about," Vincent hollers. "Shoot her in the head."

The muscles in Malachi's neck cord. He hisses and whips around. "Alder, you're out of here. Get up and go. Now." He points a finger toward the back of the theater.

Vincent winces and shrinks in his seat. "Sorry, Coach. I swear I won't say another word."

"It's too late for that. Now get out of my sight," Malachi snaps. Vincent walks out of the theater with hunched shoulders. I'm just glad to see him go. "They're not real guns," Malachi tells me, like that makes it all better.

We go through the whole charade a third time with the toy guns. I feel every bit as absurd performing dance moves, but at least it's with a group and not on my own.

"You're doing great, everyone. Now let's try it with the music."

A mix of hip-hop and rap thuds from the theater's speakers. Jan is right about it being easier to move to a beat—even if it's a zombie beat.

There's so much going on, I can barely keep up with casting blood and brains. The whole thing is a mess, but I guess that's exactly what Malachi wants.

Vincent's words come back to me about Malachi only saving me for Halloween week. I hadn't wanted to believe it, but after this freak show of a routine, I wouldn't put it past him.

"Okay, everyone. That's enough for today," Malachi announces. "Great job. Good energy. See you at the final dress rehearsal." The group clears out quickly, leaving me with my coach and Max and Jimmy, who are still filming, but I'm so used to the cameras, I hardly notice them.

I glower at Malachi. "I thought you didn't take requests."

"I don't," he says, pursing his lips.

"Then why did you pair me with Vincent?" I demand.

"Because one of you has to go, and if you're more interested in boys than casting, then maybe it should be you."

How dare he?

Something monstrous takes over my mind. "Bite me," I seethe. "Get stuffed and bite me, you blind old bat."

Malachi locks eyes with me, but it's not nice Haylee who stares back. I feel like a demon is possessing my body, one filled with hate. One who wants to burn the world down until nothing but ash remains of her enemies.

Max lowers his camera. This time he doesn't laugh.

"I'll erase that," he says, as I storm off stage and head to the fitting room to change out of the bloody cheerleader outfit and back into my street clothes.

Hopefully Anya's efforts won't be wasted. Is anyone even going to notice my awesome costume design when my freak show begins?

Does any of it matter if Malachi only saved me for Halloween week? Even if he truly believed in my talents, insulting him is another nail in my coffin. Of course Malachi believes one of his own over me. He's not actually that old, but he is a complete and utter jerk. At least I got to tell him off before he sends me home.

CHAPTER FORTY-SIX

THE WEREWOLVES ARE hanging out in the lobby of the hotel again when I arrive.

The males are spiffed up in button down shirts and slacks or nice jeans. Daphné has on a tight white top and a short burgundy velvet skirt with two gold chains clasped along the side. Multiple gold hoops and studded earrings rim her ears and lobes. Miss Mohawk is squeezed into a purple iridescent cropped tank top over skinny black jeans. She has a long purple feather earring hanging from one earlobe and a stud in the other. Izzie's dressed in a cute floral crochet tank top over a jean skirt. None of them have their wands.

I'm exhausted. All I want to do is go to my room and collapse on my bed. I don't have the stamina of a wolf or a vampire. Let's be real, even humans have more energy than me. Maybe if I'd had a chance to eat more brains at lunch and not had to wait around all day for my turn, I wouldn't feel so run-down.

I should probably thank them for defending my honor, or whatever, in the greenroom. I'm not sure what to say.

Cody and Jake wave me over to their group. Kace leans back in a chair, arms folded.

I moisten my lips before facing Kace and his pack of wolves. "Hey, thanks for having my back earlier. So, how did it go today?"

Kace stares into my eyes for several seconds before unfolding his arms slowly and leaning forward. "Never mind that. This here is an intervention."

The werewolves all stare at me.

"O-kay," I say in confusion.

"As much as we hate the fangers, wizards are worse," Kace announces, to the agreement of the group. Cody and Jake nod vigorously. "They're elitist pricks," Kace continues. "Their witches are bitches. They can't stand sharing power with anyone else. They want to take away our wands." Several of the wolves growl.

"I'd like to see them try," Mohawk wolf snarls.

A vein pulses in Kace's neck, and his eyes drill into mine. He gets up and fists his hands. "I'm not going to stand by and let that asshat Zane Barrett get his hooks into you."

My cheeks heat. "There is nothing between me and Zane."

Kace's lips puff out. "That's not the way he's telling it."

"He's a guy," I say with an eye roll. "The only thing Zane cares about is controlling the narrative."

"Tracie and Daphné said he sat down with you during break."

I shake my head. "All part of his act."

"Luke overheard him telling his friends that you were the hottest female on the show."

For a moment, I grin. I can't help myself. It's all too ridiculous, and it's not exactly insulting. Take that, Carolina.

Kace growls. "He's objectifying you. Is that the kind of asshole you want to go out with?"

I press a fist into my forehead. "Oh my gosh. For the hundredth time, I'm not *with* Zane Barrett and never will be."

But does Kace listen to me? Nope.

"He's trying to win you to his side." He looks at his group and waits for them to nod their agreement before returning his attention to me. "You're on your own in this competition, but that ends now. From this moment forward, you're one of us—part of our pack. Team Werewolf."

"Hey, if Brody steals her, she really will be part of our team," Cody says.

I know Cody means well, but that would mean losing to Vincent, which is the last thing I want.

Izzie walks up to me with her sparkly phone and asks, "What's your number? I'll add you to our group text chains." She types in my digits as I give them to her.

"Got it?" Kace asks Izzie.

"Yep," she answers.

"Good. You're just in time to join us for dinner. Most of us didn't get enough to eat after those fangers went and ruined our appetites. Noah found us a sushi bar that caters to paranormals. Their menu includes organs and brains. I tell you, California has it all! You hungry, Z?"

"Starved," I admit.

"That's my girl," Kace says, as he throws an arm around me. He smells like nice cologne.

"Do I have time to change?"

"Yeah, yeah. Tripp told our ride to hold off until we're all ready. Tracie, go up to Haylee's room with her." Kace removes his arm and flashes me a smile.

I look from him to Tracie, with her mohawk, tattoos, and purple opal and silver moon belly button ring.

"That's okay," I say. "I'll be back down in a flash."

Kace shakes his head. "That fanger already tried to attack you once. I'm not sending you to your room alone."

"Let's go," Tracie says, striding toward the elevators in purple suede heels.

"Want me to come with you?" Daphné asks.

"No, I got this," Tracie says.

"See you back down here soon," Kace says with a wink.

Well, I guess a werewolf escort isn't the worst thing in the world. Mine isn't the friendliest, though. She says nothing as we get into the elevator together. The ride up is obviously going to remain silent unless I say something, so I tell her, "You've got an awesome look going on."

Tracie smiles with closed lips. "Thanks. Did you pack any club wear?"

"I have a couple fancier tops with lace sleeves."

Tracie nods. When the elevator reaches the eighth floor, she steps off first and looks from side to side as I step into the hallway. Once seeing it's clear, she walks alongside me to my room. After unlocking my door, I walk in and hold the door open for Tracie. Then I gasp when I see my side of the room.

All of my clothes are ripped apart and strewn over my bed and the floor surrounding it. A dark, cold well tunnels straight to my core. I grip my throat, unable to take another step.

Tracie zooms ahead of me, bending in her heels to pick up a torn boho maxi dress. I was so excited when I found it online and tried it on at home. I never got a chance to wear it in public. Hot tears sting my eyes. This violation feels worse than Vincent coming at me in the hallway last week. Blair went through my personal things and destroyed them.

Tracie tosses the dress on my bed and twists around to face me. "Didn't you put a protection spell over your side of the room?"

I grimace. "I thought that being a zombie was ward enough against anyone touching my things, but clearly I was wrong." I feel so stupid right now. Part of the blame is on me for not taking extra precautions. Out of everyone, I should know better.

Tracie purses her lips and stares at the untouched side of the room. "Who is your roommate?" she asks.

"Blair Monroe."

Tracie nods. "Witch has a broomstick up her ass. I'm stuck on the same team as her. I'll deal with her later. Tonight, we party. I'll lend you something to wear."

"That's okay—" I start to say, then look down at my sweater and clench my teeth. The wolves all look beautiful and hip.

"Come on," Tracie says, leading the way out of my room. "I've got a longer torso, but most of my tops are cropped anyway."

I follow Tracie to her room and do a double take when I see Suhani Das seated at the desk in the far corner with a laptop and headphones. The vampire has on a pair of fancy floral pajamas with three-quarter sleeves and a top that matches the pants. Her hair is pulled up in a high bun. Suhani presses a key on her keyboard and removes her headphones, frowning at the intrusion.

"Don't worry, Das. You'll have the room to yourself again in a few short minutes," Tracie says without looking at the vampire. She grabs a suitcase beside the nearest bed and hefts it on the blanket before unzipping it. "Here we go," Tracie says, as she pulls out a neon-yellow halter top that's mostly a bra with fringe hanging down.

At a loss for words, all I can manage is an "Oh, wow."

Tracie sets it on the bed and pulls out a black latex bustier. "I've got this too. I don't know what style you prefer when you go out."

"Um, maybe something a little more conservative?"

Suhani watches us without saying anything or showing any emotion. She ought to play poker. No one would ever have a clue whether she was winning or losing. Except, somehow, I suspect she would always be winning no matter what.

Tracie pulls out more halters and crop tops until I spot a fuchsia halter that will cover my full front torso. It ties at the neck with a long sash.

"Mind if I change in your bathroom?" I ask Tracie.

"Go for it. Wait, I have earrings that go with that top."

"That's okay—"

"Give me a second," Tracie growls.

If it were Kace, I'd jokingly ask if werewolves were always this bossy, but Tracie intimidates me, so I keep my lips sealed and hold my hand open when she gets out a pair of teardrop fuchsia rhinestone earrings.

"These are really pretty. Thanks." I close my fingers around the earrings before darting into the bathroom, closing and locking the door, and then setting my purse on the counter. I take off my jacket and sweater and put on the halter, tying it securely at my neck. I fluff my hair out with my hands in front of the mirror, deciding I need extra help in the volume department. I pull my wand out of my purse. "*Flufufta.*" My hair thickens in an instant. When I move my head from side to side, there's extra bounce.

"How's it going in there?" Tracie calls out.

"The top fits great. Thanks. I'm coming out."

I pull out my lipstick for a quick retouch before stepping back into the room holding my jacket and sweater. Tracie's suitcase is zipped back up against the wall beside her bed.

"You can leave those here," she says. "Just toss them on my bed for now. This area is warded—obviously." She lifts her brow.

I glance at Suhani, who still shows no reaction. She's watching us like a hawk, though.

I fold my jacket and set it on Tracie's bed. There's a cramp in my stomach that Kendra's gift is safer in another contestant's room than my own.

"Is that a *ny scelta* tattooed to your shoulder?" Suhani demands.

"A what?" Tracie peers at my shoulder.

Suhani stands up and stares intently, scanning every inch of my bare skin. "What's its purpose? How many do you have?"

I nearly laugh at the thought of affording more than one wild card. Suhani frowns. I can practically see her mentally filing away this new information like it's an advantage I might use in the competition. It doesn't matter that vampires are the species controlling the largest percentage of the world's wealth when their self-healing makes it impossible to get any kind of tattoo. That thought brings a smug smile to my lips. In this moment I feel like a tattooed rebel with no master controlling me. Must suck to be a vampire's pet.

Tracie leans in to check out the moth on my shoulder. "It's so pretty."

Suhani fists her hands. "What's it for?"

"Chill out Das." Tracie struts to the door. "Come on, Haylee. It's way too early to be holed up at the hotel."

Kace is waiting for us in the lobby when we return. He grins as he looks me up and down. "That's more like it, Z, and nice tat." The lift of his brows shows a mix of surprise and approval.

Tracie struts past us to join the others. A few seconds later, Noah, Daphné, Luke, Cody, and Jake look back at me with frowns on their lips. My guess is that she's sharing how my idiocy left me with no clothes other than what I wore today.

Kace puts his arm around me once more and tugs me toward the hotel's sliding doors.

We all wait out front for rides, I assume. When a white Hummer limousine pulls in and stops in front of us, my jaw drops. A chauffeur steps out and comes around dressed in a white suit, tie, and shiny white limo driver hat.

"Tripp Peters?" he asks.

Tripp steps forward. "That's me."

"Very good. Where to first, sir?"

"Phantom Rolls," Tripp says.

The chauffeur opens a door, and the males wait for the female wolves to get in first. I'm still gaping when Kace says, "Go ahead and get in, Haylee," adding with a sly grin, "Welcome to Team Werewolf."

This is crazy!

A purple leather couch stretches along each side of the limo; the ceiling and hardwood floor are lit up with purple neon lights along the edges. There's a mini bar and shiny narrow table behind the bench seats, supplied with glasses and napkins.

Daphné squeezes into Tripp's selfie and gives him bunny ears—or maybe I should call them wolf ears. Before the limo starts rolling, most of the wolves are taking selfies with the contestants sitting closest to them.

Kace nudges my shoulder with his. "Want to get a selfie together?"

Just what I need. More rumors. But I'm over it. I want to be a part of the group and have a good time.

Kace holds out his phone as I press into him for the picture. He snaps several, and then we look through them. "Beautiful and photogenic. You look great in every one of these," he says, as he slides his thumb with the human skull tattoo across his screen.

"Thanks. You're not so bad yourself," I tease.

Kace chuckles. "Want me to take a pic of us with your phone?"

"I no longer post on Telepatch and I deleted my JingleJam account, but I'm sure my cousin Joni would love to see it," I say with a half shrug.

"No social media presence!" Kace exclaims. All conversation is cut off as everyone in the limo stares at me with their jaws hanging open and eyes wide. "You gotta be on social, Z," Kace scolds. "Here, give me your phone."

"O-kay?" I hand over my phone.

The limo is moving now, but that doesn't stop Izzie from pushing her way through legs to plop down on the other side of Kace and watch as he thumbs through my phone.

"Didn't you used to have millions of followers on JingleJam?" Cody asks.

Tripp's head snaps up, and he stares at me like he's seeing me for the first time.

"I was going on two million." I groan.

"Don't sweat it," Kace says. "Social media sucks, but it's a necessary evil in this competition. I'll get you up and running before the night is through." He says all this while setting up the apps on my phone.

Izzie shoves her head against Kace's chest as she oversees the account setups. She squeals, "Oh, I love that!"

"Love what?" I ask, leaning in on his other side to see.

Kace turns my phone away quickly so I can't see what he's doing. "Let me finish, and then I'll show you."

He finishes and then looks up with a wide grin, announcing, "Good to go. Everyone follow Haylee." He hands me my phone. I take one look and burst out laughing at the profile name he created for me on JingleJam: **@shesZbomb**

"What has Kace done?" Daphné asks.

I hold my phone, screen facing away from me, to show the wolves who lean in for a closer look. Daphné laughs and then leans into her phone—presumably to follow my new account.

By the time I turn the phone back around and take a closer look, I have fourteen new followers.

"Don't forget to follow Haylee's @HeyHeyHaylee account on Telepatch as well," Izzie instructs the group.

Kace holds his hand out. "Your first pic of the year should be with Season 13's biggest stud."

I snort and give him my phone. "Why not? Let me get my wand in there too."

"Let me take it for you," Izzie says.

"Yeah, you should hold up glasses of champagne," Jake adds.

Kace nods and hands Izzie my phone while Noah pulls out a bottle of champagne from the mini bar and pops the cork, letting it hit the ceiling before bouncing off. Luke catches it one-handed to the applause of our crowd.

"Not for me, thanks," I say, as Noah pours champagne into a flute.

The drink is passed down from one werewolf to the next until it reaches Kace. He slings one arm around me and lifts the champagne in the other.

I hold up my wand and grin as Izzie snaps pictures. She thumbs through before handing me back my phone.

While more drinks are poured and handed out, I choose my favorite of the photos to post on Telepatch, then stare at the blank text section. I chew on my lower lip, type out a sentence, and then delete it.

Don't overthink it, Haylee. Short and simple.

I try again.

> **@HeyHeyHaylee** Having the night of my life with my fellow #SpellcasterSeason13 #SuperstarContestants 🤩🪄✨ This amazing experience has been out of this world. I'm so grateful for the opportunity to perform on my all-time favorite show. Here's to an unforgettable journey! #Spellcaster #Season13 #TeamMalachi #Celebrate 🥳

Kace leans in to read what I've written. "Perfect—except for the Team Malachi hashtag."

I roll my eyes and publish the post.

Izzie is the first to like and comment.

> **@IzzieKpaws** Having fun celebrating with you and this awesome group of werewolf casters! 🖤

A like and comment from Daphné appear next.

> **@puchikoDaf** I feel the same way, cocotte. 😉🖤

I go through following back my new werewolf friends while they drink, laugh, and talk. The banter surrounding me warms my soul and makes me feel a welcome sense of security and belonging. It helps distract me from the anger of having my travel clothes destroyed by my wicked witch of a roommate.

"What soundtrack did Cleo give you, Tracie?" Noah asks.

"'She Wolf' by Shakira."

"Oh, hot. You're gonna kill it."

"I so am," Tracie boasts. "At least the witch gave me a good song. What about you?"

"Duran Duran, 'Hungry Like the Wolf,'" Noah says.

"How about you, Izzie?" Jake asks. "What song did you get from Brody?"

"You won't know it," she answers.

"What is it called?"

"It's alternative rock by singer-songwriter Fiona Apple. The song's called 'Werewolf.'"

Jake looks it up on his phone and starts playing the song.

I turn to Kace. "What song did you get?"

Amusement lights up his brown eyes. Kace lifts his brows and grins. "'Thriller' by Michael J."

Tracie laughs. "Now there's a perfect pairing."

Kace juts his chin. "Got my own dance group. The song was originally intended for a male zombie contestant, but since there weren't any, Brody thought I should do it, since I've got the moves." Kace rocks his hips over the bench seat. "We're doing the whole cemetery dance number, with the background dancers dressed as zombies. I'll have on a Z Squad uniform and dance with my ghoulish group. I mean, at the end I'm going to have to appear to kill them." He turns to me. "Sorry, Z."

I shrug. "Do what you gotta do."

"What about you? What beats are you casting to?" Kace asks.

When I tell him, he slaps his thigh and exclaims, "I love that song!"

I scowl. "It's ridiculous."

"Hey, now," Kace says seriously. "I've been catching up on past seasons, and dance numbers typically go over well with the audience."

"Yes!" Tracie exclaims with a fist pump.

"If only I could dance," I mutter, folding forward in defeat.

Kace smirks. "Good thing we're going to a dance club after dinner."

My head jerks up. "We are?"

"Yep, and you're in luck because Tracie and I can help you work on your moves."

Tracie gives a slight nod. "Sure, why not? We want Haylee to beat all the fangers on her team."

"That's right." Kace rubs his fingertips together as a smug smile settles over his luscious lips. I glance out the window, which makes Kace laugh. "There's no escape, Z. You're stuck with us now."

CHAPTER FORTY-SEVEN

EXHAUSTION, DESTROYED CLOTHING, and the nasty witch asleep next to me aren't enough to wipe the grin off my face. I just had one of the best nights ever.

Upscale dining. Clubbing. Limo. I'm hooked on the high life.

Also, after I retrieved my purple jacket and my sweater from her room, Tracie came in quietly with me, shifted, and took a dump on the side of the bed Blair gets out of each morning. I spelled it not to stink until she steps foot in the pile. It's hard to sleep or zomb out waiting for that fun moment. It's also hard to rest because I'm replaying the evening over and over in my head. I can still feel the music pulsing through my body and hear the laughter of our group living it up and sticking together like the loyalest of packs.

Why couldn't I be a werewolf?

I don't know how to love myself as I am. I used to, before I was turned into a flesh-eating freak of nature. If I can't accept myself, then how can I expect anyone else to? This is my chance to be a zombie pioneer and give my species a makeover. It's sorta my specialty, after all.

Eventually, I drift off and sleep until Blair's scream wakes me.

"Oh my god! What the hell! Is this shit? Did you shit on the floor? I'm going to throw up." Blair runs into our bathroom and slams the door behind her. I hear the shower turn on a moment later and burst into a fit of laughter.

Tears leak from my eyes as I continue to laugh. My clothes are still strewn all over the floor on my side, so I get out of bed and pick up each ruined article and toss it in the wastebasket. It's too small to hold everything, so once it's full, I start a pile beside it. I'm going to have to wear the same jeans and sweater from yesterday. Tracie said I could come by and borrow something, but I figure I can get one more wear out of my sweater, since I had to put on the cheerleader costume for most of yesterday. I don't know if my purple jacket would have withstood a witch, but Blair's lucky she didn't get the chance to shred this precious gift, or a pile of crap beside her bed would have been the least of her problems. Tomorrow, hopefully, I'll have my cool zombie costume to wear, and then I'll return home for three weeks before lives. Well, hopefully I'll be returning for lives. I feel a whole heck of a lot more confident doing my dance moves thanks to last night's outing and bonus coaching from my furry new friends.

My nose wrinkles as the poo stink becomes too much. I grab my wand and cast away the smell. The crap, on the other hand, can't be disposed of as easily.

I grab the plastic liner from the ice bucket, using it to cover my hand and as far up my arm as it will reach to pick up what I can from the smashed pile. I'm afraid Blair would leave it for the maid to clean. Once the bag is tied off, I stick it between ripped clothes in the waste basket, grabbing one of my ruined shirts and a bottle of water from the counter to do what I can for the carpet. It still needs professional product. Using my clothes to clean up crap isn't how I envisioned final rehearsal day, but at least my side of the room is now tidy—not to mention warded! Fool me once.

While Blair continues her extended shower, I get dressed and head out with my toiletries bag and purse. It's not ideal, but I head to the hotel gym's locker rooms for a shower. After all the dancing I did last night, I need it.

Happily, the showers aren't in use. I stuff my clothes and purse into one of the provided lockers with a small lock and key for use by guests. I still bring my wand with me to the shower. There's a stack of fresh towels by the mirrored sinks and countertop, along with shampoo, conditioner, and body wash in each stall.

After I'm scrubbed and washed up, I get dressed and make use of the locker room's hair dryer. It isn't until my hair is styled and have makeup on, that I check my phone. I've got several texts.

Cameron: Glad you're having a good time with the wolves. Just don't let your guard down. Good luck with rehearsal.

Haylee: I won't. Thanks! 😊

Mariana: Good luck at your next cast-off! 🪄✨

Haylee: Thank you. 😘

Tracie: Has she stepped in it yet? 💩

I snort and text back.

Haylee: I don't know if she'll ever come out of the shower. I had to use the hotel gym locker to rinse off.

Daphné: Tracie told me what that witch did to your clothes. Forgive my French, but *c'est une vraie vache*! If you need to borrow something to wear, let me know, cocotte.

Haylee: Thanks. I'm set for today.

Kace: Wanna meet for breakfast?

Followed by two more . . .

Kace: You sleeping in, Z? Getting your Zs? LOL

Kace: I got a table in the hotel cafe. Join me if you see this in time.

I check the time on his last message, which was only seven minutes ago. Purse slung over my shoulder, I rush out to meet up with Kace, excited not to eat breakfast alone. It's great that the hotel has provided meal options for *Spellcaster*'s creature contestants, but eating by myself has been anxiety-inducing every time I have to see the waitress's look of disgust when I order, and then try to hide what's on my plate from the rest of the diners by hunching over my serving of brains. Having someone to eat with who won't turn green as I chew is a rarity I don't want to miss.

I'm practically running down the hall to the elevators, until I get inside and have to wait. As soon as the steel doors open at the ground floor, I rush out and zoom straight into the cafe searching for Kace.

He grins and waves to me from a table in the middle of the room like he's been expecting me all along. I return his smile and stride straight over. This morning, Kace is wearing a black sweatshirt with white chalkboard font reading: ***NAH, I'M GOOD***. There's also a backpack beside his black-and-white-checkered high-tops.

"Last night was fun," he drawls, lifting his brows like something exotic occurred.

"So much fun," I agree, as I take off my purple jacket and hang it, along with my purse, on the chair in front of him before sitting down. "Where is the rest of the pack?"

"Probably sleeping in." Kace chuckles.

"Not you?"

The skull tattoos on his fingers dance as he rubs the bottom of his chin with his fist.

"Got a morning rehearsal. Plus, I don't like skipping meals."

"Breakfast is the most important meal of the day," I tease.

"Every meal is important," Kace returns.

"True dat," I say, setting my arms on the table and bobbing my head.

Kace laughs.

A tall, grinning waiter sweeps over. "I see your breakfast companion made it down," he says with a wink. "Do you need more time with the menu, or do you know what you want?"

"Brains," I say.

The waiter and Kace laugh. At first, I fear the waiter thinks I'm making a joke . . . until he says, "I wish all women ordered that fast." He winks at me again.

I stare open-mouthed at him, like he's the weirdo.

"Me too," Kace agrees. "I'll have my usual."

"Coming right up," the waiter says before striding away.

Kace sees me stare after him and laughs again. "That's Dylan. He's a super fanboy of the show. We're pretty much celebrities in his eyes."

I look down at the table. "I don't know that I see myself as a celebrity. I mean, I want to win, obviously, but I'm still just me."

"Hey," Kace says, reaching across the table to lift my chin. I meet the solid oak determination in his brown eyes. "You're not *just* anything. You're extraordinary."

"Thanks," I whisper, blinking several times.

Kace releases my chin and leans forward against the table, staring at me in a way that's intimate and unsettling. It makes me squirm in my chair.

"Do you want to go out with me, Haylee?"

A flush of adrenaline spreads through me and turns my head in circles. I clutch the sides of the table.

Kace is asking me out? Just like that? What do I say? Do I want to go out with him? Does he mean on a date? Or steady like boyfriend and girlfriend?

"Go out?" I ask.

He looks totally serious. "Yeah, wanna be my girl, my woman . . . my Z." Kace flashes me a grin that's all teeth and dark promises. My belly flips and cheeks flame. "What's the matter, Z? Am I not boyfriend material?" Kace challenges, rubbing his tattooed thumb against his index finger.

I chew on my lower lip, then release it and shake my head, staring at the table rather than at him as I say, "It's not that. I'm just not ready for that kind of thing. I've never gone out with anyone. I've never even held a guy's hand."

God, this is so embarrassing. Never mind kissing—I've barely even touched a boy. My cheeks feel like they're turning into candied apples.

"Haylee," Kace says firmly. "Look at me." I lift my eyes and meet the serious browns staring into mine. "I'm not looking for a hookup. I'm looking for someone special. Someone beautiful. Someone who is fun to be around. I'm looking for one-of-a-kind, makes all the other females seem stale in comparison. You're all those things and more, Z. I never met anyone like you before, and I doubt I ever will again. I'm not one to beat around the bush, so what do you say?" He grins, face relaxing as he leans back in his chair. I swallow, still too stunned to formulate thoughts, let alone words. And because it's Kace, he adds, "When it comes to my enemies, I'm a nightmare with claws. But it when it comes to my woman, I'm a gentle giant. Whoever my lady is, she gets treated like a princess. Would you like to be a pampered princess, Haylee?"

A chuckle rumbles up my throat and loosens me up. I can't even roll my eyes at him because, yeah, I would totally love to be treated like a princess. Not a rag doll. Not the walking dead. A princess.

"Will you give me a tiara if I say yes?" I tease.

"Something better." Kace's eyes light up. He scoots back and plunks his backpack onto his lap. Once it's unzipped, Kace pulls out a black hoodie and hands it to me.

"What's this?" I ask, straightening out the garment and lifting it up to read the white distressed font.

Kace grins. "A gift."

It reads: ***NOT DEAD YET***

I laugh. "Is this the surprise you were talking about?"

"Yup. You like?"

"I love it." I really do. It makes me smile, and it's the first gift a guy has ever given me—not counting my dad or Cameron. I drape the hoodie over my purple jacket on the back of my seat to take back to my room after we eat.

Kace stares into my eyes. "Tracie told me what your hag of a roommate did to your clothes, which is why I also got you this." His backpack is like a magic hat that he keeps pulling gifts from. Kace holds up a fitted V-neck T-shirt that says *Hollywood* in white script and *CA* in fuchsia. There's a stamped emblem in white with palm trees in a circle and *California Dreamin'* in smaller script below the *CA*.

"Kace!" I squeal, taking the T-shirt. The fabric is super soft. "This is so sweet of you." Thanking him isn't enough. I get up and hug him where he sits.

He chuckles and returns my hug. "The choices in the hotel gift shop were limited. I thought you'd like this one best."

"I love it," I say as I return to my seat. I hold the design side facing me and grin. Souvenir shirts aren't usually my style, but this one is fun, and the fact that Kace got it for me makes it extra special.

I turn halfway in my chair and carefully drape it on top of the clothing pile I've got going on my chair. "Now I feel bad that I don't have anything for you," I say as I face Kace again.

He shakes his head. "I don't need gifts, Z. I prefer being the giver." His brows jump, and my stomach is all a flurry.

Dylan arrives with a tray. He sets a plate of scrambled brains in front of me and then fills the space in front of Kace with multiple plates that contain an omelet, fried potatoes, bacon, a stack of pancakes, a biscuit with gravy, and pineapple slices.

"Can I get either of you anything else?" Dylan asks with a ready smile.

Kace leans over the plates and inhales.

I smile at Dylan. "I'm good, thanks. Kace might need more food, though."

"I'll start with this and see," Kace says, and we all laugh.

"You two enjoy," Dylan says, tucking the empty tray under his arm and striding away.

"Don't have to tell me twice," Kace says, as he grabs a fork and digs in.

With his attention on shoveling down his meal, I don't feel as self-conscious eating my plate of brains. I like the way the hotel cafe serves them scrambled in the morning and then prepares organs that appear steak-like in the evenings. They've made a real effort. Even though everything is served raw, it has the appearance of familiar foods.

Speed-eating comes in handy in a situation like this. I scarf down every last bit of brain, feeling energized by the time I'm finished.

Kace finishes his main breakfast just as fast, pushes the empty plate away, and pulls the stack of pancakes closer. He points his fork at me. "It's good to see a female with a hearty appetite. I'm telling you, Haylee, you fit right in with wolves, and you belong with me."

I smile. "Well, you do make a lot of good points. I'd be lying if I said your offer wasn't tempting."

Kace leans over the table, eyes shining as he speaks. "You know what they say, once you go—"

"Black?" I interject.

Kace smirks. "I was going to say wolf, but yeah, that too. Double jackpot." His brows jump.

"Wait. What's the werewolf saying?" I ask.

"It goes like this . . . Once you go were, nothing else compares."

I snort, which is very unlady—and unprincess—like but Kace is clearly fine with me being who I am. Being together feels comfortable. Natural. I like it, and I like him, but I'm not ready for a relationship. Not yet.

Still smiling, I say, "I think we need to focus on the competition."

Kace stabs the top pancake with his fork and lifts the entire thing off the plate. It hovers near his mouth as he locks eyes with me and smirks. "I wouldn't want to distract you from winning, Z."

"Maybe you'll win," I counter.

"Nah. I'd rather you win it all and show those fangers, wizards, and witches how it's done."

"You wouldn't want a werewolf to win?" I ask.

"I told you, Z. You're one of us now. You win, we win." Kace stuffs the pancake between his grinning lips, chews it up swiftly, and swallows it down before stabbing the next one on the plate. "You already won my heart. I want the queen's heart to be yours too."

My stomach turns into a hot-air balloon lifting me off my seat. "You know, you're making it really hard to turn you down."

"I can't help it if I'm irresistible." Kace shrugs and stuffs another pancake into his mouth.

"Can I keep your hoodie even if I don't go out with you?"

Kace nods. He doesn't speak until he's finished chewing and swallowing. "I told you, Z. It's a gift. But there's more where that came from, if you ever decide to take a walk on the wild side and go out with me."

"Let's get through Season 13 first," I say.

Kace smirks. "Whatever you want, Z."

A fresh blast of heat fills my chest. That light, happy feeling continues after Kace finishes eating and we head out of the cafe. I put on my jacket and hug the hoodie and T-shirt against my torso, grinning until we see a waitress leading Zane, Dominic, and Nathaniel to a table. Zane doesn't see me immediately—not until Dominic elbows him.

There's a lazy smile on his lips that turns straight down as soon as he sees me with Kace. Zane shoves his hands inside the pockets of his tailored slacks and strolls over to us. I stop. It takes Kace a moment to realize I have. Once he does, he backs up until he's by my side, arms folded, eyes narrowed on Zane. Dominic and Nathaniel hurry over, standing on either side of their friend.

"Good morning," Zane says to me casually.

"Good morning," I repeat.

"You look nice," Zane continues, as though it's just the two of us.

"Thanks."

Zane pulls his hand out of his pocket and rubs the back of his neck. "You know, if you ever want to meet up for breakfast, just let me know."

"Um—" I never know how to respond to Zane. Worst of all, I don't trust him. This has to be part of a cruel game. No doubt he's planning on humiliating me if I'm ever dumb enough to agree. I look between Dominic and Nathaniel, who have on their poker faces.

"They wouldn't have to come," Zane says.

Clearly having heard enough, Kace steps in front of Zane and sneers. "Haylee isn't some novelty doll for you to play with while you wait to be sent home. She's part of my pack, and we don't take kindly to anyone who messes with one of our own."

Dominic and Nathaniel shift on their feet and share a sidelong glance with one another. Zane slouches in place, like he couldn't feel more relaxed, when he turns his cerulean eyes from me and aims them at Kace.

"What are you going to do? Throw food at me for talking to Haylee?"

A wicked laugh rumbles from Kace's throat. He loosens his arms and flexes his fingers. "Nah, man. I would never waste good food on you. I'd rather make you my next meal." He flashes Zane a grin that's all teeth.

"You think you can take me? You don't even have your wand with you," Zane says, staring pointedly at Kace's tattooed fingers.

Kace lifts one hand and rubs a finger over his thumbnail. "I don't need a wand."

The cafe has gotten quiet. Regular human diners have put down their forks and glasses of juice and are staring. I hear whispers of "Season 13 contestants." The last thing we need is another incident getting back to Jovi—or our coaches. Mine in particular.

I place my hand on Kace's arm, giving him a gentle squeeze. "He's just making pleasantries. No need to perform an impromptu combat cast-off for the hotel guests. I'd really like to go try on my new shirt."

Kace looks at me and bobs his head. "Yeah, cool. I'll walk you to your room. I gotta get going soon for my rehearsal."

"Enjoy breakfast," I say to Zane. Even though I question his motives, I have no reason to be rude to him. He could have abandoned me with Vincent instead of offering his protection. That's something I don't take lightly.

Zane's eyebrows pull together when he frowns.

"Let's order," Nathaniel says.

"Good idea," Dominic chimes in.

The pair of wizards walk to a table where the waitress sets down three menus and pours water into their glasses.

Zane hangs back and meets my eyes. "He's dangerous, you know. The only way wolves know how to handle zombies is to tear them apart."

Kace growls at Zane before steering me out of the cafe. "Don't listen to him. I'd never hurt so much as a hair on your head," he says during our walk to the elevator.

But it's too late. Zane's words are already on repeat, infecting my mind with visions of Z Squad werewolves using their claws and fangs to rip zombies apart. How could I think for even a second that a ripper and a zombie could ever have a future together?

CHAPTER FORTY-EIGHT

BLAIR IS BLISSFULLY absent from our room. It's a relief not having to worry about any sort of retaliation ending up in my bed. Shields up!

My final rehearsal isn't until late afternoon, so I lay on top of my bed on my stomach and thumb through Telepatch, which is where the majority of the Spellcaster contestants are posting. There are loads of Carolina Bellmore sightings, which sucks. She appears posing on Hollywood Boulevard, in front of the Dolby Theatre, outside Capitol Records, with a tiger behind her at Griffith Park, and at Universal Studios with a red bow headband that matches the one on the person dressed in a Hello Kitty costume beside her. The latest snaps are at the Hollywood Wax Museum, where she's got her hand on Marilyn Monroe's wax shoulder.

Hashtag Carolina Bellmore is blowing up.

> **@tilly.harmon58** OH MY GOD YOU GUYS!!!!! You'll never guess who I just saw at the Hollywood Wax Museum! #CarolinaBellmore in the flesh! Guys, she is The Coolest!!! As you can see here, she posed with wax figures for me and anyone else lucky enough to be there at the same time as her. 😍 I can't wait for the #Spellcaster lives. #VoteCarolina #TeamMalachi #SpellcasterSeason13

I pop over to my new profile on JingleJam and see I only have fifty-two followers. My chest tightens as I'm reminded yet again that the odds of me making it to finals, never mind winning, are about as low as it gets—like bottom of the ocean, no hope of seeing the light low.

I switch back to Telepatch to see what my werewolf friends are posting. Tripp Peters has at least three reels a day. I tap one from yesterday.

"How's it going, Tele-*pack*?" Tripp greets with a friendly, megawatt grin. "I'm about to get fitted for my Halloween costume. Can you guess what I'll be going on stage as?" He chuckles in a way that makes my mouth want to laugh with him. Tripp's a natural on camera, coming off more at ease than he does in real life. Dang it!

I've been so focused on my performances that I keep forgetting how important connecting with the audience (aka voters) matters for the lives.

I turn my phone's video camera on myself. I sit up on my bed and fluff my hair with my hand, checking how I look on my phone's screen. I've got on the Hollywood tee Kace gave me, along with a pair of gold star earrings, since my jewelry was spared Blair's massacre.

I hit record.

"Hey, hey. This is Haylee recording my first reel of the year. I am so excited to be a contestant in caster, er, *Spellcaster* that is, for their critter season. It's interesting, and, uh, arg." I stop recording and delete my first attempt.

"Hey, beauties," I try again, and then promptly stop recording. I was always more of a lurker on Telepatch. I should never have deleted my account on JingleJam.

"Hello from Hollywood!" I point at my shirt and giggle, which sounds stupid, so I stop recording, delete, and try again.

"Hello from Hollywood! This is Haylee with my first reel in a really long time. Things have changed since I last posted. For starters, I now eat, um, brains. Yeah. Maybe not the best thing to lead with." I stop recording, drop my phone on the blanket, and squeeze my face between my palms.

I used to be able to do this.

I fluff out my hair, pick up my phone, and try again and again until I've recorded something postable. Then, for my own sanity, I close the Telepatch app . . . and move over to JingleJam—but only for entertainment. Last night, Kace asked Izzie to film him break dancing at the club. The video already has over eight thousand views, three thousand likes, and two hundred comments—mostly from females. My stomach hardens as I read them.

@furfriendtammy Capital A Alpha!

@shifterjane

@lunarlycanthrope I want Kace Warren so bad!

@packprowler930 Lookin 4 a hookup? DM me.

@alphabite2nt How about busting out your moves at my place?

@22howler I live near Hollywood, and I'm single.

What the hell? JingleJam isn't Tinder.

I look closer to see if Kace replied to any of these hussies, not that I'd be able to see if he DMed "Miss at Desperate and Lonely."

My phone buzzes with a new text.

Kace: Rehearsal's over. The twins and I are heading to Universal Studios. Want to come with?

Haylee: I wish but don't want to risk missing rehearsal.

Kace: Next time.

Haylee: Have fun.

Kace: You, too. Bust your moves, Z!

Haylee: Will do.

Kace:

Haylee:

Kace:

Haylee:

Kace:

Haylee: You don't have to buy me another shirt!

Kace: I know.

My hands tingle as I grin at my phone. I wish I could join Kace, Cody, and Jake at Universal Studios. It would be so much fun. I'm stuck, though.

And I wouldn't be able to relax always checking the time or worrying about missing rehearsal because of a traffic accident on the way back to the theater.

I want to make it to the lives so bad, it feels like my chest will burst.

I want to come back in three weeks and spend more time with my new friends. I want to keep performing. I don't know how to go back to a normal life after this.

So, I bring up "Zombie Delight" on my phone, get up, and set the phone on the dresser. I hit play and practice my moves in front of the mirror.

Malachi leans forward and slouches in his purple chair, watching me and my group for our final rehearsal.

My dance moves are spot-on, thanks to the practice and pointers I received from Kace and Tracie at the club after dinner last night. When I move perfectly in sync with the professional backup dancers, a smile climbs up both my cheeks. It's hard to admit that Malachi was right when he told me to have fun with it, but this time feels different, like maybe it's possible to be okay with who I am.

At the end of the number, Malachi stands up and applauds as he walks to the edge of the stage.

"Excellent control of magic and seamless choreography. You nailed it, Haylee."

If my face wasn't already flushed from all the dancing, constant movement, and casting, it would be from Malachi's compliment. It tugs at a thread of guilt within me for telling him to get stuffed. I wish I could delete it as easily as Max is able to on his camera.

I look Malachi in the eyes when I say a gracious, "Thank you." Maybe we can pretend like I never said what I did yesterday.

"Great job, everyone," Malachi says, including the extras and backup dancers.

They grin, high-five, and slap each other on the back. As with the other species, the humans form their own clique, which doesn't include me.

They stick together at the back of the stage. I suppose the opportunity to perform on national television outweighs doing so with a zombie.

Malachi takes the stairs up the stage one by one while the backup group clears out. As he approaches me, I imagine Max and Jimmy zooming in from multiple angles to capture this exchange. Malachi plants himself in front of me, jaw tight like he's expecting another outburst from me. I don't know whether to apologize for yesterday or leave it alone. I end up offering a smile—a peace offering—and say, "Thanks for all your help, Coach."

Malachi raises a brow as though waiting for a but. I keep smiling. Finally, he relaxes his shoulders and grins back. "Perform like you did just now in the final cast-offs, and you could very well find yourself casting in the lives."

My lips part in complete surprise. I can't believe Malachi is saying this with the cameras recording. Maybe he'll ask Max and Jimmy to delete it. But then, why say it at all?

I touch my lips with three fingers like that might help my mouth come up with a response. The word *thanks* whispers off my tongue.

Malachi gives me a curt nod. "Good luck tomorrow."

CHAPTER FORTY-NINE

IT'S PERFORMANCE DAY for Team Malachi and Team Brody.

Anya has painted my face, neck, and hands blue to match the bodysuit adhered to every curve and inch of my body. It's every bit as badass as she said it would be, with a comic design of bloody ribs above my chest, a spinal cord, pelvis with a heart in the center, knee, and partial leg bones in a cream color that appear exposed through the ripped blue flesh. In the chest area, it's got a blue bosom that includes rounded outlines over my breasts. At least the face paint covers the flush in my cheeks. I've never worn anything this skin-tight in my life. My body's entirely covered while fully on display.

At Anya's suggestion, I spell my hair blood red to match the drips on the costume. The effect looks incredible. The reflection in the mirror could be someone else—a comic hero. Super zombie. I turn my head from side to side, grinning into the mirror.

"After I finish your other cheek, you have to let me snap a photo for Leandro," Anya says. "He's going to have extra bragging rights for outfitting a *Spellcaster* contestant."

"He deserves every bit of praise," I say, and then hold still for Anya to paint a set of teeth on my right cheek.

I watch in the mirror through the black circles she painted around my eyes. The bridge and tip of my nose are also done in black. My red lips pop over the blue face paint. Anya outlined them in black. I'm buzzing like I'm hooked into a power plant at peak load. My muscles tremble, and I feel like throwing up.

The roller coaster inside my stomach only builds speed. It doesn't help that we have hours of waiting around. According to the flat screen, Team Malachi is performing first, but I'm going up against Vincent last. Suhani is scheduled first, performing against Teo. I won't be sorry to see him, or any other teammate, go home. Suhani is the only tolerable one in the bunch.

Izzie walks over to me in her cute wolf outfit and looks me up and down with a smile.

"That outfit is rad."

"Thanks. Anya found it for me."

Anya smiles. "Well, my work here is done. Good luck, ladies."

"Thanks," Izzie and I say in unison.

Izzie pushes her hair off her face with her furry fingerless glove.

"Nervous?" I ask.

Izzie sighs. "I wish Brody hadn't paired me against Lilly." I follow the direction of her head as she turns and looks at a blond witch dressed in a short, tight, black dress. Lilly wears tall, black boots over fishnet stockings.

I am able to relate to Izzie in an instant. I always hated dressing up in costume for the very reason of feeling less sexy and less cute than everyone else.

"I like your outfit better," I tell Izzie truthfully.

"You do?"

"Your hat is so fun."

"It is, isn't it?" Izzie grins and pats the sides of the furry hat. She lowers her arms and pushes cosmetics and body paint around on my vanity station. Her lashes remain lowered when she says, "I really want to make it to the lives."

"Me too," I say.

Izzie picks up a small can of black face paint and then sets it back down. "Each week it gets harder to see my new friends leave the show, and now our team is getting cut in half again."

I nod, wondering who will be left after Halloween week. I hope that Izzie, Kace, Tracie, Daphné, Cody, and Jake all make it through. Also, I hope Zane is back for lives. I can't help myself. Not that he needs any well wishes from me to make it all the way to the finals. The sooner he's eliminated, the better, yet I'm not ready to see him leave the competition. I don't trust him, but I can't help enjoying his attention. Not that I expect anything to come of it, obviously. If in some insane version of the world he tried asking me out, I'd give him the same answer I gave Kace. The timing isn't right, and I'm not ready.

Good thing my thoughts are private; otherwise, everyone would think I'm delusional to entertain a scenario in which a hot werewolf and a suave wizard were vying to be my boyfriend. Why not add an older, hunky vampire coach into the mix while I'm at it?

Keep dreaming, Haylee.

"Suhani and Teo to backstage," a crew member announces a bit later.

My stomach dips as I look up at the digital time at the bottom of the flat screen. I may be last, but our teams are getting smaller every week, and once the competition begins, Colt keeps everything moving quickly.

Carolina tosses her hair over her shoulder after she is called backstage for her cast-off with Clark. "Later, bitches," she says before strutting out.

It's easy to be confident when she knows Malachi will pass her through no matter what.

"Goodbye, Clark," I mutter beneath my breath. When Izzie raises her brows, I add, "I won't miss anyone who leaves my team."

She nods. "Yeah, it sucks to be on a team of all fangers. At least there won't be as many of them during lives."

"Happy thoughts," I say, and we both laugh.

Izzie squeezes her fingers. "Are you nervous?"

"Every time I'm about to go on stage," I answer.

Izzie nods. "I feel like my stomach is going to explode. Want to try some breathing exercises together?" When I give her a pointed look, she slaps her fuzzy glove against her cheek. "Sorry! I forgot. Uh, how do you prepare yourself before you preform?"

"I give myself pep talks in my mind." I tap my temple. "I used to say them out loud in front of my mirror before going live on JingleJam, but I don't want to look like the crazy zombie chick talking to herself backstage."

Izzie laughs. "Well, whatever works, right? What kind of things do you tell yourself?"

I think for a moment and then look into the mirror as I demonstrate. "I have practiced and am prepared. I will give my best performance. The audience is excited and wants me to succeed. I look awesome." I wink at Izzie in the mirror. She grins back. "I am going to win my cast-off," I continue, addressing my reflection. "Malachi will announce me as the winner."

Izzie taps her hands together in silent applause.

I'm beyond grateful for her company and distraction. The clock speeds up, and the next thing I know, I'm being called backstage.

"You got this," Izzie says.

"So do you," I reply, smiling back at her. I hold out my fist. Izzie laughs and gives me a furry fist bump. I lift my chin. "And now to have fun casting and busting a move for my adoring fans."

Izzie points two fingers at me. "You're Z bomb."

I chuckle as I head out. Each step of my blue high-tops falls heavily like the clock hand on a mechanical stopwatch. My bladder is telling me I have to pee, and my stomach says it wants to vomit. My head insists I'm about to faint. The only thing that will shut them up is getting on stage and performing.

Vincent is already waiting in his Dracula costume. As soon as he notices me, he sneers, but he doesn't say anything in front of the crew member waiting with us. Her attention is on the stage, where Malachi announces Oliver as the winner. The backup dancers and performers joining our numbers are gathered on the opposite side of the stage.

"Next up we have a cast-off between Vincent Alder and Haylee Hutchins," Colt announces into his microphone. "Here's a little behind-the-scenes look at their practice sessions."

The theater dims as clips from our rehearsals play. It's quick snippets of Malachi coaching us and of practice—starting with Vincent's. None of Vincent's insults are aired, for which I'm relieved. Nor does my outburst end up on screen—triple relief! I do have to re-listen to Malachi talking about how my soundtrack is a spoof on a zombie apocalypse and to have fun with it.

Sure thing, Coach. I'm going to make it so fun the audience is going to be jamming in their seats.

That's the plan, anyway.

Colt calls Vincent to the stage to do his sick little number. At the end, Colt thanks him and begins announcing me while Vincent and his backups are leaving the stage.

"Next up is a *fun* performance by Season 13's only zombie contestant, Haylee Hutchins." Colt puts an emphasis on "fun" like it's an amusing joke we're all in on.

Several enthusiastic howls go up in the audience, followed by more. They sound encouraging, which is unexpected.

My dance crew waits until I've taken my first steps on stage to emerge from the side and take their places.

When the first chord of music plays through the speakers, I swing out my wand arm and cast a city street filled with cracks and potholes, rubble, burnt trash, smashed windows, blood-stained fences, and knocked-over mailboxes. A performer wearing a heavy winter jacket and hat with ear flaps walks across the stage holding a handwritten sign that reads: ***THE END IS HERE***.

I swing my hips to the beat and point my wand at the first zombie victim to be set upon. "*Goretrotta expellis halluce.*" Blood appears to spurt out as the performers pretend to tear at human flesh.

I tap my sneaker against the other one and then to the side, repeating the movement with my other foot as I shimmy over to the next scene, in which the militia is gathering. A performer in a trucker baseball hat hands out the fake guns from a camouflage duffel bag. I add shoulder movement with my arms, hips, and legs, getting my groove on like never before. Next, I take side steps to keep facing the audience as I move along and cast special effects over the next scene. A rifle is aimed at a zombie performer's head. I point my wand in the same direction. "*Goretrotta expellis veed.*" Blood appears to explode, and the zombie performer drops to the ground.

My adrenaline spikes as the lyrics lead up to the dance number and my backups get into position, taking up the center of the stage. I stand in front of them, and when I join the dance, it's like an out-of-body experience. Or perhaps it's more like being possessed. My limbs are nimble. Flashes of blue from my bodysuit catch the spotlights as I move in sync and with speed to the music.

When my performance ends, the applause and howls from the crowd are deafening. I turn and smile at my backup dancers. My word of "thanks" is drowned out by the audience as the troupe exits to the side of the stage.

I face the coaches, who didn't escape the show's costume week. Malachi is draped in a long, red velvet coat with a matching ascot tucked into his black vest. A blood drip is painted at the corner of his lips, stopping just above his chin. His eyes meet mine, and he lifts a very *told you so* brow.

Colt strides on stage—dressed impeccably in his usual tux—and motions for Vincent to join us. The vampire replaces his frown with a cocky grin as he swaggers on stage. When he reaches the spot next to Colt, he tosses his cape over one shoulder and winks at the audience, earning himself several chuckles from the crowd.

While his microphone is lowered, Colt smiles at us and says, "Hey, good job, you two." Then he addresses the theater. "That was certainly fun. Two outstanding performances. What did you think, Brody?"

A wide grin reaches Brody's eyes. His hair has been teased to stick up all over his head, and he's wearing face paint to make him appear more wolf-like in human form. Furry sideburns stick to the sides of his face. The same brown fuzz covers his chest and arms beneath a red-and-black flannel shirt he wears unbuttoned.

Brody scratches his chin, taking a moment to respond. "Well, I'm a bit biased, what with Haylee being an honorary member of Team Werewolf."

"You wish," Malachi scoffs.

Brody smirks and tilts his head in Malachi's direction. "The only thing blockhead over there got right was saving Haylee. I really screwed the pooch on that one."

Malachi sets his wand in his lap and presses both palms over his eyes. "I'll never get that visual out of my head."

Cleo rolls her eyes and shakes her head and the pointy hat she's wearing.

Brody rubs his hands together and chuckles. "Then again, maybe Malachi will give me a second shot at the competition's dark horse."

This time, Cleo scoffs.

"Zen?" Colt asks.

Zen is dressed up as an Egyptian king, which is quite clever given this season's prize. A headdress covers his hair, and a large gold-toned pyramid medallion hangs from his neck. Black and metallic gold fabric covers him from head to foot.

"Vincent, you came on stage and showed us that you can create and maintain a multi-layered illusion while performing numerous tasks. You drew us into your scene and told a story through mirage and enactment that was seamlessly executed."

Vincent's chest puffs out, and his grin widens. I try not to fidget in place while my faithless former coach waxes poetic about Vincent's performance. What's worse is seeing Malachi look over at Zen and listen attentively.

Zen takes a long pause, seated tall in his purple chair like a damn pharaoh. He's still looking at Vincent when he starts talking again, which is partly why his next words take a couple seconds to catch up to my racing thoughts. "But so did Haylee, and she happened to do so slightly better in terms of complexity, engagement, depth, and diversity."

Vincent's smile falls off his face like a lost coin hitting the ground and rolling under a dresser.

"Cleo?" Colt asks.

I brace myself as the witch circles her wrist, flashing long nails painted black.

"These were two very different performances. It will be interesting to see who Malachi chooses." She looks over at him and lifts a brow.

"Two different but exceptional performances," Malachi says. "You both took what you learned in practice and fine-tuned every detail. There is no real winner here when you both did everything I asked of you, but, unfortunately, I can only choose one of you to move on to the lives." He frowns and looks at his hands, clasped in his lap.

When I try to swallow, my throat tightens. Brody made it sound like he'd steal me if given the chance, but I don't want Malachi to let me go. I don't want to be saved. And I sure as hell don't want to lose to the likes of Vincent.

My blue-painted fingers turn cold. The longer Malachi takes to decide, the more I feel the color draining from me—not that anyone can tell with all the body paint.

When Malachi looks up, I catch his eye and express a multitude of emotions without saying a single word.

I don't want to be coached by anyone else. I lean into our prolonged eye contact and somehow, my muscles relax. A soft smile loosens my lips.

Be a rebel, Malachi Rayne. I double dare you.

His gaze intensifies on me.

"Malachi, who is the winner of this cast-off?" Colt asks.

Malachi blinks and shifts his attention to Colt. "The winner of this cast-off is Haylee."

"What the f—" Vincent's curse is drowned out by the howls and cheers. When none of the other coaches lifts a wand to steal him, he storms off stage, cape billowing after him like dark smoke.

"Congratulations, Haylee," Colt says with a smile and a chuckle.

"Thank you," I say to him, and then look at Malachi. Tears well in my eyes. I blink them away quickly before I end up with black paint streaks over my blue face. I wave and smile at the audience as I walk off the stage.

It feels unreal. Like a dream. How is it possible to feel this happy when I've lost so much? But I do. The spotlight chases away the shadows . . . at least while I'm on stage.

CHAPTER FIFTY

THREE WEEKS BACK home feels like forever.

I can hardly sleep or sit still. Eating isn't a problem. I'm always up for brains. But passing the time has my stomach in a constant spin. I just want to get back to Hollywood, practice my next performance, and spend time with my new friends—the best ones I've ever had in my whole life.

"Don't forget—you've got your interview with WNV in two hours," Cameron reminds me.

I lift my head from my phone screen to where he's seated at the dining table with a glass of green gook—some kind of vegetable protein smoothie. It's Thursday morning and just the two of us after TJ left for work and Joni for school. My plate of breakfast brains is empty. I wolfed it down and have been scrolling through JingleJam and Telepatch ever since, "stalking" the other contestants.

Kace has been a busy wolf since he returned home to Missouri. Not only has he been interviewed by his local media stations, but he's visited schools to talk to kids about spellcasting. The pictures of him with little boys and girls grinning in delight are the cutest. I press "like" on all of them.

I pull one leg up on the chair and lean over my phone. I've got on black leggings and a scoop-neck Betty Boop T-shirt Kace bought for me at

Universal Studios. In silver sequins, it says: ***BREAK THE RULES***. I'm going to need to change and get ready soon, but I figure I have another fifteen minutes of free time.

I nearly drop my phone when I see a new follow from Zane Barrett.

His name enlarges as my hand jerks my phone in front of my face.

Should I follow him back? It feels rude not to. So I do. Zane's name pops into my notifications again and again as he likes my most recent posts. I go over to his account and do the same. I mean, I've already seen them, but I hadn't liked any. I suppose I can now.

Cameron clears his throat loudly.

I jerk my head up and lower my phone. "Sorry. Did you say something?" I ask sheepishly.

"Never mind," Cameron says with a shake of his head. "Are you going to turn into one of those teenagers glued to her phone all the time?"

"Not all the time. I can't be on my phone while I'm performing." I shoot him a teasing grin.

Cameron huffs, but he's grinning back. His phone buzzes, breaking his smile as he looks to see who texted.

"Hmmm. Who's on his phone now?" I smirk. Cameron sets his phone back down and drinks his smoothie in silence. "Everything okay?" I ask.

He sets his glass down, half-finished, and frowns at his phone. "Everything's fine. It's Judy—again."

My brows lift. "Who's Judy?"

"Miss Elms."

"Oh." Cameron drinks down the rest of his smoothie. I wait until he's finished to ask, "What does she want?"

"A husband." My scowl pushes a rough chuckle from Cameron's lips. "Sadly, Judy isn't getting the hint."

"Or doesn't want to," I mutter.

It hasn't been quite a year since Kendra died, but that will change next month. It's the worst kind of anniversary. Heartbreak. Anguish. Despair. How am I supposed to get through another Thanksgiving weekend without reliving the horror of that day? I worry for Joni and Cameron, too. We had no ashes to scatter. No graves to visit. How are we supposed to honor the dead?

Releasing a heavy sigh, Cameron picks up his phone and thumbs what I assume is a response to Miss Judy Elms.

"What are you telling her?" I ask, even though it's none of my business. Cameron's great about open communication with me and Joni.

"The same thing I keep telling her—that I'm busy," Cam answers.

Jeez, how many times does Miss Elms have to be turned down before she takes the hint? I feel annoyed on Cameron's behalf. There's no way I'd ever chase after a guy who kept blowing me off. I would never chase after a guy period. Not like it's an option. Being chased by a zombie isn't exactly every guy's dream.

I roll my eyes at my own idiocy and scoot away from the table. I take my plate, fork, and steak knife to the sink, where I wash them and place the dish and utensils on the drainboard.

My outfit is already laid out on my bed. Betty Boop gets replaced with a fuzzy white V-neck over baby-blue ankle pants that I plan to wear with pumps. I brush my hair in front of the bathroom mirror and part it on the left, leaving it smooth and straight as I get to work on my makeup. I go with a white shimmer in the corners of my eyes, sweeping the color over my lid and then adding soft pink and a touch of purple at the corner. Black liquid eyeliner goes on next, followed by a thick coating of mascara. I rub liquid blush above my cheekbones to add a touch of color to my light skin. Peachy pink lipstick goes on last with a glossy coating.

The face I see reflected in the mirror looks beautiful.

"Be bold, be beautiful, and always be yourself," I say to myself.

I probably should have filmed myself getting ready for the interview. Once the show goes live, the audience decides who goes forward in the competition. It's time to resurrect my old hashtags and bring the beauty brigade over to @shesZbomb. But not today. My makeup is perfect, and I'm not about to remove it and start over.

Cameron drives me to the local television studio and waits in the greenroom while Marie Jones interviews me. During a commercial break, I'm escorted onto the news stage and told to make myself comfortable on a cream couch. Marie crosses her slender legs from beneath a short pencil skirt and smiles at me from the opposite end of the couch while a crew member speedily powders her nose.

"We're back in ten," a man wearing a headset announces, holding up all of his fingers. The crew member hurries away with her makeup brush as the man silently counts the seconds with his fingers. As soon as he finishes, Marie beams at the camera.

"Joining us today is *Spellcaster* Season 13 contestant and Virginia native, Haylee Hutchins." She turns her head to smile at me. "Haylee, thank you so much for being here today."

I smile back. "Thank you for having me."

Marie lifts her hand, palm facing up. "I have to say, my daughter absolutely loved your butterfly performance."

"I'm so glad," I say.

Marie addresses the camera. "If you missed last night's performance, Haylee's display of illusions and levitation was stunning, though her coach chose to let her go. Luckily, she was saved by coach Malachi Rayne, as you can see in the following clip."

I fight a frown as I have to re-watch the rejection, followed by the images of me storming off the stage as Malachi lifts his wand before I notice.

Marie's gaze returns to me. "Haylee, how did you feel when Malachi saved you?"

I push down the humiliation and burning rage I felt when Zen picked Nathaniel over me and shove aside my annoyance over Malachi taking his sweet time saving me. When he chose me last week, I made a silent promise to be a devoted member of his team. That's what viewers expect, anyway—gracious contestants who adore their celebrity coach.

I sit up tall and smile for the camera. "Well, as you saw, I wasn't expecting Malachi to save me, but I'm so grateful he did. I've been a mega fan of his forever, so it's pretty surreal."

Marie nods her chin up and down slowly. "Haylee, you were a four-wand lift. How come you didn't choose Malachi from the start?"

I've prepared for the question of why I chose Zen in the blind auditions so that I'm not fumbling for a response.

"Zen seemed like a good choice in the moment. I mean, you can't go wrong with any of the coaches. They're all some of the best spellcasters in the country. As you know, I'm new to the whole supernatural thing, and there's a lot of dogma about species clashing. Zen felt like the neutral choice." When Marie nods again, it's with understanding. "I'm so happy I got to work with Zen," I add. "He's really cool and observant."

"And what's it like working with Malachi Rayne?" Marie asks.

Infuriating is the first word that comes to mind.

"It's a dream come true," I answer.

"I can imagine," Marie says. She straightens up and leans forward. "Next week is combat week. Is there anything you can share with our viewers about your upcoming combat round on *Spellcaster*?"

"Yeah. I won't be wearing a dress for that one."

Marie laughs. "Well, we're all excited to watch your next magical match. Thank you again for joining us, Haylee, and best of luck on Team Malachi." Marie speaks into the camera next. "Don't miss the combat rounds airing Thursday and Friday at 8:00 p.m. Eastern next week here on WNV." Her smile freezes until the countdown man announces we're clear. Marie stands. I do the same. "That was great, Haylee."

"Thanks, and tell your daughter hi from me."

Marie's straight white teeth show when her smile widens. "Thank you. She'll love that."

Shortly after my televised interview, a DM from Zane pops up in Telepatch. I'm lying face up on my bed. I was trying to zone out and recharge, but that's been nearly impossible since the competition began.

Zane: Great interview. You're a natural.

I can't help beaming.

Haylee: Thanks. You making the rounds?

He must be. It's part of our contract to appear on the network's local affiliate shows in our hometowns. All publicity is good publicity, according to Jovi, who encouraged us to accept any and all offers to make guest appearances on TV, radio, and podcasts.

Zane: It's weird getting attention for magic rather than modeling.

Haylee: Good thing it comes to you naturally. 😉

Zane: I mentioned you in my last interview.

I gape at my phone for several seconds before replying.

Haylee: Do I want to know?

Zane sends me a link. I can't not click it. The link takes me to a Los Angeles news web page. I didn't realize Zane lived in California, but it doesn't surprise me. The golden boy in the Golden State. He's lucky to have such an easy commute to Hollywood, unlike me flying all the way across the country week after week. Not that I'm complaining I get to do that!

There's a video news clip on the web page with the headline: ***Local model, wizard, &*** **Spellcaster** ***Season 13 contestant Zane Barrett sits down for an interview.***

I click play and listen to a male reporter introduce Zane, who is seated beside him on a studio couch dressed in a snazzy midnight-blue suit with a thin matching tie.

"This is the first time you've performed magic for the public," the reporter says. "Most wizards consider spellcasting for the sole purpose of entertainment beneath them. What made you decide to audition for the show?"

Zane shrugs, looking bored. "My agent set it up."

The reporter nods and waits, but Zane slings an arm over the couch and stares back at him like *next question*.

After clearing his throat, the reporter asks, "Do you think you have an unfair advantage over wand-wielding contestants?"

"If the show's producers felt that way, they wouldn't have opened auditions to witches and wizards," Zane answers.

"So, who do you think is your biggest competition at this point?"

"Haylee Hutchins," Zane answers immediately.

The reporter blinks several times and stares at Zane like he's expecting him to laugh it off as a joke at any moment. When Zane says nothing, the reporter blinks again.

"Uh, okay. What makes Haylee Hutchins a caster to watch out for?"

"Natural talent. Control. Skill. And quite frankly, a passion for magic that is sadly lacking in the wizarding community."

My mouth gapes open at the same time as the reporter's. His jaw snaps shut, and he clears his throat.

"Moving on to next week's combat rounds, do you feel like the other creatures have an unfair disadvantage against witches and wizards in this kind of a casting scenario?" The reporter sounds hellbent on getting Zane to admit his kind has an advantage.

Instead, in typical laid-back ease, Zane asks, "Why?"

"Because you don't have to worry about losing hold of your wand," the reporter says.

"If another contestant loses hold of their wand, that's their problem, not mine." Zane's back to sounding like a conceited, entitled prick. It doesn't matter, though. I scroll down to the comments below the video, where Zane is being reamed out for his praise of me.

Zane Barrett is a traitor to his kind.

I think Zane's gone in-zane. LOL

What's the big deal? Her butterfly performance was beautiful.

If you love zombies so much, how bout you marry one?

Zombie bride!!!! Ba,ha,ha

He's even got Z in his name.

Go back to modeling!

This is gross.

What's gross?

Haylee Hutchins got a 4-wand lift so ALL FOUR COACHES think she's got mad talent.

Haters suck worse than vampires!

At least it's not all bad.

I DM Zane.

Haylee: Are you crazy? Why did you say that?

Zane: Because it's the truth.

Haylee: Aren't you afraid of losing votes?

Zane: Why should I be? I'm already all-powerful.

"Oh my god," I groan at the screen. "Why are you even competing?"

I close everything on my phone and toss it beside me on the blanket. Zane's response doesn't merit one of my own. When I check again ten minutes later, it's still sitting there like a cocktail umbrella—a breezy garnish on Zane's charmed beach of a life.

I check the time. There's a little over an hour before Joni returns home from school. I've returned to scrolling through Telepatch when my phone rings, startling me so much my hand jerks, and it starts to slip out of my grip. I mean, who expects a phone to ring these days?

I squeeze the phone securely and see the name pop up: ***Uncle Al Bites.***

CHAPTER FIFTY-ONE

I SWIPE TO TALK to my uncle. "Did you find something out?" I ask.

"Hello, Haylee. Not yet," Alvan says. A heavy pause follows before his voice drops twenty degrees. "Why didn't you tell me you were going to be on TV?"

My muscles tense. "I didn't think you'd care."

"I care about your well-being and safety. Exposing yourself on national television goes against both."

"Far be it from me to deny the public the sensation that is my spellcasting."

"This isn't funny," Alvan snaps.

"Do you hear me laughing?" Sweat breaks out over my neck and beneath my arms and chest.

I'm on my feet, pacing back and forth between my bed and Joni's, gripping the phone like it's an explosive device that will blow off half my face if I release the slightest pressure before it's deactivated.

It's not enough that Uncle Alvan chose vampirism over his nieces. Now he wants to stomp all over my dreams. Well, he's too damn late. I'm already on the show, and I'm performing in the lives.

“Don’t you have more important things to do than worry about a magic competition?” I challenge.

“It’s not the competition I’m worried about.”

“Right, you’re sooo worried about your brain-eating niece.” That’s when it hits me. I stop pacing. “Oh, my god. This isn’t about my welfare at all, is it? You’re ashamed of me. You’re afraid people will find out you’re related to a zombie.” My stomach churns.

“This has nothing to do with me,” Alvan fires back. “What you are puts you at risk. That’s just the way it is, and rather than playing it safe, you’re being reckless.”

“So, I’m not allowed to have a life ever again?” I demand.

“You can have a life—just not in public.”

I kick one of my tennis shoes across the room, nostrils flaring. Alvan is acting like I should join a leper colony on a remote island.

“Let me get this straight. It’s okay for vampires, werewolves, witches, and wizards to have a public life, but not zombies.”

“People aren’t afraid of the other species,” Alvan says.

I scoff into the phone. Is he for real? People aren’t afraid of bloodsucking monsters, clawed beasts, or all-powerful wizards? It’s the stupidest thing I’ve ever heard. “If you say so,” I answer sarcastically.

“You don’t belong on *Spellcaster*,” Alvan intones.

I didn’t think he could piss me off any more than he already has. I was wrong.

“Well, Malachi thought I was worth keeping around, and *he’s* a vampire.”

Alvan huffs. “Malachi Rayne is a circus clown.”

“Excuse me?” My entire body shakes. The quakes travel up my throat. I can’t say anything more until this seismic rage levels out.

“He’s a performer—not to be taken seriously,” Alvan states.

My tears are acid burning my eyes and scorching trails down my cheeks to my chin. I grit my teeth and attempt to inhale. Breath isn’t a requirement, but I could really use some air.

“Malachi Rayne is the greatest spellcaster on the planet,” I seethe through the phone. “You’re just jealous he’s talented and famous and an elite member of Forever 23 with no master to serve—unlike you.”

"Haylee—"

"Don't call me again unless you have useful information to share on who arranged to have my family killed." I hang up on Uncle Alvan. He tries calling back, but I ignore him and the new message that pops up on my phone.

I put on the purple jacket Kendra gave me, zip it up, sit on my bed, pull my legs in to my chest, and wrap my arms around them. Sobs burst out of me.

"Haylee? What happened?" Cameron stands in my doorway, frowning. He narrows his eyes on my phone. "Who was that? Who upset you?" he demands, as he stomps into the room.

I shake my head and sniffle. "It was Alvan."

Cameron scowls. "What did he say to you?"

"He doesn't think I should be on *Spellcaster*."

Cameron's entire face turns red. "Don't listen to that inhuman lackey. You belong on the show, Haylee. You earned your place there. Four-wand lift. Saved by Malachi Rayne. Chosen to continue every week since. You're performing in the lives because of your talent. Alvan Bates is a spineless puppet who can't stand to see members of his own family succeed. He was a human underling before, and he's a vampire minion now."

I snort even though I'm still angry. I release my legs and stretch them to the floor.

Cameron takes a seat on the edge of the bed beside me. "Put that parasite out of your mind. You're going to change the world for the better by showing everyone that you're more than a stereotype. Your parents and sister would be so proud, and they're the ones who matter—not your useless uncles or anyone else."

I nod my agreement, and tears stream down my face. A watery film appears over Cameron's eyes, which he blinks away. I turn and hug him.

"Thanks, Cam."

He squeezes me back gently. "Promise to keep believing in yourself and show the world what you're made of."

"But what about my family?" I sniff. "I doubt Uncle Alvan will share any news about their killers after the argument we just had."

Cameron loosens his arms and presses his hand into my back. "We can't trust him, anyway. I've got the name of the new firm where Dora, your father's old paralegal, now works. Unfortunately, it's in DC. I don't want to question her over the phone or email. I need to figure out a good time to drive over and talk to her."

"Let's go next week," I say, sitting up straight.

Cameron shakes his head. "You have interviews scheduled all week, and your guest appearance at Harmony Hills Elementary's spellcasting class. I was actually thinking of taking TJ with me, so you and Joni don't have to worry about him while I'm gone."

"But you won't have anyone with you to spell him," I protest.

Cameron pulls his hand from my back and shrugs. "He seems motivated to find out who's responsible for his wife's death. I'll make it quick. One night, maybe two. I'll be back in time for your performance at the Curtis Magnolia Magic Center."

I chew on my lip. "Alvan found out the last time we looked into things."

"Because he was Henry's contact on the lease," Cameron answers readily.

I'm still uneasy. Cameron was right about Alvan being a puppet answering to his puppet master. If he caught wind of Cameron questioning my dad's former staff members, Alvan might be compelled to report it to his higher-ups . . . which begs the question, how is he carrying out an investigation without his master's blessing? Or maybe it's a perk of servitude—special permission to investigate and carry out vengeance against a being who has wronged you. I wish there was a way to know what Alvan's true agenda is.

"I don't like splitting up," I say.

Cameron stands up. "I know, but we're not making enough headway. I'll be fine."

That's not a promise Cameron can make. It's up to me to ensure he's safe, which is why I close myself inside the bathroom that night and text Daniel. If Cam can hire a spellcaster to train me in combat, then I can hire the same one to accompany him to DC and offer protection if necessary.

Daniel: Overnight costs extra.

Haylee: Does this mean you'll do it?

Daniel: I'll see if I can move my schedule around and get back to you.

We spell TJ into obeying Cameron first thing Thursday morning. I make Daniel repeat the spell before they head out on their road trip. A little while later, I ride the bus with Joni—an arrangement made through Cameron with the school—and spend the day with Harmony Hills's spellcasting teacher answering questions and giving demonstrations with small groups of kids from each grade.

Mrs. McCoy, the young casting teacher dressed in a long, billowy skirt and blouse, stops a fourth-grade boy with messy hair and thick glasses from entering. "Sorry, Christopher, but you can't join the group without a permission slip signed by your parents."

He peers around her and looks to where I sit, waiting for the bell to ring and Mrs. McCoy to introduce me to the next group of students seated on a thick mat on the floor. There are five of them holding wooden wands, stealing glances my way. When I smile, they smile back or flush and quickly look away.

Christopher's lower lip quivers. "But I want to see the zombie spellcaster," he insists.

"It's not up to me," Mrs. McCoy answers calmly.

"That's not fair!" he yells.

"Christopher, shouting isn't going to change anything."

The boy's eyebrows lift over the rims of his glasses. "I'll watch from the doorway."

"Sorry, Christopher, but students aren't allowed in the hallway during class. You need to return to Mrs. Jacob's room."

"I want to see! I won't tell my parents!" Christopher hollers, as Mrs. McCoy slowly closes the door on him. "Poor boy. He's so disappointed," she says to me.

All I can manage is a grimace. I'm disappointed too, because it's a reminder of how I'm seen by so much of the population. Did students need permission slips to see Kace during his school visits? Unlikely!

Mrs. McCoy moves to the front of the classroom and clasps her hands together. "All right, everyone. You're in for a special treat. Today, Haylee Hutchins is spending the hour helping you with magic. Let's all give her a welcoming wand lift."

Five enthusiastic wands are raised into the air. It's pretty cute. I wish I could get a picture with them for Telepatch, but Mrs. McCoy already explained that the parents didn't want their children appearing in public photos.

"Thank you," I say to the kids.

"You can lower your wand now, Emily," Mrs. McCoy says to a girl in pigtails.

There is only one desk in this room, pushed aside in the corner. Mrs. McCoy's skirt ripples around her ankles as she walks up to the dry-erase board and grabs a wand that is nestled between markers in the narrow tray lining the bottom of the board.

"How many of you saw Haylee's performance on TV last week?" All five wands shoot back up. Mrs. McCoy lifts her wand as well. "That's great. Now lower your wands. How many of you will be watching *Spellcaster* tonight?" They all lift their wands again. "Okay, lower your wands. Haylee, can you share a little about how you practiced some of your routines right here at Harmony Hills?"

Wand in hand, I leave the chair and stand in front of the kids with a grin. "The celestial performance I did for the blind auditions and the butterfly performance you saw last week were both choreographed inside your school's auditorium."

"Cool," one of the boys murmurs.

The girl with pigtails stands on her knees, clutching her wand.

"But my first introduction to spellcasting was inside a classroom very similar to this one," I add. The kids share eager looks with one another before returning their attention to me. "You need to master the basics to become a truly gifted caster."

Mrs. McCoy beams. "Wonderful advice, Haylee. My students will show you what we've been working on, but first, does anyone have any questions for Haylee?" All five wands go up. "Shane," Mrs. McCoy says.

A boy with neatly trimmed brown hair straightens up and lowers his wand. "Are you going to win your combat round?"

Mrs. McCoy chuckles. "You know Haylee can't share that kind of information with us." She points to another student. "Candace."

The girl with the pigtails continues holding her wand over her head as she asks, "Were those real butterflies you made appear?"

I smile and shake my head. "That would have been cool, but those were illusions."

"Great question," Mrs. McCoy says. "We're going to practice casting illusions with Haylee after we finish questions." Mrs. McCoy allows each of her students one question before we move on to practice. There is only one Lignum Vitae wand, which the students take turns using while the others practice the words and motions with their wooden practice wands until the bell rings, signaling lunch break.

When Mrs. McCoy arranged for me to be a guest in her classroom for the day, she said I could bring a sack lunch to eat in the teachers' lounge during the break. I told her I don't need to eat three meals a day, but I do accompany her to the lounge to discuss casting and what it's like being on the show.

"It's been so great having you as a guest in my class," Mrs. McCoy says.

"Thanks. I'm having a good time too."

Mrs. McCoy grins widely. She's only taken a couple bites of her egg-salad sandwich, which is placed on a piece of paper towel alongside some hard pretzel sticks and grapes. "You're a natural with the kids. You should consider offering private spellcasting lessons after you're done with the show."

I'm not sure if it's her way of saying I have no chance of winning and ought to consider teaching as an alternative, but Mrs. McCoy seems genuinely nice, so I decide to take it as a well-intentioned compliment. It's not the worst idea, especially since I had to quit my job at Raw Tasty's because of my travel and practice schedule. What happens when the show's over? It's hard to imagine life after the show, but it doesn't hurt to know there are options. Would Daniel think of me as competing with him for business? It's not like I'm interested in teaching magical combat.

Miss Elms—Judy—stops by our table, clutching a glass container with some kind of salad inside. "Hi, Haylee. Is Cameron not here with you today?"

"He's out of town," I say.

She blinks. "He left you and Joni alone with her dad?"

I don't tell her that TJ went with him. Instead, I say, "It's a quick trip."

After chewing and swallowing a bite of sandwich, Mrs. McCoy pops a grape into her mouth.

Miss Elms smiles at me with closed lips. "Well, let me know if I can help with anything while he's gone. I'd be happy to come over after school and spend time with you girls until Mr. Mullins returns home from work. I miss having Joni in my class."

"I've got it covered, but thanks," I say.

Miss Elms hugs her salad container against her chest and nods. "If you change your mind, Cameron has my number." She walks over to a corner table and joins a couple of middle-aged women already eating their lunches.

"The kids are so excited to tune into *Spellcaster* tonight," Mrs. McCoy says, as though we were never interrupted.

"Yeah, I don't know if my combat round will be aired tonight or tomorrow."

"My students and I are rooting for you," Mrs. McCoy says.

"Thanks."

Joni is in with the group of fifth graders who are part of Mrs. McCoy's first after-lunch period.

"Hi, Cousin Haylee!" Joni calls excitedly when I walk in.

"Hey, Joni."

She stands with four other girls, forming a close circle of whispered words and giggles. Three boys sneak glances from across the room as they whack one another with their wands or toss them in the air and catch them.

When the bell rings, Mrs. McCoy closes the door and clears her throat. "Okay, everyone. Have a seat so we can get started. I know you're all excited to practice casting with Haylee Hutchins from Spellcaster Season 13, Team Malachi, who also happens to be Joni's cousin."

Joni beams and is the first to sit down. The girls she was clustered around take their spots on the mat on either side of her. The boys sit behind them.

One of the girls raises her hand. Her wooden wand remains in her lap.

Mrs. McCoy lifts a brow. "Yes, Katy? Did you have a question for Haylee?"

Katy looks directly at me and asks, "Are you going out with Zane Barrett?"

My face instantly flushes. "No," I stammer, while thinking, *What the hell?*

"Oh, okay." Katy shrugs. "My sister said she read somewhere that you two were going out."

"We're just friends," I say.

"He's really cute," one of the other girls says. Her friends nod.

"Are you going out with Kace Warren?" Katy next asks. Two of the girls giggle. Joni lifts her chin and flashes a proud smile.

"Kace and I are also friends," I say.

Mrs. McCoy steps forward. "Okay, that's enough with the personal questions. Does anyone have a question for Haylee about spellcasting? Yes, Jordan?"

"Have any of the vampire or werewolf contestants tried to bite anyone on the show?"

The same two girls giggle, which makes Jordan puff up and grin behind them.

"No, that's not allowed," I say. Oh my gosh, I miss the younger groups.

Mrs. McCoy claps her hands together. "I think that's enough questions. Let's work on levitation. Whichever one of you can float the highest wins a stackable scented pencil. Who wants to go first?"

"I do," Jordan says. He practically bounces off the mat. Mrs. McCoy hands him the Lignum Vitae wand.

"Haylee, mind keeping your wand ready if anyone goes too high and loses hold of their levitation?" Mrs. McCoy asks.

"Happy to provide a safety net if needed," I say.

One by one, the students come up and cast their levitation spells. They range from a foot off the ground to three. Except for Joni. She goes all the way to the ceiling and touches it.

"Don't fall!" Jordan yells in a clear attempt to break her concentration.

"Jordan," Mrs. McCoy says in a warning tone.

"Um, I can't get down," Joni says.

"*Lantly descent*," I tell her.

She repeats the spell and floats gently back to the mat.

"Well done, everyone," Mrs. McCoy says. "And Joni, you can pick out a pencil after class." She nods in the direction of her desk with its pen cup filled with bright stackable pencils topped with acrylic stars in multiple colors.

"Good job," I whisper to Joni at the end of class.

She grimaces. "I needed help getting down."

"You'll do it yourself next time," I say.

She smiles and skips over to Mrs. McCoy's desk, studying the pencils before plucking one with a purple star on top. "See you after school," Joni chirps on her way out.

I check my text messages while the next group of students filter in from the hall.

Cameron: Brock is stopping by with dinner for you and Joni around 6. Don't open the door for anyone but him.

Haylee: What if Girl Scouts come by selling cookies?

Cameron: No exceptions.

Haylee: Got it. How's it going there?

Cameron: Just dropped our things off at the motel. TBD.

Haylee: Good luck.

CHAPTER FIFTY-TWO

THAT EVENING, BROCK texts to let me know he's on his way and again after he's pulled up, even though Joni and I can clearly see him exit his van carrying a pizza box, bag, and large bottle of Sprite from the window. His van is black with a flame design along the sides, the Raw Tasty Meat Co. logo overlapping the flames, and his website in large letters.

Joni opens the door. "Hi, Brock."

"Hey, Joni. How was school?"

"Good. Do you want me to carry something?"

"I've got it. If you could close the door behind me, that would be great." Brock walks up to the dining table and sets the pizza and soda down. He holds up the paper bag. "This is for you," he tells me.

"Thank you." I take the bag from him and stick it in the fridge for later.

"You should eat with us," Brock says.

"Yeah," Joni agrees. "I can handle it."

"I'm the last person who would ever feel squeamish around brains." Brock winks at Joni.

"A brain surgeon might beg to differ," I say.

"Meh." Brock shrugs.

"Come on, Haylee. Please eat with us." Joni heads for the fridge like she intends to plate the brains herself.

"I've got it," I say, rushing in front of her. "You can set the table." I stack two plates on the counter, followed by forks, knives, and cups. Joni whisks them away to place on the table while Brock leans his back against the counter, watching me pull out the bag he brought and unwrap the brain before setting it on my plate.

"Miss having your help at the shop," he says.

"I miss it too," I say automatically.

He snorts. "No, you don't."

I roll my eyes and shake my head. "It was a great job for someone like me."

Brock leans forward. "Someone like you is meant for better things."

"I don't know." I stare down at the brain on my plate. It's a harsh reminder of what I am. Nothing will ever change that.

The pizza—no surprise—is a meat lover supreme. Joni frowns at the piece on her plate for several seconds and then picks the meat off with her fingers, discarding the pieces into a pile on the side of her plate.

Brock lifts a piece and points the end at her. "What's the matter? You vegetarian now, Joni?"

Joni looks up and smiles sheepishly. "Yeah, sorry."

"Since when?" I ask.

"I wish Cameron had told me," Brock says.

Joni shakes her head. "I haven't told him yet. It's okay. I don't mind picking off the meat."

"Well, I'm happy to take your toppings." Brock holds out his plate for Joni to push the meat pile over with her fork.

"Are you sure you're okay with me eating a brain in front of you?" I ask Joni.

"Yeah, of course. You're the one eating it, not me," she insists before taking a bite of her slice of now cheese pizza.

I dig into the brain, using a fork and steak knife. I'd use my hands, but I get the feeling that utensils make it slightly less disturbing when dining with company. The sound of chewing and swallowing fills the dining room. Brock devours three slices in a row before chugging down a full glass of Sprite.

"What's your schedule tomorrow?" he asks me.

"I have a radio interview in the morning, and then I'm spending the afternoon with Stella at Mystic Wand Haven." It's posted on the shop's SocialSphere page as an event—a "come get your picture taken with the local *Spellcaster* contestant while you shop" kind of thing.

Brock refills his glass with Sprite and pulls a fourth slice of pizza from the box. Joni's picking meat off her second slice.

"How are you getting to the radio station and Mystic Wand Haven?"

"Uber."

"What time? Maybe I can drive you at least one way."

"It's fine," I groan. "I used Uber all on my own in California. I don't need to be picked up and dropped off like a little kid."

Brock snorts.

"Want more meat?" Joni asks him.

"Can't say no to that," Brock says. He takes Joni's plate and pushes the extra toppings over the edge with his knife, directly onto his slice of pizza, then sets the plate in front of Joni. She takes small, deliberate bites and drinks a sip of Sprite between each one.

"I hope they play your combat round tonight," Joni says.

I don't. If Brock sees me being shot at and lynched on TV, there's a good chance he'll insist on taking time out of work to drive me around. So, of course, that's exactly what happens.

Joni cries out in alarm when John Gable fires his first bullet at me. A vein throbs in Brock's neck when the rope winds around my neck.

"It looks worse than it was," I say.

Joni and Brock don't respond. Their eyes are glued to the television screen. I clench my jaw. It really looks bad. I mean, it was terrible up until the point where I attacked John. That part was fun.

"See," I say after John's rope turns into a python. "I turned the tables on that fanger."

Right after Malachi announces me as the winner on TV, my phone rings. It's Cameron. I sigh as I answer.

"Are you okay?" he demands, like everything that played out on stage just now happened to me. "You didn't tell me that bastard fired live rounds at you. How was that allowed? Did the producers know that was coming? Did Colt? Did your coach?"

"I don't know," I say.

"I'm going to have words with the producers. Maybe I'll find a lawyer while I'm out here and sue the show for reckless endangerment."

"Cam, no!" I yelp. "Please, just let it go. It wasn't like that for my Halloween performance. That was only combat. It's over now. I shielded, and I won."

I feel a panic attack coming on. If Cameron goes after the show, they'll drop me faster than a severed limb. The worst is over. I've made friends. I remind him of this fact, but it takes him several more minutes of cursing the show's director, producers, and coaches . . . and threatening to deliver a live python to John Gable.

Once he's calmed down somewhat, Cameron asks, "Is Brock there?"

"Yeah. Do you want to talk to him?"

"I'll call him." Cameron ends our call. Brock's phone rings after.

"Hey, man," Brock answers in a serious tone. "Yeah, I saw it all. Sickening." He listens a moment and nods. "Yeah, no worries. Yep. Cool. Yeah. Let me know when you're headed back."

After Brock says goodbye, I fold my arms and arch a brow. "Let me guess. You're driving me around tomorrow."

Brock smirks. "And spending the night."

I throw my back against the couch and huff. "Do what you gotta do."

It's not like he's asking permission.

Meanwhile, two new text messages come in.

Mariana: I just saw your combat round. That was horrifying! But the rope snake was pure genius.

Kace: Maybe those fangers will finally learn not to mess with you.

True to his word, Brock sleeps on the couch and drives me to the radio station, where he waits until the end of the interview before dropping me off at home. He returns three hours later to drive me to Mystic Wand Haven, where I'll be hanging out from 2:00 to 5:00 p.m.

I make a quick wardrobe adjustment, switching out my floral cardigan for my purple Team Haylee jacket, which I wear over the white V-neck I've got tucked into a pair of skinny jeans with a brown belt. My nails look amazing painted midnight blue with little stars and moon art.

"You don't have to hang around for three hours, you know," I say, as Brock pulls into a parking spot along the sidewalk, four stores down from the magic shop.

"I need to check on a few things at work, but I'll walk you in," Brock answers.

I huff, but really, I'm relieved to spend a few hours hanging out at Mystic Wand Haven without a bodyguard.

There's a small poster taped on the window from the inside of the store facing out with a photo I sent Stella of myself holding my wand and smiling. When I enter the store, the bell over the door chimes. There is a table covered in a vintage cloth printed with black cats, cauldrons, skeletal trees, bats, and witches' hats. A tall stainless-steel hot-water dispenser is set on top, along with cute little teacups, small square napkins, a wood crate filled with tea bags, and a platter stacked with star-shaped cookies that have a hole cut out of the top star and an apricot jam center.

Brock scans the table and then the store like he's looking for booby traps.

"Haylee! It is so great to see you. Thank you for taking time out of your busy schedule to make a guest appearance at our shop." Stella's bohemian skirt billows as she rushes forward to greet me.

"Happy to," I say. "Stella, this is Brock. He's a family friend and owns Raw Tasty Meat Co. He's just dropping me off."

Brock's chest and chin lift, making him appear to expand in size. "And I'll be picking her up at five," he says, adding, "Nice to meet you, Stella."

Stella smiles. "You as well. Thank you for bringing Haylee over."

He nods and turns to me. "Have fun. Be safe. And call me if you need anything, okay?"

"Yep. See you at five, boss man."

Brock snorts and shakes his head. "See you at five—probably sooner."

I roll my eyes and groan. Nothing like an adult treating me like a child to make me feel—like a child! Which I'm not.

"Do you want a cookie and some tea before you go?" Stella asks.

Brock swings around to face the refreshment table and scratches his beard. "Maybe a cookie for the road."

Stella strides over to the table, places a star cookie on a napkin, and hands it to Brock. "I made them myself. I hope you enjoy it."

Brock stares down at the cookie, now in his hand, and then looks back up at Stella with pinched brows. "There aren't any special ingredients I should be aware of, are there?"

Stella grins. "Just good old-fashioned flour, sugar, salt, butter, eggs, vanilla extract, jam, and the most important ingredient of all—love."

The look on Brock's face is priceless. I can't even describe it. Even through his beard I can see the polite smile he's trying to maintain morph into a grimace.

I stifle a laugh as he hurries out of the shop with the love-filled star cookie.

As soon as the door closes behind Brock, Stella says, "I really appreciate you doing this. There are some excited little girls coming by after school to meet you."

"I'm looking forward to it," I say. I would have flipped out—at any age—to have a local *Spellcaster* contestant make an appearance at Mystic Wand Haven. It's still surreal that I'm that contestant. Thinking of myself as a celebrity feels super weird. I slip my hands into the pockets of my jacket and then take them back out. My nails look way too fabulous to conceal for even a second.

There's a table set up near the register with a stack of *Spellcaster* Season 13 postcards Stella hired a digital artist to design. It has cute cartoon creatures (a vampire, a werewolf, a witch, and a zombie) lined up at the bottom, holding wands. Above the creatures is a full moon and, inside the moon, the *Spellcaster* logo. Beside the postcards, there are purple markers for me to autograph as a free keepsake courtesy of the shop. Stella texted me the finished design, and I'm excited to see them in print. I pick one up and grin.

"These turned out great. Do you want me to start signing them or should I wait and do it in front of customers?"

Stella moves to my side and lowers her head, staring at the postcards. "I think people would enjoy watching you sign a card for them, but it would be great if you started signing some—maybe half—that I can give out to folks who miss today's event."

"Sounds good." I take a seat, set my wand on the table, pull the cap off a marker, and sign my name over the first postcard. As I sign, I lay them down side by side, giving the ink time to dry.

High school has just ended for the day, and I wonder if anyone from Brookdale will show up. It would be really cool if Georgia came by—a zombies supporting zombies kind of thing. Maybe we need our own club. Z-23, except not 23. The Z League, or Society Z. All ages welcome.

I gather up the signed postcards, now that my signature has had time to dry, and stack them together into a "done" pile.

"Would you like a cup of tea, Haylee? Can you drink tea?" Stella goes to the refreshment table before I answer.

"I can, but I'm fine, thanks." I do not want any liquid near the pretty postcards.

I grab another and have just scrawled out the letters H-A-Y when an egg hits the shop's front window and explodes. Stella gasps. More follow. They crack apart on impact and smear yolk across the glass.

My spirit cracks apart as easily as the eggshells, and my muscles cramp.

Stella runs outside and shouts at the top of her lungs, "Get back here, and clean this up right now! Oh, you better run, cowards. You're lucky I don't have my wand on me. I'll be ready for you next time."

The marker shakes between my fingers. I put the cap back on, set it down, and stand on stiff legs. My stomach rolls with nausea. What made me think I'd be treated any differently than all of the other sentient zombies persecuted every day for what they are? Being on *Spellcaster* doesn't grant me a magical pass, but it helps me forget how ugly the world is—until I'm reminded over and over again that people suck.

Stella stomps back inside muttering, "I'd cast a shield over the store, but then customers couldn't get in. There must be some work around. I'll consult *Wards and Protection Spells: The Witch's Advanced Defense Manual.* There should be at least one copy on the shelves. But first, I want to get this mess cleaned up, so it doesn't deter customers from coming into the store. I'm not going to let those hooligans chase off true practitioners."

"I'm so sorry," I say, unable to swallow past the lump in my throat.

"This is not your fault, Haylee," Stella says sternly.

"I'll help you clean off the windows," I offer.

Stella shakes her head. "No, you won't. You're the store's celebrity guest." She looks at the window and frowns. "Maybe you should call Brock. I hate to disturb him at work, but it might be better if he sticks around for the event."

My shoulders drop. Stella's right. She's a one-woman show here at the shop and shouldn't have to add security, janitor, or bouncer to her duties.

I nod and try to swallow again to no avail. "I'll call him."

"Sorry, Haylee," Stella says. "I'll fill a bucket with hot water and soap in back while you phone him. And you might want to pour yourself a cup of the calming tea blend. It always helps me."

"Yeah, thanks." I dial Brock while Stella storms into the back room.

"What's happening?" is how he answers.

I wince. "The store just got egged."

"What? Outside or in? Are you okay?" Brock demands.

"I'm fine. It was outside. The window is covered in egg." I stare at the slimy mess as I speak. I sigh. "Stella would feel better if you were around for the event. Do you mind?"

"Of course I don't mind," Brock says gruffly. "I'm leaving now. Don't go anywhere." He ends the call, and I huff.

Where the heck does he think I'd go? I'm at my own special event. Well, currently no one has shown up to see me, but there are those little girls Stella mentioned. It's the younger ones who are the sweetest—before they grow up into judgmental, trash-talking, egg-throwing, horrid humans.

Not everyone is like that. I'm just venting.

I set my phone on the refreshment table, select the calming tea blend, and fill a teacup with steaming water. Hints of chamomile, lavender, lemon balm, and peppermint fill my nostrils as the tea steeps. The aroma is nice, and my throat could use any kind of liquid at this point. I stare at the pretty star-shaped cookies Stella made with love, wanting something nice to replace the sight of the egged window. I wonder if Brock will report this incident to Cameron right away or wait for him to return home.

My throat tightens. I can barely swallow or produce enough saliva to help. The tea hasn't had time to steep, but I could use a warming sip.

The bell jingles above the door. I set my cup down. It's great that someone is coming in despite the egged store front, but I still wish they hadn't seen it. I wish it hadn't happened to begin with.

"I'll be right out," Stella yells from the back room.

I turn to greet our event's first guest only to find Caleb pointing a gun at my face. His expression is glazed. His eyes look dead as he fires.

The blast of the bullet is deafening, though I still hear Stella's scream.

Fire burns through my left cheek and shatters half of my jaw. I stumble backward as Stella rushes in from the back room. Caleb runs out of the store.

"Haylee!" Stella yells, coming to my side.

I waver in place. Confusion washes over me. Hunger consumes me. It's a feeling like no matter how much I eat, I will never be full or whole again.

Stella looks at my face and gasps. "Oh, my god. Sit down while I call an ambulance."

I hear her words, but they don't compute. I don't know what she wants. I take a step forward, stumble, and then regain my footing. A raspy sound emerges from my throat. Stella's eyes widen. She backs away slowly, keeping me in her sights as she goes behind the counter and pulls out a wand. The spell she casts sounds familiar, but I still can't place it. Stella lifts her phone to her mouth. Her lips move and make sounds I don't understand.

I don't know which way to walk or what to do. I'm just hungry. So very hungry. And something doesn't feel right with my face.

CHAPTER FIFTY-THREE

"SLUMBER ENDS THIS *doze a fake. Thoughts emerge and come awake.*"

My body jolts as my mind turns on like it's connected to a switch in the wall. This feels more like I jammed a butter knife into an electric socket. I jerk into a seated position, my eyes flying open to find I'm tucked into a hospital bed.

"Eat this," says a young African American nurse dressed in baby-blue scrubs, her straightened hair pulled back into a ponytail. She manages not to wince as she places a plate with cut-up brain into my lap.

I grab at the lumps of brain matter with my bare hands and stuff them inside my mouth, chewing like a beaver taking down a tree.

It isn't until I've finished every last bit of brain that I take a closer look at my surroundings. For starters, there's a teddy bear on the bed with me. I've got a single room with a large window. There's an overflowing bouquet filled with pink and purple flowers in a glass vase on a counter beneath a TV. A forty-something Asian witch with short, straight hair stands beside the nurse watching me. Cameron leans against the wall with his arms folded. When our eyes meet, he drops his arms to his sides and walks over to the bed, looking grim.

My memories return in broken shards. Eggs spattering the window. Caleb's detached look. The gun. Being shot in the face.

Bits of brain rise up my throat. I swallow hard to force it all back down. I lift my hands to my cheeks, my fingers hovering just above the skin. I can't bring myself to touch my face and feel the damage. I can see, so my eyes are okay. I was able to eat, so I've got my mouth. What's missing? My nose? Oh, my god. Does this mean I'll never be able to smell again?

"Your face is fine," the witch says.

"This is Ji-Su. She's an alterationist," Cameron says. "She already repaired your face."

The nurse grabs the plate from my lap and leaves the room.

"Are you able to speak?" Ji-Su asks.

"I—uh, yeah, I guess so." I blink. I wasn't expecting words to emerge so easily. I sound like myself. My hearing is fine, too. "So, my face is back to normal?"

"It is," Ji-Su says.

"Thank you."

Ji-Su nods and then looks at Cameron. "Make sure she eats every day for the next week. She'll be fine, but extra nourishment will have her functioning better faster."

"I'll see to it," Cameron says.

When Ji-Su leaves the room, the silence is heavy with Cameron's dark mood. I can practically feel the anger and guilt wafting off him. The clothes I had on when I got shot haven't been changed. My purple jacket shimmers over my arms like magical armor. I'm still here. I'm okay. Not dead yet. I grab the stuffed bear and hug it against me.

Cameron rakes his fingers through his hair. He's going to have bald spots if he keeps tugging at it. "Haylee—" My name is forlorn on his lips.

"Please don't apologize," I say.

Cameron shakes his head. His eyes are downcast. "I should have been there with you."

I let go of the teddy bear and set it beside me again. Hugging a stuffed animal isn't going to help make me appear as an independent young adult. I wonder who sent it. Kace? Malachi? Yeah, right. And who are the flowers from? Why aren't there more flowers?

Oh, my gosh, stop being such a diva, Haylee.

But I was shot in the face, so you'd think that would earn me a dozen bouquets—at least.

"How long have I been in the hospital?" My nostrils flare in panic. I haven't missed the first week of lives, have I?

"Only overnight," Cameron says. "After you were shot, Stella called an ambulance. The EMTs sedated you. I rushed back as soon as Brock called me. He stayed with you until I got back. The doctor kept you drugged while an alterationist reconstructed your face." The skin beneath his eyes looks bruised, and his sockets are hollow as he stares miserably at my face.

I press my hands against my cheeks. "I look fine now, right? Ji-Su wasn't just saying that to keep me calm?"

"You look beautiful, Haylee, but this should have never happened to you to begin with."

I sit up straighter. "Did they catch Caleb?"

Cameron grinds his teeth. "Z Squad has that little psycho in custody, but they're already saying they won't be able to charge him with murder, since you survived."

I yank the covers off my bed. At least the nurse didn't undress me and put me in a hospital gown while I was unconscious.

"I need to talk to Sgt. Ganon," I say. "He can charge Caleb with the murder of Myles Castillo. Caleb all but admitted he killed him when he attacked me after school at the end of last year."

I step onto the linoleum and am relieved to stand upright without feeling like I'm on board a sailboat attempting to walk across the deck in the middle of a squall.

Cameron straightens. "I'll come with you, but first we need to stop by the house and show Joni you're fine. Brock is with her. He feels terrible too."

"Everyone needs to stop feeling terrible," I groan. "You can't follow me around everywhere I go. It wouldn't have mattered if you or Brock were at the shop with me. That still wouldn't stop a deranged psychopath like Caleb from coming in with a gun. At least now the Castillo family might finally get some peace and justice. Speaking of which, did Dora share anything useful in DC?"

Cameron's face is stony. "She told me I should speak to the woman who worked for Laurence before her, a woman named Evelyn Jensen." Cam fixates on the floor. He's got the look of someone who is zombing out and has entered an echo chamber of his own thoughts.

"Okay," I say slowly. "So where do we find Evelyn?"

Cameron blinks and looks back up. "She's in an assisted living facility in Long Beach, California."

This news feels like a kick to my gut. "Why is she in assisted living?"

Cameron shakes his head. "Dora didn't know. All she could tell me is that Evelyn suffered brain trauma, and Laurence paid to place her in a facility in California."

"Is Long Beach near Hollywood? Where's my phone, and my wand?" I look around the sparse room.

Cameron walks over to a chair, grabs a gift shop bag, and hands it to me. "They're both in here." I double check, confirming that my most prized possessions are intact, and pull out my phone while Cameron answers before I have time to open a search. "Long Beach is about forty-five minutes from Los Angeles depending on traffic." When a smile leaps over my lips, his brows wrinkle. "Promise me you won't look into this while you're in Hollywood." Cam's pupils drill holes into mine.

I feign exasperation. "Cam, it's the first week of live cast-offs. I honestly have no time to go investigating."

"Promise me," Cam growls. He'd make a great werewolf.

I look him dead in the eyes. "I promise." Only my promise is the one I made to seek justice for my parents and Kendra, and that vow comes before all others.

Cameron's shoulders relax a fraction, and he nods, breaking eye contact to glance toward the window and rub the back of his neck. "I'll figure out a way to contact her." He looks so beaten down, it breaks my unbeating heart. I hope that once we find out who had my family killed, Cameron can find some semblance of peace.

I clear my throat gently. "Maybe we could hire Daniel to house-sit and spell TJ so that you and Joni could come out to Hollywood with me one week. Joni could watch the show with the live audience while you talk to Evelyn."

Cameron looks at me and purses his lips, which looks gentle compared to his frown.

"Maybe," he says thoughtfully.

"I mean, as long as I make it through to next week." I shrug.

"You will," Cameron says.

"Well, extra incentive," I try to joke. But Cameron's staring off again. "We're going to find out who did this," I say more seriously. "We're getting closer to the truth." I'm not sure about that, but Cameron looks like he could use some hope. I know how that feels. It's not much, but saying it out loud makes me feel more confident.

"Yes," Cameron says. "And once we do, I am going to kill anyone who played a part in Kendra's death."

I swear the temperature in the room drops twenty degrees. With a shiver of unease, I zip up my jacket, and jut my chin, asking, "Who are the flowers from?"

Cameron follows my gaze and blinks as though just now noticing the bouquet.

"I think they're from Colt and the rest of the crew. Ji-Su said she reported the incident to one of the show's producers."

I grab the teddy bear off the bed. "And who is the bear from?"

"That's from Joni."

I nod. It's sweet and disappointing. I put it in the gift shop bag and walk over to the floral arrangement. Cameron sweeps in front of me. "I'll carry that." He grabs the vase and lifts it off the counter.

Once we reach Cam's car, I take the vase from him and rest it between my thighs for the drive home. Joni runs outside as soon as we've pulled up along the sidewalk. Cameron comes around and takes the flowers from me.

Joni bounces on her toes in front of me. "Haylee! You're back! You look great," she assures me.

"Thanks for the bear," I say, lifting the bag.

As soon as we step inside, Brock tackle-hugs me and squeezes tightly. I chuckle and pat his back. "I'm fine. Really. Supernatural, remember?"

It takes Brock several more seconds to release me. Once he does, he steps back and clears his throat. "You've got a whole shelf in the fridge filled with organs and brains."

"Thanks, Brock. That's really sweet of you."

"Thanks, man," Cameron says.

Brock sobers when he speaks to Cameron. "You guys good for now?"

"Yeah, we're headed to the Z Squad station soon. Haylee wants to give a statement."

"Want me to come with you?"

"No, we've got it, but thanks. Thanks for everything."

"I should have stayed at the shop."

"No, I should have never left," Cameron insists.

"Guys! Please." I set the bag on the dining table and throw my arms up in exasperation. "I'm a survivor."

They wrinkle their brows like nothing I'm saying is getting through.

The following day, every chair in Z Squad's press room is filled with reporters.

Sgt. Ganon asked me to stand beside him at the podium while he issued a statement. Cam wasn't happy about it but ultimately respected my decision to appear at the werewolf's side.

It turns out Alexander was right about playing nice with my local Z Squad. After I shared my suspicions about Myles, they interrogated Caleb wolf-style and got him to confess where he buried the body in a patch of woods behind his house.

They dug up Myles—in pieces. It still makes me want to puke. I knew Caleb was a sicko, but this is next-level psychotic.

The story turned national, with the attack on me front and center.

Sure enough, when Sgt. Ganon transitions from statement to question period, reporters call out, "Miss Hutchins!"

"Did your attacker cause any permanent damage?"

"Miss Hutchins, are you still in the running on *Spellcaster*?"

"Miss Hutchins, has anything new come to light about why your family was attacked last year?"

Sgt. Ganon turns to me and lifts his brow. When I nod, he steps away from the podium so I can take his place.

"Hi, everyone," I say into the microphone. "Thanks to Starlight Regional Hospital and the alterationist they called in, I am fine. I mean, I'm still a zombie." I pause for laughter, but the reporters only stare at me, holding up phones and recording devices. Alrighty then. I clear my throat and square my shoulders and stare into the faces watching me. "What happened to me at Mystic Wand Haven was awful, but at least Myles Castillo's family will finally get some justice for their son's murder. This is only the beginning. I plan to get justice for my own family, no matter how long it takes to uncover the truth." I step away from the podium.

"Miss Hutchins, do you believe a murder sentence should carry the same weight if the victim was undead?"

"Miss Hutchins, has this incident made you fearful of going out in public?"

"Miss Hutchins, any theories on who would have wanted your family dead?"

The reporters continue firing off questions, but I'm done answering them. Sgt. Ganon takes my place at the podium as Terrick escorts me out of the press room. Cameron slips out with us. He's been my shadow ever since the incident. If he didn't need to look after Joni, I know he'd follow me to Hollywood too.

"You're a natural," Terrick says as we enter the hallway.

"At surviving murder attempts," I quip.

Terrick scoffs, but he's holding back a smile. I'm about to roll my eyes when I notice a large, muscular, Black dude headed my way. I feel my entire face light up at the sight of "Chef Brains." We're tattoo twins now—not that I'll tell him.

"Maurice!" I run over and throw my arms around him like he's my long-lost uncle. I'd rather have Maurice as an uncle over TJ or Alvan any day.

"Hey there, Sparky," he says, with a chuckle that shakes me while I'm plastered to his chest.

I lean back and smile up at him. "Have you missed your all-time favorite inmate?"

Maurice's eyes squint when he laughs. Cameron folds his arms. None of this is funny to him. Nothing is and may never be, but humor helps me deal with life.

"World-famous inmate," Maurice says. "Glad you kept your spark and used it to light a fire. Me and my baby girl love watching your performances together. We'll be voting for you when you make it to the lives . . . you're making it to the lives, right?"

I shrug and wink, which sets Maurice off chuckling again.

"Maurice, this is Cameron, my brother-in-law and guardian. Cameron, this is the man who fed me my first brain."

Cameron unfolds his arms to reach out a hand and shake Maurice's firmly.

"That's a strong grip you've got there, Cameron," Maurice says approvingly.

"Nice to meet you," Cameron answers gruffly. He turns his attention to me. "We should go before the press adjourns and chases us across the parking lot."

"Smart thinking," Terrick says with a nod.

Maurice lifts his fist. "Power to you, Haylee."

I smile. "Thanks, Maurice. What's your little girl's name?"

"Annabelle." His eyes shine as he says her name.

"Tell Annabelle I said hi and that I appreciate her support."

"Will do, Haylee. Will do."

The parking lot isn't entirely clear. A reporter and cameraman run after me and Cam, but we're faster. We sprint for his car. Once inside, Cameron tears out of Z Squad's parking lot as though a tidal wave were coming.

I turn my phone off silent and spend the ride going through texts and social media. It's been a barrage since the story got out about my attack. It makes me feel better about the lack of flowers and cards at the hospital—no one knew yet.

Kace's first text to me said:

Kace: Want me to kill him?

Kace: I'm NOT kidding.

I answer back.

Haylee: Thanks for the offer, but he needs to answer for his crimes. P.S. Should you be proposing murder over text?

Kace: I was kidding about not kidding.

Haylee: Uh-huh.

Kace: Black humor.

He also sent me thirteen pink roses—delivered to the house in a wide vase with a yellow-and-white polka-dot ribbon tied in a bow.

The only flowers I received from Malachi were illustrated ones on a *Get Well Soon* card. Not that I expect a bouquet from my coach. Then again, I was shot in the face!

I haven't heard a peep from Zane. Well, if he wasn't scared off before, this most likely did the trick. I re-check my DMs just in case, followed by his Telepatch profile page. He hasn't posted anything new since my attack. My stomach sinks. What if something happened to him? A second later, I shake my head. He's golden boy Zane Barrett. He's fine. Probably hungover from partying with his model buddies—including the sexy, single variety of chicks who would jump his bones with one curl of his finger.

Whatever. If that's who he really is, then he can have at it. I'm not interested in his sympathy.

"Did someone say something bad?" Cameron demands.

I blink and look up. We're stopped at a red light, and his eyes are boring into the left side of my head.

"What do you mean?"

"You've been frowning at your phone since we passed Maple and Third."

"Oh. No, it's not that. I was just overthinking something."

"You know you can talk to me about it if you want."

"Thanks. I know. It's nothing."

Cameron opens his mouth to speak, then seems to think better of it. He frowns at the red light. Eventually, it turns green, and we arrive back home. We don't even need a key, with Joni's new butler service. She throws open the door. "How'd it go?"

Cameron excused her from school again, but he says this is the last day.

"Great," I answer. I've gotten a taste of justice, which makes me more determined than ever to do the same for my parents, sister, and aunt. Taking down Caleb is only the beginning.

I'm still disgusted by what he did to Myles. If I hadn't dropped out of school, I could have been next. It sends a chill through me that sinks all the way through to my bones. Right before he walked in and shot me, he posted a ranting manifesto on his Telepatch account. It was removed from the social media site, but not before parts of it were aired on TV. His words still haunt me.

I am going to do what that vampire sorcerer failed to during combat. I am going to shoot a zombie. They're not really alive. They shouldn't be on TV or the radio or going around thinking they're better than humans—because they're not. They're a plague on the planet. They don't even feel pain, and I can prove it.

He's got a warped brain. I wouldn't eat it even we were stranded on a deserted island together, and he died and eating him was the only thing that would keep me alive. I'd choose starvation!

Speaking of eating . . .

"I made veggie sandwiches for Cameron and me and set out a brain for Haylee," Joni announces.

"Thank you, Joni," Cameron says.

"And a package was delivered for Haylee," Joni adds.

"You didn't answer the door, did you?" Cameron asks at the same time I demand, "What package?"

Joni shakes her head. "I waited until the delivery driver drove off to bring it inside. I'll get it." She dashes into the living room and sprints back with a book-sized box in her hands.

Cameron snatches it from her like it's a grenade that's about to go off. I try to grab it from him, but he holds it away from me. "We don't know what's inside," he reminds me.

"Well, does it say who it's from?" I stand on my tiptoes, trying to get a look at the mailing label.

"It says it's from Zane Barrett," Joni offers.

CHAPTER FIFTY-FOUR

"CAMERON, GIVE IT!" I practically tackle him to get my hands on the package. I grasp the edges, but Cameron holds firm.

Our eyes lock.

"I'll open it first," he says.

"It's addressed to me," I counter. What if it's something embarrassing—like a book on the Kama Sutra? Obviously, that's not what's inside, but that doesn't mean I want Cameron to see it before me. "Please, Cam," I say. "Zane's not going to send me a booby-trapped box." Cameron's lower lip folds over. "Please," I say again.

"Please, Cam," Joni chimes in.

His fingers tighten, making my stomach sink. Then he hands it over, huffing out, "Fine, but open it on the table, and Joni, have your wand ready."

Joni nods eagerly and races off for our shared room while I groan. But Cameron's set jaw tells me that this is his final compromise.

I set my crossbody bag on the table and grab scissors from the kitchen while Joni runs back with her wand. Cameron places the package on the dining table.

Joni plants herself across the table, her feet placed hips distance apart, and announces, "Ready!"

Cameron stands beside me, which is so annoying, while I slice through the tape. Once the top seams are unsealed, I set the scissors on the table and open the box. There's a thick, leather-bound book nestled inside of black tissue paper. The title is embossed into the leather, announcing: *Fortify and Defend: Ancient Incantations for Protection*. I caress the cover and pull it out.

"What is it?" Joni asks, standing on her tiptoes and craning her neck.

"I think it's a rare book of protection spells," I say, showing it off but unwilling to hand it over for anyone else to look at. I turn it around and gasp. There's a symbol of a snake arching above an eye between two pillars on the bottom left corner of the back cover.

Cameron leans in, taking a closer look. "Does that mean something?" he asks.

I nod reverently, momentarily speechless. After moistening my lips, I say, "This symbol means the book can only be sold to witches and wizards."

Cameron folds his arms and huffs. "That sounds illegal."

Yeah, the way compulsion, mind manipulation, sucking blood, and a bunch of other supernatural behaviors are off-limits yet totally taking place. Each species seems to take the laws as suggestions they're disinclined to respect. But Cameron's missing the point. Zane got me a book that beings outside of the wizarding community would have a nearly impossible chance of possessing. This is, without a doubt, one of the best gifts ever. (Sorry, Kace.)

I don't know whether to hug the book or cart it away to my room and flip through it page by page. Oh, I should get on Telepatch and thank Zane too.

When my phone rings, Cameron, Joni, and I all stare at my purse. Did Zane spell the book to alert him when I opened it? My eyes widen on the cover as though it's a two-way mirror in which he's watching me now. Then I remember that Zane doesn't have my phone number. I reluctantly set the book back in the box and fish my phone out of my purse.

Cameron's still in my personal space, so he sees the name on the screen.

Uncle Al Bites

"Ugh, do I have to answer?" I wrinkle my forehead. "What if he found out you were digging around in DC?"

Cameron's jaw tightens. "Let's find out."

Joni chews on her lower lip while squeezing her wand in both hands.

Way to ruin the moment, Uncle Al.

I clear my throat and answer, "Hello?"

"Haylee, are you okay?" The way he asks sounds clinical.

"I'm fine. Why?"

"Because I've seen you all over the news. Why didn't you tell me you were attacked?" Anger leaches through his words.

"Oh, well, I've been busy getting my face reconstructed and bringing my attacker to justice. Never a dull moment, ya know?"

I would have thought that would have gotten a smirk out of Cameron or Joni, but they frown at my phone like it's a meteor hurtling toward Earth. They're so quiet, I wonder if they're holding their breath.

I guess the only person I'm cracking up is myself. That is, until Uncle Alvan says something that turns the blood in my veins to slush.

"Maybe now you understand why you have to drop out of the competition."

My mouth hangs open. No sound emerges. I have no words or thoughts in that moment—only complete and utter shock at what I'm hearing come out of my uncle's mouth. Is he kidding? I made it to the lives. No one drops out of *Spellcaster*. Why would they? Why would any sane caster give up the opportunity of a lifetime? And I'm good at it. Scratch that. I'm great!

Uncle Alvan seems to be waiting for my response, but I still can't get my mouth to work, so his horrid voice fills the silence.

"You had your fun. Now it's time to do the right thing for yourself and Joni. You are recklessly putting yourself in danger. There are a lot of dangerous individuals out there who don't want to see a zombie competing alongside vampires, werewolves, and wizards."

There's a lump of burning coal stuck in my throat, but I manage to ask in a low, cold voice, "You mean beings like yourself?"

"I would never hurt you," Uncle Alvan says.

My stomach tightens. How does he not comprehend that he's hurting me right now?

"I can't just drop out."

Cameron's face turns a bright, angry red at my words. He bares his teeth and curls his fingers into fists. Joni frowns and taps the tip of her wand against her cheek over and over.

"After what happened during break, they'll understand," Uncle Alvan insists.

I'm so upset, I can't even joke about disappointing my adoring fans. I look down at the book Zane sent me.

I'm not a victim. I'm a survivor. I have haters, but I also have powerful friends. "The only way I'm leaving the show is if I'm not voted through," I say firmly into the phone.

Uncle Alvan snarls. The sound makes me jerk in place. It sounds so inhuman. So . . . vampire.

"Drop out of the competition. I'm warning you, Haylee. Your father and mother didn't listen and look what happened to them."

My nostrils flare. I see red. It tinges everything within sight. Alvan knows more about that than he's willing to share. I should be the one grilling him, but that's not the plan. Instead, I fire back, "What's the worst that can happen? Someone sics a zombie horde on me? Been there, done that."

"You have no idea what you're dealing with," Uncle Alvan snarls. "You're running out of wake-up calls. Next time, you might not wake up at all."

This time, he's the one to hang up on me.

I lower my phone slowly, set it on the table, and take a step back. My earlier shock returns. I shouldn't be surprised that Uncle Alvan's gone to the dark side at this point, but it still hits me. I've lost him. Anything that was ever good in him is gone.

"I wish I could wring his neck," Cameron says, shaking his hands in the air in demonstration. He twitches all over—shaking mad.

"Uncle Alvan wants you to leave the show?" Joni squeaks out the question.

I grit my teeth. "He said I should drop out."

My cousin blinks back tears. "How could he suggest that? Do you think his master made him say that?"

"I don't care," I say. "He's dead to me either way."

Joni's lower lip quivers. She still wants to believe our uncle cares about us. I can see the internal pleading in her eyes even though he never bothers to contact her. Joni's not a threat; therefore, he has no reason to try to put a leash around her neck.

"You are not dropping out of the competition," Cameron says.

"Of course not," I answer. Especially not after being told I should. Now, I want to win more than ever.

Joni takes a shaky gulp. "You don't think Uncle Alvan would hurt you, do you?"

"He said he wouldn't."

This doesn't appear to alleviate Joni's concern. "But would someone else try? Maybe he really is concerned for your safety."

I huff. "Doubtful. And someone is always going to be trying to hurt me. But luckily, I have this handy, dandy book of defensive spells to keep me safe." I lift Zane's gift up like it's a trophy. "I'd better go study."

After all the attention from reporters at the press release, Cameron's hovering, Joni's constant anxiety, and Uncle Al's unveiled threats, I could really use some quiet time to myself. Just me, myself, and new spells to memorize and practice.

So I grab my phone, purse, and book and take them to my bed, but not before closing the door. Hopefully, Joni won't take offense. I miss having my own room. My space. My sanctuary.

I flop onto my stomach, take a picture of the book, and then send it to Zane with the message, "Thanks so much!"

JingleJam is blowing up with viral videos of people filming themselves doing the dance number from "Zombie Delight."

Overnight, I have over 100,000 new followers. It's insane.

There's a fresh round of requests from local news outlets, including our daily paper, which runs the headline ***The Unkillable Haylee Hutchins*** over my photo. It gets picked up by the Associated Press and spreads across national news.

Kace: Wow, Z. You're more famous than the rest of us combined.

Haylee: Yeah, maybe I should be thanking Caleb.

Kace: I still want to kill him . . . but I won't.

Haylee: You'll just have someone else do it.

Kace: 😗

Haylee: 🤣

Kace: 🐺 💀 🪦

What I thought was going to be a long three weeks ends up going by in a whirlwind. I've barely squeezed in the last interview before I'm packing my suitcase to return to Hollywood.

It's time for the lives.

CHAPTER FIFTY-FIVE

To: Top 20 Spellcaster 13 Contestants
Subject: Your First Week of Lives

Dear Contestants,

Congratulations on making it to Week 1 of the live cast-offs.

For your first lives, your coaches have selected a song for you to demonstrate your skills of vocal distortion. You will be asked to imitate the voice of the song's original singer using your spellcasting skills, while maintaining a static scene crafted with illusion and one real element. Viewers will be encouraged to guess which of the elements is truly on stage before your performance concludes. Keep in mind that your ability to fool the audience may help earn you votes. Once your song ends, you will expel your illusions, revealing the object left behind.

After working with your coaches, you will each have one hour to practice your song and set on the *Spellcaster* stage before your live performance on Thursday.

Whether or not you continue to Week 2 lives is now in the hands of voters.

Friday is results day. Three members from each team will be voted through to the next week of competition. The remaining eight will have one more chance to perform live in front of viewers. Whichever one of the remaining eight receives the most votes will earn the thirteenth spot and continue to the Top 13.

Attached, you will find the schedule for when your team meets for practice.

Good luck in the lives.

CHAPTER FIFTY-SIX

BACK IN HOLLYWOOD, it's just me and Malachi Rayne during our first coaching session since the three-week break.

Well, me, Malachi, Jimmy, Max, and several members of the sound and stage crew.

I'm the last member of Team Malachi to be ushered to the stage, after my coach finishes with Suhani.

Saving the best for last, is he? I snort to myself.

I'm dressed casually in sneakers, white jeans, and a light green T-shirt I had custom printed during break. I only used to wear tees to bed. Kace must be rubbing off on me.

As soon as I walk on stage, the cameras point my way, recording my movements to join my coach where he stands holding a clipboard with a thin stack of papers. He's too preoccupied marking up the sheet with a pen to immediately notice my awesome new tee.

I certainly notice Malachi, though. He has on a fitted black top that's unbuttoned at the collar and loosely tucked into a pair of snug blue jeans. Lean arm muscles press against the short sleeves of his shirt and continue to a motorcycle chain bracelet. The man's got wicked bling circling his fingers—the coolest being an onyx square with crescent moons accenting the sides.

His dark hair matches the stubble covering his cheekbones, chin, and the space above his upper lip. It reminds me that even though Malachi is young, he's most definitely a man, while I'm a teenager and always will be.

I tug at my short ponytail secured high on my head. Maybe I should have left my hair down.

Malachi clicks his pen closed and lowers it, along with his clipboard. "How are you feeling, Haylee? Are you excited about performing in the lives?"

He sounds mechanical, like he's a marionette repeating the same lines to start the session with each of his five remaining team members. I know that the show is more or less scripted—plus he's been doing this for thirteen seasons—but I was hoping for a personal greeting after taking a shot to the face. He's acting like it never happened.

The cameras are recording, and I have a part to play too.

"I'm super excited to be competing in the cast-offs," I say enthusiastically. "And I'm dying to find out what song choice my coach picked out for me this week. Let me guess . . . 'Super Freak' by Rick James."

Malachi full-on laughs, which warms me from my belly down and stretches the smile already on my face. Glad he found that amusing, because I worked on that line before leaving Virginia, searching out songs I could joke about.

"Cute, but no," Malachi drawls, staring straight into my eyes.

He is so freaking hot; I swear I can feel my insides burning whenever he's not being a total vampire douche.

I tap the tip of my wand against my open palm. "Is it 'Freakshow' by Britney Spears? Or 'Lil Freak' by Usher?"

Malachi's eyes light up with his smile. His irises appear almost fluid, like dark molasses that sticks to your soul. He's a decent male, the kind who doesn't stare at a woman's chest, so he still doesn't see what's on my T-shirt until he pulls a sheet from the back of the stack on his clipboard and begins to hand it to me.

Malachi's arm and smile freeze as he scans the four-word screen printed over my green shirt. His gaze lifts and meets mine. I smile, but he doesn't return it this time.

"You know that shirt is going to piss off a lot of vampires."

I purse my lips and shrug. "It's not my fault if they don't have a sense of humor."

"Wearing that T-shirt on national television won't win you any votes with vampires. You can run back and change in the fitting room. You're lucky you're my last coaching session. I'll let you start our session over this one time." Malachi reattaches the sheet of paper he was about to hand me to his clipboard and looks at Max, who lowers his camera.

"Nah, I'm good," I say.

Malachi looks at my shirt again and scowls.

In thick brush type, it reads: ***ZOMBIES HAVE NO MASTERS***

I think it's awesome. I should trademark this sucker. It started out as a "screw you" to Uncle Alvan for telling me to drop out of the competition, but I think the whole concept is pretty catchy.

"What do you care? You're Forever 23. You have no master," I challenge.

Malachi shakes his head. "This isn't about me. Look, I'm not going to sugarcoat this. There's a good chance the public won't vote you through to next week. Antagonizing an entire species won't do you any favors."

"Oh, please, they wouldn't vote for me even if I wore an "I love vampires" T-shirt to every practice session." I roll my eyes.

Malachi looks upward and shakes his head. "Your funeral. Let's pick this up where we left off." Once Max lifts his camera to his shoulder, Malachi detaches the sheet from his clipboard and hands it to me. "For Week 1 of the live cast-offs, I've chosen 'Unstoppable' by Sia for your vocal imitation. Are you familiar with the song?"

I shake my head as I scan the lyrics, a lump forming in my throat, clogging unshed tears because I swear the words were written for me. It makes me feel like Malachi truly sees me and believes in me more than I could have imagined. It makes me feel a bit bad about the T-shirt, but there's no turning back time—unless the wizarding community knows something and is keeping the rest of the world in the dark.

Malachi plucks his wand from a long pocket at his hip and lifts it to signal the sound team. Every time he does that, he looks like a conductor commanding an orchestra.

Instruments play from the speakers, filling the empty auditorium with the mellow opening beat. Then Sia's words pour out. My lips move along as I lower my chin and read the lyrics as she sings.

I've heard Sia's voice before while streaming music. She's one of those artists who never goes out of date, no matter how much time passes, and she possesses a unique tone. I can't believe I missed this empowering song of hers until now, though. It thrums inside my chest cavity and pulses against my bones.

Voice imitation has never interested me before. The spell is quite technical, to the point where I used to joke that it would be easier to practice mimicking the voice without magic, over and over until you got it down. Singing in someone else's voice makes the spell all the more difficult. But I love the song Malachi's selected for me so much, I'm extra motivated to master the voice of Sia and knock this one out of the ballpark.

After I've listened through the entire song, Malachi instructs me to sing along out loud. After that, it's just the music with me singing karaoke-style. It's a cringe-worthy sing-along that the audience will definitely laugh at when they air the replay of our practice session during lives. Hopefully, I don't have the worst voice in the competition. I'm a spellcaster, not a singer.

Next comes the silent chanting. I can't be casting my spell out loud while singing at the same time.

"*Mimicast Sia melousness*," Malachi chants.

"*Mimicast Sia melousness*," I repeat.

He nods. "Now silently inside your head."

Mimicast Sia melousness fills my head.

Malachi paces the stage, selecting a new spot in which to stop and observe me.

"Now sing the lyrics while silently chanting."

The first two lines emerge in my own voice. I grimace and start over with the same result. I clear my throat and try again and again. After I fail my fifth attempt, I stomp one foot against the stage in frustration. "This is impossible!"

Malachi lifts a brow and smirks. "Is the 'Unkillable Haylee Hutchins' really incapable of carrying a tune?"

So he did keep tabs on me during break. It makes me grin until he nods at my shirt and says, "Maybe you should change that to 'Zombies can't sing.'"

"Ha, ha," I say in annoyance, which brightens Malachi's eyes.

"Ready to try again, or should we ask the stage crew to hand out earplugs to our live audience?"

My mouth flies open. "Oh my gosh! You're so freaking rude."

"And you're unprepared," Malachi shoots back. "You received the email. You knew this was coming. Did you practice even a little, or were you so busy basking in the spotlight that you forgot you're competing against the country's top supernatural spellcasters?"

"Basking in the spotlight," I sputter. "Is that what you call—"

"Yes. Yes. You were shot in the face," Malachi rudely interrupts. "Believe me, I know. The whole country knows. You've survived unspeakable horrors. You're part of an oppressed minority. You're bullied and misunderstood. An underdog. An outcast. Life's unfair. Get over it."

My mouth hangs open. I clamp it shut and glare at him. "This is bullcrap. You treated your teammates on all of the previous seasons so much nicer."

Malachi huffs. "That was before the producers forced me to work with self-absorbed supernaturals. My human contestants never stood around worrying that they were human. On the set and on the show, they cared about one thing and one thing only—practicing and mastering their spellcasting skills. It's time to decide what you want to focus on. Are you merely a survivor, or are you more? Close your eyes."

"What?" So many emotions are spinning through my head. I don't know whether to feel hurt, apologetic, outraged, or motivated to prove myself.

"Close your eyes," Malachi repeats. "Stop overthinking. Stop reacting. Start chanting and sing like Sia instead of a tone-deaf teenager."

"Seriously? You're so—" I sputter and stop myself when I see Malachi lift a brow in challenge. I clear my throat softly and finish with, "Right. You're so right."

"Am I?" Malachi smirks like he doesn't believe me for a second.

I close my eyes and tunnel deep into my psyche to a place that holds no color, no emotion, no judgment, and most importantly, no inner monologue. It's not only safe here, it is serenity.

Mimicast Sia melousness.

The stage is gone. There are no cameras, no crew, and no hot and infuriating vampire coach watching me. There's no music, either, but that doesn't stop me from testing out the chorus. Sia's voice fills my ears as I sing about putting on my armor to show how strong I am.

I believe the last lyrics as I repeat them again and again, and it's as though I'm possessed by the singer herself. Maybe I should dye half my hair black.

Once I finish, I open my eyes. The first thing I see is Malachi wearing a pleased grin.

"How did that feel?"

"A lot better," I admit.

"It sounded better too," he quips. I scoff, but my smile takes all of the indignity out of it. "Try it again, eyes closed, with the music," Malachi instructs.

I run through the song without trouble, but once Malachi has me sing with my eyes open, I stumble over lyrics and cut in with my own voice.

By the time I've finished, Malachi's expression has turned hard as stone. "Well, you have a lot of practice to do before Thursday. We need to move on to your set illusion before we run out of time." He pulls a sheet of paper loose and sticks it on top of his clipboard. "I'd like you to create the landscape of a medieval tournament. I want to see a platform with a throne on which a king would sit, smaller wooden chairs on either side, old-time stalls and tents along either side of the stage, and an earthen terrain in the center for jousting and archery."

"Will I be using my wand to joust?" I ask, playfully jabbing it in front of me. Jake and Cody are going to be so jealous of my scene—unless Brody gives them a circus set with flaming hoops.

Malachi shakes his head. "Too troublesome without a horse."

"Or a horse could be my one real thing."

"If you want to be obvious about it."

"No," I say.

Malachi nods. I join his side and am handed my own copies of the color drawings for the illusions I need to create on stage.

"If you can manage, it would look extremely cool if you were able to turn your wand into a sword here and run it through the heart of a target dummy here, and then turn it into an arrow here and shoot it into a bullseye." Malachi draws a star next to two sets of lyrics and then points out two spots on the drawing of the full scene set with his pen.

I press my fingertips against my lips, wishing there was an actual chair I could sit on.

This is too much. Not only do I have to create an entire freaking medieval scene, but I also have to alter the appearance of my wand with a lightning quick duplicate illusion to leave embedded in the tournament targets since I can't leave my actual wand behind without making it all disappear. I could do all of that if I didn't have to chant inside my head and alter my voice at the same time. Not only alter my voice . . . but sing!

My head goes fuzzy. I close my eyes.

"You can do this, Haylee. I've seen you cast illusions like they're confetti."

I open my eyes, blink, and nod.

"Start with the platform." Malachi taps his pen against the drawing of the raised structure with its wooden beams, triangular roofing, and open deck. Banners hang from either side of the centermost platform.

I walk toward the back of the stage and cast, bringing the illusion into existence in an instant. Instead of a throne, I cast a purple coaches' chair then turn and smirk at Malachi. He grins back at me, his eyes alight.

"Leave it. In fact, let's get a spare up there as your real element. I'll have the set crew hang it level with the platform illusion and spell the cords holding it in place invisible."

Both of my brows lift. "Won't that be obvious?" I ask.

Malachi looks at the illusionary purple chair and rubs his chin. His smile tells me he likes the idea too much to drop.

"So obvious no one will suspect it," he says. "See if you can make one of the banners flutter slightly whenever you walk past it. Fool the audience into thinking they're clever enough to spot what they think is the real element while the obvious choice is staring them right in the face." This time, Malachi shows teeth when he grins.

I smile back. "I kinda love it." We make a great team, but that's not something I'm about to admit out loud.

I take advantage of every second I have left of our session. By the end, my spirits are soaring, and I feel like hugging Malachi. I don't, of course.

Instead, I say, "Thanks, Coach," and lift my hand for a high five. Malachi stares at my raised hand and lifts a brow, making himself appear like an arrogant F23er. It sorta sucks that he can be a prick and look hot at the same time. I keep my hand up and stare him down. "Do vampires not high five?" Malachi huffs before giving my hand an obligatory tap. "That all you got, Malachi Rayne?" I taunt, leaving my hand up. He shakes his head and then gives me a real high five, smacking his palm against mine. "Much better," I say.

He rolls his eyes, which makes me laugh. His lips quiver like he's fighting back a grin. "Bye, Haylee. Have a good evening."

"Thanks. You too. I'm unstoppable today . . . and tomorrow . . . and the next day . . . and the next. All thanks to my incredible coach—the one and only Malachi Rayne."

Oh my god, his smile is gorgeous. I can feel myself lighting up inside when he smirks at me. Do I sound too flirty? I'm just joking around. My neck heats. *Time to go, Haylee.*

I hurry past Max, who has already lowered his camera, and make my way down the stairs. Keeping my eyes on the exit, I pass row after row of empty seats. I hear steps behind me and think Malachi is coming after me. But why? My stomach twists before I do. When I turn, all is silent. No one is behind me. The stage is empty as well.

Okay, weird.

I turn and continue out of the auditorium and into the theater's quiet lobby. Once more, Team Malachi was last on the schedule. It's eerily quiet.

I pull out my phone to arrange a ride.

"Boo," a male voice says into my ear.

I scream and drop my phone.

CHAPTER FIFTY-SEVEN

THE SECOND KACE appears, I whop him on his shoulder.

"Don't ever do that again! You're lucky I'm incapable of having a heart attack."

Kace's laugh is a deep rumble. The message on his T-shirt reads, in all caps: ***I'M JEALOUS OF ME TOO***.

"You started it, Z," Kace says, as he squats to retrieve my phone from the floor and hands it back.

"Yeah, well, I think we need to find a new game."

He gives me a bright-eyed smile and juts his chin at me. "Love the shirt."

"Why, thank you." I bat my lashes playfully and press a hand to my chest.

Kace laughs. "You've got balls, Z. Way to stick it to your coach."

I shake my head. "It wasn't meant for Malachi. He doesn't even have a master, and he's actually been pretty cool."

Kace folds his arms and frowns. His voice drops an octave. "Oh, yeah?"

I tilt my head to the side. "Yeah. His coaching has been helpful, and he's picked out good soundtracks. You liked 'Zombie Delight,' remember?" I arch a brow, but Kace glowers.

"I was watching the fanger at the end of your practice session. That fool was checking you out every time your back was turned to him," Kace growls.

Wait. What? Malachi was checking me out? Heat rises to my neck like it's the spout on a teakettle that's reached boiling point. Happy butterflies enter my stomach while angry moths beat inside my head.

I take a step back and put my hands on my hips. "You were watching me practice?" I demand.

Kace's bottom lip puffs out. He shrugs. "I didn't want you to have to ride back to the hotel alone, so I stuck around."

"But your practice session ended hours ago." I gape at Kace.

He stuffs his hands inside his pockets and shrugs again, not meeting my eyes.

My heart might not beat any longer, but I feel it melt. How can I be mad at Kace when he hung around the theater for hours after he could have left just so he'd be here for me?

"What about the rest of Team Werewolf?" I ask. I haven't gotten a chance to check the group text.

"Clubbing," Kace says. "I told them maybe we'd catch up later. Unless you wanna go out just the two of us. I'm good either way."

"As fun as both sound, I kind of want to turn in for the night. Do you mind?"

"Of course not, Z. We've made it to the lives. We're here to make it all the way to the finales. If you need extra rest in order to recharge, then do what you gotta do."

I nod. "Thanks for understanding. I love hanging out with the group, but I don't have the same kind of stamina as wolves."—my cheeks flame at the thought of my words coming across as sexual—"I mean, energy," I say lamely. I circle my wrist. "You know what I mean. I get tired more easily. Not that I'm lethargic. I just need me time to zomb out." I can't look at Kace. One moment things feel so easy with him. The next, I'm Miss Awkward and Embarrassed.

Kace chuckles and steps closer until he's directly in front of me. Ever so gently, he reaches for my face and tips my head up by my chin.

"I know what you're saying, and it's all good." When I huff, he leans in, bringing his lush lips closer. "I mean it. You do you. No one else can."

"Thanks." I look from his powerful brown eyes to his full lips, and I am here to tell you that zombie hormones function just fine. Maybe too well.

They sizzle along my spine and zap at my nerves. There's a foreign ache inside my chest and at my core.

Kace grins. "You waiting for a kiss, Z?"

I swallow and take a step back. "I really need to focus on making it into the top thirteen."

"Uh-huh." Kace shows a mouth full of straight white teeth with his next wide smile.

The wolf looks way too sure of himself, which is why I say, "Also, I've never kissed anyone before, so maybe I ought to ask my coach to help me with that so I can work on my performance."

Kace doesn't just scowl. There's fury in the murderous flash of his eyes. I laugh, but his muscles bunch together like he's about to beat down an opponent. The tattooed skulls look ominous as they tighten with his fists.

"No way. That fanger isn't getting your first kiss," he seethes.

"Kace, I was kidding." He knows I was kidding, right? I wince. Maybe there are certain subjects werewolves don't handle as well—like rival males. Not that Malachi Rayne is a rival. It's laughable. There's no way he was checking me out . . . is there?

I glance down at myself. I'm wearing jeans and a T-shirt that's offensive to Malachi's kind. Carolina had on a pleated mini skort and backless halter top today for her session with Malachi.

"Promise I'll be your first," Kace says.

"First kiss?"

His dark smile and hooded gaze feel more like silk rose petals than beating butterfly wings sweeping through my belly. I don't want to make Kace a promise I can't keep. I already did that to Cameron, and it still tastes like sour milk coating my throat.

"Maybe," I say.

Kace shoots me a sly grin. "I'll make you a deal. We both make it into the top thirteen, we kiss."

"Hm, how about top five?" If Kace and I both manage to make it to the finale, that's an event definitely worthy of a first kiss.

"Top eleven," Kace counters.

"Top ten," I return.

"Nah." Kace shakes his head. "I like odd numbers."

I lift my brow. "Five's an odd number."

"Nah," he says again. "Let's go eleven. That's in two weeks. I can wait. Let the anticipation build. And don't worry—I've got enough stamina for both of us." He winks as my face fills with heat. Kace chuckles. "Our first kiss is going to be unforgettable, Z."

"Okay, but we have to make it to the top eleven, and it's just a kiss."

Kace bobs his head. "Right. We'll save the celebration sex for the finale."

"Oh my gosh. You wish!" I press my hands over my ears like that will block the full-on flames heating my body inside and out. It's not enough to cover the sound of Kace's laughter.

Once he's composed himself, Kace arranges our ride and plays the perfect gentleman by opening doors for me and walking me to my hotel room.

Outside the door of room 809, Kace flashes me one final grin for the evening and says, "Rest up, Z."

I enter my room with a smile on my lips. The room is dark. Blair is either off with her witchy friends or has turned in for the night.

As I reach for the light switch, I'm sucked into a silent wind tunnel that jettisons me into the bathroom. The door slams shut behind me, and the lock clicks from within. The force of the spell knocks me backward onto the hard floor.

"What the hell?" I yelp.

I get to my feet and storm the door. The lock is stuck. I pull out my wand. "*Entra*," I say before grabbing the knob again. It doesn't budge.

"*Translocate bedroom.*" I attempt to teleport.

"You might as well set your wand aside. You're no match for a witch," Blair says smugly from the opposite side of the door.

I pull out my phone. All I get is a black screen even though the battery was at 58% last time I looked at it. Never mind texting for help.

Demanding Blair let me out is fruitless, so I don't bother. Instead, I say, "My friends are going to come looking for me if I don't show up for breakfast."

The witch cackles gleefully. "Don't worry yourself, freak. You'll get your morning brains, but tonight you're sleeping in the bathroom in case the urge to take a crap comes over you again."

I turn on the bathroom light and look at the countertop. Unfortunately, Blair hasn't left her toothbrush or anything else I can threaten to dunk in the toilet. That's not all. She's removed all of the towels. There's no blanket or pillow, either. I'm not going to plead with her to let me out or beg for bedding.

"You can scream all you want after I put up a silencing spell," Blair adds.

I walk back to the door and narrow my eyes as I envision her standing on the other side looking pleased with her cruel spell.

"Why would I spend my time screaming when I have better things to do?" I ask tauntingly.

"What does that mean?" The change in Blair's tone from triumph to suspicion gives me a momentary jolt of satisfaction.

"I do my best revenge plotting when I'm bored and trapped." I back away from the door with a manic grin.

Blair doesn't comment. I get the last word, but I still end up stuck inside a bathroom all night in spite of every attempt to cast myself out of here. My wild card might be powerful enough to get me out of here, but no way am I wasting it on the likes of Blair Monroe. I can't even get onto social media to pass the time. Blair's spell is multi-layered and as unforgiving as the witch who cast it.

Eventually, I pad the bathtub with the shower curtain and then lie on top. I can zomb out anywhere. It's not discomfort so much as indignation that keeps me up half the night. I nod off in fits and starts, waking to a fresh wash of fury.

How dare that witch lock me up? Why won't my spells work? I thought my casting was strong enough to get me out of a situation like this. Does this mean witches are, and always will be, superior at casting?

I have to win Queen Yapsut's heart, I think over and over again. I fixate on winning. I also imagine my wolf friends shifting and pissing all over Blair's suitcase and clothing—though not her bed because that wouldn't be a nice surprise for the maid. A dark part of my mind imagines Kace's wolf taking a chunk of flesh out of the witch, which is exactly why I can't tell him. I don't want him risking his place in the competition. The other wolves have been nice to me, but only because of him. He's my only true friend here. I don't know what Zane is, but it's definitely not a friend. I don't trust him.

Plus, he's a wizard. It's kind of impossible not to hate on his species as the porcelain tub presses into my back and a crick forms in my neck. I know better than anyone not to stereotype. Plus, he gifted me that rare book, but I envy how effortless his power is and that he has a carefree, charmed life. I hate him so much.

But also, I don't.

Without my phone or a window, I don't know it's morning until I hear Blair's voice.

"I'm going to use my friend's shower," she announces. "The spell locking the bathroom door will dissolve ten seconds after I leave. I hope you learned your lesson about proper roommate etiquette."

I flip her off. It doesn't matter that she can't see. There's something oddly satisfying about giving someone the middle finger from the other side of a wall. Other than that, I hold still in the bathtub and let Blair stew in the silence. I can picture her waiting for a response of some kind. I give her nothing. I wish the witch would leave already.

Now that her silencing spell is down, I hear her shuffle around, unzip her suitcase, walk past the bathroom, and finally, slam the door after she leaves our room.

I count down slowly from ten and then hoist myself out of the tub. My bones are stiff, and my stomach growls. The first thing I do when I get out of the bathroom is order room service. There's a dark cloud hovering over my head, and I'm in no mood to talk to anyone.

I'm not letting Blair, or anyone else, get in the way of my investigation. I only have one free day before my final practice session on stage. I should be mastering the mimic spell in my room, but this is my chance to get to Long Beach and see if I can extract any useful information from Evelyn.

There's no time to waste. I reattach the shower curtain, snatch one of the towels Blair tossed on top of the dresser, and take a speed shower so that I don't miss my breakfast brains delivery. It's not as though I'm keen to spend extra time in the bathroom after being trapped in there all night. My hair is wet, but combed, and I'm dressed in a scoop-neck black cotton dress that lands above my knees when there's a knock at the door.

"Room service."

I open the door and tip the young man in the hallway before taking the tray. There's a silver dome covering the plate. I carry it to the small table in the corner of the room and remove the cover. The brains are chopped and scrambled. After devouring my meal, I brush my teeth, apply my makeup, spritz on perfume, and put on my purple jacket. I've got my phone, wand, and wallet in a black crossbody bag with a gold celestial print.

When I step into the hall, I'm not alone. Zane, Dominic, and Nathaniel are waiting for an elevator. It's quicker to dash back inside my room than dig out my wand and turn myself invisible—so that's what I do.

I stand behind the door and sigh heavily, waiting and waiting . . . and waiting some more just to be safe.

A knock at the door makes me scream in surprise.

"Haylee, it's Zane."

I grimace. Of course it is. I'm less than enthused when I open the door.

"Hi," I say, unable to mask my annoyance.

Zane's brows draw in. "Are you hiding from me?"

"I forgot my sunglasses." I glance over his shoulder, expecting to see Zane's sidekicks at his back, but they must have taken the elevator without him, because he's alone.

Zane sees me looking and says, "I told the guys to have breakfast without me."

"Well, I already ate, so you should join your friends." I remain in my room, holding the door, blocking Zane from coming in. He stands in front of me, standing between me and the hall.

"You headed someplace?" Zane asks.

"Yes, actually, and I need to get going."

"But not without your sunglasses." His brows lift. When I don't respond, he says, "We can take the elevator down together."

"Go ahead," I tell him.

"I can wait."

"Don't bother."

Zane purses his lips. "Someone got up on the wrong side of the bed."

It's the wrong thing to say. My lips draw back as I bare my teeth at him and glare. A raging zombie would scare most beings off, but Zane stays planted in front of the door like some kind of luminous sentinel guarding Heaven's golden gates.

"Zane, I'm tired, and I'm not in the mood."

"Why are you tired?" he asks suspiciously, lifting his chin to look into my room.

Not that it's any of his business, but I go ahead and tell him. "It's a little hard to sleep when your roommate locks you in the bathroom all night. Your pal Blair is a real sweetheart." I fling the words at him like he's partially responsible.

Zane looks me in the eyes and has the audacity to smile. "Well, you did defecate on her bed."

My mouth gapes open. "I did not! That was a wolf, and she did it on the floor *beside* Blair's bed, not *on* her bed. And that was after Blair destroyed all of my clothing."

"She did what?" Zane frowns.

"Whatever. It doesn't matter. I have someplace I need to be."

"You're not on the practice schedule until tomorrow," Zane says.

It seems Kace isn't the only one keeping tabs on me.

"I've got personal business," I say cryptically.

"And I've got a car parked at the hotel. I'll drive you wherever you need to go."

I snort. "Zane Barrett, chauffeur for hire."

"Free of charge." His smile is dazzling. It reminds me so much of the way Cameron used to smile at Kendra, it hurts. Not that Zane feels a fraction of the love and adoration Cam had for my sister. That's not what I'm saying.

All I know is it's a bad idea. "Thanks, but I'm good."

"At least tell me where you're going," Zane insists.

"Fine. Long Beach. You can go now."

Zane's eyes widen. "Long Beach. That will cost you a fortune." Yeah, it will add up, but a fortune is pushing it. Zane leans into my room, his brilliant blue irises as mesmerizing as oceans. "Come on. Let me drive you. It's the perfect temperature for riding with the top down, wind in your hair, sunshine all around. And I could use a break from the hotel, if I'm being honest." He sticks one hand in his pocket and shrugs his shoulder. "Or you could wait around for an Uber and get a ride from a stranger in a smelly car."

"Have you ever taken an Uber? They're not smelly." I roll my eyes and huff. "But since you need the break, fine. I'll grab my sunglasses. Stay where you are." I need to get going, and Zane is the faster option.

At least he remains put like a cute door stopper and doesn't joke about seeing my room since I saw his. I'm well and truly not in the mood.

Zane holds the door open until I place my hand below his. Carolina chooses that moment to leave her room. She's dressed in a black leather miniskirt, a fitted yellow blazer over a tight white V-neck, and tall green suede boots. Her blond hair has more volume than a shampoo commercial, with thick, straight, silken layers. Carolina's head is tilted as she stares at her phone. Naturally, it's too much to ask that she not notice Zane appearing to leave my room with me.

CHAPTER FIFTY-EIGHT

CAROLINA'S HEAD SNAPS up, and she zeros in on us. She stops, tosses her hair over her shoulder, and plants one hand on her hip. "You have got to be kidding me," she says with disgust.

All I can think is *why?* Why did Carolina Bellmore have to leave her room at that exact second? Why did Zane have to be coming from the direction of my room with me?

Why? Why? Why?

"Not that you'll believe me, but Zane was waiting for me in the hall," I say.

Carolina tosses her hair from side to side and laughs cruelly. "Oh, but I do believe you. If wonder boy Zane Barrett had boned you already, he'd be long gone. Once he starts ignoring you, I'll know he got you on your back." Zane folds his arms and glares at Carolina. She lifts one manicured hand in front of her mouth and says, "Oops. Did I ruin your chance of ticking another creature off your 'beasts to bang' bucket list? Guess you'll have to hunt down a new zombie freak to woo."

A wave of heat rolls off Zane—and I mean that literally. It's not the cozy, campfire kind of warmth. It's a volcano about to spew, run screaming for your life, scorching heat. It dissipates as suddenly as it emerged, leaving me to question whether I imagined it to begin with.

"Let's go, Haylee. Don't listen to a word she says." Zane storms toward the elevators and snaps his fingers. The light beside the nearest set of doors turns red and dings. When the doors open, a woman stumbles out, quickly followed by a man.

The woman keels over like she's about to throw up. I know how she feels. The thought that Zane is after me because he has some kind of sick monster fetish makes my stomach queasy. I can't believe I ever compared him to Cameron. It doesn't matter that Zane has no fangs or claws; he's still not human.

The man from the elevator shakes his head at Zane's approach. "Don't get in. There's something wrong with the elevator."

The poor couple doesn't realize that Zane is the one who used his powers to send the elevator hurtling to the eighth floor.

My stomach tightens, especially when Carolina flashes me a gleaming smile.

"You should watch the movie *Cruel Intentions*. It's an oldie but goodie—full of insights you could learn from." She smirks and struts over to the elevators. "I'll wait for the next one," she tells Zane in a haughty tone.

He holds the doors open with one hand and ignores her. Zane's blue eyes blaze in my direction. I don't know what else to do. I need to get to Long Beach, and I want Zane to explain himself.

As soon as the doors close behind us, the elevator rushes down to the lobby without stopping at any floors. It reaches the lobby with a jolt that makes me bump into the elevator wall.

Zane doesn't speak or look at me as he storms through the lobby and out the sliding doors, where he tells a man at the valet stand to bring his car around. Soon enough, a sleek white convertible Corvette pulls up in front of us.

Zane snaps his fingers, and the passenger door opens. I go ahead and get in while he takes his place in the driver's seat. As soon as I close my door, he speeds out of the hotel's front entrance and screeches onto the road. The light ahead turns red, only to go back to green, which has got to be Zane using his mental powers. It's completely illegal—the way compulsion is, though cops are more likely to go after wizards than vampires.

The top is down on the car, wind rushing in my hair with Zane's speed as he merges onto US-101. He steers the Corvette across lanes, zipping through traffic. If I were still human, I'd probably be a bundle of tightly wound nerves, gripping the armrest.

But I'm not even a little nervous.

Zane grips the steering wheel. I've never seen him look uptight until now, and I can't help it. I burst out laughing.

He hasn't stopped frowning since running into Carolina.

"What's so funny?" he asks, in a miffed voice that only makes me laugh harder.

I put on my sunglasses and grin at him. "I don't know, Zane. Do you ever laugh for no good reason?"

"No," he answers.

"Well, you should try it some time. It's liberating."

He briefly takes his eyes off the road to look at me before returning his attention to traffic. He doesn't laugh, but his shoulders relax, and he leans back in his seat.

"You know why Carolina said those things, right?" he asks. When I shrug, he continues. "It's because she's jealous." I laugh again. "I mean it," Zane says seriously. "She's used to being the center of attention. Now she's at the bottom of the barrel. She doesn't belong on the show. Everyone knows the only reason she made it onto *Spellcaster* is because Malachi made sure to select her."

"Well, this week the public decides whether or not she stays," I say.

Zane scoffs. "People are morons."

"Make sure to share that on camera," I laugh.

Zane glances over at me and smiles. It's boyish and maybe the first true smile I've seen on him, because for all Zane's confidence and swagger, he generally feels distant, like he's an actor in his own life.

He watches traffic ahead as he asks, "What's in Long Beach?"

"A woman who might know something about my family's deaths," I tell him.

Zane's attention snaps back to me and then returns to the highway just as quickly.

"I don't know how much she'll be able to tell me with her brain injury, but I have to at least try."

"I'll get the information from her," Zane says.

"What do you mean?" I ask.

"I can get inside her head—beyond the trauma—and find the truth."

I gape at him. I knew wizards were powerful, but I never heard of anything like this. For all their pomp, wizards are still extremely secretive about their full range of capabilities.

"Can you get inside anyone's head at any time?" I ask in horror.

It's Zane's turn to laugh. "Don't worry. Your secrets are safe. And getting inside an addled mind isn't easy." His laughter dies, and a tight frown takes the place of his smile.

Zane looks downright grim as we cruise along the highway. But whatever he can do to help, I'm not about to turn it down. I don't care if it's dangerous or illegal. I don't care if it puts him in danger. And, right now, I don't care if the only reason he's helping me is part of some sick scheme to score with a zombie chick.

Just because I'm a virgin doesn't mean I'm naïve.

I'm going to use Zane before he ever has a chance to use me.

Before reaching Long Beach, Zane pulls off the highway into a gas station to fill up, get the facility's address from me, and make a call. He leaves the car to make the call from a distance where I can't hear him.

I pinch the zipper on my jacket, watching him pace about twenty-five feet in front of the car with his phone pressed to his ear. He frowns the entire time and grips his phone as he listens to whoever is on the other end of the line.

Vampire hearing would be really handy right now.

Zane's voice rises in anger, but I still can't make out what he's saying. He paces some more, clutching his phone, lips moving then pausing to listen. Eventually, he pockets his phone and strides back to the Corvette. I don't know if he got what he wanted or not.

Zane gets in and slams his door shut.

Maybe that was a not.

"Everything okay?" I ask tentatively.

Zane runs his hand through his hair. "Yeah, all good. My doctor will meet us there."

"Your doctor?" I blink several times. "Why does your doctor need to be there? Is he some kind of wizard brain specialist?"

"No, he's a regular, human doctor, but I need his help." Zane smiles grimly. "In order to get inside a damaged mind, I have to die."

"What?" I blast. My entire body jerks forward.

Okay, so I know I just said I didn't care what it took to get to the truth, but killing Zane is not an option.

"It's okay, my doctor will bring me back," Zane says.

I slam my back against the seat and stare at him as though he's just grown a second head. "Oh, well, in that case . . . NO!" I yell.

A dude in cargo shorts, a tank top, and flip-flops looks over from where he's pumping gas into a Mini Cooper.

Zane puts on his sunglasses, starts the Corvette, and gets back on the highway.

"Zane, you can't do this."

"My body. My choice," he responds with a cheeky grin.

"That's not funny." I laugh. When he smirks, I clear my throat. "I'm serious."

"My mind's made up," Zane says, "and Dr. Managold is one of the best."

"At killing and reviving patients?" I demand.

Zane shakes his head. "He's one of the best doctors in the entire country. I trust him with my life."

"You might, but I still think this is a terrible idea," I grouse. The last thing I want is to lose someone else I care about because, for better or worse, Zane Barrett is important to me. "Why are you doing this?"

Zane turns his head my way. My parting lips are reflected back at me in his dark lenses.

"Because you deserve the truth."

My heart squeezes and chin quivers. Guilt floods me because for a moment, I'm not thinking about what happened to my family. I'm wondering what Zane's true motives are. But he just offered to die for me. Perhaps that's truth enough.

CHAPTER FIFTY-NINE

ZANE'S DOCTOR IS handsome, young, and pissed off.

After claiming to be Evelyn's nephew in town to visit his aunt, Zane secured us a private visit inside Evelyn's room. Oh, and he also said I was his girlfriend and held my hand as we were escorted through the halls to the elevator and up to Evelyn's room on the top floor at level four.

Carolina's warning about Zane becomes shapeless white noise as I stand to the side watching Dr. Managold slap a paper with typed print on a dresser in front of Zane.

"Read this and then sign and date it at the bottom." He pulls a pen out of his starched white shirt pocket and hands it to Zane, who takes it, bends over, and immediately begins to sign. "I said read it first," Dr. Managold snaps. He has thick brown hair that's trim and tidy, and a cleanly shaved face.

The pen freezes in Zane's fingers. He sighs and scans the print, making a couple of humming sounds as he goes. "Mm-hmm, got it," Zane says, and then finishes signing his name and dating the document. "I'm ready."

Dr. Managold sighs irritability. "I know it's pointless, but I still have to entreat you to reconsider."

"Mind's made up, Doc," Zane says, flashing one of his rare boyish grins.

Dr. Managold doesn't look at me. I get the sense that this isn't about me being a zombie but about him knowing Zane is doing this for me and he can't count on my help in talking sense into Zane.

Meanwhile, Evelyn dozes in bed—thanks to Zane. I tried talking to her, but it was useless and depressing. The poor woman has been reduced to a functional vegetable. Too bad there isn't a protective rune that prevents physical trauma in addition to mind manipulation. When a nurse led us into her room and announced that her nephew was here for a visit, Evelyn blinked several times from her recliner beside the ocean-facing window and said, "He is? That's nice."

She looks peaceful under Zane's sleeping spell. I expected her to be older, but she can't be more than thirty. Her shoulder-length brown hair is brushed shiny, and her skin has a healthy glow. Staring at her asleep brings tears to my eyes. I feel my dad's presence in this room, in his kindness for his former employee's care.

Zane plops down into the recliner and pulls the lever for the footrest. "Time to die," he announces.

Dr. Managold picks up his black satchel, carries it over to the window, and sets it on the table beside the recliner.

"If I lose my license over this—"

"You won't," Zane interrupts. "I warded the room so that anyone other than ourselves who even thinks about entering will find themselves with a sudden case of explosive diarrhea."

I might have laughed if it weren't for the gravity of what we're about to do. Pretty soon, I might lose count of all the illegal activities I'm involved in. I guess I really am part of the supernatural species. It's like being a celebrity with special privileges and free passes to break the rules.

I zip my jacket up to just below my neck and hug my arms around my middle. Never mind the illicit and daredevil antics about to go down in this room. I might find out who had my parents, sister, and aunt killed. It's information I want more than anything. More than winning *Spellcaster*. I have to know what really happened.

"Thank you, Zane." I say it now in case something goes wrong, and I don't get a chance to later. I don't want to think that way, but my mind's turned forever morbid since the zombie attack.

A pair of cerulean eyes latch onto mine, and that breathless but don't need to breathe feeling comes over me. Zane could ask just about anything of me right now, and I'd agree. But all he says is, "Time to uncover the truth."

Dr. Managold reaches into his bag and sets a syringe and vial on the table.

"You've got ten minutes."

"Plenty of time," Zane says, flashing his cocky public smile.

"Ten minutes!" Before I can bluster about permanent brain damage to Zane, Dr. Managold shuts me down with one hard glare.

"Witches and wizards function at a higher level than humans. He'll be fine as long as he's not dead for more than ten minutes."

"Seriously?" I gape at Zane, who smirks.

"You need to take this seriously. There are no guarantees," Dr. Managold says gruffly. He pushes a chair from the table beside Zane and then grabs one of the syringes and a vial and sits heavily beside his patient.

"I am. I promise," Zane says in earnest.

Cocky or not, he's about to die. There's a voice inside my head screaming for him to stop. I press my lips together and hold still as I watch Dr. Managold stick the needle into the vial and fill it with liquid. He doesn't bother with a last-chance appeal when he locates a vein in Zane's inner elbow and shoves the needle in. "Do not leave this room," are Dr. Managold's last words as he injects Zane.

Zane's eyes flutter closed. His chest rises and falls. Rises and falls. And then stops. With his head against the recliner, he looks like he's asleep. But he's not. He's dead, and it doesn't matter that he's coming back. Watching him die rips another gash across my soul.

Something between a whimper and a sob breaks through my lips. I want to rewind time and tell him not to do this. I should have agreed to breakfast at least once. I should have had that drink with him the first time he asked. What if he doesn't come back?

Dr. Managold sets a timer on his smartwatch and then stands up slowly and crosses his arms. His attention is on Zane, but I can practically feel his animosity toward me.

"This wasn't my idea," I say. Not that it matters, because either way, Zane's doing this for me.

Dr. Managold looks down at Zane. "Clock's ticking, Zane. Get in. Get out. And back in your body. Doctor's orders."

There's a creepy kind of reassurance to the way Dr. Managold speaks to Zane's corpse. He checks his watch again.

I loosen my arms and stuff my hands inside my jacket pockets. A soft gasp from Evelyn's lips has me spinning around to stare at her. Dr. Managold pulls his attention away from Zane to look at the woman. He purses his lips and gives a grim nod.

"Good, he's inside."

"What's happening?" I whisper.

I don't expect Dr. Managold to clue me in, which makes it surprising when he joins my side and answers.

"Most souls go straight to the light—like moths—but some linger. That's what Zane is doing. In order to access the memories of Miss Jensen's mind, Zane must take temporary possession of her."

"Possess—like a demon?" I gape at the doctor.

Evelyn makes a soft gurgling sound.

Dr. Managold glares at me. "Shh. Don't distract him."

Zane can hear us? I want to ask, but I press my lips together because despite the doctor's rude bedside manner, I definitely do not want to distract Zane while he takes control of Evelyn.

This is downright freaky. I never heard boo about wizards having the ability to come back from the dead and possess other people. I stare at Evelyn and chew on my bottom lip, bracing for her to pop up and speak to us in a discombobulated voice with glazed eyes.

She remains horizontal, eyes closed, but I keep expecting something ghoulish to happen.

Dr. Managold checks his watch every few seconds.

"No. No. I can't do that," Evelyn whimpers, as though in the grip of a bad dream. Her face tightens. "Please," she whispers.

I don't notice that I've pulled my hands out of my pockets and threaded my fingers together until I feel the pressure in my bones as I squeeze tightly.

Poor Evelyn doesn't deserve to have her mind violated and emotions abused.

"I'm so sorry, Evelyn," I whisper.

Her face relaxes. "I promise," she whispers.

And then a bloodcurdling scream erupts from her lips.

I yank my wand out of my crossbody purse and point at the door. "*Heshnad alt cho.*"

The shrieks continue, but no one beyond this room will be able to hear Evelyn's screams. Hopefully, none of the facility's staff were close enough to hear and come running. If they do, they'll be running in the opposite direction, thanks to Zane's special warding. I'd rather not attract attention to begin with.

Evelyn's scream is abruptly cut off, leaving behind a silence as unsettling as her wailing.

Dr. Managold walks over to her bedside and stares down with a tight frown.

"Is she still breathing?" I whisper. I can't tell, with the quilt covering her chest. She's so still and silent.

Dr. Managold presses two fingers to the pulse point at her neck, nods, and then walks over to Zane. I stare at his bag, expecting him to get out a fresh syringe and another vial, but the doctor checks his watch, lowers his arm, and stares at Zane.

I walk over and stop at Zane's other side. "Has it been ten minutes?"

"No, but I believe he's gotten what he needed."

"Shouldn't you be injecting him with the antidote?"

A derisive huff leaves Dr. Managold's lips. The doctor slides a dark gaze my way. "There is no antidote."

The room feels too hot. I push my jacket sleeves up to my elbows.

"But he told me he needed you to bring him back."

"He needed me to kill him," Dr. Managold says coldly. "He has to bring himself back."

"But—"

Zane jerks upright, gasping as though he's been trapped underwater and just made it to the surface for air. He grips his throat and then lowers his arms and squeezes the armrest of the recliner, blinking rapidly.

Dr. Managold steps in front of him. "Do you know who I am?" he asks.

Zane's chin lifts to look up at the doctor.

"Of course, I know who you are."

"What's my name?"

"Really?"

Dr. Managold taps his foot.

Zane stares at his doctor for a moment and then says, "You are Dr. Managold, and I am Zane Barrett . . . back from the dead." He smiles, but there's no humor in it.

"Zane, are you okay?" I ask.

He looks past Dr. Managold and meets my eyes, but his bland expression is impossible to read. Did he get any useful information out of Evelyn? I hold back, because it seems rude to ask when he literally died in order to dig through the woman's memories.

"I'm fine," Zane says. "Too bad I can't tell anyone what I'm capable of. It's . . . indescribable." He casts a distant stare in Evelyn's direction.

"Good thing it is, since you won't be telling anyone about this ever." Dr. Managold zips his bag and grabs it by the handles off the table. "Now, if you'll excuse me. I have real patients who need me."

The doctor hurries out, bag in hand.

Zane gets out of the recliner and stretches. "We should go too," he says.

I nod and look at Evelyn, who is still silent and asleep. "Will she be okay?"

Zane glances her way and shivers slightly before straightening up and snapping his attention back to me.

"She won't remember what I dug out of her memories, which is a good thing. She's at peace here staring out at the ocean and being cared for."

I chew on the inside of my cheek. "Can you do me one more favor before we go?"

Zane lifts a brow. He's probably thinking he already died for me. What more could I want? But I didn't ask him to, and I can't leave without knowing that Evelyn has a permanent place here. Since my dad was paying for her care, I don't know what it means now that he's dead. I need Zane, as her supposed nephew, to ask if the funds are going to run out.

When I explain this to Zane, his expression softens.

"Yeah, of course," he says.

After we leave Evelyn's room, a heavyset caregiver starts toward it as we're walking away. I hear a loud fart, followed by hurried steps as the poor woman races for the bathroom. I grimace.

"Um, Zane. Did you remove the ward?"

Zane frowns and slows his steps to look over his shoulder. "Oh, right."

Zane stands at the edge of the ocean, staring across the waves as though in a trance.

I'm trying to be patient as he takes time processing his out-of-body experience. At least I am comforted in the knowledge that my father wired enough funds to cover Evelyn's care for two lifetimes. Zane found out that my dad left instructions to consider anything extra a donation to the facility.

The sun illuminates Zane's blond hair while a gentle breeze sends the slightest ripple over his short-sleeved button-up shirt, and the tide reaches for his sneakers. Zane takes a step back to avoid getting his shoes wet, but his gaze doesn't leave the distant horizon.

"Are you sure you're okay?" I ask for the tenth time.

Zane finally answers in a faraway voice. "There is magic, and then there is power beyond our wildest imagination."

Great. Hopefully death and resurrection isn't the first step in turning him into a dark sorcerer.

Loose strands of hair blow into my face. I push them away.

"Wizards don't do this sort of thing very often, right? Would I know if a sorcerer had accessed my mind?" I ask.

Zane glances sideways at me. "Yes, which is another reason wizards don't practice the art. Not only would a functioning mind know of the intrusion, but it could be fought off—unlike entering a damaged brain."

"But you were still able to get past all the muddle to her memories?" I ask eagerly. Hopefully, this wasn't all for nothing.

"I got through," Zane says. He turns to me. "Let's walk down the beach."

"Or you could tell me what you discovered, and then we can walk the beach," I counter.

He looks me in the eyes, frowning. "I hate sharing something that will hurt you."

I swallow. "Is it my uncle Alvan? He's involved, isn't he?"

If Zane's surprised I suspect my own uncle, he doesn't show it. But he nods and starts walking slowly down the beach. "One of Evelyn's final memories before her injury was of her boss's brother-in-law, Alvan Bates."

Now I'm the one having an out-of-body experience as I match Zane's steps but don't feel the sand beneath my feet. It's one thing to suspect Uncle Alvan of betrayal, and another to have something so horrible confirmed.

"Exactly how involved was he?" I demand.

"He paid Evelyn a visit at her apartment and tried to get her to poison your father by slipping arsenic into his morning coffee. For her cooperation, he promised her eternal youth—courtesy of his employer. Evelyn refused."

As we walk, Zane continues looking across the ocean. It feels like he hasn't fully returned to his body, and I need him here telling me everything he possibly can.

"So he attacked her?" I ask angrily.

"She begged him not to harm her and promised she wouldn't tell a soul. Alvan said he needed an associate to compel her into silence. She was so scared and then relieved that she wouldn't have to die for doing the right thing." Zane purses his lips. "I really hate vampires."

"What happened next?" It's difficult to remove the impatience from my voice.

"Evelyn thought the rune tattoo your father got her would protect her from being compelled, but Alvan's vampire associate showed up with a baseball bat."

I abruptly stop walking, feeling sick. After swallowing, I clutch my throat. My vision goes hazy. Everything is out of focus.

"Did Alvan stick around while . . ." My voice trails off.

"No," Zane answers. "He left before the vamp started swinging."

"Coward," I spit. "I suppose when bribery didn't work to kill my father, he had to take more extreme measures by hiring a spellcaster and rounding up a zombie horde."

"That I don't know," Zane says.

"Did Alvan mention the name of his employer?"

"No."

"I guess I'll have to find out for myself so I can send him—and awful Al—a special care package . . . the kind that goes *boom*," I say darkly.

Zane inclines his head for me to continue walking with him, like the movement will help me process such revolting treachery.

"There's something else you should know," Zane says. "Evelyn thought that Alvan must have been compelled, but when she tried to get through to him, he said he was doing this so that his employer would turn him. Evelyn wanted to know how he could do such a thing."

"What did Alvan say?"

"He said he tried to warn Laurence to stop going after vampire masters and that it was his own fault for not listening. He said it was too late for his brother-in-law but not for himself and not for Evelyn." Zane pauses for a moment, staring over the ocean again before continuing. "What I experienced were not only Evelyn's memories, but her feelings and impressions as well, and Alvan Bates showed no signs of hesitation or remorse. Sorry," Zane adds.

Talk about delivering bad news.

I'm sorry too. Sorry I ever asked Alvan to be my guardian and Joni's when he's the reason we lost our mothers, my father, and Kendra. I know Aunt Chloe was a mistake. She and Joni were at the wrong place at the wrong time thanks to Uncle TJ and his fist. But at what point did Alvan decide to sentence me and my family to death by sending a horde to our house?

Scalding tears spill from my eyes and burn trails down my cheeks. Broken bits of memories cut through my mind.

During Kendra's first Thanksgiving back from college, I heard my sister telling Uncle Alvan she met the greatest guy, and Alvan teasing, "When's the wedding?"

"Not until after graduation," Kendra teased back.

"What's this now?" Mom had interjected.

"I'll help you pick out the bridesmaids' dresses," I'd immediately volunteered.

Mom said, "Let's not get ahead of ourselves."

Uncle Alvan, Kendra, and I laughed at the cringe on Mom's face. That was before she met Cameron, of course. He won us all over immediately. Now he's a man broken beyond repair. Alvan saw to that. What did Kendra ever do to Uncle Al, besides welcome him into our home at every holiday and cheer on his advancements in New York?

And what about me? I was always complimenting his chic city style and even joked that I wished I could get my dad to update his wardrobe.

I wish I could take those words back. My dad was one of a kind. The absolute best. An unsung hero. Alvan's nothing but a villain.

I kick sand.

"What are you going to do?" Zane asks.

"What would you do—if it was your family?" I want to know.

"I'd kill everyone involved," he says.

I don't doubt his sincerity. But I shake my head and say, "No. Death is not enough. It's too quick. They need to suffer. They have to pay."

And by "they," I mean Uncle Alvan, his master, and anyone else involved.

I need names.

What I really need is to win *Spellcaster*, eat Queen Yapsut's heart, become an all-powerful sorceress, and turn my enemies to dust.

CHAPTER SIXTY

SOMEHOW, I'M ABLE to perform my routine as though my world wasn't just turned upside down all over again.

After my performance, I call Cameron and Joni from backstage on an absolute high after crushing my challenge. I channeled Sia like a battle cry, and according to my coach, "blew the roof off of the room." The live audience went absolutely wild. Joni flipped out over the phone. She and Cameron would never know I went off digging up information this week. I feel like I'm leading a double life.

After the live show concludes, I party with the wolves. They're a wild bunch, howling in the club as we enter and ordering bottles of champagne, which they don't bother pouring into glasses.

Kace is the only one who sees through me. He scoots beside me in a corner booth, his gaze intense.

Tracie lifts a bottle of champagne to her lips, takes deep swallows, and then passes it to Daphné. "Time to dance," she announces.

"Yeah, it is!" Izzie agrees enthusiastically. She's the first out of the booth, quickly followed by Jake.

Kace doesn't move a muscle, so I start to scoot out the other side with the wolves, until he places his hand on my thigh.

"Haylee and I will join you in a moment. First, we need to talk."

"See you on the dance floor," Tracie says, as she struts toward the dancing masses in her high heels, tight jeans, and purple halter top.

The rest of the group follows her, taking last sips or bringing bottles with them. Tripp is the only other wolf who remains behind. He scoots away from me and Kace, his head bent over his phone.

I grab an empty bottle left behind and lift it. "So, cheers to our first live show, and here's to making it into the Top 13."

As I set the bottle down, Kace's frown deepens. It's like he can smell that I'm hiding something. He removes his hand from my thigh to place both of his arms on the table.

"Want to tell me what's up?"

My brows furrow. "What do you mean?"

"You've been avoiding me," Kace accuses.

"I'm here seated beside you right now," I huff.

"You keep blowing me off for breakfast."

"I'm not blowing you off. We talked about this. I need time to recharge, especially before a technical performance."

Kace rubs the table with his index finger. "Nah, there's something you're not telling me. Something's off."

I won't insult his intelligence by pretending everything's great. "Okay, fine, but it's personal."

Kace's fingers tighten into fists. "Is Zane still bothering you?"

"No. It has nothing to do with any of the other contestants or the competition."

Even Blair is behaving herself—though her evil glare communicates how unhappy she is about it. I'm pretty sure Zane spoke to her, not that she's sharing. She doesn't say anything to me anymore, which is great.

"You know you can talk to me about anything, right?" Kace presses.

"I know," I say, staring into Kace's eyes. "You're my best friend."

"Friend," Kace repeats gruffly, looking displeased.

"Soon to be first kiss," I remind him.

His smile looks sad and forced. "You don't owe me anything, Z."

Who knew the tough guy would be so sensitive?

I fold my arms and smirk. "Don't back out on me now, Kace Warren. I'm looking forward to our first magical kiss." Tripp looks up from his phone. I keep my attention on Kace. "For now, how about a dance?"

"Are you trying to distract me, Z?" Kace grins.

I shake my head. "I'm distracting myself. My problems can wait until later." They have to. Tomorrow is the first results show. And I'm still plotting my revenge on Alvan, his master, and the rest of his master's minions—including the spellcaster who set the horde on me and my family.

Cameron and Joni can't know. Cam will only get himself killed, and Joni's too young and fragile to know the truth. I may never tell her. Kace can't know either.

"Tell me who—or what—is troubling you, and I'll take care of them all," he vows.

A genuine smile comes over me as I stare into the earnest brown eyes of this incredibly attractive and loyal werewolf. My gaze drops to his lips. I kind of want to kiss him right now, but a deal is a deal. Top eleven. Two weeks.

"I'm really looking forward to that kiss, but tonight, let's dance."

Kace strokes the wolf tattoo on his neck while staring at me. He sits close enough for me to feel his body heat along my right arm and leg where he's pressed in. "Whatever you want," Kace says.

He scoots out first, and I push my way out of the booth behind him. We leave Tripp stuck to his phone and join the others, who howl at our approach. Poor Jake can't stop staring at Izzie as she dances and laughs with the group.

Kace wastes no time taking my hips in his hands. "This okay, Z?" he asks huskily, his lips brushing the shell of my ear.

"Yeah," I say, as I thread my arms around his neck.

Kace pulls me closer. My nerves buzz, and my smile stretches toward my ears. I know the wolves go out clubbing all the time, but I feel like such a rebel. Kace grinds against me, and I move with him—pressing my body against his without restraint. I'm surprised at how naturally it happens. Our bodies feel good together. It gets me all worked up, wanting to kiss him tonight rather than wait.

What if Kace doesn't make it to the top eleven?

I have to make it to the finale. I need all the power I can get my hands—and teeth—on in order to take down Alvan, his master, and their whole bloody organization—and protect the people I love.

For now, I dance. It feels like a dream. An alternate reality in which I'm part of the supernatural race, competing on my favorite show, and grinding with a big, Black, tattooed guy who could literally rip a person's throat out.

I think of what Kace said about "once you go were" and start to laugh.

He lifts his brows. "What's so funny, girl?"

I slide my arms to his shoulders and then back up to his neck, grinning like a fool. "Nothing else compares," I say.

Kace's eyes light up when he chuckles.

I don't tell him he's the first guy I've ever danced with. I don't technically have anyone else to compare Kace to, but I don't need experience to know he's got smooth moves. There are young women openly checking him out as they dance in their girl groups and cast hungry looks his way. Luckily, none of my new female werewolf friends have shown any interest in Kace.

Izzie bumps her way over to us and raises her voice over the techno music.

"Some of us are headed back to the hotel. Wanna catch a ride with us, or are you staying?"

Tracie shimmies over and hollers, "The night is still young!"

Izzie rolls her eyes. "We still have to be on stage live tomorrow."

"Don't have to perform, though," Tracie counters. She doesn't stop dancing as she converses.

"Unless we're in the bottom eight," Izzie says with a frown.

Tracie bats the air with a flick of her wrist. "Don't be a killjoy, Izzie."

But Izzie's right. I need my rest.

I rub my lips together and take a sidelong glance at the women who seem to have moved closer as though anticipating my departure, ready to launch themselves at Kace the second I step away. I glare at a brunette in a gold spandex minidress who has been eying Kace like he's a piece of meat. Heavy mascara doesn't hide her hazy, drunken eyes. She's just looking for a good time. Kace is so much more than that. But also, he deserves someone who can keep up—not some lethargic zombie who experiences bursts of energy followed by a crash of all-consuming exhaustion.

The thought of not being enough for Kace hollows out my chest.

He studies my face a moment before saying, "Come on, Z. Let's call it a night."

"That's okay. You can stay if you want," I say too quickly.

The brunette bumps into Kace's shoulder and giggles. "Oops, sorry about that."

"No worries," Kace answers, without looking to see who knocked against him. The brunette pouts. "Izzie's right," Kace announces. "We all need to be ready for tomorrow."

"Speak for yourselves," Tracie huffs. "I need to keep moving my body." She dances her way over to a couple of guys standing with beers beside a pillar. She grabs both of their free hands and pulls them with her to the dance floor. "Daf, get over here. I got one for each of us."

Daphné laughs. "Enjoy yourself, *cocotte*. I'm going back to the hotel to call my sister."

"As long as it's your sister you're calling and not your ex," Tracie yells after her.

Kace places his hand on my lower back as we follow Izzie and Daphné out of the club and join the rest of the wolves waiting outside. There's no limo tonight. We split up into Ubers. Kace invites us into Tripp's ride, which is the first car to arrive.

"Gotta get Cinderella home from the ball," Kace jokes.

"So now I'm Cinderella," I grouse.

Kace tilts his head back and stares at me with eyes that shine like he's just spotted the world's first unicorn. "Nah, Z. You're no Cinderella, and no princess, either. You're a queen."

For the first live eliminations show, each contestant is called on stage to recreate our illusion from the previous night.

When it's my turn, I stand with Colt Cohen in front of my tournament grounds from yesterday's performance. Anya put half my hair up in a fun bubble ponytail and left the rest loose and wavy with extensions to make my hair longer. I feel pretty in a black-and-blush patterned blouse that's tucked into a long black skirt. A thick belt with a crescent moon buckle cinches the whole look with a touch of celestial magic.

"Who here thinks that the real element in Haylee's illusion was the jester? What about the straw dummy?" Colt chuckles into the microphone.

"The flag!" someone from the audience yells.

"Or perhaps that," Colt says. "Do you think you guessed correctly? Let's find out." He turns to me with a mirthful smile. "Haylee, please reveal your non-illusion for the audience."

Grinning, I swish my wand and remove the pause placed on the tournament illusion, which leaves the purple chair hanging over the stage.

The live audience laughs and applauds.

"Well done, Haylee," Colt says. He gives my shoulder a brief squeeze and then announces Nathaniel up next.

The women's dressing room backstage is as quiet as I've ever heard it. Most contestants scroll through their phones, incessantly checking viewer comments about yesterday's performances.

Suhani stands out in a green kurta covered in embroidery and beadwork. She wears matching pants with embroidered flats over her bare feet and is draped in a gold embroidered scarf. She looks like Indian royalty with smoky eyes, jumbo chandelier earrings, and golden hair jewelry set in her midnight locks. It brings an inner smile to my lips to see her every bit as intent on checking her phone as the other contestants. This shouldn't amuse me, though. Suhani's got her head one hundred percent in the game. She's not running off in the middle of a competition solving a murder mystery.

Carolina sits atop a chair facing everyone in a short, bright red dress with ruffles along the skirt, at the shoulders, and at the ends of the long sleeves. The fabric clings to her curves. She's wearing lipstick and nail polish to match, and has her long blond hair pulled into a high ponytail that's curled at the ends. The smile doesn't leave Carolina's lips as she holds her phone up high and scrolls through with swipe after swipe of her polished finger. Every few seconds she coos, "Oh, that's so sweet. My fans are the absolute best."

Blair huddles with her witch friends. They check their phones and speak in hushed whispers, giving Carolina the evil eye from time to time. My roomie is still acting like I don't exist, which is more than fine by me.

I stand with Daphné and Tracie, who has been filling us in on her threesome from last night while I school my expression to one of interest rather than shock. Tracie doesn't need to know what a greenhorn I am.

"I usually stick to my own kind because they know how to please a female best, but if I do go out on a limb with humans, there have to be at least two to keep up with me," Tracie says.

"Wolves know how to make their lovers howl," Daphné agrees.

I try not to blush. Instead, I nod like this is a completely normal, not at all awkward conversation. As Tracie overshares, my attention drifts to her neck and the black choker with the word *WOOF* spelled out in silver letters. She looks punk rock in a fluorescent-pink and black denim vest that's frayed around the openings at her shoulders. There's nothing under the tight top, exposing bare skin of her flat tummy above her black-and-white plaid pants with suspenders hanging loosely against each hip. Her silver-tipped mohawk defies gravity in spiked peaks. It's not a style I could ever pull off, but Tracie makes it look badass and feminine. I hope that she, Daphné, and Izzie make it to the Top 13, because I enjoy their company, even though I'm trying not to flush as Tracie mentions some "back door" action last night—information I really don't need, or want, to know.

My eyes screw into my head before I can stop them.

"Hey, don't knock it until you've tried it," Tracie says.

It's a relief when Izzie returns from her stage time with Colt. She's a walking rainbow in her oversized crochet cardigan with multicolored stripes covering most of her short denim overalls. Chunky black platform shoes cover a pair of striped pink, purple, and black knee-high socks. Izzie clomps over to us and starts pulling at the loose strands of bright yarn that hang all over her cardigan. Her pink hair covers half her face when she looks down at her shoes.

"Elimination days are the worst," Izzie moans.

Daphné reaches over and gives Izzie's shoulder a squeeze. "Your rendition of Björk was flawless. The audience loved it."

"Thanks. I know you did Taylor Swift proud with your 'I Know Places' performance."

"*Merci, cocotte.*"

"And Haylee blew her coach away," Izzie teases.

I blush before I can stop myself. Luckily, my friends don't point it out.

"We gave it our all. If that doesn't get us into the Top 13, then whatever." Tracie shrugs. Izzie, Daphné, and I frown at her. "Tonight, I say we party no matter what," Tracie adds.

I force a smile because either way, I'm headed home tomorrow, and keeping what I learned about Uncle Alvan from Cameron is going to feel ten times worse when I see him in person.

Jovi enters and the room quiets. "Ladies, it's time for you to join the males and take your places on stage for the live eliminations."

CHAPTER SIXTY-ONE

CAROLINA STANDS GRACEFULLY and sets her phone down on the closest vanity table. She's the first to strut through the dressing room, giving her ponytail a toss every several steps. "Top 13, here I come," she says. Leah, the most recent addition to Team Vampire, hurries after her as though Carolina is her master. Suhani is right behind them, moving with dignity and grace. Blair is quick to lead the witches out.

Tracie has to swat at Izzie's hands when it looks as though she's going to pull the threads out of her cardigan.

"You're going to make it. The audience loves you," Tracie growls at her.

"I don't know. My prop was too obvious." Izzie grabs another thread.

"That's not what matters," Tracie says a little too loudly as we approach the stage.

"No talking." Jovi glares at us.

I wince, even though I'm not the one talking. Tracie narrows her eyes at Jovi. Good thing the show's director isn't the one picking out the finalists.

Backstage, we line up the way we practiced that morning, grouped together by teams. Once we're all in position, Jovi says "ready" into her headset.

Circus music blares through the speakers. When it ends, the audience erupts into applause.

"That was Spencer Thomas from season ten. Thank you, Spencer," Colt's voice echoes through his microphone. "And now it's time to call out our Season 13 contestants."

Spellcaster's mysterious mood music begins, putting me instantly on edge.

Here goes nothing, I think, as we file on stage and take our places facing the coaches and audience.

Colt is dressed up in his suit, standing in front of us. "It is time to announce the top three casters from each team. Remember, the contestants I don't call will have one final chance to compete for the thirteenth spot in the live performances. Here we go. From Team Cleo . . ." Colt pauses for effect, allowing the music to fill the silence. "In no particular order, the first caster you voted through to next week is . . . Zane Barrett."

The crowd goes wild. I'm standing close enough to Carolina to hear her huff and mutter, "People are so stupid." Suhani watches Zane like a monarch prepared to battle a foreign prince for sovereignty.

Zane waves to the crowd and flashes them a dimpled smile as he walks off stage.

We've barely spoken since his death-defying inquisition into Evelyn's mind. I still worry about long-term effects on his mental state, but it was his choice, and what's done is done. At least, that's what I keep telling myself.

Dominic Monroe is announced as the next member of Team Cleo to be voted through. When Colt announces Tracie next, my wolf friend throws her head back and howls. The other wolf contestants chorus, along with some of the audience members. I grin and throw in a howl of my own, thrilled that Tracie made it through, and Blair didn't.

Dare I hope that Carolina gets sent packing next?

It's about as likely as vampires trading in blood for Hawaiian Punch, but a girl can still dream.

Colt turns to the remaining members of Team Cleo and offers an encouraging smile. "The rest of you can head backstage and get ready to perform for the thirteenth spot."

Ugh, Blair could still worm her way back into the competition, but I'd say her chances are slim. She's not exactly a crowd-pleaser.

The music starts back up.

"And now, from Team Brody. In no particular order, the first caster you voted through to next week is . . . Tripp Peters."

I know I should be happy for Tripp, but we haven't bonded. Instead, I clap politely while chewing on the inside of my cheek, hoping to hear Kace's name next.

Colt waits for Tripp to leave the stage before speaking into the microphone. "Next, from Team Brody . . . Izzie King."

Izzie squeals and spins around to hug each of her teammates—starting with Jake. I bang my hands together, feeling so happy for her and Tracie. But I'm still on pins and needles. Kace has to be voted through. He just has to!

"And the third and final spot on Team Brody goes to . . . Kace Warren."

"Yes!" I fist-pump the air.

Luckily, the cheers and howls cover up my shout.

Kace looks over his shoulder and flashes me a wide grin before leaving the stage. I wish Cody and Jake had gotten Tripp's spot, but even I know that would have been too much to hope for. They still have one final shot at remaining on the show. Once the rest of Brody's less fortunate team members have been excused, Colt moves on to Team Zen, leaving me and the rest of Team Malachi in prolonged suspense.

"And now, from Team Zen. In no particular order, the first caster you voted through to next week is . . . Daphné Melanson!"

I cup my hands around my mouth and howl with the wolves.

Daphné claps her hands together in front of her face in excitement and then fist bumps the remaining wolves on the stage. I hold my hand up, and she gives me a high five before waving to the audience as she exits the stage.

Nathaniel Duke is the next member of Team Zen announced, which is mildly annoying, but at least two werewolves made it through, with Daphné called first and Luke announced third.

Team Malachi are the last casters standing. Carolina straightens her back and flutters her eyelashes, grinning widely into the cameras and live audience.

"From Team Malachi, the first member to be voted through is . . . Suhani Das." That's no surprise, nor is Colt's next announcement. "From Team Malachi, the next member to be voted through to next week is Carolina

Bellmore." The audience cheers wildly as Carolina struts her stuff across the stage, flicking her wrist to wave at the crowd. "And the final spot on Team Malachi goes to—" Colt keeps everyone in suspense for several drawn-out seconds before lifting the card to read. "Oliver Wessex."

The world stops turning, nearly throwing me off my feet.

My body jerks and then turns numb. My vision blurs. Static fills my ears.

I didn't make it.

I'm going home for good.

The audience hates me.

After Oliver swaggers off stage, Colt turns with his microphone to address Leah and me.

"You can head backstage and get ready to perform for the thirteenth spot. Good luck." He looks directly at me when he says the last part, but it doesn't matter.

If the public didn't vote for me before, what difference will one more performance make?

Blair and her friends have already changed into new outfits and are being ushered out of the dressing room by one of Jovi's assistants to return to the stage and compete for the thirteenth spot.

I walk in behind Leah, who is whisked to a vanity by Carolina who orders her to undress and get ready to give a killer performance. "The thirteenth spot belongs to Team Vampire," Carolina intones. She snaps her fingers at an assistant. "Help her get dressed."

Izzie, Tracie, and Daphné rush over and tackle-hug me. Meanwhile, Anya frantically waves me over to get changed. My wolf friends trail after me as I hustle, caught up in the urgency no matter how slim the odds.

"You've got this, *cocotte*," Daphné says.

"Damn straight she does," Tracie agrees. "I can't even believe you weren't voted through to begin with. It's totally insane. The viewers are probably in shock and getting their phones ready for the moment voting opens."

Izzie nods vigorously as I unclasp my belt and strip. Anya already has my long, sheer and gold sequined gown ready to slip over my head. She helps me smooth my dress down and then immediately gets to work on my hair, pulling out the bubble ponytail before weaving my blond locks into a braid crown.

"Eliminations suck," Izzie moans. "As much as I love Jake and Cody, they don't have Haylee's level of talent."

"You love them both? *Equally*?" Tracie lifts her brows and smirks.

"Not this again," Izzie says in exasperation.

Tracie runs a black-painted nail across her *WOOF* choker. "Fine, we'll save the 'twins are a package deal, and three is fabulous' conversation for later."

Once my hair is braided and pinned into place, Anya secures a golden crown on my head.

Izzie gasps like she's only just noticed my transformation. "Haylee! You look like a queen."

Tracie scans me from crown to golden sandals. "A sexy, golden goddess queen—I dig it."

"*Très belle*," Daphné agrees.

Well, at least I'll go out in style, I think morosely.

"Have a seat, Haylee," Anya says.

I'm careful of the gown with all of its sheer parts as I lower myself onto the edge of the seat. Anya uses makeup wipes to clean off my face and start over. She already has gold shimmer open on the vanity and gets to work immediately dusting my cheekbones. Next, she applies creamy metallic gold with a smear-on stick above my eyes, followed by liquid black eyeliner.

Izzie watches, transfixed as Anya finishes up.

Tracie pulls out her phone. "Daf, Izzie, get in here."

Daphné, Izzie, and Tracie lean in to take selfies with me on my chair. I smile confidently. That's the magic of a makeover. It allows me to flash a gorgeous grin despite the disappointment and blow to my confidence.

Tracie narrates as she taps out a post to go with the photo she snapped. "Backstage with my bitches. Ready to party all night long after making it into the Top 13."

Izzie chimes in as she types. "I am beyond grateful for your votes and support. Making it into the Top 13 is a dream come true. The amazing

Haylee Hutchins is preparing to COMMAND the stage. Remember to vote Haylee Hutchins and howl for Haylee."

Tracie bobs her head as she continues typing out her post. "Hashtag Spellcaster 13. Hashtag Top 13. Hashtag vote Haylee Hutchins. Hashtag Howl for Haylee. Hashtag single and horny."

"Tracie!" Izzie gasps.

Tracie lowers her phone and winks. "That one's for me."

It feels good to laugh. Izzie groans and shakes her head.

As soon as Blair returns from her performance, she sits at her vanity station, pulls out her phone, and frowns as she scrolls over her screen.

Anya, being a pro, has me ready with minutes to spare. She pulls a silver gown and a long iridescent cape from the costume rack and hangs them up in front of me. I don't need to memorize the pattern, since I will be performing a costume change rather than a wardrobe illusion for my performance, but I do need the actual dress to pull it off. Witches are way better at this kind of thing, but I don't have time to worry about that. Anya brings over a silver crown next and sets it on the vanity.

I look at my golden reflection in the mirror and then stare at the silver crown and gown. We all got a chance to practice our backup performances in case we weren't voted through, but I wish I could have run through the routine a couple more times—especially now that I'm waiting to compete for the thirteenth and final spot.

I try not to fidget in my seat. Tracie, Izzie, and Daphné offer me more reassurances moments before Leah and I are summoned to wait behind the curtains for Colt to announce us individually to the stage.

"Failure is not an option," Carolina calls after Leah.

Tracie cups her hands around her mouth and yells, "Take no prisoners, Haylee!"

Carolina swings her ponytail and lifts her nose, narrowing her eyes on Tracie like she's a yapping dog she'd like to kick.

Izzie's arm shoots out to give my hand a quick squeeze. "No matter what, no one can deny that you belong in the Top 13."

I wish her words made me feel better instead of reminding me that talent's not enough in this competition. Popularity counts for more.

Maybe this is it.

Or maybe I'll be lucky number thirteen.

Leah is called onto the stage first, followed by the remaining contestants competing to remain in the competition. Looks like I'm closing things out.

The second the stage dims, Jovi's assistant whispers an urgent, "You're up," to me. I hustle to my spot in the center and take my place as 'Castle' by Halsey plays from the speakers and a spotlight beams over me, making the gold sequins glitter over my dress.

When I walk forward, I cast an illusion of a rippling golden portal. It's round and just large enough to walk through. As I pass through, I squeeze my wand in one hand and snap my fingers with my other while visualizing the silver gown, cape, and crown replacing what I'm wearing.

"*Lee-va cont silv*," I cast quickly.

The portal turns from gold to silver as I step through to the other side in my silver costume.

The audience gasps in awe. I'm pretty sure I nailed the timing, but there's no time to congratulate myself. This is another complex performance with multiple moving parts, where timing is everything.

"*Acilla galont il mae*."

Ice spreads across the stage and crystallizes along the curtains. I take deliberate, regal steps toward the coaches and audiences, carrying myself like an ice queen.

"*Elis stra*."

Cleo's breath turns to fog. I lock eyes with her long enough to see a chilling look come over her face. Yet I'm the one in control, dropping the temperature in the theater. Foggy breath fills the audience.

"Oh my gosh!" someone gasps, but the words are spoken with wonder rather than alarm.

Brody puffs out purposeful breaths of air, looks over at Malachi's visual lack of breath, and laughs.

I turn my back to the audience and swirl my wand, rotating my portal to face the sides of the stage instead of the audience.

"*Lee-va cont gol*," I cast, and snap my fingers as I make another pass through the portal as it turns to gold.

The theater unfreezes in an instant as I emerge in my golden gown and crown. I spread my arms wide, and sequins appear to detach from my dress and shimmer across the stage into the theater to the "ohhs" and "ahhs" of the live audience.

I make my way through the shimmering illusion and then pivot and slowly return to the portal. Another pass through brings falling snow to the stage and theater as I'm dressed once more in silver.

I end my performance in the gold gown and crown I started in, casting an illusion of a castle behind me.

The audience goes wild. Applause thunders and howls chorus. If the thirteenth spot went to the contestant to receive the loudest cheers, it would already be mine. But voting is about to begin.

CHAPTER SIXTY-TWO

COLT STRIDES ON stage with a wide grin. He stops beside me and speaks into his microphone. "Absolutely stunning, Haylee. Now it's time to call the rest of our competing casters to the stage for this season's first live save."

The other hopeful contestants walk on stage, and we take our spots with our remaining teammate. Cody and Jake give me a thumbs-up. I smile and mouth, "Thanks."

"Incredible performances from our remaining casters," Colt says. "Unfortunately, only one of them can make it through to next week."

"Or two," one of the twins says, low enough for only those of us on stage to hear.

"You only have five minutes to vote," Colt announces. "Voting starts now."

I picture the countdown clock appearing below screens as viewers at home get on the *Spellcaster* app to vote.

Colt walks over to Team Brody and smiles. "Noah, while we wait, what has this experience meant to you?" Colt holds the microphone in front of the werewolf.

Noah clears his throat. "It's been incredible. Brody has taught me lots of new tricks, and I've made cool new friends." He runs a hand through his shoulder-length hair and grins.

Colt walks over to Team Cleo. "Blair, what can viewers expect if you make it into the Top 13?"

Blair straightens her shoulders and lifts her chin. "They can expect to see real magic."

Colt continues holding his microphone in front of Blair. When she offers nothing more, he moves on to my team with an enthusiastic, "Haylee!" My stomach drops. I'm nervous enough waiting for voting to end and the winner to be announced.

I moisten my lips as Colt asks, "As the show's first and only zombie, what would it mean to you to be voted through to next week?"

The theater goes silent. The stage lights are blinding. I can feel the cameras aimed at me—along with millions of eyes watching live across the country. Whatever I say, there are no do-overs. No edits.

My nerves are electrical currents that have me wired and anxious at this opportunity to use my voice in front of the country and world. I may not get another chance like this again. But it's not helping that I feel like I might throw up when I open my mouth. My hands shake, but I have to speak up, even if I pass out afterward. I want to make my family proud. It doesn't matter that they're no longer around to see me do this. Purpose fills my lungs. Kendra's voice echoes inside my head.

Imagine if you used your power for good.

When I speak into the microphone, I feel like I'm listening to someone else talk in my voice.

"Whether I move on to next week or not, my work is only beginning. Every species should value all life forms. Those who think they are above the law need reminding. And for all of the sentient zombies out there watching, remember that you deserve the same rights as anyone else."

Yeah, that statement isn't going to win me any votes. It might even get me killed. But right now, I feel closer to my family than I have since their deaths. And for a moment, I feel untouchable.

Colt walks over to Team Zen and continues asking questions without comment. He's professional all the way.

"We have time for one more question," he announces, returning to Team Malachi. "Leah, what have you loved most about performing on *Spellcaster*?"

After Leah answers, Colt takes his place center stage. "Voting has closed, and it is time to find out which of these remaining casters received the most votes."

Music plays, and a stagehand strides across the stage with a shimmery purple card, which she hands to Colt before walking off. Colt holds the card face down.

The remaining members of Team Brody latch onto one another, linking arms and pressing shoulder to shoulder. I've watched teammates hold hands during these nerve-racking eliminations, but I know better than to reach for my vampire teammate's hand.

Colt slowly lifts the purple card. "And now . . . the caster moving forward to next week . . ." He turns the card over in front of his face, where only he can see the name printed on the other side. Colt lowers the card. His back is to us, so I can't see his expression, only listen as he announces, "From Team Malachi . . . Haylee Hutchins, congratulations on being voted through to next week."

My mouth gapes open as Colt turns and gives me a brief sideways hug before facing the audience and cameras once more. "Tune in next week to watch your Top 13 compete live with more incredible feats of magic—"

Colt's words fade out as Cody and Jake race over and bow in front of me.

"Oh, mighty and powerful queen, we congratulate you," Jake says.

The rest of the wolves join us. I'm touched that they're all laughing and smiling despite not making it to next week. Noah lifts me off my feet, and I give a little squeal of surprise. He sets me down, and we shuffle off stage after the stage lights flash that we're no longer live on camera. Colt thanks the studio audience for coming out to watch the show.

In front of our group, Blair tells her posse, "There's no way she was voted through. The producers probably just wanted to keep a zombie around for controversy."

Cody scoffs at her back. "Someone's a sore loser."

The rest of the wolves are waiting for us backstage. I get swept up in the hugging—starting with Kace, who lifts me off my feet.

"You did it, Z. Congratulations."

"You too," I say back.

"The rest of you, don't forget you made it to lives, and we're all friends for life. *Spellcaster* class of Season 13," Tracie says to the wolves who didn't make it to next week.

"She's right," Jake says, bobbing his head. "We're all bonded for life."

Izzie's pink cheeks match her hair. She rolls her eyes, grinning at the same time.

"Ah, man. I'm going to miss hanging out," Cody says.

Kace slings his arm around me and pulls me against his side. "Listen up, everyone," he says. "Let's make a pact, right here, right now, that someone from our group wins the show."

Daphné says an enthused, "*Oui!*"

"Agreed," Tracie says.

The other wolves nod and voice their agreement. Kace turns his chin to study me from up close.

"That includes you, Z. Let's hear your agreement."

I chuckle. "I think that's up to the audience."

"Nah."

We all laugh while Kace continues his intense stare.

"Sure," I say. "Someone from our group definitely has to win."

Tracie struts forward with her chest lifted. "Great. Now that that's settled, it's time to party."

After changing, I share a ride with Kace, Tripp, and Luke back to the hotel. The guys sit in the back, blabbing the entire way.

"Six wolves in the Top 13! Our species rules!" Luke announces.

"With Haylee, our pack has the top seven spots," Kace says.

"What's the species countdown to?" Luke muses. "Six wolves, three vampires, three wizards, and—"

"One zombie queen," Kace finishes. He leans forward and gives my shoulders a brief squeeze.

Luke claps his hands and laughs. "Double their numbers."

"The public has clearly shown their preference," Tripp chimes in.

It's still light out, but it won't be for long. The streetlights and buildings are a blur, and the voices in the back seat fade as I zomb out.

I should feel happy that I made it to next week, but all I can think about is how I'll have to go through this whole humiliating charade all over again.

At the hotel, I ride up the elevator with the guys. Tripp and Luke head for their rooms with a wave and a "See you soon," while Kace lingers in the hallway. He purses his lips and studies my face.

"You okay?"

I nod. "Top 13. Yay." I don't mean for it to come out sarcastic. I'm lucky. I should be jumping up and down for joy.

Kace frowns. "You know it's bullshit you weren't voted through right away."

"It doesn't matter." I sigh.

Kace cups my chin and tilts my head back gently. "Everyone has to fight their way to the top. You've shown the world you command the stage. Tonight, you reminded them why you deserve to win this whole thing."

I pull out of his hold and shake my head. "Don't you want to win?"

Kace stuffs his hands in his front pockets and shrugs. "Nah. I auditioned for the experience and to make new friends. Didn't realize I'd meet the woman of my dreams while I was at it." He winks.

I roll my eyes while my stomach swoops. "You are such a freak; you know that, right?" I joke.

"Freaky for you," Kace says.

"Oh my gosh!" I burst out laughing, which shakes off some of my doldrums.

Kace smirks and lifts his brows. I'm not in a laughing mood, but that doesn't seem to stop him from pulling me out of my funk.

"I'll walk you to your door," Kace announces.

I shake my head. "No need. The coast is clear." I glance down the empty hallway before returning my attention to the mirthful brown eyes that shine on me. "So, see you in the lobby at seven, I guess."

"You guess?"

I smile. "See you soon."

"You can count on it." Kace stays where he is, watching that I reach my door.

Now that I've made it through and secured myself another week on *Spellcaster*, I just want to crash in my room . . . ALONE. But this is my last night to hang out with Jake, Cody, and Noah. I need to summon up some energy and set aside my revenge plots for an evening.

First, I have a little over an hour to relax before meeting back up with the wolves. All I want right now is my room to myself. Blair's never stuck around before, but it's not as though she'll be out celebrating after losing the thirteenth spot to me. It might not even be safe for me to go inside, which is why I cast a shielding spell before walking in. The last thing I'm expecting is enthusiastic applause as I enter.

My eyes bug out at the state of my room, which is filled with flower arrangements, balloon bouquets, champagne in an ice bucket next to crystal flutes, and—most shocking of all—Phoenix Starr lying on my bed, leaning against the headboard.

CHAPTER SIXTY-THREE

THE ABILITY TO think or speak is swallowed up in the open hole of my gaping mouth.

"There she is! Lucky number thirteen." Phoenix swings her long, slender legs off my bed and straightens up.

Cascading layers of silky red hair drape past her shoulders. Coin-sized silver sequins shimmer from her short, sleeveless dress. There is no material between sequins, exposing bare skin. I can just make out nude-colored underwear. She's bra-less on top.

"Phoenix Starr," I gasp.

This has to be an illusion. All of it. The flowers. The "congratulations" balloons. The champagne chilling in a bucket on top of the dresser . . . and Phoenix Starr. Her especially.

She saunters over to me on silver stilettos that make her tower over me. Her red hair is parted in the middle and falls in beachy waves.

"We did it," she announces, as she breezes right past me to get to the champagne, stopping to look over at a young woman I am just now noticing seated on a chair in the corner, scrolling through her phone. "Kelly, you'd better do the honors. I'm more likely to pop a balloon with a flyaway cork—or worse." Phoenix laughs heartily. "This is Kelly, PA extraordinaire."

Kelly walks over holding her phone and smiles. "Hi. Congratulations on your incredible performance."

"Thanks," I say, still trying to figure out what is happening as Kelly pockets her phone and uncorks the champagne effortlessly. She keeps hold of the cork in one hand and tosses it into the wastebasket.

Phoenix's personal assistant is dressed in sneakers, blue jeans, and a gray T-shirt. Her dark blond hair is pulled back in a ponytail.

"Remember to pour one for yourself," Phoenix tells her.

Kelly fills two glasses before pouring a small amount into a third glass. She hands one of the full flutes to Phoenix and then to me.

Phoenix lifts her glass. "A toast to us."

I clink glasses with her and Kelly and take a small sip to be polite. Kelly does the same before setting her glass on the dresser—in the little space not taken up by flowers.

"Maybe you should clue Haylee in as to why we're inside her room," Kelly suggests.

"Mm, right," Phoenix says, right before she guzzles down her entire flute of champagne and pours herself another. "I love champagne," she announces. "It's like a party in a glass. Best beverage ever." The light catches her sequins as she moves around the room, holding the flute with her pearly white manicured nails.

She struts past Blair's bed, which is entirely covered in balloons and flowers. That's when I notice that my former roommate's bag is gone, as is her mini gemstone statue collection.

"We told the front desk we needed to get inside your room to throw you a surprise party," Phoenix says, before taking another hearty sip of champagne. "We got rid of the witch while we were at it," she adds, swinging the arm holding the champagne over Blair's former bed. The motion is quick, but Phoenix doesn't spill a drop. "Her aura was seriously dampening the space. Kelly had to light some sage to clear the energy before the flowers and balloons could be brought in."

I nod like this all makes perfect sense. "This is such an amazing surprise." I'm not sure how to ask, so I go ahead and blurt the question burning a hole through my head. "Why are you doing this?"

Phoenix blinks and stares at me like she can't comprehend my confusion. She lifts her glass and drinks down a couple more sips before finding a place to set it down.

"Haylee, think of me as your fairy godmother, but not the old Cinderella version." She wrinkles her nose. "I'm the young, hot version in heels." She walks right up to me and smiles with pearly white teeth. Phoenix stands so close I can feel her breath on my forehead. I feel like I should take a step back, but that would be rude. Phoenix Starr is the country's most famous socialite. She's someone people clamber to get close to. They don't back away. I wait politely for Phoenix to continue talking or move out of my space. She does so with a smile, snatching her champagne flute. "As a general rule, I arrive late to parties," she announces next. "I almost missed this one, but thank god I made it in time with Kelly's help."

Kelly's head is bent, looking at her phone as she reads aloud. "Have you seen Haylee Hutchins perform on *Spellcaster*? She's my absolute favorite contestant to ever grace the stage with her beauty and talent. No one rocks a wand like Haylee. I cannot wait to see what she does (and what she wears) next! You all know what to do. Hashtag vote Haylee Hutchins. Hashtag Spellcaster Season 13. Hashtag she's Z bomb. Hashtag hottie alert. Hashtag never twenty-three."

Phoenix mouths along to the hashtags and laughs when Kelly finishes. "Never twenty-three—don't you just love it? Clever Kelly came up with that one."

Kelly inclines her head like it's no big deal. It's nice to see Phoenix compliment her assistant and include her in the drinks. You never know with celebrities and socialites. I never dreamed I would meet Phoenix Starr in person. I still feel like I'm dreaming. Yeah, I'm a contestant on a show, but Phoenix was born in the spotlight. Her entire purpose is to be famous and fabulous. I'd be lying if I said I didn't feel starstruck.

"We're going to show them all what we're made of," Phoenix says to me. "Vampires, werewolves, wizards—men. They think they call the shots. Well, we're here to shake the foundation beneath their feet. The moment I saw you storm off stage after that old codger of a coach choose a fledgling wizard over your gorgeous butterfly performance, I recognized a kindred spirit. You and I are a couple of black swans."

Suddenly, it all makes sense. This is another one of Phoenix Starr's wild and crazy stunts to piss off her father. Whatever her reason, without her help I won't make it to the finale, so if this is what it takes, I'll drink the bubbles I've been offered. Having an advantage will be a welcome change.

I moisten my lips. "Thanks for your vote of confidence."

"Absolutely! Now, let's get you changed so we can go out on the town and celebrate. Don't worry—I bought you a dress." When I gape at Phoenix, she says, "Fairy godmother, remember?" She strides over to where Kelly has seated herself back in the corner and grabs a shopping bag from the floor. What she pulls out makes my mouth hang open like a guppy's.

"But that's the same dress you're wearing." I thought women *hated* wearing the same dress. Then again, this is Phoenix Starr, and she's not known for being typical or predictable.

"I know," she says with excitement. "We're going to look so cute together. Hashtag smoking hot twins in sequins." Phoenix laughs. "The pics are going to look amazing."

Kelly nods. "Double the pleasure. It's going to be drool city. Guys will be wiping off their phone screens with the hems of their shirts."

Another laugh bursts from Phoenix's lips, which are stained a very pretty dusty rose. I like the way her laughter sounds joyful and bold. She doesn't chuckle softly or giggle. When Phoenix is mirthful, she gives it a full belly laugh.

"Drool city," she repeats. "That's hilarious, Kelly, and totally true." She sets the identical sequin dress on my bed and next pulls out a pair of silver sandals. "I wasn't sure about stilettos. I've been wearing them since I was old enough to walk, so we erred on the side of caution."

I nod gratefully. "Thanks."

Kelly lifts her head. "There's also a white tube top and boy shorts to wear underneath. Not everyone is as uninhibited as Phoenix."

My laugh is shaky, nothing like the dazzling starlet's. "Thanks. I'll, uh, try this on—in the bathroom." I take the bag Phoenix hands me, along with the dress, and dash into the bathroom. Once I've set the items on the counter, I stare into the mirror at the wild eyes staring back and mouth, *Oh my freaking God!*

Then I hold up the dress. The same thought runs through my head. There's no way I can wear something this skimpy . . . even with a tube top and boy shorts underneath. But I have to at least try it on for Phoenix. I see no other way around it. She's so excited. And . . . she's Phoenix freaking Starr! Phoenix Starr wants to be my fairy godmother/sequin dress twin. I've had a lot of surprising moments in my life lately, but this one takes the cake.

Not wanting to keep Phoenix or Kelly waiting, I hurry and change—opting for the boy shorts and tube top. After I pull the dress on over the white undergarments, I stare into the mirror. The dress is sexy and fun . . .and so not me. I cannot leave my room, let alone the hotel, in this sequin slip.

First, I'll show Phoenix I tried.

She's drinking more champagne when I step out. As soon as she sees me, she lowers her flute and says, "Yes, girl. Stunning! Not many women can pull off this dress but look at us. We're too hot to handle."

Kelly stands from where she's seated. "Let's start by the balloons with champagne."

"Great, but first I need a refill," Phoenix says. "Haylee, you're behind. Here, take your glass for pics." I take the flute from her and watch as she refills her glass before slinking over to the balloon bouquets all but obstructing the view out the windows. "Get on over here, Haylee. Don't be shy."

"Um." My ears feel like they're burning. *It's just pictures*, I tell myself. Far better to be photographed inside the sanctuary of my room than out in the open. Afterward, I can change, and hopefully, Phoenix won't mind since we'll have pictures as sequin twins.

Once I join Phoenix, Kelly looks us over. "Hold your champagne flutes hip level—loosen your grip, Haylee, like the glass is about to slip through your fingers. Don't actually drop it, of course."

I try to mirror Phoenix's effortless hold on her drink.

"Great, but switch hands, Haylee," Kelly says.

I do as she instructs, freeing up my hand closest to Phoenix.

"Want us to hold hands?" Phoenix asks.

"Yeah, try that," Kelly says.

Phoenix takes my hand without hesitation. She's way cooler about touching a zombie than I ever was. She does realize I'm a zombie, right? It would be so awkward if she thought I was a vampire.

"This is adorable," Kelly says, as she snaps pictures with her phone—or more likely Phoenix's phone. "Now turn around. Let's get you from behind." The dress is backless. I've never been this nude in front of anyone in my life. "Okay, flower shots."

Phoenix leads the way to the floral arrangements. Once those are done, she announces, "Time to shake our booties for a dance reel. Let's do this, Haylee!"

Somehow, I find myself with my arm pressed against Phoenix's as we coordinate lifting our flutes at the same time, taking a sip, and then swinging our hips in sync, side to side. My smile feels as big as hers.

Phoenix dips forward low enough to show the tops of her breasts as she says, "Spell—"

She pulls back, and I lean forward next to say, "caster."

"Season," Phoenix says.

"Thirteen," I chime in.

"Team Malachi!" we yell in unison and then clink glasses and drink champagne.

After she finishes swallowing, Phoenix points at the moth on my shoulder with the hand holding her champagne flute. "Cute tattoo."

"Thanks."

"It's a *ny scelta*. The most expensive tattoo in existence," Kelly supplies.

"Then I definitely want one," Pheonix says with a toss of her hair. "What do you think, Kel? Ankle or hip?" She juts her hip out and lifts her brows with a smirk.

"I think it would look cool on your thigh," Kelly answers.

My phone buzzes.

"Oh shoot, what time is it?" I ask, setting down the champagne flute to grab my phone. There's a group text invite to meet in the hotel bar for drinks before heading out.

"Let's do one more before we head out," Phoenix says.

I try not to wince. "Uh, I'm supposed to meet up with the other werewolf contestants."

Phoenix purses her lips. "But you're not a wolf."

"They're my friends, and it's my last chance to say bye to the ones not returning next week." My stomach knots. I don't want to blow off Phoenix or my friends. Talk about awkward—especially when Phoenix continues to pout.

Kelly clears her throat. "How about we head out now, and Haylee meets up with her friends in a couple hours."

I smile at Kelly gratefully.

Phoenix looks upward in thought for a second before a wide grin stretches up her cheeks. "Perfect," she announces. "Aaron's been begging me to make an appearance at that Malibu event tonight. Perhaps he'll get his wish after all." She flips her hair back. "Well, we'd better get going." Phoenix drinks down the champagne in her flute and sets it on the dresser.

"Here, I thought you might need this," Kelly says, pulling out a long, silver purse that will fit my wand, phone, and wallet.

I thank her as I take it. She really is an extraordinary assistant, but I would expect no less for Phoenix Starr.

The socialite isn't the type who likes to wait around, so when we head for the elevator, I text the group that I'll meet up with them later, followed by a speedy text to Kace.

> **Haylee:** So, you're not going to believe this, but Phoenix Starr was waiting in my room and wants to take me out before I meet up with you guys later.

When the elevator dings, I slide my phone back inside the purse. The doors open, and a woman in her thirties screeches like she's a teenager at a pep rally.

"Phoenix Starr!"

"Nothing to see here," a masculine voice intones. I nearly join the woman yelping in surprise when I hear Zane's voice behind us. Did he place a spell alerting him whenever I approach the elevators?

The doors close quickly on the woman as she hurries to dig her phone out of her purse.

"The next one will be empty," Zane announces.

Phoenix twists around and grins as she scans him up and down. "Zane Barrett, look at you branching out to reality TV."

Zane shrugs one shoulder, hardly looking at her. "It's a competition."

"Exactly, and my girl Haylee here is going to win." Phoenix leans against me. That's when Zane takes a closer look at what we're wearing.

I try, and fail, not to blush. After telling Phoenix I couldn't spend the entire evening with her, I felt like I was stuck wearing the dress. If I was wearing it on stage, I wouldn't feel nearly as self-conscious as I do going out and standing in the hallway under a certain wizard's scrutiny.

Zane has one of the toughest faces I've ever attempted to read.

"You both look beautiful," he finally says.

"I think you mean gorgeous," Phoenix returns.

"Yeah, that too." But his voice is flat.

When another elevator arrives, Phoenix stands in front of Zane and holds her palm in front of him to stop him from entering. "You can catch the next one, Zane. This is a ladies-only elevator."

I clench my teeth and send Zane silent apologies for Phoenix's rudeness. Maybe I can find a bathroom stall to sneak into later and message him.

Zane stays where he is. His eyes find mine as he says, "Don't let your guard down."

"Says the wolf to the lamb." Phoenix shoots Zane a haughty look and lifts her chin. "Kelly."

Kelly pushes the close button on the elevator doors. My limbs feel like jelly as Zane continues to stare into my eyes until the doors shut him out.

Phoenix huffs the moment he's closed off. "You can't trust wizards."

It's a long night. One that's totally surreal.

There's a private car waiting out front that whisks us off to a restaurant/bar on the seaside in Santa Monica. A hostess leads us to an outdoor patio with cushioned bench seating and chairs surrounded by a waist-high plexiglass railing overlooking the ocean. Heat lamps radiate warmth while candle flames glow from large glass votives.

The sign leading in reads: ***RESERVED***.

Beautiful people are already gathered and come forward to kiss Phoenix's cheeks and meet me.

"Haylee Hutchins, *Spellcaster* Season 13's winner," Phoenix announces. "You voted for my girl, right?"

"Of course. We all did!"

"Keep voting, and tell all your followers," Phoenix says.

This party is supposedly for me, but I feel like Phoenix's sparkly shadow. I'm perfectly polite as I wait until I can join my real friends.

A waiter offers Phoenix a tray of cocktails to choose from. She selects a margarita glass with a thick straw and caramelized lemon slice artfully topping the middle of the slushy beverage.

"Haylee, grab a drink," Phoenix commands before I can shake my head at the waiter.

Well, there are worse people than Phoenix Starr to be bossed around by.

I grab something light pink and icy with sprigs of rosemary at the top and hold on to it for show.

Kelly's off in a corner scrolling through her phone. Nobody interrupts her. I thought I could slink off and do the same, but I soon learn that I'm pretty much Phoenix's accessory for the evening until the conclusion of this exclusive celebration.

A buffet of appetizers is set down across a long, low table in the center of the patio. Drink glasses are brought out full and are whisked away as soon as they're emptied. Phoenix sucks each cocktail down like it's the elixir of life. She threads her arm around mine and tugs me with her on impressively steady legs, considering she's consumed half her weight in alcohol and is wearing stilettos.

"Zen is such a square. At least Haylee's on the right team now," Phoenix says to a young, preppy-looking guy in slacks and a polo with designer sunglasses propped on his head. He sips a martini beside the railing.

"I thought you said you were over Forever 23," the prep says.

Phoenix lifts her nose. "Oh, I am, but they're not over losing their chance at me. The vamps want me bad. They're offering to start a new club in my honor: Forever 28."

The prep lifts his brows and smirks. "If only Daddy would give his blessing." He takes a sip of his martini.

Phoenix narrows her eyes at him before grabbing my arm and pulling me away from the calming view of the ocean. "Come on, Haylee. I'll introduce you to Carson Montague. He has over three million subscribers on JingleJam.

I would have thought Phoenix would need to pee by now, but she keeps making the rounds—and downing more drinks—leading me around with her. When she finally does have to use the ladies' room, I plop down on the cushioned bench and pull out my phone. I have texts from Cameron and Kace, and a DM from Zane.

Cameron: Celebrate your win and be safe. When you have a chance, call me no matter how late it is.

Kace: Who?

I chuckle softly at Kace's message, which is followed by a newer one.

Kace: Never mind. Looked her up. You ditching me for a socialite, Z?

Haylee: Try kidnapped. I think she sees me as a charitable cause.

I open Zane's message next.

Zane: What are you doing with Phoenix Starr?

I chew on the inside of my cheek. First Carolina and now Phoenix have warned me about Zane. He's probably a major playboy. He looks like one. I'm not totally naïve. But I can't ignore the fact that thanks to Zane, I know who went after my family. I'd still be floundering in the dark if not for his help. At the very least, he deserves an explanation—especially after the way Phoenix treated him.

A flash of silver sequins catches my eye before I have a chance to respond to Zane's message. Right before Phoenix reaches me, a tall, thin brunette in a beige minidress heads her off, not bothering to lower her voice as she demands, "Are you sure this is a good idea? It seems extreme even for you."

Phoenix throws back her head and laughs heartily. "Which is why no one knows who you are, while I will be forever famous. Fortune favors the bold, but if you're uncomfortable, maybe you should go."

"I'm just concerned for you," the brunette whines.

Phoenix frowns at her. "You should definitely leave. This party is for rebels, and you're clearly not one of us."

"Phoenix—"

Phoenix turns her back on the brunette and lifts one slender arm in the air as she calls out to a young man in a tailored suit talking to a blond beside a heat lamp. "Eli, get over here and meet our guest of honor."

And so the evening goes until I am able to leave, or rather be dismissed by Phoenix Starr. She has Kelly arrange a separate ride back to LA for me to join the wolves at a club downtown.

CHAPTER SIXTY-FOUR

To: All Remaining Spellcaster Season 13 Contestants

Subject: Week 2 Lives

Dear Contestants,

Congratulations on making it into the Top 13!

Get ready to sweep viewers off their feet for Week 2 lives.

For your live performances, you will take your levitation spells to new heights.

After working with your coaches, you will each have one hour to practice your song and set on the *Spellcaster* stage before your live performance on Thursday.

Friday is results day. Ten of you will be voted through to Week 3's top eleven. The three contestants with the fewest number of votes will perform for the eleventh spot during the instant saves.

Attached, you will find the schedule of when you meet with your coach for practice.

Good luck!

CHAPTER SIXTY-FIVE

OVER THE WEEKEND, I gain over half a million new followers on Telepatch thanks to Phoenix Starr.

For the first time, I feel like I have a real chance at winning the show.

"Top 11, here I come," I tell Cameron and Joni, when they drop me off at the airport Sunday evening.

We've spelled TJ to stay home, keep his mouth shut, and watch TV.

Joni hugs me and starts crying. This goodbye is different. Cameron agreed that it makes more sense for me to stay in California for the remainder of the competition rather than fly back and forth across the country for the weekend. Counting this week, I have five left—if I make it to the finale.

Flight time would be better spent practicing. I'm good at levitation, but I need to be great. Amazing. The best. And who knows what they'll ask us to do next week for the Top 11 performances? Which reminds me, I have my first kiss coming up with Kace. It's going to be a memorable week.

At least all the hubbub with Phoenix Starr provided one big blazing bomb of a distraction from my detective work and terrible discovery. It even took my mind temporarily off of the terrible truth. Not completely. No way. But I haven't had a moment to myself to fully process what I learned, and maybe that's not a bad thing, since I'm pretending I'm still in the dark. For now, I need to prioritize.

On paper, it would look simple.

Priority #1, Win *Spellcaster* Season 13.

Priority #2, Get revenge on Uncle Alvan, his master, and the rest of his minions and associates.

Yeah, sure, easy.

Each goal is riddled with Herculean challenges, but Phoenix is right. I'm a rebel. Soon to be an *all-powerful* rebel. Once I win the heart, I will be unstoppable . . . and I'll make every vampire involved in my family's deaths pay.

I'll work out the details later.

I give Joni a final hug and smile at Cameron, who still looks like he's lost his grin forever. He's buffed out from his continued visits to the gym, and there's gloom in his eyes as though a gray cloud has taken up permanent residence inside his head.

He nods at me. "See you in the Top 10."

That's the other thing. Cam's planning a trip with Joni midway through my five remaining weeks on the show to visit Evelyn. At least I know he won't learn anything from her. It's not like he has a wizard willing to break the law and die for him in order to extract information. I'm already prepared to put on a show of disappointment, followed by encouragement that we'll find another way to get to the truth.

"See you in a couple weeks," I say, with enthusiasm for Joni's benefit.

We've already scheduled Daniel to come by every morning she's gone to spell TJ into not telling anyone he's under our control.

My cousin finishes swiping away her tears and grins. "I can't wait! I'm so excited!"

"Live audience," I say. Joni gives a happy squeal. "Well, I'd better make my way through security," I announce. "See you soon."

"Good luck, Haylee," Joni says.

"Be safe and call home every day," Cameron tells me.

I bob my head. "I will," I promise. "You know you can count on me for the full report." Excluding my extracurricular PI endeavors, of course. But when it comes to *Spellcaster*, I keep Cam in the loop. I mean, mostly. Some things are private—like my upcoming kiss with Kace.

I turn and hurry off before I blush and give Cameron any reason to be suspicious.

My plane lands in LA so early in the morning, it looks like night outside.

After claiming my luggage, I get a ride to the hotel and check in. I grin at Blair's empty side the moment I walk in, set my bags aside, and crawl into bed. It doesn't take long to fall asleep.

A light tapping on the door wakes me before the alarm I set on my phone. I have to pry my eyes open. There's a blurry film over my vision that takes multiple blinks to clear.

The tapping continues.

With a groan, I stumble out of bed toward the door. I look through the peephole and see Izzie in the hallway with a pink-and-black hardshell suitcase.

A smile spreads over my lips as I open the door. "Are we roommates now?"

Izzie grins back. "Thank goodness they didn't stick me with Carolina."

We share a squeal of excitement and relief before Izzie rolls her suitcase in. She's wearing a fuchsia and teal tie-dye mesh T-shirt over a black sports bra, vinyl fuchsia shorts, and tall, chunky black moon boots. A pair of dark flat-top shield sunglasses sits on top of her head of pink hair. She looks like she beamed down from some retro punk planet.

"Ready to win our way to another week?" I ask.

"I can't believe I made it this far already." Izzie pushes her case against the wall across from the foot of her bed, stretches her arms over her head, and yawns. "You want to get breakfast? I'll see if anyone else is around to join us."

"Sure."

Between my nap and a serving of breakfast brains, I should be ready for my one-on-one coaching session with Malachi, which is scheduled for one this afternoon.

Kace, Tripp, and Daphné haven't arrived at the hotel yet, which leaves Tracie, Luke, Izzie, and me sharing a booth in the hotel's cafe.

"This feels so weird without the rest of the gang," Tracie says. Her mohawk is spiked and she's wearing a white T-shirt with black graffiti underneath a sleeveless, frayed jean vest.

Izzie frowns and nods.

Luke twists a thin leather bracelet around his wrist. Both of his elbows rest on the table. "Let's make sure we're all here next week," he says.

I look across the table at Tracie and ask, "Are you still roommates with Suhani?"

She rolls her eyes and huffs. "You know she's not going anywhere, so we're stuck together. You and Izzie lucked out."

"What about you, Luke? Who's your roommate?" I ask. I haven't spoken to him much in the past, but now that our group is thinning out, it wouldn't hurt to get to know him better.

"Zane Barrett."

"Oh," I say in surprise, feeling a flush creep up my neck.

"He's all right," Luke says with a shrug. Tracie scowls and smacks him. "What? He plays cool songs on his guitar."

"Oh, really? How sweet. Maybe the two of you can hang out at a beach bonfire and weave friendship bracelets together," Tracie says snidely.

Luke's brows lift. "Well, my last two roommates were vampires, and I'm telling you Zane is a big improvement."

It's nice to hear someone who isn't a wizard say something nice about Zane. We messaged briefly over the weekend. I filled him in on Phoenix Starr, which I still haven't fully processed. He called her a spoiled rich girl pulling a publicity stunt. To which I replied that I wasn't born yesterday, but that I also wasn't too proud to acknowledge I need all the help I can get for viewer votes.

I want to believe Zane can be trusted, that he's my friend, but that doesn't make him any less clueless. He's a powerful wizard. A model. A celebrity. Wealthy and connected. He's incapable of grasping what I'm up against.

Our breakfasts arrive, and I've only taken one bite when Kace strides in.

"Yo," he says, jutting his chin at our group. "You eating without me?"

"You said you wouldn't make it in time," Izzie chides. She scoots over to make room for me to do the same and create a spot for Kace at the end of our bench.

"My bag was the first one out, and my driver made good time," Kace says, glancing at the narrow space beside me. "I'll get a chair."

He grabs a seat one-handed from a vacant table and sets it at the end of the booth before plopping down and stealing a pancake off Tracie's plate. When she growls at him, he laughs.

"Thought you said you liked sharing."

Tracie huffs. "You should ask first."

Kace holds the pancake up between two fingers. "Can I have this pancake?"

"Like I'd want it back after you've manhandled my food."

Kace grins. "Thanks," he says, and then stuffs the whole thing into his mouth. At least he chews with his mouth closed.

"So, Kace, who's your new roommate?" Izzie asks cheerfully, adding, "I'm with Haylee now."

Kace swallows the pancake down before beaming at me and Izzie. "Way to go, ladies. I have to shack up with Oliver." Kace's former smile turns deadly. "The fanger shouldn't have been voted through in the first place."

"Well, the public has another chance to do the right thing and send him home at the end of the week," Tracie says. She slaps Kace's hand when he reaches for another one of her pancakes. "Hey, order your own."

"I will, as soon as the waiter shows up."

Once Kace puts an order in and gets served, he wastes no time catching up to the rest of us. If magic doesn't work out for him, he's got a future in competitive speed-eating.

After we're all finished, our group walks into the lobby, where several guests request selfies with us.

"Team Werewolf!" the others shout for the photo.

My smile wavers, because as much as I love being a part of their group, I am not a wolf.

"And zombie," I add the next time they do it. I'm not only here to compete. I want to represent my species with pride.

"Oh shoot. I've got my session with Cleo coming up," Tracie says, before rushing for the lobby's entrance.

The rest of us take the elevator up to the eighth floor and wish one another luck.

"My session isn't scheduled with Brody until tomorrow, but I reserved studio time to practice levitating," Izzie announces in the hallway.

"Shouldn't be too difficult; you're already a lightweight," Kace jokes.

I rub my chin thoughtfully and smirk at him. "Good point. Think you can manage to manipulate gravity, big guy?"

Kace smirks. "As you know, this wolf has extra motivation to make it into the Top 11." He winks at me.

My eyes are on his lips in an instant, and my stomach belly flops. I clear my throat and move away. "Well, my coaching session is at one, so I need to get ready."

"Uh-huh, you do that, Z," Kace says in a deep, husky voice, throwing in another wink . . . followed by a chuckle.

Once we're shut inside our room, Izzie lifts her brows. "What was that about?"

I unzip my bag and search through my clothes, pulling out a pair of crimson crushed-velvet pants that are stylish and comfortable.

"Kace and I made a deal that if we both make it into the Top 11, we'll kiss."

"Kace is a big sweetie—and I bet he's a great kisser," Izzie says.

My thoughts return to Kace's lush lips and imagine what kind of kiss he has in mind. I hope he keeps it short and sweet. I'm not ready for a full-blown make out . . . or tongue. Nope. I need to work my way up to the advanced stuff. For better or worse, I trust Kace to make the experience both satisfying and respectful.

I grab a black V-neck, set it back down, select an eyelet camisole instead, and look up at Izzie.

"Sorry Jake and Cody are no longer around."

"It's the nature of the beast," Izzie says with a shrug. She smiles. "Besides, we're still in touch, and they'll be back for the grand finale group performance."

"It will be fun to see them again," I say.

Izzie nods and checks her phone. "I'd better head over to the studio. Have a great coaching session, and see you later—unless you're getting together with Phoenix Starr."

"I haven't received a summons yet."

We share a laugh before Izzie uses the bathroom and then leaves the room. I take my time getting dressed, putting on makeup, and twisting my hair into two cute buns secured behind my ears. A pair of gold-toned earrings dangle from my lobes, and I pull my circular *H* pendant over the black camisole.

My remaining time is spent lying on top of my bed with my eyes closed until the timer goes off on my phone. I get out of bed, spritz on a rosy perfume, slip into an awesome pair of rhinestone-studded ankle boots, and put on a cropped moto jacket. After checking my reflection in the bathroom mirror, I arrange a ride and head to the lobby with my wand, phone, and a few essential cosmetics zipped up in a black-and-gold evil eye clutch with a thick tassel and a strap that hangs over my arm.

When my ride pulls up in front of the hotel, I get in the back and say, "*Spellcaster* studio, please."

Brown eyes meet mine in the driver's rearview mirror.

"You a contestant?" he asks in a heavy African accent.

"I am," I say with a polite smile. "Do you watch the show?"

He shakes his head and chuckles mirthfully. "No time for TV, but my three daughters always ask me what famous celebrities I had in my car."

My smile stretches. "I wouldn't call myself a celebrity, but I am excited to be in the *Spellcaster* Top 13."

My driver whistles, sounding impressed.

"They will be very excited. What is your name?"

"Haylee Hutchins."

He bobs his head enthusiastically as he rounds the next street corner. "Very good. I will tell my girls I had Haylee Hutchins, Top 13, in my car."

My driver, Dejen, makes friendly chitchat as he drives. When we reach the theater, he says, "Good luck!"

"Thanks. Tell your girls hi from me."

"I will do that, Haylee Hutchins."

Hopefully, they won't freak out when they discover their dad had a zombie in his car.

Jovi is seated on a cushioned chair across from the show's producers, who share a couch in the theater lobby. There are papers laid across a coffee table between them, and Jovi makes marks on one of the sheets.

"Good afternoon," I say as I pass them.

Jovi looks up only long enough to tell me, "Malachi is running late, but you can go ahead and wait for him in the theater."

I stare at her, thinking, *Really? Malachi would ream me out if I was late, but it's okay if he cuts our practice short because he took too long at lunch or whatever it is that's holding him up.*

The werewolves look up from their notes and give me hard stares. Oh, right. They're probably worried I might wait in the lobby when they clearly want a private space to work.

"Okay, I'll just wait in the theater for Malachi to show up," I say.

"He shouldn't be long," Jovi says in a dismissive voice, before scratching something out roughly with her pen. "No. The Crypt Kittens are too unreliable. Remember season nine?"

One of the werewolves rubs his chin. "They've been begging us for a second chance."

The other werewolf scoffs. "You mean their agent has been begging."

"We'd get more viewers."

"Our ratings are already the highest they've ever been," Jovi says. "Season 13 has everything humans love: magic and supernaturals."

Alrighty, I'll leave them to it.

Inside the theater, I head straight for the stage. There is no sign of Max or Jimmy. I guess the guys have no reason to stand around waiting for Malachi to show up.

The auditorium is extra quiet and almost eerie with the purple pentagon glowing in the center of the stage.

I pull out my wand and set my purse off on the far side of the stage. Then I walk into the center of the pentagon. Purple lights illuminate my ankle boots. I face the empty coaches' chairs, about to jokingly address the absent judges when a sense of dread creeps over me and silences my tongue. The hairs along the back of my neck prickle.

When I look at the purple chairs, it feels like they're looking back.

I hold still and listen. It's too quiet, like sound has been sucked from the auditorium. Something thick and wrong coats the air. It's muggy without being hot.

My fingers tighten around my wand. I lift it and open my mouth to cast a shielding spell but am cut off by the earsplitting blast of bullets.

CHAPTER SIXTY-SIX

THERE IS NO time to duck as the bullets pelt me from a semiautomatic assault rifle.

Lead burns through my flesh, bones, and organs. I scream in horror. I'm a standing target, but there's no time to do anything. It all happens too quickly.

My blood and gore splatter the stage. The pentagon feels like a bullseye I stepped into.

My wand flies out of my hand—ripped away by a spell I never heard.

I'm in so much shock, I don't have the wherewithal to chastise myself for losing hold of my wand.

In the following silence, I notice a richly dressed male vampire seated in Malachi Rayne's purple chair. Five vampires hover near him, holding an arsenal of nasty weapons. Flamethrower. Ax. Katana. Spiked baseball bat. And what would a Season 13 killing spree be without a chainsaw? Shouldn't the assault rifle be enough? The rest of it seems like overkill.

A cloaked figure stands in the aisle farther away, holding two wands. I'm pretty sure one of them is mine, but the auditorium lights are off, and the ominous caster stands well outside the glow of the stage lights. Now I know how they kept themselves invisible. The caster probably has us in a silencing bubble as well; otherwise, Jovi and the wolves would have run in by now.

Or would they?

My stomach hardens to stone.

Malachi is never late. What if he set me up? These are all vampires leering at me. Even from a distance, I can sense that their caster is a vampire.

My body burns all over, but at least they didn't blow off my face. That must be what the chainsaw is for . . . or maybe the bat.

I look into the pale face of the tall, dark-haired vampire sitting straight-backed in Malachi's chair, one tailored suit leg crossed over the other. His Italian leather shoes are polished to a shine.

When our eyes meet, his glare is intense enough to burn almost as hot as the wounds seared through my flesh.

"You must be my uncle's master," I spit out the last word.

The vampire lackeys hiss and start toward me with their weapons, until their master lifts his arm from the chair's padded purple armrest and holds up his palm, stopping them in their tracks.

"What's the matter, Uncle Al?" I call out to the hooded figure. "Don't have the guts to face me—just like you didn't have the spine to go after my father or my family yourself?" I seethe, and now my mind is on fire along with the rest of my body.

My words make the master smirk. "That's not your uncle."

Not missing a beat, I lift my brows and answer, "Oh, wow. He's more of a coward than I thought—doesn't have the stomach to watch from the sidelines either." I'm not surprised that Uncle Alvan's sitting out another family murder. Also, I highly doubt he has the magical aptitude that his master's mystery caster shows.

My stomach roils, and tears swarm behind my eyeballs. I point a finger at the cloaked caster who sticks to the aisle near the back rows.

"Did you send that zombie horde after my family?" I demand. Silence weighs over the stage. I stagger, feeling a wave of wooziness. I lift my hand to my neck, noticing my earring is no longer there. When I reach for my earlobe, I find that it, too, is gone.

The master sits up taller as he addresses me. "My clan members aren't allowed to speak without my permission, and I am not here to answer your questions."

"Well, you're completely useless," I sneer.

Another round of bullets is fired into me. I cry out and stumble backward, clutching my stomach, fruitlessly trying to stop the bleeding with arms and hands that are gushing blood.

The gunman stays beside his master as the other four lackeys head for the stage.

I scan the exits. Where the hell is Malachi? A silencing bubble shouldn't be enough to keep him out, and he should be here by now. I don't want to believe that he had anything to do with this, but what other explanation is there for his absence?

I grit my teeth and manage to huff. "Seven grown vampires against one zombie girl. Kinda sad, don't you think? I mean, go ahead and bludgeon me to death, but know that my very last thought will be about how pathetic you and your species are."

The vamp with the ax lifts it as he leads the charge up the stairs.

His master stands up in a flash and raises his voice as he commands his lackeys to "Wait."

The eager vampires stop in their tracks and grip their weapons, glaring at me with twitching eyes.

I'm only slightly relieved to delay being chopped to bits on stage.

The master slowly lowers himself back into the seat before snapping his fingers. "Serafina, come forward and reveal yourself."

The cloaked figure drifts down the aisle, taking her time to reach the front rows like she's a supermodel strutting down a catwalk. The hooded crimson cloak looks like something straight out of an evil secret society. As she draws near, I see black pointed heels moving through the gap in the cloak, and my wand, which moves to join her own—leaving one of her hands free. She has a french manicure with polished nails and white curved tips. When she reaches the front aisle, the crimson caster stops.

In the brief moment of silence, I hear my blood dripping on the stage. My body tenses as Serafina pulls her hood back.

My eyes nearly pop out of their sockets. I gasp at the woman who is no stranger to me.

Serafina is Aunt Chloe, and her narrowed gaze drills into me like she's come back from the dead and blames me for being eaten alive.

Only that's not true. She's a vampire. When did that happen?

Dark liner rims her eyes, and long dark lashes curl toward her sculpted brows. Deep bronzer highlights her cheeks, and pale pink lipstick coats her lips. A slim black elastic headband keeps her light brown hair out of her face. It looks thick and healthy, with copper and blond highlights. She looks stunning in a black sleeveless jumpsuit and a princess-cut diamond pendant nestled just below her collarbone.

"You should have kept your head down and your mouth closed," she says coldly.

Words evade me. There is only darkness inside the cavity of my mind that spreads to my chest. My legs feel like rotted timber—chewed through by termites—about to collapse. Everything burns. It's too much.

When I blink, tears stream down my face. My tongue feels too thick in my throat. "Did you kill them?" My voice cracks.

Aunt Chloe doesn't bother denying her heinous betrayal.

"They put us all in danger," she snaps.

Her tone dredges up a flicker of my defiance. I glare at her through angry tears that drip into my wounds and mix with my blood.

The vampire master leans forward in his seat and threads his fingers together with a grin. This is why he called Aunt Chloe forward. After I insulted him, it wasn't enough to destroy my body. He wants to break my soul.

But it also buys me more time. Maybe Malachi was truly delayed, in which case, he has to show up at some point. NOW would be great!

"What kind of mother sends a zombie horde in after her own daughter?" I spit the question at Aunt Chloe.

She hisses and fists her free hand. "Joni was supposed to stay home that morning. She begged and pleaded, but I told her no, to wait in her room until I got back from speaking to my sister after I manipulated TJ into hitting me. I was in the bathroom for less than five minutes spelling TJ's handiwork not to heal too quickly. When I came out and grabbed my keys to leave, the door to Joni's room was closed. I thought she'd behaved and done as I instructed. I didn't know she had hidden in the back seat of my car until I pulled up to Laurence and Melanie's house and she popped up."

"Well, in that case, I guess she deserved to be attacked by zombies." Fresh tears burn trails down my cheeks as my thoughts spin out of control. I can't fathom how Aunt Chloe could do something so evil. So coldhearted. So unforgivable.

Aunt Chloe huffs. "I placed a protective spell around my daughter before we walked in. Joni's fine."

"No, she's not!" The scream erupts from my lips. "What's wrong with you? How could you do this?" My questions come out in shrieks.

The woman digging her manicured nails into my wand has lost her soul. But she's the one who chose to give it up.

She lifts her chin. "I did what I had to in order to save myself and my daughter. Melanie and Laurence had plenty of opportunities to save themselves, along with you and your sister, but they insisted on taking the moral high ground."

"How inconsiderate of them," I say sarcastically.

"Morals do you no good when you're dead," Aunt Chloe fires back.

"I can't believe you and Uncle Alvan could sit with us at Thanksgiving dinner and then attack my family the very next day."

"Alvan." Aunt Chloe sneers his name. "My brother is a spineless pawn." The master's lackeys chuckle rudely. "Alvan has me to thank for being made," my aunt boasts. "Couldn't get his own hands dirty, so big sis had to step in and take care of everything."

"Serafina is a cunning negotiator," the master vamp says proudly as he strokes his chin. "She was clever enough to convince me to turn her *before* she disposed of your family. Quite the arrangement. I had to send my best manipulator to fool her husband and child into thinking she was out of town selling her wares at a craft festival during her transformation. Both were commanded to comply with my orders not to complain or question *Chloe's* absence."

It's as though a cold hand has reached inside my stomach, squeezing, and twisting until every part of me churns with nausea and disgust. Knowing this vile vampire's lieutenant came in and controlled my cousin fills my mouth with a bitter taste.

The master wrinkles his nose. "The ruse was more elaborate than anything I've ordered in the past. My subordinate had to spend a week in Garnet convincing the humans that your aunt was having travel delays and to forget his visits or that they were ever under the influence of a vampire. It's a good thing Serafina proved her worth."

Aunt Chloe acknowledges his cynical praise with a nod, but she hasn't smiled once since pulling back her hood. She stands rigid, embodying the cold, unfeeling vampire stereotype, which only makes me angrier.

"I couldn't risk contamination when I called in the zombies."

Bile rises up my throat. "You watched them devour my mom? My dad? Kendra?" I choke on a sob. A flash of bloody flesh and nasal bone where my sister's face should have been punches through the flimsy mental wall I've tried desperately to guard.

There isn't a flicker of emotion in Aunt Chloe's sharp gaze.

"What about the body I saw wearing your plaid coat?" I ask with a watery voice. "Did you kill some innocent woman who looked like you just to throw everyone off?"

"She didn't need to," her master says. "What you and Z Squad saw was a dead zombie wearing your aunt's coat. Serafina placed herself in a protective circle while commanding the horde inside your home with her casting. When Z Squad arrived, she killed a female zombie, dressed her in her coat, and slipped out the backway while the wolves were busy tearing apart the horde."

"No one cares about inspecting zombie victims too closely," Aunt Chloe chimes in. "I knew it wouldn't take much for everyone to believe that I died in that attack—simply a familiar coat and a face destroyed beyond recognition."

Her master grins. "Serafina has earned her place as one of my newest lieutenants with her spellcasting skills. Her talent makes this show look like a three-ring circus."

"You're right about your Uncle Alvan," Aunt Chloe says. "My brother is a coward, but he also came to me with this opportunity, and so I took it and ensured his immortality—after mine."

"I suppose you didn't want to include Uncle TJ in the deal and remain married to him forever," I say bitterly.

Aunt Chloe's lips twist into a vicious scowl. "If I didn't need that imbecile to raise Joni in my absence, he'd already be dead. I'll have to wait until she's old enough to take care of herself, and then I'll deal with him once and for all."

This makes the lackeys chuckle again.

"And now you know the truth," the master says. "May it torment your final thoughts." He looks at my aunt and points to the purple chair beside him. "Have a seat, Serafina, and witness the final act." After my aunt settles into Zen Renko's seat, her master flashes me a malicious grin. "Not feeling so superior now, are you?"

I don't know if my aunt chose a new name for herself or if her master renamed her like a pet, but it reminds me that yes, I am superior. I'm my own master. And these vamps are forgetting that I'm a deadly supernatural.

Screw final thoughts and feelings!

I won't give them the satisfaction of watching me suffer.

I reach up and touch my "H" pendant one last time before removing my bloody jacket and discarding it on the stage. The vampires creep up the stairs, taking their time, like killing me is a delicacy to be drawn out strike by strike. My wild card tattoo is a mild comfort. I press two fingers against the ensorcelled moth.

The Spell of Sanity Turnabout is stuck inside my mind like sap.

I guess the *ny scelta* was meant for this final spell all along. It would be a waste not to use it.

But as the vampires close in, an angry scream builds inside my head.

I'm not ready to die!

There has to be another way out of this. Where is Malachi? If only I didn't need a wand to perform magic. Could I use the wild card rune to save, rather than destroy, myself?

I try to come up with a spell to get me out of this. If there's a silencing bubble around us, it could block me from teleporting outside of the theater, and then I'll have wasted my one chance to use the wild card to my advantage.

I could make myself invisible, but they'd sniff me out like bloodhounds. That, or Aunt Chloe would spell me visible again. One thing she can't do is reverse a sanity turnabout. Once I go full zombie, there's no turning back.

Still, there has to be another way. I have to at least get a message to Cameron. It can't end like this. It just can't.

The vampire with the ax steps onto the stage.

I turn and run in a burst of speed that likely surprises the vamps as much as me as I dive past the curtains at the back corner of the stage. My vision tunnels as I race down the deserted hallway. Of course, there's no one around to help me. My boots beat out a frantic tempo. There's nothing I can do about the blood trail that follows me. I don't have time to bandage my countless wounds.

Pounding shoes echo through the corridor at my back.

I burst ahead, running like an Olympian about to bring home the gold medal. With my last shred of hope, I run for Malachi's room. I'm a blur of bleeding limbs as I zip past Cleo's closed door . . . only to find Malachi's door is also closed.

I try the knob. It's locked.

I pound on the door in case Malachi is inside. "Malachi!" I yell. "Malachi, please!" I beg. My fist leaves bloody smears on the door. There's no answer.

The vampires thunder toward me. They've brought their weapons with them. Isn't their master afraid to miss the show?

"We've got you now," one of them yells triumphantly.

I'm already sprinting again. That's what I command of my body, at least, but it seems it's had enough. My feet drag over the light gray laminate floor, leaving behind more bloody smears.

A burst of fire singes the clothing on my back and burns through my skin. I scream and wonder if I've somehow turned back into a human to feel pain this agonizing.

Laughter follows my scream.

"Time to exterminate the zombie vermin," one of the vamps says.

"Xerxes wants to watch," another says. "Grab her, and we'll drag her back to the stage and finish this."

I stumble past Zen's closed door, hunched over in agony. The next door is Brody's, and it's open several inches. I blink several times, as though it's an illusion that will disappear before I reach sanctuary—like a mirage in the desert. Each time I blink, it remains slightly open.

Mustering the last of my strength, I propel myself forward and push through the door, slamming and locking it behind me. I'm submerged in darkness, as though I've entered a black hole. I run my hand along the wall until I find a light switch, flick it on, and hope for the sight of Brody napping on the couch against the wall, but I guess that would be asking too much from this cursed universe.

I'm all alone, and one of the vampires just started up his chainsaw.

CHAPTER SIXTY-SEVEN

METAL TEETH CHEW through Brody's door and spray sawdust in their wake.

I'm next.

I don't know if it's possible to feel any more pain than what I'm suffering already. The skin on my back feels like it's melted off. I wouldn't be surprised if I'm part skeleton—like the bodysuit I wore for my Halloween week performance.

The horrific braying of the chainsaw cuts out, but it's only to give the vampire with the ax a chance to warm up his swing. The blade hacks away until bursting through the center of the door.

It's followed by a burst of flames.

I yelp, stumble backward, and fall onto a furry rug. It rubs and bristles against my exposed back, yanking a sob of pain from my lips.

When I try to get back up, my arms give out like they've turned into gelatin.

I'm done for.

It's a reality I'm not ready for. One I don't accept.

The chainsaw grumbles and whines to life, cutting around the door handle.

Get up, I tell myself. *Get up and move that couch in front of the door. You've done this before.*

Yeah, but I had a wand that time, and even then, how did that work out? Those zombies still forced their way through the door without weapons of any kind and flew at me like freaking mutant ninjas. These are vampires I'm dealing with.

I don't stand a chance.

My limbs don't listen. The most I can manage is to drag myself across the carpet, moving away from the door like escape is still a possibility through some magic portal in the far wall just waiting to whisk me away to safety. There's a large, cushy chair with a throw blanket tossed over the cushion against the far wall. I crawl over and squeeze in between the back of the chair and the wall.

The chain saw cuts out abruptly right before I hear the heavy thud of the metal doorknob hitting the ground.

Bitter tears plaster my cheeks.

I'm sorry, Kendra. Sorry I let you and Cameron down.

I'm sorry, Mom. Sorry I didn't help out more and for being a brat the day you died.

I'm sorry, Dad. Sorry I wasn't able to avenge you and Mom and Kendra.

I'm sorry, Joni. Sorry your mother turned into an evil bloodsucking demon from hell.

I rub a bloody finger over my wild card tattoo.

Maybe I can still take out some of these parasites before I join my family. They have weapons, but the last thing they're expecting is a crazed zombie to come at them. Hopefully I can devour enough of them before they get a chance to self-heal. I saw what quick work they made of my family. Maybe it's time to fully embrace my flesh-eating side.

"She's trapped herself inside," one of the lackeys says. "I'll bring her out."

"No," a cruel, deep voice says. "You should have never allowed her to leave the stage. It is time for a reminder of why I am the master. Now step aside."

In a moment of blind panic, I touch my tattoo and whisper,

"Body. Mind. Soul. Divide.

Flesh decay. Remains waste away.

Body. Mind. Soul. Divide.

Thoughts move on. Memories gone.

Body. Mind. Soul. Divide."

Footsteps.

Slow, but close.

Food.

Hungry. So hungry.

Flesh, blood, brains moving closer. Must not let it get away.

Stuck.

Must get unstuck before food slips away. It's talking. Good. It's still here. It continues speaking and getting closer, working me into a frenzy of frustration. I'm pressed tight between a heavy chair and a wall.

The chair is yanked aside, allowing me to spring up and attack.

My food hollers. I dig my nails into its arm so it can't get away as I locate exposed flesh and bite and chew. My prey screams and thrashes, trying to dislodge me. Instinct warns me to anticipate a struggle. I hold tight, Herculean strength surging forth. I bite and chew through layers of skin until I reach the raw, bloody flesh within. The robust flavor coats my tongue and renews my energy.

If I don't devour this morsel on the spot, it might get away. And I'm starving.

This is my purpose. My nature. There is nothing else.

I consume my meal like it might be my last.

It turns out there's more where this came from, and I don't even have to share.

My next meals are pesky. They slice, bash, and cut into me. One of them accidentally roasts another with flames. The smell of cooked flesh supercharges every muscle in my battered body.

Nothing, and I mean NOTHING, is getting between me and those pounds of flesh.

I've never eaten live food until now. It makes all previous meals seem dull and tasteless in comparison. It's a thrill I can't get enough of. The challenge is managing multiple meals at once. They refuse to wait their turn. One chops through my arm below my elbow. Half of my arm falls off my body and hits the ground. I don't need it to eat, so whatever. But it does make devouring my prey more challenging.

I see no other option but to speed-eat.

Consuming this number of meals one at a time isn't working, so I alternate between them until they're no longer fighting back as hard. I'm learning quickly, like a rehabilitated shark released back into the wild. And, wow, what a weird thought. Like, where did that come from?

All this meat is filling my head with bits of coherent thought. I want more. More. More. More. It's nirvana. I want to keep hold of this high forever.

There is no me. No worry. No pain.

I am energy.

I am hunger.

I am free.

CHAPTER SIXTY-EIGHT

LIFE IS GREAT . . . until it's not.

My body erupts with pain. Tears spill from my eyes in a continuous flow down my cheeks that dribble from my chin. My stomach feels full to bursting.

I heave and try to catch myself, but I'm missing one arm!

I fall face forward into my own vomit. Sputtering, I pull away, blinking rapidly and swiping vomit off my face with the one hand I have remaining.

The air smells putrid. Burnt flesh permeates my nostrils.

Dead, charred, and devoured vampires litter Brody's dressing room. There's blood and guts smeared all over the carpet and sprayed across the walls. Gore sticks to the spikes on the baseball bat now resting beside a vampire with his skull bashed in and brains missing.

I sit in the center of it all, and standing in the broken doorframe to witness the horror is Malachi Rayne.

How is this registering?

How am I here? Coherent?

With Malachi staring at what's left of me, I wish I weren't.

His brows are drawn, and he's white-knuckling his wand. He stares into my eyes.

I literally wish I was dead.

Humiliation is only the beginning. There's the unbearable pain ravaging my entire nervous system and torching my wounded body. I've been mutilated. Attacked. Betrayed. And then spit back out into a disfigured heap on the floor.

Malachi Rayne looks at me like I'm a ticking time bomb—and he hasn't decided whether he should attempt to defuse it or sprint as fast as he can out of Brody Morgan's dressing room and run for cover.

Actually, he does neither. He keeps staring at me. I've never seen so many emotions on a vampire's face. One moment it's concern. The next, horror. Then pity. Then anger. Then panic. Followed by determination. Always landing back on uncertainty. It all mixes together like a kaleidoscope on psychological overload.

My coach's black hair is disheveled, and his short-sleeved mustard top is rumpled. It's unbuttoned, and the white shirt underneath is smeared with blood. He doesn't look any less hot. Then again, he's not missing an arm, an earlobe, or half his skin.

"Haylee, are you back?" Malachi asks uncertainly.

All I know is I don't want to be here. I'm done. Just done.

"Kill me," I whisper.

Malachi is in front of me in a flash, crouching over the floor so close our foreheads practically touch. How can he stand to be mere inches from such a disgusting, smelly mess?

When I start crying, Malachi's face crumples.

"I'm going to fix this," he vows.

A pitiful sob bursts through my lips. "Where were you?"

He should have been at our practice session. He left me at the mercy of my family's killers.

I shouldn't have to suffer this way.

It shouldn't be possible.

But here I am.

Not dead yet.

SPELLCASTER WILD CARD IS MORE THAN A STORY.

It's a message to anyone who has ever been knocked down to get back up and continue to fight, to survive, to never give up, to realize their star power and shine for the whole world to see.

You can help me (and Haylee) spread this message by posting a book review and recommending Spellcaster to other readers.

Thank you for lending your star power to this project.
If you share this book on social media, please tag me @NikkiJefford so that I can thank you . . . and give you a four-wand lift!
🪄🪄🪄🪄😉

AUTHOR'S NOTE

At first, I wanted to dedicate this book "for those loved and lost". Then I realized, no; this book is for those left behind. We are the ones who must keep going after death has taken the people and companions who brought love, laughter, comfort, and joy to our lives. Sometimes loss is change. It's instability or the end of a relationship. It's heartbreak. It's betrayal. It's someone close to you morphing into a different version of themselves. In short, it's life.

This book is for us. This book is for you.

I originally intended to complete the Season 13 competition in book one, but Haylee's journey kept expanding (like her first Teddy spell). It wasn't until I passed page 600 of my word doc that I accepted that Season 13 would need to continue in book two. Now that that's settled, I am thrilled to have the extra page space to bring you more wonder, magic, and all the rest. The good. The bad. The ugly. The beautiful. I hope you're excited to watch the All-Stars perform. I know I am!

Special thanks to my phenomenal design team. Najla Qamber put together the gorgeous cover design—and totally captured the darker vibe of the story with her skull and snakes. Nada Qamber brought her magical touch into the interior design. The Qamber sisters go the extra distance every time we work together fine-tuning multiple versions to create a beautiful book for you to enjoy inside and out.

Thank you to my wonderful editors: Kelly Hashway, editor and author (developmental editing); Liz Ferry at Per Se Editing (copy editing); and Roxanne Willis aka: Foxy Roxy's Proofread & Polish (final content editing and proofreading).

Thank you to my loyal readers for being the loveliest of humans who stick with me even when I go MIA to tackle life's ongoing battles.

Special thanks to all the rockstar ARC readers who helped spread the word. And to Daphné and Katryne for being so much fun to collaborate with on Daf's character.

Finally, I cannot end this author's note without a shoutout to Cosmo, The Wonder Westie. Me and my beloved fur companion were inseparable for nearly seventeen years until he crossed the rainbow bridge on December 10, 2022. Cosmo kept me company through all my finished book series to date and was with me to start this new series through the first 70,000 words. He was the wind in my ears as I typed through Haylee's grief of losing her family (knowing his kidneys were failing and that our precious time together was coming to an end). I could not have asked for a better writing companion.

Haylee signs off with "Be bold. Be beautiful. And always be yourself." To that, I will add, "Be strong and love with your whole heart."

Also, keep your power charged!

xo, Nikki

P.S. How the heck was Haylee able to return to her senses? My editors all speculated, but I'm not telling. There is an explanation that no one has guessed. All shall be revealed…in the next book!

SAY HELLO!

Sign up for Nikki's spam-free newsletter. Receive cover reveals, excerpts, and new release news before the general public; enter to win prizes; and get the scoop on special offers, contests, and more.

Visit Nikki's website, nikkijefford.com, to put your name on the list, then confirm your email so you won't miss out.

See you on the other side!

DO YOU LOVE ROMANCE, DANGER, AND HEROINES WHO FIGHT BACK?

Meet Aurora Sky Vampire Hunter in this gritty YA urban fantasy series.

"Full of action from the very first page, *Aurora Sky* is a book that will have the reader hanging onto every word, staying up late into the night to find out just what is going to happen next!" – Examiner.com

Thanks to her rare blood type, Aurora Sky is forced to hunt vampires for a secret government agency in Alaska while juggling school, dating, and secret missions. With the help of an undercover informant, an overzealous partner, and Mr. Tall, Dark, and Maddening, Aurora takes on the underworld and the deceitful man running the agency.

SLAYING, MAGIC MAKING, & RULING ACROSS REALMS

Discover your next fantasy fix with these romantic, coming-of-age titles by Nikki Jefford:

AURORA SKY: VAMPIRE HUNTER

Aurora Sky

Northern Bites

Stakeout

Bad Blood

Hunting Season

Whiteout

True North

AURORA SKY STORIES

Night Stalker

Evil Red

Night of the Living Dante

SPELLBOUND TRILOGY

Entangled

Duplicity

Enchantment

Holiday Magic

ROYAL CONQUEST SAGA

Stolen Princess

False Queen

Three Kings

Holiday Crown

The Golden Prince

The Dark Pretender

The Ice Twins

The Forever Princess

ABOUT THE AUTHOR

Nikki Jefford loves fictional bad boys and heroines who kick butt. Books, travel, TV series, hiking, writing, and motorcycle riding are her favorite escapes. She is a third-generation Alaskan now living in the western mountains of North Carolina. The dark side of human nature fascinates her, so long as it's balanced by humor and romance.

facebook.com/authornikkijefford
instagram.com/nikkijefford/
tiktok.com/@nikkijefford

Milton Keynes UK
Ingram Content Group UK Ltd.
UKHW042108041024
2011UKWH00078B/75/J

9 798986 976198